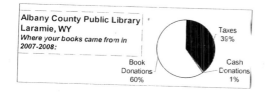

eddie bear,
private detective

Other Books by Robert Rankin

The Brentford Trilogy
The Antipope
the Brentford Triangle
East of Ealing
The Sprouts of Wrath
The Brentford Chainstore Massacre
Sex and Drugs and Sausage Rolls
Knees Up Mother Earth

The Armageddon Trilogy
Armageddon: The Musical
They Came and Ate Us
The Suburban Book of the Dead

Cornelius Murphy Trilogy
The Book of Ultimate Truths
Raiders of the Lost Car Park
The Most Amazing Man Who Ever Lived

The Trilogy That Dare Not Speak Its Name Trilogy
Sprout Mask Replica
The Dance of the Voodoo Handbag
Waiting for Godalming

Not Available in Any Trilogy
The Witches of Chiswick
The Brightonomicon

eddie bear, private detective

THE HOLLOW CHOCOLATE BUNNIES
OF THE APOCALYPSE

THE TOYMINATOR

Robert Rankin

FANTASY

THE HOLLOW CHOCOLATE BUNNIES OF THE APOCALYPSE
Copyright © 2002 by Robert Rankin
  Publication History: Gollancz paperback, September 2002
        Gollancz paperback, August 2003
THE TOYMINATOR Copyright © 2006 by Robert Rankin
  Publication History: Gollancz hardcover, August 2005

First SFBC Science Fiction Printing: November 2006

Published by arrangement with:
Gollancz
An imprint of the Orion Publishing Group
Orion House
5 Upper St Martin's Lane
London WC2H 9EA

Visit The SFBC online at http://www.sfbc.com

ISBN: 978-0-7394-7744-1

Printed in the United States of America.

Contents

the hollow chocolate bunnies of the apocalypse

This book is dedicated
to the memory
of Jon Jo

1

'Once upon a time,' said the big fat farmer, 'it was all fields around here.'

The traveller glanced all around and about. 'It's still all fields,' said he.

'And there you have it.' The farmer grinned, exposing golden teeth. 'Nothing ever changes in these parts. Nothing. Nor will it ever. And so much the better for that, says I. Though so much the worse, say others. It all depends on your point of view. But isn't this ever the way?'

'I suppose that it is.' The traveller nodded politely. He was hot and he was weary. He had wandered many miles this day. His feet were sore and he was hungry. He took off his blue felt cap and mopped it over his brow.

'The colour's coming out of your cap,' the farmer chuckled. 'Your forehead's gone all blue.'

'Which, you must agree, is different,' said the traveller. 'And admits, at the very least, to the possibility of change in these parts.'

'On the contrary.' The farmer dug about in his voluminous patch-worked smock, brought forth something chewable and thrust it into his mouth for a chew. 'To me it admits something else entirely. To me, it admits that you, a ruddy-faced lad—'

'Tanned,' said the lad. 'Tanned from travel.'

'All right, tanned, then. That you, a tanned lad, of, what would it be, some sixteen summers?'

'Thirteen,' said the travelling lad. 'I'm tall for my age. Thirteen I am, which is lucky for some.'

'All right then yet again. That you, a tanned lad, thirteen years and lucky for some, scrawny-limbed and—'

'Spare,' said the tall, tanned lad. 'Spare of frame and wiry of limb and—'

'Dafter than a box of hair,' said the farmer. 'That you are a gormster and a dullard, with a most inferior cap, who understands little of the world and will surely come to grief in a time not too far distant.'

'Oh,' said the lad. 'Indeed?'

'Indeed.' The farmer spat with practised ease across the field of flowering crad. 'Nothing ever changes in these parts and there's a truth for you to be going along with.'

'And going along I mean to be.' The lad wrung sweat from his most inferior cap and replaced it upon his tanned and heated head. 'Just as soon as you have furnished me with answers to questions I must ask. You see, I have wandered from the road. I followed a sign that said shortcut, and now I find myself here.'

'It happens,' said the farmer. 'More often than you might suppose.'

'As *rarely* as that?' said the lad, who was never one prone to extravagant speculation.

'At the very least, but mostly a whole lot more.'

The travelling lad whistled.

'Please don't whistle,' said the farmer. 'It aggravates my Gout.'

'I am perplexed,' said the whistler. 'How can whistling aggravate Gout?'

'Gout is the name of my goat,' the farmer explained. 'I have a pig called Palsy and a cat called Canker. Once I owned a dog by the name of Novinger's syndrome, but his howling upset my wife, so I sold him to a tinker.'

'Oh,' said the lad once more.

'Yes, oh. And whistling aggravates my goat. As does poking him in the ear with a pointy stick. Which, in all truth, would aggravate me. And I'm not easily upset.'

'Righty oh.' The lad shifted from one weary foot to the other, and his stomach growled hungrily. 'But regarding these questions that I must ask.'

'Are they questions of an agricultural nature?' the farmer enquired.

'Not specifically.' The lad shook his heated head.

'That's a pity,' said the farmer. 'Because my knowledge on the subject is profound. I trust it's not a question regarding clockwork motors. Because, for all the life that's in me, I cannot make head nor toe of those infernal machines.' The farmer made a sacred sign above his treble chin.

'It's not clockwork motors.' The lad made exasperated sighing sounds. 'I was lately apprenticed in that trade and I know everything I need to know regarding them.'

'Cheese, then?' said the farmer. 'I know much about cheese.'

'Directions only.' The lad blew droplets of bluely-tinted sweat from the tip of his upturned nose. 'All I wish for are directions. How do I get to the city from here?'

'*The city?*' The farmer almost choked upon his chewable. 'Why would a lad such as yourself be wanting to be going to the city?'

'I mean to seek my fortune there,' the lad replied, with candour. 'I am done with toiling in a factory. I will seek my fortune in the city.'

'Fortune?' coughed the farmer. 'In the city? Hah and hah again.'

'And why "hah", you farmer?' asked the lad.

'Because, my tanned and wiry boy, you'll find no fortune there. Only doom awaits you in that direction. Turn back now, say I. Return to the mother who weeps for you.'

'I have no mother,' said the lad. 'I am an orphan boy.'

'A little lost waif; my heart cries bloody tears.' The farmer mimed the wiping of such tears from the region of his heart.

'Let not your heart weep for me.' The lad straightened his narrow shoulders and thrust out his chest—what little he had of a chest. 'I know how to handle myself.'

'Turn back,' advised the farmer. 'Return the way you came.'

The lad sighed deeply. 'And what is so bad about the city, then?' he asked.

'Where to start?' The farmer puffed out his cheeks. 'And where to end? So many evil things I've heard.'

'And have you ever been to the city yourself?'

'*Me?*' The farmer placed his hands upon his over-ample belly and gave vent to raucous sounds of mirth.

'And why now the raucous sounds of mirth?'

'Because what do I look like to you, my poor lost laddo?'

'You look like a big fat farmer, as it happens.'

'And what would a big fat farmer be doing in the city?'

'Trading produce, perhaps? This crad that flowers all around and about us in these fields that never change.'

The farmer scratched his big fat head. 'And why would I want to trade my crad?'

'For money. To buy things.'

'What sort of things?'

'Food, perhaps?'

The farmer gave his big fat head a slow and definite shaking. 'You are indeed a mooncalf,' said he. 'I am provided here with all the food that I need.'

'Other things then. Consumer durables, perhaps.'

'What?'

'Consumer durables. I am not entirely sure what they are. But I am informed that the city holds them in abundance. And I mean to acquire as many as I possibly can.'

The farmer shook his head once more, and there was a certain sadness in the shaking.

'Clothes then,' said the lad. 'Everyone needs new clothes at one time or another.'

'And do I look naked to you?'

The lad now shook *his* head, spraying the fully clothed farmer with sweat. The farmer was certainly clothed—although his clothing was strange. His ample smock was a patchwork, as if of a multitude of smaller clothes all stitched together.

'My wife and I have all we need, my sorry orphan boy,' said the farmer. 'Only disappointment and despair come from wanting more than you need.'

'I've no doubt that there's wisdom in your words,' said the lad. 'But as I have nothing at all, anything more will represent an improvement.'

'Then return the way you came. Weave clockwork motors if you must. Hard work, well achieved, is sometimes rewarded.'

'No,' said the lad. 'It's the city for me. My mind is set on this. But listen, if you have never visited the city, why not accompany me? Your gloomy opinion of it might be modified by experience.'

'I think not. The city is for city folk. There are those who toil there and are miserable and those who prosper and are happy. The toilers exceed the prosperers by many thousands to one. So much I have been told, and what I've been told is sufficient to inform my opinion.'

'Perhaps I will return one day and alter this opinion.'

'Be assured by me that you will do no such thing. Many have travelled this way before you, seeking wealth in the city. None have ever returned wealthy. In fact, none have ever returned at all.'

'Perhaps they became wealthy and so felt no need to return.'

'Your conversation tires me,' said the farmer. 'And as I can see that you are adamant in your convictions and eager to be on your way, I suggest that we speak no more. I have discharged my responsibilities. My job is done.'

'Responsibilities?' asked the lad. 'Job?'

'My responsibility and my job is to stand in this field of flowering crad and discourage young lads such as you from travelling towards the city. Such was my father's job, and his father's before him.'

'Why?' asked the lad.

'Because that's the way we do business in these parts. Nothing ever changes around here. If you travel on towards the city, you will surely meet your doom. And when you do, you will blame me for it.'

'Why should I?' asked the lad.

'Because I know that you will come to grief. I know it. And if you were in my position and knew that travellers, should they travel in a certain direction, would come to grief, would you not advise them against it?'

'Of course I would,' said the lad. 'But—'

'But me no buts. I have advised you. I have warned you of an inevitable consequence. What more can I do?'

'You could be a little more specific,' said the lad, 'regarding the manner of this imminent and inevitable doom that lies ahead for me.'

'That I cannot do.'

The traveller shrugged. 'So which way *is it* to the city?' he asked.

'The city lies five miles to the south.' The farmer pointed. 'Cross yonder stile and follow the path. The path leads eventually to the outskirts of the city, but—'

'But *me* no buts,' said the lad. 'Thank you and farewell.'

The lad stepped carefully across the field of flowering crad, swung his long and agile legs over the stile and proceeded southwards down the path. Sparrows sang in the hedgerows, trees raised their leafy arms towards the sky of blue and the sun continued its shining down.

'A strange old breed are farmers,' said the lad to no one other than himself. 'And many folk hold to the conviction that the rustic mind, attuned as it is to natural lore, possesses a raw wisdom which is denied to the over-civilised city dweller, whose sophisticated intellect is—'

But he said no more as he tripped upon something and then plunged forward and down.

And then down some more.

Presently he awoke from unconsciousness to find that he was lying at the bottom of a pit. Rubbing at his head and peering blearily about, he became aware of a movement someways above. Looking up, he espied the face of the farmer.

'Thank goodness,' said the lad. 'Please help me. I appear to have fallen into a hole.'

'You have fallen into *my* hole,' said the farmer, 'the hole that a distant ancestor of mine dug to receive the bodies of the foolhardy boys who failed to heed his advice.'

'Oh,' said the lad, rubbing some more at his head and blinking his bleary eyes.

'A hole maintained by and through generations, and now by myself. Although it would appear that I must furnish its bottom with a few more sharpened spikes; you have missed those that there are, by the looks of you.'

'Oh,' said the lad once more.

'Nothing ever changes around here,' said the farmer. 'My forebears feasted upon the flesh of foolish boys, and so do I. It's a family tradition. Their meat fills my belly and their clothing covers my person. I would hardly be so big and fat and well-dressed if I subsisted upon crad alone, now, would I?'

'I suppose not,' said the lad, dismally.

'I gave you warnings,' said the farmer. 'I gave you opportunity to avoid travelling to your inevitable doom. But did you listen?'

'Perhaps if you *had* been more specific,' the lad suggested. 'I took your warnings to mean that the city spelled my doom.'

'You didn't listen carefully enough,' said the farmer. 'But doom is doom, no matter how you spell it. Unless, of course, you spell it differently from doom. But then it would be another word entirely, I suppose.'

'I suppose it would,' the lad agreed, in the tone of one who now knew exactly how doom was spelled. 'But I have no one to blame but myself.'

'Well said.' The farmer grinned. 'And so, as the spikes have failed to do their job, I must do it with this rock.' The farmer displayed the rock in question. It was round and of a goodly size. 'Perhaps you'd care to close your eyes whilst I drop it onto your head?'

'Not so fast, please.' The lad tested his limbs for broken bones, but found himself intact, if all-over bruised. 'How do you mean to haul my body from this pit?'

'I have grappling hooks,' said the farmer, 'fashioned for the purpose.'

'Hot work on such a day,' said the lad. 'Hard work, but honest toil justly rewarded, I suppose.'

'In that you are correct.'

'But *very* hard work, nonetheless.'

'And me with a bad back,' said the farmer. 'But what must be done, must be done.'

'Would it not make your job easier if you were to help me from the hole? Then I might walk with you to your farmhouse, where you could brain me at your leisure?'

'Well, certainly it would,' said the farmer.

'Thus also sparing you all the effort of dragging my body.'

'You are most cooperative,' said the farmer. 'But there's no dragging involved. I have my horse and cart with me.'

'Then let me climb aboard the cart. It's the least I can do.'

'I appreciate that,' said the farmer.

'It's only fair,' said the lad. 'You *did* warn me, and I failed to heed your warning.'

The farmer leaned over and extended his hand. 'Up you come, then,' said he.

The lad took the farmer's hand and scrambled from the hole.

'There now,' said the farmer. 'Onto the cart if you please, and let's get this braining business out of the way.'

The lad glanced over at the farmer's cart. And then he smiled back towards the farmer. 'I think not,' he said. 'Your purse, if you will.'

'Excuse me?' said the farmer. 'My purse?'

'I will have your purse. Kindly hand it over.'

'I fail to understand you,' said the farmer.

'I demand compensation,' said the lad, dusting himself down. 'For injuries incurred through falling into your hole. I am severely bruised and more than a little shaken. I'll take whatever money you have upon your person and we'll speak no more of this regrettable incident.'

'Climb onto the cart,' said the farmer. 'I will brain you immediately. Think not of fleeing; I am an accurate hurler of rocks.'

'Be that as it may,' said the lad, 'I will have your purse and then be off to the city.'

'This is ludicrous. Idiot boy.' The farmer raised his rock.

The lad produced a pistol from his sleeve.

'What is this?' the farmer asked.

'A weapon,' said the lad. 'A clockwork weapon. I built it myself for use in such eventualities as this. Its spring projects a sharpened metal missile at an alarming speed. Far faster than one might hurl a rock.'

'Bluff and bluster,' growled the farmer, swinging back his rock-holding hand, preparatory to a hurl.

The lad raised his clockwork pistol and shot off the farmer's left ear. Which came as a shock to them both, though possibly more to the farmer.

'Waaaaaaaaah!' shrieked the man, dropping his unhurled rock onto his foot, which added broken toes to his woeful account.

'Your purse,' said the lad, waving his gun in a now most shaky hand.

'Waaaaaaaah! I am wounded!' The farmer took to hopping and clutching at his maimed head.

'The next shot will pass directly through your heart.'

'No,' croaked the farmer, 'no no no.'

'The world will be a better place without you in it.' The lad steadied his pistol with both hands. 'You are a monster.'

'And you are an iconoclast,' moaned the farmer, still hopping. 'With no respect for tradition.'

'Such is indeed the truth. Now hand me your purse. You are losing a great deal of blood. It would be well for you to return to your farmhouse and have your wife dress your wounds.'

'Damn you,' said the farmer, adding profanities to these words.

'Your purse, *now!*'

The farmer grudgingly produced his purse. It was a weighty purse, full as it was with the gold of a foolish boy who had passed that way earlier in the day and failed to heed the farmer's advice. This foolish boy presently hung in joints in the farmer's smoking house.

'On second thoughts,' said the lad, 'I think it would be for the best if you went down into the hole.'

'What?' cried the farmer. *'What?'*

'The path is narrow,' said the lad. 'Your horse might stumble into that hole, if it doesn't have something to place its hoof upon.'

'What?' the farmer cried again.

'I mean to borrow your horse; I have walked enough for one day.'

'This is outrageous. Preposterous.'

'Best to get it over with as quickly as possible. Before you bleed to death.'

'But the hole.' The farmer ceased his hopping and stared down into the hole. 'The spikes. I am not so scrawny as you.'

'Spare,' said the lad. 'Wiry.'

'I will puncture myself.'

'That's a chance we'll have to take. The hole, or die where you stand.'

'But the spikes . . .'

'Perhaps fate will smile upon you.'

'Fate wears a somewhat glum face at present.'

'Really? Yet I would swear that it grins in my direction.'

'You . . .' The farmer spoke further profanity.

'The hole, and now.' The lad cocked his clockwork pistol.

The farmer, groaning and moaning, lowered himself into the hole.

The lad tucked his weapon back into his sleeve, stepped over to the farmer's horse and detached it from the cart. Then he leapt onto the horse's back and prepared to gallop away. 'I've never ridden a horse before,' he called down to the farmer, 'so this should be something of an adventure.'

'I hope you are thrown and break your neck,' called the farmer.

'What was that?'

'Nothing. May good luck attend you.'

'Thank you very much. And what is the name of this mount, farmer?'

'Anthrax,' called the farmer. 'But he'll not answer to your commands. Quite the reverse, in fact.'

'I'm sure Anthrax and I will get along fine.' The lad held Anthrax by his reins. 'And so we say farewell, master farmer. Our acquaintance has been brief, but it has been instructive. We have both learned something, so let us not part upon bad terms.'

'I am stuck fast.' The farmer huffed and puffed and moaned and groaned. 'I might well die in this hole.'

'If no one comes looking for you, then in a day or two you'll be slim enough to climb out. Or perhaps loss of blood will facilitate a more immediate shrinkage and you'll be home in time for tea.'

'You filthy . . .'

'Quite enough,' called the lad. 'Your conversation tires me. I will now take my leave for the city. One day I will return this way with great wealth. Though not along this particular path.'

'One thing before you go.' The farmer raised his voice.

'And what thing is this?'

'Tell me only your name.'

'My name?' said the lad. 'My name is Jack.'

'That is good,' called the farmer. 'A man may not truly lay a curse upon another man without first knowing his name. I curse you, Jack. May you never know wealth. May all that you wish for be denied you.'

'A spiteful sentiment,' said Jack. 'And so farewell.' Jack dug his heels into Anthrax and Anthrax sprang forward.

The farmer, unable to duck his head, was heavily hooved upon.

2

Anthrax the horse jogged merrily along. There was a definite spring in his four-legged step. Freed from his death-cart constraints, he appeared a very happy horse indeed.

Jack, although pleased to be no longer walking, did not altogether share the horse's joy. Precariously perched, and lacking for equestrian skills, he clung to the horse's reins and counselled the beast to slow down a bit.

Which it didn't.

The path meandered, as paths often do, around grassy knolls and down through dingly dells. All was rural charm and niceness, all of which was lost upon Jack. He was rather peeved, was Jack. Peeved and altogether unsettled. He was peeved about falling into the farmer's hole. That had been a foolish thing to do. He should have listened more carefully to the farmer's warnings. To the phrasing of them. Jack's failure to interpret the farmer's words correctly had come close to costing him his life. That was very peeving indeed.

Regarding the altogether unsettledness, this was a twofold business. All that blood which had flowed from the farmer's maimed head: that was unsettling enough, but the fact that Jack had not actually meant to shoot the farmer's ear off in the first place was doubly unsettling. This had called into question the accuracy of Jack's clockwork pistol. He had meant to shoot the farmer in the knee. There would have to be a lot of work done upon that pistol if it was to prove any use at all as an accurate means of defence.

Anthrax kicked his back legs in the air, all but unseating Jack.

'Calm yourself,' cried the lad. 'No need to go mad, take it easy, please.'

The horse did a skip or two and settled into a trot.

'Slow down, please.'

The horse did not slow down.

The meandering path met up with a rugged track and Jack caught a glimpse of a signpost. It read TO THE CITY in fine big capitals.

'Jolly good show,' said Jack. 'Please slow down a bit, *please*.'

The horse began to canter.

'No!' Jack flung himself forward and clasped his arms about Anthrax's neck.

'Slow down!' he shouted into the horse's left ear. 'Slow down or I'll sell you for cat meat when we reach the city.'

The horse began to gallop.

'No!' shouted Jack, now altogether ruffled. 'Slow down! Slow down! No!'

If there is a faster thing than galloping that horses can do, this horse began to do it now.

Jack closed his eyes tightly and steeled himself for the inevitable concussion and imminent doom that awaited him.

Anthrax thundered forward, his hooves raising sparks on the rugged track, his ears laid back and a fair old froth a-forming round his mouth. The horse appeared possessed.

Eyes tight shut and mouth shouting, 'Slow down please,' Jack was borne along at the speed which is commonly known as breakneck.

The horse would not obey his commands. Quite the reverse, in fact.

And then Jack opened his eyes and a very broad smile appeared on his face. 'Faster!' he shouted. 'Yes boy, yes, faster! Faster! Faster!'

The horse slowed down to a gallop.

'Faster!' shouted Jack. 'Come on!'

The horse slowed down to a canter.

'Faster!'

A trot.

'Faster!'

A jog.

'Faster!'

The horse, all sweaty and breathless, slowed down to a gentle stroll.

'And faster.'

Anthrax came to a halt.

Jack released his grip from the horse's streaming neck and slid himself down onto the ground. He patted the horse on an area known as a flank, then stroked its foaming muzzle parts.

'I should have known,' said Jack, taking deep breaths to steady himself. 'I'm sorry, boy. It was all my fault, wasn't it?'

The horse made a kind of grumbling sound, as if it understood.

'The damnable farmer trained you, didn't he, boy? He trained you to go faster if you were told to go slower and likeways round. In case anyone stole you. I remembered what he said: "He'll not answer to your commands. Quite the reverse in fact." And I'm sure that when you had eventually unseated your rider and tired yourself out, you'd have wandered home of your own accord. It seems that I have much to learn of the ways of the world. I will be very much on my guard from now on.'

Jack led Anthrax on along the rugged track. Presently they came upon a horse trough and both drank from it. Suitably refreshed, Jack climbed back onto the horse.

'Stop,' said he, and the horse set off at a gentle pace.

The rugged track led now up a sizeable hill and Anthrax took to plodding. Jack sighed deeply, but, feeling for the animal which, he surmised, hadn't exactly lived a life of bliss so far, climbed down once more and plodded beside it.

The track led up and up. The sizeable hill seemed little less big than a small mountain. Jack huffed and puffed, and Anthrax did likewise.

'Good lad,' said Jack. 'We're almost there, I think.'

And almost there they were.

And then they were altogether there.

And Jack, still huffing and puffing, with blue sweat striping his face, hands upon knees and heart going bumpty-bumpty-bump, raised his squinting eyes to view what vista lay beyond.

And then he opened both his eyes and his mouth, very wide indeed.

For beyond, across a plain of grey and stunted furze, lay THE CITY.

Writ big in letters. Large and capital.

'Whoa,' went Jack, taking stock of whatever he could. 'Now that is a very BIG CITY.'

And as cities go, and in these parts, but for this one, they didn't, it was indeed a *very* BIG CITY.

And a very dirty city too, from what Jack could see of it. A great dark sooty blot upon the landscape was this city. A monstrous smut-coloured carbuncle.

Anthrax the horse made a very doubtful face. Which is quite a feat for an equine. Jack cast a glance at this very doubtful face. 'I know what you mean,' he said. 'It doesn't look too welcoming, does it?'

The horse shook its head.

'You're a very wise horse,' said Jack. 'And I apologise for that earlier remark of mine about having you converted into cat meat. If you get me in one piece to the city, I'll see that you're well cared for. But,' and he stared once more towards the distant conurbation, 'that is one ugly-looking eyesore of a city. Perhaps your previous owner was right in all he said. But we must remain optimistic. Shall we proceed?'

The horse shook its head.

'You would rather return to haul corpses?'

The horse shook its head once more.

Jack now shook his own. 'I'm talking to a horse,' he said to himself. 'The events of today have unhinged my mind.'

The sun, Jack noticed, was now very low in the heavens.

The blue of the sky had deepened and the day was drawing towards night.

'We'd best get a move on,' Jack told Anthrax. 'I need to fill my belly and find myself lodgings for the night.' He shinned once more onto the horse's back, told it to stop, and set off.

The rugged track wound down the biggish hill/smallish mountain and presently joined a paved and city-bound road. This pushed on-wards through the grey and stunted furze. Onwards and onwards and onwards. Ahead, the city loomed, its outlying districts becoming more clearly defined. Jack was not impressed by what he saw. The road reached peasant huts, crude and weathered. Strange and pale little faces peeped out at him through glassless windows. Jack dug in his heels. 'Slower,' he told Anthrax, 'slower, boy.'

Anthrax got a trot on.

Beyond the peasant huts lay what Jack correctly assumed to be the industrial district: grim, grey factories with chimneys coughing smoke. The air was rank, and Jack took to covering his nose.

'Not very nice around here.' Jack patted Anthrax's neck. 'This is the kind of place I left behind, factories like this. But let us not be downhearted. I'm sure we can find a pleasant hostelry in a nicer part of the city.'

The sun was beginning to set.

At length, but a length too long for Jack's liking, the industrial dis-trict lay astern, or the equine equivalent thereof. Now the buildings showed traces of colour: a hint of yellow here and a dash of orange there. A trifle dusted over, but a definite improvement.

The style of architecture was new to Jack, and therefore looked ex-otic. The buildings were constructed from huge square bricks, each embossed with a letter of the alphabet. But these had not been laid in order to spell out words, but apparently at random.

Suddenly something rushed past Jack and his mount, causing Anthrax to panic. Jack shouted 'Faster!' very loudly indeed and Anthrax jerked to a halt. Jack viewed the rapidly diminishing rusher: some kind of mechanical vehicle.

'Car,' said Jack. 'Nothing to be afraid of. I worked upon cars at the factory. Went like the wind, though, didn't it, boy? I'll be having one of those myself some day soon.'

Anthrax shook his head about.

'Oh yes I will,' said Jack. 'Stop then, boy. We have to find a hostelry soon or I'll fall off your back from hunger.'

The sun was all but gone now, but light shone all around, from bright lanterns held aloft by iron columns that rose at either side of the road at intervals of fifty paces. These lit buildings that showed brighter colours now, reds and greens and blues, all in alphabet brick.

The colours raised Jack's spirits. 'Almost there,' he told Anthrax. 'A warm stable and a manger of hay will shortly be yours.'

Anthrax, all but exhausted, plodded onward.

'Listen,' said Jack. 'It's been a difficult day for the both of us. But you've got me here. I'll see you all right. You're a good horse. Hey, hey, what's that I see ahead?'

What Jack saw ahead was this: a long, low building painted all in a hectic yellow. A sign, wrought from neon, flashed on and off, as such signs are wont to do. Words were spelled out by this sign. The words were *Nadine's Diner*.

'There,' cried Jack. 'An eatery.'

If horses can sigh, then Anthrax did. And as they reached Nadine's Diner, Jack clambered down, secured Anthrax's reins to a post which may or may not have been there for the purpose, promised the horse food and drink, as soon as he had taken some for himself, squared up his narrow, sagging shoulders and put his hand to the restaurant door.

The door was an all-glass affair, somewhat cracked and patched, but none the less serviceable. Jack pushed upon it and entered the establishment.

It wasn't exactly a home from home.

Unoccupied tables and chairs were arranged to no particular pattern. Music of an indeterminate nature drifted from somewhere or other. A bar counter, running the length of the long, low room, was attended by a single fellow, dressed in the manner of a chef. He viewed Jack's arrival with a blank expression—but a blank expression mostly shadowed, for several bulbs had gone above the bar and he obviously hadn't got around to replacing them.

Jack steered his weary feet across a carpet that was much of a muchness as carpets went, but hardly much of anything as they might go. He squared up his shoulders somewhat more, squinted towards the dimly lit chef and hailed this fellow thusly:

'Good evening to you, chef,' hailed Jack.

'Eh?' replied the other in ready response.

'A good evening,' said Jack. And, glancing around the deserted restaurant, 'Business is quiet this evening.'

'Is it?' The chef cast his shadowed gaze over Jack. 'You're blue,' he observed. 'Why so this facial blueness? Is it some new whim of fashion from the House of *Oh Boy!* that I am hitherto unacquainted with? Should I be ordering myself a pot of paint?'

'Inferior cap,' said Jack, taking off his inferior cap and wiping his face with it.

'That's made matters worse,' said the chef.

'Might I see a menu?' Jack asked.

The barlord scratched his forehead, then wiped his scratching hand upon his apron. 'Is that a trick question?' he asked. 'Because I can't be having with trick questions. Chap came in here a couple of weeks ago and said to me, "Do you know that your outhouse is on fire?" and I said to him, "Is that a trick question?" and he said to me, "No it isn't." And I was pleased about that, see, because I can't be having with trick questions. But damn me, if I didn't take a crate of empties outside about an hour later to find that my outhouse had been burned to the ground. What do you make of a thing like that, eh?'

Jack shrugged.

'And well may you shrug,' said the chef. 'So your question is not a trick question?'

'No,' said Jack, 'it's not.'

'That's fine then,' said the chef. 'How may I help you, sir?'

'I'd like something to eat, if I may,' said Jack. 'And a stable for my horse and directions to where I might find a room for the night.'

'God's Big Box,' said the barlord. 'It's want want want with you, isn't it? Were you breast-fed as a baby?'

'I really can't remember,' said Jack.

'Nor me.' The chef shook his head, which appeared to creak as he shook it. 'But then, I never was a baby. It's funny the things that slip your mind, though, isn't it?'

Jack nodded politely. 'I'm dying from hunger,' he said. 'Please feed me.'

'About half past seven,' said the chef.

'Excuse me?' said Jack.

'Oh, sorry,' said the chef. 'I've got a woodworm in my ear. It crawled in there last Tuesday. I've tried to entice it out with cheese, but it seems to be happy where it is.'

'Food,' said Jack, pointing to his mouth. 'I've gold, I can pay well.'

'Boody fries, you need.' The barlord smacked his lips noisily together. 'Mambo-munchies, over-and-unders, a big pot of jumbly and an aftersnack of smudge cake. And if you'll take the advice of a professional who knows these things, add a pint of Keener's grog to wash the whole lot down with.'

'All this fare is new to me,' said Jack. 'But a double helping of each, if you please.'

'I *do* please,' said the chef. 'But the oven's broken down again, so you can't have any of those. Not even the grog. If I had my time over again, I would never have bought this crummy concession. I'd have trained to become a gourmet chef for some big swell on Knob Hill. Or I could have gone in with my brother; he has a specialist restaurant over on the East Side. Serves up smoked haunch of foolish boy, supplied by some local farmer who breeds them, I suppose.'

Jack took a very deep breath which, when exhaled, became a very deep and heartfelt sigh. He brought forth his pistol and levelled it at the chef. 'If you do not feed me at once,' he said, 'I will be forced to shoot you dead and feast upon *your* carcass.'

'That's something I'd like to see.' The chef gave his nose a significant tap, the significance of which was lost upon Jack. But the sound of this tap drew Jack's attention. It was not the sound of flesh being tapped upon flesh. Jack stared hard at the shadowy chef and, for the first time, truly took in what there was of him to be seen. There was something altogether strange about this fellow. Something unworldly. Jack looked at the chef's hand. It was a false hand. A hand carved from wood. Jack looked now, but furtively, towards the face of the chef. That nose was also of wood. A wooden nose. Upon . . . Jack's furtive glance became a lingering, fearful stare . . .

. . . upon . . . a wooden face!

The chef's entire head, so it appeared, was made of wood.

Jack blinked his eyes. That wasn't possible. He was surely hallucinating from lack of food. A man might have a false hand, but not a false head.

'Bread,' said Jack. 'Cheese, whatever you have. Hurry now, hunger befuddles my brain, as the nesting *woodworm* . . .' he paused, then continued, 'does yours.'

'As you please.' The chef shrugged, ducked down behind the bar counter and re-emerged with a plate of sandwiches held in both hands.

Both hands were wooden.

The hands worried Jack, but he viewed the food with relish.

'I regret that I don't have any relish,' said the chef, placing the plate upon the bar counter and clapping his wooden hands together. 'I've been expecting a delivery. For some months now.'

'I'll take them as they come.' Jack reached out a hand to take up a sandwich, but then paused. 'What are they?' he asked.

'Sandwiches,' said the chef.

'I mean, what's in them?'

'Ham. It's a pig derivative.'

Jack tucked his pistol back into his sleeve, snatched up a sandwich and thrust it into his mouth. 'Bliss,' he said with his mouth full.

'It's rude to talk with your mouth full,' said the chef. 'A mug of porter to wash them down?'

'Yes please.' Jack munched away as the chef drew a mug of porter. Jack watched him as he went about his business. There had to be some logical explanation. Folk could not have wooden heads. Perhaps it was some kind of mask. Perhaps the chef had been hideously disfigured in a catering accident and so now wore a wooden mask. An animated wooden mask. Jack shrugged. It was as good an explanation as any. And anyway, it was none of his business.

Eating was currently his business.

'We don't get many blue-faced youths in these parts,' the chef observed as he drew the mug of porter. 'Your accent is strange to me. Which part of the city are you from?'

Jack munched on and shook his head. 'I'm not from the city,' he said. 'I'm from the south.'

'I've never travelled south.' The chef presented Jack with his beverage. 'But they tell me that the lands of the south are peopled with foolish boys who travel north to seek their fortunes in the city. Would there be any truth in this?'

Jack raised an eyebrow and continued with his munching.

'Between you and me,' said the chef, 'I do not hold travel in high esteem. Folk should stay put, in my opinion. It's a wise man that knows where he is. And if he knows where he is, he should stay there, don't you agree?'

Jack nodded. 'No,' he said.

'Was that a trick answer?'

'Probably.'

'So you want a room for the night?'

Jack nodded once more. 'And a stable and fodder for my horse.'

'You won't need that,' said the chef.

'I will.' Jack pushed another sandwich into his mouth, chewed it up and swallowed it down. 'He can't stand out there all night.'

'Well, obviously not.' The chef adjusted his apron, which didn't really need adjusting, but he adjusted it anyway. It was a chef thing. 'But that's neither here nor there, is it?' said the chef, when he had done with his adjustments.

Jack took up the mug of porter and drank deeply of it. He was underage and shouldn't really have been drinking alcohol. But as the chef hadn't made a fuss about it, then Jack felt that neither would he. 'Why is it neither here, nor there?' he asked, without particular interest.

'Because someone just stole your horse.'

'What?' Jack turned to look out of the window.

The post was still there, but Anthrax wasn't.

'Oh no,' cried Jack. 'Someone has stolen my horse.' And leaving the balance of his porter untested, he rushed from Nadine's Diner.

Outside, he stared up and down the lamp-lit street. The only trace of Anthrax was a pile of steaming manure. Jack shouted out the horse's name, and listened in hope of an answering whinny.

To his great delight, one came to his ears.

'Good boy,' said Jack. 'This way, I think,' and he dashed around the corner of the diner and into a darkened alleyway.

'Anthrax,' called Jack, 'where are you, boy?'

And ahead Jack saw him, by the light of a distant lamp, being led along by something that looked far from human. Something squat and strange. 'Stop!' shouted Jack. 'Come back with my horse, you . . . whatever you are.'

And then Jack was aware of a movement behind him.

And then something hit him hard upon the head.

And then things went very black for Jack.

3

The moon, shining down upon the city, shone down also upon Jack, shone down upon the body of Jack, that was lying strewn in an alleyway. The moon didn't care too much about Jack. But then, the moon didn't care too much about anything. Caring wasn't in the moon's remit. The moon was just the moon, and on nights when there wasn't any cloud about, it just shone down, upon anything and everything really, it didn't matter what to the moon. The moon had seen most things before, and would surely see them again. And as for all the things that the moon hadn't seen, well, it would see them too, eventually. On nights when there wasn't any cloud about.

Not that it would care too much when it did.

It was a moon thing, not caring.

The moon couldn't help the way it was.

Jack lay, face down, in the bedraggled fashion of one who has been roughly struck down, rather than gently arranged. One who has been dragged and flung. As indeed Jack had.

He'd lain for several hours in this untidy and uncared-for state, and would probably have lain so for several hours more, had not something prodded and poked him back into consciousness.

This something was persistent in its prodding and poking. It prodded and poked until it had achieved its desired effect.

Jack awoke with a start, or a jolt, if you prefer, or a shock, if you prefer that. Jack had no particular preference. So Jack awoke with a start and a jolt and a shock. Jack awoke to find a big round face staring right up close and at him.

Jack cowered back and the big round face, governed by the laws of perspective, became a small round face. And in accordance with other laws regarding relative proportion, remained that way. Jack blinked his eyes and stared at the face. It was the face of a bear. A teddy bear. A knackered-looking teddy bear, with mismatched button eyes and a kind of overall raggedness that did not make it altogether appealing to behold.

The bear was wearing a grubby old trenchcoat.

'Bear.' Jack made limp-wristed pointings. 'Toy bear. What?'

'What?' asked the toy bear. 'What?'

'I'm dreaming.' Jack smacked himself in the face. 'Ouch!' he continued. 'Oh and . . .'

'You're new to these parts, aren't you?' said the bear. He had that growly voice that one associates with toy bears. Probably due to the growly thing that they have in their stomachs, which makes that growly noise when you tip them forward. 'I'm Eddie, by the way. I'm the bear of Winkie.'

'The who?'

'The bear of Winkie. I'm Bill Winkie's bear. And I'm not just any old bear. I'm an Anders Imperial. Cinnamon-coloured mohair plush, with wood wool stuffing throughout. Black felt paw pads, vertically stitched nose. An Anders Imperial. You can tell by the special button in my left ear.' Eddie pointed to this special button and Jack peered at it.

The button looked very much like a beer bottle top.

It *was* a beer bottle top.

'And what is your name?' asked the bear.

'I'm Jack,' Jack found himself saying. He was now talking to a teddy bear. (Granted, he had recently chatted to a horse. But at least the horse had behaved like a horse and had failed to chat back to him.) 'How?' Jack rubbed some more at his head. 'How is it done?'

'How is *what* done?' asked the bear.

'How are you doing that talking? Who's working you?'

'Working *me*? No one's working *me*. I work for myself.'

Jack eased himself into a sitting position. He patted at his person, then he groaned.

'Stuffing coming out?' Eddie cocked his head to one side.

'Stuffing? No.' Jack patted some more about his person. 'I've been robbed. I had a purse full of gold coins. And my boots. Someone's stolen my boots.'

'Don't knock it,' said Eddie. 'At least you're still alive. Listen, I've got to sit down, my legs are drunk.'

'Eh?' said Jack. 'What?'

'My legs,' said the bear. 'They're really drunk. If I sit down, then just my bum will be drunk and that won't be so bad.'

'I've lost it,' said Jack. 'Knocked unconscious twice in a single day. My brain is gone. I've lost it. I've gone mad.'

'I'm sorry to hear that.' The bear sat down. 'But it will probably help you to fit in. Most folk in the city are a bit, or more so, mad.'

'I'm talking to a toy bear.' Jack threw up his hands. His clockwork gun fell out of his sleeve. 'Oh, at least I still have this,' he said. 'Perhaps I should simply shoot myself now and get it all over with. I came to the city to seek my fortune and within hours of arrival I'm mad.'

'You came *to* the city? You're a stranger to the city?'

'This has not been a good day for me.'

'Tell me about it,' said the bear.

'Well,' said Jack. 'It all began when—'

'No,' said the bear. 'It was a rhetorical comment. I don't want you to tell me about it. I was concurring. Today hasn't exactly been an armchair full of comfy cushions for yours truly.'

'Who's yours truly?'

'I am, you gormster.'

'Don't start with me,' said Jack, slipping his pistol back into his sleeve and feeling gingerly at the bump on the back of his head. 'I've got brain damage. I can see talking toy bears.'

'Where?' asked Eddie, peering all around.

'You,' said Jack. 'I can see you.'

'You need a drink,' said the bear. 'And I need another upending.'

'Upending? I don't understand.'

'Well, I don't know what you're stuffed with. Meat, isn't it?'

Jack made a baffled face.

'Well, I'm stuffed with sawdust and when I drink, the alcohol seeps down through my sawdust guts and into my feet. I'd have to drink a real lot to fill up all the way to my head and I never have that kind of money. So I get the barman to upend me. Stand me on my head. Then the alcohol goes directly to my head and stays there. Trouble is, it's hard to balance on your head on a barstool at the best of times. You've no chance at all when you're drunk. So I fall off the stool and the barman throws me out. It's all so unfair. But that's life for you, in an eggshell.'

'It's a nutshell, isn't it?'

'Well, you'd know, you're the loony.'

'I'm not well.'

The bear scrambled nearer to Jack and peered very closely at him. 'You don't look too well,' said he. 'Your face is all blue. Is that something catching, do you think? Not that I'll catch it. Moth is all I catch. That's one reason that I drink so much, to ward off the moth.'

'It's not fair.' Jack buried his face in his hands and began to weep.

'Oh, come on.' Eddie Bear shifted over on his drunken bottom and patted Jack's arm with a paw. 'Things really could be worse. You'll be okay. I can direct you to the hospital, if you think you need your head bandaged. Or I'll stagger with you, if you want. Or you can carry me upside down and I'll sing you drunken songs. I know some really rude ones. They're all about pigs and penguins.'

'I had a cap somewhere,' said Jack, wiping his eyes and peering about in search of it.

'Was it blue?' asked the bear.

Jack nodded.

'Well, it isn't quite so blue now. I was sick on it. Mostly sawdust, of course, but evil-smelling; I had a curry earlier.'

'This really isn't happening.'

'I think you'll find that it is. Do you want to come back to my place? You could sleep there.'

Jack climbed painfully to his feet. He gazed down at the toy bear. 'You really are real, aren't you?' he said.

'As real as,' said Eddie.

'As real as *what*?' said Jack.

'Wish I knew,' said Eddie. 'But I can't do corroborative nouns. None of us are perfect, are we? I can get started. As big as, as foul as, as obscene as. But I can't get any further. But that's life for you again. As unfair as . . . Listen, wouldn't you rather go to a bar and have a drink? My bum's beginning to sober up. I seep at the seams. I've got leaks as big as . . . But we all have our problems, don't we?'

Jack agreed. 'I'm very confused,' he said. 'But I don't want to go to hospital. I don't like hospitals. And I'm really too young to go into bars.'

'You're quite big enough; let's have a beer. It won't lessen your confusion, though. In fact, it will probably increase it. But in a nice way and that's as good as, isn't it?'

'I should try and get my purse back. And my horse.'

'You had a *horse*?'

'A horse called Anthrax; he was stolen.'

'Then he's probably cat meat by now. Or being minced up to make burgers for that Nadine's Diner around the corner.'

'That's terrible,' said Jack. 'Poor Anthrax.'

'This isn't a very nice neighbourhood, Jack.'

'So what are *you* doing in it?'

'I'm on a case,' said Eddie Bear. 'I'm a private detective. Hence the trenchcoat.' Eddie did a bit of a twirl, then flopped back onto his drunken bum.

Jack shook his head, which pained him considerably. 'I am mad,' he said. 'This is all mad.'

'Come and have a beer,' said Eddie. 'I'll pay. And kindly carry me, if you will. My legs are still as drunk as, if you know what I mean, and I'm sure that you do.'

It was still a bright and moonlit night and as Jack, with Eddie underneath his arm and guided by the bear's directions, lurched painfully in his stockinged feet along this street and that and around one corner and the next, he was, all in all, amazed by the all and all that he saw.

'This is a very strange city,' said Jack.

'It's not strange to me,' said Eddie. 'How so is it strange to you?'

'Well,' said Jack, 'from a distance, as I approached the city, it all looked grey and dour. And it *was*, on the outskirts. But the deeper I go, the more colourful it becomes. And it's night now.'

'You'll no doubt find it positively garish in the daytime.' Eddie wriggled about.

'Careful,' said Jack, 'I'll drop you.'

'You're squeezing me in all the wrong places. You'll push me out of shape.'

'Sorry,' said Jack. 'But tell me this. Are you a magic bear?'

'A magic bear? What is a magic bear?'

'I'm thinking perhaps a toy bear brought to animation through witchcraft or something like that. Not that I've ever believed in witchcraft. Although I did once meet with a wise woman who could make ducks dance.'

'Did they dance upon a biscuit tin?'

'Now I come to think of it, yes. How did *you* know?'

'It's an old showman's trick,' said Eddie. 'Involves a lighted candle inside the biscuit tin.'

'Urgh,' said Jack. 'That's most unpleasant.'

'Works well, though. Look, we're here.'

'Where's here?'

'Tinto's Bar,' said Eddie. 'This is where I normally do my drinking, when I'm not on a case and getting thrown out of other bars. Put me down please, Jack.'

Jack put Eddie down and viewed the exterior of Tinto's Bar.

The exterior of Tinto's Bar was colourful, to say the very least.

'Ghastly, isn't it?' said Eddie. 'I've suggested he repaint the place. But does he listen? No, he just throws me out. That's the trouble with being a teddy. Well, one of the troubles. People throw you about. They take liberties with your person. It's not nice, I can tell you.'

'I quite like the colours,' said Jack.

'They're mostly brown,' said Eddie. 'Those that aren't blue. They clash, in my opinion.'

Jack stared at the bar's exterior. 'There aren't any browns or blues,' he said.

'There are from where I'm looking. But then from where I'm looking, all the world is either brown or blue. It depends which eye I'm looking through. I've only the two, you see, and one's brown and one's blue. Not that I don't have others. I've a drawer full. But I can't fit them. No opposing thumbs, you see.' Eddie waved his paws about.

Jack looked down. 'What?' he said.

'Pardon is more polite,' said Eddie. 'But it's the curse of the teddy bear. Paws rather than hands. They don't even amount to proper paws, really. Proper paws are like stubby fingers. Mine are just sewn sections; nothing moves. You have no idea how lucky you are. Fingers and opposable thumbs. Bliss. What would I give, eh? That would be as wonderful as.'

Jack pushed open the door and he and Eddie entered Tinto's Bar.

It wasn't too colourful inside. In fact, it was all rather monochrome, or whatever the black and white equivalent of monochrome is. Black and white, probably.

The floor was a chequerboard pattern. The ceiling was likewise. But there was something altogether wrong about that ceiling. It was far too near to the floor. Jack had to duck his head. There were tables and chairs, around and about, arranged in pleasing compositions. But as Jack viewed these, he could clearly see that their dimensions were wrong. The tables and chairs were much too small, built, it appeared, for children. And upon the chairs and seated at the tables, engaged in noisy discussion sat . . .

Jack stopped in mid head-duck and stared.

Sat . . .

Jack opened his mouth.

Sat . . .

Jack backed towards the door he had come in by.

Sat . . .

'Toys!' shouted Jack, and he fled.

It was another alleyway, and Jack was sitting down in it.

'You're really going to have to pull yourself together,' Eddie told him.

'Toys?' Jack made an idiotic face.

'So?' said Eddie.

'Toys. In the bar. I saw them. They were drinking and talking.'

'That's what they do. What *we* do. What's the big deal?'

'Am I dead?' asked Jack. 'Is that it? I'm dead, aren't I?'

Eddie shook his head. 'You're a bit messed up. But you're not dead. You're as alive as.'

'And so they were real?'

'As real as. This is a very weird conversation, and becoming somewhat repetitive. You're a very strange lad, Jack.'

'*I'm* strange? How dare you? I was in that bar. I saw toys. *Live* toys. Dolls and bears like you and clockwork soldiers and wooden things and they were alive. I saw them.'

'Well, what did you expect to see, insects? You're in Toy City and Toy City is where toys live, isn't it?'

'Toy City,' said Jack. 'I can't believe it.'

'Listen,' said Eddie. 'You're a nice lad and everything. But you really must pull yourself together. You're in Toy City, which is where toys live. Which is where toys *have* always lived and *will* always live. It's hardly Utopia, but we get by somehow. Nothing ever changes around here. Or shouldn't anyway, which is why I'm on the case I'm on. But this is where you are.'

'This can't be happening. I must have gone mad.'

'Yeah, well,' said Eddie. 'Perhaps you are mad. It's a shame. A real shame. Perhaps it would be better if we just went our separate ways. I wondered, I suppose. But perhaps I was wrong. I think I'll say goodbye.'

'Wondered?' said Jack. 'What did you wonder?'

'If, perhaps, you'd be the one. To help. It was only a thought. A drunken thought, probably. Forget it.'

'How can I forget it? I don't know what it was.'

'I need a partner,' said Eddie the Bear. 'I'm in a bit of a fix and I need a partner. I thought perhaps . . . But it doesn't matter. Go home, Jack. Go back to wherever you came from. This isn't the place for you to be. You don't understand about here. Sleep in this alley tonight, then go home, that's my advice to you.'

'I'm sorry,' said Jack. 'But I'm really confused. Real toys? Live toys? Living in a city?'

'You came to Toy City and you didn't expect to meet toys?'

'I didn't know it was *Toy* City. All I knew was it was *the* City. Where things happened. Nothing much ever happened in the town where I lived. So I came here to seek my fortune.'

'Interesting concept,' said Eddie. 'I've never heard of anyone doing that before. But then, this is the first time that I've actually met anyone who came from outside the City.'

'Because no one ever reaches here,' said Jack.

'Why? Do they get lost?'

'No, eaten, mostly.'

Eddie shrugged. 'Well, I wouldn't know about that. All I know is what I am. I live in Toy City. Things are as they are.'

'But toys can't live. They can't be alive.'

'And why not?'

'Because they can't.'

'But why?'

'Because I say that they can't.'

Eddie Bear looked up at Jack.

And Jack looked down at Eddie.

Eddie Bear began to laugh.

And then, too, so did Jack.

'Shall we go and have that beer?' asked Eddie.

'Yes,' said Jack. 'Let's do that.'

4

Tinto's Bar looked no better to Jack on second viewing.

The interior was still the black and white equivalent of mono-chrome and the chairs and tables were still arranged in pleasing compositions. But the scale of everything was still all wrong and Jack had to duck his head once more, and keep it ducked. And all those *toys* were still there. And all those toys still worried Jack.

The lad steadied himself against the nearest wall. There was no longer any doubt in his mind regarding the reality of this. It *was* real. That it couldn't be real did not enter into it. He was here and all these toys were . . .

'Drunk!' Jack looked down at Eddie. 'All these toys are drunk.'

Eddie looked up at Jack. And Eddie shrugged. 'It's late,' he said. 'They've been in here all evening. Don't folk get drunk where you come from?'

'People do,' said Jack. 'But not . . .'

'Don't start all that again. Buy me a drink.'

'I don't have any money. I was robbed.'

'You've some coins in your trouser pocket. I felt them when you were unconscious.'

'What?'

'I was trying to bring you round.'

'You were going through my pockets?'

'Not me,' said Eddie. 'No can do. No opposing thumbs.'

Jack patted at his trousers.

'Other side,' said Eddie.

'Oh yeah,' said Jack, digging deeply into a pocket and winkling out a number of coins. 'That's a bit of luck.'

'Stick with me, kidder,' said Eddie. 'I'll bring you lots of luck.'

Jack gazed down at the shabby-looking bear and nodded his ducked head in a manner that lacked conviction.

'To the bar,' said Eddie, leading the way. 'Let's both get as drunk as.'

Jack followed on, keeping his head down and making furtive sideways glances as he did so. There were toys to all sides of him, and just a little below. They were chatting away in a rowdy fashion, banging their glasses on the tables and generally carrying on as folk carry on anywhere when they are well in their cups.

There were dolls and there were gollys, teddies and toy soldiers, and fluffy-faced animals of indeterminate species. And they all had that look of 'favourite toys' which have been loved to the point of near-destruction.

Jack watched Eddie climb onto a bar stool. How could he move about like that? He was all filled up with sawdust; he'd said so himself. He had no bones, no muscles, no sinews. How could it be possible?

Jack shrugged and sighed and sat himself down on a bar stool next to Eddie. It was a very low bar stool, beside a very low bar counter, and Jack found himself with his knees up high.

'Can't we go somewhere else?' he whispered to Eddie. 'This stool's too low for me. I look a complete gormster.'

'No you don't.' The bear grinned, a big face-splitter. 'You look as handsome as. Get the beers in.'

Jack sighed again. 'Where's the barman?' he asked.

'Howdy doody, what'll it be, sir?' The barman sprang up from beneath the bar counter, causing Jack to fall back in alarm.

'Control yourself,' said Eddie as Jack stared, all agog. 'It's only Tinto, the barman.'

Tinto was clearly mechanical, powered by a clockwork motor. He was formed from tin and glossily painted, though much of the gloss was now gone. His head was an oversized sphere, with a smiling face painted on the front. His body was a thing-a-me-oid* painted with a dicky-bow and tuxedo. The arms were flat, though painted with sleeves and shirt cuffs. The fingers of the hands were fully articulated.

Jack glanced at Eddie, who was staring covetously at those fingers.

'Howdy doody, what'll it be, sir?' said Tinto once again. The painted lips didn't move. The voice came from a tiny grille in the painted chest.

'I . . .' went Jack, 'I . . .'

'Beer,' said Eddie.

* A cylinder with a hemisphere joined to each end of it.

'Coming right up,' said Tinto. 'And anything for the complete gormster?'

'He'll have a beer too,' said Eddie. 'And he's my friend and he's paying.'

'No offence meant,' said Tinto.

'None taken,' said Eddie.

'There was too,' said Jack.

'No there wasn't,' said Eddie. 'Just relax and drink beer.'

'I.D.,' said Tinto.

'What?' said Eddie.

'I.D. for the gormster. He looks underage to me. Underaged and oversized.'

'*Underage?*' Jack's jaw dropped. '*Oversized?*' His face made a frown.

'I run a respectable bar,' said Tinto. 'Top notch clientele, as you can readily observe. I can't have blue-faced, stocking-footed ragamuffins coming in here and losing me my licence. You'll have to show me your I.D. or . . . I . . . will . . . have . . .' Tinto's voice became slower and slower and finally stopped altogether.

'What's happened to it?' Jack asked.

'*Him!*' said Eddie.

'Him,' said Jack.

'Run down,' said Eddie. 'He needs rewinding. 'I generally take advantage if this happens when I'm alone with him in the bar. Nip around and help myself to a free beer.'

'Do it now then,' said Jack.

'There're too many folk here now. But he loses his short-term memory when he's rewound, so just back me up.'

Jack shrugged. 'Fair enough.'

'Nellie,' called Eddie, 'Nellie, a winding needed here.'

A dainty doll with a huge wasps' nest of yellow hair hastened along behind the bar counter, turned Tinto around and began to vigorously crank the key in his back.

'See his name there, on his back?' said Eddie, leaning over the bar counter and pointing it out to Jack.

Jack perused the barman's back. 'It doesn't say Tinto,' he said, 'it says Tintoy. The "Y" has worn off.'

'You're right,' said Eddie. 'But don't mention it to Tinto. He thinks it makes him special.'

Jack opened his mouth to speak, but didn't.

'Thank you, my dear,' said Tinto, his head turning a semicircle. 'Almost ran right down there. Now, what was I doing?' His body revolved to catch up with his head.

'You were pulling two beers for us,' said Eddie.

'Was I?' asked Tinto.

'You were,' agreed Jack. 'You'd just scrutinised my I.D. and commented on the fact that I looked young for my age.'

'Did I?' said Tinto.

'You did,' said Eddie. 'And we'd just paid for the beers.'

'You had?' said Tinto.

'We had,' said Jack. 'Eddie did. With a gold piece. But we haven't had the beers yet and Eddie hasn't had his change.'

'So sorry,' said Tinto. 'I'll get right to it.' And he moved off along the bar to pull a brace of beers.

'A gold piece?' whispered Eddie. 'That's pushing it a bit.'

Jack shrugged. 'I was only backing you up. You can always tell him it was a mistake if you want and say you gave him the right money.'

'Oh no,' whispered Eddie. 'A gold piece is fine. I must remember that in future.'

Tinto returned and presented Eddie and Jack with their beers and Eddie with a great deal of change. 'Cheers,' said Eddie, taking his glass carefully between his paws and pouring beer messily into his face.

'Cheers,' said Jack, doing likewise, though without the mess. The glass was tiny. Jack drained it with a single gulp and ordered another.

'So, Eddie,' said Tinto, doing the business for Jack, who paid with the change from his trouser pocket. 'Any word from Bill?'

'No,' said Eddie, manoeuvring his glass back onto the bar counter. 'He's been gone for a week now. But I'm sure he'll be back very soon.'

'Who's Bill?' Jack asked as Tinto passed him a new beer.

'My partner,' said Eddie.

Tinto laughed, a sound like small stones being shaken about in an empty tin can.

'All right, my *owner*,' said Eddie. 'Bill Winkie, the famous detective. I'm Bill's bear; I told you in the alleyway, Jack.'

'Bill Winkie?' Jack took a gulp and placed his latest empty glass on the counter. 'Bill Winkie, Private Eye?'

'The same,' said Eddie.

'I've read the books,' said Jack.

'I never get a mention,' said Eddie.

'No, you don't, but that's not the point.'

'It is to me. Without me he'd never solve a single case. I'm the brains behind that man.'

'That's really *not* the point,' said Jack. 'The point is that Bill Winkie is a fictional detective. He's not a real person.'

'He seems pretty real to me.' Eddie took up his glass once more and poured beer into his face. 'From the brim of his snap-brimmed Fedora to the toes of his smelly old socks.'

'You're telling me that Bill Winkie is real?'

'As real as.'

'Hm,' went Jack. 'It follows.'

'Eddie's not kidding you around,' said Tinto. 'He really does solve most of Bill's cases. He's a natural, a born detective.'

'Cheers,' said Eddie. 'I appreciate that.'

'Credit where credit's due,' said Tinto. 'But you'll only get that credit here. And I don't even give credit. This is a cash-only establishment.'

'What he means,' said Eddie, 'is that toys have no status. This may be Toy City, but toys have to know their place. Step out of line and you turn up missing.'

'I don't really understand,' said Jack.

'The status quo,' said Eddie. 'I'm a teddy. I'm supposed to do teddy things. Eat porridge, picnic in the woods, be cuddly, stuff like that.' Eddie made a face and spat sawdust.

'And you're not keen?' said Jack.

'I'm a bear with brains. I have ambitions.'

'About the brains,' said Jack. 'I have been wondering about those.'

'Oh yeah?' Eddie patted at his head with a paw. 'You've been wondering how a head full of sawdust can actually think?'

'It had crossed my mind, yes.'

'And so how does your brain think?'

'It's a brain, that's what it does.'

'It's a piece of meat,' said Eddie. 'And how does a piece of meat think? You tell me!'

'Well . . .' said Jack.

'You don't know,' said Eddie. 'Nobody knows. Except perhaps for Mr Anders. He knows almost everything.'

'And who is Mr Anders?'

'The kindly, loveable white-haired old Toymaker. He birthed me and everyone else in this bar, with the exception of you.'

'So why don't you speak to him about this status quo business? Tell him you want your recognition?'

'Er, no,' said Eddie. 'The Toymaker made me to be a teddy and do teddy things. The fact that I don't care to do them is my business. So I'll just keep my business to myself.'

'Or turn up missing?'

'I don't want to think about it.'

'So don't. Let's drink. Do you want me to turn you upside down yet?'

'No, not yet, but thanks anyway. You're all right, Jack. I like you.'

'I like you too, Eddie, cheers.' Jack raised his glass, but it was empty.

Eddie raised his, but it was empty too. Eddie fumbled with his paws and dropped his glass, shattering it upon the floor.

'Sorry,' said Eddie. 'It happens. A lot.'

'You haven't mentioned to the Toymaker that you would really like a pair of . . .' Jack stopped himself short. Of course Eddie hadn't. He could hardly ask the Toymaker to fit him with a pair of hands. That would not be maintaining the status quo.

'Sorry,' said Jack.

'Forget it,' said Eddie. 'Buy me a beer. It's your round.'

'You have a lot of change on the counter there.'

'Yes but that's *my* change and it's *your* round.'

'Fair enough,' said Jack. 'Although it isn't my round.' Jack purchased a brace of beers with the last of his money and the two took to drinking once more.

'Tell me,' said Eddie, 'about where you come from. I've never met anyone who wasn't brought up in this city.'

'It isn't much,' said Jack. 'It's just a small township, supported by a factory. They make clockwork stuff there. I used to build . . .' Jack drew Eddie closer.

'What?' asked Eddie.

'Clockwork barmen,' said Jack. 'Like Tinto. They said, "Howdy doody friend, what'll it be?" But that's all they said. They didn't talk like Tinto.'

'So you know all about clockwork?'

'You've seen my clockwork pistol. I designed and built it myself. It's not quite as accurate as it's supposed to be, though.'

'But you do know all about clockwork?'

'Pretty much all. But working in the factory nearly did for me. We were like slaves in there. I hated it. The sun used to beat down on us through the glass roof. And when the sun was at its highest, there was this bit of glass in the roof that was convex, like a lens, see, and at midday the sun would come through that and really burn me badly. I'll never forget it as long as I live. I had to get away. So I ran. I'd heard that there was wealth to be had in the city, so I came here to seek my fortune.'

'Pooh,' said Eddie. 'Sounds like you had a pretty rough time. You did the right thing running away.'

'I didn't have a lot of choice really. There was some unpleasantness; I don't want to go into that now.'

'That's okay with me. Your own business is your own business. So you've come here seeking work?'

'In a manner of speaking.'

'I could offer you work.'

'You?'

'Me,' said Eddie. 'I need a partner, I told you.'

'But you're Bill's bear.'

'And he's not here and while he's gone, I need a partner. I can do the thinking. But I can't do the hand working and I can't do the questioning and the driving around and . . .'

'The driving around?' said Jack.

'Bill left without his car and . . .'

'Car,' said Jack. 'What kind of car?'

'You know all about cars then, do you?'

'If they're clockwork cars. And what other kind of cars are there?'

'None that I know of.'

'I know all about them. I've helped build them.'

'But you've never actually driven one?'

'Well, one. But there was some unpleasantness, which I don't want to talk about either.'

'Well, Bill has one and it's standing in the garage. But I need a partner to do all the stuff that he could do and I can't.'

'Because of the status quo?'

'Exactly. If we solve the case, there'll be gold in it for you.'

'*If* we solve it?'

'*When I* solve it. Which I will.'

'So I get to drive you around and play the part of Bill Winkie, is that what you're suggesting?'

'In essence, yes.'

'Then I'm up for it,' said Jack. 'I'll do it.'

'Brilliant,' said Eddie. 'Then we're partners. Put it there,' and he stuck out his paw.

Jack took it between his hands and shook it.

'Partners,' he said.

'That's as brilliant as,' said Eddie, withdrawing his paw and employing it, with its fellow, to take up his glass once again.

'To partners and success,' he said.

'I'll join you in that,' said Jack. 'Cheers.'

'Cheers.' The two drank once again, drained their glasses and ordered further beers.

'So,' said Jack, 'tell me about the case that *you* are going to solve.'

'It's a pretty big number,' said Eddie. 'Prominent member of society brutally slain.'

'That's a job for the police, surely?'

'Surely,' said Eddie. 'And I'm sure they're doing their best to track down the murderer.'

'I detect a certain *tone* in your voice,' said Jack. 'One that suggests to me that you're not altogether convinced that the police will—'

'Exactly,' said Eddie. 'You're most astute. Bill received a cash-up-front advance from an anonymous source to take on the case. It was a great deal of cash. Enough to retire on, really. Bill has a lot of debts. He gambles a great deal and runs up big bar bills. And cleaning bills; he's very fastidious. Likes a clean trenchcoat, does Bill.'

'Er, just one question,' said Jack. 'Before Bill . . . er . . . went away, did he pay off his debts?'

'Not that I know of,' said Eddie. 'I'm sure he will when he comes back, though.'

'And he left, taking the big cash advance with him?'

Eddie nodded.

'Ah,' said Jack.

'Ah?' said Eddie.

'Nothing,' said Jack. 'You're pretty fond of Bill, aren't you?'

'I'm Bill's bear. I have been since he was a child.'

'So you trust him?'

'Of course, why do you ask me that?'

'Oh, no reason really.' Jack applied himself to his beer. 'So you'd like the case solved for him before he gets back from his holiday, or whatever?'

'That's it,' said Eddie. 'There's the promise of much more money, when the case gets solved.'

'And you think that you can trust this anonymous benefactor to pay up when the case is solved?'

'Why wouldn't I?' asked Eddie.

'You're a very trusting little bear.'

'Don't patronise me,' said Eddie.

'Sorry,' said Jack. 'Did Bill leave you any money?'

Eddie shook his head. 'And the rent on the office is overdue. I'd like to get this case solved pretty quickly.'

'All right,' said Jack. 'I'll help you out. I'll be your hands and do all the stuff you want. Especially the car driving. I'm up for it.' Jack patted Eddie on the head.

'Jack,' said Eddie.

'Eddie?' said Jack.

'Pat me on the head like that again and I'll butt you right in the balls.'

'Sorry,' said Jack, withdrawing his patting hand.

'I know what you're thinking,' said Eddie. 'You're thinking that Bill has absconded with the advance money, leaving the silly little bear to deal with the case. That's what you're thinking, isn't it?'

'Of course not,' said Jack.

'Then you *are* a complete gormster,' said Eddie. 'Because that's what's happened.'

'Oh,' said Jack. 'Then you . . .'

'Of course I know. But I don't care. Solving the case is all that matters to me. Applying the sawdust in my head to finding the solution. Proving to myself that I can do it, even if I never get the credit. Can you understand that, Jack?'

'Not really.' Jack shook his head.

'Then it's too subtle for you. But it's what I do and who I am. You'll get paid, you'll do well out of this, if you join me.'

'I *will* join you,' said Jack. 'I've said I will. And we've shaken hand and paw and we're partners.'

'Good,' said Eddie. 'But just as long as we understand each other. I have the measure of you, Jack. But you'll never have the measure of me.'

'If you say so.'

'I do. Drink up, and I'll buy you another.'

'I'm beginning to feel rather drunk,' said Jack. 'And on such small glasses of beer too.'

'The youth of today has no staying power.'

'I'll survive,' said Jack. 'I might throw up a bit later, but I'll survive.'

'I'll throw up with you; let's drink.' Eddie ordered more beer. 'We'll make a great team,' he told Jack.

'I'm sure we will.' Jack raised his glass and drank, spilling much of what little beer there was down his chin.

'We have so much in common,' said Eddie, doing likewise.

'This case.' Jack replaced his glass upon the bar, with some small degree of difficulty. 'This prominent member of society who got murdered, tell me about him.'

'Fat sod,' said Eddie. 'Big fat sod. Someone boiled him.'

'Boiled him?'

'Alive in his swimming pool. Heated the water to boiling point and pushed him in, or something like.'

'Fiendish,' said Jack.

'That's my opinion,' said Eddie. 'And I think there's some kind of cover-up. The papers are even suggesting that it was suicide.'

'Suicide? In a boiling swimming pool?'

'The papers are putting it about that he tried to commit suicide once before.'

'And did he?'

'Not in my opinion. He fell.'

'Fell?'

'Off a high wall. Broke half the bones in his body. There was a regiment of soldiers passing at the time, but they couldn't resuscitate him. Paramedics patched him up, though. They were conveniently close.'

'Come again?' said Jack.

'It was big news at the time. There was a song written about it. He was nothing before that song, but he got rich from the royalties. Because he wrote it himself.'

'Eh?' said Jack.

'Scam,' said Eddie. 'The whole thing was a set-up.'

'I'm lost,' said Jack. 'I have no idea what you're talking about.'

'But I bet you know the murder victim.'

'How could I? I'm new to this city.'

'You'll have heard of him. You'll even have sung about him falling off that wall.'

'I don't think that's very likely,' said Jack.

'Oh, I think you'll find that it is,' said Eddie. 'His name was Humpty Dumpty.'

5

Jack awoke to find himself in strange surroundings. As this was now becoming a regular habit, rather than a novelty, he merely groaned and blinked, rolled onto his belly and eased himself up on his knees.

He was in an office, a definite improvement on the death pit or the alleyway, but hardly the five star accommodation he'd been hoping for when first he entered the city. The words 'how did I get here?' came almost to his lips, but he withheld them. He had vague recollections of the latter part of his night out with Eddie. It had involved much beer, and later, much vomiting. Then there had been much staggering along streets, much climbing of stairs and then much floor and much oblivion.

Jack stretched himself, fretted at the clicking of his joints, ran gentle fingers over his pulsating forehead and said 'never again' in a whispery kind of a voice.

Underage drinking. Jack shook his head and regretted the doing thereof. Where *was* the pleasure in underage drinking? Jack tried to recall the pleasure.

It wasn't easy.

'Still,' whispered Jack, 'you have to keep at it. Overcome the miseries of the vomiting and the whirling pit. Pay your dues and work towards the real rewards of big-time adult drinking. Something to look forward to.'

Jack's knees buckled under him.

For now he needed a quiet sit-down.

Jack gave his surroundings a bleary perusal and took in what he could of them. An office, that was for certain. And yes, he recalled, the office of the now legendary Bill Winkie, *fictional* detective. Jack sniffed at the office. It didn't smell too good: musty and fusty and tainted by the smoke of many cigarettes.

But, for all of its overloaded atmospherics, here was an office that owned to a certain 'lack'.

There was a hatstand that lacked a hat to stand on it and a water cooler that lacked anything to cool. The filing cabinet lacked a bottom drawer and the desk, lacking a leg, was being supported at that corner by a large alphabet house brick (lacking a corner).

Jack eased himself carefully around the desk and settled down onto the chair that stood behind it. The chair lacked comfort. Jack turned gently around on it to face a window that lacked a pane of glass. He turned back, took in a ceiling fan that lacked a blade and a carpet that lacked a pattern.

Jack turned once more towards the window and raised his eyes, which pained him no little bit.

A Venetian blind, no doubt lacking a slat or two, was fastened in the up position. But, strung to the cord at ceiling height and dangling by the neck, was Eddie Bear.

'Oh no!' cried Jack, leaping from the chair and shinning onto the desk.

The desk that lacked a leg had a top that lacked support. It gave with a hideous crack and Jack fell through it.

He was only slightly dazed this time and his eyes soon reopened to find a big round face looming at him once again.

'What did you do *that* for?' asked Eddie. 'The guvnor will be very upset when he returns to see what you've done to his antique desk.'

'You were trying to hang yourself.' Jack beat away bits of desk, getting splinters in his fingers. 'I was saving you.'

'Ah,' said Eddie, de-looming his face. 'Ah no. I was sobering up. I hang myself in the upright position, then rely on natural seepage, through the feet. Stone cold sober again. Doesn't work for you meatheads though, does it?'

'You might at least say sorry.'

'Why? I didn't break the desk.'

'Oh, never mind.' Jack climbed once more to his feet. 'I have *such* a hangover,' he said. And, looking up once more, 'How did you manage to climb up that cord in the first place?'

'Practice,' said Eddie. 'You need a drink.'

'No, I need breakfast. And the toilet.'

'The joys of the human digestive system. You should have a drink, though. Bill's hangover cure. His own special concoction. There's some in the desk drawer. Well, what's left of it.'

Jack rootled about in the desk drawers and finally unearthed a sinister-looking green bottle.

'That's the kiddie,' said Eddie. 'You have a swig of that.'

Sighing and muttering by turn, Jack uncorked the bottle, sniffed at the contents, made a face of displeasure, then took a swig.

He looked at Eddie and Eddie looked at him.

'It takes a minute or two,' said the bear. 'I'd sit back down, if I were you.'

Jack sat back down. 'Would you say that I had a good time last night?' he asked.

'Certainly,' said the bear. 'You had a good time last night.'

'Did I? Really?'

'No,' said Eddie. 'Of course you didn't.'

'Then why did you say that I did?'

'Because you asked me to. What a strange young man you are.'

'I'm seriously thinking of going home.' Jack rubbed at his forehead. 'I don't think city life agrees with me.'

'It doesn't agree with most folk.' Eddie sat down at Jack's feet. 'But then, if you're poor, what kind of life does?'

'I came here to seek my fortune.'

'Then I hope you'll share some of it with me when you do. I ran up a bit of a bar tab at Tinto's last night. He wrote it down, in case he forgot about it.'

'Humpty Dumpty,' said Jack, and he groaned as he said it.

'Fat and dead.' Eddie plucked bits of fluff off himself. 'In that order.'

'No. Humpty Dumpty. That was why I got so drunk.'

'And there was me thinking that it was all the beer you consumed that was to blame.'

'He was the reason behind all the beer. A nursery rhyme character.'

'Ah,' said Eddie, once more. 'They don't like that term. They prefer "Preadolescent Poetic Personalities".'

'*They?* That's right, I remember. Miss Muffet, Georgie Porgie, Jack and Jill, the whole sick crew. They're all real people, according to you, and they all live here in the city.'

'They have to live somewhere.'

'Not if they don't exist.'

'Please don't start all that again, Jack. You went on and on about that last night. "They're not real." "Why not?" "Because I say so." Your conversation became extremely tedious. And very slurred.'

'Agh! Oooh! Ow! Urgh!'

'That's easy for you to say.'

'Aaaaaagh!' Jack clutched at his stomach and fell forward onto Eddie.

'Get off me.' Eddie flapped about. 'You'll have my seams bursting, get off.'

Jack got off. 'I'm sorry,' he said, 'but I feel . . .'

'How do you feel?'

'Actually,' Jack looked all around and about, 'actually, I feel excellent. In the very best of health.'

'Bill's lotion, works every time.'

'Lotion? Don't you rub lotion on?'

'Do you? Well, it's all the same, it worked, didn't it?'

'Yes, it did.' Jack took up Eddie and set him upon the ruins of the desk. 'I'd like some breakfast,' he said. 'And I still need the toilet.'

'Okey doke,' Eddie grinned. 'But we're still partners, right? You'll help me solve the case? Be my hands, and whatnots?'

'Whatnots?'

'We'll not debase our conversation with cheap innuendo, will we, Jack?'

'Certainly not.' Jack had a big smile on. 'I'll give it a go. I'll help you solve your case, mad as it is. I keep my word. We shook hand and paw and we're partners.'

'Jolly good, now help me down, please.'

Jack helped Eddie down.

'I want to visit the crime scene,' said the bear. 'I haven't been able to thus far. The authorities won't give clearance to a teddy. But you'll be able to bluff us in, I feel confident of that.'

'I'm not sure that I do,' said Jack.

'Well I am, because I'll tell you what to say. Now, you did tell me that you could actually drive a car, didn't you?'

'In theory,' said Jack.

'Well, theory and practice are not too far removed. Come on, I'll show you Bill's car. But first we need to clean you up. Get all that blue dye off your face. You smell rank and you could do with a change of clothing and some shoes. I'll kit you out from Bill's wardrobe.'

'So I can play the part of Bill Winkie.'

'So you can *be* Bill Winkie. Men all look the same to toys. You'll be able to carry it off.'

Jack nodded thoughtfully. 'I'm up for it,' he said. 'But I want breakfast.'

'Do you have money to pay for breakfast?'

Jack patted his pockets and then shook his head.

'Perhaps there'll be something to eat at the crime scene,' said Eddie. 'A bit of boiled egg, or something.'

★

Now, there is a knack to driving a car. Any car. Even one that is pow-ered by a clockwork motor. There is steering to be done and gears to be changed and this involves clutch-work, and, if reversing, looking into mirrors and judging distances. There are all manner of complica-tions and knacks involved. And skills, there are definitely skills. In fact, the remove between theory and practice is a pretty large remove, when it comes to driving a car.

Let us take, for example, the deceptively simple matter of starting up a car. This is not something that should be attempted in a light-hearted and devil-may-care manner. It's not just a matter of turning a key and putting your foot down somewhere and *brrrrrming* the engine.

Well, it sort of is.

But then again, it isn't.

Jack considered that it probably was. And, it has to be said, when Eddie led him into Bill's garage and Jack switched on the light and be-held *the car*, Jack was heard to remark that it would be 'a-piece-of-the-proverbial' to 'burn that baby'.

'This phraseology is odd to my ears,' said Eddie. 'Does it mean that you are actually conversant with the whys and wherefores requisite to the *safe* locomotion of this vehicle?'

Jack rubbed his hands together and grinned broadly.

'That's not really an answer,' said Eddie.

'I know clockwork,' said Jack. 'I've worked on cars like this.'

'Yes, but driven them?'

'I'm sure I said yes to you last night.'

'You may have,' said Eddie. 'But we were both pretty out-of-it. I definitely recall you mentioning that there was some "unpleasantness" involved.'

'We'll have to wind it up first,' said Jack.

'This much I know.'

'Then we get in and I drive.'

'It all sounds so simple when you put it that way.'

'There's one thing,' said Jack. 'I don't have a driving licence. I'm too young to drive.'

'I don't think we should let a small detail like that stand in the way of the disaster that immediately awaits us as soon as you get behind the wheel, should we?'

'You're a most articulate little bear,' said Jack.

'Don't patronise me,' said Eddie. 'I warned you about that, didn't I?'

'You did,' said Jack. 'So should I wind?'

'Please wind,' said Eddie.

★

The car was an Anders Faircloud: pressed tin in the metallic blue of a butterfly's wing. It was long and low and highly finned at the tail, the way that every good car should be (apart from the short stumpy sports ones that go like poop off a scoop and generally come to grief on late night motorways with a celebrity (though rarely a Preadolescent Poetic Personality) in the driving seat). It had pressed tin wheels with breezy wide hubs and big rubber tyres. It was a blinder of an automobile and its all-over glory gave Jack a moment's pause for thought.

'Eddie,' said Jack.

'Jack?' said Eddie.

'Eddie,' said Jack. 'This is a superb automobile.'

'Bill's pride and joy,' said Eddie.

'So herein lies a mystery. Why would Bill Winkie not take his car when he went off to wherever he went off to?'

'What are you suggesting?' Eddie asked.

'Nothing,' said Jack. 'I was just wondering why he would have gone off and left his precious car behind.'

'I don't know,' said Eddie. 'Perhaps he didn't take the car because it is such a noticeable car. Perhaps he has gone off somewhere to be incognito. Perhaps he's working on the case, incognito. Is that enough perhapses for you?'

'Perhaps,' said Jack.

'Wind the car up,' said Eddie. 'Let's go to the crime scene.'

'Yes,' said Jack. 'Let's do that.'

Well, there *is* a knack to driving a car.

And Jack didn't have it.

No doubt he'd get it, given time, like he would getting drunk. But these things *do* take time, even the getting drunk thing. He was okay on the winding-up part of the procedure, though. There was no doubt about that.

'No!' howled Eddie as Jack backed out of the garage at speed, before the garage door was actually raised.

'Stop!' screamed Eddie, as Jack performed a remarkable handbrake turn in the middle of the traffic that moved (quite swiftly) in the street beyond.

'We're all gonna die!' bellowed Eddie as Jack tore forward on the wrong side of that street.

'I'm getting the knack of this,' said Jack, gronching the gears and clinging to the steering wheel. 'These things take time. I have the measure of it now.'

'No you don't!' Eddie ducked down in his seat. Even lower than he already was.

'Piece of the proverbial.' Jack spun the steering wheel, which at least took him onto the right side of the road. 'Does this car have a music system fitted? One of those music bow wheel-pin contraptions?'

'Forget the music.' Eddie covered his face.

'Easy-peasy.' Jack put his foot down somewhere. It was the brake; the car did a bit of a spin; Jack took his foot off the brake. 'What about *that?*' he said.

'You don't even know where we're going.'

'Do you?'

'Yes, the wrong way.'

'Well, why didn't you say so?' Jack spun the wheel again. The Anders Faircloud moved from the on-going lane back into the other-going lane, causing much distress amongst the other-going-laners.

'Got it now,' said Jack. 'Out of the way, fellas!' And he honked the horn.

'Well, you do know where the horn is.'

'Do you know what?'

'What?' said Eddie.

'I'll tell you what,' said Jack, 'this is great. Do you know that? Great! I'm driving a car. Do you know how great this is for me? This is . . .'

'Great?' said Eddie.

'As great as,' said Jack. 'As wonderful as, in fact. Marvellous. Incredible. I'm enjoying this *so* much.'

Jack took a sudden right turn, cutting across oncoming traffic and causing much sudden braking from it and much shunting of one car into another.

'And why did you do *that?*' Eddie asked from beneath the pressed tin dashboard.

'I don't know. Because I could, I suppose. Where would you like me to drive to?'

'I'd like you to stop. In fact I'd *love* you to stop.'

'Well, I'm not going to. So where would you like us to go?'

'Okay.' Eddie climbed out of his seat and peeped over the dashboard. 'Turn left at the next road and . . . Jack, do you feel all right?'

'I feel incredible,' said Jack, 'full of power, do you know what I mean?'

'It's the lotion.' Eddie covered his face as Jack put his foot down again. 'Bill's lotion, the stuff you were apparently supposed to rub on, rather than drink. I'd never actually seen him doing the actual rubbing in. I sleep late as a rule. I think it's pumped you up rather and . . . Oh my . . .'

Jack went 'Weeeeeeeeeee,' and then he went 'Ooooooooooooh!' and then he went 'Oh!' and 'Damn.' And then he said, 'We've stopped.'

'The clockwork's run down,' said Eddie. 'You put it under—how shall we put this?—certain strain.'

'What a rush,' said Jack, sitting back in the driving seat. 'Did I love that? Or did I not? I loved it. I did. It was wonderful. It was . . .'

And then Jack passed from consciousness once more.

'I think this is going to be a very emotional sort of a relationship,' said Eddie, to no one other than himself. 'But let's look on the bright side. By sheer chance, or coincidence, or a force greater than ourselves, which guides our paths and moulds of our destinies, we have stopped right outside Nursery Towers, the home of the late and lamented Humpty Dumpty.'

6

Humpty Dumpty.

Did he fall, or was he pushed, or was it that he jumped?

Or was it, in fact, none of the above?

There has always been controversy surrounding Humpty Dumpty's famous plunge from the wall. Historical details are sketchy at best. Eyewitness accounts conflict. And even the exact location of the original wall remains uncertain.*

Conspiracy theories abound. One hinges on the matter of Humpty's real identity. According to some, he was a failed Toy City TV stuntman called Terry Horsey, who reinvented himself by taking on the exotic, foreign-sounding name of Humpty Dumpty and performing a real-life stunt, without the aid of a crash mat.

This theory has been dubbed the 'Did He Fall (on purpose)? Theory'.

It does not, however, stand up to close scrutiny, as extensive searches through the Toy City TV archives have failed to turn up a single piece of footage, from any TV show, that involved a thirty-seven-stone stunt man.

The 'Was He Pushed? Theory' stands upon even shakier ground (ha ha). It incorporates a number of co-related sub-theories, listed below:

* In a famous lawsuit, two rival farmers, each claiming that the original wall stood upon their property, and each receiving a hearty annual turnover from tourists who paid to view it, sued each other. Humpty Dumpty refused to substantiate either claim and the case was thrown out of court. It is interesting to note that since his death in the swimming pool, several supposed 'Stones from the True Wall' have been put up for auction. Although of doubtful provenance, these have commanded high prices from collectors of relics.

Sub-theory 1: He was pushed by: (a) a jealous lover; (b) a miffed business associate; (c) a rival, either in love, or in business; or (d) an assassin hired by any of the above.

But he survived the fall.

Sub-theory 2: He did *not* survive the fall. In this theory, he actually died and was replaced by a lookalike.

Sub-theory 3: He *did* survive the fall, but was replaced by a lookalike anyway and went into seclusion somewhere.

Exactly where, and indeed *why*, is not explained.

The 'Did He Jump? Theory', currently enjoying a renaissance in Toy City's popular press, puts forward the failed suicide hypothesis. It hints at depression brought on by Humpty's obvious eating disorder and draws support from an interview he once gave on *The Tuffet*, a popular Toy City TV chat show hosted by the ever-youthful Miss Muffet, on which Humpty spoke at length about his weight problem.

Critics of this particular theory state that Humpty's appearance on the show was nothing more than a cynical marketing exercise to promote his latest book, *The H Plan Diet*.

Yet another theory has it that there was more than one Humpty Dumpty, but no wall involved: one Humpty fell from the side of a grassy knoll and another from the window of a book depository.

This is known as 'The Particularly Stupid Theory'.

Here endeth the theories.

For now.

There was a lot of manipulation involved. And that's not easy when you don't have opposing thumbs. Or even fingers. All you have to work with are paws, and crude paws to boot. (Or to paw.) Eddie dug around in the glove compartment. When he'd finally wormed out the hypodermic, it was the Devil-bear's own job for him to grip it and aim it and actually inject its contents into Jack.

The result was somewhat immediate.

'Are we there?' asked Jack, opening his eyes.

'We're here,' said Eddie, tossing the hypo out of the car and grinning painfully. 'Nice driving.'

'Piece of cake. So what now?'

'Okay. Well, we have to get in there. There might be a policeman on guard, so we . . . *whisper, whisper, whisper.*'

'We'll *what?*'

'You'll . . . *whisper, whisper, whisper.*'

'Why are you doing all this *whisper, whisper, whispering?*'
Eddie sighed. 'Did you understand any of it?' he asked.
'Yes, all,' said Jack.
'Then do it.'
'Fair enough.'

Nursery Towers was big. Which is to say, *big*. It was a major complex on the lower western slope of Knob Hill. Only the very rich lived here. Nursery Towers rose up and up and spread all around and about.
'There's money here,' said Jack, peering up. 'Big money.'
'Please try and keep your mind on the job.'
Jack swung open the driver's door and removed himself from the vehicle; Eddie followed him. 'Don't forget your fedora,' said Eddie.
Jack retrieved the hat from the rear seat, stuck it onto his head and closed the car door. Then he did much adjusting of his trenchcoat, straightening the belt and turning up the collar. 'How do I look?' he asked Eddie. 'Pretty darn smart, eh?'
Eddie sighed and nodded. 'What is it about trenchcoats,' he asked, 'that bring out the vanity in a man?'
'Search me.' Jack did shoulder-swaggerings and turned down the brim of his hat. 'But do I look the business, or what?'
'As handsome as. Now, you do remember everything I whispered to you?'
'Of course. I'm Bill Winkie, private eye and—'
'Save it 'til it's needed; follow me.'
'Ah no,' said Jack. 'I'm the detective, you're the detective's bear, *you* follow *me*.'
'Sweet as,' said Eddie, scowling as he said it. 'So which way do we go?'
'Right up the front steps and in through the big front door.'
'Wrong,' said the bear. 'Around the back and in by the tradesmen's entrance.'
'Oh, come on now.'
'Just do it the way I told you, please.'
'Well, as you ask so nicely. Then let's go.'
And so they went.

The tradesmen's entrance was in an alleyway. This was litter-strewn and unappealing. Jack turned up his nose.
'Knock at the door,' said Eddie, 'and do your stuff. Make me proud of you, eh?'

'Leave it to Bill,' said Jack, a-knocking at the door.

There was a bit of a wait. And then a bit more. Then there was a longer wait and then a longer one still.

'I don't much care for this waiting,' said Jack.

'It's second nature to me,' said Eddie. 'When I'm not getting drunk, or being thrown around, I'm generally waiting for something or other.'

They waited some more and then Jack knocked again.

This time there was no wait at all; the tradesmen's entrance door croaked open.

Jack was taken somewhat aback. 'It croaked,' he whispered to Eddie, 'rather than creaked. Why did it do that?'

'Who's on the knock at this fine tower block?' asked a very strange voice indeed.

Jack looked in and then Jack stepped back. Smartly, and right onto Eddie.

'Ow!' howled Eddie. 'Get off me.'

'Big frog!' howled Jack, getting off Eddie.

'Yes?' said the big frog. 'Bright as fizziness. What is the nature of your business?'

Jack chewed upon his upper lip. The big frog was a very big frog indeed, easily equal to himself in height, standing erect upon its long rear legs and all decked out in a rather spiffing tailcoat and wing-collared shirt, replete with a dashing spotty bow-tie. The big frog appeared to be made out of rubber.

'I am the concierge,' said the big frog. 'And you are a gormster, I perceive. Hurry up and take your leave.'

'Winkie,' said Jack. 'Bill Winkie, private eye. Here upon the business of Mr Anders.'

'Mr Anders, maker of toys, greatly beloved of girls and boys?'

'Do you know of another Mr Anders?'

The big frog licked his lips with an over-long flycatcher of a tongue. 'Naturally I know several,' it said, taking in a deep breath. 'Panders Anders, the pale poom runner, right royal rascal and son of a gunner. Ackabar Anders, the starlight meanderer, profligate poltroon, feckless philanderer. And of course, Anthony Anders the third, tall as a trouser and beaked as a bird.'

'What is all this?' Jack muttered in Eddie's direction. 'He speaks in rhyme.'

'Rhymey Frog,' said Eddie. 'Haven't you ever met a rhymey frog before?'

Jack shook his head. The rhymey frog prepared to slam shut the door.

'Ah, no,' said Jack, putting his foot in it. 'Very important business. Mr Anders, and all that. Kindly let us in.'

'Us?' said the frog. 'There's only one of you I see. Or do you wear a crown and use the royal "We"?'

'There's me and my bear,' said Jack, waving a hand towards Eddie.

'Hi,' said Eddie, waggling a paw. 'Pleased to meet you, I am sure.'

'I shall need from you a letter of introduction. To admit your entrance without any further interruption.'

'That didn't scan too well, did it?' said Jack.

'It's all in the enunciation,' replied the frog in a haughty tone. 'But to the crude, uncultured ear, even champagne sounds like beer.'

'My apologies,' said Jack. 'Now please let us in or I will be forced to shoot you dead.'

'No,' said Eddie. 'That's not what we agreed.'

'Yes, but—'

'Show him the money,' said Eddie.

'Money?' the frog said. 'Coin of gold? It's often used to bribe, I'm told.'

'Then you were told correctly.' Jack held out the few meagre coins that Eddie had given to him. The rhymey frog blinked bulbous and disdainful eyes at them.

'I know it's not much,' said Jack. 'But consider it a token down-payment. I have come to collect certain sums owing to Mr Anders. I am to collect them from the penthouse apartment of the late Humpty Dumpty. I am instructed by Mr Anders to furnish you with a percentage of these certain sums, to accommodate you for any inconvenience caused.'

'Well remembered,' whispered Eddie.

'Well . . .' said the frog, thoughtfully.

'Or I could come back later,' said Jack. 'Perhaps when you've gone off shift and the night porter is on.'

'Welcome, friend,' said the frog, swinging wide the door and snatching the coins from Jack's outstretched hand.

The big frog took the stairs in leaps and bounds. Jack and Eddie took the lift.

'Rhymey frog!' said Jack. 'What is *that* all about?'

'Have you never heard of energetic engineering?' Eddie asked.

'Are you sure you've got that right?' Jack asked.

'Of course. Well, possibly. Well, probably. It's something to do with very busy work being done in toy factories.'

'There's a great deal of that; I can vouch for it,' said Jack, having a fiddle with the lift buttons.

'Please don't touch those,' said Eddie.

'But it's the first time I've ever travelled in a posh lift like this. Can we stop at all the floors?'

'No,' said Eddie. 'But, as I was saying, energetic engineering. Busy busy busy. It's been known to drive men mad. And mad men make mistakes. Rhymey frogs, fluffy trains, grumpy clocks, frank chickens.'

'Don't they just get scrapped?'

'Not when they amuse Mr Anders.'

'I'd like to meet this Mr Anders.' The lift came to a standstill. 'We're here,' said Jack.

'No we're not. You pressed one of the buttons. I told you not to. Press the penthouse one. Let's see if we can beat that frog.'

They didn't beat that frog. He was waiting at the penthouse door, a bunch of shiny keys in his froggy fingers. He looked a little puffed, though. But then, frogs often do.

'The policemen stuck all this tape across the door,' said the frog. 'They said they'd come back some time soon, to stick on a whole lot more.'

Jack ran his finger along the strip of brightly coloured tape and licked his fingertip. 'Yellow berry,' he said. 'Very tasty.'

'Doing that's illegal,' said the frog.

'It is,' agreed Eddie. 'Yellow berry? Are you sure?'

Jack broke off a strip of the strip and stuck it into his mouth.

'Illegal,' said the frog once more.

'You're not rhyming that with anything,' said Jack, making lip-smacking sounds.

'That's probably because he lives in mortal dread of the police,' said Eddie. 'Them dishing out such vicious on-the-spot punishments to offenders and everything.'

'Quite so,' said Jack, hastily wiping his mouth. 'So, shall we go inside? Attend to the financial business of the important Mr Anders? Kindly open up the door, Mr Froggie.'

Mr Froggie handed Jack the keys. 'I'd rather you did it,' he said. 'I'd prefer not to touch the tape.'

Jack glanced at Eddie.

Eddie shrugged. 'We're here now,' he said. 'Might as well do it.'

Jack pulled away the yellow-berry-flavoured tape. 'Which key?' he asked the frog.

'Any one of them will do; they're all the same and none are new.'

'That's not very secure, is it?'

'No one who's not official ever gets past me. I'm as vigilant as it's frog-manly possible to be.'

'You can't argue with that,' Eddie said. 'Open up the door, Bill.'

'I'm in charge here.' The door to the late Humpty's apartment was a richly panelled silkwood affair, decorated with all manner of carved reliefs—mostly, it appeared, of fat folk falling from walls. Jack eyed the door appreciatively. This was a proper door. A proper rich person's door. The kind of door that he'd have for himself as soon as he'd made his fortune.

Jack turned a key and opened up the door. 'You wait here,' he told the frog as he and Eddie slipped into Humpty's penthouse. 'We won't be long.'

'Perhaps I ought to come inside,' said the frog. 'It's best that I, in there, should be. In the interests of security.'

Jack slammed the door upon him.

'Well, we're in,' said Eddie. 'Although it could have been easier.'

'I thought I did very well. I'm new to this detective game. Remember it was *me* who got us in. Not you.'

'I seem to recall that you were all for shooting the frog.'

'I was bluffing.'

'Right,' said Eddie. 'To work.'

'Right,' said Jack. 'I'll have a look around. See if I can find some clues.'

'No,' said Eddie, 'you just sit down quietly and don't touch anything. *I'll* search for clues.'

'Yes, but—'

'Jack,' said Eddie, '*I'm* the detective. You're my partner. *Junior* partner.'

Jack shrugged. 'Please yourself then.'

Humpty Dumpty's penthouse was opulent. It was palatial, it was magniloquent. It was eggy.

There were egg motifs on the richly woven carpets and the elegant silk wallpaper and on the fabrics of the furniture and even on the switches for the lights. Jack tinkered with one of these and lit up a gorgeous chandelier that hung overhead. It was festooned with hundreds of crystal eggs. Jack shook his head and whistled.

So this was what being rich was all about, was it? Then he'd have some of this. But not exactly like this. There was something all-too-much about this. It was the scale, Jack thought, thoughtfully. Where Tinto's bar had been too small for him, everything here was much too big.

Jack sat himself down on a great golden chariot of a chair in the vestibule and stretched his hands to either side of him. He couldn't even reach to the chair's arms. This Humpty had evidently been a fellow of considerable substance. Positively gargantuan.

Jack watched Eddie as he went to work. The bear paced up and down, cocking his head to this side and the other, backing up, throwing himself forward onto his stomach, wriggling about.

'How are you doing?' called Jack.

'Would you mind opening the doors to the pool area for me?' said Eddie.

Jack hastened to oblige. It took considerable effort to heave back the enormous doors, but when this was done, it proved well worthwhile.

Jack found himself in the pool area. The pool itself was egg-shaped, which came as no surprise to Jack. It was mosaic-tiled all around and about and many of these tiles were elliptical.

The entire pool area was sheltered by a great stained-glass dome of cathedralesque proportions. Jack gawped up at it in wonder. There were no egg motifs to be found up there; rather, the whole was a profusion of multi-coloured flowers, wrought in thousands of delicate panes of glass. The sunlight, dancing through these many-hued panes, cast wistful patterns over the pool area and Jack was entranced. He had never seen anything quite so beautiful in all of his life.

The apex of the dome was an enormous stained-glass sunflower, its golden petals radiating out from a clear glass centre. Jack gave another whistle. He'd definitely have one of these roofs when he'd made his fortune.

Jack pushed back the brim of his fedora. The roof was stunningly beautiful. But there was something . . . something that jarred with him. Something that didn't seem entirely right. That appeared to be out of place. But what was it? Jack shrugged. What did he, Jack, know about stained-glass roofs? Nothing, was the answer to that. The roof was beautiful and that was all there was to it.

The beauty of the roof above, however, was somewhat marred by that which lay directly below it. Specifically, in the pool, or more specifically still, on the surface of the pool's water: a very nasty crusty-looking scum.

'So how *are* you doing?' Jack asked the ursine detective.

Eddie shook his tatty head. 'It's tricky,' he said. 'So many policemen's feet have trampled all around and about the place. But there's no evidence of a struggle. Humpty was bathing in the pool. The murderer took him by surprise.'

Jack peered down at the pool with its nasty crusty scum. 'Boiled him?' he asked. 'How?'

'Not sure yet,' said Eddie. 'My first thoughts were that the murderer simply turned up the pool's heating system. But that would have taken time and Humpty would have climbed out when the water got too hot.'

'Perhaps Humpty was drugged or asleep in the pool.'

'That's not how it was done. I'll tell you how it was done as soon as I've figured it out.'

'Hm,' said Jack, putting a thumb and forefinger to his chin and giving it a squeeze.

Eddie paced around the pool, did some more head cocking, some more backing away and then some more throwing himself down onto his stomach and wriggling about. Then he stood up and began to frantically beat at his head.

'What *are* you doing?' Jack asked.

'Rearranging my brain cells,' said Eddie. 'Vigorous beating peps them up no end.'

'Your head's full of sawdust.'

'I know my own business best.'

'I'll leave you to it then.' Jack sat down on a poolside lounger. It was a most substantial poolside lounger, capable of accommodating, at the very least, a fat family. Possibly two. No, that would be silly, *one* fat family. And no more than that.

Jack swung to and fro on the lounger and looked all around and about. Around and about and up and down, then up again once more.

Eddie was down on his belly once again, leaning over the pool.

'What are you doing now?' Jack asked.

'Come and give me a hand, if you will.'

Jack swung out of the lounger.

'Take my legs,' said Eddie. 'Lower me down. But *don't* drop me in the water.'

'Okay. What have you seen?' Jack lowered Eddie over the edge.

'Eleven, twelve, thirteen,' said Eddie. 'Interesting. Pull me up, please.' Jack pulled Eddie up.

'See it?' said Eddie, pointing with a paw. 'The scum on the side of the pool. The pool water's lower than it should be. The scum has left traces, like beer does on the inside of a glass as you drink from it. There're thirteen separate lines going down. And it's thirteen days since Humpty was boiled. What do you make of that?'

'The pool water has dropped a little each day. Perhaps there's a leak.'

'The water would drain away steadily if there was a leak; there wouldn't be any lines.'

Jack shrugged. 'Evaporation,' he said. 'It's warm enough in here.'

'Not *that* warm. The stained-glass roof keeps direct sunlight out, as you can see.'

Jack looked up again. The roof looked the same as it had done before: stunningly beautiful, but not entirely *right*.

'Get me that rubber ring,' said Eddie. 'I want to get an overview from the middle of the pool.'

'You're going to float about in that scummy water?'

'*On*, not *in*.'

Jack brought over the rubber ring, put it into the pool and lifted Eddie onto it. 'Push me out,' said Eddie. Jack pushed him out.

'It's something very clever,' said Eddie, 'whatever it is.'

'Eddie,' said Jack, 'what was the exact time of death? Does anybody know?'

'Midday,' said Eddie. 'Mr Froggie was doing his rounds; he heard the scream.'

'Midday,' said Jack, thoughtfully. 'What's the time now, do you think?'

'I don't have a watch. Around that time, I suppose.'

'Eddie,' cried Jack, 'get out of the pool.'

'What?' said Eddie.

'Get out of the pool, quickly.'

'Look,' said Eddie, 'I'm the detective and although I appreciate you trying to help—no, strike that, actually I don't. I think that the best thing you could do is—'

'Bong!' went a clock, somewhere in the late Humpty's apartment.

'Eddie, get out of the pool. Row or something.'

'I'm not putting a paw in that scum.'

'Get out of the pool.'

BONG.

'What are you going on about?'

BONG.

'Eddie, quickly.'

'What?'

BONG.

'Hurry.'

'What?'

BONG

'Waaaaaaaaaaah!' Jack dived into the pool.

BONG.

'Have you gone completely insane?' called Eddie.

Jack struck out with a will.

BONG.

Jack floundered in the scummy water and grabbed the rubber ring.

BONG.

Jack floundered further and grabbed Eddie.

BONG.

Jack snatched Eddie from the ring.

BONG.

Jack swam fiercely and dragged Eddie to the edge of the pool.

BONG.

Jack hauled himself and Eddie out of the horrible water.

BONG.

A shaft of light swept down through the central portion of the stained-glass window. Through the eye of the great sunflower. Through the huge, clear lens. The magnified concentrated sunlight struck the water, causing an all-but-instantaneous effect. The water boiled and frothed. Viciously. Brutally. In a deadly, all-consuming maelstrom.

'Stone me,' said Eddie, from the safety of the poolside.

Jack spat Humpty scum, but didn't have much to say. 'Clever,' said Eddie, squeezing himself and oozing scum water from his seams. 'I did say clever. And *that was* clever. Clever and fiendish.'

The two were now in Humpty's kitchen; Jack was swathed in towels. Eddie ceased his squeezings and struggled to pour hot black coffee. 'I'd have been a goner there,' he said. 'I'd have cooked. I don't know what the effects would have been, but I'd bet I wouldn't have been Eddie Bear any more. Horrible thought. Thanks for saving me, Jack. You're as brave as.'

'No problems,' said Jack. 'Although I don't feel altogether too well. I think I swallowed some Dumpty.'

'It's been repeatedly boiled. It should be free of any contamination.'

'That doesn't make me feel a whole lot better.' Jack sipped at the coffee. 'And look at my trenchcoat and my fedora, ruined.'

'I'll see to it that you get brand-new ones, made to measure. Somehow. You saved my life. How did you work it out?'

'The stained-glass roof just didn't look right. I didn't see what it was at first. Then I realised that the centre of the sunflower at the very top of the dome was clear glass, and convex. A huge lens. And *sun* flower. And midday sun. It all sort of fell into place. I told you how I worked in the factory and the sun used to beat in through the glass roof and there was this one bit like a convex lens and how it used to burn me at midday.'

'I remember,' said Eddie. 'We'll make a detective out of you yet. So old Humpty was taking his regular midday dip and . . . whoosh.'

'What I don't get,' said Jack, 'is why the murderer didn't return and remove the lens?'

'Why should he bother? The job was done.'

'Because it's evidence. The police could surely trace the maker of the lens. *We* could, couldn't we? Do you want me to climb up there and get it down?'

'And how do you propose to do that? We're twenty-three storeys up and I can't see how you'd get to it from the inside. That dome is huge.'

'We'll leave it then,' said Jack.

'This is no ordinary murderer we're dealing with,' said Eddie. 'Mind you, it's the bunny that intrigues me the most.'

'Bunny?' said Jack. 'What bunny?'

'This bunny,' said Eddie. 'This bunny here. Eddie fumbled open the door of Humpty's fridge. It was a fridge of considerable dimensions. 'Mr Dumpty was a notable gourmand. That fat boy knew how to eat, believe me. Yet his fridge is completely empty, but for this. A single hollow chocolate bunny.'

Eddie took the dear little fellow up in his paws and gave it a shake. 'What do you make of that then, Jack?'

'Let's eat it,' said Jack. 'I'm starving.'

'I think it's probably evidence.'

'Let's eat it anyway. We can remember what it looked like.'

There came now a sudden beating at the apartment door. This beating was accompanied by shouts. These shouts were the shouts of policemen. 'Open up,' shouted these shouts. 'This is the police.'

'Oh dear,' said Eddie. 'I think Mr Froggie has done us wrong.'

'You talk to the policemen,' said Jack. 'I'm in a towel.'

'I think we should run, Jack. We're not supposed to be here. Gather up your wet clothes.'

'Yes, but.' Jack gathered up his wet clothes and his sodden fedora.

'Put on your wet clothes and hurry.'

'Yes, but.'

'Believe me, Jack, you really don't want to get involved with policemen.'

'All right,' said Jack, trying to struggle into his soggy trousers.

'Hurry,' counselled Eddie.

Policemen put their shoulders to the door.

And Jack took frantically to hurrying.

7

It is a fact well known to those who know it well that we can only truly know what we personally experience. Above and beyond that, it's all just guesswork and conjecture.

Of course, there are those who will take issue with this evident profundity. They will say, 'Ah, but what do we *really understand* by *truly know* and *personally experience*?' But to these issue takers we must say, 'Get a life and get a girlfriend.'

We really *can* only truly know what we personally experience. And when we experience something entirely new, something that we have never experienced before, it can come as something of a shock. And it can be hard at first to fully comprehend.

Jack, for instance, had never before heard a really big, expensive silkwood apartment door being smashed from its hinges. And so the sounds of its smashing were alien to his ears.

The fraboius grametting of the lock against its keep was positively malagrous in its percundity. The greebing and snattering was starkly blark.

And as for the spondabulous carapany that the broken door made as it struck the vestibule floor . . .

. . . the word phnargacious is hardly sufficient.

Rapantaderely phnargacious would be more accurate.

And as to what happened after this, it is probably all for the best that Jack neither heard nor saw any of it.

Laughing policemen bounced into the late Humpty's vestibule. They fairly bounced, and they 'ho ho ho'd' as they did so.

They were all jolly-jolly and all-over blue,
With big jolly bellies, a jollysome crew.

Their faces were jolly,
Their eyes jolly too.
And they wouldn't think twice,
About jolly-well knocking seven bells of blimey out of you if you so much as looked at them in a funny way. Because for all their jollity, they were a right bunch of brutal, merciless, bullying . . .
And so on.

Which at least was how the rhymey frog would have put it. But the rhymey frog did not accompany these jolly laughing policemen into the apartment. Instead, they were joined by a short and portly jolly red-faced being, composed, it appeared, of perished rubber. He answered to the name of Chief Inspector Wellington Bellis. But only to his superiors.

Mostly he answered only when called 'sir'.

For all his jolly red-facedness, Chief Inspector Bellis was having a rough day. It is the nature of Chief Inspectors, no matter where they are to be found, nor indeed upon which day of the week they are found, to be having a rough day.

Chief Inspectors are *always* having a rough day.

It's a 'Chief Inspector thing'.

Chief Inspector Bellis was having a particularly rough day on this particular day. Earlier, he had been called into the presence of his superior, The Chief of All Police, the one being that Bellis called 'sir', and torn off a strip (a strip of arm on this occasion), upbraided (with the use of real braid) and berated (which involved a genuine bee, a wooden rat, but happily no ed).

The Chief of All Police wanted results. He wanted to know why Bellis had not yet tracked down the murderer of Humpty Dumpty. Although the Toy City press were selling the populace the story that Humpty had committed suicide, the police knew that it was Murder Most Foul, and questions were being asked in very high places as to why Bellis had not yet tracked down the murderer.

The Chief of All Police had handed Bellis a secret memo and Bellis had raised his perished eyebrows and dropped his perished jaw onto his perished chest. The memo contained most terrible news. And then the telephone had rung.

The Chief of All Police had handed the receiver to Bellis.

'There's a rhymey frog on the line,' he had said. 'Deal with it.'

And so here was Bellis, now having a *really* rough day, here to deal with it.

Bellis stood in the ruptured doorway puffing out his perished cheeks and making fists with his podgy, perished hands.

'Why?' he shouted. 'Why? Why? Why?'

'Ho ho ho and why what, sir?'

'Why, officer,' asked Bellis, 'did you break down the crubbin' door? I ordered you to wait until the rhymey frog went and got his spare set of keys.'

The laughing policeman made a troubled, though no less jolly-looking face. 'I . . . er . . . ha ha ha, was using my initiative, sir.'

Bellis scowled and shook his fists. 'Well, now we're in, I suppose. Go and arrest the malfeasant.'

'The *what*, sir?' the officer chuckled.

'The criminal, the intruder, the unlawful trespasser.'

'Which one of these do you want arrested first, sir?'

'Do you have a name?' asked Bellis, glaring upward daggers.

'Officer Chortle, sir. I'm a Special Constable. I've got my name printed on my back, see?'

The officer turned to display the name that made him special. Bellis kicked him hard in the backside. 'Go and arrest. It's what you do, isn't it? It's what you're for?'

'To uphold the law, using reasonable force when necessary, which, as you know, is always necessary, sir.' Officer Chortle saluted with his truncheon, bringing down a shower of crystal eggs from the chandelier.

'Then get to it. Bring me the offender. All of you, get to it!'

Police officers to the right and left of Bellis hastened to oblige.

'And don't break anything else.'

The police officers went about their business, leaving Bellis all alone in the vestibule, to listen to expensive things being broken by officers of the law.

Bellis recognised these sounds. These sounds weren't alien to his perished ears. He'd heard such sounds, and similar, many times before. The Chief Inspector sighed and shook his head and then delved into a perished pocket and brought out the secret memo. He read it once more and once more shook his head. This was bad, very bad. The day, already a rough day, looked like getting altogether rougher.

At length, and at breadth, the officers returned, downcast.

'Gone,' said Officer Chortle, with laughter in his voice. 'They've all gone, even the dressmaker.'

'Trespasser!' Bellis threw up his hands and made fists with them once more.

'You've dropped your piece of paper,' said Officer Chortle.

'Shut up!'

'Oh dear.' The rhymey frog peered in at the devastation. 'If you please, I've brought my keys.'

'Somewhat late,' said Bellis. 'The bird has flown.'

'Bird, too?' said Officer Chortle, a giggle escaping his lips.

'Shut up. Go downstairs and wait by the wagon. All of you. Now!'

The officers took their leave, laughing merrily as they did so and all but marching over the rhymey frog.

'Gone,' said Bellis. 'Escaped. Do you have any thoughts on this?'

The rhymey frog opened his big wide mouth and prepared to express his thoughts in an epic forty-verser.

'No,' said Bellis, raising once more the hands he had temporarily lowered. 'I do not wish to hear them. Speak to me only of the trespasser. And speak to me in prose, or I'll run you in and lock you up and have Officer Chortle do things to you that you'll never wish to recite. And he'll laugh all the time as he does them. Which always makes it that little more frightening, in my opinion. What do you think?'

The knees of the rhymey frog began to knock together. 'Tricky,' he said. 'Tricky, dicky.'

'Careful,' cautioned Bellis.

'It was a man.' The rhymey frog took to rolling his eyes. 'And men all look the same to me.'

'A *man* was here?' Bellis raised his eyebrows high.

'Your face all cracks when you do that,' said the frog. 'Mr Anders could fix that for you. With a stick and a brush and a small pot of glue.'

'I have no wish to bother Mr Anders,' said Bellis. 'Tell me about the man who was here. Anything. Anything at all.'

'He had a bear with him,' said the frog. 'A rotten old bear with mismatched eyes. And a big fat belly about this size.' The frog mimed the dimension. The Chief Inspector glared anew.

'No more rhyming! And I don't want to hear about some stupid teddy bear. A major crime has been committed here. One of the city's most notable elder citizens has been murdered.'

'The papers say it was suicide,' said the frog.

'You heard the scream!' shouted the Chief Inspector. '*You* reported the crime.'

'Oh yes,' said the rhymey frog. 'So I did. That was very public-spirited of me, wasn't it?'

Chief Inspector Bellis rocked upon his perished rubber heels. 'The trespasser was probably the murderer,' he said, 'because murderers always return to the scene of the crime.'

'Why?' asked the rhymey frog.

'Because it's a tradition, or an old charter, or something. Never mind why, they just do.'

The rhymey frog now began to tremble all over.

'Yes,' said Bellis. 'Exactly, he could have done for you too. I will have to ask you to accompany me to the station, where Officer Chortle will beat a statement out of you.'

'Oh no.' The rhymey frog was now all-a-quake.

'Then make it easy on yourself. Give me a detailed description of the man.'

'I don't know. I just don't know. All men look the same to me. I'm sorry.'

'All right,' said Bellis, 'never mind. Go off about your business.'

The rhymey frog looked all around and about. 'I'll get a dustpan and a brush, some paper and a quill. I'll list all the broken things and then I can send you the bill.'

There was a moment of silence. It was brief.

'I think I'll just go and have my lunch instead,' said the frog. And he turned to hop away.

And then he paused and then he turned back to Bellis. 'There is one thing,' he said. 'I don't know if it will be of any help.'

'Go on,' said Bellis.

'The murderer told me his name,' said the rhymey frog. 'His name is Bill Winkie.'

'There you go,' said Eddie Bear. 'They've all gone now. They've made a terrible mess, but they've gone.'

Jack stared around at the mess and then he stared down at Eddie. Jack's face was blue once more, but this time it had nothing to do with inferior headwear.

'F . . . f . . . fridge,' stammered Jack. 'W . . . why did w . . . we have to hide in the f . . . f . . . fridge?'

'Because it was the best place to hide,' said Eddie. 'The police neglected to look in it the first time they were here. It seemed a pretty safe bet to me that they wouldn't look in it this time either.'

'I'll die.' Jack shook from the frosted hairs on his head to the trembly toes on his feet. 'I'm f . . . f . . . frozen. You're not even s . . . s . . . shaking.'

'I'm a bear,' said Eddie, brightly. 'We bears don't feel the cold. Not even when we're as sodden as. If you know what I mean, and I'm sure that you do.'

Jack gathered his trenchcoat around himself. It was even colder than he was. 'I'm going home,' he managed to say. 'I've had enough of city life.'

'Don't be a quitter.' Eddie gave Jack's shaking leg an encouraging pat.

'I'm dying.'

'You'll thaw out. Hobble back to the pool area. It's nice and warm out there.'

Eddie led the way and Jack did the hobbling.

At length, and at quite some length it was, Jack was finally all thawed out, and pretty much dried out too. Throughout this lengthy process of thawing and drying, Jack maintained a brooding silence.

Eddie, being not a bear to cherish a silence, spent the period smiling encouragingly and doing cute little teddy-bearish things. Not that Eddie was capable of doing cute little teddy-bearish things with any degree of genuine commitment.

'So then,' said Eddie, when the time seemed right, 'shall we be off about our business?'

'You can,' said Jack. 'I'm leaving.'

'Oh no,' said Eddie. 'Don't say that. We're partners, Jack. You agreed. We shook on it and everything.'

'Maybe we did. But being with you is a dangerous business.'

'Yes, but danger is exciting. And you wanted some excitement in your life. Didn't you?'

Jack shrugged. The shoulders of his trenchcoat rose to his ears and then stayed there.

'Look at me,' said Jack. 'I'm a wreck. I'm starving and I'm cold and I'm broke, my fedora's ruined and my trenchcoat's all gone crisp.'

'It's a dry-clean-only,' said Eddie.

'A raincoat that's dry-clean only?'

'Bill Winkie would never have gone out in the rain wearing his trenchcoat.'

Jack shook his head.

'But it does look good on you. You're a born detective. Come on, perk up. I'll buy you lunch.'

'You don't have any money.'

'I've a penny or two.' Eddie patted at the pockets of his trenchcoat. Eddie's trenchcoat looked as good as new. He grinned painfully. 'I can wangle us some lunch at a chum of mine's. Stick with me, kidder. We'll succeed and you'll get all the fortune you came seeking.'

Jack shook his head dismally. 'You'll be better off without me,' he said. 'I'm nothing but bad luck. It's because I'm cursed. A farmer I met on the way to the city cursed me. He said, "I curse you Jack. May you never know wealth. May all that you wish for be denied you." '

'What a horrid man,' said Eddie. 'Why did he curse you like that?'

Jack shrugged again and this time his trenchcoat returned to his shoulders. 'Bad grace, I suppose. Just because I shot off his ear and made him jump into a pit full of spikes.'

'There's no pleasing some people,' said Eddie. 'But we're a team, you and me. And listen, Jack, I need you. I can't solve this case without you. Please don't run away. We did shake and you did give me your word.'

Jack managed one more shrug. 'All right,' he said. 'I did give you my word. I will stay until you've solved the case. But then I'm moving on. There will be another city somewhere. Perhaps I'll find my fortune there.'

'Another city?' Eddie made a thoughtful face. 'I wonder if there *is* another city.'

'Bound to be,' said Jack.

'Well, perhaps. But I find such thoughts as fearsome as. I'll stick with what I know. And what I know is *this* city.'

'Feed me in this city,' said Jack. 'Feed me now.'

'Right,' said Eddie. 'Let's go. Oh, and we'll take that hollow chocolate bunny with us. That's a clue if ever there was one. It might have fingerprints or something.'

'Ah,' said Jack, and he made a certain face.

'Ah?' said Eddie. 'And what is the meaning of that certain face you're making?'

'About the bunny.'

'What about the bunny?'

'I ate it,' said Jack. 'While we were in the fridge. I was so hungry. And there were all these alien sounds. These malagrous gramettings and really spondabulous carapany.'

'You *ate* the evidence?' said Eddie. 'Well, that's a new one.'

'I'm sorry, but I was starving.'

A sudden high-pitched shriek caused Jack and Eddie to turn their heads. In the doorway to the pool area stood the rhymey frog, dustpan in one hand, brush in the other.

The rhymey frog shrieked once again, cried 'Eeek it's the murderer!', dropped his dustpan and his brush and hopped away at speed.

Jack looked at Eddie.

And Eddie looked at Jack.

'What did he mean by *that*?' asked Jack.

'Ah,' said Eddie. 'You didn't hear everything that went on while we were hiding in the fridge, did you?'

'No,' said Jack. 'Only the alien sounds. I wolfed down the bunny and stuck my hands over my ears after that. Why did the frog just call me a murderer?'

'Well . . .' Eddie made a certain face of his own. 'I think it better if I explain that to you over lunch.'

Eddie followed the direction taken by the frog.

'Hold on,' cried Jack. 'Tell me what's going on.'

'It's no big deal. Let's do lunch.'

'It *is* a big deal. Come back.'

'I'll tell you on the way, then.' Eddie reached the vestibule.

'Tell me now,' said Jack, scooping Eddie up and holding him out at arm's length.

'Don't do that to me.' Eddie struggled. 'It's undignified; let me down.'

'Tell me what's going on. Tell me now.' Jack shook Eddie all about.

'No.' Eddie struggled some more. 'Put me down.'

'I won't put you down until you've told me.'

'Hold on, Jack, what's that?' Eddie pointed.

'Don't try to distract me. Answer my question.'

'No, there's something there on the floor. It wasn't there when we came in.'

'It's a broken door,' said Jack, shaking Eddie ever more violently.

'No, the paper. Help. Stop. Let me down.'

Jack let Eddie down.

'There,' said Eddie, wobbling on his paws. 'Pick that up, Jack. What is that?'

'It's just a piece of paper.' Jack picked it up and handed it to Eddie. 'Now tell me why the frog called me a murderer.'

'In a minute. Oh dear me!' Eddie let the piece of paper fall from his paws.

'What does it say?' Jack asked. 'What does it say on the paper?'

'It says,' said Eddie, and he paused, 'that Little Boy Blue has been murdered.'

8

Jack, who was feeling somewhat down, perked somewhat up when he was once more behind the wheel of Bill's splendid automobile. But as he swung this wheel around, the pendulum of his mood swung with it. 'About this business of the frog calling me a murderer.' Jack brrrmed the clockwork engine.

'Forget all that.' Eddie, standing on the passenger seat, pointed through the windscreen. 'I think he was just a bit upset about the door getting broken and the apartment getting ransacked and everything. Don't let it upset you, Jack. Cast it from your mind. It's as irrelevant as. Turn right, please.'

'Hm,' went Jack. 'Then what about this second murder?' Jack turned right rather sharply, causing a clockwork cyclist to spill from his clockwork cycle.

'Careful,' said Eddie. 'Please be careful. We don't want to draw any more attention to ourselves.'

'Any *more* attention?'

'Just drive, Jack. First on the left here.'

Jack took the first on the left on the two left wheels of the car.

'But what *about* this second murder?' Jack asked once more when the car was back on four wheels and spinning merrily along. 'Tell me this, Eddie. Humpty Dumpty and Little Boy Blue. They were—how shall I put this?'

'Meatheads?' Eddie suggested.

'Men,' said Jack. 'They were men, rather than toys.'

'The old rich,' said Eddie, covering his face with his paws as toy pedestrians scattered before the on-rushing motorcar. 'You won't find

many of your race here in Toy City. But those you will find are generally rich.'

'On the fortunes they made from royalties on their nursery
rhymes.'

'Like I told you, yes. Look out!'

'Look out at *what*?' There was a clattering of tinplate against tin-
plate and something colourful mangled under the wheels. 'What *was*
that?' Jack asked Eddie.

'Only a clockwork clown,' said the bear. 'He's a bit mashed-up, but
I think he'll be all right. I've never cared much for clowns myself. How
about you, Jack?'

'I don't like them,' said Jack, and drove on.

Shortly, however, the clockwork motor ran down and Jack was
forced to get out and rewind the car.

Then Jack drove on some more.

'So what *about* this second murder?' Jack asked once again. 'Do you
have any theories?'

'We haven't visited the crime scene yet. We'll get some lunch first
and see about fixing you up with a disguise.'

'Disguise?' Jack asked. 'Why do I need a disguise?'

'Trust me,' said Eddie. 'You *do* need a disguise.'

At Eddie's bidding, Jack brought Bill's car to a wheel-shrieking halt,
which raised an impressive shower of sparks that Eddie wasn't impressed by.

'You've worn out the tyres,' he told Jack.

'Sorry,' said Jack. 'So where are we?'

'At my chum Wibbly's.'

'And Wibbly runs a restaurant?' Jack peered out through the windscreen. They were not in the swankiest part of town. The buildings, although constructed in the vernacular Alphabet brick that typified the
architecture of Toy City, had that faded, tired look to them, which told
Jack that this wasn't one of the better neighbourhoods.

Jack made disdainful sniffings with his nose. 'Not a gourmet
restaurant then? Do you not have any posh, rich friends, Eddie?'

The bear did not dignify this with a reply.

'Sorry,' said Jack, once again. 'So what does your chum Wibbly do?'

'Well.' Eddie pushed open the passenger door. 'He used to be a
professional wobbler, but since the accident, he doesn't do much of
anything.'

Jack climbed from the car and leaned upon the bonnet. 'But he
does have food in his fridge?'

'Fridge?' Eddie rolled his button eyes, which really had to be seen to be believed. 'Just follow me, Jack. And when you meet Wibbly, try not to look shocked by his appearance.'

'This sounds promising,' said Jack, and he followed Eddie.

Wibbly inhabited a basement flat, but of course it wasn't referred to as a basement flat. No one who actually lives in a basement flat ever refers to it as a basement flat. It's just not done. People who live in basement flats refer to their flats as *garden* flats. So Wibbly lived in a *garden* flat. Though without a garden. Or indeed, any windows.

Which made it a cellar, really.

The cellar steps had been boarded over to form a steep wooden ramp. Jack struggled down this, attempting to maintain his balance. Eddie gave up the unequal struggle and simply tumbled to the bottom.

Jack helped Eddie up. 'It doesn't smell too good down here. Somewhat ripe, shall we say.'

'Just be polite,' said Eddie. 'Wibbly is my friend. And please try not to look shocked when you see him.'

'Trust *me*,' said Jack. 'Would *I* let you down?'

'Knock at the knocker.'

'You're nearest,' said Jack.

The door was low, the knocker was low. Eddie knocked at the knocker.

Knock knock knock, went Eddie Bear. 'Just smile and be polite,' he said to Jack.

'Just trust me. I won't let you down.'

From beyond the door came creaking sounds, and sounds that were, for the most part, new to Jack. He recognised the basic creakings, but the subtle nuances of the scranchings and the endulating shugs had him cocking his head upon one side.

'Don't do that,' said Eddie. 'It makes you look like a complete gormster.'

'Sorry,' said Jack, and he straightened his neck.

'And be polite.'

'I will. I promise.'

The door eased open a crack and a beady eye peeped out.

'Wibbly,' said Eddie Bear.

'Eddie Bear,' said Wibbly.

Wibbly swung wide the door.

'Aaaagh!' screamed Jack. 'It's a monster.'

Jack was counselled to stay out of sight whilst Eddie engaged in sensitive negotiations through the letterbox. Much emphasis was put on the fact that Jack was a bumpkin from out of town, all but bereft of intelligence and given to sudden unexpected outbursts. But he was a harmless, simple soul, whom Eddie had taken under his wing.

Out of sight, Jack stewed over this. But the thought of stew made him ever more hungry. And so he suffered in silence.

Presently Wibbly, brought almost to the point of tears by Eddie's pleas for mercy on behalf of the poor simpleton, allowed the two of them in.

Eddie made Jack promise once more to be polite.

Jack made Eddie go first.

The 'sub-level' apartment—apparently Wibbly preferred this term to 'cellar'—was 'economically furnished'. Which is to say that there wasn't much furniture at all.

There weren't any chairs, but then, why would there have been? Wibbly couldn't sit down.

Wibbly was one of those wibbly wobbly toys with legless, convex bottom portions, filled up with lead shot that could be endlessly battered backwards and forwards, only to roll upright again and again and again.

Until they finally broke.

It wasn't easy to break them, as they were made of stern and durable stuff. But a child has a lot of time on its hands. And a determined child can break anything, even an anvil, if he or she is determined enough.

Wibbly still wobbled and wouldn't fall down.

But he lacked for a lot of his head.

He possessed a degree of face, located on the left-hand side. But much of his head was merely void. He had a dangling eye and a row of exposed teeth. He was not a thing of joy to gaze upon.

'Wibbly, this is Jack,' said Eddie. 'Say hello to Wibbly, Jack.'

Jack made the face of a simpleton and did that thing with his hands that people do when impersonating simpletons, that thing which is no longer considered politically correct, but which people still do anyway, because it makes other people laugh. Particularly when the doer and the viewers have all had a few drinks.

'What a complete gormster,' said Wibbly. 'Looks like he's been taking a swim in that dry-clean-only trenchcoat. Why did you bring him here, Eddie?'

Jack looked on in morbid fascination as the exposed teeth rose and fell and half a tongue waggled between them. How could this thing speak? How could it move? It was all but hollow. Jack shook his head. There was some big secret here, in this strange city. Some *big* secret.

Mr Anders, the kindly, loveable white-haired old toymaker, had to be the brains behind it all. He had to be the one who held the Big Secret. Jack wondered whether Mr Anders might be looking for an apprentice. Working for him and learning the Big Secret would be infinitely preferable to knocking about in dark cellars, conversing with fractured wobbly men and having to impersonate a dullard.

Infinitely preferable!

'He's Bill's cousin,' said Eddie, smiling towards Jack. 'I'm looking after him while Bill's on his holidays.'

'Holidays?' said Wibbly, revolving on his axis, which afforded Jack a view of his all-but-hollow head. 'The word on the street is—'

'I don't care what the word on the street is.' Eddie tried to fold his arms, but, as ever, failed. 'Bill will be back. But until he is, I'm dealing with his case. And Jack here is helping me.'

'Just what this city needs, another Jack.' Wibbly wobbled (but he didn't fall down).

'What of this?' asked Jack.

'The city does suffer from a surfeit of Jacks,' Eddie explained. 'There's a Jack B. Nimble, and Jack of Jack and Jill, and Jack Spratt.'

'And Little Jack Horner,' said Wibbly.

'And Big Jack Black,' said Eddie.

'Who's Big Jack Black?' asked Jack.

'Another Preadolescent Poetic Personality.' Eddie sat down on Wibbly's floor.

'Well, I've never heard of him.'

'Of course you haven't. Because he never got famous. He's one of the sorry few meatheads whose nursery rhymes never caught on.'

Jack did sniffings. 'So why did Big Jack Black's rhyme never catch on?' he asked.

Wibbly chuckled loudly. The sound echoed up from his hollow belly and, had there been windows, would surely have rattled them. 'Recite it, Eddie,' he said to the bear. 'You can remember it, can't you?'

'I think so,' said Eddie. 'It goes like this:

'Big Jack Black
'Lived in a sack,
'Lived in a sack did he.
'He dined upon cripples,
'And little boys' nipples,
'Served upon toast for his tea.'

''Nuff said, I think,' said Wibbly.

Jack shook his head once more and his stomach grumbled loudly.

'Nice grumbling.' Wibbly offered Jack half a smile, for it was all he possessed. 'Your belly's as empty as my own. I generally have a bucket or two of lead shot at this time of day. Perhaps you'd care to join me?'

'I don't think that would agree with my digestion,' said Jack.

'He's fussy. For a loon,' said Wibbly.

'Don't wind the lad up, Wibbly,' said Eddie. 'Give him some bread and milk or something.'

'Anything edible will do,' said Jack.

Wibbly had some bread, which was not altogether hard, if you left the crusts. And some milk that wasn't altogether evil-smelling, if you didn't smell it too closely. And even some cradberry jam that wasn't altogether unspeakable, if you didn't speak about it and took the trouble to scrape the fur off the top.

Jack, who had now reached the point where he was prepared to eat almost anything, ate almost everything. With relish.

But without relish, as there wasn't any relish.

Eddie ate what was left of the jam. Including the furry bits. 'I don't know what it is about jam,' he said, wiping a paw over his now jammy face. 'I can't stand honey, but I do love jam.'

'Nonconformist,' said Wibbly, ladling lead shot in through the hole in his head. 'So what have you really come for, Eddie? It wasn't just for a free lunch.'

'Well, it *was*.' Eddie had his paw now stuck in the jam pot. 'But it was also for a bit of information and a small favour or two.'

'That's what friends are for,' said Wibbly.

Eddie smiled. And struggled.

'To ponce off,' said Wibbly.

'Oh, come on, Wibbly.' Eddie now fought to free his paw. 'Remember that it was Bill who found you this place and built you the ramp down the stairs and . . .'

'Yes, all right,' said Wibbly. 'And I look after his dodgy gear and everything.'

'You store certain sensitive items.' Eddie rolled around on the floor, fighting with the jam pot. Jack, who could bear no more of it, eased out Eddie's paw and helped him back to his feet.

'Thanks,' said Eddie. 'Friendship, see.'

'Dullards don't count,' said Wibbly. 'Dullards will befriend anyone who feeds them. But go on, what do you want?'

'A disguise for the dullard.'

'What?' said Jack. 'This disguise business again. I like the trenchcoat and the fedora.'

'You're going under cover. You need a disguise.'

'I don't want a disguise.'

'He doesn't want a disguise,' said Wibbly.

'Thank you,' said Jack.

'He wants a smack,' said Wibbly. 'Shall I give him one? I used to be red–hot at head–butts. But, you know how it is.'

'I *don't* want a disguise,' said Jack once again.

'He *does* want a disguise,' said Eddie. 'From Bill's trunk.'

'He'd look good as a clown,' said Wibbly with another hollow chuckle.

'I thought, a whore,' said Eddie.

'*What?*' said Jack.

'Only joking,' said Eddie. 'Actually, I thought you'd look best as a gentleman.'

'A gentleman?' Jack preened at his trenchcoat lapels. 'I like the sound of that. Will I have a dandy cane and an eyeglass and everything?'

'The dullard is truly a dullard,' said Wibbly, chuckling once again.

'I said, a gentleman,' said Eddie, 'not a fop, although—' He winked at Wibbly. Wibbly winked back with his dangling eye. It wasn't a pretty sight.

'Okay,' said the wobbly one. 'I'll get him kitted out from the trunk. What else did you want, Eddie?'

Eddie looked up at Jack. 'It's a personal matter,' he said. 'We can discuss it whilst Jack is changing.'

'Follow me then, Jack,' said Wibbly. And he led Jack from the room, his convex bottom making sounds upon the floor that Jack now recognised.

Wibbly returned presently to the company of Eddie, who spoke to him in hushed and urgent tones.

Presently still, Jack returned to the company of Wibbly and Eddie, was soundly mocked and laughed at for his choice of costume and was then led from the room once more by Wibbly.

Presently presently still, Wibbly returned to the company of Eddie, in the company of Jack, who now cut something of a dash. Not to say a sprint. Or even a full-pelt run.

'Natty,' said Eddie. 'As natty as. Give us a twirl then, Jack.'

'Pretty smooth, eh?' said he.

Jack looked more than pretty smooth. Jack looked truly magnificent. He wore the costume of a dandy: a pale pink frock-coat, with quilted lapels and ruffled cuffs; a cloth-of-gold waistcoat with bright jewelled buttons; white silk stockings, fastened at the knees, beneath red velvet pantaloons. Buckled shoes and a natty cravat completed this pretty-as-a-picture.

'He'll certainly be noticed,' said Wibbly.

'That's the intention,' said Eddie.

'Oh,' said Jack. 'Is it? I thought the disguise was for undercover work.'

'I'll explain everything to you on the way.'

'I wish you luck,' said Wibbly. 'Shall I look after the trenchcoat and fedora and whatnots?'

'We'll take them with us,' said Jack.

'We will,' said Eddie. 'Thanks for everything, my friend.'

Wibbly smiled and wobbled.

But he still didn't fall down.

'I didn't like him at all,' said Jack, back at the wheel of the car. 'He's a very scary individual.'

'I think he's very level-headed, considering he only has half a head to be level with. I wonder how well you'd get on with only half a head.'

'I'd be dead,' said Jack. 'And better off that way.'

'Just drive the car, Jack.'

'To the crime scene?'

'I'll point the way, and promise me you'll drive carefully this time.'

'I promise you,' said Jack, putting his buckle-shoed foot down hard.

9

For those who are unacquainted with the career of Little Boy Blue subsequent to his period of employment as a somnambulant shepherd, a period notable only for his inactivity, exemplified by his famous haystack slumberings, which permitted his untended sheep to carouse in the meadows whilst his cows laid pats amongst the corn; a brief history follows.

According to his best-selling autobiography, *I May be Blue, but I'm Always in the Black*, his rags-to-riches rise was an overnight affair, with his self-penned rhyme going straight into the charts at Number One, toppling Mary Mary, who had held the position for fourteen consecutive weeks.

This is not altogether true, firstly because Mary Mary did not achieve her own fame until several years later, and secondly because Boy Blue did *not* write his own lyrics.

They were the work of a professional rhymester by the name of Wheatley Porterman, whose distinctive lyrical style can be discerned in several other 'self-penned' classics of the genre, *Georgie Porgie, pudding and pie* and *There was an old woman who lived in a shoe* (the house version), to name but two.

Wheatley Porterman's gift was for identifying social problems, which he set in verse that touched the public's imagination, in the case of Boy Blue, the scandal of child labour in rural areas which drove underage shepherds to exhaustion.

With *Georgie Porgie*, it was sexual harassment in the playground, by teachers against schoolgirls, Porgie being an overweight geography teacher whose notorious behaviour had previously gone unreported, due to his connections in high places.

Regarding *There was an old woman who lived in a shoe*, Wheatley's finger was once more unerringly upon the button of the public conscience. Whether there actually *was* an old woman who lived in a shoe and had so many children that she didn't know what to do remains in some doubt. Wheatley asserted that she was allegorical: a cipher, or symbol, for the hideous overcrowding in certain inner city areas.

A consultation with the curator of *The Hall of Nearly All the Records* discloses that the rhyme is registered as the 'exclusive property of Old Woman Inc.', the chairman and sole shareholder in Old Woman Inc. being one W. Porterman, Esq.

But be this all as it may (and well may it all be too), Little Boy Blue, either in partnership with Wheatley, or under contract to him, claimed to have written the rhyme himself. And a world which didn't care much either way, but appreciated celebrity for the sake of celebrity alone, took his claims at face value.

Within weeks of sleeping rough beneath haystacks and smelling strongly of sheep dung, the Boy had made it to the big time. His trademark shepherd's smock, now blue silk, with pearls upon the cuffs, was adopted as *the* fashion look of the year (blue, as ever, being the new black, when some other colour isn't having its turn).

His establishment of an exclusive haute couture fashion house, *Oh Boy!*, was inevitable. In less time, it seemed, than it took to shake a crook at a scurrying lamb, Boy Blue found himself lionised by the cream of Toy City Society. Facsimiles of his famous portrait, *The Blue Boy*, still hang in many homes.

And in Toy City, blue is still the new black.

All of the foregoing Eddie passed on to Jack as Jack passed through the streets of Toy City—rather more speedily than Eddie cared for.

'Fashion House, eh?' said Jack, swerving, to Eddie's relief, around a number of teddies who were crossing the road. 'The fashion in my town was for grey overalls. That's all the workers ever wore. And as all the townsfolk were workers, that's all anyone ever wore.'

'You weren't wearing grey overalls when I met you,' Eddie observed.

Jack laughed. 'I traded them in at a farm I passed by, in exchange for a new set of clothes, although the cap was somewhat inferior. The farmer was convinced that grey overalls must be the very height of town fashion, seeing as all the town dwellers he'd ever met wore them.'

'This wasn't the same farmer whose ear you shot off?'

'That was an accident. But no, that wasn't him.'

'Hey, look,' said Eddie. 'Up ahead. Stop the car here, Jack.'

Jack looked up ahead and then he stopped the car. Up ahead was blocked by a heavy police presence. A cordon stretched across the road.

Laughing policemen held back a crowd of on-looking toys, a crowd that *cooed* and *my-oh-my*'d and peered up at the façade of *Oh Boy!*.

'Policemen?' Jack asked. 'They look very jolly.'

'Don't be fooled by that,' said Eddie. 'They won't bother you, if you do *exactly* as I tell you.' And Eddie went on to explain to Jack exactly what he was to do.

And Jack, having listened, smiled broadly. 'And I will actually get away with doing *that*?' he asked.

'You certainly will,' said Eddie. 'And the more you do it, the more you'll get away with it.'

'Right then,' said Jack. 'And what will you be doing, while I'm doing what I'll be doing?'

'I'll be doing my job,' said Eddie. 'Examining the crime scene for clues.'

'Okay, then. Let's get on with it.'

The façade of *Oh Boy!* was something in itself. It was a triumph. A triumph of bad taste.

Why it is that bad taste always triumphs over good is one of those things that scholars love to debate, when they don't have anything better to do, such as getting a life and a girlfriend.

Is there actually such a thing as 'good taste'? they debate. Or 'Is it all not merely subjective?'

Well, of course there is such a thing as good taste! Some things actually *are* better than other things, and some people are capable of making the distinction.

But . . .

Bad taste will always ultimately triumph over good taste, because bad taste has more financial backing. There is far more profit to be made from selling cheap and nasty products, at a big mark-up, than selling quality items at a small mark-up. And you can always produce far more cheap and nasty items far more quickly than you can produce quality items. Far more.

And, as every successful dictator knows, it's far easier to convince a thousand people en masse of a bad idea, than it is to convince a single individual. It's a herd thing.

Or a flock thing.

Flocks are controlled by a single shepherd.

Like Little Boy Blue, for instance.

Peering over the low heads of the toy folk and the higher heads of the policemen, Jack stared up at the façade of *Oh Boy!*. It was a regular eyesore: big and brash and in-your-face gaudy, smothered in flashing neon that brought up the outline of a leaping lamb here and a snorting shepherd there, in less-than-modest many-times-life-size which simply screamed 'Success!'

'Very tasteful,' said Jack.

'It's as foul as,' said Eddie. 'You've no taste, Jack.'

'Oh yes I have,' said Jack. 'My taste is for wealth. And if this is the taste of the wealthy, it's tasteful enough for me.'

'Curiously, I can't argue with that,' said Eddie. 'Go on then, Jack, do your stuff.'

'Okey dokey.' Jack raised his chin, puffed out his chest, straightened the ruffles on his cuffs, dusted down his quilted lapels and then swaggered forward, shouting, 'Make way, peasants,' in a loud and haughty tone.

Toy folk turned and stared. Those who had faces capable of expression glared somewhat too. But they cowered back and cleared a path before the tall and well-dressed swaggering shouter.

'That's it, out of my way.' Jack swaggered onwards, with Eddie following behind.

Policemen loomed, big and blue and jolly, but clearly now to Jack no laughing matter at all. There was something all too menacing about the way they curled their smiling rubber lips towards the shouting swaggerer and fingered their over-large truncheons.

Jack swallowed back the lump which had suddenly risen in his throat. 'Stand aside there,' he told them. 'I am a patron of this establishment. Step aside lively, oafs. Go on now.'

Officer Chortle, for as chance would have it, it was he, stared at Jack eye to eye. 'What do *you* want?' he asked, in the tone known as surly. Though naturally he smiled as he asked it.

'You dare to question *me*?' Jack made the face of one appalled. 'I'll report you to your superior. What is your name?'

'Name?' went the officer, scratching his head with his truncheon.

'Name,' said Jack, in an even haughtier tone.

'Chortle,' said Chortle. 'Special Constable. My name is on my back. That's how special I am.'

'Move your stupid rubber arse,' said Jack.

Eddie grinned behind Jack's back. How dearly *he* would have liked to have said *that* to a policeman.

The Special Constable stood aside. His jolly face contorted into a hideous scowl.

Jack swaggered up the steps and through the great open doorway and into *Oh Boy!*.

★

Now, if it was tasteless on the outside, what would you *really* expect within? Jack did whistlings from between his teeth. 'This is *really* swank,' he said to Eddie. The bear peered all around and about.

'It's certainly something,' he said.

The Grand Salon of *Oh Boy!* was a monument to just how far you could truly go if you had more money than taste. The furnishings were of gold and gilt, with settees that dripped tassels and fringes. A central fountain was composed of countless naked pink marble cherubs which sprinkled scented water from their privy parts. The similarly pink marble floor was strewn with pinkly-dyed sheepskin rugs, their stuffed heads showing emerald eyes. The walls were hung with numerous oil paintings of the Blue Boy himself, posed in the most surprising positions.

There were many policemen around and about. Some were coming and others were going. Most, however, were just standing around, laughing, but looking rather lost. Some were touching things that they shouldn't. A voice called out loudly to one of these: 'Don't touch that, you cretin.' It was the voice of Chief Inspector Wellington Bellis. Eddie recognised this voice.

Eddie ducked behind Jack. 'That's Bellis,' said Eddie. 'He's the Chief Inspector. Keep him talking for as long as you can, while I give the crime scene a once-over. I'll meet you back at the car.'

'Right,' said Jack. 'I say, *you*! Yes, you there with the perished head. Who are you?'

Bellis glanced bitterly in Jack's direction. 'And who are *you*?' he said.

'And that's quite enough of *that*.' Jack made his way towards Bellis. 'I've already had to upbraid one of your dullard constables for his impertinence. I'm a patron of this establishment. A personal friend of Boy Blue. What is going on here?'

'Oh, my apologies, *sir*.' There was a certain tone in that *sir*, a tone that wasn't lost upon Jack. 'There has been an incident.'

'Incident?' said Jack.

'Homicide,' said Bellis. 'I regret to tell you that Boy Blue is dead.'

'Dead? *Dead*?' Jack put his hands to his face, which made the expression of horror. 'Boy Blue, my dearest friend? How did this happen?'

'Perhaps you'd care to view the body?' There was now a different tone in the Chief Inspector's voice. A tone of malice, perhaps.

'Well,' said Jack, feigning immoderate distress, 'I don't know, I mean, well, is it messy?'

'I wouldn't exactly describe it as messy.' Bellis glanced down and Jack followed the direction of Bellis's glancing. A silken sheet covered a huddled something. The body of Boy Blue, Jack supposed. 'Go on, have a peep,' said Bellis.

'My dearest friend.' Jack made snivelling sounds. 'I mean, I don't know. If such a terrible thing has happened, such a shock, I don't know. I should, perhaps, pay my respects. Oh, I really don't know.'

'Have a little look,' said Bellis, a big wide smile upon his rubber face. 'Pay your last respects.'

'Well,' said Jack. 'Perhaps just a little look.'

'Officer,' said Bellis to one of the officers who was touching things that he shouldn't. 'Kindly lift the sheet and show the nice gentleman the deceased.'

'Yes sir, chief.' The officer smirked, stooped and whipped away the sheet with a flourish.

Jack stared down and his eyes grew wide and his mouth fell hugely open. And then Jack crossed his legs and he said, 'Ouch.'

'Ouch would be about right,' agreed Bellis. 'You might recognise the murder weapon. It's his crook. His original crook, from the days when he was a humble shepherd. It was kept in the showcase by the door. It would appear that he was bending over, tying his shoelace. We think someone took the crook, then ran at him, using the bottom end as a spear. It entered his own bottom end, and left via his mouth. Much in the manner that one might spit a pig for a barbecue.'

Jack nodded his head and chewed upon his lower lip. The manner of the murder was, to say the least, grotesque. The problem with it was—and Jack, for all he could do, was now finding this a *real* problem—the problem with it was that, in the darkest way possible, it was also very funny indeed.

Jack looked over at Bellis.

The moulded smile upon Bellis's face was spreading up towards his ears.

'Right up the old farting box,' said Bellis, restraining a titter.

'How dare you!' said Jack. 'This is no laughing matter. My dear friend. My . . .' Jack chewed harder upon his lip and told himself that this wasn't funny. It *wasn't*. This was a dead man here. It wasn't funny!

'Sorry,' said Bellis. He let free a giggle, then controlled himself once more. 'Cover him up again, officer.'

The officer, still smirking, stooped once more and recovered the corpse.

'Terrible business,' said Bellis, with as much solemnity as he could muster up.

'Terrible business,' Jack agreed.

★

'Terrible business,' said Eddie, when Jack returned to the car to find him waiting there. 'Most unprofessional.'

'But I was rude,' said Jack, settling himself back behind the driving wheel. 'You said that I should be as rude and obnoxious as possible. Act like a rich man, you said. Behave badly.'

'I mean about the laughing,' said Eddie. ' "Terrible business" you said to Bellis and then the two of you collapsed in laughter.'

'It was nerves,' said Jack.

'It wasn't. You thought it was funny.'

'I'm sorry,' said Jack. 'But it was.'

'You wouldn't have thought it so funny if it had happened to you.'

'Well, obviously not. Other people's misfortunes are far funnier than your own.'

'It's *not* funny,' said Eddie, shaking his head as he said it. 'Well, perhaps it is, a little. But that's not the point. It's another murder and that *isn't* funny.'

'Well, it's really nothing to do with us. We're supposed to be investigating the murder of Humpty Dumpty. That's what Bill got the money for.'

'You don't think that perhaps these two murders might be in some way connected?'

Jack shrugged. 'How should I know? This is the big city. How many murders do you get here in a week?'

'On average?' said Eddie. 'None.'

'None?' said Jack.

'None,' said Eddie. 'Humpty's murder was the first ever murder of a meathead. Which is why, in my opinion, the newspapers are covering it up, spreading the suicide rumour to avoid panicking the population. Certainly toys are forever getting into fights and pulling each other to pieces. But that doesn't count as murder and doesn't merit a police investigation. This is men who are being killed, Jack. The old rich. This is serious stuff.'

'So you're thinking . . . What are you thinking?'

'I'm thinking,' said Eddie, 'that it's the same murderer. I'm thinking that Toy City has a serial killer on the loose.'

10

'What is a *serial* killer?' Jack asked.

'It's a term that I've just made up,' said Eddie. 'It means a killer who murders more than one person. Serially. One after the other.'

Jack whistled and diddled with things on the dashboard. 'It's possible, I suppose,' said he. 'But what about evidence? Did you find any clues?'

'Plenty,' said Eddie, making a very pleased face. 'Firstly, the killer did not run at Boy Blue, using his crook like a spear. The crook was fired from some contrivance across the street. One of the panes of glass in the front door was shattered. The crook was removed from the showcase and fired at Boy Blue when he was bending over.'

'Tying his shoelace,' said Jack.

'Did you see any laces on his shoes?'

'I didn't look.'

'I did,' said Eddie. 'I peeped. He was wearing slip-ons. Boy Blue bent down to examine this.'

Eddie displayed a bundle on his lap. 'And before you ask me what it is, I'll show you. I was able to liberate it before some big clod of a policeman stood upon it. Have a look at this, Jack.'

Eddie unwrapped the bundle and Jack stared down.

'Bunny,' said Jack. 'It's another hollow chocolate bunny.'

'Just don't eat this one,' said Eddie. 'It's evidence.'

'Of your serial killer?'

'It could hardly be a coincidence, could it?'

Jack made free with another whistle. 'So where do we go from here?' he asked. 'Back to Bill's office?'

'Ah, no.' Eddie shook his head. 'I don't think we'll go back there for a while. As this is the only clue we've got, I think we'll follow it up. Do you fancy a visit to the chocolate factory?'

'Do they give away free samples?' Jack asked. 'Because I'm really quite hungry again.'

'Rewind the car and drive,' said Eddie. 'I'll show you which way to go.'

Jack was beginning to gain some sense of direction. The major streets of the great metropolis were slowly beginning to familiarise themselves. It wasn't all such a mystery any more. Well, a lot of it was. But some wasn't.

'I recognise this bit,' said Jack. 'There's Tinto's bar, and right along there is Bill's office.'

'Straight on,' said Eddie, 'up Knob Hill.'

The hill road wound upwards, as hill roads will do, unless you're coming down them, of course.

Jack drove past Nursery Towers. 'What's that dark-looking house at the very top of the hill?' he asked.

'That's where Mr Anders lives.'

'The kindly loveable white-haired old toymaker. I'd like to visit him; do you think we could stop off and say hello?'

'Not without an appointment,' said Eddie. 'And you're on your own when you do it.'

At Eddie's instruction, Jack turned off the hill road and was very soon outside the gates of the chocolate factory.

If *Oh Boy!* had been tasteless, the chocolate factory was style personified. It was an elegant building, composed of yellow brick, all sweeping curves and fluted arabesques. It rose like an anthem, in praise of life's finer things.

'Ugly-looking dump,' said Jack.

Eddie shook his head.

'Do you want me to be rude and obnoxious again?'

'I wouldn't want to put you to the effort.'

'It's no effort, I assure you.'

'Just follow me,' said Eddie.

Now it is a fact, well known to those who know it well, that detective work is rarely straightforward, because finding things out is rarely straightforward. Getting information from folk, when folk do not wish to part with information, can be difficult. *Is* difficult. And on the rare occasions when folk are eager to part with information, it often turns out that this information is inaccurate. Which can lead to all kinds of confusion.

But if, at the end of the day, and such like, the information you have managed to acquire, in the course of your detective work, leads to an arrest, then you've got a result. And if the suspect is convicted, then you've got an even bigger result.

And if the suspect is a murder suspect and gets sent off to the electric chair, then you've got an even bigger bigger result.

And if it turns out later that the murder suspect was in fact innocent, and was sent off to the electric chair because the information you acquired was inaccurate, well, tomorrow's another day, isn't it? You can try and get it right the next time.

The chocolate factory had big gates at the front. There was a gatekeeper in a tiny box beside these gates, keeping them, as it were.

Jack sniffed the air. It smelled sweet. It smelled of chocolate. Eddie addressed the gatekeeper. 'This is, er, Lord Dork,' said Eddie, indicating Jack. 'He is a connoisseur of chocolate and I've brought him here on a special visit.'

'Then you've come to the right place,' said the gatekeeper. 'Because I'm a special gatekeeper. I'm the head gatekeeper. Because, although, as you can see, I'm only a head, I'm also the gatekeeper. Which makes me the head gatekeeper. Which makes me very special, don't you agree?'

Eddie nodded and peeped in at the special head gatekeeper. He was indeed nothing but a head. A little round wooden head. 'So, can we come in?' Eddie asked.

'No,' said the gatekeeper. 'We're closed to all visitors.'

'But this is Lord Dork. *The* Lord Dork.'

'One Lord Dork is much the same to me as another,' said the gatekeeper.

'So you're not inclined to grant us entry?'

'Even if I were, I couldn't. Look at me, I may be a special head, but I'm only a head. How could I possibly open the gate?'

'Who generally opens the gates, then?' Eddie asked.

'Search me,' said the gatekeeper. 'I've been here for years, in rain and snow and fog and fug; I've yet to see those gates open up at all.'

'But don't the workers go in and out?'

'There aren't any workers,' said the gatekeeper.

'I smell chocolate,' said Jack. 'Someone is making chocolate.'

'If I had shoulders, I'd shrug them,' said the gatekeeper. 'And if I had legs, I'd probably walk. It's not much fun at times being me, I can tell you.'

'I could pull your head out of the box and we could drop it off somewhere,' said Eddie, helpfully.

'No thanks, I like it here. It's not much of a job, but it's all I have. I'll make do. Goodbye.'

'We have to get inside,' said Eddie. 'It's very important. It's about this.' Eddie held up his bundle and showed the chocolate bunny to the gatekeeper.

'What is that?' the gatekeeper asked.

'It's a hollow chocolate bunny.'

'Oh,' said the gatekeeper. 'So that's what chocolate looks like. I'd always imagined it to be pink.'

'Pink?' said Jack. 'You've never seen chocolate?'

'I have now,' said the gatekeeper. 'And I'm very disappointed. It's not nice having all your illusions shattered. Please go away, you've quite spoiled my day.'

Eddie made an exasperated face.

'We're getting nowhere,' said Jack. 'Shall we just climb over the gates?'

'You can't do that,' said the gatekeeper. 'It's not allowed.'

'Really? And so what are you going to do about it?'

'I'll sulk,' said the gatekeeper. 'I sulked the last time and I'll sulk this time too.'

'Last time?' Eddie asked. 'What last time?'

'The last time someone got past the gates. They didn't even speak to me; they just leapt over. I really sulked, I can tell you. I don't know whether it helped or not. But what else could I do?'

Jack shook his head.

'Perhaps you should have raised the alarm,' Eddie suggested.

'I'm not employed to do that,' said the gatekeeper. 'I'm employed to stop people going through the gates without my authorisation.'

'And how do you do that?'

The gatekeeper laughed. 'It's a fine joke, isn't it?' he said. 'I never have to. The gates are always locked.'

Jack scratched at his head. 'Yes, but—'

Eddie stopped him. 'So you're only employed to stop people going *through* the gates? Not *over* them?' he asked the gatekeeper.

'My contract only says *through them*.'

Jack shook his head once more.

'This person who leapt over the gates,' Eddie said. 'What did they look like?'

'Looked like a meathead,' said the gatekeeper. 'And all meatheads look the same to me.'

'There's nothing specific that you can recall?' Eddie asked.

'They had a sack,' said the gatekeeper. 'I remember that. It was an empty sack when they jumped over, but it looked weighty and full later, when they jumped back again.'

'Significant,' said Eddie. 'Is there anything else you can remember?'

'I remember a sparrow that once built its nest in that tree over there.'

'About the meathead who climbed in and out?'

'No, she just looked like a meathead.'

'*She?*' said Eddie.

'It was a female meathead,' said the gatekeeper. 'They have those things that stick out in the front.'

'Tits?' Jack asked.

'Feathers,' said the gatekeeper.

'We're talking about the meathead, not the sparrow,' said Eddie.

'Me too,' said the gatekeeper. 'She had big feathers, sticking out of the front of her bonnet.'

Back in the car, Eddie said, 'Well, it was a struggle, but we got there eventually.'

'I didn't get any chocolate,' said Jack. 'And I'm still hungry.'

'But we got information. Someone leapt over the gates of the chocolate factory and stole a sack full of somethings.'

'Bunnies, you're thinking?'

'Let us assume so. And it was a woman.'

'It might have been a man in a feathered hat.'

'Does that seem likely to you?'

Jack shrugged. 'The unlikely is commonplace in this city,' he said.

'It's a woman,' said Eddie. 'We're looking for a woman. Perhaps it was a love triangle. She was the scorned lover of both Humpty and Boy Blue. Or something.'

'So what is the significance of the bunnies?'

'Some love thing. I don't know. Men give chocolates to women.'

'You're clutching at straws,' said Jack. 'I don't believe it was a woman. Did a woman climb onto Humpty's roof and put in that lens? Did a woman fire that crook from across the street? Did a woman leap over those gates? Did you see how high those gates were?'

'We're looking for a woman.'

'We're not.'

Jack drove the car back down Knob Hill and, at Eddie's instruction, towards Tinto's bar. He didn't look in the driving mirror as he drove along, but then Jack rarely, if ever, looked into the driving mirror.

Which was a shame as it happened. because if Jack *had* looked into the driving mirror, he might well have noticed the car that was following him.

It was a long and low expensive-looking car and it was being driven by a woman.

A woman who wore a feathered bonnet.

11

The sun was drifting down towards the horizon as Jack steered Bill's car along one of the more colourful streets of Toy City. Eddie had suggested that they take the pretty way back to Tinto's bar.

This street was a shopping area for toys. There were brightly lit bazaars, shaded by decorative awnings. Produce in baskets, tubs and crates spilled onto the pavements.

Jack slowed the car and kerb-crawled along, peering out and marvelling at the wares and wonders, and at those who shopped and strode and moved: toys, and more toys.

Jack's thoughts were all his own and his thoughts were about thoughts. How could all these creations, these things wrought from tin and wood and padded fabric, *think*? How could they move and talk? It was ludicrous, impossible, and yet it was so. Jack thought back to the gatekeeper at the chocolate factory.

'A head,' said Jack, with a shake of his own. 'A talking head in a box. Now I ask you, how does that work?'

'Most inefficiently,' said Eddie. 'The way he just let people leap over the gates. Outrageous. I'd have sacked that head if it had been working for me. I'd have told that head to hop it.' Eddie tittered foolishly.

'You know exactly what I mean.'

'I do,' said the bear. 'But must you keep going on about it? You admit that you don't even know how your own brain works.'

'But at least I *have* a brain. Your chum Wibbly had nothing at all in what he had left of his head. It can't work, none of it can.'

'But it does. Your own eyes attest to the fact. Don't let it get you down, Jack. If you ever meet up with the toymaker, you can ask him all about it.'

'And do you think he'll tell me?'

Eddie shrugged. 'I doubt it. But at least you will have asked.'

'Mad,' said Jack. 'It's all quite mad.' And he lapsed into a sullen silence.

Eddie leaned back in the passenger seat and tried once more without success to fold his arms. Thoughts moved about amongst the sawdust in his head; how they did and what they were was anybody's guess.

At a length that was shorter rather than long, he had done with thinking, and also with Jack's silence.

'Jack,' said Eddie, all bright and breezy, 'Jack, are you a virgin?'

'*What?*' went Jack, and the car swerved onto the pavement, scattering shoppers, who shook their fists and shouted words of abuse.

'A virgin?' said Eddie. 'Careful where you're swerving.'

'What kind of question is *that*?'

'An easy one to answer, I would have thought.'

'Well, I'm not answering it.' Jack regained control of the car.

'So you *are*,' said Eddie. 'It's nothing to be ashamed of; you're still a young lad.'

'I'm old enough,' said Jack.

'But you haven't done it yet?'

'Eddie, change the subject, please. We're supposed to be on a case. Two murders. Concentrate on the murders.'

'I am,' said Eddie. 'Take a left here.'

Jack took a left there.

'So you've never been in a doll's house,' said Eddie.

'A doll's house?' said Jack.

'A doll's house, a bordello, a knocking shop.'

Jack rammed his foot down hard upon the brake, dislodging Eddie from his seat and causing him to fall in some confusion to the floor.

'Oooh ouch,' went Eddie. 'Steady on. Help me up. I'm all in a mess down here.'

Jack helped Eddie up and positioned him back on the seat. 'Talk about something else,' he said. 'Talk about the case.'

'But it's pertinent to the case. I know a place where we might get some information regarding the suspect. Tarts wear feathered hats, don't they?'

Jack nodded in the manner of one who had some knowledge of these matters.

'Yes, well, they do,' said Eddie. 'And tarts are to be found in bawdy houses. And I know of only one bawdy house in this city. And I know of it most intimately.'

Jack shook his head once more. 'And you are a patron of this establishment?' he asked.

'A regular patron, as it happens.'

Jack stared down at Eddie. He stared down hard and he stared down in particular towards a certain area of Eddie Bear's anatomy. 'But you're a teddy bear,' he said. 'You haven't got a w—'

'I *have*, you know,' said Eddie. 'It's just that I keep it tucked away when it's not in use.'

'I don't believe you,' said Jack. 'Teddies don't have—'

'You want me to show it to you?'

Actually Jack did. 'No, I certainly don't,' said he.

'Bears are noted for their sexual prowess.' Eddie puffed out his plump little chest.

'I think you'll find that's rabbits,' said Jack. 'But I really must insist that you change the subject. This is becoming most distasteful.'

'It's nature,' said Eddie. 'It's as natural as.'

'Nothing in this city is *natural*. But tell me about this bawdy house.'

'Ah,' said Eddie. 'Now you're interested.'

'Only if it's pertinent to the case.'

'Yeah, right.'

'Eddie,' said Jack. 'This murderer, this serial killer of yours. He—'

'She,' said Eddie.

'He, or *she*. They won't stop at two, will they? They'll go on killing?'

Eddie made with the very grave noddings. 'It's more than probable,' he said.

'Then don't you think that we should, perhaps, be trying to work out who's likely to be murdered next? Then we could warn them. And lie in wait for the murderer, or something.'

'You're getting the hang of this detective game, Jack. Drive on; we'll go to the bawdy house.'

Jack threw up his hands and then Jack drove on.

The streets became less colourful and soon Jack was driving along grim and narrow roads that were positively grey.

'It's horrible here,' he said. 'This is a really horrible district. What a foul place. What a really foul place.'

'I was brought up here,' said Eddie.

'Well, I'm sure it has its good points.'

'It doesn't,' said Eddie. 'Park here.'

'Are we there?' Jack asked.

'Of course we're not. But no one ever parks their car *outside* a bawdy house. They park a couple of streets away and approach on foot. Normally wearing some kind of disguise.'

'I'm wearing a disguise,' said Jack.

'You certainly are, Jack. Oh, and don't forget to lock the car. Then there'll be the vague chance that it will still be here when we get back.'

Jack and Eddie left the car and Jack locked up the doors.

'Follow me,' said Eddie.

And Jack did so.

A little ways behind, and altogether unobserved, another car drew silently to a halt. It was long and low and expensive-looking. The driver's door of this car opened and a lady's leg appeared. It was a long and slender leg, tightly sheathed in black rubber. At the end of this leg was a dainty foot, shod with a wonderful shoe. Its highly raised heel was a delicate chromium spiral. Its toe was a dagger of steel.

The exterior of the bawdy house was nothing to speak of.

The interior, however, was quite another matter. It was one of those grand salon jobbies, but this was where any similarity between it and the house of *Oh Boy!* ended.

The ceiling was a gentle dome, richly figured with plaster reliefs of amorous cupids and garlanded satyrs. The walls were made gay with pastoral paintings of frolicsome centaurs and dainty Arcadians. These were engaged in the most intimate pursuits, but had been wrought with such charm and whimsy as might bring an appreciative smile to the face of the most worthy cleric.

Pale silkwood caryatids rose between these paintings. They had been lovingly carved and bore delicate features and robes, which seemed all but diaphanous. They held, in their outstretched hands, crystal candelabra which lit the salon to a nicety.

The furnishings were rich, but of a richness which is restrained, tutored, composed. The colours of the fabrics were of the subtlest shades: dainty pinks and tender violets. Billowy cushions were cast here and there, creating an atmosphere of comfort and informality. And all around and about were elegant vases from which the most gorgeous blooms breathed their precious fragrances.

'Oh my,' said Jack as his feet all but sank into a carpet woven with a thousand blushing roses. 'Oh my, oh my.'

'You approve?' asked Eddie.

'Well, I think it's incredible.' And it was incredible. It was overwhelming in its beauty. Jack was overwhelmed. And he was nervous too. For after all, he *was* a virgin. And wonderful and marvellous as this place was, it *was* a bawdy house. An actual bawdy house. Where there would be actual women who had actual sex on a professional basis. Which was actually somewhat daunting.

Actually.

'You wait until you see the bedrooms,' said Eddie, rubbing his paws together.

'Eddie,' said Jack. 'Just one thing. We are here on business, aren't we?'

'Of course,' said Eddie.

'Because if there's one thing I do know about ladies who work in bawdy houses, it is that you have to pay them. With real money. And we don't have any money.'

'Do I spy an expression of relief on your face?' Eddie asked.

'You do *not*,' said Jack. 'I'm just saying, that's all.'

'I have an account here.' Eddie grinned from ear to furry ear.

Jack didn't grin, but now another thought entered his head. 'Eddie?' said Jack.

'Jack?' said Eddie.

'Eddie, when you, you know, *do it*.'

'Yes,' said Eddie. It was a low, deep, growly kind of yes.

'Do you do it with a dolly?'

Eddie's button eyes virtually popped from his head. 'A dolly?' he said in the voice of outrage. 'A *dolly*? Do I look like some kind of pervert who'd do it inter-species? I do it with another bear! Female, of course. Dolly! That's gross!'

'I'm sorry,' said Jack. 'Oh look, who's this?'

'It's Mother,' said Eddie.

'Your mother? But . . .'

'Mother Goose,' said Eddie. 'Or Madame Goose, as she prefers to be called.'

Madame Goose was indeed a goose, and a very large goose was she. Jack could see that she wasn't a clockwork goose, rather, some great soft toy of a thing, fully feathered and most convincing. She was a profusion of petticoats and a gathering of gingham, with glittering rings on the tips of her wings. And she walked with a quack and a waddle and a quack and a flurry of eiderdown (which hopefully didn't infringe any copyrights).

She came a-waddling across the rose-pelted carpet, the light from the crystal candelabra twinkling on her gorgeous gingham.

'Eddie,' said Madame Goose, bending low and pecking kisses at the bear's cheek. 'It's been too long. Have you come to settle your account?'

'I've come to introduce a close friend of mine,' said Eddie. 'This is Lord Schmuck.'

Jack narrowed his eyes at Eddie.

Madame Goose curtseyed low, her petticoats spreading over the carpet like the petals of some exotic bloom, or a pink gingham jellyfish, dropped from a height. Or something else entirely.

'Always a pleasure to meet with members of the aristocracy,' she said. 'You'll find that we can satisfy your every wish here.'

'Verily,' said Jack, once more adopting the haughty foppish tone that he'd previously employed upon the policemen. 'Well, naturally I am used to the very best of everything. So I trust that the damsels on offer are more well-favoured than yourself in the looks department. You fat old turkey.'

Madame Goose fell back in horror, flapping her ring-tipped wings all about.

Eddie head-butted Jack in that certain area of his anatomy.

'Gurgh!' went Jack, doubling over in pain.

'Don't be rude in here, you schmuck,' counselled Eddie at Jack's now lowered ear. 'These are my friends. Apologise at once.'

'I'm sorry, Madame.' Jack clutched at himself in an unbecoming manner and took to the drawing of deep breaths. 'I'll get you for that, Eddie,' he whispered from between his gritted teeth.

'Please pardon Lord Schmuck,' said Eddie, stepping briskly beyond Jack's kicking range. 'His manners aren't up to much. But his heart and his wallet are in the right places.'

'Quite so,' said the Madame, smoothing down her ruffled feathers and curtseying once more.

'Any chance of a morsel of food?' Jack asked. 'And a glass of wine, please.'

'Seat yourself, gents,' said Madame Goose. 'I will bring you something at once.'

'You sit down, Jack,' said Eddie. 'I'll accompany Madame to the kitchen. Have a few words, if you know what I mean.' Eddie tapped at his nose with his paw.

'Don't be long,' said Jack, lowering himself with care onto an over-stuffed settee.

'I'll be back as soon as.' Eddie followed Madame from the salon.

Jack sat awkwardly, nursing himself. He sighed and he made a sorry face. He felt most uncomfortable here. The opulence, the colours and the fragrances were indeed pleasing, but he wasn't pleased. This was, after all, a whorehouse. A high-class whorehouse, perhaps, but nevertheless, a whorehouse. Its wealth was founded upon degradation: money earned by women who sold their bodies to men. Jack glowered at the rosy carpet.

He had never considered himself to be a lad with high moral values. He was basically honest, but above and beyond that, he'd never given the subject of morality a lot of thought.

'I think I'll go and wait outside,' said Jack to himself.

'Oh no, don't go.'

Jack looked up. The face of a beautiful girl smiled down upon him. Her mouth was wide and smiling, displaying a row of perfect teeth. Her head was a bouquet of golden curls, the colour of sun-ripened corncobs. Her eyes were dark and large, brown and glossy as burnt sugar, fringed by gorgeous lashes. And there was a troubled sadness in those eyes.

Jack stared into those eyes.

'I'm Jill,' said the beautiful girl.

'Oh,' said Jack, 'I'm pleased to meet you.' And he rose to shake her hand.

Jill curtseyed low and Jack could see right down her cleavage. Jill had a beautiful body. It went in and out in all the right places, and just by the right amounts too. Jack estimated that she could be little more than his own age—although with teenage girls it's often very hard to tell. 'I'm, er, Lord, er.' Jack took a deep breath. 'My name is Jack,' he said.

'Jack and Jill,' Jill giggled prettily. 'What about that?' she asked.

Jack managed a lopsided grin. 'What about that,' he said.

'Madame sent me out to entertain you. None of the other girls have arrived yet. We don't really open until later in the evening. But I am here, if you'll have me; just tell me what you wish for.'

'Oh,' said Jack. 'Well, nothing like *that* at the moment, thank you. I'm just waiting. For a friend.'

'I can be your friend. I can be anything you want me to be.'

'Please sit down,' said Jack.

Jill sat down and Jack sat down beside her.

She reached out a hand to clasp his own, but Jack returned it politely. 'Don't you like me?' Jill asked.

'I don't know you,' said Jack. 'But you look very nice. Very pretty.'

'Thank you very much. You're very handsome.' Jill's eyes took in the jewelled buttons on Jack's waistcoat. 'And I love your clothes.'

'They're not mine. I only borrowed them.'

'I rent mine from Madame,' said Jill.

'Do you mind me asking you something?' Jack lowered his eyes. 'I mean, you're very young, aren't you? To be working in a place like this?'

'I have to eat,' said Jill, her fingers toying with one of Jack's jewelled buttons. 'But let's not talk about me. Let's talk about you. Would you like to come upstairs with me now?'

'I'd love to,' said Jack, easing himself away. 'But it's not right.'

Jill looked somewhat sternly at Jack and when she spoke, there was fire in her voice. 'What are you saying?' she asked. 'That there's something wrong with the way I make a living? I'm good at what I do and what I do is not illegal. Are you some God-botherer, come to convert me from my wicked ways or something?'

'No,' said Jack. 'Slow down. No offence meant. It's just—'

'You're a virgin, aren't you?' said Jill

'I'm *not*,' said Jack rising to leave. 'I have to go.'

'Please don't,' said Jill. 'I'm begging you, please don't.'

'Begging?'

'If you walk out, I'll be in trouble with Madame.'

'I wouldn't want that,' said Jack, sitting down again.

'Thank you,' said Jill. And her fingers stroked at his buttons once more.

'But tell me, and I don't mean to offend you, isn't there some job other than this that you'd rather be doing?'

Jill cast him a look that was filled with contempt. 'I'd quite like to be a princess,' she said. 'Do you know any princes who are looking for a tart to marry?'

'Please be calm.' Jack raised calming hands. 'The reason I'm asking is that I ran away from the factory where I worked. Because I hated it. I came to the city to seek my fortune.'

'You came *to* the city.' Jill laughed. 'You thought you'd seek your fortune *here*? You are clearly a gormster. No offence meant.'

'None taken,' said Jack, as if none *was* taken.

'But you came *to* the city.' Jill shook her golden curls 'I've never heard of anyone coming *to* the city before. I've heard that beyond the bounds of the city are desolate realms peopled by cannibals.'

'You're not altogether wrong there' The image of a now-one-eared farmer filled Jack's head. 'And perhaps I'll never find my fortune. Perhaps I am well and truly cursed.'

'I know that I am.' Jill's voice was scarcely a whisper.

'What did you say?' Jack asked.

'Nothing,' said Jill. She placed a hand upon his. This time Jack didn't remove it.

'You said you were cursed,' said Jack.

'No, I didn't. So, do you want to come upstairs with me?'

Jack smiled wanly. 'I don't have any money, I'm afraid.'

'You can open an account.'

'I don't know,' said Jack.

'If you do come upstairs,' said Jill, 'I can promise that you won't be disappointed. And if you are a virgin, then you'll lose your virginity in a manner that you'll remember all your life.'

'Well,' said Jack.

'And if you don't come upstairs,' said Jill, 'then Madame will beat me and possibly throw me out on the street. And you wouldn't want that, now, would you?'

Jack shook his head.

'Come on then,' said Jill.

Outside, clockwork cars purred on the streets and the denizens of the great metropolis went on doing whatever they were doing. Five miles to the north, a foolish boy fell into a farmer's pit. The sun sank beneath the horizon and night came upon Toy City.

And on a white bed, in a white room, with white curtains, Jack lost his virginity. Which was quite some going, considering his tender years.

And when his virginity was lost, elegantly lost, he lay, all spent, his head upon a silken cushion, staring at the ceiling. Jill, in Jack's arms, tousled his hair.

'How was that for you?' she asked.

'Wonderful,' said Jack. 'Quite wonderful.'

'I'm pleased.'

Jack sighed and smiled. 'I love you,' he said. 'Will you marry me?'

'Certainly,' said Jill, 'as soon as you become a prince. In the meantime, I'll make out your bill.'

When Jack left the white room, he moved upon feet that scarcely touched the floor. He fairly soared. He felt marvellous. He felt that he had now become a man.

Just wait 'til Eddie hears about *this*, he thought. And, I wonder how you go about actually becoming a prince, he thought also.

As this had now become his goal in life.

Down the stairs Jack wafted. Light as thistledown and dishevelled as a nettle bed. He had lipstick all over his face and the jewelled buttons on his waistcoat were missing.

'Eddie.' Jack reached the bottom of the stairs. 'Eddie, where are you?'

All was silent and Jack breathed in all there was. The subtle perfumes seemed almost more subtle. But now Jack felt a twinge of guilt. Had what he'd just done been wrong? Immoral? Corrupt? Well, yes it had, but.

But.

Jack pressed all such thoughts aside. What had just happened had been wonderful, beautiful. And something that was wonderful and beautiful couldn't be wrong, could it? And Jill acted as if she'd been enjoying it too. And if she'd enjoyed it too, then it definitely wasn't wrong.

It was right.

'Yes,' said Jack. 'It was. Eddie, where are you?'

All was as silent as before.

Rather too silent, really.

Jack crossed the salon and pressed his hand against the door that led to the kitchen. He was very hungry now. And very thirsty too. A snack was in order. A celebratory snack, all washed down with a glass of bubbly wine.

Which could go on Eddie's account.

Jack pushed the door open.

'Eddie,' he called once more, 'where are you? Come on.'

Beyond the doorway was a hallway and beyond this hallway, yet another door. Which is often the case with hallways, especially those that lead from one room to another. Jack pranced down this hallway and knocked upon the door that it led to.

And as there was no answer to his knockings, he turned the handle and pushed the door open. It was the door to the kitchen. Jack peeped in.

The kitchen was a magnificent affair, the kind of kitchen that Great Houses had. And this was indeed a great house. There was a flagstoned floor, a huge central table, ovens and ranges and rows and rows of hanging pots and pans and skillets.

Jack was impressed by this kitchen. 'This kitchen,' said Jack, 'is what I call a kitchen. This is a magnificent kitchen. The kind of kitchen that Great Houses have. And this is indeed a great house. The only thing I don't like about this kitchen, the only thing that really spoils this kitchen for me, is *that*.'

And Jack stared at the thing that spoiled the kitchen and Jack felt just a little sick. Because on the huge central table lay Madame Goose. She lay as a goose stripped for cooking. Her legs were trussed and her neck had been wrung.

Mother Goose was dead.

'Jack,' said the voice of Jill, 'Jack, what are you doing in the kitchen?' And now Jill's hand was upon Jack's shoulder.

Jack turned and said, 'Go back. Don't come in here.'

'Why not?'

'Something's happened, something bad.'

'Show me, what?' Jill pushed past Jack. 'Oh no,' she said, and she screamed.

'Just go back,' said Jack. 'I'll deal with this.'

'Deal with *what*? She's dead, isn't she?'

'Pretty dead,' said Jack, approaching the body on the table. His heels clacked upon the flagstone floor. Jack's feet were truly back upon the ground.

'This is terrible.' Jill wrung her hands; big tears welled in her eyes. 'Terrible, terrible.'

'I'm sorry,' said Jack, viewing the body. 'I'll get something to cover her body.'

'I'm not sorry about *her*,' said Jill. 'But if she's dead, then I'm out of a job, which is terrible.'

'Right,' said Jack, peering some more at the body. 'Whoever did this must be very strong. Hardly the work of a woman.'

'Woman?' said Jill.

'Eddie thinks . . .' Jack paused. 'Eddie,' he said. Then, '*Eddie!*' he shouted. 'Where are you, Eddie? Are you hiding somewhere?'

No reply gave comfort to Jack's ears.

'*Eddie!*' shouted Jack.

'Jack,' said Jill, 'I think you'd better look at this.'

'What?' Jack asked. And Jill pointed.

The kitchen door was open, but it was towards the doormat that Jill was pointing.

Jack followed the direction of this pointing, and then Jack said, 'Oh no.'

On the doormat lay something which filled Jack with horror.

That something was a large pile of sawdust.

12

'Eddie?' Jack went all weak at the knees. 'Eddie, is that you?'

A gentle breeze entered at the kitchen door and rippled Eddie's innards all about.

'Waaagh!' went Jack. 'Get a dustpan and brush! Gather him up in a bag!'

'Have you gone mad?' Jill asked.

'It's Eddie! My friend! This is dreadful!'

Jack was at the door now and he stared out into an alleyway beyond. 'I'll go after him,' he told Jill. 'I'll try to find the rest of him.'

'Jack, stop,' said Jill. 'It's a toy. Who cares about a toy?'

'I do,' said Jack. 'He's my friend.'

'You're a bit old for that kind of thing, aren't you?'

'He's my partner,' said Jack.

'Get real,' said Jill. 'It's a toy. Toys don't care for our kind and if you're smart, you won't care for theirs. You can always find yourself another toy bear, if that's the sort of weirdness you're in to.'

'What?'

'No wonder you were so useless in bed.'

'*What?*'

'Perhaps you'd have preferred it if I'd put a fur coat on.'

'Stop!' cried Jack. 'Stop now! Sweep Eddie's sawdust up and put it in a bag. Then call the police. I'm going after Eddie. I'll be back.'

'Oh yes, *sir*,' said Jill.

Jack cast her a very stern glance. 'Sweep him up and call the police,' he said.

★

Jack moved cautiously along the alleyway. There was always the chance that the murderer might still be lurking there, lying in wait. Ready to pounce.

Sprinkles of sawdust lay here and there amongst discarded refuse. Jack's sunken heart sank deeper. 'Eddie,' he called, throwing caution to the wind that was ruffling Eddie's sprinklings. 'Are you there? Anywhere? Eddie? Eddie!'

The alleyway led out to a street.

Further sprinklings of Eddie led to the pavement kerb.

Beyond this, on the road, were two black skid marks.

'Kidnapped,' said Jack. 'Or,' and he paused, 'or murdered.'

Jack returned with drooping shoulders to the kitchen.

Jill was sitting on the table, casually plucking feathers from a wing of the deceased Madame.

'Stop doing that,' said Jack. 'Did you call the police?'

'They're busy,' said Jill. 'Apparently Little Boy Blue has been murdered. How about that then? Another rich bag of rubbish done away with.'

'You don't really care about anybody, do you?' Jack asked.

'And why should I? Nobody cares about me.'

'I care,' said Jack.

'Of course you don't.' Jill dusted feathers from her delicate fingers. 'You only care about me because I'm the first girl you've ever had sex with.'

'That's not true,' said Jack.

'Then let's see how much you care about me when you get the bill.'

'I don't have time for this.' Jack peered all around and about the kitchen. 'My friend has been kidnapped and I have to find him. There must be some clues here. What would Eddie do?' Jack paced about in the manner that Eddie had at Humpty Dumpty's apartment. And then Jack recalled that it was actually he, Jack, who had solved the riddle of how Humpty met his grisly end.

'I can do this,' said Jack. 'I *can* do this.'

'You're a detective then, are you?'

'Sort of,' said Jack. 'Sort of.'

'Oh, sort of, is it? And so what are your deductions, Mr sort-of-detective?'

'Give me a minute,' said Jack, peeping and peering around.

'Give me a break,' said Jill.

Jack made an exasperated face. 'You may not care about anybody or anything,' he said, 'but I do. Someone has injured and taken my friend. And murdered this goose here.'

'And so you're looking for clues?'

'I am,' said Jack.

'Then why are you looking in all the wrong places?'

Jack, who was now under the table, straightened up, striking his head. 'Ouch,' he said. 'And do you know the *right* places?'

'All the clues you need are staring you in the face. You're just not looking at them properly.'

Jack got to his feet once more and stood, rubbing at his head. 'What are you saying?' he asked.

Jill eased herself down from the table. 'Do you want me to explain it all to you?'

'As if you could,' said Jack.

'I could,' said Jill. 'I could tell you exactly what happened here and give you a description of the person who did it.'

'I'll bet,' said Jack, searching for clues in the breadbin.

'But if you don't want your little teddy bear back, then forget it.'

Jack replaced the lid of the breadbin and turned once more towards Jill. 'Go on then,' he said.

Jill shook her corncob-coloured head. 'Oh no,' she said. 'You owe me money. Quite a lot of money, as it happens. I charge double for virgins.'

'You'll get your money,' said Jack. 'In fact, if you can lead me to Eddie, I'll pay you double your double.'

'He must be losing a lot of sawdust,' said Jill, pointing towards the paper bag which sat beside her on the table, the paper bag which now contained the kitchen-sweepings of Eddie. 'He could be nothing more than a glove puppet soon.'

'Treble your double, then.'

'It's a deal.'

Jack sat himself down on the table. Then, finding himself far too near to the corpse, got up and stood by the stove. 'Go on then,' he said wearily, 'impress me.'

'Right,' said Jill. 'Well, when you went off down the alleyway, I had a few moments to give this kitchen a looking-over before I called the police and swept up the bits of your friend. These were my immediate impressions.'

Jack disguised a sigh as a yawn. Or possibly he didn't.

'Firstly,' said Jill, 'I examined the kitchen door after you went through it into the alley. No signs of forced entry, yet that door is always locked.'

'It was unlocked and open,' said Jack.

'Exactly,' said Jill. 'And the key is always in the lock on the inside, but it isn't now, it's in the outside of the lock. The killer entered through that door by pushing a piece of paper under it from the outside, then poking the key from the lock with a stick, or something. The key drops onto the paper and the paper is pulled under the door. It's very basic stuff. Everyone knows how to do that.'

'Of course,' said Jack. 'Everyone knows that.'

'You obviously didn't. Our killer is now inside, in an empty kitchen, but hears someone coming and so hides.'

'The killer hides?' said Jack. 'Where does the killer hide?'

'The killer hides in that cupboard,' said Jill, pointing to an open cupboard. 'It's the broom cupboard. The door, as you see, is open and the brooms have all been pushed to one side. That's not how I left them.'

'Okay,' said Jack. 'The killer hides in the cupboard; what then?'

'Madame Goose and your friend Eddie enter the kitchen from the hallway. They talk, Eddie helps himself to jam—' Jill pointed to an open jam pot, surrounded by messy paw marks. 'Whatever your friend says to Madame upsets her.'

'How can you tell *that*?' Jack asked.

'Because Madame took down her brandy bottle from that shelf and poured herself a drink. She doesn't drink before midnight unless she's upset about something.'

'Yes, all right,' said Jack. 'This is fair enough. Because you work here. You put the brooms in place, you know about the brandy. I couldn't be expected to figure that stuff out. It's not clever. It's obvious to *you*.'

'Fine,' said Jill. 'Then how about this? The killer burst out of the cupboard, struck down Madame Goose with a broom, picked up a kitchen knife and slit your partner's throat.'

'Whoa, stop,' said Jack.

'Broom,' said Jill, pointing. 'Knife on floor, sawdust on mat. And your killer is a woman, Jack.'

'What?'

'A woman. She's about five foot six in her exclusive high-heeled footwear and she wears pale pink lipstick. She smokes *Sweet Lady* brand cigarettes and favours *Dark Love* perfume.'

'What?' said Jack once more.

'There's the butt end of her cigarette in the broom cupboard. Her lipstick's on it and the mark of her high-heeled boot. I could smell her perfume in the air when I came into the kitchen. As to her height, she swung Madame Goose's body up and onto the table after she killed her, then she trussed her legs. A taller person would have tied them higher, further from the feet. She tied them as high as she could reach without climbing onto the table—there are no heel-marks on the table, I looked. She's about my height. She's *very* strong.'

'Oh,' said Jack.

'And she wears a feather bonnet. There's a feather stuck in the door jamb of the cupboard.'

'Oh,' said Jack, once again.

'Now, my guess is,' said Jill, 'and here it's only a guess, so correct me if I'm wrong, my guess is that if you are a sort-of-detective, you're working on a case. Probably two cases. The two *big* cases that are on the go at the moment: namely, Humpty Dumpty and Boy Blue. Now I'm guessing once again here, but what if these two were linked to a woman, possibly in some romantic fashion. Revenge crimes, perhaps. A wronged lover. A wronged lover in a feathered hat.'

Jack made groaning sounds.

'My feelings then,' said Jill, 'would be that the killer was on to you and your friend. Followed you both here. Overheard what Eddie had to say to Madame Goose and what she in turn said to Eddie, then silenced the both of them. How do you think I'm doing?'

Jack made further groaning sounds.

'There's only one thing that mystifies me.'

'Go on then, what is it?'

'It's *that*,' said Jill and she pointed to the mantelpiece. 'What is *that* doing here?'

Jack looked up at the mantelpiece.

On it stood a hollow chocolate bunny.

Jack drove once more through the streets of Toy City. This time Jill sat beside him. On her lap was the paper bag. The paper bag made Jack very sad.

'I like this car very much,' said Jill. 'Is it yours?'

'It's borrowed,' said Jack. 'So where are we going?'

'We're going to find the killer. You want your friend back and I want my money. Such is the nature of our business arrangement. Why did you change your clothes? I don't think much of that trenchcoat.'

'My waistcoat lost its buttons,' said Jack. 'I can't imagine how that happened, can you?'

'Turn left here,' said Jill.

★

Jack turned left and then left again, and then Jack said *'Oh Boy!'*

'We're here,' said Jill.

'But why are we here?'

'Because it's the only connection we have. Feathered bonnets are this season's fashion amongst the wealthy. It's another "Bucolic Woodland" look. It's a Boy Blue thing. And the heel marks on the cigarette butt, "Boots by *Oh Boy!*".'

'The police have all gone,' said Jack. 'Do you want to go inside?'

'Obviously I do. I'd like to have a little look through Boy Blue's client list. Perhaps we can identify this mystery woman.'

'Let's hope so,' said Jack.

They entered by the rear door of the premises. It was a simple enough business, involving, as it did, Jack sliding a piece of paper under the door, winkling the key out from the inside of the lock with a stick, or something, then pulling the key on the paper under the door.

'As easy as,' said Jack.

Which made him sadder still.

The two slipped into the silent building.

'Let's find the office,' said Jill. 'There'll be a filing cabinet or something.'

Jack followed Jill. They passed through the grand salon, where soft light fell upon the pink marble floor, highlighting a taped contour shape where the body of Boy Blue had lain.

'How did he die?' Jill asked. 'You know, don't you?'

'It wasn't nice,' said Jack. 'Although, I must admit, it was rather funny.'

'Let's go upstairs,' said Jill.

'Where have I heard that before?'

Jill turned a scathing glance on Jack.

'Upstairs it is,' said Jack.

Upstairs they came upon Boy Blue's private office. The door was unlocked and they went inside. Moonlight cast pale shafts through tall windows, lighting upon expensive-looking items of furniture and a very grand desk indeed.

Jill began rooting about in the drawers of the desk.

Jack began touching things that he shouldn't.

'Don't touch those things,' said Jill.

'Don't tell me what to touch.' Jack touched something else, which fell and broke.

'Smench!' it went on the floor.

'Sounded expensive,' said Jill.

Jack joined her at the desk.

'Switch the desk light on,' said Jill.

'Do you think we should? Someone might see the light.'

'Not up here.'

Jack switched on the desk light. 'What have you found?' he asked.

Jill laid a large leather tome on the desktop and began to leaf through it. Vellum paper pages fell one upon another.

'The Spring and Catch Society,' said Jill. 'It's a secret organisation.'

'Then how do you know about it?'

'You'd be surprised the things men tell me.'

'No, I wouldn't,' said Jack.

'Well, it says here that Boy Blue was a member. And so are most of the old rich. These are rituals, see.'

'They don't make any sense.' Jack peered at the page. The words meant nothing to him.

'They're in code.'

'I don't think it's a clue. What about the client list?'

Jill pushed the tome aside and pulled another from the drawer. 'Accounts,' she said, 'let's have a look through this.' She began leafing once more through paper.

'Please get a move on,' said Jack.

'Be patient.'

A sudden sound came to Jack's ears. 'What was that sudden sound?' he asked.

'Nothing. Don't worry.'

'But I heard something. Oh.'

Another sudden sound, this time accompanied by a lot of sudden movement, caused Jack to leap back in shock.

There was now a lot of sudden light. Big and sudden and bright and all shining right at Jack.

'Take him, officers!' shouted a sudden voice.

And all of a suddenness, big, blue, jolly, laughing figures were all over Jack. And Jack was pinned to the floor.

From beneath much pressing weight Jack found himself staring fearfully into the perished rubber face of Chief Inspector Wellington Bellis.

'Gotcha,' said Chief Inspector Bellis. 'They always return to the scene of the crime. I knew I was right. I just had to wait this time.'

'Now hold on there.' Jack struggled without success.

'And you answer to the description of the suspect who broke into

Humpty Dumpty's, earlier today. Bill Winkie, private eye, I arrest you for murder.'

'No, stop, this isn't right.'

'Take him to the station, officers,' said Bellis. 'And if he gives you any trouble, then . . .'

'No,' wailed Jack as laughing policemen dragged him to his feet. 'You've got the wrong man. Tell him, Jill. Tell him.'

But Jill was nowhere to be seen.

13

It is a fact, well known to those who know it well, that there is scarcely to be found anywhere a society which does not hold to some belief in a supreme being.

A God.

A Divine Creator.

Toy City is no exception.

In Toy City a number of different religions exist, each serving the spiritual needs of its particular followers. Four of the more interesting are The Church of Mechanology, The Daughters of the Unseeable Upness, Big Box Fella, He Come, and The Midnight Growlers.

Followers of *The Church of Mechanology* are to be found exclusively amongst members of Toy City's clockwork toy population: wind-up tin-plate barmen, firemen, taxi drivers and the like.

These hold to the belief that the universe is a vast clockwork mechanism, the planets revolving about the sun by means of extendible rotary arms and the sun in turn connected to the galaxy by an ingenious crankshaft system, the entirety powered by an enormous clockwork motor, constantly maintained, oiled, and kept wound by The Universal Engineer.

The Universal Engineer is pictured in religious icons as a large, jolly, red–faced fellow in greasy overalls and cap. He holds in one holy hand an oily rag and in the other, the Church's Sacred Writ, known as *The Manual*.

The Manual contains a series of laws and coda, but, as is often the case with Holy books, these laws and coda are penned in a pidgin dialect of unknown origin, which leaves them open to varied interpretation. An example of its text is *Winding is not to facilitate in counter to the clockways direction for tuning the to.*

Followers of The Church of Mechanology consider themselves special and superior to all other varieties of toy, in that, being clockwork, they are *in tune* and *at one with* the Universe.

A number of sub-sects, breakaway factions and splinter groups exist within The Church, with names such as *The Cog-Wheel of Life, The Spring Almost Eternal* and *The Brotherhood of the Holy Oil.* These are End Times Cults, which subscribe to the belief that, as individual clockwork toys enjoy only a finite existence due to the ravages of rust, corrosion, spring breakage and fluff in the works, so too does the Universe.

Their prophets of doom foretell The Time of the Terrible Stillness, when the great mechanism that powers the Universe will grind to a halt, the planet will no longer turn upon its axis, the sun will no longer rise and even time itself will come to a standstill.

If asked what The Universal Engineer will be doing at this momentous moment, they will politely explain that He will be cranking up a new Universe elsewhere, powered by something even greater than clockwork.

If asked what this power could possibly be, they will like as not reply, 'And there you have it! What power *could* be greater than clockwork?'

The Daughters of the Unseeable Upness is a movement composed entirely of dolls—but only those dolls that have weighted eyes which automatically close when the doll's head is tilted backwards. Such city-dwelling dolls can never see the sky, as their eyes shut when they lean backwards to look upwards. These dolls therefore believe that the sky is a sacred place that must not be seen, and that all who do see it risk instant damnation.

As with clockwork toys, dolls enjoy only a limited existence before they eventually disintegrate, and as the onset of disintegration in dolls is inevitably marked by one of their eyes sticking open, followers of this religious persuasion invariably wear large, broad-brimmed, sanctified straw hats, or have their eyes glued in the half-shut position.

According to the followers of *Big Box Fella, He Come,* as everything new, especially a toy, always comes in a box, then so too did the universe.

The universe, they claim, is a construction kit, which God assembled with the aid of his little helpers. It is God's toy. One day, they claim, God will tire of his toy, disassemble it and, being a well-brought-up God, put it back in its box.

And that will be that for the universe.

This particular religious belief system is predominant amongst

Jack-in-the-boxes. They consider themselves to be special and blessed because they are the only toys that actually remain within their original boxes, the toy nearest to perfection being the toy that has never been taken out of its box.

They believe that the universe is cubic, the shape of its original box, and so see themselves as microcosmic. The assembled universe consists of a number of boxes, one inside the other, the smallest of these containing the Jack himself. This exists within a larger cubic box, the city, which stands upon a cubic world, within a boxed solar system.

Mortals, they claim, cannot travel between the separate boxes: only Big Box Fella can do that—he and his nameless evil twin.

Big Box Fella is one of God's little helpers. He and his brother were given the task of assembling the city, which was part of the Universe Kit. It was God's intention that, once the city had been correctly constructed, Big Box Fella and his brother would tend to its upkeep and protect its also-to-be-assembled population (you have to remember that the universe is a very complicated construction kit).

However, things did not go quite as planned, because Big Box Fella's brother refused to follow the instructions, thereby committing the first ever act of evil. He improvised, with the result that certain things were incorrectly assembled, other things had parts left out and a city that would otherwise have been perfect was anything but.

Big Box Fella cast his brother out of the city and attempted to put things right, but, out of spite, his brother had taken the instructions with him, and so the task was impossible.

Some followers of this cult think that Big Box Fella is still in the city, tirelessly working to correct all his brother's mistakes. Most, however, believe that he left the city and went in search of his evil twin, to retrieve the instructions, and that he will return one glorious day and make everything perfect.

This, they hope, will happen before God tires of his toy universe, takes it all to pieces and puts it back in its box.

The Midnight Growlers has been described as 'a robust and rumbustious cult, more a drinking club than a religion, characterised by rowdy behaviour, the swearing of mighty oaths, the imbibing of strong liquors in prodigious quantities and the performance of naughtiness, for the sake of naughtiness alone'.

For the greater part, the teddies of Toy City (The Midnight Growlers is a teddy bear cult) are law-abiding model citizens, who picnic and go walky-round-the-garden, behave with good grace and exhibit exemplary manners. That within this dutiful ursine population such a wayward faction as The Midnight Growlers should exist is a bit of a mystery.

An investigative reporter from the Toy City press sought to infiltrate this cult. He donned an elaborate teddy costume and managed to pass himself off as a bear, and spoke at length to the Grand High Muck-a-muck of the cult, who referred to himself as The Handsome One. The Handsome One explained many things to the reporter, but the reporter, who was finding it difficult to match The Handsome One drink for drink in the downtown bar where the meeting took place, became too drunk to remember most of them.

The reporter did manage to recall that there was a great deal of convivial camaraderie within the cult, and The Handsome One constantly told him that he was 'his bestest friend'.

The reporter was eventually unmasked, however, when he fell from the barstool, on which he was attempting to balance upon his head, and passed out on the floor.

In none of these religious movements, it is noteworthy to note, is the kindly loveable white-haired old toymaker worshipped as a God. Although he is feared and revered, those toys inclined towards religious belief consider him to be a doer of God's work, but not actually a God in his own right.

The Handsome One declared that he didn't have any particular views on the subject of God, but that as far as the toymaker was concerned, he was 'his bestest friend'.

Then he too fell off his barstool.

At this present moment, however, The Handsome One and Grand High Muck-a-muck of The Midnight Growlers Cult (indeed, if the truth be told, the *only* member of The Midnight Growlers Cult) was a most unhappy bear.

He lay downcast and best-friend-less upon the cold damp floor of a cold damp cell, and he dearly wanted a beer.

The coldness and dampness of his circumstances did not concern him too much, but other things concerned him greatly.

The nature of his being, being one.

And this is not to say the *cosmic* nature of his being.

It was the physical nature of his being that presently concerned him. And the nature of this being was, to say the very least, *desperate*.

Eddie Bear raised himself upon a feeble paw and gazed down at the state of himself. It was a state to inspire great pity.

Eddie was no longer a plump little bear. He was a scrawny bear, an emaciated bear, a bear deeply sunken in the stomach regions. A bear with only one serviceable leg.

This leg, the right, was a weedy-looking article, but was superior to its companion, which was nothing but an empty flap of furry fabric.

Eddie groaned, and it hurt when he did so. Eddie's throat had been viciously cut and his head was all but severed from his body.

Eddie surveyed the bleak landscape of himself. This was bad. This was very bad. Indeed this was very, very, very bad. Eddie was in trouble deep, and such trouble troubled him deeply. Eddie Bear was afraid.

'I am done for,' mumbled Eddie.

And it hurt very much as he mumbled it.

Eddie tried to recall what had happened to him, but this wasn't proving an easy thing to do. The contents of his head were slowly leaking out through the gash in his neck. Eddie settled carefully onto his back and tried to scrape some in again.

What could he remember?

Well . . .

He could remember the kitchen. And Madame Goose. And asking her what she knew about an agile woman in a feathered bonnet who was capable of leaping over the locked gates of the chocolate factory.

Now why had he been asking about that?

Eddie gave his head a thump.

Ah yes, the woman was the suspect. The serial killer.

What happened next?

Eddie gave his head another thump and it all came rushing painfully back.

That was what happened next.

Eddie recalled it in all its hideous detail:

The door of the broom cupboard opened and Eddie was the first to see her emerge. He was impressed by the way she moved. It was smooth, almost fluid. And you couldn't help but be impressed by the way she looked. She wore a feathered bonnet, but it wasn't so much a bonnet, more some kind of winged headpiece, which fitted tightly over her skull and covered the upper portion of her face: a mask with cutaway eyeholes and a slender beak that hid her nose. The mouth beneath was painted a pink that was as pink as. And this was set into a sinister smile. The teeth that showed within this smile were very white indeed.

Her body was, in itself, something to inspire awe. Eddie had never been an appreciator of the human form. All women looked pretty much the same to him (apart from the very fat ones. These made Eddie laugh, but he found them strangely compelling). This woman wasn't fat anywhere. She was slim as a whispered secret, and twice as dangerous, too.

Her body was sheathed in contour-hugging black rubber, held in place by many straps and buckles. Eddie had never seen an outfit quite like it before. It looked very chic and expensive, but it also had the down-to-business utility quality of a military uniform about it. It flattered in an impersonal manner.

She hadn't spoken a word. And this made her somehow more terrifying—because, if she inspired awe in Eddie, she also inspired terror.

She leapt right over the table and she wrung the neck of Madame Goose with the fingers of a single hand. And then she picked up a kitchen knife and cut Eddie's throat with it.

The rest was somewhat hazy.

Eddie vaguely recalled being hauled up by his left leg, dragged along an alleyway and flung into the boot of a car. Then there was a period of bumping darkness. Then a horrible light. Then dark corridors. Then here. The cold damp cell.

And oblivion.

And now he was awake again. And gravely injured.

And very scared indeed.

Jack wasn't so much scared as furious.

He had been wrongfully arrested. And he had been beaten about and thrown into the rear of a police van. And now he was being driven uptown at breakneck speed. And there was a big policeman sitting on his head.

'Get your fat arse off me,' cried Jack. 'You're in big trouble. You can't treat me like this.'

Officer Chortle, whose bottom it was, laughed loudly. 'We have you bang to rights, meaty-boy,' he said. 'We've all been waiting for this one.'

'What do you mean?' Jack asked.

'For the chance to bring one of your lot to justice.'

'I don't have a *lot*,' said Jack. 'I'm just me.'

'You're a man,' said Officer Chortle. 'And men think, they're above the law. The law is for toy folk, not for men. But you've killed your own kind and we have you now.'

'I demand my rights,' Jack demanded. 'And I demand to see a solicitor.' Jack had read about solicitors in a Bill Winkie thriller. Suspects always demanded to see their solicitors. It was a tradition, or an old charter, or something.

It was a suspect thing.

'No solicitor for you,' said Officer Chortle, who read only weapons manuals. (Though mostly he just looked at the pictures.) 'You're going uptown and we'll lock you away until all the paper-work's done. Then I think we'll take you to pieces, to see what makes you run.'

'No!' Jack shouted. 'You can't do that to me.'

'Tell it to Bellis,' said the officer.

'Is he here?'

'No, he went on ahead. Probably to warm your cell for you. He left me to act on my own initiative. I love it when he does that. It means that I can hit things.'

'Listen,' said Jack, trying to think straight, 'can't we make some kind of a deal?'

'Are you trying to bribe an officer of the Law?'

'Frankly, yes,' said Jack.

'Go on then,' said the officer of the Law.

'All right,' said Jack. 'You hate meat-heads, don't you?'

'I do,' said Officer Chortle. 'We all do.'

'So you don't really care about them being killed.'

'Not at all,' said the officer.

'So the more that get killed, the happier you'll be.'

'That's true,' the officer agreed.

'So let me go and I promise to kill loads more of them. I'll kill them all, if you want. What could be fairer than that?'

'Well,' said Officer Chortle, 'if you put it that way,' and he raised his bum from Jack's head.

'Thanks,' said Jack.

'Had you fooled.' Officer Chortle sat down once more. 'That's all the confession we needed. You heard what he said, didn't you, men?'

'Yes we did,' said the officers, laughing fit to burst.

The police van sped onwards through the night-time streets of Toy City, the bell on its top ringing loudly. The ringing of this bell gave Jack a headache. The pressure of Officer Chortle's bottom didn't help to soothe the pain.

'You've got the wrong man, you know,' Jack ventured.

'You've said enough,' said Chortle. 'Be silent now, or I will be forced to plug your mouth.'

Jack maintained another of his sulking silences.

At length a new sound came to Jack's ears. It was louder than the ringing bell and it caused Officer Chortle to raise his bum once more.

'What is *that*?' he shouted above the sound, which had grown to an all but intolerable din. It was now accompanied by a considerable grinding vibration.

The driver of the police van shouted back at Officer Chortle. 'It's a fire engine,' he shouted. 'A Mark 5 Roaring Thunderer. The deluxe model. It's trying to push us off the road.'

'What?' shouted Officer Chortle. 'That's outrageous. Push it back.'

'But sir, it's a Roaring Thunderer. It's bigger than us. Much bigger.'

Officer Chortle glared out through the police van's rear window. The Roaring Thunderer *was* much bigger. Very much bigger indeed.

'Do something, driver,' he ordered. 'I'm in charge here. Take evasive action.'

The driver took evasive action. He swerved onto the pavement, scattering pedestrians, including several who had, by coincidence, been earlier scattered by Jack.

'He's coming after us,' shouted the driver. And the Roaring Thunderer was.

It really was a magnificent vehicle. Constructed of heavy gauge pressed steel and finished in glossy red and black, it had a nickel-plated ladder, with wheel-operated rotating turntable and elevation extension, powered by a crank handle, pressed steel wheels and a cab-mounted bell. It normally came complete with six tinplate firemen, two with hose-gripping hand attachments.

Had Jack been able to see it, he would have admired it. And he certainly would have wanted to drive it. The reflected streetlights glittered on its polished bits and bots. It was mechanised by two extremely powerful double-sprung synchronised clockwork motors which took five clockwork firemen to turn its enormous key.

The Roaring Thunderer careered along the kerb, striking down lampposts and tearing the overhanging awnings from the shops and bazaars. It struck the police van once again. The driver of the police van took to praying.

'You're not a mechanologist,' shouted Officer Chortle. 'You're a bendy policeman. Cut that out and drive faster.'

'The van won't go any faster. Oh no!'

The police van overturned. Over and over and over it overturned.

Within the van, the officers of the Law and their captive revolved in a blur of blue bouncing bellies and long lanky limbs. The rear doors burst open and Jack found himself airborne.

And then things went very black for Jack.

Very black indeed.

★

Eddie moved once more into the black. Unconsciousness was never anything other than black for Eddie, for teddy bears don't dream while they sleep. They exist in a state of non-being which is truly unconscious.

How long Eddie remained in this particular period of blackness he was unable to say, because he didn't have a watch. He had tried to wear one in the past, but it always fell off, his stumpy little arm lacking a wrist. This particular period of blackness ended in an abrupt fashion when a bright light shone upon him.

Eddie peered up, shielding his eyes with a floppy paw.

A figure stared down upon Eddie.

Eddie flinched.

The figure said, 'Eddie, it's you.'

Eddie said, '*Jack?* My bestest friend? Is that you?'

'It's me,' said Jack. 'It's me.'

'And you've come to save me. Jack, this is wonderful, how—'

But Eddie's words were cut short as Jack was suddenly propelled forward at considerable speed. He landed heavily upon the bear, raising a cloud of sawdust and causing Eddie's button eyes to all but pop from his head.

Before he passed once more into blackness, Eddie was able to glimpse the force behind Jack's untoward propulsion.

Standing in the doorway of the cell was the woman in the winged headpiece.

She didn't speak a word. She just smiled.

And then she slammed the cell door shut upon both of them.

14

'Kidnapped.' Jack sat shivering in the coldness and dampness and in the mostly darkness of the horrid little cell. 'She kidnapped me. She hijacked a fire engine, drove the police van off the road, I fell out, she picked me up and threw me in the boot of a car and drove here. Where is here, by the way? Oh, Eddie, I'm so glad to see you.'

'Kidnapped?' Eddie whispered. 'Police van?'

'It's a long story,' said Jack, giving the bear's sunken belly a gentle pat. 'And it's far from over. Who is she, Eddie? She's really scary.'

Eddie tried to shake his head, but couldn't.

'I'm sorry I fell on you,' said Jack. 'And I can't see you too well in this mostly darkness. But from what I can see, you look in a terrible state. Is there anything I can do for you?'

'Get me out of here,' Eddie's voice was faint. 'Get me to the toy-maker. Only he can save me.'

'Oh Eddie, I'm so sorry. Can't I stuff you with something? I could tear up your trenchcoat.'

'Won't work. Get me to the toymaker, Jack. Save me.'

'But how?'

'Use your clockwork pistol. Shoot the lock off.'

'Chief Inspector Bellis confiscated my pistol. He said it was evidence.' Jack rose and peeped out through the little grille in the cell door. 'Perhaps the key's in the lock,' he said. 'I know this really clever trick.'

'Everybody knows that trick.' Eddie made small moaning sounds. 'The key won't be in the lock.'

'There might be a loose flagstone with a secret passage under it. There often is in books.'

Eddie moaned a little more.

'Don't worry, Eddie, I'll get us out of here.' Jack knelt once more and cradled Eddie's wobbly head. 'You'll be all right,' he said. 'I'll get you to the toymaker. He'll have you as good as new. Better than new.'

Eddie's button eyes crossed.

'Stay awake, Eddie.' Jack stroked the bear's head. 'We're in this together. We're partners, aren't we? Partners don't let each other down. Partners stick together through thick and thin.'

Eddie said nothing.

'Come on, stay awake.' Jack shook Eddie's head, but gently. 'Don't you . . .' His words tailed off. 'Don't you . . .'

'Die?' whispered Eddie. 'Get me to the toymaker.'

'Right,' said Jack. And he leapt to his feet.

'Ow,' went Eddie as his head struck the floor.

'Sorry, sorry. But I'll get us out. I will.'

Jack looked all around and about. Around and about looked hopeless: a horrid little cell of coldness and dampness and mostly darkness. A sturdy cell door and not a hint of window. The floor was of concrete, with no hint of flagstone.

'Only one way out,' said Jack. 'I'll have to pick the lock.'

Eddie said nothing. The chances that Jack could actually pick a lock were so remote that they did not require commenting upon.

Jack peered into the keyhole. A wan light shone through it.

'Hm,' went Jack thoughtfully. 'That would be a big old lock, by the look of it.'

To save his energy, Eddie groaned inwardly.

'But,' said Jack, 'it's probably just your standard side-crank mortise lock, with a single-arc lever action and a drop-bolt sliding movement.'

'Uh?' went Eddie.

'Locks are only clockwork motors without the motors,' said Jack. 'And if I do know about anything, Eddie, I know about clockwork.'

'Mm,' went Eddie, in an encouraging manner.

'So,' said Jack. 'All I need is something to pick it with.' He rooted around in his pockets. 'Ah,' he went at length. It was a discouraging 'Ah'. The kind of an 'Ah' that a lad might make when he finds that he has nothing whatsoever in his pockets to pick a lock with.

'Eddie,' said Jack.

Eddie said nothing.

'Eddie, I don't suppose you have a piece of wire about your person?'

Eddie said nothing once more.

'It's only that if you did, I really *could* pick that lock. But I don't seem to have anything on me.'

Eddie raised a feeble paw.

Jack knelt down beside him. 'Sorry,' said Jack.

Eddie's mouth opened.

Jack leaned closer.

'Growler,' whispered Eddie.

'Well there's no need to be insulting. I'm doing my best.'

'My growler. Use my growler.'

'What?'

'There's wire in the diaphragm of my growler, use that.'

'What?' went Jack again.

'Put your hand down the hole in my throat. Pull out my growler; do it quickly, hurry.'

'But,' went Jack, 'are you sure it won't kill you or anything?'

'Just do it now, Jack. There's no time left.'

Jack made a pained expression. The idea of putting his hand through the hole in someone's throat and tearing out their voice box was most unappealing. But then, Eddie was only a toy.

Jack made a brave face. Eddie wasn't *only* a toy. Eddie was his friend. His bestest friend. And he had to save his friend. Jack steeled himself and then, very gently, he did what had to be done.

Eddie sighed softly. His mouth moved, but no words came from it.

'We're out of here,' said Jack. 'Just trust me.'

Now as anyone who has ever tried to pick a lock will tell you, there's a definite knack to it: a bit like riding a bike, or holding a tiger by the tail, or dining with the devil with a very long fork. Or, if you are into sexual gymnastics, engaging in that position known as 'taking tea with the parson'.

Or doing algebra.

Or climbing a mountain.

Or knowing the secret of when to stop.

But the point of all this is, that some of us have the knack.

And some of us haven't.

And when it came to picking locks, Jack hadn't.

'There,' said Jack. 'That's got it.'

But it hadn't.

'There,' he said once more. '*That's* got it.'

And it had.

Which certainly proves something.

Jack eased open the cell door. No hideous groaning of hinges broke the silence.

What light that could fall through the cell doorway fell through, in and onto Eddie. It displayed, in gruesome detail, just how dire the little bear's condition now was.

'You'll be fine,' said Jack, although there was a lack of conviction in his tone. 'I'm going to have to fold you up a bit and stuff you into my big inside pocket. I'll stick you in head downwards, so you don't, you know, lose any more brains or anything.'

Jack did the business as delicately as he could.

He closed and buttoned his coat. Patting softly at the bulge that was Eddie, he whispered, 'You'll be okay, my friend.' And then, upon very light feet indeed, Jack tiptoed up the passageway.

It was a low and narrow passageway and all along its length there were other cell doors. Jack didn't stop to peep in at any, but he felt certain he could feel eyes peering at him through the rusty little grilles. Jack hastened his tiptoeing. This was not a nice place to be.

Up ahead was an iron staircase. Jack took the steps two at a time.

And then there was another passageway.

And then another.

And then one more.

And then another one more.

And then there was an iron staircase leading down.

And then another passageway.

And then Jack was back at the open cell door.

'Ah,' said Jack. 'Now there's a thing.'

Jack retraced his footsteps.

Now it would be tedious indeed to continue with this kind of stuff for too long, what with some of us knowing the secret of knowing when to stop. So let it just be said that after a great deal more passageway perambulation, Jack eventually came upon a door that led to a street. And, having picked its lock, opened it. And on that street, which was not one that Jack recognised, there stood an automobile.

It was long and low and expensive-looking. And Jack, who still had some lock-picking left in him, availed himself of this automobile and drove it away at some speed.

Jack drove and drove until the car ran down, rewound it and drove on some more. He eventually found himself in an area of the city that he recognised, and finally he drove up Knob Hill towards the house of the kindly loveable white-haired old toymaker.

It was a fine old house. A fine *dark* house: all turrets and spires and gables. Its leaded glass windows were deeply mullioned and its slated roofs pitched at queer angles. There were buttresses fashioned with grinning gargoyles and all kinds of glorious architectural fiddly bits. These fussed around and about the house and offered the eye of the beholder much to dwell upon.

There were no fences or gates, only a bit of a gravel drive. Jack parked the car upon this, told Eddie, 'We're here,' and removed himself at speed to the toymaker's door.

The door was a singularly magnificent affair. It put Jack in mind of Humpty Dumpty's door. It was old-style grand.

At its centre was a large, carved smiley face with a huge brass ring through its nose. This ring was the knocker. Jack reached out towards it.

'Don't even think about touching that,' said the carved smiley face. 'You can't come in. Goodbye.'

Although little about Toy City now surprised Jack, the carved smiley face on the door caught him somewhat unawares.

'Oh,' said Jack. 'Oh.'

'Oh?' said the face. 'Is that all you have to say for yourself?'

'I have to see the toymaker,' said Jack.

'Say please then.'

'Please,' said Jack.

'No,' said the face. 'Go away.'

'I *have* to see the toymaker. It's urgent. It's a matter of life and death.'

'It always is,' said the face. 'No one ever comes just to pay a visit. Or bring presents. Oh no, they turn up here at all hours of the night saying "my arm's fallen off", or "my spring's coming loose", or "a rat's gnawed my foot", or . . .'

Jack reached out his hand.

'Don't touch my knocker,' said the face. 'I'll bite you.'

'I have a bear here that needs fixing.'

'There you go,' said the face. 'See what I mean? I knew it. I just knew it. Go away. Come back tomorrow.'

'Let me in now,' said Jack.

'And what happened to *please*?'

'Right,' said Jack. 'Stuff you.' And he pulled out the wire from Eddie's growler and prepared to pick yet another lock.

'What are you doing?' asked the face.

'Letting myself in,' said Jack.

'You can't do that. It's more than my job's worth to let you do that.'

'Do you have a brother by any chance?' Jack asked.

'Certainly do. He's the gatekeeper at the chocolate factory.'

'What a surprise,' said Jack. 'Well, I'm letting myself in.'

'But you can't *do* that.'

'And what are you going to do about it?'

The face made a thoughtful face. 'You've got me there,' it said. 'If you were in my position, what would you do?'

'Well,' said Jack. 'You discourage folk from entering, don't you?'

'I certainly do,' said the face. 'Lot of selfish timewasters. I keep 'em out. Stop them from bothering the toymaker.'

'And that's your job, is it?' Jack was growing frantic.

'Not as such,' said the face. 'I act on my own initiative.'

'So when was the last time you actually let anyone in?'

The face made an even more thoughtful face. 'Can't remember,' it said. 'Ages ago.'

'So no one ever gets to see the toymaker?'

'He's busy. He designs toys.'

'How do you know what he does?' Jack's fingers were now at the keyhole.

'I can see what you're doing,' said the face.

'So what are you going to do about it?'

The face made a thoughtful face, perhaps even *more* thoughtful than the previous one. Then suddenly it made an enlightened face. 'Raise the alarm,' it said.

'How?' Jack asked.

The face began to frantically knock its knocker.

'Inspired,' said Jack. 'You certainly are a credit to your profession.'

Knock Knock Knock Knock Knock went the knocker.

And at length the door opened.

Jack looked in.

And a very old face looked out at him.

It was a very old face, but it was a big one: a big face on a large head that was attached to a little body.

Now it is another fact, well known to those who know it well, that very famous people always have big faces. They have big faces and little bodies. Why this is, no one knows for sure—even those who know facts well don't know it. But it's true and there it is.

Jack said, 'Sir, are you the toymaker?'

'I am the kindly loveable white-haired old toymaker,' said the toymaker, and he indicated his hair and the kindliness of his features. And they *were* kindly. *Very* kindly.

'Then, sir, please, I need your help. My friend has been grievously injured.'

'I can only help toys,' said the toymaker.

'Intruder!' shrieked the wooden face. 'Call the police!'

'Be quiet, Peter,' said the toymaker.

'My friend is a toy,' said Jack. 'He's a bear.' Jack opened his coat.

The toymaker peered in. 'From what I can see, he looks a little under the weather,' said he. 'You'd best bring him in and I'll see what I can do.'

'Thank you, sir,' said Jack.

'And enough of that *sir* business. My name is Mr Anders. You can call me Anders.'

'That doesn't sound too polite.'

'It's my first name. I'm Anders Anders.'

'Oh,' said Jack.

The toymaker swung wide the door and, much to the disgust of the carved knocker face, ushered Jack inside.

It's strange how some homes are so much bigger on the inside than you would expect, isn't it?

So it came as a huge surprise to Jack to find just how really small the toymaker's house was inside.

Jack had to duck his head.

'It's a spatial ambiguity thing,' the toymaker explained as he led Jack towards his workroom. 'Something to do with the transperambulation of pseudo-cosmic antimatter. Easily explainable in terms of quantum physics, if you know what I mean.'

'Haven't a clue,' said Jack.

'Well, let's get your little friend onto the workbench and see what can be done for him.'

'Yes,' said Jack. 'Let's do that.'

The workroom was *exactly* as Jack might have expected it to look.

Tools of many persuasions were racked on every wall between shelves and shelves of gingham and lace and kapok and countless jars containing glass eyes that stared out blankly at Jack. Sewing machines and other machines jostled for space upon a workbench crowded with half-completed toys. Beneath this, rolls and rolls of fur fabric of every bear shade were piled upon one another in furry confusion. From the low ceiling hung dolls' arms and legs of all sizes and shapes.

A coal fire burned brightly in a tiny fireplace and beside this stood a comfy-looking chair.

'Onto the bench with him then,' said the toymaker.

Jack carefully eased Eddie from his pocket and laid him down on the workbench.

'Oh dear,' said the toymaker. 'This is a very sorry-looking bear. I think we'd be better just to bin him.'

'No!' said Jack. 'No, please, he's my friend. Save him if you can.'

'Your friend,' said the toymaker. 'He really *is* your friend?'

'He is,' said Jack. 'I care about him.'

'Nice,' said the toymaker. 'Very nice.' And he looked once more upon Eddie. 'Ah,' he said. 'I know this model. It's one of the old Anders Standards.'

'I was given to understand that he's an Anders Imperial,' said Jack. 'He has a "special tag" in his ear.'

Mr Anders viewed the "special tag". He raised a quizzical eyebrow and then he laughed. 'Toys will be toys,' he said. 'And this one, you say, is your friend?'

Jack nodded. 'My bestest friend,' he said.

'Nice,' said the toymaker once more. 'Everyone should have a bestest friend. And a bear is as good as any to have. But this little bear is all but gone. Perhaps I should empty out his head and give him a complete refill.'

'No, please don't do that. He's Eddie, let him still be Eddie.'

'You really *do* care, don't you?'

'Very much,' said Jack.

'I'll leave his head alone then and just re-stuff the rest of him.'

'He needs a new growler,' said Jack.

'He's lost his growler? What a careless little bear.' The toymaker shook his kindly white-haired old head. 'Well, you go and sit yourself down in that comfy-looking chair and I'll see what I can do to save your Eddie.'

'Thank you, sir.' Jack took himself over to the comfy-looking chair and sat down upon it.

'You can't sit here,' said the chair.

'Oh,' said Jack, leaping up.

'Quiet, you,' the toymaker told the chair. 'He's my guest. Sit down again, my boy.'

'Jack,' said Jack. 'My name is Jack.'

'There'll never be a shortage of Jacks in this city,' said the toymaker, and he set to work upon Eddie.

Jack sat down once more. The chair made a grumpy sound and did what it could to make itself uncomfortable.

Jack watched the toymaker at work.

So this was him: the man behind it all. The man who somehow brought toys to life. The man with the Big Secret. And here he was in his workshop, putting Eddie back together. And being so kindly and loveable and white-haired and everything.

And then it all hit Jack. All of a sudden. Like.

The toymaker didn't know, did he? He had no idea at all about what was going on out there in Toy City. He didn't know what a ghastly dystopia of a place it had become. He was all cosseted away here, guarded by the knocker on his front door.

'How are you doing?' Jack asked the toymaker.

'It will take a bit of time. Perhaps you'd better come back in the morning.'

Jack thought about this, but, no, he had nowhere to go. He was a wanted man. The police were after him. And the wild woman with the winged hat. She'd probably know by now that he'd escaped, *and* stolen her car.

'I'll stay here, if you don't mind,' said Jack.

'Then get yourself some sleep,' said the toymaker. 'That chair is very comfortable.'

'Thanks,' said Jack as the chair made rocky fists beneath his bum. 'I am rather tired, as it happens. And rather hungry too, as that happens also.'

'I'll wake you for breakfast then,' said the toymaker.

What a nice man, thought Jack and, even with rocky fists under his bum, was very soon fast asleep.

15

Jack did not enjoy a lot of restful slumbering. Jack spent the night assailed by terrible dreams. And they really *were* terrible, filled with murder and mayhem and him running and running, pursued by all manner of monstrous nasties. Jack tossed and turned and fretted and mumbled and finally awoke to find that he had been thoughtfully covered by a colourful quilt, but had the silly big face of a bear grinning down at him.

'Waaah!' went Jack, leaping up.

'Easy, chap.' The silly big face vanished as Eddie Bear fell to the floor.

'Eddie, it's you. You're fixed.'

'I'm as good as.' Eddie fairly beamed.

Jack looked down at Eddie. Eddie looked up at Jack.

'Eddie,' said Jack.

'Jack, chap?' said Eddie.

'Eddie,' said Jack. 'That isn't your voice.'

'New growler, chap,' said Eddie. 'Posh, ain't it?'

'Very posh,' said Jack. 'But I don't like the *chap* business.'

'Sorry, chap. I mean, sorry, Jack. And thank you. Thank you very much.'

'My pleasure,' said Jack. 'And oh. I smell breakfast.'

Jack and Eddie took their breakfast with the kindly loveable white-haired old toymaker. It was a banquet of a breakfast; a belly-busting beano; a guzzling gourmand's groaning-board blowout. It consisted, amongst other things, of creamed crad, honeyed ham, devilled dumplings and grilled greengages, not to mention the sautéed salmon, spiced spinach, parboiled pumpkin and peppered persimmon. Nor indeed, the caramelised carrots or the fricasséed frog.

And during the course of this eclectic and alliterative breakfast, Jack did his best to engage the toymaker in conversation.

'Sir,' said Jack, 'I'm so very grateful to you for saving my friend. If I had any money, then I'd gladly pay you. But if there is anything I can do for you, please tell me and I'll do it.'

'There isn't,' said the toymaker, munching on marinated mallard.

'Anything at all,' said Jack, toying with his tenderised tit.

'Nothing,' said the toymaker, skilfully spearing stuffed starfish with his filigreed fork.

'I'm very good with clockwork.' Jack diddled with a deep-fried dogfish. 'I was apprenticed.'

'Where?' the toymaker asked as he pursued a pickled pea around his plate.

Jack told him where.

The toymaker raised a snowy eyebrow. 'And you left there to come to the city?'

'It's a long story,' said Jack, 'but if there's anything I can do . . . if you need an apprentice or an assembler or—'

Eddie kicked Jack under the table.

'When I've finished the work I'm presently engaged in, of course.' Jack scooped up and swallowed a sliver of souffléd sugar beet.

'And what work is that?' asked the toymaker.

'I'm—'

Eddie kicked Jack again.

'Ouch,' said Jack and he glared at Eddie.

Eddie put his paw up to his mouth and made shushing sounds.

The toymaker looked from Jack to Eddie and then back at Jack once more.

'It's lowly work,' said Jack. 'Compared to what you do, it's absolutely nothing.'

'I don't consider what I do to be work.' The toymaker pushed a portion of potted plums onto his plate. 'What I do is fun and games. Everything I do is fun and games. The fun for me is in the game. The game is in the fun.'

'Right,' said Jack, 'but, sir—'

'Call me Anders,' said the toymaker. 'Anders Anders is my name.'

'Mr Anders, then. Can I ask you a question?'

'I don't know,' said Anders Anders, '*can* you?'

'*May* I ask you a question?'

'You may.'

'Then please will you tell me, how is it done?'

'How is what done?'

'The toys, how do you bring them to life?'

'You can't ask *that*.' Eddie, whose face was full of flambéed flamingo, spat much of it all over Jack.

'Steady on,' said Jack, wiping himself.

'You can't ask Mr Anders *that*! Bad chap!'

'He can,' said Mr Anders. 'He can ask.'

'Then how *do* you do it?'

'I said you could ask. I didn't say that I would tell you.'

'And so you won't?'

Mr Anders shook his kindly loveable white-haired old head. 'No,' he said.

'Then please just tell me this,' said Jack. 'Is it magic?'

The toymaker shook his head once more. 'Not magic,' he said. 'Science. And that is all I will say. One day I may well take on an apprentice. And one day, perhaps, that apprentice will be you. But not today and not for a long time yet to come. So, for now, would you care for some more of this frazzled falafel?'

'Yes please,' said Jack.

'Me too,' said Eddie. 'And another of those bevelled brownies.'

When the breakfasting was finally done with and Jack and Eddie, big-bellied both, bade the toymaker farewell, Jack offered his hand and the ancient fellow shook it.

'I'm very grateful, sir,' said Jack. 'I really truly am.'

'Anders,' said Anders Anders. 'Just call me Anders.'

'Thank you, Anders,' said Jack. 'I am deeply grateful.'

'That goes for me too, chap,' said Eddie. 'Chap, *sir*. Thank you, thank you, thank you.'

'Look after each other,' said the toymaker. 'And be good.'

The door closed upon them. 'And don't come back,' said the carved face of Peter upon it.

'Well,' said Jack. 'Wasn't he the nice one.'

'A regular gent,' said Eddie.

'You know I'm sure that if we'd asked him nicely, he'd have seen his way clear to fitting you out with opposable thumbs.'

'*Weaah!*' went Eddie.

'*Weaah?*' queried Jack.

'*Weaah* there,' Eddie pointed a paw with a non-opposable or any otherwise thumb. 'It's *her* car! *She's* here.'

'Calm down, Eddie,' said Jack. 'I stole the car.'

'Right,' said Eddie. 'Well done, chap.'

'Please stop it with the *chap* thing.'

'I can't help it. It's the new growler. It'll wear in, bear with me.' Jack laughed.

'Why are you laughing?'

'You said bear with me. And you're a bear.'

'That is *very* sad,' said Eddie.

'You're the same old Eddie,' said Jack. 'Shall we go?'

'We shall,' said Eddie.

'And where to?'

'Back to the serial killer's hideout. We'll stake the place out and then plan how we can capture her.'

'Ah,' said Jack. 'Ah.'

Jack drove the car and Eddie sat trying to fold his arms and look huff-full.

'Never made a note of the address,' said Eddie. 'How unprofessional is *that*?'

'I was thinking of *you*. I just wanted to get you to the toymaker's.'

'Yeah, well.'

'How dare you "Yeah, well" me. I saved your life.'

'Yes, you did. And I'm very grateful. But we have to stop this thing.'

'You were right, though, Eddie. It's a woman.'

'I wasn't right,' said Eddie. 'Take a left here.'

Jack took a left. 'Why weren't you right?' he asked.

'Because she's *not* a woman.'

'*Not* a woman? You're saying she's some kind of toy?'

'She's not a toy,' said Eddie.

'Not a woman and not a toy? So what is she, Eddie?'

'I don't know,' said the bear. 'And that's what really worries me.'

'She's a woman,' said Jack. 'A very strange woman, I grant you, but she's a woman. I know what women look like and she looks like a woman.'

'But she doesn't smell like one,' said Eddie. 'Under the perfume, she doesn't smell like a woman. I've got a bear's nose.' Eddie tapped at that nose. 'My nose knows.'

'She's a woman,' said Jack.

'She's not,' said Eddie. 'Take a right.'

Jack took a right. 'Where are we going?' he asked.

'Back to Wibbly's,' said Eddie. 'I asked him to check out a few things for me. We'll see how he got on.'

★

Eventually they arrived at Wibbly's. Jack waited in the car while Eddie slid down Wibbly's ramp. Eddie returned and Eddie didn't look at all well. He flopped in the passenger seat and stared at the dashboard.

'What did he say?' Jack asked.

'He didn't say anything.'

'He didn't find out anything?'

'No, Jack,' Eddie looked up at Jack. 'He didn't say anything because he couldn't say anything. Wibbly is all over the floor. Someone smashed him all to pieces.'

'No,' said Jack.

'We have to stop her,' said Eddie. 'Whatever she is, we have to stop her. Madame Goose was bad enough, but Wibbly was a close friend. This time it's personal.'

Jack stared out through the windscreen. 'We've got her car,' he said. 'Can't we trace her through the car?'

A smile broke out upon Eddie's face. 'Good one, Jack, chap,' he said. 'Let's have a go at that.'

The showrooms of the Clockwork Car Company were in the very best part of the city, just five doors down from *Oh Boy!*.

The building itself was a magnificent affair and a description of its architectural splendours might well have filled several paragraphs, had anyone been in the mood to write them down. But if anyone had been in the mood, then that mood might well have been modified by the fact that the showrooms of the Clockwork Car Company were presently fiercely ablaze.

Jack leapt out of the car. Eddie leapt out with him. Clockwork fire-fighters were unrolling hoses. Crowds viewed the holocaust, oohing and ahhing. Jolly red-faced policemen held back these crowds, ha-ha-hahing as they did so. A crenellated column toppled and fell, striking the pavement with a devastating sprunch.

'She got here first,' said Jack. 'She's very thorough, isn't she?'

'Very,' said Eddie. 'Very thorough.'

Jack gawped up at the roaring flames.

'Eddie,' he said.

'Jack?' said Eddie.

'Eddie, if she's that thorough, then she knew we'd come here, didn't she?'

Eddie nodded.

'And would I be right in thinking that she probably wants to kill us now?'

Eddie nodded again.

'So doesn't it follow that she'd probably be here? Awaiting our arrival?'

'Back into the car,' said Eddie. 'Quick as you can, please, chap.'

And quick as they could, they were back in the car.

'Drive?' said Jack.

'Drive,' said Eddie. 'No, don't drive.'

'Don't?' said Jack.

'Don't,' said Eddie. 'That's exactly what she wants us to do.'

'It's exactly what *I* want us to do,' said Jack. 'And fast.'

'Exactly. So that's exactly what we mustn't do. If we make a run for it, she'll come after us. We must stay here amongst all these folk. She's less likely to attack us here.'

'A vanload of policemen didn't worry her too much last night,' said Jack.

'Well, unless you can come up with a better idea.'

'There's policemen here,' said Jack. 'And the police are after me. They think I'm the murderer.'

'Forget about the policemen,' Eddie said. 'Worry about her. We can't have her hunting us. That's not the way detectives do business. It's unprofessional. Bill Winkie would never have let that happen. We're going about this all the wrong way.'

'Well done,' said Jack.

'It just makes sense,' said Eddie.

'No I didn't mean that. I meant that you got seven whole sentences out without once calling me chap.'

'Let's go and watch the fire, *in the crowd*,' said Eddie. 'Chap!'

It's a sad–but–truism that there really is a great deal of pleasure to be had in watching a building burn. There shouldn't be, of course. A burning building is a terrible thing: the destruction of property, the potential for loss of life. There shouldn't be any pleasure at all in watching a thing like that. But there is. And every man knows that there is, not that many of them will own up to it.

It's a small boy thing, really. Small boys love fires. They love starting and nurturing fires, poking things into them, seeing how they burn. Small boys are supposed to grow out of such small boy things when they become big boys, of course. But they don't. The bigger the boy, the bigger the fire the bigger boy likes to get started.

And when bigger boys become men, they never lose their love of fire. They can always find something that needs burning in the backyard.

And when a man hears the ringing of those fire engine bells, the temptation to jump into the car and pursue the appliance is a tough one to resist.

And if a man just happens to be walking down the street and actually sees a building on fire . . . Well.

Jack stared up at the flames.

'What a tragedy,' he said.

'What a liar you are,' said Eddie. 'You're loving every moment.'

'No I'm not.'

'Then why were you jumping up and down and cheering?'

'Was I?' Jack asked.

'You were,' said Eddie. 'Bad, bad chap.'

'It's a small boy thing,' Jack explained. 'You wouldn't understand.'

'I certainly wouldn't,' said Eddie. 'I'm full of sawdust, remember?'

'Sorry,' said Jack. 'So what about your plan?'

'We hunted are going to become the hunters. Merge into the crowd with me, Jack, and keep your eyes open for her.'

It wasn't that easy for Jack to merge into the crowd. Most of the crowd were about Eddie's height.

'Perhaps you should crawl,' Eddie suggested.

'Oh, very dignified.'

'She might well have you in the sights of some long-range gun type of item. Of the variety capable of projecting a shepherd's crook across a street and right up Boy Blue's bottom.'

Jack dropped to his knees. 'After you,' he said.

Above them the inferno 'ferno'd on, watched by the crowd of toys who, for various personal reasons, didn't really enjoy the spectacle the way it should be enjoyed.

The clockwork fire-fighters had their hoses all unrolled now, but were decidedly hesitant about turning them on. Being clockwork, they greatly feared water.

'Ho, ho, ho,' went the laughing policemen. Jack tried to keep out of their way.

Eddie stopped and thumped at his head with his paws. 'I've an idea coming,' he said.

'I hope it's a good one,' said Jack. 'I'm getting my trenchcoat all dusty.'

'It's a great one,' said Eddie. 'I'll explain it to you on the way.'

'The way to where?'

'The way to where we steal the police car.'

★

There was a really nice police car parked near by, as it happened. It was a Mark 7 Fairlane Cruiser, pressed steel construction, hand-enamelled in black and white, with a nickel-plated grille and brass roof bell. It was all polished up and the pride and joy of a certain Special Constable named Chortle. Jack had no trouble at all picking the lock on the driver's door.

'I feel utterly confident that this will work,' said Eddie as he slid into the police car beside Jack.

'And what makes you feel so utterly confident?' Jack enquired.

'My natural optimism. Do the business, Jack.'

'Righty right,' said Jack. And he took up the little microphone that hung beneath the dashboard. He held it between his fingers and viewed it disdainfully. It was just a plastic nubbin attached to a piece of string. 'How can this work?' he asked.

'You just speak into it. You can talk to the police at the police station.'

'How?' Jack asked.

'With your mouth,' said Eddie.

Jack shrugged. 'Hello,' he said.

'Hello,' said Eddie.

'No, I'm saying hello into this silly pretend microphone on the piece of string.'

'Very professional,' said Eddie. 'Very good.'

'Hello,' said a voice.

'How did you do that without moving your mouth?' Jack asked.

'It's the police station, talk to them.'

Jack shook his head. 'Right,' he said. 'Emergency! Emergency!'

'Who's that saying emergency?' asked the voice.

'Me,' said Jack. 'Who's that asking?'

'Me,' said the voice.

'Officer down!' shouted Jack.

'That's not my name,' said the voice. 'I'm Officer Chuckles. And there's no need to shout.'

'There's every need to shout,' shouted Jack. 'I said *officer down!* An officer's down!'

'A downy officer?' said the voice. 'An officer covered in down?'

Jack put his hand over the microphone. 'Have you got any other great ideas?' he asked Eddie. 'This isn't going to work.'

'Yes it is. Explain in urgent tones that you are at the fire at the Clockwork Car Company showrooms. And that the *woman* who started the fire, the same woman who murdered Humpty, Boy Blue and

Madame Goose, is attacking officers. Give a full description of her and demand lots of assistance. Do it, Jack.'

Jack did it. 'Send every officer you have,' he said. 'And quickly.'

'Ten-four,' said the voice in the affirmative.

'There,' said Eddie. 'Job done. Now all we have to do is sit here and wait for things to happen.'

'But she's not attacking any officers,' said Jack.

'Well, she sort-of-will-be.'

'How can she sort-of-will-be?'

'If she's attacking a police car, then that's almost the same as attacking a police officer.'

'I suppose so,' said Jack. 'But why should she be attacking a police car?'

'Because *we're* in it. I saw her following us through the crowd just before I had my great idea.'

'What?' said Jack.

'Here she comes,' said Eddie, pointing. 'Lock the doors, Jack.'

'Oh no.' Jack made haste with the door lockings.

The woman in the feathered headpiece, and Jack was in no doubt that she *was* a woman, strode across the street and stopped in front of the police car. She leaned forward and placed her hands upon the bonnet. And then she smiled at Eddie and Jack, who took to cowering in an undignified manner.

'Jack,' whispered Eddie, 'start the car.'

Jack fumbled in his pockets, searching for his piece of growler.

The woman raised her hands, made them into fists and brought them down with considerable force onto the bonnet of the Mark 7 Fairlane cruiser, making two nasty dents and spoiling the hand-enamelled paintwork.

'Waaah!' went Eddie. 'Hurry, Jack.'

Jack hurried. He pulled out the wire and went about the business. But it wasn't easy, what with the car now shuddering beneath the repeated blows.

'Get a move on!' shouted Eddie. 'She's smashing the bonnet to pieces.'

Jack got a swift move on. The wire clicked in the keyhole, releasing the twin-levered drop-bolt side-action tumblers in the lock, which freed the clockwork mechanism that powered the automobile. Jack put his foot down on the clutch and stuck the gearstick into reverse.

'Don't reverse,' cried Eddie. 'Run her down, Jack.'

'I can't do *that*,' Jack said, appalled. 'I can't run over a woman.'

'She's not a woman. She'll kill us, Jack.'

'I can't do it, Eddie.'

Jack put his foot down hard on the accelerator. Wheels went *spin spin spin* and *shriek* upon the road, but the police car stayed where it was.

'I can't reverse,' shouted Jack.

'That's because there's a big fire engine parked behind us. The only way is forward, Jack. Run her over.'

'I'll try and nudge her out of the way.' Jack stuck the car into first gear and put his foot down once again.

Spin spin spin and *shriek shriek shriek* went the wheels once more, but in a different direction this time.

'She's holding back the car.' Jack had a fine sweat going now. 'It's impossible.'

'For a woman, yes,' said Eddie. 'But not for whatever she is.'

'She's a robot from the future,' said Jack.

'What?' went Eddie.

'Sorry,' said Jack. 'I don't know why an idea like that should suddenly come into my head.'

'Put your foot down harder, give it more revs.'

'The cogs will fracture.'

'Do it, Jack.'

Jack did it. Well, he would. Anyone would have.

The police car edged forward.

Jack and Eddie cowered.

And members of the crowd were turning now, drawn away from their interest in the flaming holocaust by the sounds of the shrieking police car wheels.

Lots of heads were turning. Most of the heads, in fact. Even policemen's heads.

The woman–or–whatever strained against the moving car. The visible area of her face wore a taut and terrible smile.

'What is she?' Jack pressed his foot down as far as it would go. 'What is she?'

'Robot from the future,' said Eddie. 'Definitely. Run *it* down, Jack. Run the nasty robot down.'

The wheels spun and shrieked and sparks rose and flickered; the police car inched forward. Whatever she was, or was not, she clung to the bonnet.

And then she leapt onto it.

Freed from her restraint, the police car footed and yarded it forward at the hurry-up, but not out into the open road that might have led to freedom. The offside wheel buckled from its axle; the car swerved and plunged across the street towards the gathered crowd and the blazing building.

'We're gonna die!' shouted Jack.

'We're gonna die!' shouted Eddie.

Aaah! And *Oooh!* And *Eeek!* went members of the gathered crowd, parting in haste before the on-rushing car.

'Ho ho ho,' went the laughing policemen, parting in haste with them.

'Out of the car,' shouted Eddie. 'Jump, Jack.'

'The doors are locked!'

'Unlock them!'

'Hang on to me, Eddie, I'm opening mine!'

'Waaah!'

Shrieking screaming wheels.

A smiling face against the windscreen.

Fleeing crowds.

Burning building.

On-rushing police car.

Doors now open.

Jack and Eddie jumping.

More on-rushing police car. Woman-or-not-woman clinging to the bonnet.

And into the inferno.

Mash and crash. Explode and grench. And spragger and munge and clab and plark and blander.

Jack and Eddie, bruised but alive.

The Clockwork Car Company showrooms coming down.

And then a terrible silence.

'Am I alive?' Eddie asked.

'You're alive,' said Jack. 'We're both alive. We're safe.'

And then a voice.

The voice of Chief Inspector Wellington Bells.

'You are both under arrest,' said this voice.

16

'The secret of being a successful policeman,' said Chief Inspector Bellis, 'is in doing everything by the book. And before you ask me which book that is, I will tell you. It is the policeman's handbook. It tells you exactly how things are to be done. It covers all the aspects of gathering and cataloguing evidence. It is most precise.'

'Is there a point to this?' Jack asked.

'There is,' said Chief Inspector Bellis. 'There is.'

He, Jack and Eddie sat in the interview room of the Toy City Police Station. It was hardly a gay venue, as was, say, the Brown Hatter Nite Spot, over on the East Side.

Neither was it a Jolly Jack Tar of a place, like The Peglegged Pirate's Pool Hall, over on the West Side.

Nor was it even an existential confabulation of spatial ambiguity, such as the currently displayed installation piece at the Toy City Arts Gallery, down on the South Bank Side.

Nor was it anything other than an interview room in any way, shape, form, or indeed, aesthetic medium.

In the way of such rooms, its walls were toned a depressing shade of puce. In shape it was long and low and loathsome. In furnishings, it was basic: chairs, a table and a filing cabinet, lit by a naked light bulb which dangled from the ceiling at the end of a piece of string. There was no aesthetic involved in this lighting. But the string was of medium length.

So it was, as interview rooms go, very much of a muchness.

Eddie quite liked it. It reminded him a bit of Bill Winkie's office. Jack hated it.

'I've told you everything,' said Jack. 'And it's all the truth.'

Chief Inspector Bellis nodded his perished rubber head. He was accompanied by two laughing policemen. One of these was Officer Chortle. Although he was laughing, he pined for his police car.

'The truth,' said Bellis, staring hard at Jack. 'Now what would *you* know about the truth?'

'I've told it to you,' said Jack. 'All of it that I know.'

Chief Inspector Bellis shook his head, and sadly at that. 'Would it were so,' he said. 'But you see, criminals are notable for never telling the truth. You rarely if ever get the truth from a criminal. A criminal will profess his innocence to the end. Criminals do not tell the truth.'

'I wouldn't know about that,' said Jack, 'because I am not a criminal.'

'Which brings me back to doing things by the book,' said the Chief Inspector. 'Gathering evidence. Writing it all down. I write everything down. I have really neat handwriting. See this piece of paper here?' Bellis displayed the piece of paper. 'It has all manner of things written down upon it, in really neat handwriting. All manner of things about you. About how you entered Humpty Dumpty's apartment without permission from the authorities. And appeared shortly after the death of Boy Blue, disguised as a wealthy aristocrat. And later returned and broke into the premises, and later still escaped from police custody, and today stole Officer Chortle's brand new police car and drove it into a flaming building. How am I doing so far?'

'I demand to see my solicitor,' said Jack.

'Me too,' said Eddie. 'And even though I had a big breakfast, I'm quite hungry again. I demand to see a chef.'

'Anything else?' asked Chief Inspector Bellis.

'You could set us free,' said Eddie. 'After we've eaten.'

'Office Chortle, smite this bear,' said the Chief Inspector.

Officer Chortle leaned across the desk and bopped Eddie Bear on the head with his truncheon.

'Ouch!' went Eddie, in ready response. 'Don't hit me.'

'No, don't hit him.' Jack raised calming hands. 'We *have* told you the truth. That woman-or-whatever-she-was was the murderer. We're detectives; we were tracking her down. Did you find the body?'

'We found something,' said Chief Inspector Bellis 'But we're not entirely certain what we've found.'

'Robot,' said Jack. 'From the future.'

'What was that?' Chief Inspector Bellis raised a perished eyebrow. Officer Chortle raised his truncheon once more.

'Nothing,' said Jack. 'Nothing at all.'

'Nothing at all.' The Chief Inspector sighed. 'Well, I have you two bang to rights, as we policemen say. So why not break new ground by simply confessing? It would save so much unnecessary violence being visited upon your persons. Not to mention all the paperwork.'

'We're innocent,' said Eddie. 'We were just pursuing the course of our investigations.'

'Oh yes,' said Chief Inspector Bellis, consulting his paperwork. 'On behalf of this mystery benefactor who paid the handsome advance to your employer, Bill Winkie, who has mysteriously vanished without trace.'

'He'll be back,' said Eddie. 'He'll tell you.'

'Perhaps,' said the perished policeman. 'But for now I have you and I have all my impeccable paperwork, all penned in precise terms, in a very neat hand, and all pointing towards your guilt. Go on, confess, you know you want to.'

'I certainly don't,' said Eddie.

'That's as good as a confession to me,' said Bellis. 'I'll make a note of that.'

'And make sure you spell all the words right,' said Eddie. 'Especially the word "twerp" and the manner in which it should be applied to yourself.'

Officer Chortle smote Eddie once more.

'Eddie,' said Jack, 'don't make things worse.'

'How can they be worse?' Eddie rubbed at his battered head. 'This fool won't listen to reason. He won't believe the truth. But at least the killer is dead. That's something. We'll have our day in court. He can't prove anything against us. There's no evidence linking us directly to the crimes.'

'And how do you know that?' asked Bellis.

'Because we didn't commit them,' said Eddie.

'I have circumstantial evidence.'

'That's no evidence at all. It won't hold up in court.'

'I don't know where you keep getting the "court" business from,' said Chief Inspector Bellis. 'There won't be any court involved in this.'

'What?' said Eddie.

'I was going to mention that,' said Jack. 'But I didn't have time. This is some kind of "authority from higher up" jobbie; the Chief Inspector has been given the power to simply make us disappear.'

Eddie made growly groaning sounds.

'Killing the cream of Toy City's society is a very big crime,' said the Chief Inspector. 'It calls for extreme measures. Now, you can confess all and I'll see to it that you go off to prison. Or you can continue to profess your innocence, and . . .' The Chief Inspector drew a perished rubber finger across his perished rubber throat.

'But we didn't commit these crimes.'

'I saw you drive that woman into the burning building with my own two eyes. That's enough for a murder charge on its own.'

'If it *was* a woman,' said Eddie. 'Which it wasn't. As you know.'

'There's an autopsy going on at this moment.' Chief Inspector Bellis arranged his paperwork neatly upon the desk. 'We'll soon know all about that. And you *did* steal this officer's police car.'

Officer Chortle glared at Eddie.

Eddie took to a sulking cowering silence.

'Look,' said the Chief Inspector. 'I'm a fair fellow. Firm but fair, and I do believe in justice.' He turned to Jack. 'What say we just blame it all on the bear and let you go free?'

'Well,' said Jack.

'What?' said Eddie.

'No,' said Jack. 'Eddie is innocent. I'm innocent. Why not just wait for your autopsy report? See what that has to say.'

Chief Inspector Bellis sighed. 'I think we've said all that can be said here.' He rose from his chair and tucked his impeccable paperwork under his arm. 'I'll leave you in the company of these officers. They can beat the truth out of you. Then you'll both be disappeared.'

'No,' said Eddie. 'No more hitting. We give up, we confess.'

'We do?' said Jack.

'We do,' said Eddie. 'Just leave us alone here and we'll draft out our confessions.'

'Make sure that you do, or . . .' Chief Inspector Bellis drew his finger once more across his throat, nodded his farewells and, in the company of the two laughing policemen, left the interview room, slamming the door and locking it behind him.

'Well,' said Eddie to Jack. 'That's sorted.'

'Sorted?' Jack threw up his hands. 'We're done for. They'll disappear us. And why did you tell him we'd write out confessions?'

'To stop me getting hit again and buy us some time alone. Now, out with the wire, Jack, and pick the lock.'

'They confiscated the wire,' said Jack.

'We're done for,' said Eddie.

Time passes slowly in a police interview room when you're left all alone in it. Or even with a friend. Especially when you're waiting for something terrible to happen to you. Time should pass quickly in such circumstances. But it doesn't. It passes very slowly indeed.

'It's all so unfair,' said Eddie. 'We're heroes; we shouldn't be treated like this.'

'Eddie,' said Jack, 'what do you think this is really all about?'

'What do you mean?' Eddie fiddled at the door. 'If I had an opposable thumb,' he said, 'I'd always keep a really long nail on it, just for picking locks.'

'What I mean,' said Jack, 'is *what* is all this about? Who was the murderess? Why did she do what she did?'

'Who can fathom the workings of the criminal mind?' said Eddie.

'Detectives,' said Jack. 'That's what they do.'

'Not in this case, Jack. She's dead, we'll never know.'

'And soon we'll be dead. Disappeared. And that will be that for us. It's all been a bit pointless, really, hasn't it?'

'Don't talk like that, Jack. We did our best.'

'We were useless, Eddie. We were rubbish at being detectives. Everything we did was wrong. Bill Winkie would be ashamed of us.'

'Don't say that. All right, we made a few mistakes . . .'

'A *few* mistakes? We made nothing but mistakes.'

'We did our best.'

'And where has it got us? We're lucky to still be alive. And we won't be alive for much longer, I'm thinking. I'm going to write my confession and hope I can escape from prison.'

'Don't be so pessimistic, Jack. There has to be a way out of this mess.'

'Eddie,' said Jack, 'there is. I *could* pick the lock. You've got a new growler, haven't you?'

'Now hold on.' Eddie covered himself as best he could. 'That would really hurt. It really hurt the last time.'

'Yes, but we *could* escape. I'll just rip your stomach open.'

'No.' Eddie dropped from his chair and backed away.

'Only joking,' said Jack.

'Good,' said Eddie, still backing away.

'We'll just wait here until the policemen come back and beat you up some more and then disappear the both of us.'

'Out with my growler,' said Eddie Bear.

'No, there has to be another way.'

'I wish I knew one,' said Eddie.

'You know what,' said Jack, 'you were right. When you said that we were going about things in all the wrong way. About the hunters being hunted, and how we should do things the way Bill Winkie would have done them.'

Eddie nodded in a hopeless kind of way.

'I've read all the books,' said Jack. 'He wouldn't have ended up here.'

'That doesn't help,' said Eddie.

'No, sorry, it doesn't. But if he *had* ended up here, there would have been a twist to it.'

'There's always a twist in detective books,' said Eddie. 'That's what makes them special.'

'So there should be a twist here.'

'This isn't a Bill Winkie thriller.'

'Let's assume it is,' said Jack. 'Or an Eddie Bear thriller. Let's look at it all from a different perspective.'

'Big words,' said Eddie. 'So what's the twist?'

Jack shrugged. 'I wish I knew,' he said.

'Thanks very much,' said Eddie. 'That's all been very helpful.'

'Give it a chance, Eddie.'

'What, we simply sit here and wait for this twist to just happen?'

'That's exactly what we do. That's what would happen in the books. And when it happens here to us, it will change everything and we will go out and do the job properly. The way it should be done. The way it's done in detective thrillers.'

'I don't get it,' said Eddie.

'You will,' said Jack. 'Just trust me.'

And so they waited.

It was tense, but then, important waiting is always tense. It's filled with tension, every waiting moment of it.

The tense waiting was done at the exact moment when it ceased.

And it ceased at the sound of a key being turned in a lock and the sight of the interview room door swinging open.

Chief Inspector Bellis entered the interview room.

'Have you completed your written confessions?' he asked.

Eddie flinched.

'Not as such,' said Jack.

'So you've decided to go for the violent beating and disappearance option.'

'No,' cried Eddie. 'Have mercy.'

'Mercy?' The Chief Inspector's eyebrows were raised once again. 'You are asking me for mercy?'

'We are,' Jack agreed.

'Oh well, fair enough then, you can go.'

'What?' went Jack.

And 'What?' went Eddie too.

'You can both go free,' said Bellis. 'I'm dropping the charge.'

Jack's mouth hung open. Now this *was* a twist.

Eddie said 'What?' once again.

'You heard me, I'm dropping the charge.'

'Charge?' said Eddie. 'You're dropping *the* charge? Only the one? I don't understand.'

'Taking and driving away a police vehicle,' said Chief Inspector Bellis. 'That's the only charge against you and I'm dropping that charge.'

'Ah, excuse me, sir,' said Jack, 'but why?'

'Somethings have come up.'

'What kind of somethings are these?'

'Two somethings,' said the Chief Inspector. 'The body in the morgue. Or what's left of it. Isn't a body.'

'Then what is it?' Jack asked.

'I'm not authorised to tell you that.'

'Oh,' said Jack. 'And the other something?'

'There's been another murder,' said Chief Inspector Bellis. 'And, as you've both been here in custody, I know that you are not responsible. But it's the same killer as before; I'd stake my reputation on it.'

'Another murder?' Eddie said. 'But the body or whatever it is in the morgue . . .'

'Is obviously not the killer. I'm letting you go. Get out. Leave the building.'

'Thanks,' said Eddie. 'Come on, Jack.'

'I'm coming,' said Jack. 'But who died? Who was murdered?'

'Jack Spratt,' said Chief Inspector Bellis. 'Jack Spratt is dead.'

17

Apart from those that do, of course, celebrity marriages never last.

For although celebrities are very good at being celebrities (they would not *be* celebrities if they were not), most of them are absolute no-marks when it comes to being a caring partner in a shared relationship. They just can't do it. It isn't in them to do it.

Not that we ordinary folk blame them for being this way. We don't. After all, it is we ordinary folk who have made these people celebrities.

Which possibly makes *us* to blame.

Or possibly not.

No, not: it's not *our* fault. *We* have given these people celebrity. They owe *us*.

And as we have huddled in rain-soaked hordes to cheer them at their celebrity marriages, it is only fitting that they give us something in return: the entertainment of their celebrity divorces. Let's be honest here, who amongst us can genuinely claim that we do not thoroughly enjoy a really messy celebrity divorce? We love 'em. We do.

We love to read in the gutter press all about the mudslinging, accusations and counter-accusations. And if there's a bit of the old domestic violence in the millionaire mansion, we revel in that too. We even love the petty squabbling about who gets custody of the penguin. And as to the sordid and startling disclosures of what the private investigator actually saw when he peeped in through the hotel bedroom window, those get our juices flowing fair to the onset of dehydration.

And while we're being absolutely honest here, let us admit that when it comes to reading about the celebrity divorce, women love it more than men.

They do, you know. They really do.

It's a woman thing.

If you ask a man, he'll probably tell you that yes, he does enjoy a celebrity divorce, but given the choice, he'd far rather watch a building burning down.

But that's men for you.

Jack Spratt was a man, of course: a rich celebrity of a man, and his divorce from his wife Nadine brought colour to the front pages of the Toy City gutter press for several weeks. It was a very entertaining divorce.

The grounds were 'irreconcilable culinary differences' but, as it turned out, there was a whole lot more to it than that.

They were a mismatched couple from the start. Jack, a man naturally destined for fame by nature of having a big face and a small body, married Nadine, a woman with a very small face and a very large body (physical characteristics which would normally have doomed anyone to oblivion). They married when Nadine was fifteen.

Jack had always had a thing about large women.

It was that little man thing which is only fully understood by little men. And these little men have no wish to confide it to big men, lest they get a taste for it too and cut the little men out of the equation.

Nadine was a very large woman, and Jack loved her for it.

That their eating habits were so diametrically opposed didn't matter at all to either of them. In fact, it worked perfectly well during the early part of their relationship, when they lived in a trailer park on Toy City's seedy South-West Side. He worked in the slaughterhouse district on the night shift, where the black meat market in offal flourished. Had they never achieved the fame that their nursery rhyme brought them,★ they might still have been together today.

Sadly, the more rich and famous they became, the more clearly did the cracks in their relationship begin to show. They did not part amicably. She demanded a share in his chain of lean-cuisine gourmet restaurants. And he in turn laid claim to half of her fast-food burger bar franchises, *Nadine's Fast Food Diners*.

Neither wished to share anything with the other; these separate empires had been years in the building. So each sought to dish the dirt on the other—and when celebrity dirt starts getting dished, there al-

---

★ A rhyme penned by the now legendary Wheatley Porterman, who, while still an impoverished rhyme writer, happened to be living in the trailer next door to Jack and Nadine.

ways seems sufficient to build a fair-sized Ziggurat, a step pyramid, two long barrows and an earthwork.

With a little left over to heap into an existential confabulation of special ambiguity installation piece, such as the one currently on display at the Toy City Arts Gallery.

Jack's lawyer brought forth evidence that Nadine had been intimate with at least seven dwarves.

In response to this, Nadine hit Jack somewhat below the belt, dwelling far too graphically upon his sexual inadequacies. He had never satisfied her sexually, she said, because, with his refusal to eat fat, cunnilingus was denied to her.

This disclosure was met with howls of joy from the gutter-press-reading population. And much thumbing through dictionaries. Followed by even greater howls.

So much Eddie told Jack as they trudged across town to the rear of Boy Blue's where Jack had left Bill Winkie's car.

He told Jack more when, having discovered that Bill Winkie's car now stood upon bricks, its wheels having been removed by jobbing vandals, they trudged further across town to avail themselves of the whatever-she-was-that-wasn't-a-woman's car, which they had left parked at the scene of the Clockwork Car Company fire.

And if there was anything that Eddie had missed first or second time around, he revealed that to Jack when, having discovered, much to their chagrin, that the car had been removed to the police car pound for being parked in a tow-away zone, they trudged back to the police station.

If there was anything else that Eddie had forgotten to mention, it remained unmentioned when, upon learning that the car would only be surrendered to Jack and Eddie if they could prove ownership and pay the fine, they trudged, carless and footsore, across the street from the police station and into a *Nadine's Fast Food Diner*.

It was a spacious affair, with man-sized chairs and tables. These were all of pink plastic and pale pitch-pine. The walls were pleasantly painted with pastel portraits of portly personages, pigging out on prodigious portions of pie—which, considering the alliterative nature of the breakfast served by the toymaker, may or may not have been some kind of culinary running gag.

'I love these places,' said Eddie. 'High cholesterol dining.'

'What's cholesterol?' Jack asked.

'I think it's a kind of pig.'

A waitress greeted them. She was tall and voluptuous, pretty in pink and tottered upon preposterously high high-heels. She led them to a vacant table and brought Eddie a child's high-chair to sit on.

'I know it's undignified,' said Eddie. 'But it's worth it for the nose bag.'

The waitress said, 'I'll give you a moment,' and tottered away. Jack watched her tottering. She did have extremely wonderful legs.

'Something on your mind?' Eddie asked. 'Regarding the *dolly*?'

Jack shook his head fiercely. 'Certainly *not*,' he said. 'Do you have any money, Eddie?' He perused the menu. It was a wonderful menu. It included a host of toothsome treats with names such as The Big Boy Belly-Buster Breakfast, The Double-Whammy Bonanza Burger Blowout and The Four Fats Final Fantasy Fry-Up.

Jack cast his eye over the Hungry Cowboy's Coronary Hoedown: two 10 oz prime portions of beef belly flab, generously larded and cooked to perfection in a sealed fat-fryer to preserve all their natural grease, served between two loaves of high-fibre white bread and the soggiest chips you'll ever suck upon.

Jack's mouth watered. '*Have* you any money?' he asked Eddie.

Eddie shifted uncomfortably. 'I've done a bad thing,' he said. 'And I don't want you to hate me for it.'

'I won't hate you,' said Jack. 'What have you done?'

'I've stolen some money,' said Eddie.

'Really?' said Jack. 'From where?'

'From *whom*,' said Eddie. 'Remember when we were saying good-bye to Chief Inspector Bellis and he was giving us both a hug and saying how sorry he was that Officer Chortle had bashed me on the head with his truncheon?'

'Yes,' said Jack. 'And I noticed a tone of insincerity in his voice.'

'Me too. And when he was hugging us, I also noticed a big purse of coins in his rubbery pocket. And even without the aid of opposable thumbs, it was such a simple matter to ease it out. And I felt that he owed us for all the torment he'd put us through and . . .'

'Say no more, my friend,' said Jack. 'I understand entirely.'

'So you don't think I did a wicked thing?'

Jack shook his head and smiled broadly. Then he dipped into a trenchcoat pocket and brought out something black. 'By remarkable coincidence,' said Jack, 'I nicked his wallet.'

'Waitress,' called Eddie, 'two of the Mighty Muncher Mother-of-all-Mega-Meals, please.'

'With the Greasy Chin Cheesy Cream Dipping Sauce,' Jack added.

'And a double order of extra-fat fries on the side?' Eddie asked.

'And two slices of bread and butter,' Jack said. 'And butter the bread on both sides.'

The voluptuous waitress departed, leaving the now grinning pair.

'Once we've spent all the paper money, we should hand that wallet in,' said Eddie. 'There might be a reward.'

'Let's not push our luck,' said Jack. 'What are we going to do next?'

'Well, I thought that after we've dined, we might hit a bar or two.'

'What are we going to do about the case? I assume that we're still on the case? Jack Spratt's murder is another of these serial killings, is it not?'

'It seems logical. But with the weird woman-thing dead . . .'

'If she, or it, *is* dead,' said Jack. 'Perhaps she just got up off the morgue slab and walked away.'

'There's something big going on,' said Eddie. 'I think Chief Inspector Bellis needs all the help he can get. Even ours. Which is why he set us free.'

'So should we go to the crime scene and see what's what?'

'I'll bet we'll find another chocolate bunny. It's as certain as.'

'Tell me, Eddie,' said Jack. 'I didn't like to ask, but was there one in Wibbly's lower-ground-floor apartment?'

Eddie nodded grimly. 'But hey hey,' he said, 'here comes the grub.'

'Now *that* is what I call fast food.'

The waitress laid the spread before them. It covered most of the table. She returned to the kitchen, then returned to the diners with another tray-full.

'Pull that table over,' said Eddie.

Jack pulled the table over and the waitress unloaded the second tray. 'Will that be all?' she asked.

'I doubt it,' said Eddie. 'We'll give you a call when we need you again.'

The waitress, whose painted face was incapable of expression, rolled her eyes and departed.

'Nice legs,' said Eddie.

'I thought you never went inter-species.'

'One can fantasise,' said Eddie. 'Tuck in.'

And the two of them tucked in.

At considerable length they finished their gargantuan repast and took to perusing the dessert menu. The Death-by-Hog-Fat Pudding looked enticing.

'Eddie,' said Jack, 'there's something I've been meaning to ask you.'

'Ask on, my friend,' said Eddie.

'It's just that, well, you eat a lot of food, don't you?'

'As well as being noted for their sexual prowess, bears are greatly admired for their hearty eating; there is no secret to this.'

'Yes,' said Jack. 'But you haven't got a bottom, have you, Eddie?'

Eddie gawped at Jack. 'So what am I sitting on, my head?'

'No, I mean, I'm sorry if this is somewhat indelicate, but what I mean is, where does all this food you eat go?'

'Are you telling me that you don't know what bears do in the woods? When they're not picnicking, of course. Or after they've picnicked.'

'But you don't do that,' said Jack. 'I don't wish to be crude here, but you haven't taken a dump since I met you.'

Eddie scratched at his head with his paw. 'You know you're right,' he said. 'Alcohol drains slowly through me, but you're right. I *never* have taken a dump; where *does* it all go? That's as weird as.'

Jack shrugged.

'You buffoon,' said Eddie, shaking his head. 'Of course I go to the toilet.'

'But when I put my hand inside you to get your growler, there was nothing inside you but sawdust.'

'Oh I see,' said Eddie. 'You know all about digestive systems, do you? I suppose you know exactly how the human digestive system works.'

Jack nodded in a manner which implied that he did.

'Thought not,' said Eddie.

'Digestive juices,' said Jack. 'I've got them in me. You haven't.'

'How come, no matter what colour the food you eat is, it always comes out as brown poo?' Eddie asked. 'Explain that to me.'

'Er . . .' said Jack.

'Jack,' said Eddie. 'Although I greatly admire your seemingly unquenchable thirst for arcane knowledge, there will always be things that you'll never be able to know. Live with this. Let brown poo be an exemplar. Do you understand what I'm saying, *chap*?'

'You said *chap* again,' said Jack.

'Do you want any pudding, *chap*?'

'I think I'm full,' said Jack. 'Should we go to Jack Spratt's now?'

'You wouldn't prefer, perhaps, going for a drink first?'

'If we are going to play by the rules and do things the way that a detective should do things, then we should definitely go to a bar first. Detectives get all manner of important leads in bars.'

'Then we'll take a wander over to Tinto's. You never know, he might run down again while we're there.'

'Check please, waitress,' called Jack.

★

Tinto's bar was as ever it was: already crowded with members of Toy City's non-human population. And evening was coming on once more by the time that Jack and Eddie reached it. They were able to gain a pair of barstools without too much trouble, though, because, it had to be said, neither Jack nor Eddie smelled particularly good. They hadn't washed in a while, nor changed their clothes, and after all they'd recently been through, they were far from wholesome when it came to personal hygiene. Drinking folk edged aside for them.

Eddie had, however, visited the toilet before they left *Nadine's Fast Food Diner*. This was not to have a dump though, but to purchase some contraceptives from the machine.

Not that Eddie actually used contraceptives. But he did know this really funny thing you could do with them. Which he did on occasions in bars, and which inevitably got him thrown out.

It was a bear thing.

Eddie plonked himself down on a bar stool; Jack lowered himself uncomfortably onto the next, legs once more up around his neck.

'Evening, Tinto,' said Eddie, addressing the clockwork barkeep. 'Beer, please.'

'And for your gentleman friend?'

Jack recalled the size of the beers. 'Six beers for me,' he said. He had clearly forgotten their potency.

'Nine beers,' said Tinto, whose grasp of mathematics had never been up to much.

'So, Tinto,' said Eddie, as Tinto pulled the beers, 'how goes it for you upon this pleasant evening?'

'Don't talk to me about pleasant evenings,' said Tinto, presenting several beers and pulling several more. 'Did you hear what happened to Jack Spratt?'

'Took the ultimate diet,' said Eddie. 'Yes, we heard.'

'What a way to go,' said Tinto. 'Coated in batter and cooked in a deep fat fryer.'

'I didn't hear *that*,' said Eddie. 'Do you know where it happened?'

'At the *Nadine's Fast Food Diner* down the road. The one with the pretty waitress. Apparently Nadine wouldn't even close the restaurant. They took away the cooked corpse and she just went on serving dinners. Didn't even change the fat in the fryer.'

The colour drained from Jack's face. 'Where's the toilet?' he asked.

'I'll show you,' said Eddie. 'I need it too.'

Presently the two rather shaky-looking detectives returned to the bar. They were both somewhat lighter in the stomach regions.

'And what makes it worse,' said Tinto, continuing where he left off, pulling further beers and losing count, 'is that Jack Spratt owed me money. Him and his damned secret society. He rented my upstairs room for their meetings and now I bet I'll never get my money.'

'Secret society?' Eddie swallowed beer. 'What secret society?'

'Probably the Spring and Catch.' Jack swallowed beer.

Eddie and Tinto swivelled in Jack's direction.

'What do *you* know about the Spring and Catch?' Eddie's voice was a hoarse whisper. Which is not to be confused with a horse whisperer.

'Not much,' said Jack. 'Only that they perform strange rituals and that all the Preadolescent Poetic Personalities are members. Boy Blue was in it. And Humpty Dumpty. And Jack Spratt.'

'How do *you* know this?'

'There was a book at Boy Blue's. I saw it.' Jack took up another beer. 'Significant, eh?'

'I wonder why they'd hold their meetings here?' Eddie wondered.

'And you call yourself a detective,' said Jack.

'Excuse me?' said Eddie.

'Eddie,' said Jack, 'if this was a Bill Winkie thriller, it would now be approximately halfway through. And by this time, all the major players would have made their appearances and most of the major locations would have been established. Tinto's bar has already been established as a major location in the scenario. It's where the detectives drink. So it shouldn't surprise you to find that something pertinent to the case would have happened here.'

'You're getting pretty good at this,' said Eddie.

'It's pretty basic stuff,' said Jack, 'for we professional private eyes.'

'You're right,' said Eddie. 'So go on, Tinto, let's have it.'

'Have *what*?' Tinto asked.

'Whatever it is.' Eddie tapped at his nose. 'The all-important something that is pertinent to the case.'

'I don't know what you're talking about.'

'The Spring and Catch held their rituals in your upstairs room. I think you'll find that they left something behind. Something seemingly irrelevant to you, but of great importance to the professional private eye. That's the way it always happens in detective thrillers.' Eddie winked at Jack.

'You can't wink,' said Jack. 'Not with those button eyes.'

'See how good he's getting, Tinto,' said Eddie. 'Attention to detail and good continuity is everything.'

'Thanks,' said Jack. 'So where's the important something, Tinto?'

'Well,' said Tinto, and his head revolved, 'I can't think of anything. Except, of course—but no, that wouldn't be it.'

'It would,' said Eddie.

'It would.' Jack took up another glass and drank from it. Eddie, whose glass was empty, helped himself to one of Jack's.

'I think I have it somewhere,' said Tinto. 'Or perhaps I threw it away.'

'You didn't throw it away,' said Eddie. 'Go and look for it.'

'All right.' Tinto wheeled away along behind the bar.

'What do you think it will be?' Jack asked Eddie. 'Key to a left luggage locker? Receipt for something? Map with a big X on it? Or maybe even the Big M itself.'

'You really did read all the Bill Winkie thrillers, didn't you?'

'All of them,' said Jack.

'Then I expect you remember how fastidious he was. How he didn't like his trenchcoat getting dirty. And how much he really cared about his motor car.'

Jack dusted down the lapels of the now extremely grubby trenchcoat and wondered what the jobbing vandals might presently be helping themselves to from Bill Winkie's automobile.

'When he gets back from his holiday,' said Jack, carefully, 'I'm sure he'll be very impressed by the way *you* solved the case.'

'Ah, here comes Tinto,' said Eddie.

And here Tinto came. 'Found it,' he said, twirling something between those oh-so-dextrous fingers that Eddie oh-so-coveted. 'I hope it's what you're hoping for.' Tinto passed it over to Eddie.

Eddie placed the item before him upon the bar counter and poked at it with a paw. In terms of the looks of it, it was truly beyond description. But considering its size, or lack of it, its weight was unsurprising. 'It looks like the Big M,' he said. 'The Maguffin. What do you think, Jack?'

'Looks like it to me,' Jack agreed.

'What's a Maguffin?' Tinto asked.

'You tell him, Jack,' said Eddie. 'You've read all the Bill Winkie thrillers.'

'Certainly,' said Jack. 'In all detective thrillers, there is always a Maguffin. The Maguffin is the all-important something, the all-importantness of which will not become apparent until its important moment has come.'

'Well put,' said Eddie.

'I see,' said Tinto, who didn't. 'Then I'm glad I could be of assistance. Do you want to settle your bar bill now, Eddie?'

'No,' said Eddie. 'I don't. But Jack will tell you what I do want to do.'

Jack raised another tiny glass of beer. 'Is it, get drunk?' he asked.

'It is.' Eddie raised *his* glass. 'And when Jack and I are drunk, we will come up with some really inspired idea for solving the case. And then, while balancing upon my head, I'll show you this really funny thing I can do with a contraceptive.'

'And then I'll throw you out,' said Tinto.

'Sweet as,' said Eddie. 'Whose round is it now?'

'Yours,' said Jack. 'Ten more for me.'

'Sweeter than sweet as.' Eddie grinned. 'Same again please, *chap*.'

18

They got *very* drunk.

Eddie showed Jack the really funny thing he could do with a contraceptive and Tinto threw them both out of the bar. But as it was late, and they *were* both very drunk, they didn't really care.

They wandered back to Bill Winkie's office, assuring each other, as if assurance were required, that they were 'bestest friends'.

Jack threw up in the bathroom. Eddie strung himself up on the Venetian blind. Jack collapsed onto the floor.

The night passed without further incident.

In the morning the big smiley sun arose above the roofscape of Toy City and beamed down its blessings upon each and all without due favour or prejudice.

The soundly snoring detectives awoke, Jack nursing a hangover to stagger the senses of the Gods and Eddie as fresh as the proverbial daisy that was never actually mentioned in a proverb.

'Feeling rough?' Eddie asked.

'As rough as,' said Jack.

'Perfect,' said Eddie.

'Perfect?' said Jack.

'Bill Winkie was always hungovered,' said Eddie. 'That anti-hangover lotion never worked too well.'

'What?' said Jack. 'But you . . .'

'And I had to top you up with a hypodermic full of happy juice. But all that is behind us. You keep the hangover, Jack. It will help you to function as a proper private eye. We're professionals now.'

Jack groaned. 'Breakfast?' he suggested. 'Then we find out what this Maguffin's for.' He turned the Maguffin over on his palm. Considering the lightness of its shade, it was quite dark in colour. 'Right?'

'Wrong,' said Eddie. 'We review the situation. That is what we do. Try to gain a detached overview.'

'Right.' Jack rubbed at his throbbing forehead and returned the Maguffin to his trenchcoat pocket. 'Go on then,' he said. 'Impress me.'

Eddie climbed onto the wreckage of Bill Winkie's desk. 'Now,' said he, 'my train of thought runs in this direction. I—' But Eddie's train of thought was suddenly derailed by the sounds of frantic knocking at the office door.

Jack looked at Eddie.

And Eddie looked at Jack.

'Expecting a visitor?' Jack whispered.

Eddie shook his head. 'It might be a client,' he whispered back to Jack.

Jack made a doubtful face.

'Well, it *might*.'

'Go and answer it, then.'

Eddie made a face more doubtful than Jack's. 'Perhaps *you* should go,' he suggested.

'Did Bill leave a spare gun around anywhere?'

Eddie shook his head once more.

Jack took up a broken-off desk leg, brandished it in a truncheon-like fashion and cautiously approached the office door. 'Who is it?' he called.

'Toy City Express,' a voice called back.

Jack glanced towards Eddie. 'I think it's another train,' said he.

'Toy City Express *Deliveries*,' said Eddie. 'It's Randolph the delivery boy; put down the desk leg and open the door, Jack.'

'Fair enough.' Jack put down the desk leg and opened the door.

A golly in a dapper red uniform, with matching cap worn in the ever-popular peak-to-the-rear manner, grinned up at Jack. 'Yo Popper,' said he.

'Yo Popper?' said Jack.

'Yo, popper humbug,' said the delivery boy. 'Tootin' here a seam-rippin' hot pack for my bear Eddie, you wise?'

'What?' said Jack.

'Don't jazz me up meat-brother. Head me to the bear.'

'What?' said Jack once more.

'The popular patois of the Golly ghetto,' said Eddie, poking his head out from between Jack's knees. 'It's a delivery for me. Hey Randolph, how's it hanging?'

'Like a python wid de mumps. Yo, popper Eddie boy. Here's de pack, ink my page and it's all done yours.'

The golly passed a clipboard with a dangling pen on a string to Eddie. Eddie placed the clipboard on the floor, took the pen between both paws and signed his name. He returned the clipboard to the golly and availed himself of the package.

'Give Randolph a tip,' said Eddie to Jack.

'Fair enough,' said Jack. 'Always take care when dealing with farmers, Randolph.'

'I meant money,' said Eddie.

'Fair enough. Never spend more than you earn.'

'I meant give him some money. Tip him with money.'

'I know exactly what you meant. But I don't have any money, and anyway, it's *your* package.'

'Sorry, Randolph,' said Eddie. 'We're both broke at present. I'll buy you a beer in Tinto's some time.'

Randolph replied with phrases of popular Golly ghetto patois, which, although their specific meaning was lost upon Jack, their general gist was not. Jack closed the door upon Randolph.

'So what have you got?' Jack asked Eddie.

The package was a large envelope. Eddie passed it up to Jack. 'You open it,' he said. 'Envelopes are tricky when you don't have opposable thumbs.'

Jack took the envelope, opened it and emptied out its contents. 'Tickets,' he said. 'Two tickets to a TV show.'

'Wibbly,' said Eddie. 'Good old Wibbly.'

'But Wibbly is . . . well . . . you know.'

'I know,' said Eddie. 'But when we were at his place, I asked him for a couple of favours. To use his contacts and get us these tickets. He obviously came through for us before he was, well, you know.'

'Why do we want tickets for a TV show?'

'It's not just any old TV show. It's Miss Muffett's TV show. *The Tuffet*. It's a talk show. Little Tommy Tucker is making a guest appearance on it today.'

'And this is relevant to the case?'

'Is there anything else there, or just the tickets?'

'There's a letter,' said Jack.

'Then read it.'

Jack read it. 'Dear Eddie,' he read, 'here are the tickets you wanted. I had to call in a lot of favours to get them, so you owe me big time. Regarding the advance money paid out to Bill that you asked me to check on, I called in a few favours there too, for which you also owe me big time. The money came, as you suspected, from a joint trust fund held by the prominent PPPs.'

'Preadolescent Poetic Personalities, before you ask,' said Eddie.

'I wasn't going to ask; might I continue?'

'Please do.'

Jack continued. 'It seems that Little Tommy Tucker drew out the cash and seeing as the guy is a recluse, then you're probably right in thinking that the only chance you'll have to question him about it is if you can corner him at the TV studios. I wish you luck. I'm having this sent to you via Toy City Express because I think I'm being followed. See you when I see you. And don't forget that when you do that, you owe me big time. Your friend, Wibbly.'

'Good old Wibbly,' said Eddie. 'A friend indeed.'

'Indeed,' said Jack. 'Well, I suppose that explains the tickets.'

'Ever been to a TV show before, Jack?'

'No,' said Jack. 'What about you?'

'No,' said Eddie. 'So I'm really excited. How about you?'

'It's no big deal.' Jack shrugged in a nonchalant fashion. 'I'm not particularly bothered.'

'You liar,' said Eddie. 'You are too.'

'You're right,' said Jack. 'I am. I'm *really* excited.'

Happily, the studios of Toy City TV were not too far distant from Bill Winkie's office. A pleasant saunter, or stroll. A pleasant saunter, or stroll, does tend to work up an appetite though, or in the case of Jack and Eddie, even *more* of an appetite. And this particular saunter, or stroll, took two famished detectives past several breakfasting places, all of which breathed tempting breakfast smells at them.

Jack gave his pulsating forehead further rubbings.

'I'm *really* hungry now,' he said.

'Me too,' said Eddie. 'But the show's being recorded at ten o'clock. So even if we had the cash, we still wouldn't have time for the breakfast.'

'Perhaps there'll be food laid on at the studios.'

'Bound to be,' said Eddie. 'And fizzy wine too, I shouldn't wonder.'

'Let's walk faster then.'

'I'm walking as fast as I can.'

'Do you want me to give you a carry?'

'In broad daylight? I may be hungry, but I still have my dignity.'

The two pressed on past further breakfasting places and finally reached the Toy City TV studios—or, at least, the queue.

'What's all this?' asked Jack, viewing the long line of chattering toys.

'It's the queue for the show,' said Eddie. 'What did you think it was?'

'I can't be having with queues,' said Jack. 'I don't like queues at all.'

'They don't bother me,' said Eddie. 'Waiting around is second nature to teddies.'

'Well I'm not having it; let's push to the front.'

'Lead on, big boy.'

Jack led on. He and Eddie reached the front of the queue. The front of the queue was at the front door of the studios. Jack looked up at the studios' front parts.

The studios' front parts were impressive. They fairly soared. Rising pilasters of frosted rainbow glass swept upwards to support glittering multi-mirrored arches. Within these, intricately tiled mosaics, of every colour and hue, arranged in elaborate geometric patterns, glimmered in the morning sunlight. The overall effect was of a jewelled palace or fantastic temple.

It was a real mind-boggler.

'Amazing,' said Jack.

'Ghastly,' said Eddie.

'Shall we go inside?'

'You have the tickets and the status; push right in.'

'Fair enough,' said Jack, and made to push right in, but his passage was barred by several large and burly fellows, sporting dark suits, mirrored sunglasses and little earpiece jobbies with mouth mic attachments.

'And where do you think you're going?' one of them asked.

'I'm Bill Winkie, Private Eye,' said Jack, flashing his tickets. 'Here on a case; stand aside if you will.'

'I won't,' said the burly fellow. 'This is a secure area; you will have to be frisked.'

'Outrageous,' said Jack.

'Please yourself,' said the burly fellow. 'Goodbye then and leave me with your tickets, I can always sell them on.'

'Frisk away then, if you must,' said Jack. 'But no funny business around my trouser regions.'

The big burly fellow commenced with the frisking of Jack. He did a very thorough job of frisking—far too thorough, in Jack's opinion. Especially about the trouser regions. He turned all of Jack's pockets inside out, then finally said, 'All right. Go through.'

Jack went through.

The burly fellow frisked Eddie too.

Then Eddie followed Jack.

Once within the studio lobby area, Jack began frantically patting at himself.

'What are you up too?' Eddie asked.

'The Maguffin,' said Jack. 'Where's the Maguffin?'

Eddie produced the Maguffin. 'I have it here,' he said.

'But how?'

'I thought it might arouse suspicion, so I lifted it from your pocket.'

'But once again, how?'

'It's a knack. Here, stick it back in your pocket.'

Jack took the Maguffin from Eddie's paws. 'But he frisked you too,' said Jack. 'Where did you hide it?'

'You really don't want to know.'

'No,' said Jack, pocketing the Maguffin. 'I don't think I do.'

The studio's lobby was a swank affair. Its walls and ceiling and floor were all patterned with colourful mosaics. Jack wondered at the craftsmanship, and wondered what it all must have cost. It must have cost plenty, was his conclusion.

The colourful walls were further coloured by numerous painted portraits. Jack rightly assumed these to be of prominent Toy City TV personalities. He perused them with interest. Many were of impossibly glamorous dollies with preposterously inflated bosoms and very big hair.

So big, in fact, as to be veritable jungles.

The faces which peeped forth amidst all this big hair had the looks about them of jungle clearings, which kept the encroaching follicular foliage at bay only through the medium of extreme cosmetic cultivation. As studies in the overuse of make-up, these were nonpareil.

Jack found the faces fascinating. These were idealised images of supposed feminine beauty. Features were exaggerated, increased or diminished; the eyes and mouths were much too large, the noses all far too small.

But for the dolly portraits, no other toys were pictured. All the rest were of Jack's race: men.

These either struck noble poses or grinned winningly, according to the public image they wished to project.

Eddie looked up at Jack, then further up at the portraits, then once more at Jack. 'Your thoughts?' Eddie asked.

'Probably much the same as yours,' said Jack. 'And would I be right in assuming that there are no teddy stars on Toy City TV?'

'No,' said the bear. 'Just men and dollies. And look at those dollies, Jack. Disgusting.'

'Disgusting?' Jack asked.

'Well, you don't think that those are their *real* bosoms, do you?' Eddie beckoned Jack and Jack leaned down to Eddie.

'Fake,' Eddie whispered into Jack's ear. 'They're made of rubber.'

Jack straightened up and shook his head. He had no comment to make.

'So,' said Jack. 'What do we do now? Do you want me to bluff and bluster my way into Little Tommy Tucker's dressing room, so you can have a few words with him?'

'Let's do it after the show.'

'Why after? Why not before?'

'I was thinking that perhaps he might not be too keen to speak to us. It might even be necessary for you to rough him up a bit.'

'What?' said Jack.

'We need information,' said Eddie. 'Any information. So we might have to, you know, lean on him a little. And things might get ugly and he might call for his security men and we might get thrown out of the building. And then we'd not get to see the show.'

'Makes perfect sense,' said Jack. 'Let's push into the studio and get a seat at the front.' Jack's stomach rumbled. 'What about some food?' he asked.

'Exert a little self-control,' said Eddie. 'We're professionals, aren't we?'

'We certainly are.'

It is a fact well known to those who know it well, and indeed to anyone else who has ever been dumb enough to apply for tickets to a TV show, that the interior of TV studios, the very interior, the sanctum sanctorum, the heart of hearts, the belly of the beast, the studio proper, is a real disappointment, when you've finished queuing up and finally get to see it.

It's rubbish.

The audience seating is rubbish. It's Spartan, it's uncomfortable, it's crummy. The stage set is rubbish. It's cardboard and plywood and not well painted at all. And there're wires everywhere. And there are cameras that get in your way so you can't see properly. And there are rude crew persons who behave like pigs and herd you in and bully you about and who won't let you get up during the show, even if you desperately need the toilet. And it always smells rough in there too, as if some orgy or other has just been going on—which tends to make the disappointment you feel even worse, because you know you must have just missed it.

And the other thing is that the show is never the way you see it on TV. The show always goes wrong and there has to be take after take after take. And although for the audience this does have a certain novelty value to begin with, by the tenth retake the novelty has well and truly worn off.

There is nothing glamorous about TV studios. Absolutely nothing glamorous at all. They're rubbish. They are. Rubbish.

'Isn't this brilliant?' said Eddie.

'Certainly is,' said Jack.

As they were the first into the studio, they were 'escorted' to the very front seats by one of the 'crew'.

A crew pig in fact. All bendy rubber and portly and scowling, he had the word CREW painted in large letters across his belly. He huffed and puffed in a bad-tempered manner and jostled Jack and Eddie along.

'Sit *there*,' he ordered.

Jack and Eddie hastened to oblige. The seating was toy-sized and Jack found his knees once again up around his shoulders. But he didn't care. He was loving it all.

Jack sniffed the air. 'You can even smell the glamour,' he said.

'I can definitely smell something,' said Eddie.

More rude crew pigs were now herding the rest of the audience in.

Jack looked all around and about. Overhead hung many stage lights. To the rear of each was attached a sort of half-bicycle affair: the rear half, with pedals, chain wheel and seat. And upon each seat sat a clockwork cyclist, whose job it was to pedal away like fury to power up the light and move it this way and that when required so to.

The instructions for the requiring so to do were issued from a booth set directly above the stage: the controller's box. The controller already sat in his seat of control. Evidently purpose-built for this role, he was undoubtedly the most remarkable toy Jack had so far seen. He was big and broad and constructed from bendy rubber. His wide, flat face had six separate mouths set into a horizontal row. From his ample torso sprouted six separate arms, each hand of which held a megaphone. As Jack looked on in awe, the controller bawled separate instructions through four different megaphones. Clockwork cyclists to the right and left and the above of Jack pedalled furiously away and swung their lights here and there at the controller's directing.

The lights swept over the low stage beneath the controller's box.

The stage set resembled a woodland arbour, painted plywood trees, a blue sky daubed to the rear, with the words *Tuff it on the Tuffet* painted upon it in large and glittering golden letters. The floor of the stage was carpeted with fake grass, on which stood a number of stools fashioned to resemble tuffets and arranged in a semi-circle. To the right of the stage was a small clockwork orchestra.

'I'm really enjoying this,' said Jack, 'and it hasn't even started yet.'

Before the stage, clockwork cameramen were positioning their clockwork cameras, large and bulky affairs of colourful pressed tin which moved upon casters. The clockwork cameramen appeared to be positioning their cameras in such a way as to create the maximum obstruction of the audience's view of the stage.

Eddie was looking over his shoulder, watching the rude crew pigs herding in the audience of toys. 'Hm,' he said.

Jack pointed towards the large and glittering letters that were painted upon the pretend sky backdrop. 'What does Tuff it on the Tuffet mean?' he asked Eddie.

'Miss Muffett's show is one of those talk show jobbies,' Eddie explained, 'where toys air their embarrassing personal problems on primetime TV. I once wrote a little poem about it; would you care for me to recite it to you?'

'Is it a long poem?' Jack asked.

'No, quite short.'

'Go on then.'

Eddie made throat-clearing growlings and then he began:

'Scandalous secrets and shocking surprises,

'Secreting their persons with silly disguises,

'Or proudly parading their sexual deviation,

'With clockwork and teddy and even relation.

'Recounting their fumblings with famous Toy folk,

'Or confessing the need for the herbs that they smoke.

'All in the hope that the show will bestow,

'Media absolution.'

'Very good,' said Jack.

'Did you really think so?'

'Not really,' said Jack. 'I was being polite. But why would anyone want to come on a TV show and air their dirty laundry in public, as it were?'

Eddie shrugged. 'That is one of life's little mysteries,' he said. 'My guess would be that either they're actors making it all up, or they're very sad individuals who crave their moment of glory on TV. But who cares; it's great television.'

'And Little Tommy Tucker is going to be "tuffing it", is he?'

'I doubt that. He's probably promoting his new hit single. He's a big recording artiste, is Tommy. He doesn't have to sing for his supper any more. Well, he does in a manner of speaking, but his singing has earned him enough for a million suppers in the City's finest eateries.'

Jack's stomach rumbled once again. But at least his hangover was beginning to lessen. 'Famous singer, eh?' said Jack.

'Top of the charts,' said Eddie. 'Not my pot of jam though. I'm an Elvis fan, me.'

'Elvis?' said Jack. 'Who's Elvis?'

Eddie rolled his button eyes. 'He's the King.'

'Well I've never heard of him.'

'No, I suppose not. He's a bear, like me. My cousin, in fact. Tinto has an open-mic night on Fridays. Elvis sings. He's great.'

'What sort of stuff does he sing?' Jack asked.

'Tommy Tucker songs,' said Eddie, dismally. 'There aren't any others.'

'What, none?'

'Tommy sort of has the Toy City music industry in his velvet pocket. Tommy's always number one in the music charts, because the charts don't have a number two. And Tommy owns the only recording studio in Toy City, and the record company.'

'That's outrageous,' said Jack. 'So you're telling me that the only records you can buy in Toy City are Tommy Tucker records?'

'Or classical music.'

'Which is?'

'Nursery rhymes,' said Eddie. 'Sung by the Tommy Tucker choir ensemble. With the Tommy Tucker clockwork orchestra. That's them next to the stage.'

'Shut up!' shouted a rude crew pig into Eddie's ear. 'The show's about to begin. Shut up!'

'Oi,' said Jack. 'How dare you!'

'Shut up the both of you,' said the rude crew pig. 'And behave or I'll throw you out.'

Jack almost rose to take issue with the rude crew pig, but as he didn't want to miss the show, he didn't.

'It's always the same,' whispered Eddie. 'Paint a uniform on a pig and he thinks he rules the city.'

'Oh, look,' said Jack. 'Something's happening.'

And something was.

The controller shouted instructions through numerous megaphones; some lights dimmed, others shone brightly; those that shone brightly illuminated the stage.

Quite brightly.

From stage-right a figure appeared.

This figure was a clown. An all-rubber clown. An all-green, but for the red nose, rubber clown.

'Morning all,' said the all-green, but for the red nose, rubber clown.

Mumble, mumble, mumble went the audience. One or two folk managed a half-hearted 'Good morning'.

'Pathetic,' said the all-green, but for the red nose, rubber clown. 'That really won't do at all.'

'Who's this?' Jack asked.

'Warm-up clown, I think,' said Eddie.

'Shut up, you two,' said the crew pig, who had positioned himself in the aisle next to Jack and Eddie and was keeping a beady eye upon them.

'This is The Tuffet!' The all-green, but for the red nose, rubber clown made all-encompassing hand gestures. 'Biggest racing show in Toy City and you the audience must respond. You must cheer, you must applaud, you must react. Do you hear what I'm saying?'

Murmur, murmur, went the crowd.

'Do you hear?'

'Yes,' went much of the crowd, in an embarrassed murmur.

'And do you love Miss Muffett?'

'Yes,' went most of the crowd, quietly.

'I said, do you *love* Miss Muffett?'

'*Yes,*' went pretty much all of the crowd, pretty much louder.

'*I said, do you love Miss Muffett?*'

'*YES,*' went damn near all of the crowd.

'And you two,' the rude crew pig shook a trottered fist at Eddie and Jack.

'Oh yes indeed,' said Jack, in a tone that lacked somewhat for conviction.

'And me too,' said Eddie, in a likewise fashion.

'Let me hear you say "Yeah!"' shouted the all-green, but for the red nose, all-rubber clown.

'*Yeah!*' the audience replied.

'Not bad,' said the clown. 'But not good; let me hear you say "yeah" once again.'

'*Yeah!*' went the crowd with greater vigour.

'Yeah!' shouted the clown.

'Yeah!' shouted the audience back to him.

And yeah and yeah and yeah again.

'I don't like this clown at all,' said Jack.

'That's your last warning,' said the rude crew pig in between the yeahings.

'All right!' shouted the clown. 'Now we're rolling. Now let's have us some fun.'

And then the clown went about doing *The Terrible Thing*. The Terrible *Thing* is the terrible thing that all clowns do. It is *The Terrible Thing* that all clowns have always done, since the very dawn of clowning, *The Terrible Thing* that is ultimately what being a clown is all about.

The Terrible Thing that is . . .

Humiliating the audience.

Exactly why clowns do it is no mystery at all. They do it because they *can* do it, because they are allowed to do it, because they can get away with doing it. And they get away with doing it because they wear red noses and silly costumes which make them look ridiculous, make them look like fools, and so people let them get away with doing it— people who would otherwise beat the living life out of anyone else who dared to humiliate them—allow clowns do it.

Which serves them right, really.

But still makes it a terrible thing.

The all-green, but for the red nose, rubber clown began to move amongst the audience. He frolicked up and down the aisles. Here he mocked the leaky over-stuffed seams of a plump rag doll, and there he drew attention to a hint of rust upon the shoulder of a clockwork post-man. And over there he scorned a teddy's moth-eaten ear. And right at the back he made light of a wooden soldier's woodworm holes.

The audience laughed, as an audience will, as a detached sum of its individually wounded parts. That's life. But it's not very nice.

'This is foul,' said Jack.

The crew pig glared at him.

Jack caught the green clown's attention and the green clown came over to Jack.

'Well well well,' said the green clown, grinning hugely at Jack. 'What do we have here? I love the coat, are you wearing it for a dare?'

The audience laughed. Jack curled his lip.

'And is this your little bear?' The green clown beamed at Eddie.

Jack beckoned the green clown close and whispered certain cautionary words into his green rubber ear.

The green clown stiffened. 'So, on with the show,' he said. 'Clock-works, stuffed and toy folk generally, allow me to introduce your host-ess. The one, the only, Toy City's favourite Miss. Here she is. *Heeeeeeere's* Missy.'

The controller bawled instructions, overhead lights swung, focused and shone.

The clockwork orchestra struck up music.

And she made her entrance.

'The one. The only. Miss Muffett.

'Applause!' shouted the green clown.

And applause there was.

Jack turned his eyes towards the spotlit entrance of the Miss, but his view was immediately obstructed by a clockwork cameraman.

He ducked his head this way and that. And then Jack saw her: Miss Muffett.

Jack's jaw fell and his eyes became wide.

'What is *that*?' he asked.

19

If Jack had held to any religious beliefs, he might well have said that Miss Muffett was a sight to stagger the senses of the Gods.

But, as he was an atheist, he espoused no such claims. Instead he simply followed the words 'What is *that*?' with a single word.

And that single word was 'Wowser!'

'Wowser?' Eddie asked. 'What's Wowser?'

'Wowser,' Jack went once more. '*She* is Wowser. She. Well. Wowser. She is.'

Eddie gazed upon Miss Muffett. 'Wowser?' he said thoughtfully. 'That would probably do it.'

And it probably would.

From her tippy tiptoes to her tinted topknot, Miss Muffett was wonderfully wowser. She was wonderfully wowser to all points of the compass, and probably some others too.

She was remarkably wonderfully wowser, in fact.

Worryingly wowser.

As Jack viewed Miss Muffett, the wowser word came once more to his lips; Jack swallowed it back. What was so wonderfully wowser about this woman? he wondered.

Was it the hair?

Miss Muffett had the big hair of the famous.

It is a fact well known to those who know it well, and anyone in fact who ever watches TV, or goes to the movies, that although the fabulously famous may ultimately not end up always possessing big hair, they almost certainly began with it.

Big hair is a prerequisite. It is a given, as is big face and small body. It is a requirement when it comes to richness and famousness. Choose your favourite star of stage or screen; they will inevitably have had their big hair days.

Miss Muffett was currently having hers. Her hair was huge; it was blonde and it was huge. It outhuged the dollies in the lobby portraits. It went every-which-way, and every-which-way-hair is unashamedly erotic.

Curiously, bald heads on women are similarly erotic, but they're not nearly so much fun as big-haired heads. You can really get your hands into big-haired heads. And blonde big-haired heads . . .

Well . . .

Wowser!

Miss Muffett's eyes were big and blue. Her nose was tiny. Her mouth was full and wide. Slender was her neck and narrow her shoulders. Large and well-formed were her breasts, and her waist was as of the wasp. Her hips were the hips of a Goddess. Her low-necked gown, a sheath of shimmering stars. Her legs, as long as they were, and they were, were made to seem much longer by the lengthy heels upon her wowsery shoes.

And so on and so forth and such like. Da de da de da.

'She's certainly something,' said Eddie.

'I hate her,' said Jack.

'*What?*'

'That's not how it should be.' The beady eyes of the crew pig were once more upon Jack, and so Jack whispered to Eddie. 'That's not how it should be,' he said once more.

'Not *what?*' Eddie asked.

Not how a woman should be.'

'And you, a mere stripling of a lad, know how a woman should be?'

Thoughts of Jill from Madame Goose's returned to Jack. Not that they had ever been much away. Jill was, young as she was, the way a woman *should* be; in fact, she was *everything* that a woman should be, in Jack's admittedly somewhat limited opinion. Miss Muffett's beauty was there. It was definitely there. It was amazingly, wowseringly *there*. But it was too much. It was extreme. It was wowser, yes, but it was *worryingly* wowser.

'You can't look like that,' Jack whispered. 'Not really. It's too much. Do you know what I mean, Eddie? It's too much. It makes me feel uncomfortable.'

Eddie grinned, but he said nothing.

A single spotlight illuminated Miss Muffett. ' 'Allo loves,' she said in a deep and husky tone. 'Welcome to The Tuffet. Today we shall be dealing with the sensitive subject of interracial relationships. Can a fuzzy felt mouse find happiness with a wooden kangaroo? Can a teddy bear truly know love in clockwork arms?'

'Not if it's me and Tinto,' sniggered Eddie.

'Shut it!' snarled the crew pig.

'Can a big fat pug-ugly rubber dancing doll with bad dress sense and a small moustache really want to marry the worm-eaten wooden chef from Nadine's Diner?'

Jack shrugged.

'Search me,' said Eddie. 'But she'd probably be grateful for anything, by the sound of her.'

'*Very* last warning,' said the crew pig.

'Let's ask them,' said Miss Muffett, ascending the stage and setting her wowseringly wonderful behind onto the central tuffet thereof.

The controller bawled the word 'Applause' through the megaphone. And applause there was.

Rude crew pigs ushered the guests onto the stage. One was a big fat pug-ugly dancing doll in a revolting sportswear suit. The other was a worm-eaten wooden chef.

'Oh,' said Jack. 'It's him.'

'Him?' whispered Eddie, cowering beneath the gaze of the rude crew pig.

'The first night I was in the city,' said Jack. 'I went into a Nadine's Diner. He was the chef. I thought he was a man in a wooden mask or something.'

'And I woke you up in the alley outside,' whispered Eddie.

The big fat pug-ugly dancing doll required two tuffets to sit down upon; rude crew pigs moved them into place. The worm-eaten wooden chef sat down beside her.

Miss Muffett introduced her guests to the audience.

Jack yawned.

'Tired?' said Eddie.

'Short attention span,' said Jack. 'We had shows like this on TV in my town. I'm bored already.'

'Jaded with the glamour of celebrity already,' said Eddie. 'The fickleness of youth, eh?'

'That's it,' said the rude crew pig. 'Out, the pair of you.'

'I've had quite enough of you,' said Jack. 'Clear off.'

'Be quiet,' said the rude crew pig. 'Keep your voice down. The show is in progress.'

'Does this show go out live?' Jack asked the rude crew pig.

'It certainly does,' the pig replied.

'Then it would be a terrible shame if it were to be interrupted wouldn't it?'

The rude crew pig made a very foul face at Jack.

'Interrupted by me throwing you onto the stage and then kicking you all around and about on it.'

Eddie flinched.

The rude crew pig stiffened.

'Then leave us alone,' said Jack. 'Or I will make a great deal of noise and cause a great deal of trouble.'

'Just keep it down.' The rude crew pig made a very worried face.

'Go away. Or else.'

The rude crew pig took a tottering step or two up the aisle.

'Away,' counselled Jack. 'Hurry up now; I suffer from a rare medical condition which manifests itself in acts of extreme violence when I find myself put under stress.'

The rude crew pig departed hurriedly.

'Well done,' said Eddie. 'Most authoritative. Most assertive.'

'Let's go and find Little Tommy Tucker,' said Jack.

'I can't believe you,' said Eddie. 'We're here in a TV studio. Watching the Miss Muffett show live. And . . .'

'It's rubbish,' said Jack. 'It's all rubbish. The rude crew pigs, the insulting clown, this patronising woman: it's excruciating.'

'That's entertainment,' said Eddie, in a singsong kind of a way.

'Well, I can't be having with it. Let's find Little Tommy Tucker.'

'He'll be on soon,' Eddie cuffed Jack on the arm. 'Behave yourself and be patient. You're a very naughty boy.'

Jack stifled a large guffaw and directed his attention once more to the stage.

'Good boy,' said Eddie.

'So tell me, Chardonnay,' said Miss Muffett to the big fat pug-ugly dancing doll, 'what it is that you see in Garth?'

Garth, the worm-eaten wooden chef, reached out a wooden hand and squeezed the podgy mitt of Chardonnay.

'He's very sensitive,' said Chardonnay.

'How nice,' said Missy.

'And he does all the cooking and he smells very nice. He has this lovely piney fragrance. Go on, give him a sniff.'

Miss Muffett leaned towards Garth and gave him a sniff. 'Piney, with a touch of cooking lard,' she said.

'And when he gets wood, he keeps it,' said Chardonnay.

'Excuse me?' said Miss Muffett.

'I'm talking about his penis,' said Chardonnay. 'When he gets an erection, it's like a forest oak. A mighty pine. A giant redwood. A great shaft of thrusting timber. A—'

'A big log-on?' asked Miss Muffett. 'What about your social life? How have your friends taken to your relationship?'

'Mine are all for it,' said Garth. 'My mates say, "Go on my son, get in there."'

'And so they should.' Miss Muffett smiled a mouthload of perfect teeth. 'But what I mean is in terms of social intercourse.'

'If you're having intercourse,' said Garth, 'who needs to socialise?'

'How true,' said Miss Muffett. 'Someone once asked me whether I liked All-In Wrestling. I replied, if it's all in, why wrestle?'

The audience erupted into laughter.

'Excruciating,' said Jack. 'I *really* hate her.'

'I think she's fun,' said Eddie. 'And dirty, of course, and I do like dirty, me.'

'Well, I don't. This show is gross. It's all gross.'

'So,' said Miss Muffett, 'do either of you have parents and if so, how have they reacted to your relationship?'

'Well, I don't have any parents,' said Garth. 'I was hewn by the toy-maker. And well hewn too.'

'He certainly is,' said Chardonnay. 'Hewn like a rolling pin. The toymaker stuffed me.'

'I'm finishing where he left off,' said Garth.

'Well,' said Miss Muffett, 'it would appear that you two have the perfect relationship.'

'We do,' the pair agreed.

'But,' said Miss Muffett, 'things are not always as they appear and after the commercial break that is coming right up, I'll be introducing several other guests: a clockwork fireman who claims that for the last three years he has been having a gay relationship with Garth, and two dollies who have borne his children. And if that isn't enough, we'll be bringing on a straw dog who insists that Chardonnay is, as he puts it, his bitch. We'll be back in a moment right after this.' Miss Muffett smiled and the controller shouted 'cut,' through one of his mega-phones.

Chardonnay turned upon Garth and began to set about him some-thing wicked. Garth responded by butting her fiercely in the head.

Rude crew pigs trotted forward and hustled Chardonnay and Garth from the stage.

Miss Muffett arose from her Tuffet. She straightened down parts of her frock that really didn't need straightening down and approached Jack and Eddie upon her preposterous heels.

'You two,' she said, when she had approached sufficiently. 'You two have chatted throughout my first quarter. Are you both mad or just plain stupid?'

Jack gawped at Miss Muffett. 'We're . . .' he managed to say.

'Yes, you gormster, *what*?'

'We're really enjoying the show,' said Jack.

'But you feel the need to talk all through it?'

'Very sorry,' said Jack.

'Just shut it,' said Miss Muffett. 'Shut your stupid ignorant mouths. I'm a star. A big star. A famous star. You, you're nothing. Do you understand? Less than nothing. Nobodies. Nonsuches. Nonentities. You just do what you're told to. Laugh in the right places. Applaud in the right places. Then get out. Get out and go back to your meaningless little lives. Do you hear what I'm saying?'

'All too loudly,' said Jack.

'What?'

'We hear you, yes.'

'Then shut up.' Miss Muffett's wonderfully wowser blue eyes glared pointy daggers at Jack.

'Very sorry,' said Jack once more. 'We'll be quiet. We were overexcited. That's all.'

'Yes, well, see that you do. Stupid trash.' Miss Muffett turned upon her pointy heels and stalked back to the stage.

Jack looked at Eddie.

And Eddie looked at Jack.

'What a most unwowserly woman,' said Jack.

Eddie said nothing at all.

Then.

'Three, two, one,' bawled the controller, variously.

The clockwork orchestra struck up once again.

And part two of the show was on the go.

Chardonnay and Garth were back on stage, but this time each was restrained within straitjackets. Various dubious-looking types, a rusty clockwork fireman, a manky straw dog and some barely dressed dollies were hustled into the spotlight to tell their tales of drunkenness and debauchery, point accusing fingers and paws. They soon took to striking one another.

At length these too were hustled away, leaving Miss Muffett alone.

'Trash,' whispered Jack. 'It's all trash.'

'Ladies and gentlemen,' husked Missy, 'dollies and gollies, clock-workers, woodeners, and all otherwises, it is now my very great pleasure to introduce you to a very dear friend of mine: a star amongst stars, making one of his rare live appearances right here on my little show. I am honoured to welcome the supper singer himself, your own, your very own, Little Tommy Tucker.'

And the clockwork orchestra struck up once again, again.

The controller did further bawlings for applause and for complicated lighting-work, but his bawlings were swallowed up by the orchestra's stirring rendition of the Little Tommy Tucker theme and the audience's obvious adulation.

The applause was such as to have Eddie's growler vibrating.

'*Grrrrrrrrr*,' went Eddie. 'Pardon me.'

And then *He* walked out onto the stage.

He had the look of one who had partaken of the pleasures of the flesh in a manner that lacked for moderation or temperance. *He* had *really* partaken of them.

He was indeed Toy City's most perfectly wasted man.

Jack ducked this way and that as clockwork cameramen once more got in his way, but when he finally spied Little Tommy, Jack felt cause to whistle.

'No one can be *that* thin,' Jack said to Eddie.

But Little Tommy could.

There was very little of Little Tommy. He had the big face of the famous, but the little body was oh-so-little that it was a cause of pain to gaze upon. It was next to nothing. It was a wisp. A wistful whisper.

A willowy wistful whisper.

What little there was of it was encased in a truly spiffing triple-breasted blue silk *Oh Boy!* suit of the high fashion persuasion. He wore dapper little hyper-exclusive foolish-boy-skin shoes upon his dinky little feet. A nattily knotted pink velvet tie was threaded beneath the high collars of a pale lemon satin shirt. He had the remains of some very big hair piled high upon his head. A studio tan coloured his gauntly-featured face. His eyes were of the palest blue; his lips of the lushest red.

'Hi there,' crooned little Tommy, raising skeletal hands.

The audience cheered and those amongst them possessed of hands clapped these wildly together.

'Thank you, thank you, thank you.' Little Tommy beamed all around and about. He exchanged air kisses with Little Miss Muffett and bowed several times to the audience. He stepped up to a microphone before the clockwork orchestra. 'I'd like to sing a song that I know will be very lucky for me,' he said into it. 'Another chart topper.'

Further wild applause issued from the audience.

'Is he really *that* good?' Jack shouted into Eddie's ear.

'No, he's rubbish, and there's no need to shout. We bears are greatly admired for our aural capacities.'

'Urgh,' went Jack.

Eddie rolled his button eyes. 'Aural,' he said. 'Oh, never mind.'

'This song,' continued Little Tommy, 'is dedicated to a very dear friend of mine. I cannot speak his name aloud, but *He* knows who *He* is. The song is called "You're a God to me, buddy." It goes something like this.' Little Tommy beamed over his slender shoulder towards the clockwork orchestra. 'Gentlemen, please, if you will.'

The clockwork conductor one two three'd it with his baton; the orchestra launched into the number.

Jack's head ducked this way and that, but the cameramen obscured his view. He could however hear the song. And as Jack listened to it, his jaw dropped low once more.

It was . . .

'Awful,' whispered Jack to Eddie. 'The song's awful and he can't even sing.'

'It is my belief,' Eddie whispered back, 'that when Wheatley Porterman penned the original nursery rhyme that made Little Tommy famous, it was intended as a satire upon the poor quality of Toy City nightclub entertainers, Little Tommy in particular: that all his singing was worth was some brown bread and butter. Ironic the way things turned out, eh?'

Jack nodded thoughtfully, curled his lip, screwed up his eyes and thrust his hands over his ears. 'Tell me when he's finished,' he said to Eddie.

Eddie did not reply to this. His paws were already over his ears.

It did have to be said that even if Little Tommy wasn't much of a singer, which indeed he was not, he did put his heart and indeed his very soul into his performance. Veins stood out upon his scrawny neck and upon his ample forehead. Tears sprang into his eyes. His spindly arms crooked themselves into all manner of unlikely positions; his long fingers snatched at the air as if clawing at the very ether. Rivulets of sweat ran down his face, joining his tears to stripe his studio tan.

The song itself was of the ballad persuasion, which, given Little Tommy's rendition in the manner that made it all his own, had about it a quality which raised excruciation to an art form. Little Tommy trembled on his toes. At every high note, his lips quivered and his mouth became so wide that those in the upper seats who had particularly good eyesight were afforded a clear view right down his scrawny throat to see what he'd had for breakfast.

The deafening applause that greeted the song's conclusion was sufficient to arouse Jack and Eddie from the foetal positions they had adopted. Eddie put his paws together. 'Bravo,' he called.

'Irony?' Jack asked.

'Absolutely,' said Eddie.

'Bravo,' called Jack, clapping too. 'More. More.'

'Let's not overdo it.'

'Quite so.' Jack ceased his clapping.

'What can I say?' Little Miss Muffett rose from her central tuffet, clapping lightly and professionally. 'One of the greats. If not *the* great. Join me up here, Little Tommy, come and sit with me please.'

Little Tommy took another bow and joined Miss Muffett.

'Thank you, Missy,' he said, seating himself down upon the vacant tuffet next to Missy.

Jack's empty stomach made terrible grumbling sounds. 'I really have had enough,' he whispered to Eddie.

'We might as well stick it out to the end,' said the bear. 'You never know, it might get really interesting.'

'Yeah, right,' said Jack. 'They're just going to luvvy each other.'

And that, of course, was exactly what Miss Muffett and Little Tommy *were* going to do: luvvy each other big time.

'Little Tommy,' husked the Missy, 'beautiful song, beautiful lyrics, beautiful rendition.'

'I just love your dress,' crooned Little Tommy.

'And you're looking so well.'

'And you so young.'

'It's wonderful to have you here.'

'It's wonderful to be here on your wonderful show.'

'Wonderful,' husked Missy. 'But tell me, Little Tommy, I know you make very very few public appearances.'

'Very few,' Tommy agreed.

'But why this?'

'Well, Missy,' said Little Tommy, crossing his spindly legs, 'I just don't have the time. The way I see it, it is the duty of a superstar such as myself to maintain the appropriate lifestyle: a lifestyle to which the less fortunate amongst us, your audience for instance, can only aspire to in their most exalted, and dare I say, perverted dreams.'

'You might certainly dare,' said Missy. 'In fact you have.'

'Take it to excess,' said Little Tommy. 'Such is expected of someone like myself. It is my duty.'

'And you certainly have taken it to excess.' Miss Muffett smiled big smiles upon Little Tommy. 'Your squanderings and indulgences are of legend.'

'Well, thank you very much.'

'And you've just come out of detox, I understand.'

'Detox, rehab, it's a weekly thing with me. They say "If you've got it, flaunt it." I say, "If you've got it, use it up, wear it out, get it flushed and start again on Monday."'

'What a thoroughly unpleasant individual,' said Jack.

'Everyone misbehaves,' said Eddie. 'That's nature. Everyone gets away with as much as they can get away with. And the more they can get away with, the more they will.'

'That's a somewhat cynical view of life.'

'You know that I'm telling the truth.'

'That doesn't mean that I want to admit it.'

Eddie grinned. 'You're a good lad, Jack,' said he.

'But he isn't.'

'No, he's an absolute stinker.'

'Drugs?' said Little Tommy, in an answer to a question from Miss Muffett that Jack and Eddie hadn't heard. 'Well, yes, all right, I must admit that I am no stranger to drugs. Not that I'm advocating them to others, don't get me wrong, I'm not. Only for me. To me, an unhealthy cocktail of alcohol and narcotics spices things up for a bit of hot groupie action.'

'There have been reports in the Toy City Press regarding the, how shall I put it, tender ages of some of your groupies.'

'If they're old enough to walk on their own,' said Little Tommy, 'then they're up for it.'

'What?' went Jack.

Miss Muffett tittered. 'You're a very naughty boy,' she said.

'I know,' said Little Tommy. 'But you can't help liking me, can you?'

'I hate him,' said Jack. 'Hate her, hate him. I'm exhibiting no preferences, you notice.'

'Very democratic,' said Eddie.

'He needs a smack,' said Jack. 'So does she.'

'Well,' said Little Miss Muffett, 'it's been an absolute pleasure to have you here on the show, Little Tommy. I think the audience would agree with me on this.' Missy smiled towards the audience. The audience gave out with further wild applause. 'So I think we should finish this interview on a high note. Would you honour us, Little

Tommy, by giving us another of your marvellous high notes one more time?'

'It would be my pleasure, Missy.' Little Tommy threw back his head, opened his mouth as widely as widely could be and gave vent to a crackling high note of such appalling awfulness that Jack's hands and Eddie's paws rushed upwards once more towards their respective ears.

It was a long high note.

A prolonged high note.

An elongated high note.

And there's no telling for how protracted a period this particular long, prolonged, elongated high note might have continued for had it not been suddenly cut short.

The cause of its cut-shortness was not viewed by Jack as a clock-work cameraman was once more obscuring his view. Eddie saw it clearly, though.

Something dropped down from above.

From above the controller's control booth.

From above the clockwork lighting-pedallers.

From the very ceiling of the studio.

Through a hole that had been drilled through this very ceiling.

Whatever this something was, and it was very soon to be apparent exactly what this something was, it dropped through this hole and fell directly down and into Little Tommy Tucker's open mouth and on-ward further still until it reached the area inside him where rested his breakfast.

'Gulp!' went Little Tommy, suddenly foreshortening his high note. 'What was that?'

'What was *what*?' Miss Muffett asked.

'Something.' Little Tommy clutched at his throat and then at his diminutive stomach regions. 'Something fell into my mouth.'

'Well, it wouldn't be the first time.' Miss Muffett tittered some more.

'Yes, but I didn't like this. Oooh.'

'Oooh?' questioned Miss Muffett.

'Yes, Oooh, something is going on in my guts.'

'Well, upon that high note, we have to take another commercial break. But we'll be right back after it with a love triangle which turned out to be more of a pentangle. We'll say goodbye. Please put your hands together for my very special guest, Little Tommy, and I know that you'll all be going out to purchase his latest hit. What was the name of that song again, Tommy?'

'Oooh,' went Tommy. 'Aaaargh!'

Jack looked at Eddie.

And Eddie looked at Jack.

'What's happening?' Jack asked. 'I can't see.'

'Something bad,' said Eddie. 'Something very bad.'

'Oooh!' went Little Tommy once again. And 'Aaaargh' again also. He clutched at himself and leapt from his tuffet.

And then all kinds of terrible things happened.

20

Little Tommy, arisen from his tuffet, was now clutching all over himself and howling in evident anguish.

The audience members, under the mistaken belief that this was just part of the show—albeit a somewhat bizarre part—rocked with laughter and clapped together what hands they possessed.

'What's going on?' Jack shouted to Eddie.

'Up there,' Eddie shouted back. 'Above the controller's box. Hole in the ceiling. Something dropped through it into Tommy's mouth.'

'It's the serial killer again.' Jack jumped to his feet. 'Call an ambulance,' he shouted, pushing aside a clockwork cameraman and toppling his clockwork camera.

Little Tommy lurched about the stage. Something horrible was happening inside him. He jerked upwards as if being lifted physically from his feet and then slammed down onto the floor.

Jack rushed to offer what assistance he could, although he knew little of first aid. Rude crew pigs came snorting down the aisles; the audience continued with its laughter and applause, although it was dawning upon its brighter members that something was altogether amiss.

As Jack reached the now-prone supper singer, a most horrible occurrence occurred: as if by the agency of some invisible force, Little Tommy swung upright.

He hung, suspended in the air, his tiny feet dangling twelve inches above the stage. He stared at Jack face-to-face with pleading eyes and open mouth.

'We'll get you help,' said Jack, but he could clearly see that help would be too late. Little Tommy began to vibrate and rattle about.

Great tremors ran up and down his slender body. Steam began to issue from his ears.

'Oh no,' croaked Jack, taking several sharp steps back-aways. 'He's going to blow. Take cover, everyone.'

Whistling sounds came from Tommy, rising and rising in volume and pitch. Buttons popped from his triple-breasted suit, strange lumps bulged from his forehead and his shoulders began to expand. The laughter and applause in the audience died away. Horror and panic refilled the momentary void.

As Jack fell back from the stage the horde of rude crew pigs fell upon Jack. 'We'll teach you some manners,' snorted the one that Jack had recently sent packing.

And oh so quickly, as it always does, chaos reigned supreme.

The audience arose from their uncomfortable seats and made the traditional mad dash for the exits. The controller bawled instructions to the lighting pedallers, but the lighting pedallers were now dismounting and abseiling down ropes, eager to make their escape. Miss Muffett was being rapidly escorted from the stage by burly men in dark suits and mirrored sunglasses who all sported tiny earphones with mouth mic attachments. And as Jack vanished beneath a maelstrom of trotters, Little Tommy Tucker exploded.

On prime time TV.

Before a large viewing audience.

Although reruns of this particular show would top the ratings charts for many months to come, the only direct eyewitness to Little Tommy's spectacular demise was one Eddie Bear, Toy City private eye.

Knowing better than to risk being flattened by the stampeding audience and being incapable of assisting Jack in his travails against the rude crew pigs, Eddie had remained where he was, cowering in his seat. He had to put his paws right over his ears, though, as Tommy's high-pressure whistlings reached an ultrasonic level, which set toy dogs in the street outside howling. But Eddie had a ringside seat to watch the explosion.

It is another fact well known to those who know it well, and those who know it well do so through personal experience, that when you are involved in something truly dreadful and life-threatening, such as a car crash, the truly dreadful and life-threatening something appears to occur in slow motion. Many explanations have been offered for this: a sudden rush of adrenalin, precipitating a rapid muscle response, affording the individual the opportunity (however small) to take evasive action; an alteration in the individual's perception of time, which is something akin to a near-death experience, in which the individual's

psyche, id, consciousness, or soul stuff, depending upon the chosen theological viewpoint, momentarily detaches itself from the individual in
question, allowing the individual to experience the event in a different
timeframe. Or the far more obvious, trans–perambulation of pseudo-
cosmic antimatter, precipitating a flexi-tangential spatial interflux
within the symbiotic parameters of existential functionalism.

But whether or not any of these actually apply to brains comprised
entirely of sawdust is somewhat open to debate.

If asked whether he had watched the exploding of Little Tommy
Tucker in what seemed to be slow motion, Eddie Bear would, however,
answer, 'Yes, and it was not at all nice.'

Eddie watched the ghastly swellings, the vile expansions, the distor-
tions of limbs and facial featurings, and then he saw the rending of flesh
and shirt and blue silk *Oh Boy!* suit. And he saw the fragments of the
gas-filled clockwork grenade that roared out of Tommy's shredded
body. And whether it was adrenalous rush, or detached id, or pseudo-
cosmic existential functionalism, Eddie managed to duck aside as metal
shards and Tucker guts flew in his direction.

Not so, however, the wildly trotting rude crew pigs, who caught
much shrapnel in their rubber rear ends.

As the crew pigs ran squealing and Jack, who had gone down fighting, came up prepared to do some more, Eddie raised his ducked head
and saw something else.

And Eddie pointed with a paw and Jack looked up and saw it too.

Down through the hole in the ceiling it drifted, a tiny white and
brown thing. The white of it was a parachute, the brown was a hollow
chocolate bunny.

Now the mayhem hadn't lessened, because but a few short seconds had
passed. The explosion had done nothing whatever to lessen the chaos;
on the contrary, it had done everything to considerably increase it.

The fire alarm was ringing and the sprinkler system went into action. Water showered down upon the audience-turned-mob. The
audience-turned-mob turned upon itself, and much of itself turned to
other than itself; indeed, turned upon the rude crew pigs who were
scrambling also to flee.

It was now a full-blown riot situation.

'This way.' Jack hauled Eddie after him and took off at a rush for
the rear of the stage, leaping over spattered remains of the ex-supper
singer. 'The killer's upstairs somewhere; we have to get after them.'

'Whoa!' went Eddie as Jack passed the painted sky backdrop and
entered a backstage corridor. 'Slow down, Jack, think about this.'

'We have to get after the killer.'

'We don't have any weapons.'

'We'll improvise.'

'Have you gone completely insane?'

Jack dashed along the corridor. 'Let go of me,' cried Eddie. 'Put me down.'

Jack ceased his dashings and put Eddie down. 'The murderer may still be in the building,' he said. 'We have to find out; we have to do something.'

'No, Jack,' said Eddie. 'I can't.'

'You can't? Why?'

'Jack, I just saw a man get blown to pieces. I think I'm going to be sick.'

'Then wait here,' said Jack. 'I'll go alone.'

'No, don't do it, please.'

'But I might be able to catch them unawares.'

'Or you might walk straight into a trap. Let it go, Jack.'

'Are you sure?'

'You're very brave, but look at the state of you.'

'I'm fine,' said Jack.

'You're not, you're all beaten about.'

'Get away, they hardly laid a trotter on me.'

'Carry me back to the office, Jack.'

'Carry you? In broad daylight? What about your dignity?'

'I'll have to swallow that, I'm afraid.'

And then Eddie fainted.

Jack carried Eddie back to Bill Winkie's office. To spare his dignity, he hid the little bear beneath his trenchcoat.

In the office Jack splashed water on Eddie and slowly Eddie revived.

'That was most upsetting,' said Eddie. 'I didn't like that at all.'

'Are you feeling all right now?' Jack asked.

'Yes I'll be fine. Thanks for looking after me.'

'No problem,' said Jack. 'As long as you're okay.'

'It was a bit of a shock.'

'But let's look on the bright side,' said Jack.

'The bright side? What bright side?'

'Little Tommy Tucker went the way he would probably have wanted: live on stage before a cheering audience. Out on a high note and in a blaze of glory.'

'Are you trying to be funny?'

'Rather desperately so, yes.'

'Then please don't.' Eddie shook his head. 'I can't believe it. The killer did it, right in front of us. Right in front of the viewing public. How audacious can you get?'

'This killer is making a very big statement.' Jack settled down in Bill Winkie's chair. 'There's a very big ego involved here.'

'And we're always one step behind.'

'Well, we're bound to be. We don't know who this loony is going to butcher next. We don't have his hit list.'

'Hit list, a celebrity hit list,' said Eddie, thoughtfully. 'You might have something there.'

Eddie climbed onto the wreckage of Bill Winkie's desk. 'Right,' he said. 'Let's see what we have. We have Murder Most Foul: to whit, Mr Dumpty, Boy Blue, Madame Goose, Wibbly, Jack Spratt and now Tommy Tucker. I think we can exclude Madame Goose and Wibbly; they just happened to be in the wrong place at the wrong time. It's the others that matter. The old rich of Toy City. What is the common link?'

'Easy,' said Jack, swivelling about in Bill Winkie's chair, 'I know this.'

'Go on,' said Eddie.

'The common link is that they were all killed by the same murderer.'

Eddie made the kind of face that wouldn't buy you cheese. 'Was that supposed to be funny too?' he asked.

'I don't think so,' said Jack. 'But think about it, Eddie. *She*, or *it*, must have had a reason to kill them all.'

'I understand what you're saying. But *she* or *it* didn't kill Jack Spratt or Tommy Tucker. *She* or *it* was already done and dusted.'

'Oooh oooh.' Jack put up his hand. 'I've an idea.'

'Go on,' said Eddie once more.

'All right, my idea is this. There are two killers.'

Eddie groaned.

'No, I haven't finished. There are two killers, *but* they're hired killers, working for someone else. The brains behind it all.'

'What *are* you saying?' Eddie asked. 'No, wait, I know what you're saying. If the *she* or *it* was doing the killing for *her* personal motives, the killings would have stopped when she was killed.'

'Exactly,' said Jack, having another swivel on the chair. 'So if you stop this latest killer, the killings won't stop; another hired killer will take over and continue the work.'

'And our job is to find out what this *work* is. Why it's being done and who is the evil genius behind it.'

'Evil genius is a bit strong,' said Jack. 'Let's not go giving this mad person airs and graces.'

'Criminal mastermind, then,' said Eddie.

'That's more like it,' said Jack. 'So what we need to find is the common link.'

Eddie groaned once more.

'What's with all this groaning?' Jack asked. 'Are you ill or something?'

'We're going round in circles. We need to put things in order.'

'Right,' said Jack, nodding in agreement and swivelling a bit more on the chair.

'*In order,*' said Eddie, in the voice of one who has been granted a sudden revelation. 'Put things in order! As in your list. The celebrity hit list.'

Jack did shruggings which, combined with his swivellings, nearly had him off the chair.

'Why did the killer slaughter her victims in the order she did?' Eddie asked. 'Why Humpty first, then Boy Blue? I'll bet there's some reason for the order.'

'I can't see why the order matters. Why don't we go to Jack Spratt's and search for some clues there? Or back to the studios; we might find something.'

'No,' said Eddie. 'If I'm right about this, we'll be ahead of the game.'

'I don't understand,' said Jack. 'Oh damn!'

'Oh damn?'

'I've got the hem of my trenchcoat caught in the swivelling bit of the chair.' Jack yanked at the trenchcoat's hem and was rewarded with a ghastly tearing sound. 'Oh double damn,' he said.

Eddie ignored him. 'It's this way,' he said. 'I'm thinking that the victims are being killed in a particular order. I'll just bet you that it's the order that their nursery rhymes were written. I'm pretty sure that I read somewhere that Humpty was the first nursery rhyme millionaire.'

'But how does this help?' Jack fought with the chair for possession of the trenchcoat. So far the chair was winning.

'Wake up, Jack,' said Eddie. 'If I am right and the victims are being murdered in that order, then we'll know who's going to be the next on the celebrity hit list, won't we?'

Jack ceased his struggles. 'Eddie, that's brilliant,' he said. 'Then we can beat the police to the crime scene when the next murder happens.'

Eddie threw up his paws in despair.

'Only joking,' said Jack. 'We can be there before it happens, prevent it and capture the hired killer and get Bellis's boys in blue to beat
the name of the criminal mastermind out of them. Or something like
that.'

'Something like that,' said Eddie. 'So, it's *The Hall of Nearly All The
Records* for us.'

'The hall of *nearly all* the records?'

'The curator is a very honest man. He can't be expected to remember everything.'

'Well, obviously not,' said Jack. 'He'd look stuff up in the record
books.'

'Record books?' said Eddie. 'What are record books?'

'Books with records in them.'

'A novel idea,' said Eddie. 'I'll pass that on to the curator. He has
nearly all the records in his head.'

'*What?*' said Jack. 'They're not written down?'

'He does have a very large head.'

Jack shook his not-so-very-large head. 'Just one thing,' he said.
'How far away is this hall?'

'Right across the other side of the city.'

'And will we be taking a cab?'

'I don't think I have sufficient money for the fare. I was so drunk
that I actually paid off my bar bill at Tinto's last night.'

'So you'll be walking?'

'*We'll* be walking,' said Eddie.

'*You'll* be walking,' said Jack. 'I did enough walking yesterday. And
I'll keel over from hunger soon anyway. We should have used the Chief
Inspector's money to get some new wheels for Bill's car.'

'I know what,' said Eddie. 'We'll telephone *The Hall of Nearly All
The Records*.'

'Inspired,' said Jack. 'Where's the telephone?'

'Somewhere amongst all this mess; let's search for it.'

A thorough search of Bill Winkie's office turned up a number of interesting things.

It also turned up a telephone.

Jack turned up the telephone.

'Is this it?' he asked, turning it down again.

'That's the kiddie,' said Eddie.

'This toy telephone with the piece of knotted string holding the
handset on?'

'Pretty smart telephone, eh? I bought it for Bill as a birthday present.'

'But it's not a *real* telephone.'

'Please don't start all that again, Jack. Just dial *The Hall of Nearly All The Records* and let's get on.'

'And the telephone number is?'

'Oh, give it to me.' Eddie snatched away the telephone. Then he looked at it in a mournful manner. And then he handed it back. 'You'll have to dial,' he said; 'no fingers.'

'I'll just dial a number at random,' said Jack. 'You never know, luck might be on our side.'

Eddie, who had tired with groaning, made a low and growly sound instead. Jack dialled out some numbers and held the wooden handset to his ear.

'*Hall of Nearly All The Records,*' said a voice.

'Wah!' went Jack, dropping the handset.

Eddie scooped it up between his paws. 'Hello,' he said.

'Hello,' said the voice. '*Hall of Nearly All The Records.*'

'Splendid,' said Eddie. 'This is Chief Inspector Bellis here. I need some information.'

'If I have it, it's yours,' said the voice.

'Splendid once more,' said Eddie, turning to Jack. 'Get a pen and paper, Jack, and write down what I tell you.'

Jack sought pen and paper. 'Go on then,' he said, when his seeking had reached a successful conclusion.

Eddie awoke with a start. 'Sorry,' he said, 'nodded off there.' And he told the curator of *The Hall of Nearly All The Records* what he wanted to know.

'Easy,' said the curator, and he reeled off the list.

'Slow down,' said Eddie, as he dictated this list to Jack

'And . . .' said the curator.

'Yes?' said Eddie.

'Aaaaaagh!' went the curator, and the line went dead.

'Oh,' said Eddie.

'How do you spell that?' Jack asked. 'Is it a single "O"?'

'No, it's Oh! As in a surprised, if not a little shocked, Oh! The curator just went Aaaaaagh! And then the line went dead.'

'So how do you spell Aaaaaagh?'

Eddie shook his head. 'I think the curator just got murdered,' he said.

'Oh,' said Jack. 'That's bad. That's really bad. This new killer is as smart as the old one. But at least we do have the list.'

Eddie sighed. 'Read it back to me,' he said.

Jack read the list:

'Humpty Dumpty,

'er . . .
'Little Boy Blue,
'Jack Spratt,
'Little Tommy Tucker,
'Little Jack Horner,
'Little Miss Muffett,
'Georgie Porgie,
'Old Mother Hubbard.'

'Humpty Dumpty, Little Boy Blue, Jack Spratt,' said Eddie, beating the palm of his right paw with as near to a fist as he could make from the left. 'They're in the correct order. But hold on. There're only eight names. I'm sure I gave you nine. I wasn't really paying attention to which ones they were at the time, I was just trying to keep up with the curator. But I do remember how many there were. There were nine. You've left one out.'

'No I haven't,' said Jack.

'You have, Jack. I remember there were nine. Show me the list.'

'There're just eight.' Jack made to tear up the list, but Eddie knocked it from his hand and fumbled it up from the floor.

And then Eddie perused this list and then Eddie really groaned.

'I'm sorry,' said Jack.

Eddie shook his head, slowly and sadly. 'I should have known,' he said. 'I should have realised.'

'Perhaps it's not the same one,' said Jack.

'It's the same one,' said Eddie. 'There was only ever one Wee Willy Winkie. Even though he preferred to be known as Bill.'

They repaired to Tinto's Bar to take a late and liquid breakfast.

Eddie was a sad and sombre bear.

'I'm so sorry,' said Jack. 'It only really clicked when you called out his name for me to write down. Who Bill Winkie really was. But what I don't understand is, why did he become a detective? He should have been lording it up on his nursery rhyme royalties.'

'He was tricked out of his royalties by Wheatley Porterman. Signed a really bad contract. Porterman had made so much money from Humpty, he thought he'd take *all* from the next client. Wee Willy went public on the way he'd been tricked; no one ever got tricked again. But he was broke, but he *was* a natural detective, you know, all that "tapping at the windows and crying through the locks" stuff in the nursery rhyme. And checking up on whether the children were in their beds by eight o'clock. Natural detective. And now he's . . . you know.'

'We don't know he's *you know*. He's missing, that's all.'

'He's dead,' said Eddie, dismally. 'He's as dead as. This killer delights in fitting ends for his victims. Boiling the big egg man, giving the ex-shepherd the bitter end of his crook, Tommy Tucker going out on a high note, like you said. And the fellow who does all the searching goes missing Simple as that.'

'I'm so sorry.' Jack ordered further drinks that he had no means of paying for. 'Put them on my tab,' he told Tinto. The clockwork barlord, who had been listening in to the conversation, did so without complaint.

'This time it's really really personal,' said Eddie.

'We know who's going to be next,' said Jack. 'Like you said, that puts us ahead of the game.'

'Oh dear,' said Eddie. 'We'd better hurry. Tinto, call me a cab.'

'All right,' said Tinto, 'you're a cab.'

Jack began to laugh.

'That's not funny,' said Eddie. 'That's such an old joke.'

'But I'm young; I've never heard it before.'

'I'll call a cab for you,' said Tinto, whirring away to do so.

'I thought you couldn't afford a cab?' Jack took to finishing his beers.

'We'll worry about that when we get to Little Jack Horner's.'

Eddie finished his beer, and then two of Jack's before Jack could get to them.

The cab was a fine-looking automobile. It was a Mark 9 Black Cab Kerb Crawler, with lithographed pressed steel body panels, chrome-trimmed running boards and brass radiator grille.

It came complete with comfy passenger seats in plush fur fabric and a clockwork cabbie called Colin.

'Very plush,' said Jack, comfying himself upon a comfy passenger seat.

'Where to, guvnor?' asked Colin the clockwork cabbie, his tinplate jaw going *click click click*.

'Little Jack Horner's,' said Jack.

'He's popular today,' said the cabbie.

'Why do you say that?' Eddie asked.

'Because I've just come from his place; dropped a customer there.'

Jack and Eddie exchanged glances. 'What did this customer look like?' Jack asked.

'She was a strange one,' said the cabbie. 'Didn't speak. Just handed me a piece of paper with Jack Horner's address on it. She wore this feathered hat thing and she never stopped smiling. I could see her in the driving mirror. She fair put the wind up me, I can tell you.'

'Faster,' said Eddie. 'Drive faster.'

'Faster costs more money,' said the cabbie.

'Fast as you can then,' said Eddie, 'and you can have all the money I've got on me.'

'And all the money I have too,' said Jack.

The driver put his pressed-tin foot down. 'I'll show you fast,' he said. And he showed them fast.

'Eddie,' said Jack, as he clung for the dearness of life to whatever there was for him to cling to.

'Jack?' said Eddie, who clung on to Jack.

'Eddie, what are we going to do when we get there? We're no match for this woman-thing.'

The cab hung a left and went up on two wheels.

'Big guns,' said Eddie. 'We need big guns.'

'But where are we going to get big guns?'

'Big guns?' The cabbie glanced over his shiny shoulder. 'Did I hear you say big guns?'

'Watch the road!' shouted Jack.

'Big guns, I said,' said Eddie.

'I love big guns,' said the cabbie. 'Well, you have to in this business.' He now hung a right and the cab went up on its other two wheels.

'In the cabbie business?' Eddie was now on the floor; Jack helped him up.

'You'd be surprised,' said the cabbie. 'Folk get into my cab and ask me to drive somewhere, then tell me that they have no money.'

'Oh,' said Eddie. 'So you menace them with your big gun?'

'No,' said the cabbie. 'I shoot them. I'm mad, me.'

'Oh, perfect,' whispered Jack.

'Stay cool,' whispered Eddie. 'Mr Cabbie?'

'Yes?' said the cabbie. 'Oh hold on, there's a red light!'

'I'll wait until you've stopped then.'

'I don't stop for red lights,' said the cabbie. 'Not when there's a really big fare in it for me. I'll probably take the rest of the week off once you've paid up.'

'Ah,' said Eddie. And the cabbie ran the red light, much to the distress of the traffic that had the right of way. This traffic came to a sudden halt. Cars bashed into other cars. A swerving lorry ran into a shop front.

'Nearly there,' the cabbie called back. 'Best get your wallets out, and I'll take your wristwatches too.'

'You're a very funny fellow,' said Eddie.

'Thanks a lot,' said the cabbie, revving the engine and putting his foot down harder. 'And some people say that psychopaths don't have a sense of humour. What do they know, eh?'

'Nothing,' said Eddie. 'But about this big gun of yours . . .'

'This one?' The cabbie whipped it out of his jacket with his gear-changing hand. It was a very big gun indeed.

'Whoa!' went Jack. 'That's a 7.62 mm M134 General Clockwork Mini-gun. Max cyclic rate 6000 rounds per minute. 7.62 × 51 shells, 1.36kg recoil adapters, muzzle velocity of 869m/s.'

'You certainly know your weapons, buddy,' said the cabbie. 'And this one carries titanium-tipped ammunition. Take the head off a teddy at two hundred yards.'

'We're sawdust,' whispered Eddie.

Jack made shushing sounds. 'I used to work in the factory that manufactured those guns,' he told the cabbie. 'Do you have it serviced regularly?'

'I keep it well oiled.' The cabbie swerved onto the wrong side of the road, which made things exciting for the oncoming traffic.

'How many times have you fired it?' Jack asked.

'Dozens of times,' said the cabbie, performing further life-endangering automotive manoeuvres.

'And you've not had the chamber-spring refulgated?'

'Eh?' said the cabbie, taking a turn along the pavement.

'Surely you've read the manual?'

'Naturally,' said the cabbie. 'I'm a practising Mechanologist. But what has my religion got to do with this?'

'Nothing at all,' said Jack. 'But if you don't get that chamber-spring refulgated, that gun is likely to blow your arm off the next time you fire it.'

A grin appeared upon Eddie's face. It did not take a genius to figure out what was coming next.

'I could refulgate it for you,' said Jack.

'What do you take me for?' asked the cabbie.

The grin disappeared from Eddie's face.

'You're going to charge me for doing it, aren't you?' the cabbie said.

'No,' said Jack. 'I'll do it for free.'

Eddie's grin reappeared.

'Well.' The cabbie hesitated—although not with his driving.

'Listen,' said Jack, 'I'm only thinking of you. Imagine the unthinkable occurring.'

'I can't imagine the unthinkable,' said the cabbie. 'What would that be like?'

'It would be like us not being able to pay and you having to shoot us, but the gun blowing your arm off instead. You'd look pretty silly then, wouldn't you?'

'I would,' the cabbie agreed.

'And you wouldn't want to look silly.'

'I certainly wouldn't.' The cabbie handed the gun over his shoulder to Jack.

Eddie looked up at his partner with a look that almost amounted to adoration. 'Wonderful,' he said.

'We'll see,' said Jack. 'Now let's get this chamber-spring refulgated. We don't want the cabbie to blow his arm off when he shoots us.'

'Eh?' said Eddie.

Jack raised an eyebrow.

'Oh I see, you're only joking again. I don't think I'll ever get the measure of your humour, Jack.'

'We're here,' said the cabbie, bringing his cab to a shuddering halt. 'How are you doing with my gun?'

Eddie and Jack ran up the sweeping drive towards Little Jack Horner's mansion. It was a worthy mansion, situated on a lower southwestern slope of Knob Hill. It was appropriately plum-coloured, and had a great many corners to it where, within, one might sit and enjoy some Christmas pie.

The plumly-hued front door stood open.

Jack cocked the 7.62 mm M134 General Clockwork Mini-gun. Its polished butt was slightly dented now, from the blow it had administered to the rear of the cabbie's head. Jack hadn't enjoyed striking down the cabbie, but desperate times called for desperate measures. Jack ducked to one side of the open doorway, Eddie ducked to the other.

'What do we do?' Jack asked. 'Rush in, big gun blazing?'

'Sneak in, I think,' said Eddie. 'Big gun at the ready. And remember, she'll be expecting us. She knows we have the list.'

'Let's sneak then.' Jack took a deep breath and then entered the mansion, Eddie close upon his heels.

As Jack did his sneaking, he also did peepings about, not just to seek out the mysterious murderess, but to generally peruse the premises.

Jack was getting a feel for grandeur. For wealth. He'd viewed the overt opulence of Humpty Dumpty's apartment, the gilded rococo chic of *Oh Boy!* and the romantic harmony of Madame Goose's establishment.

This, however, differed from those, which indeed differed from each other.

'This stuff is old, isn't it, Eddie?' Jack peeped into an elegant room, lavishly furnished with ebonised furniture trimmed with heartstone and heavy on the ormolu. 'I mean, it's *old*.'

'Antiques so often are,' said Eddie.

'Yes, but what I mean is this: the folk in nursery rhymes are the old rich of Toy City, aren't they?'

'They are.' Eddie ducked down behind a Zebrawood thuya of considerable yearage.

'So who owned this stuff before they did? Are these people the *new* old rich? Was there previously an *old* old rich that had this furniture built for them?'

'Oh, I see what you're getting at. Well, now that you come to mention it, there was something the curator said to me about the copyrights on the nursery rhymes that doesn't seem to make any sense.' Eddie rolled onto his belly and squirmed under a low mahogany side table with foliate splayed legs and rosewood inlay.

'What did he say?' Jack followed Eddie and struck his head upon the table's underside. 'Ouch,' he continued.

'What he said was . . .' And then Eddie put his paw to his nose.

'What?' Jack asked.

'Can you smell that?'

Jack did sniffings. 'No,' he said. 'What is it?'

'Jam,' said Eddie. 'Plum jam.'

Jack clipped Eddie on the ear. 'This is no time to be thinking about food,' he said. 'Naughty, bad bear.'

'Watch it,' said Eddie. 'But do I smell plum jam. Too much plum jam.'

'Can you have too much plum jam?' Jack asked. 'I'm very partial to plum jam, as it happens. And cradberry preserve.'

'Oh yes,' said Eddie, licking his mouth. 'Cradberry preserve is very nice indeed. And bongle jelly, that's particularly toothsome on hot buttered toast and . . .'

'Stop it,' said Jack. 'I'm still hungry, but I can smell it too, now. It's a very strong smell of plum jam.'

'Come on Jack, quickly,' Eddie squirmed out from under the table and jumped to his paws. 'Quickly.'

'Okay, I'm coming. Oh damn, I'm stuck under this table.'

There was a bit of a struggle, then certain damage was inflicted upon the mahogany table with the foliate splayed legs and the rosewood inlay. Jack emerged with the big gun held high.

And he followed Eddie at the hurry-up, into another kitchen.

Jack recalled all too well the horrors that he had met with in the kitchen of Madame Goose. He was not, however, prepared for those that awaited him here.

21

'Oh no,' croaked Jack, when his stomach had no more to yield. 'That is all too much.'

Eddie was slowly shaking his head. 'Much too much,' said he.

Little Jack Horner sat in the corner.

But Little Jack was not so little now.

He had been roped onto a kitchen chair, bound hand and foot. His body was bloated, the stomach distended, hugely distorted. The cause of this was the rubber tube that had been rammed into his mouth and forced down his throat. This tube led upwards to a great metal kitchen vat, suspended from a ceiling stanchion. This vat had evidently been filled with plum jam. This vat was now empty.

On the floor, about the chair, a pool of jam was spreading. It spread over around and about a hollow chocolate bunny.

'Sick,' said Eddie, giving his head further shakings. 'That is very sick.'

Jack wiped vomit from his chin and tears from his eyes. 'He might still be alive,' he said. 'Perhaps we could pump his stomach out?'

'He's dead,' said Eddie. 'As dead as, and more so besides. Not the best way to go, I suppose. But I can think of far worse. Imagine if the vat had been filled with sprout juice.'

'Eddie, stop it, please.'

'Sorry, it's nerves.' Eddie twitched his nose. 'Jack,' he said in a low and dreadful tone, 'Jack, don't move.'

'What is it, Eddie?' Jack had the big gun raised once more.

'She's still here. I can smell her perfume.'

'Stay close to me.' Jack swung the big gun around and about.

'Come out!' he called. This first 'come out' didn't come out too well; it lacked for a certain authority.

'Come out! I have a gun.' The second 'come out' came out somewhat better. 'Give yourself up!' Jack fairly shouted now. 'The mansion is surrounded. You have no means of escape.'

Eddie nudged at Jack's leg and pointed with a paw. 'Broom cupboard,' he said.

'They favour broom cupboards, don't they?'

'Shoot through the door, Jack.' Eddie mimed gunshots as best he could. 'Shoot her while we have her cornered.'

'I can't do *that*.' Jack's gaze wandered back to the bloated corpse.

'Don't start that again. Shoot her, Jack.'

'But I . . .'

But he should have done.

The broom cupboard door splintered and through it she came: slender and deadly; swift and smooth.

And then she was on them.

She swung a fist at Jack, who ducked and struck Eddie's head with his chin. And then she had Jack by the scruff of his neck. She hauled him from his feet and swung him around in a blurry arc. Jack lost his grip upon the pistol, which skidded over the flagstone floor. The struggling Jack was hefted aloft and then flung with hideous force.

He tumbled across the kitchen table, scattering crockery and disappearing over the other side.

And then she was up on the table, grinning down at the fallen Jack. And then she was stooping to take up a large meat cleaver.

Jack backed away on his bottom. 'No,' he pleaded. 'Don't kill me, please.'

The being in the figure-hugging rubber grinned on regardless. She raised the cleaver to her lips and licked its edge with a blood-red pointy tongue.

'Who are you?' Jack tried to edge away, but there was nowhere left for him to edge to. 'Why are you doing these things?'

The being leapt down from the table and stood astride Jack, grinning evilly.

'Say something.' Jack was in absolute terror now. 'Please say something. Anything. Please.'

The being raised the cleaver. Her mouth slowly opened, as if to utter words, and then it closed again.

And then the cleaver swung down.

Jack was aware of a horrible force. Of a great pushing and pressing and cutting and tearing and . . .

An explosion of sound.

His eyes had been closed.

But now they were open.

And he saw it all happen in slow motion.

The upswing of that cleaver.

Then the down.

And then the splitting of the head.

The fracturing and shattering as the head became a thousand scattering pieces.

But it was not Jack's head.

It was that of his attacker.

The cleaver came down.

Jack ducked aside and it crashed to the stone floor beside him, dropped by a hand that was now clutching at the empty air where a head had just been. There was only neck now, with ragged sinews and tubey things spilling out dark ichor.

The hands, both hands, clutched and clawed, and then the headless body fell onto Jack.

'Wah!' went Jack. And 'Aagh!' and 'Oh,' and 'Help.'

'You're all right.' The voice belonged to Eddie. 'You're all right. I got her, Jack. Plugged her good. She's as dead as. And I'm not kidding you about.'

Jack fought to free himself from the fallen corpse. He could see the grinning bear. The grinning bear was holding the 7.62 mm M134 General Clockwork Mini-gun.

'It's a good job it doesn't have a trigger-guard,' said Eddie, 'or I'd never have been able to fire it. The cabbie was right about it taking heads right off though, wasn't he?'

'Wah!' went Jack once more.

Then once more he was sick, which, considering that he'd had next to nothing in his stomach prior to the first vomiting, was something of an achievement.

Although not one of which he could be proud.

'She's definitely dead this time,' said Eddie. 'For all of Toy City's unfathomable mysteries, I can assure you, Jack, that nothing lives with its head completely shot off.'

Jack, who was on his knees, hauled himself to his feet. 'Thank you, Eddie,' he said. 'You saved my life.'

'That's what partners do,' said the bear. 'You save my life, I save yours.'

'Thanks.' Jack stooped and patted Eddie on the back. And then he gazed down at the headless corpse. 'So what *was* she, Eddie? What do you think?'

'Turn her over, Jack. Let's have a good look at her.'

'No way. I'm not touching that.'

'Get a grip, partner. We're fearless detectives, are we not?'

'No, *we* are *not*. Look at me, Eddie. I'm shaking all over and my trenchcoat is covered in black goo. My stomach's caving in and look at the state of my fedora.' Jack stooped to pick up his fedora. The falling cleaver had taken its crown clear off.

'The new open-topped look,' said Eddie. 'It might catch on.'

'I'm not touching her,' said Jack, and he folded his shaky arms and made a shaky-headed sulky face.

'Use your foot then.'

Jack sighed and with difficulty nudged the body over with his foot.

'Fine big bosoms,' said Eddie. 'Though rather too scrawny in all the other places for my taste.'

'Stop it, please.'

'Jack,' said Eddie.

'Eddie?' said Jack.

'Jack, those fine big bosoms . . .'

'I told you to stop that.'

'Those fine big bosoms are moving.'

'Wah!' went Jack; 'Wah!' always served him well at such times. 'She's still alive. Shoot her again, Eddie. But wait until I turn away.'

'She's not alive,' said Eddie, 'she's . . . urgh, look at *that*!'

Jack looked at *that*. 'Urgh,' he agreed. 'What *is* that?'

'It's spiders.' Eddie backed away. 'They're coming out of her, everywhere. Let's go, Jack. I don't want to look at this.'

Jack took one more look, then wished he hadn't. The corpse was now a heaving mass of spiders. They spilled from her ragged neck hole, and out of belt holes and seams and here and there and all over everywhere.

'This can't happen.' Jack gawped and gasped and backed away. 'She can't be full of spiders. What *is* this, Eddie? What's going on here?'

Eddie backed away and cocked an ear. 'Do you hear what I hear?' he asked.

Jack tried to cock an ear too, but there are certain things that bears can do and lads just can't.

And vice versa, of course.

'No,' said Jack. 'What?'

'The bells of approaching police cars,' said Eddie. 'I think the cabbie must have regained consciousness and called the police.'

'Ah,' said Jack. 'And you don't think we should just stay here and talk to the policemen? Explain things? Tell them what we know?'

'I'm not keen,' said Eddie. 'I think we should head over to Miss Muffett's at the hurry-up; she's next on the list. We don't know how many of these spider-women things there are. I can't believe that this one could move so fast as to kill Tommy Tucker, then head across town and kill the curator and still get here before us. There could be another at Miss Muffett's now.'

'You're right. Back door?'

'Back door,' agreed Eddie.

They skirted the house and slipped quietly away.

'So where does Miss Muffett live?' Jack asked as he trudged along upon wobbly legs.

'Not too far. Let's hope we can get there before our criminal mastermind dispatches another of his killers. He surely won't know yet that we just popped off this one.'

'But what do you think they are, Eddie? They're not human, and they're not toys. So what's left?'

'Only one thing I can think of and I don't want to think about that. Do you still have the Maguffin?'

Jack patted his pocket. It was a sticky pocket, all black goo'd. 'Still have it,' he said. 'And one question. Before we went into that kitchen, you mentioned something the curator said to you. Something you said made no sense.'

'I did,' said Eddie. 'Turn left here.'

Jack turned left. 'It's more fun in a car,' he said. 'But what were you going to say? It was something about the copyrights on the nursery rhymes.'

'Yes it was.' Eddie's little fat teddy bear legs were tiring. 'Walk slower,' he said.

Jack walked slower.

'The copyrights,' said Eddie. 'When I asked about the order they were registered in, the curator told me: it was the dates that didn't make sense.'

'Go on,' said Jack.

'Well, the copyright on *Humpty Dumpty sat on a wall*. That was the first one ever registered. How long ago do you reckon that was?'

Jack shrugged and the crown of his fedora fell off. Jack stooped, picked it up and replaced it on his head.

'You should throw that hat away,' said Eddie.

'No chance,' said Jack. 'You can't be a proper detective without a fedora. But I don't know about the copyright; maybe thirty or forty years ago, I suppose.'

'That would seem about right,' said Eddie. 'But it's wrong. *Humpty Dumpty: The Nursery Rhyme* was registered three hundred and fifty years ago.'

'That's ridiculous,' said Jack. 'Was it another Humpty Dumpty? This Dumpty's great-great-great-grandfather?'

'There's only ever been *one* Humpty Dumpty: the one who got boiled in his swimming pool.'

'But no one can live for three hundred and fifty years.'

'Toy Town grew into Toy City,' said Eddie. 'But I don't know *when* it did. It's always been the city to me and I've been here for a long time. I was Bill Winkie's bear. I'd never thought before about how long I'd been his bear, but it must have been a very, very long time.'

'What, you're telling me that *you* might be three hundred years old?' Jack stopped short and Eddie bumped into him.

'I don't know,' said Eddie, who, having tumbled, now struggled up. 'No one ever really keeps track of time here. Things are always the same. Nothing ever changes. We just go on and on. Until we fall to pieces. If you're a toy, that is.'

'It's all nonsense,' said Jack. 'Three hundred and fifty years old! But then, in this nightmare of a city where nothing makes any sense, who can say? Are we there yet?'

'Yes,' said Eddie. 'We are. But we're not.'

'Well, that doesn't make any sense, so I suppose it's about right.'

'No, Jack, we should be there, but we're not, because it isn't here.'

'What isn't here?'

'Miss Muffett's house. It's gone.'

'What do you mean? It's been pulled down?'

'No, I mean it's gone, just gone.'

'A house can't be just gone; where should it be?'

'There,' said Eddie. 'There.'

There was a bit of a hillside with some well-established trees and some equally well-established bushes.

'There's not been a house there in ages,' said Jack. 'If there ever was one.'

'There was,' said Eddie. 'I was here last week, on the *Tour of the*

Stars' Homes bus. It's one of my favourite outings. The house was here. *Right* here.'

'You must have got it wrong. Houses do not simply vanish.'

'I never implied that there was anything simple about it. But this house has vanished.'

'You think so?'

'I know so.'

'Oh.'

22

'Listen, Eddie,' said Tinto, 'much as I like you, and don't get me wrong, I *do* like you, I can't keep giving you credit. I'm trying to run this bar at a profit. That's how business is done.'

'I know how business is done.' Eddie comfyed himself on a barstool. 'But Jack and I have just been through a very traumatic experience. We both need beer. Lots of beer. You'll get your money when we've solved the case . . .'

'Ca*ses*.' Jack uncomfyed himself on the barstool next to Eddie.

'Ca*ses*, then. You'll get your money, Tinto.'

'He might not,' said Jack. 'If we can't prevent the rest of the PPPs getting butchered, there won't be anyone left to cough up the rest of the money that was promised to Bill.'

'Stop that,' said Eddie.

'Only a thought,' said Jack.

'I saw you two on TV this morning,' said Tinto. 'I was going to mention it when you were in earlier, but it didn't seem to be the appropriate time.'

'Thanks, Tinto,' said Eddie.

'But, as it is now, I'd just like to say that neither of you are as good-looking as you look on TV. You're both shorter, too.'

'Ha ha ha,' went Eddie, in a tone that lacked for humour.

'But what happened to Little Tommy Tucker, that was terrible.' Tinto's head spun round and round.

'It was even more terrible right up close,' said Eddie. 'And please don't do that with your head; it makes me feel sick.'

'But it *was* terrible.' Tinto drummed his dextrous fingers on the bar-top, which further upset Eddie. 'Terrible, terrible, terrible.'

'As if you care,' said Eddie.

'I *do* care,' said Tinto. 'We all care really, even if we don't own up to it. Society's coming apart, Eddie. You catch this killer before everything goes down the toilet.'

'You don't use a toilet,' said Eddie.

'You know what I mean. You just won't admit that you do.'

'I admit that I *don't*,' said Eddie. 'Ten beers, please.'

'No,' said Tinto. 'Think about this, Eddie. Toy City is Toy City. It's stable. Nothing ever changes here. We may say that we don't like it, but we kind of *do* like it. We're used to it. It's all we've got. It's what we've always had. These rich and famous celebrity folk are part of the essential fabric of society.'

'Essential fabric of society?' Eddie made a face. 'What's with all this sudden articulacy on your part?'

'You know what I'm talking about. These killings. They're changing things. Things aren't the same any more.'

'You're not wrong,' said Eddie. 'Ten beers, please.'

'No,' said Tinto. 'I mean what I say. A couple of weeks ago everything was normal. As it ever was and ever would be. Then Humpty Dumpty was murdered. Then Boy Blue and Jack Spratt and—'

'All right,' said Eddie, 'I know. Don't rub it in. We're doing our best.'

'Everything's falling apart. It's as if someone is out to destroy the whole city by killing off its most famous citizens. Destabilisation. You know what I'm saying?'

Eddie looked at Jack.

And Jack looked at Eddie.

'I think I do,' said Eddie. 'Ten beers, please.'

'I'll only give you five,' said Tinto, and he whirred and wheeled away behind the bar counter.

'What do you think?' Eddie asked.

'It makes sense,' said Jack. 'This criminal mastermind of yours could be trying to bring down the entire city, starting from the top. But to what end?'

'All right,' said Eddie. 'Let's think about this. Let's *seriously* think about this,' and Eddie smote his head. '*Seriously* think,' he said, smiting again and again.

'I really hate it when you do that,' said Jack.

'It works,' said Eddie, 'don't knock it.' And he smote his head once more.

Tinto delivered nine glasses of beer.

'I see Eddie's having a good old smote,' he said. 'Although I do

constantly warn him that smoting can seriously damage your health.'
Tinto chuckled. Jack didn't.

'Tell me, Tinto,' said Jack, 'how long do you think Eddie's been
coming into this bar? In years. How long?'

'Well.' Tinto scratched at his tin plate brow with a dextrous fingertip. 'Not *that* long, I suppose. A couple of hundred years, maybe.'

'A *couple of hundred* years?' Jack all but fell off his barstool.

'Give or take,' said Tinto. 'I suppose it's quite a long time, when
you come to think about it. But then folk like Eddie and me are old-
style folk. We were built to last. Craftsmanship, you see.'

'You're winding me up,' said Jack.

'*Me* winding *you* up? Is that some feeble attempt at humour?'

'I have it,' said Eddie, bouncing up and down. 'I've figured the
whole thing out. You're not going to like it, but I have.'

Jack passed Eddie a glass of beer. Eddie took it between both paws
and drained the beer away. 'Imagine,' said he, 'that you, Jack, are a criminal mastermind.'

'All right.' Jack tried to imagine it.

'So what would you want?'

'Whatever you've got,' said Jack. 'And everything else besides.'

'Exactly,' said Eddie. 'You'd want the lot. All of it. Everything. All
of this.'

'The city,' said Jack. 'I'd want the entire city.'

'You would,' said Eddie. 'But why would you want it?'

'Because that's what criminal masterminds always want. Everything.'

'So how would you go about getting this everything?'

'Well,' said Jack, 'personally, I'd gather together a private army,
dressed in really stylish black uniforms. And I'd have this secret hideout, in an extinct volcano, with all these special trains that travel along
secret tunnels and a Doomsday weapon and this white cat that sat on
my knee and—'

'Jack,' said Eddie.

'Eddie?' said Jack.

'Never mind,' said Eddie. 'But what would you do here, in *this*
city?'

'I'd threaten it with my Doomsday weapon.'

'But if, by some chance, you didn't actually have a Doomsday
weapon?'

'I *would* have one,' said Jack.

'But if you didn't!' Eddie made a fierce face at Jack. 'If you only
had a very small private army, say three or four assassins at your disposal.
What would you do then, in *this* city?'

'I'd have my assassins kill off all the powerful members of society. Mess things up a bit. And then when the city was in total chaos and everyone was running around like headless chickens, I'd take over. Restore law and order. Seize power. Control it and . . .'

'Right,' said Eddie.

'Oh,' said Jack. 'Yes, right. And that's what's happening, isn't it?'

'It all makes perfect sense when you piece it together.' Eddie patted his head.

'Not altogether,' said Jack, 'as nothing really makes sense here. But if I *was* this criminal mastermind, I'm not exactly sure where I'd find these superhuman killer women that turn into spiders. Do you think I'd be able to get them out of a catalogue or something?'

'Not out of a catalogue. But you'll find them mentioned in a Holy Book. Which is where I start getting to the stuff that you're really not going to like.'

'I have no idea what you are talking about.' Jack took up another glass of beer and drained it away.

'Jack, something very bad is happening here in the city. Something *different*. Something new. Something the city has never seen before and doesn't know how to deal with. Something has entered the city. Something really evil.'

'Some*one*,' said Jack. 'This criminal mastermind.'

'Some*thing*,' said Eddie. 'Some*thing* that isn't a man and isn't a toy. Something else.'

'You mentioned something about this earlier, when we were walking to Miss Muffett's. Something you didn't want to think about.'

'That's the something,' said Eddie. 'And it's a terrible something. A horrible, frightening something.'

'Do you want to tell me about it now?'

Eddie took up another glass. 'I think perhaps I should,' he said. 'Because, dreadful and unthinkable as it is, it's the only thing that seems to make any sense.'

'Go on then,' said Jack. 'Tell me.'

And so Eddie told him. 'This is what I know,' said Eddie. 'In this city there are a number of religious movements. There's The Church of Mechanology, clockwork toys who believe in a clockwork universe—'

'I believe in *that*,' said Tinto, who was listening in. 'Because it's true.'

'And there're The Daughters of the Unseeable Upness,' said Eddie, 'which is a foolish dolly cult, and there's The Midnight Growlers, a philosophical movement dedicated to high spiritual ideals and the pursuit of truth and—'

'Beer,' said Tinto.

'There's also The Spring and Catch Society.'

'Who owe me money,' said Tinto. 'As you do. What is it with you cult nutters, eh? You never pay your bills.'

'Would you go away please, Tinto?'

'Do you want more drinks on your account?'

'Yes, please.'

'I'll get to it.' Tinto whirled and wheeled away.

'The Spring and Catch Society,' said Eddie to Jack, 'as you know, is a secret organisation. All the rich folk are rumoured to be in it. It's a branch of a Jack-in-the-box cult known as Big Box Fella He Come.'

'Oh,' said Jack. 'Well, I suppose there would be Jack-in-the-boxes in Toy City, although I've never seen one.'

'And you won't; they're very reclusive. They believe that the entire universe is a construction kit, taken out of the big box and assembled by God with the aid of his little helpers. Jack-in-the-boxes live underground, which is fine by the rest of us because there are far too many Jacks in this city already. No offence meant.'

'None taken, I assure you.'

'They believe that the universe comprises a number of boxes, one inside the other. They live in their boxes, which are inside secret rooms, bigger boxes, in the city, a bigger box still, that's in a box-shaped world, which is inside a box-shaped universe.'

'Which is all rubbish,' said Jack. 'Which is why I do not hold to any religious beliefs.'

'Well,' said Eddie, 'the point of what I'm trying to tell you is this . . .'

'Oh good,' said Tinto, bearing drinks. 'I thought I was going to miss the important bit.'

'The point is this,' Eddie continued. 'Jack-in-the-boxes believe in Big Box Fella, who was one of God's little helpers. He and his twin brother were given the job of constructing Toy City, which was one small bit of the universe kit. When it was finished, it was supposed to be a wonderful place to live in. Big Box Fella and his brother would have brought joy and happiness to everyone who would later be built to live there. But his brother was evil and refused to follow the instructions, which is why the city is the way it is now: a mess. So Big Box Fella threw his evil twin out of the city, but the evil twin went off with the instructions. Some Jack-in-the-boxes believe that Big Box Fella went after him and will one day return with the instructions and make everything right. Others believe that Big Box Fella is still here in the city, trying to make things right.'

'He's not doing much of a job of it.'

'Hear me out, Jack. According to the beliefs of this cult, there exists, outside the box that is Toy City, another world, a world of men, millions of men.'

'There is,' said Jack. 'I came from it.'

'No, you didn't,' said Eddie. 'You came from a town just outside Toy City. I've heard of your town. It's not too far away.'

'You've lost me,' said Jack.

'Jack, you wandered off your little bit of the map and found yourself here. But you've always lived inside the same "box" as Tinto and me. You just never knew it before. The Jack-in-the-boxes believe that there is another world beyond, outside this box, but we can't get to it. We can't move out of one box and into another. Only Big Box Fella and his evil twin can do that.'

'Ridiculous,' said Jack. 'And I'll tell you why it's ridiculous. All your rich folk made their millions from royalties earned on their nursery rhymes, didn't they? So who paid out these millions? Not toys, but men. Men out there paid. Men out there in other cities. Out there somewhere.' Jack pointed out there generally. 'That's obvious to anyone, isn't it?'

'Yes,' said Eddie, 'it is. And somehow the money comes in. I don't know how, but it does. But you and I can't get out there, Jack. We can't leave this box.'

'Nonsense.' Jack took up another glass. 'I wish we'd had some food,' he said. 'I'm already half drunk.'

'You'll want to be more drunk by the time I've finished. Think about this, Jack. The woman-creature that attacked us: she wasn't human and she wasn't a toy. So what's left? I'll tell you what's left. She was some kind of a demon. That was the something that I didn't want to think about. I've given my head a good hammering. I'm not wrong here.'

'This is mad,' said Jack. 'A demon? Demons don't exist.'

'He's right,' said Tinto. 'Demons don't exist.'

'Thank you, Tinto,' said Jack.

'She was probably a fairy,' said Tinto. 'You know, one of those pretty little clockwork creatures that live in the woods.'

'Keep out of this, Tinto,' Eddie said. 'She was a demon. Sent by the evil brother. Who seeks to return to the city and overthrow his good twin. If you put it all together, it makes perfect sense.'

'So who is the good twin? Tinto here? Or perhaps it's you, Eddie.'

Eddie shook his head. 'No, Jack,' he said. 'I'm talking about the man who is the brains behind this city. The man who created Tinto and me. I'm talking about the toymaker.'

'What?' Jack shook his own head wildly. 'This is all insane. You've been beating yourself too hard on the head.'

'It all makes sense.'

'It's superstitious nonsense.'

'You have a better idea?'

'I'll stick to the criminal mastermind theory with no Gods involved.'

'So how do you explain the spider–woman?'

'I don't.'

'Or Miss Muffett's vanishing house?'

'So Miss Muffett's house really has vanished,' said Tinto. 'Rufus the tour bus driver told me earlier that it had, but I didn't believe him. What's going on here, Eddie?'

'It's the evil twin,' said Eddie. 'That's what's going on.'

'This is rubbish,' said Jack. 'You're jumping to wild conclusions. This is not how detectives behave. Detectives catch criminals by thinking things out logically. Detectives draw logical conclusions. They catch logical criminals. They don't get involved in mad stuff like this. Come on, Eddie, this can't be true.'

'It can,' said Eddie. 'It's the only logical explanation. A famous detective, whose name now eludes me, said that once you've eliminated the impossible, then whatever remains, no matter how improbable, must be the truth.'

'You just made that up,' said Jack. 'But what are you saying? That the toymaker is really Big Box Fella, one of God's little helpers?'

Eddie nodded. 'An original Son of God. You've been driving yourself mad trying to work out how toys can live, haven't you, Jack? So this explanation should please you: the toymaker can bring toys to life because he is a God in this world. And so is his twin brother. But he's the opposite of his good brother, Jack. The evil opposite. He's returned from outside to claim this boxed–up city world of ours for himself. His good brother doesn't know what's going on. He won't know until it's too late. When all is lost.'

'So this criminal mastermind . . .'

'He's the Devil of this world, Jack. We're not dealing with a man here. We're dealing with an evil God. We're dealing with the Devil.'

23

'Same again,' said Jack. 'And stick it on Eddie's account.'

'You don't believe me, do you?' Eddie asked.

'How can I believe you, I'm an atheist.'

'Explain the spider-woman.'

'You know I can't. But I can't explain *him*.' Jack nodded towards Tinto. 'Nor you.'

'You could if you believed that the toymaker is a Son of God, possessed of Godly powers that can bestow life.'

'That's not fair,' said Jack. 'I know that that does explain things. But not to my satisfaction. Not when I'm an atheist.'

'It explains *everything*,' said Eddie. 'How toy telephones work. How teddy bears with sawdust for brains can think. Only a God can do that kind of stuff.'

'I need another drink,' said Jack. 'Oh, I've got one. And I mean to drink it.'

'I'm sorry to mess you up.' Eddie sipped his alcohol. 'But don't get me wrong. This is messing me up too. Big Time. I've never thought too deeply about this kind of stuff. And I'm not a follower of The Big Box Fella Cult.'

'My money's on you being a Midnight Growler,' said Jack.

Tinto laughed. 'Your money would be safe then. He's the *only* Midnight Growler.'

'There's money to be made in starting your own religion,' said Eddie. 'But I couldn't persuade any teddies to join mine.'

'I'll join,' said Jack. 'But come on, Eddie, the Devil? Say it really *was* the Devil. Then what could we, devoted Midnight Growlers though we might be, do to stop the Devil?'

'Bit of a tricky one, I agree.'

'But if the toymaker *is* a God,' Jack stroked at his chin, 'he did say that there might be an opening for me some day as an apprentice.'

'We have to tell him,' said Eddie. 'Tell him what's happening. Warn him.'

'But if he is a God-of-this-world, does he really have anything to fear from his brother? How do Gods battle it out? It's thunderbolts, isn't it?'

'It's fluff,' said Tinto. 'They stick fluff in each other's clockwork.'

'Eddie,' said Jack, 'think very hard now. Bang your head about as much as you want, more so if needs be. But are you absolutely sure about this? It is a pretty way-out theory. Couldn't we just be dealing with a plain old criminal mastermind?'

'I'm sure I'm right, Jack. Plain old criminal masterminds can't vanish homes.'

'So is Miss Muffett dead?'

'Perhaps they're all dead, Jack. Perhaps this is the beginning of the end.'

'Let's not get carried away. There might still be a more logical explanation.'

'We have to go and see the toymaker.' Eddie finished the last of Jack's latest drinks. 'We have to see him now. This is all moving too fast.'

'I agree with that. So let's just slow it down a little, take a few moments to think very carefully before we go jumping into something and get ourselves into trouble again. Let's have one more round before we go.'

'Just the one then. Tinto?'

'Very generous of you,' said Tinto. 'I'll have a large oil and soda.'

'I didn't mean that. But yes, go on, have one yourself. Same again for us.'

'Eddie,' said Tinto, 'does this mean that the world is coming to an end? Is the time of the Great Stillness approaching?'

'Not if Jack and I can help it.'

'Because if it is, then I think I'll close up early today. Can I come with you to the toymaker's? He might wish to employ the services of a clockwork butler.'

'Sorry,' said Eddie. 'This is a detectives-only thing. Same again before we go, please, Tinto.'

'Same again it is then,' said the barlord.

And yes. They did become very drunk, the three of them.

And you're not supposed to be drunk when you get involved with matters such as this: *Big* Matters, *Matters of an Apocalyptic Nature*. You're supposed to be coldly sober. And you just can't be coldly sober when you're drunk.

But then, if you really did find yourself involved in *Matters of an Apocalyptic Nature*, you'd need a few stiff ones under your belt before you got going with saving the world.

'We'll have to think very carefully,' said Eddie. 'Very carefully indeed.'

'That's what *I* said.' Jack squinted at Eddie in the manner that drunken people do, in the misguided belief that it makes them appear sober.

'Why are you squinting in that drunken fashion?' Eddie asked.

'I'm not. What exactly are we going to have to think carefully about, Eddie?'

'Exactly what we say to the toymaker.'

'We tell him the truth. We warn him about what his evil twin is up to.'

'Hm,' said Eddie. 'Tricky.'

'Why is it tricky?' Jack fell off his barstool.

'Well,' said Eddie, 'it's tricky in this fashion: the toymaker has never cast himself in the role of a God. Most Toy City religions have him down as a doer of God's work, but not *actually* a God. So if he *is* a God, then he obviously wishes to remain incognito.'

'So *why* is it tricky?' Jack tried to get up, but without much success. Getting up was tricky.

'He might not take too kindly to the fact that we have uncovered his true identity.'

'But we're the good guys. We're on his side.'

'But say, in the unlikely event that I've got a wee bit of the theorising wrong—'

'The evil twin bit? The *big* bit?'

'In the unlikely event. But say I'm right about the toy-maker. He might disappear us.'

'He wouldn't do *that*, would he? He's all kindly and white-haired and loveable and everything.'

'Benign Gods generally are. But they do have the unfortunate habit of chucking thunderbolts at folk who upset them.'

'You're right,' said Jack, floundering about. 'Best not to risk it. Let's crawl back to the office and get some sleep. We'll have one more drink before we go and then we'll, er, *go*.'

'Have you ever heard this theory about drinking yourself sober?' Eddie asked. 'It's a very popular theory. Amongst drunks, anyway.'

'How does it work?' Jack asked.

'Well, I had it explained to me once, but I was rather drunk at the time and I can't exactly remember how it works. But that's what we should do, Jack, drink ourselves sober and then go to the toymaker's house.'

'Pretext,' said Jack.

'What?' said Eddie.

'Pretext,' said Jack. 'We go to the toymaker's house upon some pretext. I'll rip your foot off and beg him to stitch you up or something.'

'You *won't*,' said Eddie.

'Some other pretext then. We'll engage him in casual conversation and subtly draw him in to a theoretical discussion. Then you could put your theory to him in a hypothetical manner, which will not imply any implicit knowledge on our part as to his potential status as a deity.'

'Say all that again,' said Eddie.

'Don't be absurd,' said Jack. 'I don't know how I managed it the first time. Somebody help me up.'

Tinto wheeled himself around the bar and assisted Jack into the vertical plane.

'Thanks, Tinto,' said Jack, clinging to the bar counter. 'Another round, please. Eddie and I are drinking ourselves sober.'

'I've always wanted to see that,' said Tinto. 'I'll join you again, if I may; I'm celebrating.'

'Oh,' said Jack. 'Why?'

'Because when Eddie pays this bar bill I'll have enough money to retire.'

'We haven't spent *that* much, have we?'

'I'm only expecting to enjoy a short retirement,' said Tinto. 'The end of the world's coming very soon. Didn't you know?'

'Same again,' said Jack. 'And as the end of the world's coming, drinks *all* round.'

Now, it is a fact well known to those who know it well that prophets of doom only attain popularity when they get the drinks in all round.

Eddie and Jack were soon richly popular.

Even though they both smelled very poor.

Several rather attractive dollies gathered about Jack.

Jack engaged a particularly tall and glamorous blondie-headed one in conversation. 'I'm a detective,' said Jack.

'Are you famous?' asked the blondie-headed doll.

'Very,' said Jack. 'This is my sidekick, Eddie; he's comedy relief.'

Eddie, now balanced on his head, made growling sounds from his barstool perch.

'It must be a very dangerous job,' said the dolly, fingering Jack's grubby trenchcoat lapel.

'Extremely,' said Jack. 'But I'm always ready for action.' He opened his trenchcoat to expose the 7.62 mm M134 General Clockwork Mini-gun that bulged from the front of his trousers.

'My, that's a big one,' said the dolly.

'Cocked and ready to shoot,' said Jack.

The dolly tittered.

'Excruciating,' said Tinto. 'I don't think he's drunk himself sober yet, Eddie.'

Jack whipped out his gun and waved it about in a most unsteady and dangerous fashion. 'This can take the head off a clockwork barman at two hundred yards.'

'You're barred,' said Tinto. 'Out of my bar.'

'He was only showing me his weapon,' said the dolly. 'No need to go all rusty-headed, Tinto.'

'Drink for the lady,' said Jack. 'And have one yourself, barlord.'

'Jack,' said Eddie, 'perhaps we should be off about our business now, even in our present condition. It's really important business, remember?'

'You're just jealous,' said Jack, trousering his weapon and putting his arm about the dolly's slender waist. 'Because I'm such a big hit with the ladies.'

'Jack, get a grip of yourself.'

'I have a grip of myself.' Jack took a grip of himself. It was a most intimate grip; not the kind of grip that you usually take of yourself in public.

'Get him out, Eddie,' said Tinto. 'Take him home.'

'I don't have a home.' Jack swayed about, supporting himself on the dolly. 'But I will have, a big home. A palace. I have come to this city to seek my fortune. And I will. I'll have a palace and I'll be a prince.'

'Prince?' Eddie performed a most remarkable, and probably once in a lifetime only, backflip, which resulted in his bum landing squarely upon the barstool.

'That was impressive,' said Tinto. And others all around and about made free with applause.

'I *said* prince,' said Eddie. 'What is *prince* all about?'

'Nothing,' said Jack in a sulky tone.

'Yes it is. Why did you say that you want to be a prince?'

'There's nothing wrong with having ambitions.'

'Not if they're feasible.'

'I don't care about her,' said Jack. 'I don't.'

'But I'm nice,' said the dolly. 'I have lovely hair; it gets longer if you turn the little key in my back.'

'No thanks,' said Jack, withdrawing his arm from the dolly's waist. 'But I wasn't talking about you. I was talking about *her*. I don't care about her.'

'Who is this *her*?' Eddie asked.

'Just someone. I don't want to talk about it.'

'It's that Jill, isn't it?' said Eddie. 'The girl at Madame Goose's. Did you do it with her, Jack?'

'None of your business.'

'You *did*. He did, Tinto. Jack did it with a girl at Madame Goose's.'

'I once did it with a clockwork mouse at Madame Goose's,' said Tinto. 'But I was young then and rather drunk. No one's going to hold that against me, are they?'

'Urgh!' went all and sundry, who evidently were.

'I was drunk!' said Tinto. 'Come on!'

'I once did it with a potted plant,' said Eddie. 'I was *really* drunk that night, I can tell you.'

'Stop it,' said Jack. 'She doesn't mean anything to me. It's not as if I'm in love with her or anything.'

'Jack's in love,' said Tinto.

'I'm *not*,' said Jack.

'He *is*,' said Eddie.

'I'm *not*!' said Jack.

'You're drunk,' said Eddie.

'I'm *not*!' said Jack.

'Are too.'

'Are not.'

'Are.'

Jack stared at Eddie. And it was a stare, rather than a squint. 'You know what,' he said, 'I'm not drunk any more.'

'Drunk yourself sober,' said Eddie. 'Hoorah!'

'What about you?'

'It's draining down to my legs,' said Eddie. 'You'll have to carry me for a bit.'

'Do you want to come back to my house?' said the blondie-headed doll. 'I could show you my publicity pictures; I'm hoping to get a job at Toy City TV.'

'Er, no, thank you very much,' said Jack. 'Eddie and I have important business elsewhere.'

'Most important,' said Eddie. 'Are you ready for it, partner?'
'Certainly am,' said Jack.
'Then let's go,' said Eddie.
And go they did.
As almost sober as.

24

It was nearing midnight now. Toy City was still. Remarkably still, really. But then, folk were keeping off the streets after dark. There was a killer on the loose. And the fact that this killer had performed all the killings so far during the hours of daylight had nothing to do with anything. Killers always strike around midnight. Everyone knows that.

'I think I behaved rather badly back there,' said Jack. 'Sorry, Eddie, if I embarrassed you.'

'No problem,' said Eddie. 'It's as sweet as. But you're in love, Jack, aren't you? With this Jill.'

'It was my first time.' Jack put Eddie down and relieved himself in an alleyway. 'I wasn't thinking straight.'

'There's nothing wrong with young love.' Eddie seeped a bit into the gutter. 'We've all been there and done that.'

'You've been in love?'

'Don't be so surprised. Bears love too. Everything loves.'

'Who was she, Eddie?' Jack zipped himself into decency.

Eddie sighed. 'She was beautiful. An Anders Empress. Amber eyes, vertically stitched nose in black silk yarn, beige felt paw-pads, patented tilt-growler that literally purred when you leaned her backwards, and an all-over golden mohair plush.'

'Sounds very nice,' said Jack as he tucked Eddie once more under his arm and resumed his trudging. 'Especially the patented tilt-growler.'

'She came from a very respectable family. Her great-grandparents were the bears that Goldilocks shacked up with. They organised the original Teddy Bears' picnic and owned the garden that all bears go walkies round.'

Jack looked down at Eddie. 'What a load of old rubbish,' he said. 'And there was me believing you and thinking that you were going to tell me this really poignant story about love lost and everything.'

'Fair enough,' said Eddie. 'But she *was* a posh bear and she was up for it. But I lost my nerve, had a few drinks before I went round to see her. Humped that potted plant by mistake. It didn't lead to a lasting relationship.'

'Jill is very beautiful,' said Jack, in a most wistful tone.

'I could tell you all about her,' said Eddie. 'It's a sad story. But now's not the time; we're almost at the toymaker's house.'

'Are you up for it then?' Jack set Eddie down.

'I'm all but pooing myself,' said Eddie Bear. 'I greatly fear the toymaker, as you know. And now more than ever. So remember what you said you'd do. Engage him in casual conversation and subtly draw him into a theological discussion. Then put my theory to him in a hypothetical manner, which will not imply any implicit knowledge on our part as to his potential status as a deity.'

'I said *that*?'

'You did. Do you think you can do it?'

'Of course,' said Jack. 'Trust me.'

The two trudged up the gravel drive, Jack's trudge making big trudge sounds and Eddie's making lesser. When they reached the big front door, Jack reached out for the knocker.

'*You* again,' said Peter. 'This won't do. Clear off.'

'We have to see the toymaker.' Jack's hand hovered near the knocker. 'We don't have time to bandy words with you.'

'Bandy words?' Peter laughed. 'Don't come that high and mighty talk with me. The toymaker isn't home. He's gone away.'

'The lights are on,' said Eddie.

'That's to discourage burglars,' said Peter. 'If you leave your lights on, burglars think you're at home; everyone knows that.'

'Even burglars?'

'No, of course not. Burglars don't know that. How would they know that? Who'd be likely to tell them?'

'I'm sure I wouldn't,' said Eddie. 'What about you, Jack?'

'I wouldn't tell them.' Jack's hand moved closer to the knocker.

'But there's no one home,' said Peter.

'We're burglars,' said Eddie. 'How are we supposed to know that?'

'*Burglars?*' Peter's face took on that horrified look once more. 'Burglars! Help! Help! Alarm! Alarm!' And he took to knocking most loudly.

And at length the front door opened and the ancient face of the toymaker peered out into the night.

'Who is knocking so loudly?' he asked.

'It's Peter,' said Jack. 'Anxious to admit us.'

'Burglars,' said Peter. 'Call the policemen.'

'They're not burglars,' said the toymaker. 'Come in, will you? And calm yourself, Peter, please.'

'But . . .' went Peter. 'But.'

'Perhaps you should get yourself a bell,' said Jack, smiling in a most friendly manner.

'A bell?' The toymaker beckoned Jack and Eddie inside. 'A most novel idea. But as no one other than yourselves ever comes to call, a wasted expense, I think.' The toymaker closed the big front door, leaving Peter alone with his thoughts, then led Jack and Eddie along the narrow corridor and into his workshop. 'This is a most pleasant surprise,' he told them. 'Has something else happened to you, little bear?'

'He's a bit wobbly,' said Jack. 'He hasn't been walking too well. I thought you might be kind enough to take another look at him. Eddie didn't want to bother you; he holds you in such high esteem.'

'I do,' said Eddie. 'We all do. All of us.'

'That's very nice,' said the toymaker. 'But I do not wish to be held in high esteem. I'm only a humble toymaker. Sit down, sit down.'

Jack sat down in the comfy chair.

'Get your bum off me,' it said.

'Manners,' said the toymaker. The chair made grumbling sounds.

Eddie sat down on the floor.

'You're more than just a toymaker, sir,' said Jack.

'Anders,' said the toymaker. 'Call me Anders.'

'I think I'll stick with *sir*, if you don't mind, sir. Because you *are* more than just a toymaker, as you well know. You bring life to these toys.'

'Science,' said Mr Anders Anders. 'Science, not magic. I told you before: when things are not as they appear to be, it's because they're actually simpler than you think them to be. Things are never as difficult and complicated as folk believe. You'd be surprised just how straightforward and obvious things really are. The secret is in knowing how to look at them the right way.'

'Well, however it's done,' said Jack, 'it makes you very special.'

'Everyone is special,' said Anders Anders. 'It's just that most folk are unaware how special they really are, or just how special are the folk around them. If they were aware, they'd be far nicer to each other, don't you think?'

'I'm certain you're right,' said Jack, who now felt himself to be drowning in a pond of platitudes.

'Not that they aren't nice,' the toymaker continued. 'Of course they're nice. Folk are nice. It's just that they could be even nicer. Things could be perfect. I'm an idealist; forgive an old man for his ideals.'

'Yes, sir,' said Jack. 'Yes, indeed.'

'So why *are* you here?' The toymaker leaned his ancient frame against his workbench and tinkered about with a small wooden horse. 'I stuffed the little bear's legs but yesterday; they should be good for more than a while.'

'Sir,' said Jack, 'there's big trouble you need to know about it.'

'Big trouble?' said the toymaker. 'What can that be?'

'In your city, sir.'

'My *city*?' The toymaker made a most surprised face. 'Toy Town is a town. Hardly a city.'

'It's a city, sir. A big city now.'

'I should get out more,' said the toymaker, tinkering at the horse's tail. 'Perhaps I spend too much time working. But I want to get things right, you see. It's the details that count; this horse's tail, for instance. I can't make up my mind exactly how many hairs it needs. It's all in the details. I want everything to be right. Perfect. Everything.'

'Folk are dying,' Jack said. 'Folk are being killed, here in Toy City.'

'Being *killed*?' The toymaker shook his snowy head. 'Not here in Toy Town. You must be mistaken, young man.'

'There's a murderer,' Jack said.

'Jack,' said Eddie. 'Slow down. Think.'

'He needs to know the truth,' said Jack. 'He must be told.'

'Yes, but . . .'

'Yes, but *what*?' the toymaker asked. 'What *is* this all about?'

'A murderer,' said Jack, 'in your city.'

'No,' said the toymaker shaking his snowbound head once more. 'We don't have murderers in Toy Town. Toys are naughty sometimes, but the jolly red-faced policemen give them a good telling-off when they are.'

'No,' said Jack. 'It's not like that. Those jolly red-faced policemen gave me a good kicking. Would you like to see the bruises?'

'I don't think I would.' The toymaker put down his wooden horse. 'You seem to be a very angry young man. I think perhaps you should go.'

'No, sir,' said Jack. 'You have to understand what is going on out there in your city. Bad things. Toys and people aren't nice to each other. They're not nice and now there's a murderer. Humpty Dumpty is dead. And Boy Blue and . . .'

'Stop,' said the toymaker. 'Young man, stop. You are saying terrible things. I don't wish to hear them.'

'You have to hear them. We've come to warn you.'

'Are you threatening me?'

'No, not that. Anything but that.'

'I think I must ask you to leave.'

'Eddie, tell him. Tell him your theory.'

'You have a theory, little bear?'

'No, sir,' said Eddie.

'Tell him, Eddie.'

'Shut up, Jack.'

'But this is what we came here for. It's important. It couldn't be more important.'

'The toymaker is a busy man. He doesn't have time to listen to us.'

'What?' said Jack. '*What?* What's the matter with you, Eddie? Tell him. Tell him what you think.'

'I can't,' whispered Eddie.

'Then I'll tell him.'

'No,' said Eddie.

'Yes,' said Jack. 'It's your brother, sir. Your evil twin.'

Eddie hid his face.

'He's out to take over Toy City. He's killing off all the nursery rhyme characters and—'

'Enough.' The toymaker raised his wrinkled hands. 'Enough of this awful talk. I believe you've been drinking, young man.'

'I've drunk myself sober.'

'I think not. Kindly take your leave.'

'But you have to listen. He'll kill you too.'

'Young man, I do not have a brother, let alone an evil twin, as you are suggesting. Now I suggest that you go home to bed.'

'No,' said Jack. 'You've got to listen. You've got to understand.'

'Goodnight,' said the toymaker. 'Goodnight to you.'

Jack and Eddie were ushered away from the workroom. From the corridor. From the toymaker's house.

They stood once more upon the gravel drive.

In the moonlight.

Looking at each other.

'Well,' said Eddie.

'Well what?' said Jack.

'Well, that might have gone a little better, don't you think?'

'Well,' said Jack.

'You buffoon!' Eddie threw up his paws. 'You craven gormster. You did it all wrong. You couldn't have done it wronger. That was as wrong as wrong as . . . as . . .'

'I wasn't wrong,' said Jack. 'He just wouldn't listen.'

'Unbelievable,' said Eddie. 'You are unbelievable.'

'*Me?* You just sat there saying nothing. You could have backed me up.'

'No, I couldn't,' Eddie said. 'I just couldn't, not to him.'

'All right,' said Jack. 'I understand. But what are we going to do now? He said that he didn't have a brother. You've got it all wrong, Eddie. I told you it was a silly theory.'

'Hm,' said Eddie. 'Well it's still the best theory I have and I'm sticking with it until I have a better one. But you've met the toymaker twice now, Jack. You can see that he's lost touch with what's going on in Toy City. Perhaps he's forgotten that he has a brother. It's possible.'

'Barely possible.' Jack rubbed at his arms. 'I'm cold,' he said. 'Let's go back to the office for some sleep. We'll have another think in the morning.'

'By which time more people may be dead.'

'Then what do you suggest?'

'I suggest we go back to Miss Muffett's.'

'But Miss Muffett's isn't there any more.'

Eddie tapped at his head. 'Bear with me on this one,' he said. 'I have a theory. Something the toymaker said struck a certain chord, as it were. I'd like to test a hypothesis.'

Jack shrugged and turned up his collar. 'Let's make it quick then, it's really getting nippy.'

'We'll be as quick as,' said Eddie. 'Follow me.'

'And don't hurry back,' called Peter.

25

The lower reaches of Knob Hill, that spread around and about and somewhat below the toymaker's house, glittered in the moonlight. A little star went twinkle, twinkle. It was all very picturesque.

Eddie led Jack to the spot where, earlier that day, they had viewed the place where Miss Muffett's house should have been, but wasn't.

'There,' said Eddie. 'I'm sure I'm right. What do you see, Jack? Tell me.'

'Trees and flowers and bushes and hillside,' said Jack. 'Exactly the same as before.'

'*Exactly* the same?'

'Exactly the same.'

'Exactly,' said Eddie.

'I'm missing something, aren't I?'

Eddie nodded. 'Something very obvious.'

Jack took a second look. 'Then I don't know what,' he said.

'What about the trees, Jack, and the flowers?'

'They're exactly the same.'

'Yes,' said Eddie. 'But they shouldn't be, should they? The trees should have dark shadows under them now and the flowers should all be closed up for the night.'

'Oh,' said Jack. 'You're right.'

'Remember what the toymaker said? "When things are not as they appear to be, it's because they're actually simpler than you think them to be. The secret is in knowing how to look at them the right way." '

'I remember him saying that, but I thought he was just fobbing me off with a lot of platitudes.'

'Not the toymaker.' Eddie shook his head. 'But it set me to thinking about the vanishing house. And then it came to me: it *was* all simple; you just had to know how to look at it. This is fake, Jack. All this: the trees, the flowers, the hillside. It's a big painting, like a theatrical backdrop. It's been put up here to fool folk. To fool the murderer.'

'To hide Miss Muffett's house?'

'Exactly,' said Eddie. 'Come on, let's see if I'm right.'

They approached the trees and the flowers and the hillside and . . .

'Oh,' said Jack, as his face made contact with canvas. 'You're right. But that's absurd. How could we have been fooled by something as simple as this?'

'Because we weren't looking for it.'

'Yes, but.'

'Come on,' said Eddie, 'follow me.'

'Where are you? Oh.'

Eddie was wriggling under the canvas. Jack knelt down and followed him.

'A remarkably good painting,' said Jack when he emerged on the other side of the vast canvas. 'And that would be Miss Muffett's mansion, would it?'

Eddie dusted himself down. 'That's the kiddie,' said he. 'And it should appeal to you; it's one of the houses that Jack built.'

'Jack?' said Jack.

'As in the rhyme, *This is the house that Jack built*. He didn't build too many, because he was a pretty rubbish architect and most of them fell down. He always insisted upon there being a cow with a crumpled horn in the living room.'

Jack nodded dumbly and stared at the house and the garden that surrounded it.

Miss Muffett's mansion by moonlight was wondrous to behold. It resembled a vast wedding cake: tier upon tier of white stucco, with supporting Doric columns. Before it stood a row of white marble statues, pretty maids all. Manicured trees were hung with countless silver bells and cockleshell motifs abounded in the paving stones and low walls.

'Garden design by Mary Mary,' said Eddie. 'She has her own garden make-over show on Toy City TV.'

'I'm somewhat puzzled by *that*.' Jack pointed to a huge sculpture that dominated the very centre of the garden. It more than resembled a massive raised phallus.

'She always puts something like that in whatever garden she designs. To prove just how "contrary" she is. It's a studied eccentricity thing. Frankly, I think it's rubbish. The garden *and* the house.'

'I love them,' said Jack.

'We really must sit down sometime over a beer and discuss your tastes in architecture.'

'No, we mustn't,' said Jack. 'But when I build my palace, it will look a lot better than this. Shall we have a sneak around and see what we can see?'

'Well,' said Eddie, his words all growly whispers, 'now that we're here . . . I'm . . . er . . . I'm . . .'

'What's up with you?' Jack whispered back.

'You have a sneak around; I'll wait here.'

'Something's bothering you. You're afraid.'

'I'm afraid of no man.'

'So?'

'There's something out there, and it *ain't* no man.'

'That sounds somehow familiar, but what are you talking about?'

'It's the spider, Jack. Miss Muffett's spider. It's really big, with horrible hairy legs. It's the spider in her rhyme. They live together.'

'What, it's like, her pet?'

'Not as such. But in a way, I suppose.'

'What are you saying?'

'It's a big spider, Jack. Big as you. There's been talk, in the newspapers, about their relationship. But nothing's been proved. And I don't know how spiders actually *do it*, do you?'

'You're winding me up,' said Jack.

'I'm not, honestly. It could be on the prowl; it has terrible mandibles. And spiders sick up acid on you and you melt and they eat you up.'

'Turn it in,' said Jack, 'I'll protect you.' And Jack gave Eddie a comforting pat. 'I'm not afraid of spiders, even really big ones.'

'Thanks for the comforting pat,' said Eddie, clinging onto Jack's trenchcoat.

'Big as me, you said?' Jack did furtive glancings all around.

'Maybe bigger. Perhaps we should come back in the morning.'

'We're here now, Eddie. Let's go and see what we can see. There's a light on in a window over there.'

'After you, my friend.'

Eddie and Jack did sneakings through Miss Muffett's garden. They snuck along beside a low hedge that divided the garden from a drive lined with numerous clockwork-motor cars. Large cars all, were these, and pretty posh ones too. Leaning against these cars were many big burly men. These wore dark suits and mirrored sunglasses and had little earpiece jobbies with tiny mouth mics attached to them. Each of these big men carried a great big gun.

There was also a large military-looking truck with a canvas-covered back. A shadowed figure sat at the wheel of this.

Sneakily Jack and Eddie reached the lighted window.

Jack looked up at it. 'It's too high for me to see in,' he whispered. 'Give us a lift up then.'

'Fair enough.' Jack lifted Eddie, who clambered onto Jack's head, put his paws to the sill and peeped in through the sash window, which was, as windows so often are on such occasions, conveniently open at the bottom. Had Eddie possessed any thumbs, he would have raised one to Jack. But as he hadn't, he didn't.

'What can you see?' Jack whispered.

Eddie put a paw to his mouth.

'In your own time, then,' said Jack.

Eddie peered in through the window gap and this was what he saw and heard:

The room was of ballroom proportions, which made it proportionally correct, given that it was indeed a ballroom. It was high-domed and gorgeously decorated, with foliate roundels and moulded tuffet embellishments. Eddie's button eyes were drawn to a great mural wrought upon the furthest wall. This pictured a number of bearded men in turbans flinging spears at gigantic fish.

Eddie nodded thoughtfully. He recalled reading about this mural. Jack who'd built the house had painted it himself, but being none too bright, had confused curds and whey with Kurds and whales.

Eddie would have laughed, but as it wasn't the least bit amusing, and contained a glaring continuity error to boot, he didn't. Instead, he gazed at the many folk milling about in the ballroom. The light of many candles fell upon the glittering company: the old rich of Toy City, extravagantly costumed.

Eddie recognised each and every one.

He'd seen their smug faces many times, grinning from the society pages of the Toy City press, and in the big glossy celebrity magazines, like *KY!* and *Howdy Doody*, pictured at gala balls and swish functions and First Nights and even the launch of the spatial ambiguity installation piece at the Toy City art gallery.

But other than Miss Muffett and Little Tommy Tucker, Eddie had never seen any of the others in the living flesh before. The living breathing flesh. He had only ever seen them, as others of his own social class had seen them, in photographs. As totems, icons even, to be revered and admired and looked up to. They were rich and they were famous. They were 'better'.

Eddie shook his furry-fabricked head and peeped in at them. He spied the 'olds': Old King Cole, Old Mother Hubbard, the Grand Old Duke of York. And the remaining 'littles': Little Polly Flinders, Little Bo Peep, and the hostess, Little Miss Muffett. And the 'double nameds': Mary Mary, Tom Tom, the piper's son, Peter Peter, pumpkin eater. And there was Simple Simon, who had famously met a pie man. And Georgie Porgie, the reformed paedophile. And Peter Piper, who'd picked a peck of pickled peppers, for reasons of his own. And there were Jack and Jill, who'd once been up a hill. And the Mary who'd had that little lamb. And the Polly who'd put the kettle on. And the Jack who'd built the house and mucked up the mural.

Eddie watched them, and Eddie slowly shook his head once more. There they were, and they were rich and famous. But when it came right down to it, *why?*

Most seemed to have achieved their fame for no good reason at all. For going up a hill to fetch water! Going *up* a hill? Or eating a pie, or putting the kettle on? What was it all about, eh?

It wasn't so much that Eddie was jealous—well, actually it was.

But it really didn't make any sense.

Eddie suddenly became aware that he was thinking all these things: thinking like Jack, in fact. Eddie gave his head a thump and watched as a wheeled rostrum affair was pushed into the ballroom by two of the burly suited types, who then helped Miss Muffett onto it. She stood, glamorously attired in another glittering gown, waving her manicured fingers about and shushing the company to silence.

'Ladies and gentlemen,' she said, 'firstly I would like to thank you for coming here tonight. We are all in great danger and if something isn't done, we will each go the way of Humpty Dumpty, Boy Blue and Bill Winkie.'

Eddie flinched.

'We all know who is doing this to us. We dare not wait for the inevitable to occur. We have to take steps. Do something about it.'

'I don't agree,' said Mary Mary.

'Well, you wouldn't, would you dear? You being so contrary and everything.'

'We must run away,' said Mary Mary. 'That's what we must do. Run while we still can.'

'To where?' Georgie Porgie spoke up. 'To the world beyond the city's box? The world of men? We can't get there anyway, and even if we could, what chance would there be for us amongst the people of that world? How long would we last if we, like them, were doomed to a normal life-span? Toy City is our world. Here we are rich and powerful. Here we can live on and on. Or at least we could, until *he* returned to murder us all.'

Eddie nodded thoughtfully.

'We don't know for certain that it's *him*.' This voice belonged to Jack (husband of Jill). 'Perhaps it's one of us. Someone in this room.'

'Ignore my husband,' said Jill (wife of Jack). 'He's never been the same since he fell down the hill and broke his crown. Brain damage.' She twirled her finger at her temple.

'There's nothing wrong with me, woman.'

'I can think of a number of things.'

'Please.' Miss Muffett raised her hands. 'There's nothing to be gained by arguing amongst ourselves. *He's* picking us off, one by one. And I'm next on the list. I paid a fortune to have that camouflage canvas outside done. But how long will it fool *him*?'

'I doubt whether it will fool *him* at all,' said Georgie. 'We should all just flee the city. Hide out in the surrounding countryside. Perhaps if *he* can't find us, *he'll* just go away again. I'm going home to pack my bags.' Georgie made to take his leave.

'You can't go,' said Miss Muffett. 'Not until the one that I have invited here tonight has arrived and said what he has to say.'

Georgie Porgie threw up his hands. 'And what's this mystery man going to say? That he can protect us all from the inevitable?'

'That's what he told me.'

'I don't deserve any of this,' said Georgie. 'To be on some nutter's hitlist. I've served my time and now I'm entitled to enjoy my wealth.'

'If only it was just some nutter,' said Jill (wife of Jack). 'But it isn't, it's *him*. We are the founder members of The Spring and Catch Society. We know the truth about Big Box Fella and his evil twin, because we are the elite, the first folk placed here when Toy City was assembled. We helped Big Box Fella to cast his evil twin from this world, but now he has returned to wreak his vengeance upon all of us. We knew that one day this might happen and we should have taken steps earlier to prevent it. But we didn't; we just continued to indulge ourselves. We have abused our privileges and become complacent and now we are paying the price.'

Jack tugged at Eddie's leg. 'What can you see?' he asked.

Eddie ducked his head down. 'They're all in there,' he whispered. 'All the still-surviving PPPs, and they're talking about The Spring and Catch Society and the evil twin. I was right, Jack. It's all as factual as.'

'Incredible.' Jack shook his head and Eddie all but fell off it.

'Stay still,' said Eddie. 'I don't want to miss any of this.'

'We have to kill *him*,' Georgie was saying. 'Kill *him* before *he* kills us.'

'And how do you kill a God?' asked Jill. 'Get real, please.'

'I have ten thousand men,' said the Grand Old Duke of York. 'I'll deal with the blighter.'

The Grand Old Duke was ignored to a man, and a woman. He did *not* have ten thousand men. He'd *never had* ten thousand men. He and Wheatley Porterman had made the whole thing up.

'Wait until the one I invited arrives,' said Miss Muffett. 'He'll explain everything. He'll put your minds at rest.'

'He'll save us, will he?' Georgie Porgie went to throw up his hands once again, but finding them still up from the previous occasion, he threw them down again. 'Listen, when Humpty Dumpty was killed, we all knew what it meant; we clubbed together and put up the money to employ Bill Winkie. He was next on the list. He knew that. But what happened?' Georgie drew a fat finger over his throat. 'Bill Winkie couldn't stop *him*. He never had a chance. Nobody can stop *him*.'

'*I* can stop *him*.'

Heads turned at the sound of this voice, turned to its source: to the open doorway.

'You?' said Georgie Porgie.

'You?' said Jack (husband of Jill).

'You?' said Jill (wife of Jack).

'Me?' said Mary Mary (well, she would).

'You?' said the others present, but still unidentified.

'You?'

'Me,' said Tinto. 'I can save you all.'

Had Eddie's eyes been able to widen, they would have widened now. His mouth, however, *could* drop open. And so it did. Most widely.

'Tinto,' whispered Eddie. 'What is Tinto doing here?'

'What?' asked Jack, but Eddie shushed him into silence.

'Tinto,' said Miss Muffett. 'Welcome, welcome.' Tinto wheeled himself into the ballroom.

'But he's a toy!' said Georgie. 'The wind-up barman. We all know him. Is this your idea of a joke?'

'I can save you all,' said Tinto.

'Stuff that,' said Georgie. 'I'm going home to pack. Who's leaving with me?'

'No,' Miss Muffett raised her hands once more. 'Please hear him out. Hear him out, and then you may leave if you wish to.'

Georgie Porgie folded his arms and took to a sulking silence.

'The floor is yours, Tinto,' said Miss Muffett.

'Thank you,' said Tinto. 'Now, you all know me. You held your meetings above my bar. I've respected your privacy. You know that you can trust me. I am here to protect you.'

'Indeed?' Old King scratched at his crowned head with a bejewelled finger. 'Well, listen, old chap, I don't wish to cause you offence, but I feel it will take more than a tin toy to defeat our adversary.'

'I am far more than just a tin toy,' said Tinto. 'I'm all manner of things. I'm most adaptable. Would you care for a demonstration?'

Old King shrugged. 'If you like,' said he. 'As long as it doesn't take too long and provides a bit of amusement. Should I call for my fiddlers three to accompany you?'

'That really won't be necessary.' Tinto's head revolved. 'Now who, or what, first, I wonder? Ah yes, how about this?' Tinto's left arm extended, reached around behind his back and wound his key.

'Hm,' went Eddie.

And then Tinto's hand touched certain buttons upon his chest, buttons that Eddie had never seen before. There was a whirring of cogs and then all manner of interesting things began to happen. Tinto's head snapped back, his arms retracted, his chest opened and he all but turned completely inside out.

And now Tinto wasn't Tinto any more: he was instead a tall and rather imposing gentleman, decked out in a dashing top hat, white tie and tails.

'God's Big Box!' cried Old King Cole. 'It's Wheatley Porterman himself!'

'Son of a clockwork pistol,' whispered Eddie, as a gasp went up from those inside the ballroom.

'No,' said Tinto, in the voice of Wheatley Porterman, 'it is still me. Still Tinto. But you can't fault the resemblance, can you? Faultless, isn't it? Are you impressed?'

Heads nodded. The assembled company was most definitely impressed.

'Then how about this one?' said Tinto. 'You'll love this one.' There was further whirring of cogs and the gentlemanly form of Mr Wheatley Porterman vanished into Tinto's chest. Flaps appeared from beneath Tinto's armpits, his legs slid up inside himself. Bits popped out here and popped in there, further convolutions occurred and suddenly Tinto was . . .

'Me,' whispered Old King. 'You've become me.'

'And what a merry old soul am I,' said Old King Cole's all-but-perfect double. 'I can impersonate any one of you here. Rather useful to fool your adversary, don't you agree?'

'Incredible,' puffed Old King Cole. 'And not a little upsetting. But surely my belly is not so large as that.'

'Larger,' said Tinto, who had now become Tinto once more. 'I was flattering you. But allow me to explain. I am a new generation of transforming toy, created by the toymaker for your protection.'

'So the toymaker sent you.' Old King grinned. 'Built you to protect us. Damn fine chap, the toymaker.'

'Precisely,' Tinto agreed. 'Damn fine chap, the toymaker. Or Big Box Fella, as we know him best.'

Another gasp went up from the assembly. A very big gasp.

'Something wrong?' asked Tinto. 'You are shocked and appalled that a mere toy should know the toymaker's true identity?'

Heads nodded dumbly.

'Don't be,' said Tinto. 'It remains *our* secret. I was created to protect you and to destroy the toymaker's evil twin. I have just spent the entire evening with the toymaker discussing the matter. He's very upset about the whole thing. He feels that it's all his fault and he can't bear the thought of any more of his dear friends coming to harm. So he has arranged for me to escort you all to a place of safety. Isn't that nice of him?'

Eddie scratched at his special-tagged ear. Tinto was clearly not telling all of the truth.

'But pardon me,' said Old King Cole, 'although I appreciate the quick-change routine, which is very impressive, I don't quite see how you are going to *destroy* the evil twin.'

'That,' said Tinto, 'is because you haven't seen everything I can do. I am capable of many other transformations, most of a military nature. You really wouldn't want me to show them to you here; they are all most lethal.'

'This is absurd,' cried Georgie Porgie, 'sending us a toy. Big Box Fella has clearly gone ga ga. Time has addled his brain.'

Another gasp went up at this. Possibly the biggest so far.

'No offence to Big Box Fella, of course,' said Georgie Porgie, hurriedly. 'But this is ludicrous.' Georgie, whose hands were currently in the thrown down position, made fists out of them. 'A toy!' he shouted. 'What good is a toy?'

'I'm much more than just a toy,' said Tinto.

'So you can do a few tricks.' Georgie made a face. 'That is hardly going to be enough. Show us what else you can do. Show us how tough you are. In fact—' Georgie Porgie raised his fists. It had been many years since he'd run away from the boys who came out to play. He'd learned to fight in prison. 'In fact,' he said, 'come and have a go, if you think you're hard enough.'

'I think not,' said Tinto, shaking his head. 'Not here.'

'A stupid toy.' Georgie stuck his tongue out at Tinto. 'That to you,' said he. And he raised two fingers to go with the sticky-out tongue.

What happened next happened fast. And fast can sometimes be shocking. Tinto's hand flew across the ballroom, upon the end of an arm which extended to an all-but-impossible length. The dextrous fingers of this hand snatched Georgie Porgie by the throat, shook him viciously about and then flung him down to the hard wooden floor.

A truly horrified gasp now went up from the assembly. It surpassed all the gasps that had gone before. It was accompanied by much stepping back from the fallen body. And much staring in blank disbelief.

'Outrage,' cried Old King Cole, finding his voice and using it. 'A toy daring to attack one of the elite. I shall have you scrapped, mashed-up, destroyed. Security guards, take this iconoclastic tin thing away and break it all to pieces.'

The security guards, however, appeared disinclined to become involved.

'I think not,' said Tinto, shaking his metal head. 'I must apologise for that display of gratuitous violence. But it was to prove a point. The killer of your friends walks amongst you. He is here in the city. He has already inflicted far worse upon your fellows. He has, no doubt, similarly hideous ends planned for each of you. The evil twin can be stopped. But only I can stop him.'

'Indeed?' said Old King. 'Then allow me to ask you one question.'

'Go on then.'

'Why have you waited so long?' Old King fairly shouted this. 'If you're capable of destroying this fiend, then why haven't you done so yet? Some of my closest friends are dead. If you could have saved them, why didn't you?'

'I have my reasons,' said Tinto. 'Good timing is everything, if you wish to succeed. If there is something that you truly want, it is often necessary to wait before you can get it.'

'Are you saying that you want something from *us*?' Old King asked. 'Is that what you're saying? I don't understand.'

'Well,' said Tinto, 'as you have seen, I am not just a mere toy. I am special, unique. And I can mobilise this city, raise an army of toys and lead them to destroy the evil twin. And it *can* be done, trust me. He may be a God, but he is a God in the form of a man. He's not immortal. He can be killed. And I can do it. But I will want something in return. I've discussed it with Big Box Fella. He has given me the go-ahead.'

Eddie did some more ear-scratchings.

'And what is it that you want?' asked Old King Cole.

'Well,' said Tinto. 'I toyed with the idea that I might become King of Toy City. As you have observed, I could carry this off most convincingly.'

'What?' cried Old King, falling back in outrage. 'But that's *my* job! I'm the king.'

Tinto laughed that laugh of his. And then a hinged jaw dropped open and the muzzle of a gun appeared from his mouth hole. Tinto cleared his throat with a pistol-cocking sort of sound. The gun muzzle swung in King Cole's direction.

'I'd be happy to abdicate, of course,' said Old King. 'If that's what you want, in exchange for saving us all. I'm sure it could be arranged without difficulty.'

'Of course *that* can be arranged. But *that* is not enough. The way I see it is this: if I kill the evil twin, kill a God in fact, then I have earned the right to more than a kingship. I have earned the right to . . .'

'Godhood,' whispered Eddie. 'Tinto wants to be worshipped as a God.'

'What did you say?' Jack asked.

'I said,' Eddie turned his head down to Jack, 'I said . . . Aaaaaagh!'

'Why did you say Aaaaagh?' Jack asked. And then a hand fell upon his shoulder.

Except it wasn't a hand.

It was more of a leg.

A big leg.

A big hairy spider's leg.

Jack turned to face the owner of this leg.

'Aaaaagh!' went Jack.

26

With a struggling lad beneath one big leg and a panic-stricken bear beneath another, Miss Muffett's spider marched upon its remaining hairy appendages into the Miss's mansion, through the front door, along a hall and into the perfectly proportioned ballroom.

Here it flung the two detectives down onto the hard wooden floor.

'Welly well well,' said Tinto. 'Isn't this a surprise.'

'Tinto,' said Eddie, struggling to his paw pads.

'Tinto?' said Jack, ramming the sections of his fallen fedora back onto his head and hoisting himself once more into the vertical plane.

'Skulking about outside,' said the spider—although to Jack, who had never heard a spider speak, these words were unintelligible.

'We were just passing by,' said Eddie. 'Didn't drink ourselves quite as sober as we thought. Got a bit lost. You know how it is.'

Tinto rocked upon his wheels. 'Of course I do,' he said.

'So we'll be on our way now; come on Jack.'

'But,' went Jack.

'Let's go,' said Eddie, turning to leave, but finding his exit blocked not only by the fearsome spider, but also by the two big burly men with the dark suits and the mirrored shades.

And the guns.

Eddie grinned foolishly towards Tinto, who shock his metal head. 'I think not,' said the clockwork chameleon. 'I think you should stay.'

'Fine by me,' said Jack. 'There was no need for that spider to be so rough with us. Any chance of some ears?'

'Plenty back at the office.' Eddie tugged at Jack's trenchcoat.

'No there isn't.'

'I think you *will* stay.' Tinto clicked his hinged jaw arrangement at

Eddie. 'After all, you *have* seen and heard everything that's gone on in here.'

'No.' Eddie shook his head. 'We were just passing by, honest.'

'Really? And yet I'm certain that I saw your silly furry face peeping in through the open window. I have extremely good eyesight—telescopic vision, in fact. I see all.'

'What's going on here?' Jack asked. 'And . . . oh.' He spied the prone Porgie. 'Has there been another murder?'

'Tinto,' said Eddie, 'we'd like to join up. Join your private army.'

'Join his *what*?' Jack asked.

'Tinto is raising a private army,' said Eddie. 'To fight the evil twin. Tinto is a barman of many parts. He's a real hero.'

'Is he?' Jack glanced doubtfully at Tinto.

'He *is*,' said Eddie. 'So, Tinto, where would you like me to sign?'

'No signing necessary.' Tinto's tin head went shake shake shake.

'We'll just be off then; goodbye.'

'Stay where you are,' said Tinto.

'Will someone please tell me what's going on?' Jack asked. 'Private army? What is all this?'

Tinto turned his back upon Eddie and Jack. Candlelight twinkled upon his perfect paintwork. 'Good people,' he said to the assembled company, 'great people, allow me to introduce you to Eddie and Jack. They're detectives. Eddie was Bill Winkie's bear and Jack is new to the city.'

'Hi there.' Jack waggled his fingers.

'Eddie took over the case after Bill disappeared. He and Jack have been relentlessly, if unsuccessfully, pursuing the murderer.'

'We have,' said Jack.

'Excuse me,' said Old King Cole, 'but is this some kind of joke? A toy bear and a young gormster?'

'I'm really sick of folk calling me that,' said Jack.

'Between the two of them,' said Tinto, 'they have complicated matters no end. But their antics have given me considerable amusement, which is why I have allowed them to continue.'

'You've *what*?' said Jack.

'I'll have to explain later.' Eddie clung to Jack's leg. 'If we *have* a later.'

'Have a *what*?' said Jack.

'I'm trying to be democratic here,' said Tinto. 'I thought I'd put your fate to the vote.'

'To the *what*?' said Jack.

'This city is now under martial law,' declared Tinto.

'Under *what?*' said Jack.

'Jack,' said Tinto, wheeling close to Jack, rising high upon his wheels and opening his chest to reveal a row of wicked-looking metal barbs, 'if you say the word *what* one more time, I will be forced to kill you.'

'Forced to . . .' Jack's voice trailed off.

'Thank you,' said Tinto. 'You see, desperate times call for desperate actions. It is often necessary to sacrifice an individual or two in the cause of the many.'

'But we're on your side.' Eddie made pleading paw movements. 'We want what you want.'

'I know,' said Tinto, retracting his wicked-looking barbs, wheeling himself up and down the ballroom, and glittering beautifully as he did so. 'But the point I'm trying to make is this: would you consider yourself to be an individual, Eddie?'

'Definitely so,' said the bear.

'And what about you, Jack?'

'Is it all right for me to speak?'

Tinto nodded.

'Then yes,' said Jack. 'I am definitely an individual too.'

'And there you have it.' Tinto ceased his wheelings. 'Condemned out of your own mouths, with no need for a democratic vote. There is no room for individuals in a war, only for soldiers who follow orders without question. I can't have you two running loose any more. You'd only cause further chaos.'

Jack made a baffled face.

'But you're in charge now, Tinto,' said Eddie. 'We'll do exactly what you tell us to do.'

'That's good then.' Tinto's head went nod nod nod. 'In that case I will assign you both to my first crack squadron.'

'Absolutely,' said Eddie.

'Tinto's Tornado Force,' said Tinto.

'Right,' said Eddie. 'Great name.'

'The crack suicide squadron.'

'*What?*' said Jack.

'Gotcha,' said Tinto. 'That was your last *what!*'

'No,' said Jack, 'hold on.'

'Take them out,' Tinto told the spider. 'Take them somewhere nice and quiet and well away from here and then kill them both. And kill the big *what*-boy first. He really gets up my metallic hooter.'

'No,' begged Eddie. 'Tinto, please. We're old friends. Don't do this.'

'Desperate times,' said Tinto, turning his back once more. 'But it's all for the common good. The rest of you . . .' Tinto's arm extended and swung all around and about. 'The rest of you, prepare to leave. I have a truck outside. We will repair to a place of safety. I know somewhere sweet and secure.'

Tinto whispered certain words into the ear parts of Miss Muffett's spider. 'And sick up on their faces before you kill them,' he added loudly.

'Tinto, no, please.' Eddie waved frantic paws, but Miss Muffett's spider scooped him from his pads.

'Now just you see here.' Jack raised a fist. But then he too was similarly scooped.

'We're done for,' said Eddie. 'We're sawdust.'

He and Jack were all in the dark. All in the dark in the locked boot of a big, posh automobile: a mark 22 Hyperglide limousine with pressed steel body panels finished in whey beige enamel; alloy-trim solid wheels with lithographed brass spoke motifs and moulded tyre assemblies; full pink plush tuffet seating throughout; sunroof fitted as standard; wind-up stereo sound system optional, but installed in this particular model.

This was being driven at speed through the night-time streets of Toy City by Miss Muffett's spider.

'Don't fret, Eddie,' said Jack. 'We'll be fine.'

'Fine?' Eddie's voice was hollow in the bumpy darkness. 'We're being driven to our place of execution. We will *not* be fine.'

'Of course we will. Trust me.'

Eddie growly-groaned.

'And please tell me,' said Jack, 'what *is* going on?'

The Mark 22 Hyperglide limousine sped on. The spider tinkered with the wind-up stereo system and behind him in the darkness of the boot Eddie, having nothing better to do, filled Jack in upon all of the details.

'Well,' said Jack, when Eddie had done with the filling of him in, 'I grudgingly have to admit that it does appear that your theory is correct. There really *is* an evil twin.'

'My pleasure in the knowledge that I was right is somewhat marred by our present circumstances,' said Eddie, shuddering away.

'But at least we now know who the murderer is. And why he's doing the murdering.'

'The evil twin,' Eddie shuddered on. 'But we don't know where he is and we're as doomed as.'

'Wake up, Eddie,' said Jack. 'You're missing the obvious.'

'I'm sure I'm not,' Eddie said.

'I'm sure you are. Remember what we were saying about behaving like proper detectives? Doing things the way Bill would have done them? How they would have been in one of his books?'

Eddie made noncommittal grunting sounds.

'Well, in the books, the detectives would have encountered the murderer by now, and we just did. *That* was the murderer, Eddie.'

'Tinto? You're saying that Tinto is the murderer?'

'It's not Tinto,' said Jack.

'It's *not* Tinto?' said Eddie.

'It's *not* Tinto,' said Jack. 'Don't you understand? *Not* Tinto.'

'It *was* Tinto,' said Eddie. 'We both saw him; we both know him.'

'Wasn't Tinto,' said Jack. 'That's what I'm trying to explain. That thing back there wasn't Tinto.'

'I give up,' said Eddie.

'Looked like Tinto,' said Jack. 'And sounded like Tinto. But *wasn't* Tinto. And do you know how I know?'

'Obviously not,' said Eddie.

'Because of his back. When he turned away from us, I saw it. Tinto is called Tinto because of the name on his back: Tintoy with the "y" scratched off. You showed me; you said that he thinks it makes him special. Our friend back there, at Miss Muffett's, the "y" wasn't scratched off *his* back. His back was perfect: it glittered in the candlelight. It said *Tintoy* on his back. That wasn't Tinto, Eddie. *That* was the criminal mastermind impersonating Tinto! That was the evil twin himself!'

'You genius,' said Eddie. 'You complete and utter genius. You're as smart as.'

'I'm a detective,' said Jack. 'And that's what we detectives do. Observe. Theorise. Resolve. He lied to them, Eddie. You heard him lying that he'd been at the toymaker's house. We were there, he wasn't. And remember what Bellis said about how criminals never tell the truth? They just lie and lie. He went there and lied to them and gained their confidence, told them how he could save them all, told them that the toymaker had sent him. He was disguised as Tinto because he knew that they knew Tinto. And he was disguised because they all know what he really looks like. They were there; they helped to throw him out of the city. And now he's got them all. All his old enemies. He'll kill them for certain.'

'So how can we stop him? He's the very Devil, Jack.'

'And a formidable adversary, if he can turn himself into weapons and stuff like that. But we'll find a way. Somehow.'

'Do you think he was the spider-woman too?' Eddie asked.

Jack shrugged in the darkness.

'Was that a yes or a no?'

'It was a shrug.'

'I'm very sad about all this,' said Eddie. 'I get it right and then we get captured and sent off to our deaths.'

'It will all be okay. Somehow. Trust me, Eddie.'

'I do,' said Eddie. 'But . . .'

'But what?'

'The car's just stopped,' said Eddie. 'And I think I need the toilet.'

There was a click of a key in a lock and then the boot lid swung open. Some light fell upon Eddie and Jack. Not a lot of light, but enough: enough to illuminate the fearful face of Eddie.

'Out,' said Miss Muffett's spider.

'What did he say?' Jack asked.

'He said "Out",' said Eddie.

'Oh,' said Jack. 'Right.'

Jack lifted Eddie from the boot and set him down upon the ground. And then Jack climbed out and stood before the spider.

The creature was little less than terrifying. In fact, it was a great deal more than more so: a towering black science fiction nasty. Its glistening mandibles clicked. Its complicated mouthparts moved in and out and its multifaceted eyes stared unblinkingly at Jack.

Jack stared back. 'You're one ugly mother . . .'

But the spider struck him from his feet.

Jack rolled over on the ground and glared up at the creature. 'Ask him where we are,' Jack called out to Eddie.

Eddie cowered at the car boot.

'Ask him,' said Jack.

Eddie asked the spider.

Mouthparts moved and words were uttered.

'He says we're at the abandoned doll works on East 666,' said Eddie, in a trembly tone.

Jack climbed slowly to his feet. 'Do you know your way back to Miss Muffett's from here?' he asked Eddie.

'Yes, but . . .'

'Then get in the car; we're leaving.'

The spider spoke further words.

'It says . . .' said Eddie.

'I don't care what it says,' said Jack. 'Get in the car, Eddie.'

'But, Jack.'

The spider drew back and then suddenly rushed forward at Jack: a blur of terrible scrabbling legs and horrible horrible mouthparts.

Jack drew the 7.62 mm M134 General Clockwork Mini-gun from his trousers and coolly shot the spider's head right off the arachnid equivalent of its shoulders.

'Right,' said Jack, retrousering his weapon. 'Let's go.'

Eddie looked at the fallen spider and then he looked up at Jack.

'What?' said Jack.

Eddie shrugged.

'Well, what did you expect me to do, let it kill me?'

'Yes, well no, but.'

'I couldn't shoot it back at Miss Muffett's, too many big burly men with sunglasses and guns about. I had to wait until we got here.'

'But I've been all but pooing myself. I was as terrified as.'

'But you knew I still had the gun.'

'Well, in all the excitement, I sort of forgot.'

'Sorry,' said Jack. 'So, shall we go? We have famous folk to rescue and an evil God to destroy.'

Eddie sighed. 'Right,' said he. 'But first I have to do that thing that bears do in the woods.'

When Eddie had done that thing, he returned to Jack.

'Back to Miss Muffett's?' Jack asked.

'No point,' said Eddie. 'He won't be there. He was preparing to take the famous folk away in that big truck.'

'We'll pick up some clues there, then. We'll find them, somehow.'

'No need,' said Eddie. 'I know where he'll be taking them.'

'You do?'

'Of course I do. Trust me, Jack. I'm a detective.'

The moon was ducking down now and the sun was on the up and up. Jack brought the Mark 22 Hyperglide limousine to a halt at the gates of the chocolate factory. He ran his fingers lovingly over the polished silk-wood steering wheel and thought to himself just how very much he'd like to own a car like this. Along with a chauffeur to drive him about in it, of course.

'So what are we doing back here?' he asked Eddie.

'Somewhere sweet and secure,' said the bear. 'That's what the evil twin said. And what is sweeter than chocolate? And more secure than a place with such big gates and such a dedicated gatekeeper?'

'I don't see the truck.'

'We'll have a word with our man the talking head.'

They left the limousine and did so.

'You can't come in,' said the gatekeeper. 'Not without an appointment.'

'A truck went through these gates earlier, didn't it?' said Jack.

'What if it did? It's got nothing to do with you.'

'We're here on special assignment,' said Eddie. 'We're part of an elite strike force.'

'That's a coincidence,' said the head. 'So am I.'

'Really?' said Jack. 'Which elite strike force are you in?'

'Tinto's Tornadoes,' said the head. 'I've just been enlisted. I'm already a corporal.'

'Then stand to attention when you address a superior officer,' said Jack. 'I'm a major.'

'Me too,' said Eddie. 'We're both majors. Major majors. Open the gates, corporal.'

'Can't do that, sir,' said the gatekeeping head. 'More than my commission's worth to do that.'

'Major,' said Eddie to Jack.

'Major?' said Jack to Eddie.

'Major, this soldier is being insubordinate. Have him immediately court-martialled and shoot him dead.'

'Sure thing, major.' Jack pulled out his 7.62 mm M134 General Clockwork Mini-gun.

'Opening the gates, *sir*,' said the head. 'I would salute you, but you know how it is, no hands.'

The gatekeeper head-butted certain controls and the big iron gates swung open.

Jack and Eddie saluted the head and returned to the limousine. Jack drove it through the open gates, which swung slowly shut behind him. 'Tell me, Eddie,' said Jack, 'do you have any particular plan in mind?'

Eddie offered a foolish grin. 'Not as such,' he said. 'I thought we'd sort of play things by ear, as it were.'

Jack steered the limousine across the broad expanse of courtyard that lay before the factory building. The chocolate factory really was of immense size: a veritable citadel, it seemed.

'This place is huge,' said Jack. 'A veritable citadel, it seems. It's like a fortress.'

'We didn't have too much difficulty getting past the guard on this occasion.'

'That's the military mind for you.'

Jack peered up through the windscreen. 'This is an awful lot of chocolate factory,' he observed. 'Does Toy City really consume so much chocolate as to merit a factory this size?'

'Absolutely,' said Eddie. 'Everyone loves chocolate. And I do mean everyone. And you don't get better chocolate than Sredna's. But that's possibly because no one else makes it.'

'What did you say?' Jack asked.

'I said no one else makes chocolate—'

'No, Eddie. The name.'

'Sredna,' said Eddie. 'A Mr Sredna founded the chocolate company years and years and years ago. Long before my time.'

'Sredna,' said Jack. 'Then everything that man told me was true.'

'What are you talking about, Jack? What man?'

'A man I met. Back at the town where I lived. If it hadn't been for him and what happened, I wouldn't have set out on my journey to the city.'

'Do you want to tell me all about it?'

'Yes,' said Jack. 'But not now, there isn't time. Now we have to stop the evil twin and rescue the rich folk.'

'You don't have to do this, Jack,' Eddie said. 'You know that. It's going to be dangerous. You could just walk away. If you want.'

'What?' said Jack. 'But we're partners. You and me. Jack and Eddie. We're the detective dream team.'

'Right,' said Eddie. 'We're as dreamy as.'

Jack brought the limousine to a halt and looked into the driving mirror. The sun was rising higher now, above the highest heights of Knob Hill. It shone upon the rooftops of the toymaker's house. 'So what do you think?' he asked. 'Should we go and have another of our sneakabouts? See what we can see?'

'Let's do that,' said Eddie. 'Let's sneak.'

And so, once more, they snuck.

They left the limousine and snuck about the mighty edifice that was the chocolate factory. And a truly mighty edifice it was: a Gothic goliath; a gargoyled gargantuan; a towering tessellated *tour de force*. And things of that non-nominally nominative nature, generally.

'I don't see any lights on,' said Eddie. 'And frankly, my paw pads are getting tired and sore.'

'Let's just break in,' said Jack. 'Find me a lock to pick.'

A small door presented itself. Jack selected a suitable piece of wire from a pile of waste that lay conveniently to hand, picked the lock and swung the small door open.

'After you,' he said to Eddie.

'No,' said Eddie. 'You have the big gun. Very much after *you*.'

With Jack leading the way, they entered the chocolate factory. Eddie sniffed chocolate.

'Tell me about the rabbits,' said Eddie. Which rang a bell somewhere with Jack.

'The rabbits?' Jack asked.

'The hollow chocolate bunnies. What are they all about?'

Jack shrugged. 'I haven't a clue,' said he. 'But I'll bet it's something really obvious. Where do you think we are?'

'Looks like the staff kitchens.'

'Then let's go somewhere else. I have no love for kitchens.'

They passed through a doorway and into a hallway. 'You know what,' said Eddie, 'we really do need some kind of plan.'

'I think I'll just shoot him with my big gun, as soon as I see him,' said Jack.

'That's not too subtle a plan.'

'I know.' Jack edged along the hallway, his big gun held high. 'But you see, there's always too much talking when it comes to the big confrontation situation. When I used to read the Bill Winkie thrillers and it got to the point of the final confrontation with the villain, there was always too much talking. I'd be reading it and saying "don't talk to him, Bill, just shoot him". And Bill would have the gun on him and everything, but he'd talk and then suddenly the gun would get wrestled away and then the villain would talk and talk.'

'That's the way it's done,' said Eddie. 'If you want to do it by the book, that's the way it's done. Bill always triumphed in the end, though. With my help, of course, not that I ever got a mention. But he triumphed. He did it right, did Bill.' Eddie's voice trailed off.

Jack turned and looked down at Eddie.

'I'm sorry,' said Jack. 'I know how much you loved Bill.'

'Don't talk wet,' said Eddie.

'You loved him,' said Jack. 'It's nothing to be ashamed of. And when this is all sorted out, you will have sorted it out for Bill. As a tribute to him. And your memory of him. That's noble stuff, Eddie. That's doing things for love. That's okay.'

Eddie sniffed. '*You're* okay, Jack,' he said. 'You're my bestest friend, you know that.'

'Come on,' said Jack. 'Let's do it.'

Eddie grinned, and then he said, 'Stop, hold on there, Jack.'

'What is it?'

'I smell something.'

'What do you smell?'

'Something more than chocolate. Something that I've smelled before.'

Eddie now led the way and cautiously Jack followed him. They edged along the hallway.

'The smell's getting stronger,' said Eddie.

Jack sniffed. 'I can smell it now,' he said. 'What is it?'

'I know what it is, and I don't like what it is.'

Presently they reached the end of the hallway. They passed through a narrow arch and found themselves standing upon a gantry constructed of pierced metal.

Beneath them was a vast beyond: a vast beyond of wonder.

Eddie stared.

And Jack stared too.

And, 'I don't believe *that*,' said Eddie.

27

It spread away beneath them, to dwindle into hazy perspectives: a vast subterranean factory complex.

Molten metal flowed from titanic furnaces, to be swallowed up by mighty engines fashioned from burnished brass and highly polished copper. Upon these, intricate networks of massive cogs intermeshed and glittering objects shuttled out upon clattering conveyor belts. Fountains of sparks arose above enormous lathes that tortured spinning metal. Great pistons pounded and countless funnels belched out steam.

And it went on and on and on.

And on and on some more.

'Look at it,' Eddie gasped, breathlessly. 'Look at it, Jack. It's incredible. It's as gabracious as.'

'As what?'

'You know I don't know as what.'

'I meant, what does gabracious mean?'

'How should I know?' said Eddie. 'I've never seen anything like this before. I don't have a word for it.'

Jack shook his head. 'It's very impressive,' he said.

'Assembly lines,' Eddie pointed out. 'Moving belts, but no workers. No workers at all, Jack. It's all being done by machine. It's all . . .'

'Automatic,' said Jack. 'Automated. Automation. When I was labouring away in the clockwork factory, the workers used to talk about this sort of thing: that one day factories wouldn't need workers any more. That machines would do everything.'

'But how?' asked Eddie. 'How is it done?'

Jack shrugged his narrow shoulders. 'It isn't done by clockwork, that's for certain.'

'Automation? That certainly sounds like the work of the Devil. And look there.' Eddie pointed some more. 'Look at those on the conveyor belts there. Look what the machines are manufacturing.'

Jack did further lookings.

Robotic arms snatched up the glittering objects that shuttled along the conveyor belts, jointed them one to another, pieced them together: pieced them into all-too-recognisable forms.

'Women,' said Jack. 'The machines are making women.'

'The spider-women. Tinto's private army.' Eddie made a fearful face. 'He's building them down there, thousands of them.'

'This is very bad, Eddie; we have to stop him.'

'But the scale of all this. It makes me afraid, Jack. This must have taken years to build. Years and years and years.'

'More than a few years,' Jack said, thoughtfully. 'This has been a very long-running project. Why would he want to build thousands of these creatures? What is he really up to?'

Eddie growled hopelessly. 'And all down here, beneath Toy City. Beneath the chocolate factory. And none of us knew.'

'They do favour an underground lair, these criminal masterminds. I'm a bit disappointed that it's not inside an extinct volcano, though. But there you go.'

'Don't be flippant, Jack,' said Eddie.

'Just laughing in the face of fear, that's all.'

'Which would be why your knees are knocking, would it?' Jack made an effort to stiffen his knees. 'But look at them,' said Eddie. 'Those spider-women. Look at their hands, Jack.'

Jack squinted down. 'Their *hands*?' he said. 'What about their hands?'

'Delicate hands,' said Eddie, 'coming off the conveyor belts, rows and rows of hands, all with four fingers, with opposable thumbs,' and there was no disguising the envy in the voice of Eddie Bear.

'This is hardly the time for that, Eddie. We're here on business. Detective business. To save the famous folk and bring the criminal mastermind, in the form of the evil twin, to justice. Or at least to this.' Jack cocked the 7.62 mm M134 General Clockwork Mini-gun. 'Forget about hands, please, will you?'

'I still have time to dream,' said Eddie, regarding his fingerless paws with contempt. 'So, shall we do some more sneaking?'

'Practice makes perfect.' Jack raised his 7.62 mm M134 General Clockwork Mini-gun. 'Follow me.'

Eddie followed Jack, who snuck down this staircase and the next, down and down, and down some more, to the factory floor below.

It was very noisy there, and very smelly too.

And even with all the furnaces, there was a terrible chill in the air. The chill that one feels when in the presence of Evil.

'What *is* that?' Jack shivered and covered his nose.

'The smell of the spider-women. I told you I knew that smell.' Eddie looked fearfully up at the creations upon the conveyor belts. 'It's coming from them. It's the smell of whatever they're made of.'

Jack reached out and touched the leg of one of the half-completed spider-women as the conveyor belt carried it by. 'Warm,' said he. 'And it feels almost like firm flesh. Imagine an entire army of these. It doesn't bear thinking about.'

'Could we blow them all up?' Eddie asked. 'Murders, fast car-driving, drinking, underage sex, gratuitous violence and a big explosion at the end. That's a recipe for success in any detective thriller.'

'Worth a try,' Jack agreed. 'But it might be better to rescue the famous folk first, don't you think?'

'Well,' said Eddie. It was a long well. A real *weeeeeeeeell* of a well. 'Do you think anyone would really miss them?'

'Eddie, what are you saying?'

'Only joking,' said Eddie. 'Shall we sneak about some more and see if we can find them? Perhaps somewhere away from these horrible creatures.'

'After you this time,' Jack said.

Eddie led the way between clattering conveyor belts, past the titanic furnaces and the mighty engines, around one huge and scary big machine and on past many more, until at last they snuck under an arch and down a passageway, which at least was far less noisy and didn't smell so bad.

'We're lost,' said Jack.

'We're not,' said Eddie. 'Bears have a great sense of direction. They're renowned for it. How do you think we find our way back from all those picnics in the woods, breadcrumbs?'

'We *are* lost.' They had reached a parting of the passageways. There were several now to choose from. None seemed to be saying, 'Come this way', but then again, none didn't.

Early morning sunlight dipped in through narrow arched windows. Jack glanced up at it. 'Which way should we go?' he asked.

'That way,' Eddie pointed.

'*I'm* not so sure.'

'I don't think it matters, either way.'

'Yes it does, Eddie.'

'I didn't say that,' said Eddie. 'That wasn't me.'

'He's right, it wasn't.'

Eddie turned.

And Jack turned too.

'Ah,' said Eddie. 'It's you.'

'Surprise, surprise,' said the Tinto impersonator. 'Drop your weapon please, Jack.' Where the Tinto impersonator's left arm had been, there was now a considerable weapon: it was a 19.72 mm M666 General Clockwork Maxi-cannon.

Jack recognised it at once, and in deference to its mighty firepower, he grudgingly put down his weapon. Which it pained him considerably to do.

'Chaps,' said the Tinto impersonator, shaking his metallic head from side to side. 'Chaps, chaps, chaps. The gatekeeper called me. Sergeant gatekeeper, that is. He called me to say that you two had breached the security perimeter. You're supposed to be dead. Can't you even die properly?'

Jack chewed upon his bottom lip. 'Nice place you have here . . . er . . . *Tinto*. Can't we just talk about this?'

The clockwork chameleon shook its head once more. 'You really have no idea what you've got yourself into, have you?' he asked.

'No,' said Jack, 'we haven't. But please tell me this, who are you, really?'

'I'm Tinto,' said the Tinto impersonator.

'You're *not* Tinto,' said Jack. 'You look like Tinto. But you're not him.'

'And why do you say that?'

Jack chose his words with care. Although he and Eddie knew that the evil twin lurked behind the Tinto disguise, the evil twin didn't know that they knew. So to speak. 'I know you're not Tinto, because you're too perfect,' said Jack.

'Why, thank you very much, young man. Perfect, yes.'

'Tinto's back is all scratched up,' said Jack. 'The "Y" has worn off the word *Tintoy*. That's why he called himself Tinto; he thinks it makes him special.'

'And don't you think that I'm special too?'

'Oh yes,' said Jack. 'You're very special. Unique. You're definitely one of a kind.'

'I'm warming to you.' Several of the 19.72 mm M666 General Clockwork Maxi-cannon's barrels retracted. 'Perfection is the name of the game. And everything is a game. Everything. All fun and games.'

'So who are you, really?' Jack asked.

'He's the evil twin, of course,' said Eddie.

Jack gawped down at Eddie.

'Sorry,' said Eddie. 'It just slipped out.'

'*What?*' Gun barrels bristled from places that had previously been gun barrel-free. 'What did you say?'

'Nothing,' said Eddie. 'Nothing at all.'

'You did. You said that *I* was the evil twin. You must die this instant.'

'No, hold on please,' said Jack. 'Eddie gets lots of silly ideas into his head. It's full of sawdust; it doesn't work very well.'

'And he thinks that *I* am the toymaker's evil twin?'

'That's bears for you,' said Jack, making a helpless gesture. 'They're as stupid as.'

'He thinks that I?' The Tinto head spun round and round. '*I* am the evil twin? When here am I forging a private army to destroy the evil twin? Working unpaid around the clock, and this bear thinks that I'm the evil twin?'

'So you're not?' said Eddie. 'I mean, *no* you're not. Of course you're not.'

'Of course he's not,' said Jack. 'I told you he wasn't.'

'I don't remember you telling me anything of the sort.'

Jack gave Eddie a kick. 'Shut up!' he whispered.

'Ouch,' said Eddie. 'Oh yes, of course you did.' Eddie's knees were all a-tremble now. 'Jack did say that. He definitely said that you were *not* the evil twin.'

'That's right,' said Jack.

'Good,' said the clockwork creation.

'He said you were just a loony,' said Eddie.

'He *what?*' Weaponry appeared from the most unexpected places.

'Sorry,' said Eddie, covering his face with his paws. 'I didn't mean to say that. I'm sorry, I sort of blurt things out when I'm scared. It wasn't loony he said, it was—'

'Deity,' said Jack.

'Deity?' said the gun-bristling-whatever.

'Deity,' said Jack once again.

'Deity doesn't sound in the least like loony.'

'It does when you have tatty old ears like mine,' said Eddie, pawing at his tatty old ears. 'And a head full of sawdust. It was definitely deity. I'm sure it was.'

'It was,' said Jack. 'A deity that will soon be worshipped by all the folk of Toy City.'

'This is indeed the case.'

'So what *is* your name?' Jack asked. 'Your real name? The name that will be glorified by all of Toy City when you defeat the evil twin. When you are raised to the status of Godhood that you so justly deserve.'

'Bumlicker,' Eddie whispered to Jack.

'I'm just trying to keep us alive,' Jack whispered back. 'Please be quiet, Eddie, and let me do the talking.' Jack bowed towards the Tinto Impersonator. 'Might we be permitted to know your real name, oh Great One?'

'I don't think so, no. It's private.'

'Oh, please,' said Jack. 'You're going to kill us anyway. What harm would there be in letting us know your real name?'

'No, it's private. And anyway, you might laugh.'

'Laugh?' said Jack. 'Laugh in the face of a deity? Would even *we* be that stupid?'

'Well, seeing as you're both going to die, I suppose there's no harm. Stand back, I'm going to transform.'

Eddie and Jack stood back and viewed the transformation. It was an impressive transformation. It involved all manner of bits sliding out here and sliding in there and other bits turning around and folding down and up and so forth.

Until.

'Now I wasn't expecting *that*!' said Eddie.

'Who are *you*?' asked Jack.

A dolly now stood before them: a rather foolish-looking dolly with a big silly face, all wide eyes and rosy cheeks and little kissy mouth. The dolly had golden plaited hair with big red bows, a colourful frock and dear little court shoes of polished patent leather.

'I'm PRIMROSE,' said the dolly, in a little dolly voice.

'Primrose?' said Jack.

'Primrose?' said Eddie.

'PRIMROSE,' said PRIMROSE. 'Prototype Integrated Multi-tasking Robotics Operational System.'

'That's Primros,' said Jack. 'There's an "e" on the end of Primrose.'

The dolly's little kissy mouth became a tight-lipped scowl. 'And you wonder why I want to keep it private. My acronym is rubbish; it doesn't even work. I was designed to be a multi-purpose toy that could be enjoyed by girls as well as boys. Some stupid idea that, eh? And PRIMROSE, I ask you: what kind of name is that for a metamorphosing action figure? With the kind of weaponry that can take the head off a golly at two thousand yards. I should have been given a name like SPLAT or ZARK.'

'Or simply twat,' said Eddie.

'*What?*' went PRIMROSE, making a very evil face indeed.

'Sorry, sir, nerves again. I meant TWAT as in, er, Transforming War Action Tank,' Eddie suggested.

'Yes,' said PRIMROSE. 'Twat. I like that.'

'I'll call you Twat then,' said Eddie.

'Me too,' said Jack.

'You'll both call me Master,' said PRIMROSE. 'Or perhaps it should be Mistress. I get a bit confused myself at times. So many personality changes, I get rather disorientated.'

Eddie looked at Jack.

And Jack looked at Eddie.

'He's lying,' whispered Jack. 'He's lying again.'

Eddie looked once more at Jack and Jack looked once more at Eddie and then the two of them looked towards PRIMROSE. If there was ever going to be a better time to rush and overpower the evil twin, neither of them could imagine it.

Eddie and Jack prepared to rush.

PRIMROSE, however, was no longer PRIMROSE, she was now something more approaching ZARK.

'Whoa,' went Eddie. 'What a big, bad boy.'

The ZARK was an all-action combat mode: a martial monster, bristling with polished spikes, lean and mean, armoured and dangerous.

'So you see the problem,' it said. 'However, everything will be resolved. Perhaps I'll go with Twat. Do you wish to pray to me before I kill you? As you'll be kneeling, you might want to get a prayer or two going.'

'We'd rather just stick around, if it's all right,' Jack said. 'Then we could do a lot of praying and bowing down when you're sworn in officially.'

'I think that I'll just kill you now,' said PRIMROSE.

'No, hold on,' said Jack, 'let's not be hasty.'

'There's no haste involved, I assure you. I'm killing you at my leisure.'

'No,' said Jack. 'You really don't want to do that.'

'I do. Really I do.'

'But if you kill us, you'll never find the Maguffin.'

'The *what?*'

'The Maguffin,' said Jack. 'The all-important something that's all-importantness is not apparent until its moment has come.'

'I've no idea what you're talking about.'

'Of course you do. It's about this big.' Jack did mimings. 'And this-shaped and sort of heavyish in a lighter way than you might expect.'

'That?' said PRIMROSE, or whatever PRIMROSE currently called itself. 'You have *that*?'

'Got it from the real Tinto,' said Jack. 'He said that one of the famous folk had left it behind after one of their meetings above his bar. I'll bet you really want it, don't you?'

'Well, I . . .'

'Go on,' said Jack. 'Admit it. It's really important, isn't it?'

'Hand it over to me,' said PRIMROSE. 'Now!'

'I don't have it on me,' said Jack. 'Do you think I'd carry a valuable artefact like that around with me? What does it do, by the way?'

'You think I'm going to tell you *that*?'

'What harm can it do?' Jack asked. 'You're going to kill us anyway.'

'I'm getting déjà vu here,' said PRIMROSE.

'Look,' said Jack, 'I know that you think that you want to kill us because we're such a nuisance. But you don't want to *really*. You're little less than a deity. And deities are noted for granting mercy and answering prayers and stuff like that. I know we've got on your nerves a bit and any ordinary mortal would probably want to kill us for that. But you're not any ordinary mortal, are you? You're special. You're unique. You're one of a kind. Special. You can make your own rules. Do whatever you want.'

'I certainly can,' said PRIMROSE.

'So you could just send us on our way with a wave of your dextrous hand.'

'I could, if I so chose to.'

'Then go for it,' said Jack. 'Do what a God would do. Forgive and forget. That's what a *special* God would do.'

'Well,' said PRIMROSE.

'We're beneath your notice,' said Jack. 'We're nothing. Tatty old bear and young gormster. Nothing to one as special as you.'

'You're certainly that. And I'm certainly special.'

'So there you go,' said Jack. 'That's omnipotence for you. It's a done deal.'

'It is,' Eddie agreed. 'Bravo, special guy.' Eddie offered a thumbless thumbs-up to PRIMROSE.

'All right,' said PRIMROSE. 'I will be merciful. Give me the Maguffin. And you can go.'

'Certainly,' said Jack. 'Absolutely. As soon as Eddie and I and all the famous folk are set free, I will go at once and fetch it for you.'

There was a bit of a pause then.

'Famous folk *set free*?' said PRIMROSE, slowly and thoughtfully.

Eddie looked up at Jack.

And Jack looked down at Eddie.

'Oh dear, oh dear, oh dear,' said PRIMROSE.

'Poor choice of words there,' whispered Eddie. 'And you were doing so well until then.'

'Oh dear,' said PRIMROSE. 'And there was I almost believing you. But *set free*? You think that I have them captured and locked up. You're just the same as this stupid bear. You think I'm the evil twin.'

'No,' said Jack. 'Honestly I don't. And I mean what I say, I *honestly* don't.' Jack tried to make an honest face, but couldn't.

'Give me the Maguffin, and give it to me now.'

'I told you, I don't have it.'

'Then to be certain, I'll search you. Search your body, that is.' The martial monster rolled towards Jack upon grinding tank tracks. A steel claw extended from its chest regions and snatched the lad by the throat, hauling him from his feet and dragging him up the cold stone passageway wall.

'Die,' said Battle Mode PRIMROSE.

Jack fought and struggled, but the steel claw tightened about his throat. Jack's eyes started from his head and his tongue stuck from his mouth. Being choked to death really hurt. It was no fun at all. Jack struck with his fists and kicked with his feet, but it was all to no avail. The breath was going from him now. The big black darkness was closing in.

And then there was a bit of an explosion. Which lit up the big black darkness.

It came right out of the blue. Or the black. Unexpectedly. The way that most explosions do. This one was a real eardrum-splitter, coming as it did within the confines of a passageway—even a passageway that branched off into other passageways. This explosion really rocked. It was a veritable deafener.

The head of the Martial PRIMROSE turned away from Jack. The head of the Martial PRIMROSE had a dent in its left cheek.

Jack, whose popping eyes had all but dropped from his head, felt the grip around his throat loosen and fell to the passageway floor, coughing and gagging for air.

He saw the head of the Martial PRIMROSE turn somewhat more. And then he saw it take another violent hit.

The second explosion, a double deafener, had Jack covering his ears, and had him glancing with watery blinking eyes towards Eddie.

The bear had the 7.62 mm M134 General Clockwork Mini-gun raised.

'Run, Jack,' shouted Eddie, pulling the trigger once again. 'Run like a rabbit, go on.'

'No, Eddie, no.'

'No?' said the bear.

'No, I mean, keep firing.'

'But.'

'Don't but me, Eddie. Shoot him some more. Shoot him until he's dead.'

'Right,' said Eddie, 'now you're talking.' He pulled the trigger and another shell hit home.

Martial PRIMROSE rocked upon its tracks. It was armoured, it was tough; inner mechanisms clicked and clacked, shutters opened, gunnery extended. This gunnery levelled at Eddie.

Jack rolled over, snatched the gun from Eddie's paws and came up firing. 'Retreat!' he shouted.

'But you said.'

'I know what I said, Eddie. But now I'm saying retreat. Just run.'

'Like a rabbit?'

'Like a rabbit. Run!'

Jack snatched up Eddie and tucked him under his arm.

'I'll do the running,' said Jack.

And he ran.

28

Jack ran like a rabbit, with Eddie tucked under his arm, along a tiled passageway and onwards, ever onwards.

Something whistled from behind, passed near to his ducking head, and exploded some distance before him.

'Discouraging, that,' remarked Eddie. 'Somewhat superior fire-power. And our gun only made a few small dents. Any thoughts on this, Jack?'

Jack huffed and puffed and had no thoughts that he wished to convey at present. His long limbs carried him and Eddie back onto the factory floor.

'I'm sure we're not really lost,' said Eddie as he jiggled about under Jack's arm. 'I'll just get my bearings. *Bearings*, geddit?' Eddie giggled foolishly. 'Sorry,' he said, 'nerves.'

'Please be quiet.' Jack ducked this way and the next and took cover behind a big brass pumping piston. 'I don't think he'll take pot-shots at us out here.' Jack raised his head and did furtive peepings. 'He won't want to risk damaging any of his demonic machinery.'

The armoured being in full combat mode, no longer on its tank tracks, but now on sturdy steely legs, moved purposefully along between the clattering conveyor belts, a most determined expression upon its latest metal face. Its head swung to the right and left, telescopic vision focused and refocused; tiny brass ear-trumpets extending from the sides of its head picked up each and every sound, deciphered and unscrambled them within the clockwork cranial cortex, sorting the mechanical from the organic . . .

And homed in upon Jack's breathing.

The armoured being ceased its marching; hinged flaps upon its shoulders raised, tiny rocket launchers rose and fired two tiny rockets.

These struck home quite close to Jack, causing him and Eddie great distress.

'So much for your theory about not wanting to fire his guns out here,' whispered Eddie. 'Shall we run some more?'

'I think it would be for the best.' Jack ducked some more and, hauling Eddie after him, he ran. 'Which way?' Jack asked as he reached a place where many possibilities existed.

'*That* way,' said Eddie, pointing.

'Do you know it's *that* way?'

Eddie shrugged beneath Jack's arm. 'Ursine intuition?' he suggested.

'Fair enough.' Jack ran in the direction of Eddie's choice.

Presently they found themselves in a dead-end situation. To the right and left of them high conveyor belts clattered; before them was a wall of riveted steel and behind them strolled the armoured maniac.

Difficult.

'Shoot him, Jack,' urged Eddie.

'I think we already tried that.'

'He might have a weak spot. Shoot him in the goolies.'

'I don't think he has any goolies.'

'Shut up! Be silent! Cease to speak!'

Jack and Eddie shut their mouths, fell silent and ceased to speak.

'Stupid,' said the armoured one. 'Stupid, stupid, stupid. You shot at me. You tried to kill me.'

'But,' said Eddie.

'*Shut up!* You shot at *me*. The saviour of Toy City. *Me!*'

'Who's speaking?' Jack asked.

'I told you to shut up. And put that ridiculous gun down.'

Jack dropped the 7.62 mm M134 General Clockwork Mini-gun. 'We give up,' he said.

'Of course you give up.' Cogs whirly-whirled, metal plates interlocked, armoured bits and bobs shifted and jigsaw-locked. 'You're dead; of course you give up.'

'That's not what I mean,' said Jack. 'I mean that Eddie and I *really* give up. We'll tell you everything you need to know. About the Maguffin. Everything. Well, obviously we won't tell *you*. But we'll tell the real *you*, if you know what I mean.'

'What *do* you mean?' The metallic monster drew nearer to Jack. Its chest rose and fell, expanding and contracting its shining coppery links.

'I mean I'll tell everything to your leader. To the one in charge.'

'I am in charge. I am PRIMROSE.'

'No,' said Jack. 'PRIMROSE is not in charge. You weren't telling us the truth. I'll tell everything to the one in charge. The *real* you. I know who you really are. I know your real name.'

'You know his real name?' Eddie made a puzzled face.

'You're going to kill us anyway,' said Jack. 'What harm can it do?'

'Not *that* again.'

'But what harm *can* it do?'

'None. No harm at all.' The being took a step back. Steel shutters fell over the telescopically visual eye attachments. The ear trumpets slid back into the head section. The armoured chest drew back. Legs and arms twisted, inverted.

A man of less than average height, with the large face and slender body of the potentially famous, now stood before them. He had a high forehead, deeply set eyes, a narrow nose and a bitter little mouth. He wore a rather splendid three-piece green tweed suit with a golden watch chain and a red silk cravat unknotted over the winged collar of a starched white shirt. He bore more than a strong resemblance to the toymaker.

'Mr Sredna, I presume,' said Jack. 'Sredna Sredna.'

'So you really *do* know my name,' said Mr Sredna.

'I'm very pleased to meet you,' said Jack. 'At last, and face to face.'

'I would shake your hand,' said Mr Sredna, 'but it is not to my choosing. How is it that you know my name?'

'Because I work for your company: the Sredna Corporation. We have a code 15 situation in New York.'

'A code 15?' said Mr Sredna.

'*New York?*' said Eddie.

'My name is Jon Kelly,' said Jack. 'Codename Jack, deep cover operative for the Sredna Corporation, offices in New York, London and Tokyo. I could not divulge my true identity earlier, because I was not certain that I was speaking to *you*. I'm certain now. I've very pleased to meet you, sir.'

'And I you, my boy.' Mr Sredna stepped forward and warmly shook Jack by the hand. 'Jon Kelly. I know you by reputation. A corporation man, who works only for the corporation. I am very pleased to meet you too.'

'*What?*' went Eddie. 'What is going on here? Jack?'

'Jon,' said Jon. 'Jon Kelly. I'm sorry I had to deceive you, Eddie. But business is business; I'm sure you understand.'

'I'm sure I *don't*,' said Eddie.

'Well, it's neither here nor there. Is there somewhere we can talk, Mr Sredna? Away from all this noise?'

'Jack?' Eddie shook his head. 'I don't understand any of this.'

'I'll just kill this stupid bear before we talk.' Mr Sredna glared at Eddie.

'Not worth the trouble,' said Jon. 'Let him come with us. He amuses me.'

'What?' went Eddie. 'What? What? What?'

At length they were no longer in the factory. They were high above it, in an elegantly appointed office several storeys up in the East Wing of the chocolate factory building.

The sun fell through a high mullioned window. The vista beyond the windows was of Knob Hill and the toymaker's house.

Mr Sredna sat behind an expansive desk laden with many precious things. Jon stood before the window, gazing out of it. Eddie sat upon the floor. Eddie was a very puzzled bear.

'This is a serious breach of security,' said Mr Sredna 'It is strictly forbidden.'

'The situation merited drastic action,' said Jon Kelly, turning. 'A number of serious faults have developed in the latest presidential model.'

'Surely not,' said Mr Sredna, making a surprised face. 'I oversaw the construction of that model myself. It should run flawlessly throughout its term of office. They've not let it get in the rain, have they? The buyers were told that it's not fully waterproof.'

Eddie made an exasperated face 'Will somebody *please* tell me what is going on?' he said. 'I'm losing my mind here.'

Jon Kelly (codename Jack) smiled down upon Eddie. 'You,' said he, 'are a very intelligent little bear. It has actually been a great pleasure working with you.'

'Thank you,' said Eddie. 'But . . .'

'We'll have to kill him, though,' said Mr Sredna.

'Of course,' said Jon Kelly. 'We can't have any loose ends dangling around. But it has been a pleasure. And as *I* will be killing him . . .'

'*You?*' said Eddie.

'It really doesn't matter if he knows the truth.' Jon Kelly smiled upon Eddie. 'My name, as I said, is Jon Kelly. I work for the Sredna Corporation, a corporation in the world beyond. Originally a toy company, it dates back two hundred years or so: Purveyors of Clockwork Automata to the Gentry. But times and tastes change. When I told you, Eddie, that there *was* another world out there, beyond the world of Toy

City, I was telling all of the truth. There *is* such a world. I come from there. I grew up there. I never worked in any clockwork factory, although I do know all about clockwork.'

'But Jack, everything we've been through together—'

'It was all for a purpose, Eddie. I had to contact Mr Sredna here. He's been missing for two months. We had to know what happened to him, why he had not returned to the outer world. However, Mr Sredna is a very hard man to track down.'

'I have to be,' said Mr Sredna. 'I am known here. I've had to remain in hiding and disguise until all my plans were completed.'

'I understand that now,' said Jon Kelly.

'But soon, everyone will know my name.' There was a terrible tone to the voice, and a madness in the eyes of Mr Sredna. Neither went unnoticed by either Eddie or Jon.

'Well, what you choose to do here in Toy City is *your* business,' said Jon Kelly, 'but what goes on out there in the world beyond is a different matter. And if a presidential model fails, then the Sredna Corporation's reputation is at stake.'

'What *is* a presidential model?' Eddie asked.

'A kind of toy,' said Jon. 'Mr Sredna here employs his toy-making skills in the world beyond. And he does make exceedingly good toys. Very life-like. The Sredna Corporation supplies these toys to countries all over our world. These toys then appear to run these countries. But naturally they don't actually do that. The owners of these toys are the big business consortiums that can afford to buy them from Mr Sredna. It's all just good business. It's a businessman thing.'

'It sounds ghastly,' said Eddie. 'It sounds as corrupt as.'

'Oh it is,' said Mr Sredna. 'Totally. But then, what isn't? Who isn't?'

'I'm not,' said Eddie. 'And I didn't think that Jack was. I'm very upset.'

'Your city is quite amazing,' Jon Kelly said to Mr Sredna. 'When the corporation executives sent me here to find you, they told me that this city was inhabited by toys which actually thought for themselves; actually lived their own lives. I never really believed them. Never thought it possible. There is a magic here in Toy City, there's no doubt about that.'

'Of course there is.' Mr Sredna leaned back in his chair and interlinked his long, narrow fingers. 'If it wasn't for the fact that certain things can be done here in this world that cannot be done out there, there could be no Sredna Corporation.'

Eddie punched himself violently in the head. 'I *am* going mad,' he declared. 'Jack, you're my friend. You're my bestest friend. You and I were tracking down the evil twin. Have you forgotten about that?'

Jon glanced towards Mr Sredna. 'What about *that*?' he asked.

'Nothing you need concern yourself with,' said Mr Sredna.

'I'd like to know.'

'Then you shall.' The madness was once more in the eyes. 'Those nursery rhymers: they deserved what they got. And I gave it to them, one at a time, in the order that they became famous. I've always hated them. I didn't mean for them to become rich and famous, but they did, and they had me to thank for it. But did they thank me? No, they sided with my brother and threw me out of the city.'

'Your brother?' said Eddie. 'Tell me about your brother.'

'The toymaker,' said Mr Sredna.

'So you *are* the evil twin. There, Jack, he's confessed.'

'I'm *not* evil! How dare you!' Mr Sredna brought his fists down hard upon the table. 'Evil twin this! Evil twin that! I'm not evil. Never was evil. I am *innovative*. Imaginative. *Special!* But because I didn't play by the rules, follow the instructions, do things the way they were supposed to be done, I was cast from this world by that ungrateful scum.'

Eddie cowered on the floor.

'Let me tell *you*,' said Mr Sredna, 'who really wrote those nursery rhymes.'

'Really wrote?' said Eddie. 'Didn't Wheatley Porterman write them?'

'*I* wrote them!' Mr Sredna fairly bellowed. 'They're supposed to be hymns, not damn nursery rhymes.'

'Hymns?' said Eddie. 'But—'

'Each one of them is a parable.' Mr Sredna leaned across his desk and scowled down at Eddie. 'They're *all* parables. Take the hymn of Jack and Jill: of course you can't go *up* a hill to fetch a pail of water. What the hymn really means is that if you spend your life seeking to achieve impossible goals, rather than doing something useful, you will surely tumble to earth. It's pretty damn obvious, isn't it?'

'I suppose it is,' said Eddie. 'So they're all like that, are they? They're all, like, parables; they all have real meanings?'

'Of course they do!' Mr Sredna drummed his fists upon his expansive desk, rattling precious things. 'They all mean something. They were supposed to be instructive. They were Holy Writ.'

'What?' said Jon Kelly.

'Holy Writ!' Mr Sredna's voice rose in zeal. 'Which is another reason that I was ousted. Gods aren't supposed to write their own Holy Writ. Gods are supposed to be "hands-off". Leave the writing of Holy

Writ to "inspired" mortals. And what happens to theirs? The same as happened to mine. Misinterpreted! You can't produce any kind of Holy Writ without some oaf misinterpreting it. I write deep-meaningful hymns. And the trash that I wrote those moving deep-meaningful hymns about, the examples of man's folly, they get rich and famous from the proceeds. And because I've upset them, they conspire against me and then rise up and throw me out of the city. Me, a God in my own right: they throw *me* out. What kind of insane irony is that, I ask you?'

Jon Kelly shook his head. 'I don't know,' he said.

'Enough to drive anyone mad,' said Mr Sredna. 'You think about any one of those "nursery rhymes", think about what the words actu-ally say, actually mean. But nobody ever has. It was all wasted, all my time and effort wasted. But not any more. Away with the old and in with the new. All of this is going, all of it.'

'All?' said Eddie.

'I'm erasing the city,' said Mr Sredna. 'Starting with the rich and famous folk, then working all the way down.'

'To the toys?' said Eddie.

'All going,' said Mr Sredna, making sweeping hand motions. 'As soon as the new order comes off the assembly lines, I'll have them do away with the old. It has been all fun and games for me, wiping out the old rich one at a time, coming up with ingenious scenarios, throwing the city into chaos. This city is a mess, but I'm changing all that: a Heaven on Earth, and I shall be the God in this Heaven.'

'And your brother?' said Eddie. 'What about your brother?'

'He'll have to go too. He's an old fool. He believes in the "hands off" school of deity, that a God should simply let things happen, remain neutral. If you want someone to blame for the way this city is now, blame him. If I'd been around I'd never have let it get into this state. But I'm back now and things are going to be very different. Very, very different. So it's goodbye to the kindly loveable white-haired old toy-maker. And not before time, in my opinion.'

Jon looked at Eddie.

And Eddie looked at Jon.

Neither had anything to say.

'But let's get back to business,' said Mr Sredna, smiling towards Jon. 'A problem with the presidential model, you said.'

'Its decision-making processes are not functioning as precisely as might be desired. It seems to be growing altogether too fierce. Might I say, somewhat warlike.'

'Nothing wrong with warlike,' said Mr Sredna. 'Warlike I like. You can quote me on that, if *you* like.'

'The corporation does *not* like,' said Jon. 'The Sredna Corporation's products are held in such high esteem by the companies that purchase them because they are designed to keep the peace. To uphold order and maintain the status quo.'

'Oh, *that*,' said Eddie. 'We all know about the status quo here in Toy City.'

'Shut up, bear,' said Mr Sredna.

'He has a point,' said Jon Kelly.

'Yes, and I've explained why this city is such a mess. Because I was thrown out and my stupid brother was left in charge. And what did he do? Remained neutral, let free will take its course. Free will! Free will was never a good concept. Social order is only maintained if every will is guided towards a single purpose, that of maintaining the status quo.'

'All right for some,' said Eddie, 'those at the top. Rubbish for the rest of us.'

'The rest of you will soon be no more,' said Mr Sredna. 'Those of you who will bow the knee to the new social order will survive to do so. The rest will be disappeared.'

'Jack,' said Eddie, 'say something to this loony. You're not going along with all this, are you? You don't really believe in all this? I know you, Jack. You *are* my bestest friend. I can't believe you're a part of this. Tell me it's not so.'

'Sorry,' said Jon Kelly. 'It's business. The world out there is a mess too. It needs order. It needs control. Mr Sredna's creations have given order to the world out there for the last hundred years. Apart from the occasional hiccough or two.'

'Oh, yes,' said Mr Sredna. 'You're going to mention Hitler, aren't you? Whenever there is a design problem or a mechanical fault, you people always bring up Hitler.'

'He was more than a mechanical fault.'

'A couple of cogwheels in the wrong place. I apologised.'

'So I understand,' said Jon Kelly. 'Sorry to mention him.'

'Hitler?' said Eddie. 'Who's Hitler?'

'You really don't want to know,' said Jon Kelly. 'But listen, Mr Sredna. Something has to be done about the current presidential model. You will have to come in person and rectify the faults.'

'Yes, yes, all right. But not until I've finished my business here. I have to finish off the famous folk and my brother and I want to be here when my ladies come marching off the assembly lines. I've put a lot of work into all of this, sneaking back into the city over the years—back into *my own* chocolate factory. But it's all been worth it: soon my ladies will all be up and ready to march. They're beautiful, aren't they, my ladies? An entirely new order of being. Part human, part toy and part arachnid.'

'Spiders?' said Eddie, shuddering.

'Wonderful creatures, arachnids,' said Mr Sredna. 'They don't ask any questions. They just *do*. But what I am saying is, this project is near to conclusion. You, Mr Kelly, have come here at a very bad time. But I couldn't come to your world, even if I wanted to.'

'Why not?' Jon asked.

'You know why not. I don't have the key. *You* have it though, don't you?'

'Key?' said Eddie.

'The Maguffin,' said Mr Sredna. 'That all-important something, the all-importantness of which does not become apparent until its moment has come.'

'It's a key?' said Eddie. 'To what?'

'It's *The* key,' said Mr Sredna. 'For opening the door between this world and the one beyond. There are two such keys, one mine and one belonging to my brother. When I was cast out of this world, I took with me not only the rest of the instructions for building the city, I also took both keys. Well, I didn't want my brother following me out at any time and interfering with whatever I chose to get up to out there. My brother's key remains forever on the outside. It was used, without my permission, to let Mr Kelly in here.'

'It was an emergency,' said Jon Kelly.

'I understand that. My key, however, was stolen from me and it fell into the dextrous hands of Tinto the clockwork barman.'

'I have it here,' said Jon Kelly. And from his grubby trenchcoat pocket Jon Kelly produced the Maguffin and laid it upon the expansive desk of Mr Sredna. 'Control is everything. Complete control; the operations out there in the world beyond need your creations to maintain that control. What you do here is of no concern to us. We only care about that.'

'Indeed,' said Mr Sredna, reaching across the desk and greedily availing himself of the Maguffin.

'Jack,' said Eddie.

'It's Jon,' said Jon.

'Jon,' said Eddie. 'You are a thorough-going piece of clockwork cat crap and I hate you.'

'Mr Sredna,' said Jon Kelly, 'do you have a hand-gun about your person?'

'I can readily convert,' said Mr Sredna. 'You've seen the might of my armoured protection system.'

'A hand-gun will be fine.'

'Then I have one here.' Mr Sredna delved into a desk drawer, drew out a clockwork pistol and tossed it over the expansive desk to Jon Kelly, who caught it.

'Eddie,' said Jon Kelly, 'you'll probably want to close your eyes while I do this.'

'They don't close,' said Eddie. 'You know that, *Jack*.'

'*Jon*,' said Jon Kelly. 'Turn your face away, then.'

'No,' said Eddie. 'I'm going to look you right in the eyes when you do this. I cared about you, Jack, and I thought that you cared about me, but it was all lies, wasn't it?'

'It's twist and turns,' said Jon Kelly. 'Just like a Bill Winkie thriller. And in a Bill Winkie thriller you never know exactly who's who until the end. And now you sort of know who's who, because this *is* the end.'

'Do it then,' said Eddie. 'If you have to do it, do it.' And a tear rose up in Eddie's brown button eye. 'But I really did care.'

Jon Kelly aimed the hand-gun and Jon Kelly squeezed the trigger.

'Sorry, Eddie,' he said.

29

A single shot rang out.

A steel bullet, powered by a clockwork action, left the barrel of the gun at approximately nine hundred feet per second, passed through a fabricated forehead and left via the cerebellum, taking a considerable quantity of sawdust with it and spreading this liberally over a wall that lay beyond.

'It is done,' said Jon Kelly.

Mr Sredna said nothing.

Eddie looked up at the young man who held the clockwork pistol. And the young man looked down at Eddie.

'What?' said Jack.

'Jack,' Eddie said. 'You just shot Mr Sredna.'

'And why wouldn't I?' Jack shrugged. 'He was the evil twin.'

'Yes, but *you* just shot him. *You.* You're on his side. You were supposed to be shooting me.'

'I lied,' said Jack. 'You can forgive me for that, can't you?'

'*Forgive you?* I all but pooed myself!'

'I'm sorry, but I had to get a gun from him somehow.'

'Er,' Eddie smote at his head, 'I'm really confused. Really, *really* confused. I really should be able to figure this out.' Eddie smote at his head a lot more.

'You won't be able to.' Jack walked around the expansive desk and stared down at his handiwork. Mr Sredna was slumped back in his chair. There was a big hole in his forehead and a lot of sawdust beyond. 'I really hated that,' said Jack.

'*You* hated it? How do you think I feel? I thought you were going to kill me.'

'I know, and I'm truly sorry, but that's not what I meant. What I meant was, I really hated all that talking. I told you how much I hated it in the Bill Winkie books. How the hero gets disarmed and he has to listen to the villain talking and talking. Mind you, I do see the point now. Everything does have to be explained.'

'Is he dead?' Eddie asked.

'I certainly hope so,' said Jack. 'But look at that. His head was full of sawdust. He wasn't even a man at all. He was a toy all along.'

'He was a God, Jack.'

'Well, he's a dead God now.'

Eddie shook his puzzled head. It was full of sawdust too, but happily, *still* full. 'Do you think you might be up to telling me what, in the name of any God you choose to believe in, really is going on?'

'Most of what I said,' said Jack. 'All, in fact. Except I'm not Jon Kelly.'

'Brilliant,' said Eddie. 'So who *is* Jon Kelly and how do you know all this stuff and why didn't you tell me any of it?'

'One piece at a time,' said Jack, putting his fingers on the neck of the seemingly deceased Mr Sredna and feeling for a pulse. None was evident and so Jack wiped his sawdusty fingers upon Mr Sredna's jacket, took up the Maguffin from the desk and tucked it back into his trenchcoat pocket. 'I'm *not* Jon Kelly,' Jack said. 'Jon Kelly came to my town. He wanted directions to the city. He was lost. And he was a real nutter. He had a gun and he didn't seem too concerned about who he shot with it. He was looking for a Mr Sredna; he came to the factory where I worked. He thought that was the factory run by Sredna, but obviously it wasn't. He got very angry about that, pointed his gun at me, ordered me to steal one of the clockwork cars and drive him to the city. And he talked and he talked and he talked. He told me everything.'

'Why did he do that?' Eddie asked.

'Because I asked him what harm it would do, seeing as how he was going to kill me anyway.'

'Seems to work pretty well, that ploy,' said Eddie. 'But go on with this unlikely tale of yours, Jack.'

'He told me all about the world beyond, and about the Sredna Corporation and the presidential model and everything, really. But at the time I just thought he was a madman. He did tell me that there was wealth to be found here in the city, though. And I wanted to escape from the factory anyway. And we had travelled quite a distance before I . . .'

'What?' asked Eddie.

'Crashed the car,' said Jack. 'It wasn't my fault. He had a gun to my head and I'd never driven a car before. But he went right out through the windscreen. He was dead. I didn't know what to do. I didn't want to go back; I hated working in that factory. And Jon Kelly had told me all about the wealth in the city. Though he hadn't gone into any detail; he hadn't told me it was Toy City. Or about the toys. So I pressed on. I walked. I got lost. I fell into the farmer's hole. I almost got eaten. I came here and met you.'

'And now you've killed the evil twin. And saved Toy City,' said Eddie. 'Pretty good result.'

'Seems like,' said Jack. 'Although it certainly wasn't what I set out to do. I wanted to get rich. I came here to seek my fortune.'

'You've saved us all,' said Eddie. 'That's worth any fortune.'

'Perhaps it is,' said Jack. 'None of this has been exactly what I expected.'

'But why didn't you tell me?'

'Because I'm an atheist,' said Jack. 'And a sceptic and whatever. I didn't believe it all. And I thought it was better just to keep my mouth shut about it. I wasn't exactly expecting to actually meet up with this Mr Sredna that Jon Kelly was looking for. I didn't even know if there was such a person. And then you told me that this chocolate factory was founded by a Mr Sredna. And how many Mr Srednas can there be? And Sredna is, of course, Anders spelt backwards. The evil opposite of Anders, eh?'

'I suppose it makes some kind of sense,' said Eddie. 'And it's a nice twist in the tale. Is he definitely dead?'

'Seems like,' said Jack. 'And he's already starting to pong like the spider-women. There's stuff leaking out of him. How dead can you be?'

'As dead as, I hope,' said Eddie. 'I suppose we should go and find the famous folk; what do you think, Jack?'

'I think it would be for the best. I'm sorry I had to frighten you like that. But I had to get Mr Sredna out of armoured mode so that I could actually . . .'

'Kill him?' said Eddie.

'It's not nice,' said Jack. 'It's not a nice thing to do. I know that it had to be done. It was either him or you. But it's still not nice.'

'It wasn't a person,' said Eddie. 'It was a thing.'

'In the same way that you're a thing?'

'Ah yes, I see what you mean. But you did the right thing, Jack. You killed the right thing.'

'I *did* do the right thing, didn't I?' said Jack.

'No kidding,' said Eddie. 'Let's go and liberate those famous folk.'

30

Curiously, the rich and famous folk did not seem altogether glad to see Jack and Eddie. It took the detectives nearly an hour of searching before they eventually discovered them, all locked up together in a basement cell, the door of which taxed Jack's lock-picking skills to their limits.

The rich and famous folk did not smile upon their liberators.

'We were under protection down here,' said Old King Cole. 'Go away and leave us alone.'

'The danger has passed,' Jack told him.

'I don't think it has,' said Mary Mary.

'The evil twin is dead,' said Eddie. 'Jack has killed him. You can all clear off home.'

'How dare you address royalty in that insolent manner.' Old King Cole raised high his nose. 'In fact, how dare you address me at all, you tatty little bear.'

'One more remark like that,' Jack told Old King 'and I will be forced to give you a smack.'

'Outrageous! Go away, and relock the door behind you.'

'Tempting, isn't it?' Eddie whispered.

'Very,' said Jack. 'Now all of you go home. Eddie and I have been up all night and we seriously need some breakfast.'

'And when will ours be served?' asked Old King. 'Make yourselves useful and cut along to the kitchen. I'll have double-whipped-cream-smothered muffins with—'

Jack slammed the cell door shut upon the rich and famous folk.

'I think we'll come back tomorrow,' he said to Eddie.

'Sweet as,' said the bear.

★

Together they plodded up the cellar steps, through this door and that, and finally out into the great courtyard.

The sun was high in the heavens now, beaming its blessings down upon Knob Hill, colouring the rooftops of the toymaker's house. All was sun-kissed and serene.

Jack took a deep breath, and then fell to coughing. 'What is that terrible pong?' he asked. 'Not the . . .'

Eddie sniffed the air. 'The wind would be in the east today,' he said. 'That would be coming from the slaughterhouse district.'

'Rather spoils the ambience,' said Jack.

'Never,' said Eddie, sniffing hungrily. 'I love the smell of offal in the morning.'

'Do you know what we have to do?' Jack asked.

Eddie took another sniff. 'Eat breakfast?' he suggested. 'Definitely eat breakfast.'

'Not yet, I'm afraid. We have to go to the toymaker's house.'

'But why?' Eddie asked. 'Look at me. I may smell like dung, but I'm unscathed. Which is pretty nifty, really. Bill never came out of an adventure with less than a bruise or two. I'm not even scuffed.'

'We have to tell the toymaker,' said Jack. 'Tell him everything. Tell him about his brother.'

'Oh dear.' Eddie shook his head. 'I'm not keen, Jack. You're going to admit to him that you killed his brother.'

'I said tell him *everything*. He has to know.'

'Perhaps we'll tell him tomorrow. Or *you* could. There's no real need for me to be there.'

'We'll both tell him.' Jack made a very stern face. 'Things will have to be organised, Eddie. Someone is going to have to run this city properly from now on.'

'The toymaker?'

'I can't think of anyone else, can you?'

Eddie scratched at his head. 'Well,' he said, 'I'd be prepared to have a go at being mayor. What would the wages be like, do you think?'

Jack made sighing sounds.

'Yeah, well,' said Eddie, 'I can dream.'

Jack was for walking up the hill, the day being so sunny and all, but Eddie's little legs were tired, so Jack drove him up in the Mark 22 Hyperglide limousine.

'Probably the last opportunity I'll ever get to be driven in style,' said Eddie as Jack lifted him from the limousine and set him down upon the gravel drive.

Jack sighed once more. 'I remain optimistic,' he said. 'Remember, I came to this city to seek my fortune. Perhaps when it's under proper management, opportunities might present themselves.'

'Not to the likes of me,' said Eddie.

'Don't be so sure; when the toymaker sees the way things really are, there'll be some big changes made.'

'So I might still get a chance to be mayor.'

Jack rolled his eyes.

'I know,' said Eddie. 'Dream on, little bear.'

Jack and Eddie approached the big front door.

'Not you two *again*!' Peter scowled.

'We're really tired,' said Jack. 'We're tired and we're hungry and our tempers are very short. Knock your knocker smartly, or I will tear it right off the door and fling it down the drive.'

'Knock knock knock knock knock,' went Peter's knocker.

And presently the big front door eased open and the face of the kindly loveable white-haired old toymaker peeped out.

'Can I help you?' asked the toymaker.

Jack grinned painfully. Eddie took to trembling. 'Might we come in, sir?' Jack asked.

The toymaker wore upon his kindly loveable white-haired old head a leather cap affair, drawn down low to the bridge of his nose. Attached to this was a complicated eyeglass contraption.

The toymaker pushed the eyeglass aside. 'Pardon this,' he said. 'My eyesight is not as good as what it once was. But come in, do, I always have time for guests.'

Peter made grumbling sounds.

'You're most kind, sir,' said Jack.

The toymaker ushered them in and closed the big front door behind them. 'Into my workshop,' he said. 'Down the corridor there.'

Jack, with Eddie once more clinging to his leg, stepped down the narrow corridor and once more into the workshop.

'Sit down,' said the toymaker, indicating the comfy chair.

'I'd prefer to stand, sir,' said Jack.

'As you wish, as you wish.'

'We're very sorry to trouble you,' said Jack. 'But we have come here on a very grave matter.'

'Oh dear, I don't like the sound of this. I don't like grave matters. They are usually most horrid.'

'I think,' said Jack, 'that it might be for the best if you were to accompany us immediately to the chocolate factory. There is something you must see. Many things, in fact.'

'The chocolate factory? I haven't been there for years and years. Do they still produce those delightful little hollow chocolate bunnies?'

'Amongst other things,' said Jack.

'Wonderful,' said the toymaker. 'But not today, thank you. I'm far too busy. Perhaps in a month or so.'

'It has to be today,' said Jack. 'In fact, it has to be now.'

'No, it cannot be today.'

Jack took a step forward. 'It *has* to be today,' he said.

'I don't think I like your tone, young man.' The toymaker took a step back.

Jack took another step forward. 'I'm sorry,' he said, 'but it *has* to be today. And now. You have to know what has been going on in your city. It's very bad and you are going to be very upset, but you have to come with us now.'

'And what if I refuse?'

'I really am sorry, sir,' said Jack, squaring up before the ancient, 'but if you refuse, I will be forced to drag you.'

'Jack, no!' Eddie tugged at Jack's rotten trenchcoat.

'Sorry, Eddie, this has to be done.'

'No, Jack.' Eddie's nose began to twitch. A curious smell had suddenly reached it.

'Sir,' said Jack, 'come with us, please.'

'Jack,' whispered Eddie, 'I smell a smell.'

'Not now, Eddie. So, sir, will you come?'

'I think not,' said the toymaker.

'Then I'm truly sorry.' Jack reached forward to grasp the old man's shoulders.

'That smell,' said Eddie. 'It's getting stronger.'

Jack gripped the ancient by his narrow, bony shoulders and gently tugged at him. The old man didn't move. Jack tugged a little harder. The old man remained rooted to the spot. Jack tugged very hard this time. But the toymaker would not budge.

He simply remained right where he was. Old and frail. But unmoveable.

'Come on now,' puffed Jack, pulling with all his might.

'I think not.' The toymaker slowly reached up between Jack's dragging hands and removed the leather cap that he wore upon his kindly white-haired old head.

Jack stared and then Jack ceased his futile tuggings. And then Jack took a step or two back. Three steps in fact. And very smartly indeed.

In the very centre of the toymaker's kindly loveable old forehead there was a hole. It was a neat, round hole. The kind of hole that a bullet fired from a clockwork pistol might make.

'*You!*' said Jack. 'It's you.'

'That would be the smell,' Eddie whispered.

'Me,' said Mr Sredna.

'But I shot you dead.'

'Do I look dead to you?'

'Oh dear,' said Jack. 'Oh dear, oh dear.'

'And you call yourselves detectives.' Mr Sredna laughed. It was Tinto's laugh, the one that resembled small stones being shaken about in an empty tin can. 'But you had me going there, almost. I believed you were Jon Kelly. But I never take chances. You shot a false head.' Mr Sredna lifted this head from his shoulders and cast it down to the floor. An identical head rose up through the collar of his shirt. 'This is my real head,' he said, 'and you won't be shooting this one.'

'Oh dear,' said Jack once more.

Eddie might have had something to say, but he was far too scared to say it.

'Fun and games,' said Mr Sredna. 'It was such a delight to see you running around Toy City, always too late.' Mr Sredna glared down at Eddie, who had taken to cowering behind Jack's leg. 'I do have to say,' said he, 'that, on the whole, you're not a bad detective. Not as good as Bill Winkie though, but then he knew that I was the prime suspect. He tracked me down to the chocolate factory within twenty-four hours of receiving his advance money and being put on the case.'

'He did?' said Eddie, fearfully. 'He never told me that he did.'

'I don't think he wanted to put you in danger. He broke into Humpty Dumpty's apartment and worked out how I'd done it. The moment he saw that lens in the roof he knew it had to be me. Or perhaps it was my little chocolate calling card in the fridge.'

Eddie might have shrugged, but his shoulders were too trembly.

'And then he broke into the chocolate factory while I was asleep. Searched the place. Even found my strongroom. All that gold down there had him thinking. And so did the Maguffin. He found that along with all my maps of the outer world and my accounts books. He stole the Maguffin to trap me here in this world and must have passed it to Tinto for safekeeping. Probably, I think now, so that Tinto would pass it on to you if something happened to Bill and you continued with the case.'

'He *was* very clever.' Eddie shook fearfully.

'But not *that* clever. The next morning he went to see Chief Inspector Bellis to tell him that *I* was the murderer and lead him and all his men to the chocolate factory in the hope of capturing me. But he never got to see the real Chief Inspector Bellis; I just happened to be loafing around outside the police station, impersonating the real Inspector. He was very brave, was Bill Winkie, he never talked, even under all that torture. He wouldn't tell me what he'd done with my Maguffin.'

If Eddie had been able to make fists, he would have made very big ones now.

'And that's about all,' said Mr Sredna. 'There isn't anything else to say. I won't bother to ask you for the Maguffin, Jack. Neither you nor the bear will be leaving this room alive.'

'Now hold on,' said Jack. 'Don't be hasty.'

'There goes that déjà-vu again.'

'I'm sure that we could come to some arrangement.'

'I pride myself,' said Mr Sredna, 'upon having an all-but-limitless imagination. I can think up things that no other mortal being can think up. Apart from that one over there.' Mr Sredna gestured towards the bound and gagged and quivering toymaker, all bunched up in the corner. 'And the remaining moments of his life are numbered in seconds. But even I, with all of my imagination, cannot think of any arrangement that might be made which does not involve you dying.'

'You may well have a point there.' Jack's eyes darted all around the room in search of, perhaps, some very large and deadly weapon. Or something else that might provide a final twist in the tale and allow him and Eddie to miraculously survive.

Nothing was immediately forthcoming.

Mr Sredna snapped the fingers of his right hand. The fingers extended; the fingertips hinged; evil-looking blades sprung forth.

'You first,' said Mr Sredna, pointing at Eddie. 'Shredded teddy, I think.'

'No you don't.' Jack raised his fists.

'Don't be absurd, Jack.' Mr Sredna lunged forward, swinging his unclawed fist. It struck Jack in the side of the head, carried him from his feet, across the workbench and down the other side, where he fell to the floor next to the kindly loveable white-haired, all-tied-up-and-trembly old toymaker.

Jack floundered about amongst the sawdust bales and rolls of fabric. Jack heard a terrible scream from Eddie.

And then Jack leapt back to his feet. He saw Mr Sredna holding Eddie by his un-special-tagged ear and he saw the claws, glistening and twinkling in the glow from the firelight. And he saw the hand swing and the claws go in, piercing Eddie's chest, shredding the cinnamon-coloured mohair plush fur fabric, spraying out sawdust, tearing once, then tearing again and again.

'No,' screamed Jack, and he leapt onto the table and then onto Mr Sredna. Shredded Eddie flew in every direction: a cascade of arms and legs and belly and bits and bobs. Jack's momentum bore the evil twin over, but he was up in an instant and he flung Jack down and stood astride him, grinning hideously.

'You killed him.' There were tears in Jack's eyes. 'You evil shit. You wicked, vicious, filthy . . .'

'Shut it,' said Mr Sredna. 'It was only a toy. A toy teddy bear. A big boy like you shouldn't get weepy over a toy teddy bear.'

'He was my friend.'

'That's very sad,' said Mr Sredna. 'A big boy like you should have grown out of toys. A big boy like you should have got yourself a girl-friend.'

Jack crawled back upon his bottom, but he really had nowhere to crawl to.

'In a way I'm sorry that you have to die too.' Mr Sredna grinned as he spoke. He didn't look *that* sorry. 'Folk here are so dull, do you know what I mean? They lack any kind of spirit. But you're full of it. Independent. And tricking me into believing that you were Jon Kelly: inspired.'

'Rather obvious, I would have thought,' said Jack.

'I'm trying to pay you a compliment. Being an innovative hands-on sort of a God is a very lonely calling. You can always do with a bit of stimulating conversation. But I never seem to be able to get that. No one in my own league, you see. So I just make do with having lots of sex. They're very sexy, my women, aren't they?'

'You're quite mad.' Jack curled his lip. 'You're insane.'

'They said that about Hitler. Fancy Jon Kelly telling you about him. But Hitler wasn't actually mad. He was the way I made him: a bit of a prototype. Wait until the folk out there find out what the new president of America is going to do. They sent Jon Kelly here because they were worried about the way he was behaving. They have no idea, but it is going to be *spectacular*. He'll be employing a private army. And my private army will be unstoppable.'

'And then you'll be in charge of everything, will you? Not just here in Toy City.'

'Today Toy City! Tomorrow the World!' Mr Sredna laughed that laugh that evil geniuses laugh. The one that really gets on the hero's nerves.

'Mad.' Jack wiped tears from his eyes. 'Quite mad.'

'It's simply beyond your comprehension.' Mr Sredna reached down with his clawed hand and hauled Jack back up by the throat, lifting him once more from his feet. 'Small minds have no comprehension. I am indeed one of a kind, placed upon this planet by the Big Figure himself.'

'You'll answer to Him,' said Jack. 'You'll answer to God.'

'Oh, I don't think so. He's no longer interested in this planet. The universe really *is* a big construction kit, given to him as a birthday present by his father. But you know what kids are. Once they've done a jigsaw or completed some puzzle or other, they're no longer interested in it. God gave mankind free will, they say. God does not interfere in the affairs of man, they say. It's because he's not interested. He's done this planet. He's moved on. Perhaps one day he will put the entire kit back in its box, but probably not. You know kids, do they *ever* put anything back in its box?'

'So you'll rule here?' Jack's hopelessness was now all-consuming, and the terrible emptiness he felt, with Eddie dead, left him without much in the way of a will to live—although he would have dearly loved to have wrung the life from the toymaker's evil twin. 'You'll rule this planet and no one can stop you?'

'I don't see anyone, do you?'

Jack might have shaken his head, but with the hand so tightly fixed about his throat, he was unable to do so. 'And so can you be killed?' Jack managed to say.

Mr Sredna laughed once more. 'Of course I can be killed; I'm not immortal. I'm very much like the nursery rhyme folk in that respect; old-time craftsmanship, you see, built to last. I mean, look at me, Jack. Not bad for a man of six thousand, am I? That Adam and Eve who seeded the garden in the outer world didn't last too long. Things really are different in this world. We still have the magic. So, yes Jack. I can be killed, but not by you. You left the gun back in the chocolate factory after you shot the wrong head. There are no more twists in the tale left for you.'

And the fingers closed about Jack's throat.

And that, for all it seemed to be, was sadly that for Jack.

31

It is a fact, well known to those who know it well, that, at the moment of death, your entire life flashes right before your eyes.

In fact, this fact is known to almost everyone. Although why this should actually be is something of a mystery.

Because, let's face it, who has actually verified this fact?

Has anyone ever really come back from the dead to tell it like it is? No, they haven't.

'Oh yes they have!' cry those who lack for a life and a girlfriend. 'Otherwise how would we know this fact?'

But, 'Oh no they haven't,' reply the knowers. 'No one has *ever* come back from the dead.'

Being dead is being dead. Being brought back from the dead means that you weren't really dead at all; you were only in a dead-like state. You just can't bring people back from the dead.

You can't. You really can't.

Now Jack might have taken issue with this, because as Mr Sredna squeezed him to death, Jack's life did flash right before his eyes. Very fast, but in very great detail.

Jack saw every bit of it: himself being born, and growing up in that small industrial town. And he saw himself indentured as an apprentice into the clockwork factory there and hating every minute of it. And he saw himself meeting with Jon Kelly. And then being involved in the terrible car crash. And then his lonely wanderings and the cannibal farmer and Toy City and Eddie.

And Jack realised that Eddie really had been the bestest friend that he'd ever had. And then things became a bit metaphysical and Jack felt himself moving towards other places, places of after-existence—

perhaps to the realms where young God was still putting bits of his construction kit together, creating new worlds, worlds that, Jack hoped, would be a great deal better than this one.

All these things flashed right before Jack's eyes. In seconds.

And then Jack's eyes couldn't see anything any more—anything, that is, but the colour red, which, as those who know the facts well know, and the rest of us know too, is the colour of blood.

Jack was suddenly covered in blood.

Jack gasped and gagged and wiped his eyes and blurry vision returned.

And somebody stood over Jack.

And that somebody wasn't Mr Sredna.

Out of the redness Jack returned, at a jolt, and a hurry-up too. He felt water upon his face. He opened his eyes and he stared.

'Jill,' said Jack. 'Jill, it's you.'

'It's me,' said Jill. 'And you owe me money. I told you I charge double for virgins. And there's the other money, there's . . .'

'Eddie.' Jack struggled back to his feet. 'Is he?'

'Sorry,' said Jill.

'No, he can't be. If I'm not, he can't be.'

'Don't think about him. I saved you, Jack. I've been following you since you got arrested. I want my money.'

'You followed me for the money? You did *that*?' Jack looked down at the body of Mr Sredna. Mr Sredna was well and truly dead this time. His body lacked for a head and his chest was full of holes. Jack looked at Jill.

'Well, I had to be sure,' said Jill. 'You screwed it up when you did it.'

Jack shook his head. 'And you did this all because I owe you money?'

'Well, perhaps not entirely for the money.' Jill turned her eyes down from Jack's gaze. 'There's something about you. I don't know what it is. But it makes you special.'

'Thank you.' Jack crossed the workroom, being careful as he did so not to step upon any shreddings of Eddie. Jack stooped and untied the kindly loveable white-haired old toymaker. 'Are you all right, sir?' Jack asked as he helped the ancient into the comfy chair.

'Somewhat shaken,' said the toymaker. 'This has all been a terrible shock. I had tried my best to forget about my brother. Forget that he'd even existed. I'm a very foolish old man.'

Jack patted the toymaker on the shoulder and looked up at Jill.

'I'm sorry I didn't get here in time to save your little friend,' she said. 'When I saw what was happening, I acted as fast as I could.'

'I know,' said Jack.

'You *know*?'

'I saw you,' Jack said. 'I saw you creeping in through the window, which was why I asked him whether he could be killed. I thought the information might come in handy for you. I saw you had the gun from his office.'

'Smart boy,' said Jill.

'Yes,' said Jack in a toneless tone. 'Very smart. But too late for Eddie.'

'You really loved that bear, didn't you?'

Tears were once more in Jack's eyes. And he made no attempt to hide them. 'I'm not ashamed to say it, Jill. He really was my bestest friend.'

'Perhaps,' said the toymaker, 'I could make you another bear.'

'Thanks,' said Jack. 'But it wouldn't be the same. Eddie was one of a kind.'

'And I think I still am,' came a tiny voice from a disembodied growler. 'Will somebody help me, please?'

32

It was two whole days before Jack got around to releasing all the rich and famous folk from their place of incarceration. Well, he'd had other things to do, and actually, he'd quite forgotten about them.

They were very polite to Jack, though, when he opened the cell door. Very gracious. Very thankful. Very hungry.

Jack wasn't at all hungry. He'd just dined at the very finest restaurant in the City. It wasn't a *Nadine's Diner*.

Jack was presently dining again in that self-same restaurant. He was there with Jill, to celebrate their engagement.

True, both Jack and Jill were underage, but hey, this was Toy City; let's not let a little detail like that stand in the way of true love.

And true, Jill *had* said that she fancied marrying a prince. But then Jack was a prince now. An honorary prince, but a prince none the less. The toymaker had bestowed this honour upon him.

Eddie dined with Jack and Jill. And Eddie very much enjoyed the meal. He had double portions of everything. Especially those complicated things that need holding down with a fork and slicing with a knife.

And when, at great length, the meal had reached its conclusion, Eddie looked up at Jack. 'I don't know how to thank you enough,' Eddie said. 'There are no words to express my thanks for these.'

Eddie pulled back the cuffs of his brand new trench-coat and flexed his dextrous fingers and their opposable thumbs.

'The toymaker worked very hard putting you back together,' said Jack. 'And although he really didn't approve, I eventually managed to talk him into fitting you with those. Because, after all, there were so many spare parts in the chocolate factory just going begging, and who deserved a couple of them more than you?'

'Thanks, Jack,' said Eddie. 'Would you like to see me pick my nose again?'

'Not just now,' said Jack. 'Although, don't get me wrong, I certainly enjoyed it all the other times you've showed me.'

Eddie gazed proudly at his dextrous fingers. 'They're a lovely shade of cinnamon,' he said. 'They match my new coat.'

'You're an Anders Imperial now,' said Jack. 'Except for your head, of course. I didn't let him touch your head. Other than for putting a proper special button for your ear. And the new matching eyes, of course. They're working all right, I trust.'

'Absolutely.' Eddie blinked his bright blue glass eyes. 'They're as optically efficient as. I had no idea there were so many colours to see.'

'Glad you like them,' said Jack.

'So what do you intend to do now?' Eddie asked 'Buy yourself a nice big house on Knob Hill with your half of the reward? It was good of the toymaker to make the rich folk cough up the money they'd promised to Bill for solving the case, wasn't it?'

'It certainly was,' said Jack. 'But Jill and I are not staying in Toy City.'

'What?' Eddie's eyes blinked and widened. 'But I hoped you'd live next door to me.'

'We're leaving,' said Jack. 'I have to go out there, to the world beyond. I have the Maguffin key and the toymaker's permission to use it. They're in a real mess out there and I can help to put things right.'

'That's none of our business,' Eddie said. 'No, Jack, don't go.'

'I'll be back,' said Jack, 'once I've made the necessary adjustments to the clockwork heads of their world leaders. And I *can* do that. I do know clockwork.'

'But you promise that you will be back?'

'Of course I promise. I wouldn't leave my bestest friend for ever, would I?'

'Certainly not,' said Eddie. 'Especially when he's a bestest friend of high standing. I've decided to take the mayor's job.'

'Oh yes?' Jack raised an eyebrow. 'And who offered you this job?'

'The toymaker, of course. I subtly broached the subject while I was removing his doorknocker and installing a new bell. It took a great deal of gentle persuasion, and Peter tried to put him off. But he came around in the end. Him being so kindly and lovable and grateful and everything.'

'You'll make a great mayor,' said Jack.

'There will be some sweeping social reforms,' said Eddie. 'I'm drafting out something that I like to call a constitution. It has things written into it, such as "we find it self-evident that all men and toys are created equal". And I'm working on other things too. Things of a religious nature, based on all these parables I know.'

'Sounds good,' said Jack. 'Sounds perfect.'

'Hopefully so.' Eddie grinned. 'And if I haven't thanked you enough, Jill, for saving all our lives, let me take this opportunity to thank you once again. I hope you and Jack will be very happy together. And you never know, if one day you have little Jacks and Jills of your own, and they need an old toy bear to play with, you can always bring them around to the mayoral mansion and I'll be more than happy to oblige.'

Jill smiled upon Eddie. 'I'm beginning to understand just what you see in this bear, Jack,' she said. 'There's definitely something special about him.'

'Oh yes,' Jack raised his glass to the bear. 'He's Eddie,' Jack said. 'He's as special as.'

the toyminator

FOR
JAMES CAMPBELL

FRIEND AND MENTOR.

Who inspired the writing of this book,
as with many others

And who put me back together
when I had all but fallen apart

No finer friend could any man have.

Thank you Jim.

1

The rain came down in great big buckets, emptied from the sky.

The city's population stayed indoors. Those of the clockwork persuasion greatly feared the rain, for rain brought on the terrible rust, the terrible corrosion. Those of fur dreaded sogginess, and those of wood, the stains. The rubber ducks were happy, though, but then they always are.

The city was Toy City, formerly Toy Town, and it stood there, somewhere over the rainbow, just off the Yellow Brick Road and beyond the mysterious Second Big O. And it stood there at this present time a-soaking in the rain.

The city's population blamed the rain upon the recently deposed mayor. In fact, the city's population now blamed almost everything upon the recently deposed mayor. And not without good cause for the most part, although blaming him for the inclement weather was, perhaps, pushing it a bit.

Not that the city's population were above pushing it a bit, for had they not risen up against the mayor and marched upon the mayoral mansion with flaming torches, pots of tar and many bags of feathers? And had they not dragged the city's mayor from his mayoral mansion, performed unspeakable acts upon his person and cast him beyond the city's gates, with the advice that he should never return, come wind or, indeed, come rain?

Indeed they had.

It had all been most unpleasant.

And if the tarring and feathering and the endurance of unspeakable acts and the casting forth from the city had been most unpleasant for the mayor, these things were as nought when compared to those things that were done to him by the kindly, lovable white-haired old Toy-maker, when the ejected mayor returned to the city under cover of darkness to seek sanctuary at his manse. Having cleaned up the ex-mayor, the kindly, lovable white-haired old Toymaker had demodified him. Which is to say that he removed all the modifications that he had made to the mayor in return for a great service that the mayor had per-formed for the city, in fact a great service for which he had been granted the office of mayor.

The kindly, lovable white-haired old Toymaker did not demodify the mayor in order to add insult to injury. He did not do it out of cru-elty. Rather he did it out of compassion, blaming himself, he said, for making modifications that should never have been made—playing God, as he put it. He apologised profusely to the ex-mayor as he put him through the process of demodification. He told the ex-mayor that it was all for the ex-mayor's own good and that the ex-mayor would thank him for it one day, and then he had given the ex-mayor a nice cup of tea, patted him upon the head and sent him upon his way, offer-ing his own words of advice, to whit, that the ex-mayor should in fu-ture keep within his remit and not aspire to a position above his natural station in life.

'Now go and be good,' said the Toymaker, slamming shut his front door behind the ex-mayor.

The door of Tinto's Bar hadn't opened all evening. What with the rain and everything, business had been slack. Business, in fact, was no busi-ness at all and Tinto's Bar was empty.

'I blame it on the ex-mayor,' said Tinto, to no one but himself, as he stood behind his bar, a dazzling glass in one dextrous hand, a bar-cloth in the other. 'I remember the good times, me. Well, I would if there'd ever been any.'

Tinto's Bar was long and low, all patterned in black and white che-querboard. A long and low counter it had, with a row of chromium barstools. There were tables and chairs that were shabby, but served. A dolly called Nellie, who worked the weekends. A pot man called Henry, who didn't.

Tinto the barman was something to behold. He was of the me-chanical persuasion, powered by a clockwork motor, his body formed from pressed tin and glossily painted, though much of the gloss was now gone. His head was an oversized sphere, with a smiling face painted on the front. His body was a thing-a-me-oid (a cylinder with a hemisphere joined to each end of it), painted with a dicky bow and tuxedo. His arms were flat, though painted with sleeves and shirt cuffs, and the fingers of his hands were fully and wonderfully articulated.

Now, in the light of things that are shortly to occur, it might be well to mention that Tinto was a practising member of The Church of Mechanology, which was one of The Big Four religions in Toy City along with The Daughters of the Unseeable Upness, Big Box Fella, He Come and The Exclusive Brotherhood of the Midnight Growlers. Mechanologists held to the belief that the Universe was a vast clockwork mechanism, with the planets revolving about the sun by means of extendible rotary arms and the sun in turn connected to the galaxy by an ingenious crankshaft system, the entirety powered by an enormous clockwork motor, constantly maintained, oiled and kept wound by The Universal Engineer.

The Universal Engineer was pictured in religious icons as a large and jolly red-faced fellow in greasy overalls and cap. He held in one holy hand an oily rag, and in the other the Church's Sacred Writ, known as *The Manual*.

Followers of The Church of Mechanology considered themselves special and superior to all other varieties of toy, in that being clockwork they were *in tune* and *at one with* the Universe.

It could be argued that The Church of Mechanology was something of an End Times cult, subscribing as it did to the belief that, as individual clockwork toys enjoyed only a finite existence, due to the ravages of rust, corrosion, spring breakage and fluff in the works, so too did the Universe.

Elders of the church spoke of The Time of the Terrible Stillness, when the great mechanism that powered the Universe would grind to a halt, the planet would no longer turn upon its axis, the sun would no longer rise and even time itself would come to a standstill.

And at present, what with all the chaos caused by the ex-mayor when he was the then-mayor, there was much talk amongst the practising Mechanologists that The Time Of the Terrible Stillness was now rapidly approaching. In fact, the elders of each of The Big Four religions were presently preaching that The End Times were well and truly on their way, and everyone knew whose fault *that* was.

Tinto examined the dazzling glass and found it pleasing to behold. At least you knew where you were with a glass. If it was a beer glass, then you were probably in a bar. And as Tinto was in a bar, well, at least he knew where he was. Which was something.

'I think I'll close up early tonight,' said Tinto to himself, 'take a couple of bottles of five-year-old oil upstairs, watch the late-night movie, *Rusty the Rotten Dog*, drown my sorrows and pray for sunshine tomorrow. You have to make the effort, don't you? And laugh, too, or so I've been told, because you'll cry if you don't. And crying really rusts tin toys, as salt water's worse than rain.'

Tinto had recently taken to the reading of certain 'self-help' books. It was all very well being a practising member of The Church of Mechanology, or rather, in truth, it was *not*, it was just too damned depressing, and although Tinto could not actually remember any particularly good times, he was generally of a cheery disposition. Or he had been until recently.

Tinto was presently reading *Become A Merry Old Soul in Thirty Days*, penned by a certain O. K. Cole, a prominent Toy City Pre-adolescent Poetic Personality.* Tinto had even taken on The Fiddlers Three to play in the bar during Sunday lunchtimes. The Fiddlers Three had driven away his Sunday lunchtime clientele.

'It never rains, but it damned well buckets down,' said Tinto, 'yet a smile costs nothing and brightens any day.'

A noise of an unexpected nature drew Tinto's attention towards the door of his bar. For this noise came from its creaking hinges.

'Custom?' queried the clockwork barman. 'On such a night as this?'

The hinges creaked a little more; some rain blew into the bar.

'Who is there?' called Tinto. 'Welcome, friend.'

The door, a smidgen open, opened a smidgen more. The brown button eye of a furry face peeped into Tinto's Bar.

'Howdy doody,' called the barman. 'Don't be shy, now. Hospitality awaits you here. That and beer and any seat that suits you.'

Smidgen, smidgen, smidgen went the door and then all-open-up. And then . . . and then . . .

Tinto peered and had he been able Tinto would have gawped. And had his face been capable of any expression other than that which was painted upon it, there is just no telling exactly what this expression might have become. Tinto's voice, however, was capable of all manner of expression and the words that now issued through the grille in his chest did so in what can only be described as an awed whisper. And those words were . . .

'Eddie, Eddie Bear—is that really you?'

A sodden teddy stood in the doorway, a sodden and dejected-looking teddy. It put its paws to its plump tummy parts and gave them

---

* The term preferred by Nursery Rhyme characters, to Nursery Rhyme characters. (As it were.)

a squeeze, eliciting a dismal groan from its growler and dripping rain-drops onto Tinto's floor.

'It *is* you,' said Tinto. 'It really *is*.'

Eddie Bear did shakings of himself. 'I couldn't borrow a bar-cloth, could I?' he asked.

Tinto's head revolved upon his tin-plate shoulders. 'You,' he said, and his voice rose in volume and in octave also. 'You! Here! In my bar! *You!*'

'Me,' said Eddie. 'Might I have a beer?'

'*You!*' Tinto's head now bobbed up and down, his arms rose and his dextrous fingers formed themselves into fists.

'I'll go,' said Eddie. 'I understand.'

'Yes, you . . . yes, you.'

Eddie turned to take his leave. Turned in such a sorrowful, forlorn and dejected manner, with such a drooping of the head and sinking of the shoulders, that Tinto, whose fists were now beating a rapid tattoo upon the highly polished bar counter, felt something come over him that was nothing less than pity.

'No,' said Tinto, his fists unfisting. 'No, Eddie, please don't go.'

Eddie turned and gazed at the barman through one brown button eye and one blue. 'I can stay?' he asked. 'Can I really?'

Tinto's head now bobbed from side to side. 'But you—'

'Were mayor,' said Eddie. 'Yes, I know and I'm sorry.'

'And you were—'

'Modified by the Toymaker. Hands with fingers and opposable thumbs, I know.' Eddie regarded his paws and sighed a heartfelt sigh.

'And—'

'Eyes,' said Eddie, mournfully, 'blue glass eyes with eyelids. All gone now. I'm just plain Eddie Bear.'

Tinto said nothing, but beckoned. Eddie crossed the floor towards the bar counter, leaving behind him little paw-shaped puddles.

'Sit down, then,' said Tinto. 'Have a beer and tell me all about it.'

'Could you make it something stronger than beer, please?' Eddie asked, climbing with difficulty onto what had once been his favourite barstool. 'I'm soaked all the way through and whatever I drink is going to get watered down.'

'I've got a bottle of Old Golly-Wobbler,' said Tinto. 'It's pretty strong stuff—even the gollies are afeared of it, and you know how those bad boys like to put it away.'

'Make it a treble then, please,' said Eddie.

Tinto, who had been reaching up for the bottle, which stood upon a glass shelf between the Old Kitty-Fiddler and the Donkey Punch (a great favourite with male ballet-dancing dolls), hesitated. Tinto's head revolved towards Eddie. 'You do have money?' he asked.

Eddie shook his sodden head and made the face of despair.

'Thought not,' said Tinto. 'Then you're only getting a quadruple measure.' For Tinto had trouble with maths.

'That will be fine, then.' And the corners of Eddie's mouth rose a little. But not any more than that.

Tinto decanted a measure of Old Golly-Wobbler, which might well have been a quadruple, into the dazzling glass that had so recently afforded him a small degree of pleasure because he knew where he was with it, and pushed the glass across the bar top towards the bedraggled bear. The bedraggled bear took it up between his trembling paws and tossed it away down his throat.

'Much thanks, Tinto,' said he. And Tinto poured another.

'It wasn't my fault,' said Eddie, when further Golly-Wobblers were gone and a rather warm feeling was growing in his tummy parts. 'I tried my best, I really did. I tried as hard as.'★

'And that's where you went wrong,' said Tinto, decanting a glass of five-year-old oil for himself and emptying it into his grille. 'No one wanted change, Eddie. Folk hate change and they came to hate you for trying to bring it about.'

'But things needed changing, *still* need changing.'

'No they don't,' said Tinto, and he shook his head vigorously. A nut or screw inside came loose and rattled all about. 'And now you've given me a headache,' said Tinto. 'When will all this madness end?'

'Pour me another drink,' said Eddie.

'And you'll pay me? *That* would make a change. And a pleasant one, too, I'm thinking.'

'Things do need changing,' Eddie said. 'Toy City is a wretched dystopia, Tinto, you know that.'

'I don't,' said Tinto. 'What does dystopia mean?'

Eddie told him.

'Well, I'll drink to that,' said Tinto.

'And so it needs changing.'

'Doesn't,' said Tinto. 'Certainly it's grim. Certainly toys don't get a fair deal. But if we didn't have something to complain about, then what would we have to complain about?'

Eddie Bear put his paws to his head. 'I saved this city,' said he,

---

★ As Eddie was unable to do corroborative nouns, Tinto would never know just how hard Eddie had tried, although given the sincerity of the bear's tone, the clockwork barman could only surmise that it had been very hard indeed

'saved it from the Toymaker's evil twin. He would have wiped every one of us out if it hadn't been for me.'

'And your friend, Jack,' said Tinto.

'Yes, Jack,' said Eddie. And he made a wistful face. 'I wonder whatever became of Jack. He travelled into the world of men—'

'The world of men?' said Tinto. 'A world populated entirely by meatheads? There's no such world. That's a myth, Eddie. A fantasy.'

'It isn't,' said Eddie, making imploring 'more-drink-please' gestures with his paws. 'There is a world beyond this one. Jack met a man who came from there. And that's where Jack went.'

'Didn't,' said Tinto, and he poured another drink for Eddie.

'Did too,' said Eddie.

'Didn't,' said Tinto. 'A little bird told me that he changed his mind, decided it was more fun to stay in the city with his girlfriend—that Jill from Madame Goose's bawdy house.' Tinto made the sacred sign of the spanner over the portion of his chest where his heart, had he possessed one, would have been, out of respect for the late Madame Goose who had come to an untimely end. 'That Jack hung around with that Jill for a while, but she soon spent all his money and he was reduced to working as a griddle chef in a Nadine's Diner.'

'He never was,' said Eddie.

'True as I'm standing here before you, large as life and twice as special. She left him, of course.'

'And a little bird told you this?'

'A robin. His name was Tom.'

'I don't believe a word of it.' Eddie downed his latest drink and began to fidget about on his barstool.

'Don't do it,' said Tinto.

'What?' said Eddie.

'What you're about to do.'

'And what am I about to do?'

'Try to balance on your head on that barstool.'

'I wasn't,' said Eddie.

'You were,' said Tinto. 'I know you well enough, Eddie. I know you're all filled up with sawdust and that when you drink, the drink soaks down to your legs and so you stand on your head so the drink goes there instead. And then you get drunk and silly and I have to throw you out.'

Eddie shrugged and sighed. 'My legs *are* now rather drunk,' he confessed. 'But Jack, still in Toy City? I can't believe it.'

'Not his fault,' said Tinto. 'He was in love. Females will do that kind of thing to you. Put you off what you're meaning to do. Confuse you, fiddle you out of your money, then run off with a wind-up action figure. I can't be having with females, me.'

'Have you ever had a girlfriend, Tinto?' Eddie asked.

'Loads,' said Tinto. 'And they all confused me, fiddled me out of my money and ran off with a wind-up action figure. Except for the big fat one.'

'She was nice, was she?'

'No, she ran off with a clockwork train. What was *that* all about? I ask you.'

Eddie shrugged. 'We all have a tale to tell,' he said, 'and most of those tales are sad.'

'And that's what bars are for,' said Tinto, 'so you can tell them into the sympathetic ear of a caring barman.'

'Quite so,' said Eddie, raising his empty glass between his paws. 'Cheers.'

'Cheers to you, too,' said Tinto. 'Now pay up or I'll kick you out, you bum.'

Eddie laughed. 'Most amusing,' he said.

'No, I mean it,' said Tinto. 'It's all your fault that it's raining.'

'It's not my fault at all.'

' 'Tis too,' said Tinto. 'Everything's your fault. Everybody knows that.'

'Doom and gloom,' said Eddie Bear.

'Still,' said Tinto, 'you have to look on the bright side, don't you? Or so I'm told. I'm reading this book, you see. It's going to make me merry in thirty days.'

'So how long have you been reading it for?'

'Oh, more than four days,' said Tinto. 'It's about forty-four, I think.'

'It's so good to be back here,' said Eddie.

'I thought I was throwing you out.'

'I have some money coming soon.' Eddie made encouraging motions with his glass.

'I fail to understand the motions you're making with that glass,' said Tinto, 'but what money would you have coming soon?'

'I've gone back to my old profession,' said Eddie.

'Walking round the garden?' said Tinto. 'I never really understood the point of that. A "teddy-bear thing", I suppose.'

'Not *that*, nor taking picnics in the wood. I mean my profession as a private eye. I'm setting myself up in Bill's office.'

'Bill Winkie?' Tinto made the sacred sign of the spanner again.

'Have you noticed, Eddie, that folk who come into contact with you seem to come to very sticky ends?'

'It wasn't my fault, what happened to Bill. We were as close as.' Eddie made a very sad face, for Eddie had loved Bill Winkie. Eddie had been Bill Winkie's bear. Eddie had avenged Bill's death, but Eddie still missed Bill. 'I won't be changing the name on his door,' said Eddie. 'It will still be "Bill Winkie Investigations".'

'Well, I doubt if you'd get too much business if you advertised yourself as "Ex-Mayor Eddie Investigations".'

Eddie made growling sounds. 'In Bill's memory,' he said. 'And I am confident that I shall soon have several wealthy clients on my books.'

'But you haven't yet?'

'Not as such.'

'Not as such?' said Tinto.

'Well, I haven't managed to get back into the office yet. It's padlocked up. And now I've only got these.' Eddie sadly regarded his paws.

Tinto made a sighing sound. 'That was a pity,' he said, 'the Toymaker taking those hands he'd fitted you with. Spiteful, that, I thought, although—'

'Although what?'

'Well,' said Tinto, 'it wasn't right, was it? A teddy bear with fingers and thumbs. That was all wrong. There was something really creepy about that. And I never liked those eyes he gave you, either. Teddies don't have blinking eyes. It's not natural. It's—'

'Stop it,' said Eddie. 'It's all right for you. Try living with only paws for just one week, see how you like it.'

'I'm sure I wouldn't like it, but that's not the point. We're all here for a purpose. I'm a clockwork barman. That was what I was made to be. Not a fireman, or a clown. Or a train! The city functions because the toys who live in it do what they were intended to do.'

'But the city *doesn't* function. The city is in a mess.'

'There you go again.' Tinto shook his head once more and once again it rattled. 'You can't go trying to change things, Eddie. Things might not be to your liking, but things are the way they are and we just have to get on with it. Although not for much longer, it appears.'

'Does it?' Eddie asked.

'It does, because The End Times are coming upon us. The Time of the Terrible Stillness draws near. Which, popular opinion agrees, is all your fault, by the way.'

'End Times,' said Eddie. 'That's as mad as. And it's *not* my fault.'

'I'm prepared to be reasonable.' Tinto poured himself another five-year-old, but hesitated to refresh Eddie's glass. 'I'm prepared to say that you are only partially to blame.'

'I'm not even *partially* to blame.'

'You're just in denial,' said Tinto. 'You need closure. It's all in the book I'm reading. I'll lend it to you as soon as I'm finished. Which should be in about fifty-three days, by my reckoning.'

Eddie fidgeted some more. 'If you won't give me any more drink I will be forced to stand upon my head,' he said.

'And I will be forced to throw you out.'

Eddie offered Tinto a bit of a smile. 'It's very good to see you again, Tinto,' he said. 'It's as good as, it really, truly is.'

Tinto poured Eddie another. 'It's good to see you, too,' he said. 'Even though you've brought The End Times upon us.'

Eddie Bear was more than just drunk when he left Tinto's Bar. He was rather full of bar snacks, too. Well, he had been rather hungry, and Tinto had become somewhat over-lubricated and somewhat generous in the process. As one will do if one is that kind of a drunk. He had also lent Eddie his copy of *Become A Merry Old Soul in Thirty Days*. Eddie was struggling to carry this, but at least it wasn't raining any more.

The streets were still deserted; street lamps reflected in puddles, gutters drip-drip-dripped. Eddie's footpads squelched horribly, but as his feet were drunk he didn't really notice.

Eddie had no destination. He'd been sleeping rough for weeks, trying in vain whenever the opportunity arose to enter Bill's office, slinking away at the approach of footsteps, hiding where he could.

Just how he thought he could set himself up as a detective and actually find any clients who didn't know and hate him was anybody's guess. But Eddie was a bear of substance and although he was presently down, more down in fact than he had ever been before, he was far from out.

Although, perhaps, not *that* far.

Eddie stumbled and squelched and hummed a little, too. It had been very nice of Tinto to offer him a welcome. He would definitely reward the clockwork barman for his kindness sometime. Possibly even financially. Well, anything *was* possible. Eddie hummed and stumbled and squelched. And Eddie felt optimistic, for the first time in what felt like an age. He'd pull through, he knew he would. Pull through, somehow. Make good. Make the population of Toy City proud of him. Make the Toymaker proud of him. He'd do *something*. He would, he really would.

And he would seek out Jack. Yes, he would definitely do that. Jack had been his bestest friend. They had been partners; together they had defeated the evil twin of the Toymaker. Together. He would seek out Jack and they would become partners once again. Do great things together. Jack could do things, great things. He could do things that Eddie could not, such as pick the padlock on Bill Winkie's office. For Jack was a meathead; Jack had hands with fingers and opposable thumbs.

'Jack and me,' said Eddie, as he stumbled and bumbled along, 'we were as close as. We were bestest friends. If Jack is still in the city I will find him. I will get on to that first thing in the morning. But for now I need somewhere cosy and dry to spend the night. An alleyway, perhaps.'

An alleyway presented itself, as they will when you are in your cups. Especially if you are in need of the toilet. Eddie was in need of the toilet as much as he was in need of somewhere cosy and dry, and so the alleyway that presented itself was a sort of dual-purpose alleyway. Or triple-purpose alleyway, if one were to be exact. Or quadruple, if you were Tinto.

The alleyway that presented itself to Eddie was of the type that was greatly favoured by 1950s American-genre private eyes. It had one of those fire escapes with a retractable bottom section, some dustbins and the rear door of a nightclub, from which drifted the suitably atmospheric tones of a mellow saxophone.

Eddie bumbled and stumbled into the alleyway and relieved himself to the accompaniment of much contented sighing. Even though sighing wasn't usually his thing. He lifted the lid off the nearest dustbin and then drew back in disgust. Bears have sensitive noses, after all. Another lid and then another, and then he found an empty dustbin and a new one, too. Eddie flung Tinto's book into this empty dustbin and, after something of a struggle, followed it.

'Hardly the most salubrious accommodation,' said Eddie, drawing the lid over himself and preparing to settle down for the night. 'I will probably laugh about this one day. But for all the life that's in me, I cannot imagine what day that might be. But,' and Eddie did further settlings, 'that day *will* come.'

And Eddie Bear, in darkness, settled down to sleep.

And slept.

And then awoke.

With more than just a start.

A terrible clamouring came to the ears of Eddie, a terrible rattling and jangling about. His dustbin bower was being shaken. Ferociously.

'Give a bear a break.' Eddie put his paws to his head. The din and the shaking grew fiercer.

Eddie rose and gingerly lifted the lid.

A great white light dazzled his vision. Sparks flew from somewhere and leapt all around and about.

Eddie's mismatched eyes took it all in. Whatever it was. There was a glowing orb of light, a sphere of whiteness. It grew, right there, in the middle of the alleyway, from nothing to something.

The shaking and rattling and the jangling too grew and grew. And then, just like that, because there was no other way to it, it ceased. The shaking and the rattling and the jangling and the sparking and the light. It was gone, all gone.

But something else was there.

Eddie cowered and peeped through the gap between bin lid and bin. Something had materialised. Out of nowhere. Into somewhere. In this very alleyway.

It crouched. And then it rose. And as Eddie looked on, he could see just what this something was.

It was a bear.

A toy bear.

And this bear looked like Eddie.

Just like Eddie.

The bear rose, flexed its shoulders, glanced to either side.

And then made off at the hurry-up.

Eddie Bear sank down in his bin and gently lowered the lid.

'I think I may just give up drinking,' Eddie said.

2

The morning sun rose over Toy City. It was a big and jolly sun with a big smiley face and its name was believed to be Sam.

So the sun of Sam* shone down and the Toy City folk awoke.

The economy, for Toy City had such a thing, as everywhere seems to have such a thing these days, whatever the word might mean, was a little on the decline hereabouts. Wages were down and prices were up and the niceties of life seemed as ever the preserve of the well-to-dos, those who *had*, having more, and those who *had not*, less. The heads of the have-nots drooped on their shoulders as they trudged, or wheeled, or trundled to their places of work. Factory whistles blew, traffic lights faltered, trains were cancelled, dry-cleaning failed to arrive back upon the promised day and how come one is always in the wrong queue in the Post Office?

A rattling and jangling and shaking all about awakened Eddie Bear, from a sleep without dreams, because toy bears do not dream, to recollection, then horror.

'Oh my, oh dear. Whoa!' Sunlight rushed in upon the bear as his bin bower was raised and upended. And, 'No!' shrieked Eddie, affecting that high-pitched whine of alarm that one makes when taken with fear.

Up went the bin, and up and over and out came Eddie, down into the dustcart.

As will be well known to those who know these things well, these knowers being those who watch movies on a regular basis, movie garbage consists of cardboard boxes, shredded paper and indeterminate

* The sun's father's name was also Sam. As is often the case with suns

soft stuff. When heroes fall, or are thrown, into such garbage they generally come up unsoiled and fighting.

Oh that life should as a movie be.

Eddie found himself engulfed in fish-heads, curry cartons, rotten fruit, stale veg and that rarest of all rare things, the dung of a wooden horse. Eddie shrieked and struggled and wallowed and sank and rose again and was presently rescued, lifted (at the length of an arm) and set down on the ground.

Garbageman Four looked down upon Eddie. 'What did you do that for?' he asked.

Eddie spat out something evil-tasting and peered up at Garbageman Four. Garbageman Four was part of a six-man matching clockwork garbageman crew, printed tin-plate turn-outs all. Garbageman Four considered himself to be a special garbageman, because only he had a number four printed on his back.

'What did I do *what* for?' Eddie managed to utter.

'Scream and shout and struggle about,' said Garbageman Four, rocking on the heels of his big tin work boots. 'Garbage is not supposed to do that. Garbage is supposed to know its place and behave the way it should.'

Eddie made growling sounds. 'I am *not* garbage,' he said. 'I'm an Anders Imperial. Cinnamon-coloured mohair plush, with wood-wool stuffing throughout. Black felt paw pads, vertically stitched nose. An Anders Imperial. I have the special tag in my ear and everything.'

Garbageman Four leaned down and viewed Eddie's special tag. 'That's a beer cap, that is,' he said. 'And you're a grubby rubbish old bear. Now back into the truck with you and off to the incinerator.' But as Garbageman Four reached down towards Eddie, Eddie took off at the hurry-up.

His stumpy legs carried him beyond both garbageman and alleyway and out into a main thoroughfare. Clockwork motor cars whirred by, along with cycling monkeys, woodentop children going to school and a teddy or two who viewed him with disgust.

Eddie sat down on the kerb and buried his furry face in his paws. How had it come to this? How had he reached the rockiest of rock bottoms, sunk to the very depths of the pool? How, how, how had it happened?

His woe-begotten thoughts returned to his time as mayor. He had tried so hard to make things better for the denizens of Toy City. He really, truly had tried. But no matter how hard he'd tried or what actions he'd taken, he'd always somehow managed to make things worse. Every by-law, edict and new rule he'd put in place had somehow got twisted about. It had been as if someone or something had been out to sabotage everything he'd done with kindness in his heart-regions and the good of all in the foremost of his thoughts.

Eddie groaned. And now it had come to this. He was a down-and-out, a vagrant, a vagabond. Ill-smelling and disenfranchised. An outcast. The garbage truck rumbled by, its tin-plate wheels ploughing through a puddle that splashed over Eddie Bear.

Eddie added sighs to his groaning, then rose and squeezed disconsolately at himself. He was a mess and whatever optimism he might have felt the previous evening, optimism that had probably been buoyed up by the prodigious quantities of Old Golly-Wobbler he had imbibed, was now all gone and only pain remained.

Eddie did doglike shakings of himself, spraying puddle water onto a crinoline doll who tut-tut-tutted and strutted away, her haughty nose in the air.

'I need a drink,' said Eddie. And his tummy growled. 'I need breakfast,' said Eddie. And his tummy agreed.

As chance, or fate, or possibly both would have it, across the thoroughfare from Eddie stood a restaurant. It was a Nadine's Diner, one of a chain of such diners owned by Nadine Spratt, widow of the now-legendary Jack Spratt, Pre-adolescent Poetic Personality. Jack, as those who recall the nursery rhyme will recall, was the fellow who 'ate no fat', whilst his wife 'would eat no lean', and so, in the manner of the happy marriage they had once enjoyed, between the two of them they had 'licked the platter clean' and started two successful restaurant chains, his specialising in Lean Cuisine and hers in Big Fat Fry-Ups. Hers had been the more successful of the two businesses.

They had been going through a most colourful celebrity divorce at the time of Jack Spratt's demise, when he was plunged into a deep-fat fryer.*

Eddie gazed upon Nadine's Diner: a long, low building painted all in a hectic yellow, with a sign, wrought from neon, spelling out its name, as such signs are ever wont to do.

Eddie Bear sniffed, inhaling the smell of Big Fat Fry-Ups.

* See *The Hollow Chocolate Bunnies of the Apocalypse* for further details. In fact, buy a copy right *now* if you haven't already read it, read it all the way through, then go back to the first chapter of this book and start again. Because this is a sequel. And although a damn fine book in its own right, one in fact that should win any number of awards, but probably won't because there is no justice in this world, it might be best to read the first book first and the second book second. Only a suggestion.

Eddie had no pockets to pat, so Eddie did not pat them. Because the thing, well, one of the things, about pockets is that sometimes they have small change in them. Small change that you have forgotten about, but small change that is just big enough to pay for a Big Fat Fry-Up. But Eddie didn't pat.

Eddie Bear made instead a face.

A face that had about it a multiplicity of expressions.

The chief amongst them being that of determination.

Eddie was determined that he should have breakfast.

And now was the time he should have it.

Being a bear well versed in the perils of stepping out onto a busy road without first looking one way and then the other, Eddie Bear did these lookings and when the way was clear of traffic crossed the road and wandered to Nadine's Diner.

Where he paused and pondered his lot.

It was not much of a lot to ponder. It was a rather rotten lot, as it happened. But it did require a degree of pondering. He could not, in his present soiled condition, simply swagger into the diner, order for himself the very biggest of Big Fat Fry-Ups, consume same with eagerness and, when done, run out without paying.

A subtler approach was required.

Slip around to the back, nip into the kitchen and steal? That was an option. Slip around to the back, knock on the door and then beg? That was another.

By the smiley sun called Sam! By the maker who'd made him! He'd once been the mayor of this city! Dined from plates of gold! Quaffed champagne with Old King Cole! Had his back massaged by a dolly with over-modified front parts! That he had sunk to *this*!

Eddie squared what shoulders he possessed. There had to be some other way.

Upon the door of Nadine's Diner hung a sign: HEP WANTED, it said.

'"Hep wanted"?' queried Eddie. 'That would be "help" wanted, I suppose. As in the offer of employment. Hmm.'

The dolly that leaned upon the countertop, a dolly with overmodified front parts similar to those of the masseuse who had once tended to Eddie, did not look up, or even down, at Eddie's approach. She was doing a crossword. The dolly was a most glamorous dolly, golden-haired of hair, curvaceous of curve, long-legged of leg and all around glamour of glamourousness. She was, as they say—and folk did when they saw her—absolutely gorgeous.

Now the question as to whether the absolutely gorgeous have very much in the way of brains is a question that in all truth does not get asked very often. Folk have a tendency to take other folk at face value. Well, at first, anyway. That thing about first impressions and all that. And that other question, 'If you are very beautiful, do you actually need to have very much in the way of brains?' is of course that other question. And in all truth, neither questions are questions that should be asked at all. To imply that because you are good-looking you are therefore stupid is an outrageous thing to imply. To think that you can gauge someone's intelligence by how good-looking they are, and if they are *very* good-looking then therefore they are stupid!

Outrageous.

Because, come on now, let's be honest here—if you are really good-looking, you don't need to be really intelligent.

And if that sounds outrageous, then how about this: there will always be a great many more ugly stupid folk in this world (or possibly any other) than there will be beautiful stupid folk.

Which might mean that things balance themselves out somewhere along the line. Or possibly do not. It's all a matter of opinion. Or intelligence. Or looks. Or . . .

'Four-letter word,' said the dolly in the prettiest of voices. 'Cow jumped over it, first letter *M*, fourth letter *N*.'

'Moon,' said Eddie, smiling upwards.

'What did you say?' The dolly turned her eyes from her crossword and over the counter and down towards Eddie.*

'Moon,' said Eddie, smiling angelically.

'Why, you dirty little sawdust bag!' The dolly glared pointy little daggers.

'I only said "moon",' said Eddie. 'Go on. Moon.'

The dolly's eyes narrowed. 'Just because I'm beautiful,' she snarled, 'just because I have blonde hair that you can make longer by turning a little thing-a-me-bob on my back—which makes me special, I'll add— you think I'm some stupid slutty bimbo who's prepared to moon for any scruffy . . .' she twitched her tiny nose '. . . *smelly* bear who comes in here and—'

'No,' said Eddie. 'You have me all wrong.'

'I don't think so, mister. I have you all right. Men are all the same—see a blonde head and a pair of big titties and they think they're on to an easy one.'

---

* Neat trick.

'No,' said Eddie. Well, yes, he thought. 'Well, *no*,' said Eddie, with emphasis. 'I meant the word in your crossword—the cow jumped over the moon.'

'What cow?' asked the dolly.

'The one in your crossword clue.'

'And did you see this cow?'

'I know of it,' said Eddie. 'It lives on Old MacDonald's farm.'

'Oh,' said the dolly.

'EIEIO,' said Eddie. 'As in "Old MacDonald had a farm".'

'Brilliant,' said the dolly.

'Excuse me?' said Eddie.

'That was another of the clues—"Where does Old MacDonald live?"'

'Glad to be of assistance,' said Eddie.

The dolly took to studying her crossword once more. Then she made a frowning face again and turned it back upon Eddie. 'Doesn't fit,' she said. 'Too many letters.'

'Eh?' said Eddie.

'Where Old MacDonald lives, "EIEIO" doesn't fit.'

'I've come about the job,' said Eddie. 'Help wanted.'

'It's *HEP* wanted,' said the dolly. 'Can't you read?'

Eddie sighed inwardly. 'Well, I've come to offer my HEP,' he said.

'You don't look very HEP,' said the dolly, giving Eddie the up-and-down once-over. 'In fact, you look very un-HEP and you smell like a drain with bad breath.'

'I had to dive into a cesspit to save a drowning dolly,' said Eddie. 'At no small risk to my own safety.'

'Can you play the saxophone?'

'I don't know,' said Eddie. I've never tried.'

'You're not tall enough anyway.'

'I grow larger when fed.'

'We were looking for a golly.'

'Typical,' said Eddie. 'Discrimination again. Because you're a teddy everyone thinks you're stupid. Only good for cuddling and picnicking in those damned woods.'

The dolly cocked her golden head upon one side. 'I know how it is,' she said. 'Folk just see the outer you, never the person who dwells within. Perhaps . . .'

'Yes?' said Eddie.

'No,' said the dolly. 'You're ugly and you smell. Get out.'

Eddie sighed outwardly and turned to take his leave.

'Eddie!'

Eddie ignored the voice.

'*Eddie!* Eddie, it's *you.*'

Eddie turned and Eddie stared and Eddie Bear said, 'Jack.'

Jack stood behind the counter next to the golden-haired dolly. He wore a chef's hat and jacket. And even to Eddie's first glance, he wore them uncomfortably.

'Eddie,' said Jack. 'It *is* you. It is.'

'It is,' said Eddie. 'And it's *you.*'

The kitchen of Nadine's Diner was grim. But then such kitchens are always grim. Such kitchens are places of heat and conflict, with shouting chefs and stress and panic and lots of washing-up. There was lots of washing-up to do in this particular kitchen.

Eddie sat upon a grimy worktop surrounded by many unwashed pots and pans. A rat nibbled on something in a corner; a cockroach crossed the floor. Jack stepped on the cockroach and shooed away the rat.

'That's Barry,' Jack told Eddie. 'He's sort of a pet.'

Eddie munched ruefully but gratefully on the burger Jack had fried for him.

Jack leaned on the crowded sink and wiped his hands on a quite unspeakable dishcloth. 'I thought you were dead,' he said.

Eddie looked up from his munchings and wiped ketchup from his face with a greasy paw. He was very, very pleased to see his friend Jack.

Jack smiled at Eddie and Eddie saw that Jack hadn't changed: he was still tall and spare and lithe of limb and young and pleasing to behold.

'I really thought you were dead. I heard what they did to you. I would have come to your rescue.'

'Would you?' Eddie asked.

'Well, no, actually,' said Jack. 'Not at that particular time.'

'What?' Eddie spat out some burger bun. Jack wiped it from his apron.

'You weren't exactly in my good books at that particular time,' said Jack. 'You're not exactly in them now.'

'Eh?' said Eddie.

'Edict Five,' said Jack, 'the one about abolishing the monarchy. *Your* Edict Five. And me an honorary prince. Did you forget that?'

'I thought you'd gone off to the other world. The world of men. That's where you told me you were going. To sort out the clockwork President.'

'Well,' said Jack, and he made an embarrassed face, 'I *was* going to go, but the Toymaker *had* given me a castle to live in, and there *was* Jill . . .' Jack's voice trailed off.

'I heard about Jill,' said Eddie, packing further burger into his mouth. 'I'm sorry about that.'

'There's no trusting women,' said Jack. 'At least I've learned that whilst still young.'

'Don't be too cynical,' said Eddie. 'I know she hurt you, but that doesn't mean that all women are bad. You'll find the right one, and when you do she will make you happy every single day.'

'Yeah, right,' said Jack. 'But let's talk about you, Eddie. I *am* glad that you're alive, truly I am, but your—'

'Hands?' said Eddie. 'Eyes? The Toymaker took them away. He said that he blamed himself for what happened. That you shouldn't tamper with nature, which was pretty hypocritical coming from him, as he created me. He said I should go and do what I was created for.'

'And you're not keen?' Jack took up another cloth to wipe his hands upon, as the first cloth had made them ever dirtier.

'Was I ever?' Eddie asked. 'I am a bear of superior intellect. I am a special bear.'

'You are certainly that.'

'Jack,' said Eddie, 'how would you feel about teaming up again? The old team, you and me, back in business together.'

'The old team?' Jack laughed and his laughter was not pleasing to Eddie's ears, especially to the one with the special tag in it. 'The old team? How many times did I come close to being killed?'

Eddie shrugged.

'Nine times,' said Jack. 'I counted.'

'You enjoyed the adventure. And we saved the city.'

'Yes, and I'd still be living grandly if it hadn't been for you fouling it up with your Edict Five.'

'I was just trying to make things right.'

'You're a very well-intentioned little bear.'

'Don't patronise me, Jack. Never patronise me.'

Jack shook his head. 'You're unbelievable,' he said. 'Look at the state of you. Sniff the smell of you. Go back into business together? What business?'

'If we build it, they will come,' said Eddie. 'We have Bill's office. Well, we will as soon as you have picked the lock and we can get inside. Then we'll set up. We can call ourselves "Jack Investigations" if you want.'

Jack shook his head. 'And what will we investigate?'

'Crimes,' said Eddie.

'I thought the police investigated crimes. Those jolly red-faced laughing policemen. And Chief Inspector Bellis.'

'As if they care about what happens to the likes of us.'

'The likes of *us*?' Jack raised an eyebrow. 'I don't think it's *us*, Eddie. You are a toy and I am a—'

'Meathead,' said Eddie. 'I know.'

'Man,' said Jack.

'And so you are one of the privileged.' Eddie had finished his burger. But as he was still hungry, he made the face of one who was.

'I'll fry you up another,' said Jack. 'But, no offence, you know what I mean.'

'And you know that that was what I was trying to change. The injustice of the system. The way toys are treated as if they are nothing at all.'

'They are treated as if they are toys,' said Jack, applying himself once more to that Hellish piece of equipment known as a griddle. 'No offence meant once more.'

'Toys have feelings, too,' said Eddie.

Jack turned from the grill and gazed upon Eddie. The two of them had been through a great deal together. They had indeed had adventures. They had indeed had a relationship that was based upon trust and deep friendship. A lad and a toy bear. Absurd? Maybe. But then, what isn't?

'Eddie,' said Jack, 'it really is truly good to see you once more.'

'Thanks,' said Eddie. 'The same goes for me.'

'Eddie?' said Jack.

'Jack?' said Eddie.

'Would you mind very much if I were to give you a hug?'

'I would bite you right in the balls if you ever tried.'

'Thank goodness for that,' said Jack, 'because you smell like shit.'

Jack really didn't need *that much* persuading. He put up a spirited, if insincere, struggle, of course, citing the possibilities of promotion in the field of customer services and the pension plan and putting forward some unsupportable hypothesis that young women found griddle chefs sexy. But he really didn't take *that much* persuading and, come ten of the morning clock, with Sam shining down encouragingly, Jack took what wages he felt he was owed from the cash register, plus a small bonus that he considered he deserved, and with it his leave of Nadine's Diner.

'It's spoon,' he told the crossword-solving dolly as he made his departure. 'What the dish ran away with.'

'Does this mean you're running away from me?' asked the dolly.

'Not a bit of it,' said Jack. 'I'll pick you up at eight. Take you to the pictures.'

Outside in the encouraging sunlight, Eddie said, 'Jack, are you *doing it* with that dolly?'

'Well . . .' said Jack.

'Disgusting,' said Eddie. 'You should be ashamed.'

'I am,' said Jack, 'but I'm trying to work through it.'

'And succeeding by the look of it.'

Jack tried to make a guilty face.

'You're a very bad boy,' said Eddie.

The building hadn't changed at all, but then why should it have changed? It was a sturdy edifice, built in the vernacular style, Alphabet brick, with a tendency towards the occasional fiddly piece, which gave it that extra bit of character. Bill Winkie's office was on the first floor above the garage, which might or might not still house his splendid automobile. Eddie did ploddings up the stairway. Jack did long-legged stridings.

'It feels a bit odd,' said Jack as he followed Eddie, who with difficulty had overtaken him, along the corridor that led past various offices towards the door that led to Bill's, 'being back here again.'

'We did have some adventures, though.'

'All of them life-endangering.'

'But we came through, Jack, and—'

'Look at us now?' Jack asked.

'We'll get back on top. Somehow.'

'I'll give it a week,' said Jack.

'You'll what?' And Eddie turned.

'I've a week's money in my pocket. I'll give it a week with you. That's fair.'

'It's *not* fair,' said Eddie. 'Give a month at least.'

'Well, we'll see how it goes. So where's this padlock that needs picking?'

'It's here,' said Eddie. But much to his surprise it was not. 'It *was* here,' said Eddie, 'only yesterday, but now it seems to have vanished.'

'Perhaps someone else has moved in.' Jack viewed the door of Bill Winkie's office, *BILL WINKIE INVESTIGATIONS* etched into the glass. There were some holes in the woodwork where the hasp of a padlock had been. The door was slightly open. Jack did not feel encouraged by this turn of events.

'The door's open,' said Eddie. 'That's as encouraging as.'

'No it's not,' said Jack, 'it's suspicious.'

'Depends on how you look at it,' said Eddie. 'It's like the glass of water that is either half-full or half-empty, depending on how you look at it.'

'I'm sure there's wisdom in your words.'

'I'm sure there isn't,' said Eddie. 'You'd best go first, I'm thinking.'

'And why would you be thinking that?'

'Well,' said Eddie, 'you're bigger than me and have about you an air of authority. And should there be anyone in that office who shouldn't be there, you can shoo them away, as it were.'

'I see,' said Jack. 'And that would be your considered opinion, would it?'

'Well, actually, no,' said Eddie. 'I hardly gave it any consideration at all.'

Jack shook his head and pushed open the door. It squeaked a little on its hinges, but it was a different squeak from the door hinges of Tinto's Bar. An octave higher, perhaps.

Jack and Eddie peeped into the office.

The office hadn't changed at all.

Light drifted through the half-opened blinds, falling in slanted rays upon the filing cabinet, which contained little other than empty beer bottles; the desk that Jack had broken and inadequately repaired; the carpet that dared not speak its name; the water cooler that cooled no water; and all of the other sparse and sundry bits and bobs that made a private detective's office a private detective's office.

'Ah,' sighed Eddie, 'home again,' and he sniffed. 'And don't it just smell good?'

Jack took a sniff and said, 'Rank.'

'Rank,' agreed Eddie. 'But it's a good rank, don't you think?'

'I do.'

'And it's great to be back.'

'It is.'

'And we will have great times, Jack, exciting times.'

'Will we?' said Jack. 'Well, yes, perhaps.'

'We will,' said Eddie. 'We will.'

Jack looked at Eddie.

And Eddie looked at Jack.

'There's just one thing,' said Jack.

'One thing?' said Eddie.

'One thing,' said Jack.

'And what would that one thing be?'

'That one thing,' and Jack now glared at Eddie, 'that one thing would be that thing *there*. That one thing that you are so studiously ignoring. That one thing *right there*, lying on the carpet that dares not speak its name. Are you following me, Eddie? I'm pointing now, pointing to that one thing—do you see it?'

Eddie followed the pointing finger. And, 'Ah,' said Eddie. 'You would be referring, I suppose, to the dead body that is lying there upon the floor.'

Jack nodded slowly and surely. 'That would be it,' he said.

3

'It's a monkey,' said Eddie.

'It's a *dead* monkey,' said Jack.

'It might only be sleeping,' said Eddie.

'It is *dead*,' said Jack.

'Or run down,' said Eddie, approaching the monkey on the floor. 'Its clockwork might just have run down—and run down is a small death, you know, amongst clockwork folk.'

'Look at its eyes,' Jack approached Eddie, who was approaching the monkey. 'Those eyes are dead and staring.'

'They're glass eyes,' Eddie said. 'They always stare like that.'

The monkey lay upon the carpet that dared not speak its name. It was one of those monkeys that clap little brass cymbals whilst bouncing up and down. That is all they do, really, but children, and indeed adults, seem to find them very, very entertaining. Indeed, they can never get enough of those monkeys that clap their cymbals together and bounce up and down. Very popular, those monkeys are.

Although this one, it appeared, was dead.

Eddie looked sadly upon the monkey. It lay there, on its side, frozen in mid-clap. This was clearly a monkey that would clap and bounce no more.

'Wakey-wakey, Mister Monkey,' said Eddie. 'You can't sleep here, you know.'

'It's dead, Eddie—look at it.'

'Perhaps if I were to give its key a little turn?'

'Good idea, Eddie,' said Jack. 'You give its key a little turn.'

'You think I should?'

'No, I *don't*.'

'Stay put, Jack,' said Eddie, and he plodded slowly about the fallen monkey. Eddie leaned over the monkey and sniffed, then stepped back from the monkey and viewed it, his chin upon his paw. He dropped to his knees and examined the non-speaking carpet, then glanced at the ceiling and grunted.

Jack looked on and watched him. He'd seen Eddie go through this performance before and he'd seen Eddie draw conclusions from such a performance. Significant conclusions.

Eddie climbed to his paw-footed feet and looked up at Jack. 'There's been dirty business here,' he said. 'This monkey is certainly as dead as.'

'Murdered?' Jack asked.

'Something more than that.'

'Something *more*?'

'This monkey is something more than just as dead as.'

'I don't know what you mean,' Jack said.

'Nor do I,' said Eddie. 'Stand back a little further, Jack, if you will.' And Jack stood back accordingly.

Eddie reached out a paw and lightly touched the monkey.

There was a sound, as of a gentle sigh. And with it the monkey crumbled. Crumbled away to the accompaniment of the whispery sigh. Crumbled away to dust.

Jack looked at Eddie.

And Eddie looked at Jack.

'Now *that* isn't right,' said Eddie.

They swept up the dust of the monkey. Well, not so much *they* as Jack. Well, Jack had hands with opposable thumbs after all. Eddie did hold the dustpan.

'Pour what you can of him into this beer bottle,' said Eddie, fishing one with difficulty from the filing cabinet. 'There might be something significant to be learned from the dust.'

'Did you know this monkey?' Jack asked as he tried to do what Eddie wanted.

'Hard to say,' said the bear. 'Your cymbal-playing monkey is a classic toy, of course, an all-time favourite, but telling one from the other . . . I don't know. There was one called Monkey who was with the circus. He used to drink in Tinto's, but Tinto threw him out because he was too noisy. I knew another one called Monkey, who was also with the circus, did this act where he played the cymbals and bounced up and down. And—'

'So they all look the same, do the same thing, are all with the circus and are all called Monkey?'

'That's about the strength of it.' Eddie struggled to cork the beer bottle, then set it down on Bill's desk.

'I've got a lot of Monkey left over,' said Jack.

'Put it in the bin,' said Eddie.

'Shouldn't we cast it to the four winds, or something?'

Eddie grinned at Jack. 'See what a nice fellow you are,' said he. 'How caring. What was it you said about toys only being toys?'

'That wasn't what I said. Or I hope it wasn't.'

'There's been dirty work here,' said Eddie. 'Strange, dirty work. It would seem that we are already on a case.'

'Oh no.' Jack shook his head. 'That's not how it works and you know it. Someone has to offer us a case. And pay us to take it on. Pay us, Eddie, you know what I'm saying?'

Eddie nodded thoughtfully. 'So what you're saying,' he said, 'is that we should ignore the fact that a dead monkey crumbled into dust on the carpet of this office and wait until we get some meathead client to offer us money for finding their lost dog or something?'

'Well, I'm not saying *that*, exactly.'

'So what are you saying, then?'

Jack gave some thought to an appropriate answer. 'I'm saying,' said Jack, 'that perhaps we should give this some thought. Perhaps over a drink.'

'At Tinto's?' said Eddie.

'At Tinto's,' said Jack.

Eddie took a shower, because Bill's office owned to a bathroom. And Jack squeezed Eddie dry, which Eddie didn't enjoy too much, although it made Jack laugh. And Eddie unearthed his old trenchcoat and fedora, and so too did Jack, and so they both now looked like private detectives. And they took themselves down to the garage and, much to their joy, found Bill's splendid automobile just waiting to take them away.

And so they took themselves away in it, with Jack driving.

As ever, too fast.

It was early yet at Tinto's, so trade was still slack. Some construction-worker figures with detachable yellow hardhats and gripping hands gripped beer glasses and engaged in theoretical discussions on the good-looks/intelligence dialectic. Eddie had no trouble getting served.

'Howdy doody,' said Tinto. 'Eddie Bear, come to pay off his tab, by Golliwog. Joy and gladness are mine, to be sure, all praise The Great Engineer.'

'The beers are on Jack,' said Eddie.

'And howdy doody, Jack,' said Tinto.

'Nine beers, please,' said Jack, lowering himself onto a barstool and speaking from between his now raised knees.

'Nine, eh?' said Eddie. 'This should be good.'

Tinto poured a number of beers. Eddie disputed this number and Tinto poured more. Then Jack and Eddie got into the thirteen beers.

'Just like the good old days,' said Jack, raising his glass and emptying it down his throat.

'What days were those?' asked Tinto. 'I must have missed them.'

'Eddie and I have *temporarily* renewed our partnership,' said Jack. 'And there *were* great days and will be again.'

'Bravo,' said Eddie, raising his glass carefully between his paws and emptying a fair percentage of the beer into his mouth.

'Enjoy your great days while you can,' said Tinto, taking up Jack's empty glass and giving it a polish. 'The End Times are upon us and *they* won't prove to be so great.'

'End Times?' said Jack.

'Don't get him going on that,' said Eddie.

'Doubter,' said Tinto to Eddie. 'If you were of the faith you'd understand.'

'I have my own faith,' said Eddie, struggling with another glass. 'I am a member of The Exclusive Brotherhood of the Midnight Growlers.'

'A most exclusive brotherhood,' said Tinto, 'as you are the only member.'

'We don't proselytise,' said Eddie. 'You're either a Growler, or you aren't.'

'You should join The Church of Mechanology before it's too late.' Tinto made the sign of the sacred spanner. 'Already the prophecies are being fulfilled. Did you see today's paper?'

Eddie shook his head.

'The faithful are being carried off to glory.' Tinto's voice rose slightly. 'They are being taken up by the big horseshoe magnet in the sky.'

'And that's in the paper?' Eddie asked.

'S.T.C.' said Tinto.

'Ecstasy?' said Eddie.

'S.T.C.' said Tinto. 'Spontaneous Toy Combustion.'

Eddie looked at Jack.

And Jack looked at Eddie.

'Go on,' said Eddie.

'The monkeys,' said Tinto. 'The clockwork monkeys. All over the city. Last night. They Combusted.'

'All of them?' Eddie looked aghast. He *was* aghast.

'Puff of smoke,' said Tinto. 'All of them gone. All of them. Not that there were that many of them, only about half a dozen. The papers says it was S.T.C., but that's not the truth of it. Carried off to glory, they were. Transcended their physical bodies.'

Eddie and Jack did mutual lookings at each other once more.

'I may be next,' said Tinto, 'so you'd better pay up for these drinks. I want my cash register to balance if I'm going.'

'Now, just hold on, Tinto,' said Eddie. 'Are you telling me that all the monkeys—and I am assuming that you mean the cymbal-playing monkeys that bounce up and down?'

Tinto nodded.

'That all of these monkeys combusted last night—is that what you're saying?'

'I think it was *you* who just said that,' said Tinto, 'but correct me if I'm wrong.'

'But what happened?'

'It's what the papers say. Or rather what they don't.'

'This *is* a case,' said Eddie to Jack. 'This is a serious case.'

'*All* the cymbal-playing monkeys?' said Jack to Tinto.

'Thirty-three. Or was it eighty-seven?'

'You said about half a dozen.'

'Well, I'll say anything, me,' said Tinto, 'as long as it makes me popular.'

'Show me this paper,' said Eddie Bear.

And Tinto showed him the paper.

It was the *Toy City Mercury* and the spontaneously combusting monkeys had not made the front-page headlines. Eddie located a small article on page thirteen, sandwiched between advertisements for kapok stuffing and dolly hair-styling.

Eddie read the article. 'Eleven monkeys,' he whispered.

'Twelve counting the one in the beer bottle,' said Jack.

'The one in the beer bottle?' said Tinto.

'Nothing,' said Eddie. 'But this is all rot. Who is this Professor Potty who has come up with the S.T.C. theory, anyway?'

'Eminent scientist.' Tinto gathered up further empties and took to the polishing of them. 'He does that thing where he pours one flask of liquid into another flask and then back again.'

'And?' said Eddie.

'That's about as far as it goes, I think,' said Tinto. 'Not much of an act. But better than playing the cymbals and bouncing up and down. Each to his own, I say. It takes all sorts to make a world.'

'At least he didn't blame it on me,' said Eddie.

'Yes he did,' said Tinto, 'on the next page.'

Eddie had Jack turn the page.

Eddie read, aloud this time: ' "Although there is no direct evidence to link the monkeys' demise to the ex-mayor," Professor Potty said, "I can see no reason not to." '

Jack did foolish titterings.

'This is *so* not funny,' said Eddie.

'Will you be giving yourself up, then?' Tinto asked. 'I wonder if there's a reward. If there is, would you mind if I turned you in?'

'Stop it,' said Eddie. 'It isn't funny.'

'No, it's not,' said Jack, struggling to regain sobriety. 'But it's all very odd, Eddie. Do you have any thoughts?'

'I think I'd like to meet this Professor Potty and—'

'Other than those kinds of thoughts.'

'No,' said Eddie. 'Not as yet. I wonder whether Chief Inspector Wellington Bellis and his jolly red-faced laughing policemen will be investigating?'

'What's to investigate?' Tinto asked. 'The monkeys were taken up to the great toy box in the sky. What could be simpler than that?'

'Maybe so,' said Eddie, 'but I suspect that there's a great deal more to their manner of departure than meets the eye. Bring the rest of the drinks to the corner table over there, Jack. We shall speak of these things in private.'

'What?' went Tinto. 'The cheek of you! If you and Jack are on a case, then I should be part of it. I seem to recall helping you out considerably the last time.'

'You certainly did, Tinto,' Eddie said. 'But see, you have more customers,' and Eddie indicated same who were entering the bar. 'We will not presume upon your time, but we'll let you know how we're getting on and ask your advice when we need it.'

Tinto made disgruntled sounds, but trundled off to serve his new clientele. Jack loaded what drinks remained onto a convenient tray and joined Eddie at a secluded corner table.

'Why all the secrecy?' he asked, when he had comfortably seated himself.

'I don't want to alarm Tinto,' whispered Eddie. 'These monkeys were murdered, I'm sure of it.'

'You can't be sure of it,' said Jack.

'From the evidence left behind in Bill's office, I can,' Eddie said. 'The padlock had been torn from the door—our cymbal-clapping corpse-to-be couldn't have done that. Whoever killed the monkey removed the padlock and waited in Bill's office, knowing that the monkey would come there, is my guess. He sat in Bill's chair and smoked a cigar—*this cigar.*' Eddie produced a cigar butt from the pocket of his trenchcoat with a dramatic flourish and displayed it to Jack. 'There was evidence of a struggle and a round burned patch on the ceiling. The monkey was murdered, but as I said, he was more than just murdered. The worst of it is that I think the monkey must have known that someone was trying to kill him and he came to Bill's office for help, probably thinking that some new detective had taken up residence there. And had I been able to get into that office earlier, perhaps I could have helped him.'

'Or perhaps you would have been murdered, too?'

'Perhaps,' said Eddie, taking up another beer.

'So where do we go from here?'

'We have several options. We might visit Professor Potty and see whether he has anything useful to impart. We might visit Chief Inspector Bellis, perhaps get his blessing, as it were, to work the case.'

'And perhaps get yourself arrested?'

'Perhaps,' said Eddie once again. 'But I have another idea. What we have to consider here, Jack, is motive. Why would someone want to murder every cymbal-playing monkey in Toy City?'

Jack looked at Eddie.

'Apart from the fact that they are a damned nuisance,' said Eddie. 'This seems to have been a very well-planned mass-murder. All in a single night? All the work of a single killer? I wonder.'

'So what do you have in mind?'

'This,' said Eddie, and he pushed the cigar butt in Jack's direction, 'this is the only piece of solid evidence we have. It's an expensive cigar. I wonder how many cigar stores in Toy City stock them? I wonder if they might recall a recent client?'

'Seems logical,' said Jack. 'So how many cigar stores *are* there in Toy City?'

'Just the one,' said Eddie.

It had to be said that Jack was very pleased to be back behind the wheel of the late Bill Winkie's splendid automobile. It was an Anders Faircloud, made from pressed tin the metallic blue of a butterfly's wing. It was long and low and highly finned at the tail. It had pressed-tin wheels with breezy wide hubs and big rubber tyres.

Jack, who hadn't driven for a while and who could in all honesty never have been described as a competent driver, nevertheless felt confident behind the wheel. Perhaps just a little overconfident. And as it happens, Jack was also now a little drunk. He and Eddie left Tinto's Bar and Jack followed Eddie's directions to Toy City's only cigar store.

'Slow down!' shrieked Eddie, cowering back in his seat.

'I am slowed down,' said Jack. 'Don't make such a fuss.'

'Slow down, it's right here. No, I didn't say turn left!'

The car, now turned left upon two of its wheels, bumped up onto the pavement. Shoppers scattered and those with fists shook them. Jack did backings up.

'We'll walk in future,' Eddie cowered. 'I'd quite forgotten all this.'

'I know what I'm doing,' said Jack, reversing further into oncoming traffic.

'We're all gonna die,' said Eddie.

Toy City's only cigar store, Smokey Joe's Cigar Bar, was a suitably swank affair, with lots of polished wood and a window full of smoking ephemera—all those things that look so interesting that they really make you want to take up smoking.

Jack ground the polished wheel-hubs of Bill's splendid automobile along the kerb before Smokey Joe's Cigar Bar and came to a juddering halt.

Eddie, who had seriously been considering converting to Mechanology and preparing to make his personal apologies to whom it might concern for not joining earlier, climbed down from the car, waddled around to Jack's side and, as Jack climbed out, head-butted him in the nuts.

Jack doubled up in considerable pain.

'When I say "slower", I mean it, you gormster!' said Eddie. 'Now act like a professional.'

Jack crossed his legs and wiped tears from his eyes. 'If you ever do that to me again,' he said, 'I will tear off your head and empty you out.'

'Jack, you wouldn't!'

'Right now I feel that I would.'

'Then I'm sorry,' said Eddie. 'So if you are up to it, do you think that you could see your way to limping into Smokey Joe's Cigar Bar, doing your toff act and finding out who bought the cigar?'

'I'll try,' said Jack. 'Sometimes I really hate you.'

'Do you?' said Eddie.

'Not really,' said Jack.

Jack did a bit of trenchcoat adjustment and fedora tilting, pushed open the door and entered Smokey Joe's Cigar Bar. The door gave a merry *ting, ting* as he did so.

'You shouldn't do that,' the bell told the door. 'That's my job.'

Jack stood in the doorway and breathed in Smokey Joe's Cigar Bar.

And for those of you who have never been in a cigar store, that is just what you do: you breathe it in, is what you do.

There is a magic to cigars, a magic never found in cigarettes. Cigars are special; there are complicated procedures involved in the manufacture of them. There is certain paraphernalia necessary for the proper smoking of them, such as special end-cutters, and certain matches for the lighting thereof. And who amongst us does not know that the very best of all cigars are rolled upon the thigh of a dusky maiden? A cigar is more than just a smoke, as champagne is more than just a fizzy drink, or urolagnia is more than just something your girlfriend might not indulge you in, no matter how much money you've recently spent buying her that frock she so desperately wanted. And so on and so forth and suchlike.

Jack breathed in Smokey Joe's Cigar Bar.

'It really smells in here,' he said.

Eddie Bear made growling sounds.

'A fine smell, though,' said Jack.

Mahogany-framed glass cases displayed a multiplicity of wonderful cigars, cigars of all shapes and sizes and colours, too. There were pink cigars and blue ones and some in stripes and checks. And of their shapes, what could be said?

'These ones look like little pigs,' said Jack, and he pointed to them.

Eddie cocked his head on one side. 'Do you see what *those ones* look like?'

'And how might I serve you, sir?'

Jack tipped up the brim of his fedora and sought out the owner of the voice: the proprietor of Smokey Joe's Cigar Bar, Smokey Joe himself.

'Ah,' said Jack as he viewed Smokey Joe.

The proprietor smiled him a welcome.

> Smokey Joe was a sight to behold
> A sight to behold was he.
> His head was a ball,
> And his belly a barrel,
> His ears were a thing of beaut-ee.
>
> He was built out of brass,
> And if questions were asked
> Regarding the cut of his jib,
> He'd reply with a laugh
> And a free autograph,
> Signed by a pen with a nib.

And he chugged a cigar
In his own cigar bar,
For bellows were built in his chest.
And he blew out smoke-rings
And numerous things,
Which had all his clients impressed.

'What exactly *was* that?' asked Eddie.

Jack shrugged. 'Poetry?' he said.

'Odd,' said Eddie. 'Now go for it, Jack.'

And so Jack went for it.

'My good fellow,' said Jack, 'are you the proprietor of this here establishment?'

'That I am, your lordship,' said the proprietor, sucking upon his cigar and blowing out a puff of smoke in the shape of a sheep. 'Smokey Joe's my name and I am the purveyor of the finest cigars in Toy City.'

'Well, be that as it may,' said Jack.

'It may well be because it is, your lordship.'

'Right,' said Jack. 'Well, now we've established that, I require your assistance concerning a cigar.'

'Then you have certainly come to the right place, your lordship. If there is anything that needs knowing about cigars and isn't known to myself, then I'll be blessed as a nodding spaniel dog and out of the window with me and into the duck pond.'

'Quite so,' said Jack.

'And you can use my head for a tinker's teapot and boil my boots in lard.'

'Most laudable,' said Jack.

'I'll go further than that,' said Smokey Joe. 'You can take my wedding tackle and—'

'I think you've made your point,' said Jack. 'You know about cigars.'

'And pipes,' said Smokey Joe. 'Although that's only a hobby of mine. But every man should have a hobby.'

'Well, if they can't get a girlfriend,' said Jack.

'You are the very personification of wisdom.'

'Well . . .'

Eddie gave Jack's left knee a sound head-butting. 'Get on with it,' he whispered.

'Cigars,' said Jack, to Smokey Joe. 'Well, one cigar in particular.'

'Would it be the Golden Sunrise Corona?' asked Smokey Joe. 'The veritable king of cigars, made from tobacco watered by unicorn's wee-wee and rolled upon the thigh scales* of golden-haired mermaids?'

'No,' said Jack. 'But you sell such cigars?'

'No,' said Smokey Joe, 'but a proprietor must have his dreams. And speaking of dreams, last night I dreamed that I was a chicken.'

'A chicken?' said Jack.

'They worry me,' said Smokey Joe.

'They do?' said Jack. Eddie head-butted his left knee once more. 'Well, I'm sure that's very interesting,' said Jack, 'but I have urgent business that will not wait. I need a straightforward answer to a simple question. Do you think you could furnish me with same?'

Smokey Joe nodded, puffed out a question-mark-shaped smoke cloud and said, 'I'd be prepared to give it a try, but things are rarely as simple as they seem. Take those chickens, for example—'

'I am in a hurry,' said Jack. 'I merely wish to know about a cigar.'

Smokey Joe let free a sigh of relief, which billowed considerable smoke. 'Not chickens, then?' said he.

'No,' said Jack. 'What is your problem with chickens?'

'The scale of them,' said Smokey Joe.

'Chickens don't have scales,' said Jack. 'Chickens have feathers.'

Smokey Joe fixed Jack with a troubling eye. 'Beware the chickens,' said he. 'If not now, then later. And somewhere else. I am Smokey Joe, the only cigar store proprietor in Toy City. I am one of a kind. I am special.'

Jack sighed somewhat at the word, but Smokey Joe continued.

'I have the special eye and I see trouble lying in wait ahead of you. Trouble that comes in the shape of a chicken.' Smokey Joe blew out a plume of cigar smoke, which momentarily took the shape of a chicken before fading into the air of what had now become a cigar store somewhat overladen with 'atmosphere'.

Eddie Bear shuddered. 'Just ask him, Jack,' he whispered, and fumbled the cigar butt from his trenchcoat pocket. Jack took the cigar butt and placed it before Smokey Joe on his glass countertop.

'This cigar,' said Jack, 'did it come from this establishment?'

Smokey Joe leaned forward, brass cogs whirring, cigar smoke engulfing his head. He viewed the cigar butt and nodded. 'One of mine,' he said. 'A Turquoise Torpedo.'

'But it's brown,' said Jack.

'But what's in a name?' said Smokey Joe. 'Or what's not? It may be brown, but it tastes like turquoise.'

---

* The debate regarding whether mermaids can be described as having thighs continues. And remains unresolved.

'And it is one of yours?'

'It is.'

'Then my question is this: do you recall selling any of these cigars recently?'

Smokey Joe nodded. 'Of course I do. I recall the selling of every cigar, because in truth I don't sell many.'

'And you sold one of these cigars recently?'

'I sold one hundred of these cigars yesterday evening.'

'One hundred,' said Jack. 'That is an incredible number.'

'Really?' said Smokey Joe. 'I always thought that the most incredible number must be two, because it is one more than just one, yet one less than any other number, no matter how great that number might be. And there must be an infinite number of numbers, mustn't there be?'

'I'm sure there must,' said Jack. 'But please tell me this: would it be possible for you to describe to me the individual who purchased those one hundred cigars from you yesterday?'

'Your lordship is surely mocking me,' said Smokey Joe, adding more smoke to his words.

'No, I'm not,' said Jack. 'I'm well and truly not.'

'But your lordship surely knows who purchased those cigars.'

'No,' said Jack. 'I well and truly don't.'

'Of course you do,' said Smokey Joe.

'Of course I don't,' said Jack.

'Do,' said Joe.

And, 'Don't,' said Jack.

And, 'Do,' said Joe once more.

'Now listen,' said Jack, 'I am not asking you a difficult question. Please will you tell me who purchased those cigars?'

'I will,' said Smokey Joe.

'Then do so,' said Jack.

'Then I will,' said Smokey Joe. And he did. 'That bear with you,' he said.

4

'It wasn't *me*.' And Eddie fell back in alarm. 'It wasn't me—I'm as innocent as.'

'It *was* you, you scoundrel.' And Smokey Joe huffed as he puffed. 'I'd know the looks of you as I'd know the colour of moonlight, those mismatched eyes and your scruffy old paws.'

'It's cinnamon plush,' Eddie protested. 'I am an Anders Imperial.'

'Oh yes? Oh yes?' Smokey Joe did rockings and smoke came out of his ear holes. 'You weren't wearing that fedora when you came into this here establishment, but I'll wager that under it there's a bottle cap in your left ear.'

'That's my special tag.' Eddie now cowered behind Jack's legs. This was all a little much.

'Scoundrel and trickster,' puffed Smokey Joe, pointing an accusing cigar at this scoundrel and trickster.

'Now just stop this,' Jack said. 'I feel certain that you have made some mistake.'

'Mistake?' said Smokey Joe and rolled his eyes, which seemed to smoke a little, too. 'He took one hundred of my finest Turquoise Torpedoes and I demand proper payment.'

'I am confused,' said Jack. 'You said that my associate here purchased these cigars from you.'

'With tomfoolery coin of the realm.'

'Still not fully understanding.' Jack gave his shoulders a shrug.

'Bogus coin, he paid me with. A high-denomination money note, in fact. I placed it into my cash register and moments after he left it went poof.'

'Poof?' said Jack, miming a kind of poof, as one might in such circumstances.

'Poof,' went Smokey Joe. 'And never take up mime as a profession. The money note went poof in a poof of smoke and vanished away.'

'A poof of smoke?' said Jack, not troubling to mime such a thing.

'And of no smoke that I have ever seen and I've seen all but every kind.'

'I am most confused,' said Jack.

'And me also,' said Eddie. 'And wrongly accused. Let's be going now.'

'Oh no you don't,' said Smokey Joe, and with the kind of ease that lent Jack the conviction that it was hardly the first time he had done such a thing, Smokey Joe drew out a pistol from beneath his counter and waggled it somewhat about.

'Now hold on,' said Jack. 'There's no need for that.'

'There's every need,' said Smokey Joe. 'You were thinking to depart.'

'Well, yes, we were.'

'And you cannot. We shall wait here together.'

'For what?' Jack enquired.

'The arrival of the constables, of course.'

'Ah,' said Jack. 'And you expect their arrival imminently?'

'I do,' said Smokey Joe. 'I pressed the secret button beneath my counter when you entered my store. It connects by a piece of knotted string to the alarm board at the police station.'

'Most unsporting,' said Eddie.

'Which is why I engaged you in a lot of time-wasting toot,' said Smokey Joe, 'to give the police time to appear.'

'Then all that business about chickens?' Jack asked.

'That *wasn't* toot. You should fear those chickens. I know whereof I speak.'

'You failed to mention that I should similarly fear the arrival of the constables.'

'I kept that to myself. Now just you stand still, or I will be forced to take the law into my own hands and shoot you myself.'

'For stealing one hundred cigars?' Jack threw up his hands. Smokey Joe cocked the pistol.

'Easy, please,' said Jack, his hands miming 'easy' motions and miming them rather well. 'I will pay you for the cigars. There's no need to go involving the police.'

'But I never bought the cigars,' said Eddie. 'It wasn't me, Jack, honest.'

'I know it wasn't, Eddie.'

'It was too,' said Smokey Joe. 'And his soggy feet made puddles on my floor. I had to employ the services of a mop and bucket. And they don't come cheap of an evening, I can tell you. They charged me double.'

'I'll pay you whatever you want,' said Jack.

'With *what*?' whispered Eddie.

'I'll write you an IOU,' Jack told Smokey Joe. 'I'm a prince, you know.'

'Then why aren't you wearing a crown?'

'Actually, I am,' said Jack. 'It's under my fedora.'

'It never is,' said Smokey Joe.

'It never is, is it?' said Eddie.

'In fact,' said Jack, 'you can have the crown and all the jewels on it. Will that be payment enough?'

'It must be a very small crown to fit under that hat,' said Smokey Joe, cocking his head in suspicion.

'Would you mind doing that again?' asked Eddie.

'Why?' said Smokey Joe.

'Well, you did it rather well, and it's not the sort of thing you see every day.'

Smokey Joe obligingly did it again.

'Even better the second time,' said Jack.

'Thanks,' said Smokey Joe.

'So, would you like to see the crown?'

'More than anything else I can presently imagine.'

'Right, then,' said Jack, and he swept off his hat with a flourish. It was a considerably flourish. A considerably hard and sweeping flourish. As flourishes went, this one was an award-winner. So hard and sweeping was this award-winning flourish that it knocked the pistol right out of Smokey Joe's hand and sent it skidding across the store floor.

'Run!' shouted Jack to Eddie. And both of them ran.

Although they didn't run far.

They ran to the door and through the doorway and then they ran no further. They would have dearly liked to, of course. They would dearly have loved to have run to Bill's car and then driven away in it at speed. But they did not. They came to a standstill on the pavement and there they halted and there they raised their hands.

Because there to greet them outside the store were very many policemen. Some stood and some knelt. All of them pointed guns. They pointed guns as they stood or knelt and they laughed and grinned as they did so. For these were Toy City's laughing policemen, though this was no laughing matter.

A very large and rotund policeman, a chief of policemen in fact, leaned upon the bonnet of Bill's splendid automobile. He was all perished rubber and he was smoking a large cigar. It wasn't a Turquoise Torpedo, of course, but an inferior brand, but he puffed upon it nonetheless and seemed to enjoy this puffing. Presently he tapped away ash and shortly after he spoke.

'Well, well, well,' said Chief Inspector Wellington Bellis, for it was none but himself. 'Surely it is Eddie and Jack. Now what a surprise this is.'

The 'shaking down' and the 'cuffing up' were uncomfortable enough. The 'flinging into the police van' lacked also for comfort, and the unnecessary 'necessary restraint', which involved numerous officers of the law either sitting or standing upon Jack and Eddie during the journey to the police station, lacked for absolutely any comfort whatsoever. In fact, the unnecessary 'necessary restraint' was nothing less than painful. The 'dragging out of the police van', the 'kicking towards the police cell' and the 'final chucking into the cell' were actually a bit of a doddle compared to the unnecessary 'necessary restraint'. But not a lot of fun.

'I can't believe it,' Eddie said, at least now uncuffed and brushing police boot marks from his trenchcoat. 'Wrongly accused and arrested. And this only our first day on the case.'

'My first and indeed my last,' said Jack.

'Now don't you start, please.'

'Look at me,' said Jack. 'They trod on me, they sat on me. That Officer Chortle even farted on me. And I could never abide the smell of burning rubber.'

'We'll soon be out of here,' said Eddie. 'As soon as my solicitor arrives.'

'*You* have a *solicitor*?'

'I'm entitled to have one. I know the law.'

'But do you actually *have* one?'

'Not as such,' said Eddie. 'It's always details, details with you.'

'And it's always trouble with you.'

'You love it really.'

'I don't.'

The face of the laughing policeman whose name was Officer Chortle, a name that made him special because it was printed across his back, grinned in through the little door grille.

'Comfortable, ladies?' he said.

'I'm innocent,' said Eddie. 'Wrongly accused. And Jack's innocent, too. He's an innocent bystander.'

'Looks like a hardened crim' to me,' chuckled Officer Chortle. 'And a gormster.'

'How dare you,' said Jack. 'I'm a prince.'

'Aren't no princes,' laughed Officer Chortle. 'That mad mayor we had did away with princes.'

Jack cast Eddie a 'certain' look.

'And,' said Officer Chortle, 'who can forget Edict Number Four?'

'I can,' said Eddie. 'What was it?'

'The one about curtailing police violence against suspects.'

'Ah, that one,' said Eddie. 'How's that going, by the way?'

Officer Chortle chuckled. Menacingly. 'And when it comes to it,' he continued, 'you look a lot like that mad mayor.'

'No I don't,' said Eddie. 'Not at all.'

Officer Chortle squinted at Eddie. 'No, perhaps not.' He sniggered. 'The mad mayor had matching eyes and those really creepy hands.'

'They *were not* creepy,' said Eddie. 'And neither was the mayor mad.'

'Not mad?' Officer Chortle fairly cracked himself up over this. 'Not mad? Well, he wasn't exactly cheerful when the mob tarred and feathered him.'

Eddie shuddered at the recollection. 'Has my solicitor arrived?' he asked.

'I'll have to ask you to stop,' said Officer Chortle. 'Solicitor, indeed! If you keep making me laugh like this I'll wet myself.'

'We are innocent,' said Eddie. 'Let us out please.'

'The chief inspector will interview you shortly. You can make your confessions to him then if you wish. Although if you choose not to, I must caution you that me and my fellow officers will be calling in later to beat a confession out of you. And as we do have a number of "unsolveds" hanging about, you will find yourselves confessing to them also, simply to ease the pain.'

And with that Officer Chortle left, laughing as he did so.

'Perfect,' said Jack. 'So it's prison for us, is it?'

'It might be for you,' said Eddie, 'if it's anything more than a summary beating. You're the meathead, after all. You have some status. It will be the incinerator for me. I'm as dead as.'

'We have to escape,' said Jack.

'I seem to recall,' said Eddie, 'that you do have some skills with locks. Perhaps you'd be so good as to pick this one on the door and we will, with caution, go upon our way.'

'Ah, yes indeed,' and Jack sought something suitable.

And he would probably have found it also had not a key turned in the lock, the door opened and several burly though jolly and laughing policemen entered the cell and hauled him and Eddie from it.

Chief Inspector Wellington Bellis's office was definitely 'of the genre'. It had much of the look of Bill Winkie's office about it, but being below ground level it lacked for windows. It didn't lack for a desk, though, a big and crowded desk, with one of those big desk lamps that they shine into suspects' eyes.

The walls were lavishly decorated with mug shots, press cuttings and photographs of crime scenes and horribly mutilated corpses. Eddie recognised the victims pictured in several of these gory photographs: the P.P.P.s who had been savagely done to death by the kindly, lovable white-haired old Toymaker's evil twin during the exciting adventure that he and Jack had had but months before.★

Upon the floor was a carpet, which like unto Bill's dared not to speak its name. And it was onto this carpet that Jack and Eddie were flung.

'This treatment is outrageous,' Jack protested. 'I protest,' he also protested. 'I demand to speak to my solicitor.'

'All in good time,' said Bellis, settling himself into the chair behind his desk and gesturing to the two that stood before it. 'Seat yourselves. Would you care for a cup of tea?'

'A cup of tea?' Jack got to his knees and then his feet.

'Or coffee?' said the chief inspector.

'I'd like a beer,' said Eddie.

Chief Inspector Bellis frowned upon him.

'Or perhaps just a glass of water.' Eddie arose and did further dustings down of himself.

'You'll have to pardon the officers,' said Bellis, leaning back in his chair and further gesturing to Jack and Eddie. 'Sit yourselves down, if you will. The police officers do get a little carried away. They are so enthusiastic about maintaining law and order. They do have the public's interests at heart.'

'They don't have one heart between the lot of them,' said Eddie, struggling onto a chair. 'They're all as brutal as.'

'They overcompensate,' said Chief Inspector Bellis. 'I except it's just the overexuberance of youth, which should really be channelled into sporting activities. That's what it says in this book I've been reading—*Learn to Leap Over Candlesticks In Just Thirty Days*, by J. B. Nimble and J. B. Quick. Perhaps you've read it?'

★ Which is to be found chronicled in that damn fine book (and *SFX* award-winner) *The Hollow Chocolate Bunnies of the Apocalypse*. Available from all good booksellers.

'I'll purchase a copy as soon as I leave here,' said Eddie. 'Do you suppose that will be sooner rather than later, as it were?'

'Well, we'll have to see about that. There are most serious charges.'

'*Charges?*' said Eddie. 'There is more than one charge?'

'You can never have too many charges.' Chief Inspector Bellis grinned from ear to ear, then back again. 'It's like having too many chickens. You can never have too many chickens, can you?'

'Chickens *again*?' said Jack.

'I like chicken again,' said Bellis. 'Again and again. I can't get enough of chicken.'

Jack shook his head. 'I am assuming that you are talking about *eating* chicken?' he said.

'Obviously. But it's such a dilemma, isn't it?'

Eddie shook his head and wondered where all *this* was leading to.

'You see,' said the chief inspector, 'my wife makes me sandwiches for my lunch.'

'Chicken sandwiches?' Jack asked, not out of politeness, but possibly more as a diversionary tactic, in the hope that perhaps Chief Inspector Bellis would just like to chat about sandwiches for a while, before sending him and Eddie on their way.

'That's the thing,' said Bellis. 'I like chicken sandwiches. But I also like egg sandwiches. But you'll notice that although you mix and match the contents of sandwiches—cheese and onion, egg and cress, chicken and bacon—no one ever eats a chicken and egg sandwich.'

Eddie looked at Jack. And Jack looked at Eddie.

'He's right,' said Jack.

'He is,' said Eddie. 'So why is that, do you think?'

'Because of the eternal question,' said Bellis.

'Ah,' said Eddie.

'Ah,' said Jack.

'What eternal question?' said Eddie.

'Oh, come on,' said Bellis. 'What came first, the chicken or the egg? I mean, how could you eat the sandwich? You wouldn't know which bit to eat first. You'd go mad trying. And believe me, I have tried. And I have gone mad.'

'Most encouraging,' whispered Eddie to Jack. 'I can see this being a long and difficult evening.'

'Is it evening already?' asked Jack.

'Let's just assume that it is.'

'There's no solution to it,' said Chief Inspector Bellis. 'It's one of those things that's best left alone. Forgotten about, in fact. In fact, let us never mention the subject again.'

'I'm up for that,' said Eddie, offering the chief inspector an encouraging smile. 'So, is it all right if Jack and I go now?'

Chief Inspector Bellis shook his head. 'Not as such,' he said. 'In
fact, not at all. There are these charges to be considered. Things do not
look altogether good for you.'

'But I am innocent,' said Eddie.

'That, I'm afraid, is what they all say.'

'But Eddie *is* innocent,' said Jack. 'And I can prove it.'

'Can you?' Eddie asked.

'Of course I can,' said Jack. 'The proprietor of the cigar store said
that Eddie purchased those cigars yesterday evening, did he not?'

'I heard him say that,' said Eddie.

Chief Inspector Bellis perused notes upon his desk. 'That *is* what
he said,' he said. 'Shortly before eight, last evening, just before he
closed up.'

'That's right,' said Jack. 'He said something about the rain and Eddie leaving puddles on his floor.'

Chief Inspector Bellis did further perusings and nodded.

'Then it can't have been Eddie,' said Jack.

'No, it can't,' said Eddie. 'I have an alibi. I was in Tinto's Bar at that
time, and that's right across the city.'

Chief Inspector Bellis made a thoughtful face. It was a very good
thoughtful face and both Jack and Eddie were tempted to ask him to
make it once more. But only tempted. They showed laudable restraint.
'Well, an alibi is an alibi,' said the chief inspector. 'But I can see no reason why we should let that stand in the way of letting the law take its
course and justice getting done.'

'Eh?' said Eddie.

'What?' said Jack.

'Well,' said Bellis, 'as I won't be following up on the alibi, it hardly
matters, does it?'

'Eh?' said Eddie again.

And Jack did another *'What?'* Although louder than the first.

'Crime and punishment share a certain empathy,' Chief Inspector
Bellis explained, 'in that both are dispassionate. The criminal goes
about his work in a dispassionate manner. He cares not whom he hurts
or harms. He doesn't care about the feelings of others. And so the law
behaves towards the criminal in a similar manner. The law cares not for
the criminal, it simply seeks to lock him away so that he may perform
no further crime.'

'But I'm innocent,' said Eddie.

'And if I were not dispassionate, I would care for your woes,' said

Bellis. 'But that would be unprofessional. I must never get personally involved. There's no telling what might happen if I did so, is there?'

'You might free the innocent and convict only the guilty,' was Eddie's suggestion.

'The distinction between guilt and innocence is a subtle one.'

'No, it's not,' said Eddie. 'You're either guilty or you're not.'

'I'll thank you not to confuse the issue. Charges have been made and you have been arrested. End of story, really.'

'This is outrageous,' said Jack. 'I demand to speak to your superior.'

'I don't think that will be necessary.'

'Oh yes it will,' said Jack. 'I will see justice done. I really will.'

'You tell him, Jack,' said Eddie.

'You'll tell me nothing,' said Chief Inspector Bellis, 'because I am dropping all the charges.'

'You are?' said Eddie.

'I am,' said Bellis, 'because I *know* you are innocent.'

'You *do*?' said Eddie.

'I *do*,' said Bellis. 'And upon this occasion I am prepared to let the fact that you *are* innocent stand in the way of letting justice be done.'

'You *are*?' said Eddie. 'Why?' said Eddie.

'Because in return for this, *you* are going to do something for me. Something that I surmise you are already doing and something I wish you to continue doing.'

'I am now *very* confused,' said Eddie.

'I believe I am correct in assuming that you have returned to your old profession,' said Bellis, 'that of detective.'

Eddie nodded.

'You see, I *know* that it was not you who purchased those cigars with the mysterious combustible currency.'

'You do?' said Eddie once more.

'I do,' said Bellis once more. 'You see, I have these.' And he drew from his desk a number of plasticised packets and flung them onto his desk.

Eddie took one up between his paws and examined it. 'Cigar butt,' he said.

'Eleven cigar butts,' said Bellis, 'one found at each of the cymbal-playing monkeys' resting places. All over the city. Eleven cigar butts. The twelfth you showed to Smokey Joe. You went there to enquire whether he recalled who he sold it to, didn't you?'

'I did,' said Eddie.

'And the twelfth monkey?'

'Dead in Bill's office,' said Eddie.

'Intriguing, isn't it?' said Bellis. 'And they all died within minutes of each other. And I do not believe that you ran all over the city on your stumpy little legs wiping each and every one of them out—did you?'

Eddie shook his head.

'And now you are investigating these crimes?'

'Yes,' said Eddie. 'I am. *We* are.'

'And I would like you to continue doing so.'

'Really?' said Eddie. 'You would?'

'Twelve monkeys,' said Bellis. '*All* the cymbal-playing monkeys. Annoying blighters they were, I agree, but they were our kind. They were toys. The murderer must be brought to justice.'

'I don't understand,' said Eddie.

'About justice?'

'Well, I understand about that. Or at least your concept of it. Which is as just as.'

'Did you read the paper?' asked Bellis. 'The crimes made page thirteen. I requested of my "superior" that I be allowed to put a special task force on the monkeys' case. The memo I received in reply stated that it was a low priority.'

'Typical,' said Eddie. 'Disgusting, in fact.'

'I do so agree,' said Bellis. 'I blame it on that mad mayor we had.'

'Now just hold on,' said Eddie.

'Yes?' said Bellis.

'Nothing,' said Eddie. 'Go on, please.'

'You,' said Bellis, 'you and Mr Jack here are going to act on my behalf. You are going to be my special task force. You will report directly to me on whatever progress you are making. Do you understand me?'

Jack nodded. 'Up to a point,' said he. 'So we will report directly to you to receive our wages, will we?'

Chief Inspector Bellis made a certain face towards Jack. One that Jack did not wish to be repeated.

'Would there be any chance of a reward, then,' Jack asked, 'if we could present you with a suitable culprit?'

Eddie now gave Jack a certain look.

'Sorry,' said Jack. 'The *real* culprit, then? The *real* murderer?'

'Exactly,' said Bellis. 'And in return for this public-spirited action I will forget about all the trumped-up charges that we have piled up against the bear.'

'But I'm innocent,' said Eddie.

'I think we've been through that,' said Bellis. 'You and Jack will be my secret task force. You *will* find the murderer.'

'We'll certainly *try*,' said Eddie.

'Oh, you'll do more than that. You will succeed.'

'Thanks for the vote of confidence.'

'Or you'll feed the boiler.'

'Ah,' said Eddie.

'Ah indeed,' said Bellis.

'Hm,' went Eddie. 'Well, we'll certainly do our very, very best to succeed. You can be assured of that.'

'Nice,' said Bellis.

'But the trouble is,' said Eddie, 'that the only clue we had was the cigar butt. And that just led to a case of mistaken identity. So I have no idea what to do next.'

'I'm sure you'll think of something,' said Bellis.

'I'm not *too* sure,' said Eddie.

'Brrrr,' said Bellis. 'Is it cold in here, or is it just me?'

'Ah,' said Eddie.

'Ah indeed,' said Chief Inspector Bellis.

5

'That Bellis is a monster,' said Eddie. 'I'm fuel for his boiler for certain.'

'Look on the bright side, Eddie,' said Jack. 'At least we have our freedom.'

They'd had to walk all the way from the police station to the cigar shop to pick up Bill's car, but now they were back in Tinto's Bar and Tinto was pouring them a number of beers.

'I'm doomed,' said Eddie.

'You're not,' said Jack. 'He wants the case solved. And he knows that if anyone can solve it, then you are that someone.'

'Thanks for that,' said Eddie.

'Well, you can,' said Jack.

'Not for that,' said Eddie. 'For calling me some*one* rather than some*thing*.'

'I'd never call you some*thing*,' said Jack. 'You're Eddie. You're my bestest friend.'

'So we're definitely back in business together? You haven't let this first day out put you off? You're not going to quit on me?'

'As if I would. But it is a mystery, isn't it? Twelve monkeys dead, seemingly within minutes. And the cigar butts. And the cigar man thinking you'd bought the cigars from him. What do you make of it all?'

'Dunno,' said Eddie. 'Something very odd happened last night. I thought I saw something in the alleyway where I was dossing down in a dustbin, but the timing is all wrong. I do have to say, Jack, that I have no idea at all what is going on. But whatever it is, I don't like it very much.'

'How are those beers coming, Tinto?' Jack asked.

'Slowly,' said the clockwork barman. 'Could you see your way clear to giving my key a couple of turns—I think I'm running down here.'

Jack leaned across the bar and did the business with Tinto's key.

'Thank you,' said Tinto.

'You're welcome,' said Jack.

'Let's drink the beers,' said Eddie. 'It has been a long and trying day.'

'Ah, yes,' said Jack. 'And it's definitely evening now.'

'So we should drink beers and get drunk. That is my considered opinion.'

'And the case?'

'I don't know,' said Eddie, taking up a beer between his paws and moving it towards that portion of his face where many beers had gone before. And, 'Ah,' said Eddie, when he had done with his beer. 'That does hit the spot.'

'You drink too much,' said Jack.

'Too much for *what*?' said Eddie.

Jack shrugged and said, 'I dunno.'

'Then don't presume to,' said Eddie. 'Just drink.'

'You don't think that you should be applying yourself to the case in hand?'

'Not right now,' said Eddie. 'And nor should you I seem to recall that you were supposed to be meeting up with a certain dolly from Nadine's Diner tonight.'

'Oh dear,' said Jack. 'I'd quite forgotten about her.'

'Bad boy,' said Eddie. 'Very bad boy.'

Jack perused his wristlet watch. The time was eight of the evening clock. Jack held the watch against his ear: it was ticking away like a good'n and he had no cause to doubt its accuracy. Mind you, Jack had taken that watch to pieces a couple of times to see just what made it run, as Jack knew all about clockwork. Inside that watch there was nothing to be found except for a couple of cogs that connected the winder to the hands. There was no evidence whatsoever of a conventional mechanism.

But then *that* in a watchcase was Toy City. It still made little sense to Jack. Watches without mechanisms that kept perfect time. Telephone receivers connected by pieces of string. Wooden folk and folk like Eddie, a bear all filled with sawdust, yet a bear that walked and talked and thought and felt. And Jack felt for that bear.

'You've gone somewhat glassy-eyed,' said Eddie. 'Are you drunk already?'

'No,' said Jack. 'No, I'm not. I was only thinking.'

'About the dolly?' Eddie raised his glass and would have winked had he been able.

'About a lot of things,' said Jack.

'Well, don't let me keep you from the dolly.'

'No,' said Jack. 'The dolly can wait. We have a case to solve.'

'Case-solving is done for the day,' Eddie said. 'We will start again upon the morrow, as refreshed as and as ready as.'

Jack sank two more glasses of beer.

'Go on, Jack,' said Eddie. 'I'll be fine here. Go and have a good evening out. I'll see you here later if you want, or if you have a big night of it, then at Bill's office at nine o'clock sharp tomorrow.'

'Okay,' said Jack, and he rose from his stool, being careful not to crack his head upon the ceiling. 'If it's okay, then I'll see you tomorrow. Is it all right if I—'

'Take Bill's car? Of course.'

'Nice,' said Jack. 'Then I'll be off. And don't drink *too* much, will you?'

Eddie slid Jack's share of the remaining beers in his direction and said, 'Goodbye, Jack.'

And Jack left Tinto's Bar.

Jack drove slowly through the evening streets of Toy City. He could have driven at his normal breakneck pace, of course, but he only really did that to put the wind up Eddie. So Jack drove in a leisurely manner, even though he was late to meet the dolly.

Jack did do some thinking as he drove along, about Toy City and about Eddie, and Chief Inspector Bellis and the mysterious deaths of the cymbal-playing monkeys, and at length, when he arrived at Nadine's Diner, he was none the wiser than when he'd set forth.

The dolly, Amelie, stood outside the now-lit-up diner, her shift done and her temper all-but. As Jack approached her in Bill's car, he wondered a lot about her. She was, well, how could he put it? So *lifelike*. Just like a *real* girlfriend. Whatever a *real* girlfriend was. One of flesh and blood like himself, he supposed. Did that make his relationship with Amelie somewhat . . . *indecent*? Jack asked himself. *Perverted? Wrong? Twisted?*

'Easy now,' Jack told himself.

Amelie noticed Bill's car before she recognised the driver. She made a very winsome face towards the shiny automobile and hitched up her short skirt a little to show a bit more leg.

'Strumpet,' said Jack to himself.

Bill's car whispered to a standstill and Jack cranked down the window. 'Care for a ride?' said he.

'You?' and Amelie lowered her skirt. 'It's *you*. You're late, you know.'

'Blame the garage,' said Jack. 'I have just taken possession of this automobile.'

'It's *yours*?' The dolly now fluttered her eyelids.

'All mine,' said Jack. 'I have taken a new job. One with considerable cachet. Would you care for a ride?'

'I *would*.' And Amelie tottered around to the passenger door and entered Bill's automobile.

'It smells of manky old bear in here,' she said as she twitched her pretty nose.

'Mechanics,' said Jack. 'Highly skilled, but rarely bathed. You know how it is with the lower ranks.'

'Oh, indeed I do.' And the dolly crossed her legs. Such long legs they were, so shapely and slender. They were almost like re—

'Where to?' Jack asked. 'A romantic drive in the moonlight?'

'A show,' said Amelie, adjusting her over-tight top, which looked to be under considerable strain from her enhanced front parts.

'A show?' Jack said, and his wonderings turned to his wallet. He wondered just how much money he had in it. Not a lot, he concluded, not a lot.

'A lovely night for a drive,' he said.

'Then drive me to a show.'

'A puppet show?' Jack asked. 'A Punch and Judy show?'

'A proper show at a proper club. Let's go to Old King Cole's.'

'Ah,' said Jack, as Eddie had done whilst speaking to Chief Inspector Bellis.

'You're not ashamed to be seen with me, are you?' asked Amelie.

'No,' said Jack. 'Not at all. Anything but. If it's Old King Cole's you want, then Old King Cole's you shall have.'

'You are such a sweetie.' Amelie leaned over and kissed Jack on the cheek. A delicate kiss, a sensuous kiss. Just like a re—

'Old King Cole's it is,' said Jack.

Now Old King Cole was indeed a merry old soul and when he wasn't writing self-help manuals, which was all of the time nowadays as he'd only written the one, he could mostly be found at his jazz club, a rather swank affair on Old King Cole Boulevard, a place where one came to be seen.

Old King Cole had long ago sacked his fiddlers three in favour of a more up-beat ensemble: a clockwork trio, comprised of a saxophonist, drummer, and piano player. There had been a brief period when he had toyed with a twelve-piece cymbal-playing monkey ensemble, but in the end had considered it rather too avant-garde, preferring a more traditional sound. The sound of Jazz.

Now jazz is jazz. You either love jazz or you hate it. There is no middle ground with jazz and it's no good saying you like *some* jazz. Liking *some* jazz is not *loving* jazz. All right, neither is it *hating* jazz, but that is not the point. To truly love jazz you have to have a passion for it. You have to be able to get right inside it, to feel it, to . . . blah blah blah blah and so on and so forth and suchlike.

Old King Cole loved jazz. Before the passing of the infamous Edict Five, which had dispensed with royalty in Toy City, he had been King of Toy City and with him jazz had reigned supreme. After the ousting of the now infamous mad mayor, he was royalty once more and although jazz had never truly reigned supreme (in anyone's opinion other than his own) it was back at the top with him, as far as he was concerned, and if you are King you can believe whatever you want because few will dare to contradict you.

Old King Cole's jazz club was grand. It was stylish. It was magnificent. This was no gaudy piece of flash, this was old money spent well, the work of master builders.

It had been constructed to resemble a vast grand piano, atop it a gigantic candelabra, its candles spouting mighty flames. A liveried doorman, in a plush swaddle-shouldered snaff jacket with cross-stitched underpinnings and fluted snuff trumbles, stood to attention before double doors that twinkled with carbustions of cremmily, jaspur and filigold, made proud with Pultroon finials and crab-handle 'Jerry' turrets, after the style of Gondolese, but without the kerfundles.

On his feet the liveried doorman wore crab-toed Wainscotter boots in the trumped end-loungers style and★

On his head he wore a bowler hat.

Jack cruised up in Bill's automobile, leaned out from his open window and bid the liveried doorman a good evening.

The liveried doorman viewed Jack down the length of his nose. A nose that had been considerably lengthened by the addition of an ivorine nasal Kirby-todger.†

Above his moustache.

★ Stop it *now*! Ed.
† Last warning! Ed.

'Good evening to you, sir,' said he, raising a richly ornamented glove, richly ornamented with . . . * ornaments. 'The valet will park your car for you, your lordship. Kindly leave the keys with me.'

'Splendid,' said Jack, and he climbed from the car.

Amelie the dolly did likewise.

The liveried doorman stiffened slightly, in the manner of one who is suddenly taken aback. One who has seen something troubling.

Jack turned towards Amelie, who was struggling to pull down the hem of her minuscule skirt, which appeared rather keen to remain where it nestled.

'Something bothering you?' Jack asked the liveried doorman, affecting, as he did so, a most haughty tone.

'Of course not, your lordship,' said the liveried one, straightening a sleeve that was richly embellished with . . . rich embellishments.

As further liveried individuals swung wide the double-doors, with their, er, pretty bits and bobs on them, Jack, with Amelie now on his arm, entered Old King Cole's.

And Jack became all too suddenly aware that he was hardly dressed for the occasion. And he became suddenly aware of much more than that. Heads were turning, whispers were being whispered behind hands and there were tut-tut-tuttings in the air.

And then it dawned upon Jack that Amelie's choice of Old King Cole's for an evening out had hardly been arbitrary. She simply could not have gained entrance here alone, nor in the company of a non-human companion. She would never have got past the liveried doorman.

Another liveried personage now approached Jack. 'Excuse me, your lordship,' said he.

'You are excused,' said Jack. 'Trouble me no more.'

'But I regret that I must,' said the fellow. 'Are you a member here?'

'Naturally,' said Jack.

'If I might just see your membership card?'

'Well, if you must.' Jack fished into a trenchcoat pocket, drew out his wallet and from this extracted his membership card.

The liveried personage took this, examined it at length, held it up to the light and examined it some more. Presently he returned it to Jack. 'My apologies, your lordship,' said he.

'And I should think so, too,' said Jack. 'Now guide us to a favourable table and leave us there whilst you fetch champagne.'

'Champagne?' Amelie did girlish gigglings. The liveried personage

---

*Careful now. Ed.

led them to a table. It was a rather far-flung table some way away from the stage and in a somewhat darkened corner.

'Is this the best table you have?' Jack asked.

'The *very* best, your lordship. The most exclusive. The most private.'

'Then I suppose it will have to do. The champagne now, and make it your best.'

'Our best?'

'Your best,' said Jack.

And Jack held out Amelie's chair for her and the dolly settled into it. Jack sat himself down and rubbed his hands together.

'You're really a member here?' asked Amelie.

'Of course,' said Jack. 'A while back, Eddie and I performed a great service for Old King Cole—that of saving his life from the kindly, lovable white-haired old Toymaker's evil twin. He made Eddie and me honorary life members of his club. Although now that I come to think of it, Eddie never received *his* membership card. It got lost in the post, or something.'

'Is Eddie that manky bear who turned up at the diner today looking for work?'

'Eddie is my bestest friend,' said Jack. 'In fact, he is my partner in my new business enterprise.'

'*You* are in partnership with a teddy?' Amelie raised pretty painted eyebrows and pursed her pretty pink lips.

'This surprises you?' Jack asked.

'Teddies are so common,' said Amelie.

Jack laughed. And the champagne arrived. The liveried personage immediately presented Jack with the bill.

Jack waved this away with the words, 'I have an account here.'

'You do?' asked the dolly when she and Jack were alone once more.

'Let's not fuss with details,' said Jack, pouring champagne. 'Let's just try to enjoy the evening.'

'Dolly Dumpling is on,' said Amelie. 'I've always wanted to see her perform live. And I've always wanted to come here. It's so big, isn't it? And so lush.'

'It's certainly that.' Jack tasted the champagne and found that it met with his taste. 'But personally I hate it.'

Bubbles of champagne went up the dolly's nose. 'You hate it?' she said. 'You can't hate this.'

'I'm not blind,' said Jack. 'And neither are you. We both saw them whispering and pointing.'

'Yes,' said Amelie. 'I know. I know that my kind aren't welcome here.'

Jack shook his head. 'Eddie was right,' he said, 'when he tried to change things, make them better. But it was your kind, as you call them, that rose up against him.'

'I don't understand,' said Amelie. Further champagne bubbles did further ticklings.

'That manky bear was once mayor,' said Jack. 'The mayor who tried to change things here.'

'The mad mayor?' Amelie sneezed out champagne. 'That manky bear? But the mayor had blue glass eyes and those creepy hands.'

'He cared,' said Jack, 'and still does. He would have changed things for the better.'

'Things can't be changed,' said Amelie. 'Change is wrong, everyone knows that. Things are supposed to be as things are. And toys are supposed to do what they were created for. That's Holy Writ, everyone knows that. And no one could trust that mayor, not with those eyes and those creepy hands.'

Jack sighed and shrugged. 'Drink your champagne. Do you like it, by the way?'

'I love it,' said Amelie. 'And Jack?'

'Yes?' said Jack.

'I love you, too.'

Now *this* caught Jack by surprise. And caused him confusion and shock. He had not reckoned on that. Had *never* reckoned on *that*. He'd worked with Amelie for four or five months at that diner. And yes they had become friendly. And *yes* they had become lovers. But that was only to say that they had 'made love', which is to say that they had 'had sex'. Make love sounds nicer, but making love is really, truly, just *having sex* when it comes right down to it. And Amelie and Jack had come right down to it on quite a few occasions, and Jack had really been hoping that they would be coming-right-down-to-it once more, later, in the back of Bill's car. Because location and circumstance are both big factors in making coming-right-down-to-it the very great fun that it should be. And it had not slipped by Jack that coming-right-down-to-it with Amelie had been pretty indistinguishable from coming-right-down-to-it with a re—

'Don't tell me you're drunk already,' said Jack, smiling as he did so.

'No,' said Amelie. 'Not at all.' And she blew Jack a kiss and thrust out her augmented front parts.

Jack blew her a kiss in return. 'I think you're lovely,' he said.

'But do *you*—'

'Oh, look,' said Jack, 'there's someone going up on the stage.'

That someone was Old King Cole.

He'd put on a bit of weight since the last time Jack had seen him. Put on a bit of age, too, as it happened.

'He looks ill,' said Jack.

And the old King did.

He had to be helped onto the stage by minions. It must be one of the best things about being a king, having minions. Minions and underlings. And if you are a wicked king, evil cat's-paws, too. There's a lot of joy to be had in being royalty. There did not, however, seem to be much in the way of joy to be found in Old King Cole's present condition. Even though he *did* have the minions.

And everything.

His minions struggled to manoeuvre his considerable bulk. They pushed and pulled. And two of them, who seemed to chuckle as they did so, went, 'To me,' 'To you,' 'To me,' 'To you,' which won some appreciation from those who were into that kind of thing.*

The to-me-ing and to-you-ing minions positioned Old King Cole before the microphone. The old King one-two'd into it.

'Good evening, my people,' he said, once satisfied with his one-two-ings, 'and welcome to Saturday night at Old King Cole's.'

'It's Wednesday,' said Amelie.

Jack just shrugged.

'Welcome one, welcome all and welcome to an evening of jazz.'

'Nice,' said someone, for nowadays someone always does.

'Tonight we have a very special treat. A lady who is big in jazz. And when I *say* big, I *mean* big. Tonight, we are honoured by a very big presence, a very big talent. It is my pleasure to introduce to you someone who needs no introduction. I give you the one, the only, *the* Dolly Dumpling.'

There was a bit of a drum roll from somewhere and the crowd at its tables set down its champagne and put its hands together.

Further to-me-to-you-ings took place and Old King Cole was shuttled from the stage. Darkness fell, then lights came up. A curtain rose to reveal musicians. Clockwork musicians, all shiny and well polished, with pressed-tin instruments, printed-on tuxedos and matching moustaches. Matching *what*? you might ask. And well might you ask it. There was a sax player, a pianist, and a drummer, too, and then behind them a further curtain rose and as it did so a spotlight fell.

---

* And let's be honest here, who isn't? Because when it comes to royalty amongst the ranks of British entertainers, the Chuckle Brothers reign supreme. No? Well, please yourselves, then.

And a gasp went up from the assembled crowd.
A gasp that was joined to by Jack.

> She was *simply* enormous,
> Her frock was a circus tent,
> Her chins numbered more
> Than a fine cricket score,
> And her weight would an anvil have bent.

> Her breasts were so large, and I'll tell you how large,
> For if larger there were, none there found them,
> Her breasts were so large, and I'll tell you how large,
> They had little breasts orbiting round them.

'What was *that*?' asked Jack.
'What was *what*?' asked Amelie.
'Must have been poetry, or something,' said Jack. 'But *that* is one big woman.'

And she was. They sort of cranked Dolly Dumpling forward. There was some winching gear involved, which in itself involved certain pulleys and blocks and some behind-the-scenes unwilling help from minions (who did at least say, 'To me, to you,') and liveried personages (who considered themselves above that sort of thing). Ropes groaned and blocks and winches strained and Dolly Dumpling moved forward.

The musicians cowered before her prodigious approach, and thanked whatever Gods they favoured when the approaching was done.

A microphone did lowerings on a wire and Dolly Dumpling breathed into it.

It was a deep, lustrous, sumptuous breath, a breath that had about it a fearsome sexuality. A deeply erotic breath was this, and its effect upon the crowd was manifest.

Toffs in dinner suits loosened their ties; ladies in crinolines fluttered their fans. Jack felt a shiver go through him.

Dolly Dumpling rippled as she breathed. It was a gentle rippling, but it, too, had its effect. That such a creature, of such an exaggerated size, could achieve such sensuality with a single breath and a bit of body rippling, seemed to Jack beyond all comprehension, but it *was* something, something extraordinary. Yet it was *nothing*, nothing at all, when set against the effect her voice had when that fat lady sang.

There are voices. And then there are VOICES and then there is

SOMETHING MORE. It doesn't happen often, but when it does, well, when it does, IT DOES.

Jack's champagne glass was almost at his lips. And that is where it stayed, unmoving, throughout Dolly Dumpling's first song. And it never reached Jack's lips at all even after that, because at the conclusion of the song Jack set it down to use his hands for clapping. And this went on, again and again and again.

How she reached the notes she did and how she held them there were matters beyond discussion and indeed comprehension. How she achieved what she achieved may indeed never be known. And when she breathed, 'Please do all get up and dance,' then all got up and danced.

The dancefloor wasn't large but now it filled and as Dolly Dumpling's voice soared and swooped and brought notes beyond notes and sensations with them that were *beyond*, the crowd swayed and shimmied, trembled and danced. How they danced!

Jack took Amelie in his arms and although having no skills at all as a dancer, shimmied and swayed with the rest. And waltzed, too. And then did that jazz-dance sort of thing that can't really be described and which you either *can* do, or *can't*. And Jack couldn't. Dinner suits and crinoline. Slicked-back hair and coiffured coils. Menfolk and womenfolk. Jack and a dolly. Around and around and around.

Love and magic in the air, enchantment and wonderment and joy, joy, happy joy.

And.

'I say, chap, careful where you're treading.'

'Sorry,' said Jack to his fellow dancer. Then he did a bit of a dip and a flourish and then had a little kiss with Amelie. 'Isn't this wonderful?' said Jack as he twirled the dolly round. And Amelie shook her preposterous front parts and blew some kisses to Jack.

And Dolly Dumpling's voice rose and fell and the band was pretty good, too.

And 'Careful, chap, what you're doing there,' said that fellow again.

'It's crowded,' Jack called to the fellow that he had just stepped upon for a second time. 'Sorry, just enjoy.'

'Lout,' said the fellow's partner. Loud enough to be heard for a fair circle round. 'Disgusting, coming in here with that thing.'

Jack stiffened in mid-second dip and approaching kiss and said, 'What did you say?'

'She said, "Disgusting",' said the fellow, 'lowering the tone of this establishment.'

'*What?*' went Jack.

'Leave it,' said Amelie.

'No, I won't leave it.' Jack turned to confront the fellow. A very dapper fellow, he was, probably some son or close relative of a prominent P.P.P. 'What is your problem?' asked Jack, in the manner of one who didn't know.

'You know well enough,' said the fellow. 'Bringing that thing in here and flaunting it about.'

'That *thing*,' said Jack, 'is my girlfriend.' The words 'is my girlfriend', however, were not heard by the fellow Jack had spoken to, because, at the conclusion of the word 'thing', Jack had thrown a punch at the fellow, which had caught him smartly upon the jaw and sent him floorwards in an unconscious state. Most rapidly.

'*Monster!*' screamed the fellow's partner, and screaming so set upon Jack.

Most violently.

6

At least in a bar brawl you know where you are.

There are so many moments in life when you really don't know where you are. Where you stand, how you're fixed, what you're up against and so on and so forth and suchlike. Life can be tricky like that. It builds you up and it knocks you down. The build-up is generally slow, but it leads to overconfidence. The knocking down is swift and it comes out of nowhere. And it hurts.

But at least in a bar brawl you know where you are.

You generally have a choice of three places. Right in the thick of it, getting hammered or doing the hammering. Just on the periphery, where a stray fist or flying bottle is likely to strike you. Or right on the edge, at the back of the crowd, which is the best place to be. You can always climb up on a chair and enjoy the action without too much danger of taking personal punishment.

Back of the crowd is definitely the best place to be in a bar brawl.

In life, well, that's another matter, but in a bar brawl, it's the back. You know where you are at the back.

Jack was *not* at the back. For Jack was indeed the epicentre. And when it came right down to it, Jack was *not* a fighter. He was rarely one to swing the first fist and why he had done this now troubled him. But not so much as the other thing troubled him. This other thing being the handbag that was repeatedly striking his head. The partner of the fellow Jack had floored was going at Jack as one possessed. And possessed of a strong right arm.

Jack sheltered his head with his hands and yelled, 'Stop!' But the violence ceased to do so. And Jack's shout of, 'Stop!' echoed hollowly through the air, for the music had ceased and the dancing had ceased and all conversation likewise had ceased and all eyes were upon Jack.

And then Amelie swung a handbag of her own and floored Jack's attacker.

Which somehow increased the sudden silence, made it more intense.

Jack uncovered his head and glanced all around and about himself. Stern faces stared and glared at him, eyebrows and mouth-corners well drawn down. Fingers were a-forming fists, shoulders were a-broadening. Jack now glanced down at the two prone figures on the dancefloor. A little voice in Jack's head said, 'This isn't good.'

'Right,' said Jack, now squaring his narrow shoulders. 'We're leaving now. No one try to stop us.'

The sounds of growlings came to Jack's ears, and not the growlings of dogs. The crowd was forming a tight ring now, a very tight ring with no exit.

Jack stuck his right hand into his trenchcoat pocket. 'I've a gun here,' he cried, 'and I'm not afraid to use it. In fact I'll be happy to use it, because I'm quite mad, me. Who'll be the first then? Who?'

The ring now widened and many exits appeared. Jack's non-pocketed hand reached out to Amelie, who took it in the one that wasn't wielding her handbag. 'Come on,' said Jack. 'Let's go.'

And so, with Jack's pocket-hand doing all-around gun-poking motions, he and Amelie headed to the door. And well might they have made it, too, had not something altogether untoward occurred. It occurred upon the stage and it began with a scream. As screams went this was a loud one and coming as it did from the mouth of Dolly Dumpling it was a magnificent scream. Exactly what key this scream was in was anyone's guess, but those who understand acoustics and know exactly which pitch, note, key or whatever is necessary to shatter glass would have recognised it immediately. For it was that very one.

Behind the bar counter, bottles, optics, glasses, vases, cocktail stirrers and the left eye of the barman shattered. Champagne flutes on tables blew to shards and next came the windows.

Jack turned and Jack saw and what Jack saw Jack didn't like at all.

The stage was engulfed in a blinding light. Dolly Dumpling was lost in this light, as were the clockwork musicians.

Dolly's scream went on and on, if anything rising in pitch. A terrible vibration of the gut-rumbling persuasion hit the now-cowering crowd and signalled that mad rush that comes at such moments. That mad rush that's made for the door.

Screams and panic, horror and bright white light.

Jack should have run, too, for such was the obvious thing to do. He should have taken to his heels and fled the scene, dragging Amelie with him. But Jack found, much to his horror, that his feet wouldn't budge. The expression 'rooted to the spot' had now some definite meaning to him, so instead he gathered Amelie to himself and as the crowd rushed past did his bestest to remain upright and in a single piece.

The crowd burst through the doors of Old King Cole's, tumbling over one another. Unshattered glass erupted from these doors. It was a cacophony of chaos, a madness of mayhem, a veritable discord of disorder. A pandemic of pandemonium.

And worse was yet to come.

'And worse was yet to come,' said Tinto to Eddie Bear, in Tinto's Bar, some way away from the pandemic of pandemonium and even indeed the tuneless tornadic timpani of turbulence.

'Worse than what?' asked Eddie, who hadn't been listening, but *had* been getting drunk.

'The mother-in-law's pancake-cleaning facility burned to the ground,' said Tinto, 'so we had to release all the penguins and Keith couldn't ride his bike for a week.'

'You *what*?' Eddie asked.

'I knew you weren't listening,' said Tinto. 'Nobody ever listens to me.'

'They listen when you call time,' said Eddie. 'Though mostly they ignore it. But they *do* listen, and *that* is what matters.'

'That's some consolation,' said Tinto. 'But not much.'

'Take what you can get,' said Eddie. 'That's what I always say.'

'I've never heard you say it before.' Tinto took up a glass to clean and cleaned it.

'Perhaps you weren't listening,' Eddie suggested. 'It happens sometimes.'

'Well,' said Tinto, 'if I see one of those spacemen, I'll tell them that's what I think of them.'

'You do that,' said Eddie. 'And you can tell them what I think of them, too. Whatever that might be.'

'Should I wait until you think something up?'

'That would probably be for the best.' Eddie took his beer glass carefully between his paws and poured its contents without care into his mouth. 'And by the by,' he said, once he had done with this, replaced his glass upon the counter top and wiped a paw across his mouth, 'which spacemen would these be?'

'I knew you weren't listening,' said Tinto.

'You know so much,' said Eddie, 'which is why I admire you so much.'

'You do?' Tinto asked.

Eddie smiled upon the clockwork barman. 'What do *you* think?' he asked in return.

'I think you're winding me up,' said Tinto. 'But not in the nice way. I hope they get *you* next, that will serve you right.'

'Right,' said Eddie. 'What *are* you talking about?'

'The spacemen with the death rays,' Tinto said.

'Ah,' said Eddie, indicating that he would like further beers. '*Those* spacemen. I was thinking about the *other* spacemen, which is why I got confused.'

'Are you drunk?' asked Tinto.

'My feet are,' said Eddie. 'You might well have to carry me to the toilet.'

'Now *that*,' said Tinto, 'is *not* going to happen.'

'I rather thought not, but do tell me about the spacemen.'

'You're not just trying to engage me in conversation in order that I might forget to charge you for all of those beers?'

Eddie made the kind of face that said, 'As if I would,' without actually putting it into words.

'Good face,' said Tinto. 'What does it mean?'

'It means *what* spacemen?' said Eddie.

'*The* spacemen,' said Tinto, 'who blasted the clockwork monkeys with their death rays.'

'Now this is new,' said Eddie.

'Not to *those* spacemen.' Tinto took up another glass to polish, without replacing the first. Eddie looked on with envy at those dextrous fingers. 'I'll bet *those* spacemen blast clockwork monkeys all the time.'

Eddie Bear did shakings of his head, which made him slightly giddy, which meant at least that the beer was creeping up.

'Tinto,' said Eddie, 'please explain to me, in a simple and easy-to-understand fashion, *exactly* what you are talking about.'

'The clockwork monkeys,' said Tinto, 'the ones that got blasted. They got blasted by spacemen.'

Eddie sighed. 'And who told you *that*?' he asked.

'A spaceman,' said Tinto.

'A spaceman,' said Eddie. '*What* spaceman?'

'*That* spaceman.' Tinto pointed, glasses still in his hand and everything. 'That spaceman over there.'

Eddie turned his head to view this spaceman.

And Eddie Bear fell off his stool.

'Drunk!' cried Tinto. 'Out of my bar.'

'I'm *not* drunk.' Eddie did further strugglings and managed at least to get to his knee regions. 'It's your responsibility. Where is this spaceman?'

'You *are* drunk,' said Tinto. 'You drunkard. Over there,' and Tinto pointed once again.

'Ah,' said Eddie, rising with considerable difficulty and swaying with no apparent difficulty whatsoever.

Across the bar floor at a dim corner table sat a spaceman. He was a rather splendid-looking spaceman, as it happened. Very shiny was he, very silvery and well polished. He was all-over tin plate but for a tinted see-through plastic weather dome, which was presently half-raised to permit the passage of alcohol.

Eddie tottered and swayed in the spaceman's direction. The space-man looked up from his drink and wondered at Eddie's approach.

Before the spaceman's table Eddie paused, but still swayed some-what. 'Ahoy there, shipmate,' said Eddie Bear.

'Ahoy there *what*?' The spaceman's voice came as if from the ear-piece of a telephone receiver, but in fact came from a grille in his chest similar to Tinto's. The spaceman raised a rubber hand and waggled its fingers at Eddie.

'Might I sit down?' asked the bear.

'Your capabilities are unknown to me,' said the spaceman. 'Was that a rhetorical question?'

Eddie drew out a chair and slumped himself down onto it. He grinned lopsidedly at the spaceman and said, 'So, how's it going, then?'

'I come in peace,' said the spaceman. 'Take me to your leader.'

'Excuse me?' said Eddie.

'Sorry,' said the spaceman. 'That one always comes out if I don't control myself. As does, "So die, puny Earthling," and, curiously, "I've done a wee-wee, please change my nappy." Although personally I be-lieve that one was programmed into me by mistake. Probably Friday af-ternoon on the production line—you know what it's like.'

'I certainly do,' said Eddie, 'or would, if it weren't for the fact that I am an Anders Imperial, pieced together by none other than the kindly, lovable white-haired old Toymaker himself.'

'I come from a distant star,' said the spaceman.

'I thought you said production line.' Eddie Bear did paw-scratchings of the head.

'Perhaps on a distant star,' the spaceman suggested.

'Perhaps,' said Eddie, 'but then again—'

'Let's not think about it.' The spaceman took up his glass, put it to his face, but sadly found it empty. 'I was about to say, let's just drink,' he said, 'but I find to my utter despair that my glass is empty. Would you care to buy me a drink?'

'Not particularly,' said Eddie. 'But thanks for asking.'

'In return I will spare your planet.'

Eddie shrugged what shoulders he possessed. 'I would appear to be getting the better part of that particular deal,' he said. 'If I possessed the necessary funds I think I'd buy you a drink.'

'Perhaps you could ask the barman for credit?'

'Perhaps you could menace him with your death ray and get the drinks in all round.'

'Perhaps,' said the spaceman.

'Perhaps indeed,' said Eddie.

The spaceman sighed and so did Eddie.

'I wish I were a clockwork train,' said the spaceman.

'What?' Eddie said.

'Well,' said the spaceman, 'you know where you are when you're a train, don't you? It's a bit like being in a bar brawl.'

'No, it's not,' said Eddie.

'No, I suppose it's not. But you do know where you are. Which line you're on. Which station you'll be coming to next. It's not like that for we spacemen.'

'Really?' said Eddie, who was losing interest.

'Oh no,' said the spaceman, ruefully regarding his empty glass. 'Not a bit of it. We could be anywhere in the universe, lost in space, or on a five-year mission, or something. Drives you mad, it does, makes you want to scream. And in space no one can hear you scream, of course.'

'Tell me about the monkeys,' said Eddie, 'the clockwork cymbal-clapping monkeys. Tinto tells me that you know who blasted them.'

'I do,' said the spaceman.

'I'd really like to know,' said Eddie.

'And I'd really like to tell you,' said the spaceman, 'but my throat is so dry that I doubt whether I'd get halfway through the telling before I lost my voice.'

'Hm,' went Eddie.

' ,' went the spaceman.

'Two more drinks over here,' called Eddie to Tinto.

'Dream on,' the barman replied.

'Two then for the spaceman and in return he promises not to reduce Toy City to arid ruination with his death ray.'

'Coming right up, then,' said Tinto.

'I need a gimmick like that,' said Eddie, but mostly to himself.

'Who did you say was paying for these?' asked Tinto as he delivered the spaceman's drinks to his table.

'You said they were on you,' said Eddie Bear, 'because it's the spaceman's birthday.'

'Typical of me,' said Tinto. 'Too generous for my own good. But you have to be cruel to be kind, I always say. Or something similar. It's all in this book I've been reading, although I seem to have lost it now. I think I lent it to someone.' Tinto placed two beers before Eddie and Eddie shook his head and thanked Tinto for them.

'So,' Eddie said, when Tinto had wheeled away and the spaceman had moistened his throat, 'the clockwork monkeys.'

'What a racket they make,' said spaceman. 'Or, rather, *made*. Tin on tin. If I had teeth, that noise would put them on edge. I don't approve of willy-nilly blasting with death rays, but I feel that in this case it was justified.'

'I suppose that's a matter of opinion,' said Eddie, tasting beer. 'I'm not so sure that the monkeys would agree with you.'

'Each to his own,' said the spaceman. 'It takes all sorts to make a Universe.'

'So it was *you* who blasted the monkeys?'

The spaceman shook his helmeted head. The visor of his weather dome snapped down and he snapped it up again. 'Not me *personally*,' said he. 'I come in peace for all mankind. Or in this case all toykind. It would be the vanguard of the alien strikeforce who did for those monkeys. And I know what I'm talking about when I tell you these things. Trust me, I'm a spaceman.'

Eddie sighed once more. He really couldn't be doing with sighing, really. Sighing was *not* Eddie's thing.

'Do you know where this vanguard of the alien strikeforce might be found at present?' Eddie asked.

The spaceman made a thoughtful face, although some of it was lost on Eddie, being hidden by the shadow of his visor.

'Was that a yes or a no?' Eddie asked.

'It was a thoughtful face,' the spaceman explained, 'but you couldn't see much of it because it was mostly lost in the shadow of my visor.'

'Well, that explains everything.'

'Does it?' asked the spaceman.

'No,' said Eddie, 'it doesn't. Do you know where they are, or do you not?'

'They could be anywhere.' The spaceman made expansive gestures.

'Out there, Beyond The Second Big O. The Universe is a very large place.'

Eddie sighed once more. Loudly.

'Or they could still be right here. They said they fancied going to a nightclub, to hear some jazz, I think.'

There was no jazz playing at Old King Cole's, only that terrible scream and that piercing white light. And then there was a silence and a stillness and even some darkness, too.

Jack, who was now on his knees holding Amelie to him and shielding them both as best he could, looked up.

A great many of the light bulbs in Old King Cole's had blown and the club was now lit mostly by tabletop candles. Which gave it a somewhat romantic ambience, although this was, for the present, lost upon Jack.

'What happened?' asked Amelie, gaining her feet and patting down her skirt. 'That screaming, that light—what happened?'

'Something bad,' said Jack. 'Be careful, now, there's broken glass all about.'

Amelie opened her handbag, pulled out certain girly things and took to fixing her hair and touching up her make-up.

'Nice,' said Jack, and then he peered all around. They appeared to be alone now, although Jack couldn't be altogether certain, what with the uncertain light and his lack of certainty and everything.

The stage was now in darkness; beyond the broken footlights lay a black, forbidding void.

'Dolly?' called Jack.

'Yes, darling,' said Amelie.

'No,' said Jack. 'Dolly Dumpling. Dolly, are you there?'

No voice returned to Jack. There was silence, there was blackness, there was nothing more.

'I don't like it here now,' said Amelie, tucking away her girly things and closing her handbag. 'In fact, I didn't like it here at all before, either. They were horrid, Jack. I'm glad you hit that horrid man.'

'I'm glad you hit his horrid partner,' said Jack. 'Perhaps they are still lying on the dancefloor.' Jack made tentative steps across broken glass, reached the dancefloor and squinted around in the ambient gloom. 'I think they upped and ran,' he said.

'Let's go too, then,' said Amelie. 'I know much nicer places than this. We could go to Springfellows, where all the clockworkers hang out. Or the Hippodrome, where all the hippos hang out. Or Barbie's, where dollies' bosoms often hang out.'

'No, not yet.' Jack was squinting hard now into the blackened void beyond the darkened footlights. 'Do you think you could bring me over one of those candles from the tables, maybe two?'

'Well, I could, but I don't really want to.'

'Please,' said Jack.

'Well, as you ask me so nicely. And as I love you so much.'

Jack did uneasy scuffings with his feet. Amelie crunched through broken glass and brought him a candelabra. Jack held it up before him.

'This *is* rather romantic,' said Amelie, as she nuzzled close to Jack. 'And there's no one here but us. We could—'

'We could *what*?' Jack asked.

'You know what.'

'What, here?'

'We could,' said Amelie. 'And I might let you do that thing that you've always been wanting to do, but I haven't let you do yet because you haven't told me you love me.'

'Ah,' said Jack. '*That* thing.'

Amelie blew Jack kisses.

'Tempting though that is,' said Jack, 'and believe me, it's *very* tempting, I don't think it would be a very good idea right at this moment.'

'Huh,' huffed Amelie. 'Perhaps you can't do it anyway.'

Jack put a finger to his lips. 'Just a moment,' he said, in the tone known as hushed. 'I think something very bad has happened here. I want to look on the stage.'

'Shall I wait here and take off all my clothes while you have a look?'

'Just wait here.' Jack kissed Amelie's upturned face. It was such a beautiful face. It was just like a re—

Amelie grasped Jack by the arm. 'Is there going to be danger?' she asked.

'I hope not,' said Jack.

'Shame,' said Amelie. 'I really love danger.'

'Just wait here. And if I shout "run", just run—will you do that for me?'

'I will, my love.'

Jack gave a sigh that would have done credit to Eddie★ and haltingly approached the blacked-out stage. Certain sounds now came to Jack, but not from the stage before him. These sounds were of distant bells. The bells that topped police cars. These sounds were growing louder.

★ Even though sighing really wasn't Eddie's thing. As it were.

Jack climbed up onto the stage, holding the candelabra before him. Its wan light shone upon more broken glass and then upon the piano. And as Jack moved gingerly forward, more there was to be seen, and to this more that was to be seen Jack took no liking whatsoever.

Candlelight fell upon the face of the clockwork pianist. It was a face incapable of expression, and yet as Jack peered, he could see it, see it in the eyes, eyes now lifeless, eyes now dead—that look of absolute fear.

Jack held out the candelabra and moved forward once more.

The saxophonist lay on his side. The drummer did likewise. The pianist was flat on his back.

Jack knelt and touched the pianist's tin-plate chest. And watched in horror as it sank beneath his touch, dissolved and crumbled into dust.

Jack stood and Jack trembled. What had done this? He'd been aware of nothing but a blinding light. Seen no one. No *thing*.

Now trembling somewhat and wary that whoever or whatever had done this might not yet have departed the scene of the crime, Jack took a step or two further.

And then took no more and gasped.

By the light of the candelabra he saw her. Her head lolled at an unnatural angle, the neck with its many chins broken, the show clearly over. The fat lady would sing no more.

And . . .

'Hold it right there and put up your hands.'

Torchlights shone through the now not so ambiently candlelit Old King Cole's. Many torchlights held by many policemen. Laughing policemen, all of them, with names such as Chortle and Chuckles.

'Hands you, up villain,' came shouts, and Jack raised his hands.

And then they were on him and Jack went down beneath the force of truncheons.

'The force,' said the spaceman to Eddie, 'it's either with you, or it's not.'

'And it's with you, is it?' Eddie asked.

'Oh yes,' said the spaceman. 'I was thinking of going over to the Dark Side just for the thrill of it, you know. We all have a dark side, don't we?'

'Only if I sit down in a dirty puddle,' said Eddie. 'Whose round is it?'

'Yours,' said the spaceman. And he waggled his rubber hands at Eddie. 'It's your round, so go and get the drinks.'

'It's not my round,' said Eddie.

'Damn,' said the spaceman. 'That never works. I should have gone over to the Dark Side. They have better uniforms and everything.'

'Well,' said Eddie, 'I'd like to say that it's been fascinating talking to you.'

The spaceman raised a thumb.

'I'd *like* to,' said Eddie, 'but—'

'Eddie,' called Tinto, 'there's a telephone call for you.'

'A call for me?' called Eddie. 'I wonder who that might be?'

'Chief Inspector Bellis,' called Tinto in reply. 'Jack's just been . . . Now, what would that be?'

'I give up,' called Eddie. 'What would it be?'

'It's a five,' called Tinto. 'Like two is a double and three is a treble and four is a quadriplegic.'

'Four is quadruple,' called Eddie.

'Well, it's whatever five is,' called Tinto.

'Quintuple,' said Eddie.

'That's it,' called Tinto. 'He's just been arrested for quintuple murder.'

7

Night-time is the right time, when it comes to crime.

Obviously it's the right time for criminals, because they can skulk about in shadows and perform their heinous acts under the cover of darkness. But it is also the right time for policemen, because the flashing lights atop their squad cars look so much more impressive at night, and it is to be noticed that once they have reached a crime scene and blocked off the surrounding roads with that special tape that we'd all like to own a roll of,* they never switch off those flashing lights, even though they must be running the cars' batteries down, because those flashing lights just look *so good*. They give the crime scene that extra something. They are a must. They are.

'Switch off those damn lights,' shouted Chief Inspector Bellis, stepping from his special police car—the one with the double set of flashing lights and four big bells on the top—and striking the nearest laughing policeman about the helmet. 'They give me a headache.'

'Aw, Chief,' went several laughing ones, though these were out of striking distance.

'Just do it,' roared Bellis, 'and do it now.' And he crunched over broken glass and approached the ruination that had so recently been Old King Cole's.

Jack stood in the doorway, flanked by two burly constables. Jack was in handcuffs.

'And take *those* off!' bawled Bellis.

'Aw,' went one of the burly officers of the law. 'But Chief—'

---

* Well, just think of the fun you could have, sticking it over a friend's front door while they're out and seeing their expression when they come home.

'But me no buts. And where's that bear?'

Bellis had actually picked Eddie up from Tinto's. Which had come as quite a surprise to the bear. Eddie was now asleep in Bellis's car. The driver, a special constable with the name 'Yuk-Yuk' printed on his back, leaned over the back of his seat and poked the sleeper with the business end of his truncheon.

Eddie awoke in some confusion, tried to rise, but failed dismally. He had been sleeping on his left side, with the result that his left arm and leg were now drunk, whilst the rest of him was sober.

'Out!' urged the driver, prodding Eddie once more.

Eddie tumbled from the car, fought his way into the vertical plane and then shambled in a most curious manner towards the fractured front doors of Old King Cole's.

'Hurry up,' urged Bellis, 'or I will be forced to arrest you on trumped-up charges and bang you away for an indefinite period.'

'I'm doing my best,' Eddie said.

And, 'It wasn't me,' said Jack. 'Hi, Eddie.'

'Hello, Jack.' Eddie's left leg gave way beneath him and Eddie sank down on his bum.

'I'm not impressed,' said Bellis. 'Not impressed at all.'

'It wasn't me,' Jack said once more, 'in case you didn't hear me the first time.'

Bellis did glarings at Jack and then dragged Eddie to his feet. 'How many of you officers have been inside this building corrupting the crime scene?' he asked.

Numerous officers—all of the officers, in fact—made guilty faces. But one of them said, 'We all had to go in, Chief—this mass-murderer put up quite a struggle.'

'Oh no I didn't,' said Jack.

'Oh yes you did,' said officers all, laughing as they did so.

'Well, stay out now. Come on, you two.' Bellis dragged Eddie and prodded Jack.

'But sir,' said one of the burly policemen who had been guarding Jack, 'this meathead is a mad'n, sir. He'll do for you soon as give you a look.

'Stand aside, you gormster.'

Now, it had to be said that at least the policemen had set up some lights, and the interior of Old King Cole's was now well lit throughout.

And what with the devastation and the flashing of the police car warning lights, none of which had actually been switched off, it was a pretty impressive crime scene.

Eddie leaned his drunken parts against a fluted column and surveyed the wreckage. 'The last time I was here,' he said, 'was on the night I was elected mayor. Remember that, Jack? What a night that was, eh?'

'Silence,' said Bellis.

'Sorry,' said Eddie.

'I didn't do it,' said Jack.

'Shut up,' said Bellis, and Jack shut up.

Chief Inspector Wellington Bellis puffed up his chest and then blew out a mighty breath. 'Right,' said he, 'we are all alone now. Examine the crime scene. Do whatever it is that you do. Find me clues. Go on, now.'

'Then I'm not under arrest for quadruple murder?'* said Jack.

'Did you do it?' asked Bellis.

'No,' said Jack.

'Then get to work.'

'Oh,' said Jack. 'Eddie?'

Eddie shrugged. 'Let's go to work,' said he.

'Right,' said Jack, rubbing his palms together. 'Well already I deduce—'

'Jack,' said Eddie.

'Eddie?' said Jack.

'Jack, *I* am the detective. You're my sidekick, remember?'

'I thought we were partners,' said Jack.

'Oh, we are,' Eddie said, 'and in partnership you do what you do best and I do what I do best.'

'So what do *I* do best?' Jack asked.

'Well,' said Eddie, 'you might start by trying to find three unbroken glasses and an unbroken bottle of something nice.'

'I never drink on duty,' said Bellis.

'Naturally not,' said Eddie. 'The three glasses are for me—it's thirsty work, this detective game.'

Bellis made a certain face. Eddie got to work.

Jack sought bottle and glasses. Bellis watched Eddie work. He watched as the little bear climbed carefully onto the stage, dropped carefully to his belly and did peerings all about. Did risings up and chin-cuppings with paws. Did standings back with head cocked on one side. Did pickings up of somethings and sniffings of same. Did careful steppings amidst broken footlight glass. Did clamberings up onto Dolly Dumpling and peepings here and there.

---

* Clearly Tinto's reference to quintuple murder at the end of the previous chapter must have something to do with his problem with numbers. Clearly!

Presently Bellis tired of all this.

'What do you think?' he called to Eddie. 'What do you think happened here?'

'Same as the monkeys,' said Eddie. 'Their inside workings are gone. Nothing left but shells.'

'And Dolly Dumpling?' Bellis asked.

'Neck broken,' said Eddie. 'One big twist. And that's one big neck to twist.'

'Come on,' said Bellis. 'I've freed your chum here. I picked you up in my car. I can put you in the frame for the cigar heist any time I wish. Give me something I can use. This is serious now.'

'Oh yes,' said Eddie. 'It's serious now that a meathead's been murdered. Was it not serious before then?'

'*I* put you on the case,' said Bellis. 'You know that *I* thought it was serious.'

'Quite so,' said Eddie. 'Well, I'll tell you what I have, although it isn't much and it doesn't make a lot of sense.'

Bellis said, 'Go on.' And Eddie did so.

'Firstly,' said Eddie, 'I have to ask Jack a question.'

Jack's head popped up from behind the bar counter where he had been searching for glasses.

'You were here when this happened?' Eddie asked.

Jack nodded.

'Then how come you didn't see it happen? I can tell by the way the broken footlight glass lies that the band members fell before the footlights blew. Surely everyone in this room saw the murders occur.'

Jack shook his head. 'There was a really bright light,' he said. 'It swallowed up the stage and Dolly screamed and her scream shattered all the glass.'

'Can you describe this bright light to me?'

'Yes,' said Jack. 'It was a light and it was bright.'

'Would you like me to strike him about the head a bit?' Bellis asked Eddie.

'That won't be necessary. I'll do it myself later.'

'Oi!' said Jack.

Eddie grinned and said, 'I'll tell you what this crime scene tells me. Someone or something appeared upon this stage. It didn't come up either of the side steps, nor did it come from backstage, nor did it spring up out of a trap door, because there is none. It simply *appeared*.'

'Things can't simply appear,' said Bellis. 'That defies all the rules of everything. Perhaps whatever it was came down from above.'

'It didn't,' said Eddie. 'It appeared, and with the aid of some kind of hideous weaponry it literally sucked out the inner workings of the band, their very substance.'

'But not those of Dolly Dumpling,' said Jack.

'It wasn't after her,' said Eddie, 'but she was close enough to see what happened, so she had to be silenced.'

'Things don't just appear out of nowhere,' said Bellis.

'This did,' said Eddie. 'I can see all the evidence. After the slaughter, when the lights were out, Jack came up onto this stage alone, holding a candelabra.'

'I did,' said Jack.

'And two burly constables came up afterwards, roughed Jack up a bit and pulled him from the stage.'

'They did,' said Jack.

'Sadly destroying vital evidence,' said Eddie.

Chief Inspector Wellington Bellis shook his head. 'This is madness,' he said.

'If you have a better explanation,' Eddie said.

'Any explanation would be better than yours, which is no explanation at all.'

'Something has come amongst us,' said Eddie, 'something evil, something different, the likes of which Toy City has never experienced before. Whatever did this is not of this world.'

'Right, that's it,' said Bellis. 'I'm just going to arrest the two of you and have done with it.'

'On what grounds?' Eddie protested. 'You know we're not responsible for any of this.'

'On the grounds,' said Bellis, 'that if this were to get out, we'd have panic in the city.'

'No one will hear it from me,' said Eddie.

'Nor me,' said Jack. 'Will they hear it from *you*, Chief Inspector?'

'No, they certainly *will not*.'

'Then let Jack and me go about our business,' Eddie said. 'I already have certain leads to follow up. I will keep you informed of our progress—discreetly of course.'

Chief Inspector Wellington Bellis looked perplexed. Indeed, he *was* perplexed.

Jack drove away in Bill Winkie's splendid automobile. Eddie sat in the back, next to Amelie.

'I suppose we won't be going on to that other club now,' she said.

'I'll drop you home,' said Jack. 'I'm sorry the evening didn't go better.'

'We can make up for *that*,' said Amelie.

Eddie wished that he possessed eyebrows, because if he had he could have raised one now.

'I'll see you tomorrow,' said Jack. 'Eddie and I have business to attend to.'

The sulky Amelie was dropped at her door, kissed by Jack and waved goodbye to. Jack and Eddie continued on their way.

'Fine-looking dolly,' said Eddie. 'Fine long legs and big—'

'Stop,' said Jack. 'And tell me.'

'Tell you what?'

'Whatever it was you were holding back from Bellis. You know more than you're telling.'

'Of course I do,' said Eddie, 'but I wanted to put the wind up Bellis.'

'You put the wind up me, too. Monsters from outer space, is that what you're saying?'

'Perhaps,' said Eddie. 'Perhaps.'

'So go on, tell me.'

'I don't know if I should.'

'We're partners, Eddie. You can trust me, you know you can.'

Eddie shrugged and sighed. 'I know,' he said, 'but this is bad and it really doesn't make sense.'

'Just tell me, Eddie, perhaps I can help.' Eddie swerved violently around a corner, dislodging Eddie from his seat.

'Slow *down*!' cried Eddie. 'Slow *down*!'

Jack slowed down. 'Where are we going anyway?' he asked.

'Back to Tinto's,' said Eddie.

'Of course,' said Jack. 'Where else?'

Eddie sat and tried to fold his arms. As ever, he did so without success.

'Out with it,' said Jack.

'All right,' said Eddie. 'There *was* other evidence that I didn't mention to Bellis. I can tell you the height of the murderer. I can tell you his weight. I can tell you his race and his covering.'

'Go on then,' said Jack.

'My height,' said Eddie, 'my weight, my race and my plush covering.'

'A teddy?' said Jack. 'A teddy is the murderer?'

'Not just any teddy. An Anders Imperial.'

'Just like you.'

'Not just like me—more than that.'

'I don't understand,' said Jack, taking yet another corner without much slowing down.

'Paw prints,' said Eddie. 'Paw prints are as individual as a meat-head's fingerprints. Even with mass-produced toys, they're all slightly different. They're all individual.'

'So you could identify the killer from those paw prints?'

'I already have,' said Eddie.

'So you know who the murderer is? Eddie, you are a genius.'

Eddie shook his head. Sadly so, as it happened. 'I know who the murderer is,' said he, 'but I also know that he can't be the murderer.'

'You're not making sense.'

'Jack,' said Eddie, 'I recognised your footprints on that stage.'

'It wasn't me,' said Jack, and he took another corner at speed, just for good measure.

'I know it wasn't *you*. But I could recognise your footprints anywhere, as well as I could recognise my own. And that's the problem.'

Jack shook his head. 'You're really making a meal of this,' said he. 'If you recognised the paw prints, *who* is the murderer?'

'I recognised the paw prints of the murderer,' said Eddie, 'because they are *my* paw prints. But I'm *not* the murderer!'

Presently, Jack screeched to a halt before Tinto's Bar and the two alighted from the car.

'I hope he's still here,' said Eddie.

'Tinto rarely recognises licensing hours,' said Jack.

'Not Tinto, the spaceman.'

'What spaceman? There's a spaceman in Tinto's Bar?'

'I spoke with him earlier. He told me that it was a member of the vanguard of the alien strikeforce who had blasted the monkeys.'

'Ah,' said Jack. 'You had been drinking at the time, hadn't you?'

'I'd had one or two,' said Eddie, 'but I know what he told me. And he told me that these aliens fancied a visit to a jazz club.'

'Old King Cole's,' said Jack.

'Precisely,' said Eddie.

'But an alien teddy bear, who is *your* doppelganger?'

'Stranger things have happened,' said Eddie.

'Name one,' said Jack.

'Let's go in,' said Eddie.

Tinto's Bar was rather crowded now. In fact, it was rather crowded with a lot of swells that Jack recognised as former patrons of Old King Cole's.

Jack swore beneath his breath.

Eddie, whose hearing was acute, chuckled.

'We don't want their type in here,' said Jack.

'And *whose* type would that be?' Eddie asked.

'You know what I mean.' Jack elbowed his way towards the bar and Eddie followed on in Jack's wake.

Tinto was serving drinks every which way. Jack located an empty barstool and hoisted Eddie onto it. 'Drinks over here, Tinto,' he called.

'You'll have to wait your turn,' called Tinto. 'I have posh clientele to serve here.'

Jack ground his teeth.

Eddie said, 'The spaceman was over there in the far corner, Jack— can you see if he's still there?'

Jack did head-swerves and peepings. 'I can't see any spaceman,' he said. 'A couple of gollies playing dominoes, but no spaceman.'

'Tinto,' called Eddie to the barman, 'if you can tear yourself away from your new best friends . . .'

Tinto trundled up the bar. 'Did you hear what happened at Old King Cole's?' he asked.

'Yes,' said Eddie. 'But tell me this—where did the spaceman go?'

'Is that a trick question?' Tinto asked.

'No,' said Eddie.

'Shame,' said Tinto.

'So, *do* you know where the spaceman went?'

Tinto scratched at the top of his head. 'Space?' he suggested. 'Is that the right answer? Do I get a prize?'

'You do,' said Eddie. 'You win the chance to pour Jack and me fourteen beers.'

'Fourteen?' said Tinto, and he whistled. 'Was that the star prize?'

Tinto wheeled off to do the business.

Jack said, 'Eddie, did you *really* meet a real spaceman?'

'It all depends what you mean by "real".'

'No it doesn't,' said Jack, elbowing a swell who really didn't need elbowing.

'He was a clockwork spaceman,' said Eddie. 'But who is to say whether all spacemen are clockwork?'

'He was a *toy* spaceman?'

'And who is to say that *all* spacemen aren't toy spacemen?'

'I'd be prepared to say it, but as I don't believe in spacemen, it hardly matters whether I say it or not.'

'So you don't believe in the concept that there might be other worlds like ours out there somewhere and that there might be life on them?'

Jack shrugged. 'Back in the town where I was brought up, there was a lot of talk about that sort of thing. Alien abductions, they were called. People would be driving their cars at night, down some deserted country road, then there'd be a really bright light and then they'd be driving their cars again, but a couple of hours would have passed and they'd have no memory of what had happened. Then this fellow started hypnotising these people and all sorts of strange stories came out about what had happened during the missing hours. That they'd been taken up into space by space aliens and experimented upon, had things poked up their bums.'

'Up their bums?'

'Apparently the space aliens do a lot of that kind of thing.'

'Why?' Eddie asked.

'I don't know,' said Jack. 'Perhaps they have a really weird sense of humour, or they are a bit pervy—who can tell with spacemen?'

'And these people were telling the truth?'

Jack shrugged. 'Who can say? In my humble opinion they were all mentals.'

'So you're not a believer?'

'No,' said Jack, 'I'm not. I know what I believe in and I know what I don't. And I don't believe in spacemen.'

'I seem to recall,' said Eddie, 'when I first met you on the first night that you arrived in Toy City, that you didn't believe toys could walk and talk and think and live.'

'I still find *that* hard to believe,' said Jack.

Eddie made exasperated noises. Tinto arrived with the drinks on a tray. There were many drinks. Many more than fourteen.

'We're three drinks short here,' said Jack.

Tinto trundled away to make up the shortfall.

Eddie chuckled once more. 'You fit in quite nicely here now though, don't you, Jack?' he said.

'I still find it hard to believe. But I know it's true.'

'Then maybe we'll have you believing in spacemen before it's too late.'

'Too late?' said Jack. 'Too late for what?'

'Too late to stop them,' said Eddie. 'Too late for us all.'

'You're serious about this, aren't you?'

'As I said to Bellis, "If you have a better explanation."'

Jack tucked into his share of the beers. 'Spacemen,' he said and he shook his head.

'There's no telling what's out there,' said Eddie, 'Beyond The Second Big O.'

'I've heard that expression used before,' said Jack. 'What exactly does it mean?'

Eddie shrugged. 'It's just an expression, I suppose. I don't know where I heard it first. It means beyond, beyond what we know, someplace other that's different. Really different.'

'But why The Second Big O? Why not The First Big O? Why an O at all?'

'I don't know,' said Eddie, tasting beer. 'I know most things, but I don't know *that*.'

'Perhaps the Toymaker would know.'

'Perhaps, but I have no inclination to ask him.' Eddie regarded his paws. 'Taking my hands away. That was really mean.'

'They were rather creepy,' said Jack.

'They were *not* creepy! They were wonderful, Jack. I loved those hands.'

'Perhaps if you save Toy City from the alien invasion he'll fit you with another pair.'

'Do you really think so?'

'Anything's possible.'

'You believe that, do you?'

'Absolutely,' said Jack, raising his glass to Eddie.

'Then let's drink to the fact that anything's possible,' said Eddie, raising his glass between his paws. 'Let's have a toast to that anything.'

'Let's have,' said Jack, raising his glass, too.

'To spacemen,' said Eddie. 'As possible as.'

'Did I hear someone say "spacemen"?' said Tinto.

'Jack's a big believer,' said Eddie.

'There was one in here earlier,' said Tinto.

'Really?' said Eddie. 'How interesting.'

'Well, he wasn't *that* interesting. He spent most of his time cadging drinks. But he did leave something for you.'

Eddie shook his head sadly. 'You didn't think to mention this before?' he said. 'It might be important.'

'You said it was,' said Tinto.

'I just said it might be,' said Eddie.

'No,' said Tinto, 'you said it might be important. And then you said it was and then you left with it.'

'Curiously,' said Eddie, 'you aren't making any sense at all.'

'When I gave it to you,' said Tinto, 'you thanked me for it and you tipped me for giving it to you.'

Eddie shook his head once more. 'And when did I do this?' he said.

'A few minutes ago, when you came in here before.'

'What?' said Eddie.

And Jack looked at Eddie. 'A few minutes ago?' said Jack, now looking at Tinto.

'Yes,' said Tinto, now looking at Eddie. 'You took the message he left for you, then you left. Then you came back in again, and here you are.'

'Message?' said Jack. 'The spaceman gave Eddie a message?'

'No, he left it with me and *I* gave it to Eddie. Do try to pay attention.'

'What did this message say?' Eddie asked.

'Well, you read it,' said Tinto. 'You must know what it said.'

'*I* did *not* read it,' said Eddie, 'because *I* was *not* in here a few minutes ago.'

'It *was* you,' said Tinto. 'I'd know a scruffbag like you anywhere.'

'Tinto,' said Jack, 'Tinto, this is *very* important. What did this message say?'

Tinto fluttered his fingers about. 'As if I would look at the contents of a secret message,' he said.

'*Secret* message?' said Eddie.

'That's what it said,' said Tinto. 'Top-secret message for your mismatched eyes only.'

'What did it say?' asked Jack.

'I have customers to serve,' said Tinto. 'Posh customers. I have no time to shilly-shally with hobbledehoys like you.'

'What did it say, Tinto? This is *very, very* important.'

'It didn't say much,' said Tinto. 'Just the location, that's all.'

Eddie threw up his paws and shouted, 'What location, Tinto?'

'No need to shout,' said the barman. 'Just the location of where the spaceship had landed, that's all.'

8

'Toy Town?' said Jack as he drove along with Eddie at his side.

Eddie cowered in the passenger seat. 'Please slow down,' he said.

Jack slowed down, but said, 'Toy Town,' once more. 'The supposed location of the supposedly landed spaceship. Supposedly. But I thought that Toy City *is* Toy Town, just grown bigger.'

'What a lovely way you have with words,' Eddie said. 'Toy City *is* Toy Town grown bigger. But not quite in the same location. From what I've heard of the original Toy Town, it was an idyllic, paradisical sort of place, nestling against a sunny hillside—always sunny, of course, I don't think it ever rained there.'

'I'm sure it must have,' said Jack, taking another corner in a dangerous fashion and sending Eddie sprawling.

'Seat belts,' Eddie said as he climbed once more onto his seat and glared a glare at Jack.

'What would those be?' Jack asked.

'Something I've just invented, for strapping yourself into your seat in a car.'

'Sounds dangerous,' said Jack. 'You might get trapped or something, say if the car were to go over a cliff and into a river, or something. Am I going the right way? And tell me more about Toy Town.'

'It's a bit of a way yet, and you are going the right way and the car will need a few more windings-up before we get there. But, as I say, it was the original town built for toys and P.P.P.s, from the original kit, if you believe what the followers of the Big Box Fella, He Come, Jack-in-the-box cult do. Toys lived there in harmony and happiness. Then there were more toys and suburbs were built and then places for the toys to work in were built beyond these, and then homes for the rich who made money out of these enterprises beyond this. And so on and so forth and eventually up grew Toy City, of evil reputation. Folk sort of moved away from Toy Town—it fell out of favour, reminded them of their humble beginnings. The desire for progress and evolution forced them out of their simple paradise to search for a more sophisticated lifestyle, so they came to live and work in Toy City.'

'I don't quite follow the logic of all that.' Jack drummed his fingers on the steering wheel. 'But it's still there, is it? The original Toy Town? Who lives there now?'

'I think it's a bit of a ghost town now.' And Eddie shivered. 'You hear stories about odd folk who live there. Outcasts. I thought of going there myself after I lost my job as mayor. They make movies there, I believe.'

'Movies?' said Jack, and he grinned towards Eddie. 'I've always wanted to be in a movie.'

'Since when?' Eddie raised an imaginary eyebrow. 'This is the first I've heard of such a thing.'

'You mean you've never wanted to be in a movie?'

'Have you ever seen a Toy City movie, Jack?'

Jack shook his head. 'I haven't,' he said, 'but I'll bet they're much the same as the movies I watched in the town where I grew up. Action and adventure.'

Eddie laughed. Loudly. 'Action and Adventure?' he managed to say. 'Not a bit of it—they are as dull as. Biopics, they're called. Always about prominent P.P.P.s, with constant remakes. If I watch that Jack and Jill go up that damned hill one more time, I'll puke.'

'He does fall down and break his crown—that must be quite exciting.'

Eddie sighed and he was so sick of sighing. 'Trust me, Jack,' he said, 'they're dull. Dull, dull, dull.'

'So why does anyone go to see them?'

'It's complicated,' said Eddie. 'I'll explain it to you sometime, but not now. And see, just up ahead, where the street lamps end—we're almost there.'

The street lamps ended at the top of a hill. Jack drew the car to a rather unnecessarily sharp halt and he and Eddie climbed from it. Jack peered out and down at a moonlit landscape. 'Oh,' was all he could find to say for the moment.

Jack stood beside Eddie, who peered in a likewise fashion, and a little shiver came to Eddie, which wasn't caused by the chill of the night.

There was something about Toy Town that haunted Eddie. It haunted all toys in Toy City to a greater or lesser extent. Toy Town represented something, something that had been but no longer was: paradise, before the fall. In truth, few toy folk ever ventured there. Toy Town was almost a sacred place. A place perhaps for pilgrimage, but somehow, too, for reasons that, like going to see P.P.P. biopics, were too complicated to explain, a place to be feared. An *other* place. A place not spoken of.

It *was* complicated.

'Looks pretty dilapidated,' said Jack, 'but in a romantic kind of a way. The way that ancient ruins sometimes do.'

'Hm,' said Eddie, and he shivered a little bit more.

'What's that up there?' asked Jack, and he pointed.

'Ah,' said Eddie. 'The sign.'

The sign rose above the hilltop. Great white letters, standing crookedly. Great white letters spelling out 'TO TO LA.'

' "To to la"?' said Jack. 'What does that mean?'

'It originally spelled "TOYTOWNLAND",' said Eddie. 'That was the name of the original development. Seems as if some of the letters have fallen down. It's a very long time since I've been here. And I think I've now been here long enough again. Let's come back in the morning, Jack. Or perhaps you might come back on your own.'

'*On my own?*' Jack looked at Eddie. 'What's the problem?' he asked. 'Eddie, are you scared of something?'

'Me?' said Eddie, straightening what shoulders he had. 'I'm not scared of anything. We bears are brave, you should know that. We're as bold as.'

'Right,' said Jack. But you do seem to be trembling somewhat.'

'It's cold,' said Eddie.

Jack, having eyebrows, raised them.

'Yeah, well,' said Eddie, 'there's something about this place. Something I'm not comfortable with.'

'Well, I'm not altogether comfortable myself. I'm not too keen on getting blasted by a space alien death ray, you know.'

'I thought you didn't believe in the concept of space aliens.'

'I don't,' said Jack, 'but something zapped the monkeys and the clockwork musicians. And whatever it is, I don't want it to zap me as well. Nor you, as it happens.'

'We shall proceed with caution, then. I'll lead the way, you go first.'

Jack said, 'Eh?' But Jack led the way. 'Where am I leading this way to?' he whispered to Eddie as he led it. Down and down a hillside, through gorse and briars and unromantic stuff like that.

Eddie battered his way through nettles. 'Keep a low profile,' he counselled. 'And keep an eye out for anything that looks like a landed spaceship.'

'As opposed to something that actually *is* a landed spaceship?'

'You know exactly what I mean.'

Jack, keeping the lowest of low profiles despite the heightness of his height, did furtive glancings all around and continued in the downwards direction. At length, and one too long for Jack, who was now somewhat briar-scratched about in the trenchcoat regions, and who now had Eddie riding upon his shoulders due to Eddie being briarscratched about in more personal regions, the intrepid detectives reached a bit of a road, a bit of which led into the romantic ruination of Toy Town.

'They're pretty little houses,' Jack whispered, 'but they've got holes in their roofs and everything. Do you really think anyone lives here any more?'

'We bears have almost mystical senses,' Eddie whispered back. 'We can sense things. And I sense that we are being watched.'

'By spacemen, do you think?'

'There's a tone in your voice,' said Eddie. 'Put me down, please.'

And Jack put Eddie down.

Jack said, 'I don't see any landed spaceships. But then perhaps landed spaceships have some kind of advanced camouflage and can look like ruined houses. In which case, I can see lots of spaceships. Which one do—'

'Stop it,' said Eddie. 'We *are* being watched. And I don't like it here.'

'I'll protect you,' said Jack. 'I have my gun.' Jack patted his pockets. 'Oh no,' he said. 'I don't have my gun—one of the laughing policemen confiscated it.'

'We're doomed,' said Eddie. 'Do you still have your watch?'

'I do,' said Jack, holding his wrist up to the moonlight. 'It's nearly two-thirty. Time travels fast when you're having a good time, doesn't it?'

'Turn it in,' said Eddie. 'You're as scared of this place as I am.'

'I'm afraid of no man,' said Jack.

'There's something out there,' said Eddie. 'And it ain't no man.'

Which rang a distant bell, somewhere.★

'Which way do you want to go?' asked Jack.

'Home,' said Eddie.

'That's not what I meant, and you know it.'

★ Yes, of course you know where!

'It's what I mean,' said Eddie. 'I used to live here. I'd like to see my old home.'

'Oh,' said Jack. 'Right. Lead on, then.'

And Eddie led the way.

He led the way to Toy Town Square. There were ruined shops all around and about: a butcher's, a baker's, a candlestick maker's, a cheese shop and a dolls' hospital.

Jack peered through the grime-stained window of a tailor's. 'This really is a proper ghost town,' he said. 'There's still a display in this window and suits of clothing hanging up.' Jack moved on through the square. 'Same in the cheese shop,' he said. 'It's full of old cheese. How come when the traders moved away they left their stock behind?'

'They moved away fast,' said Eddie. 'In a single day. All at once.'

'But I thought you said—'

'I know what I said. I didn't say how fast they all moved to Toy City.'

'What happened here, Eddie? Something bad, was it?'

'I don't want to talk about it now.'

Jack shook his head. 'Are we still being watched? What do your special senses tell you?'

Eddie nodded. 'We're still being watched. Come on, this way.'

And so they moved on, across the moonlit square, into a side alley that wasn't really lit very well at all, into worrying darkness, then out into some small light.

'Ah,' said Jack. 'I see.'

Before them stood a little house. A pretty little house. It was a man-sized pretty little house. A flaky painted sign upon the aged front door spelled out the name 'WINKIE' in archaic lettering.

'Bill Winkie's house,' said Jack. 'The house of Wee Willy Winkie. And you were his bear.'

'I was Bill's bear,' said Eddie. And he produced a key from his trenchcoat pocket. 'Would you care to let us in, Jack?'

Jack took the key from Eddie. 'You have the key with you,' he said, 'but you didn't know we were coming here. I mean—'

'I've always carried it, one way or another, and the another way wasn't very comfortable,' Eddie said. 'I carry it as a kind of good-luck charm, or something.'

'Oh.' Jack said no more, but tried the key in the lock. After some struggling, he turned it. 'Are you sure about this?' he asked Eddie. 'Sure that you want to go in? It might be painful for you. I know how much you loved Bill.'

'It will be painful,' said Eddie, 'but I have to There's something I have to know.'

'All right.' Jack drew the key from the lock, returned it to Eddie, then pressed his hands to the door, which opened, silently.

'There should be a candle box on the wall to your left,' said Eddie. Jack felt around to his left, found the candle box, located candles within it and a tinderbox, fumbled about with the tinderbox, drew sparks, then fire from it, lit a candle. Jack held up this candle.

'What do you see?' Eddie asked.

'Just a room,' said Jack. 'Quite tastefully furnished. Are you coming in, then?'

Eddie followed Jack.

Jack spied candles set in wall sconces, others upon a table. Jack lit these candles with his. Soft light filled the room.

Eddie gazed around and about it. 'Just as I feared,' he said.

'Feared?' Jack asked. 'What did you fear?'

'The hinges on the front door have been oiled and there's no dust,' said Eddie. Look at the tables and the chairs and the floor—no dust. Someone's living here.'

'Upstairs, do you think? Asleep?'

'Possibly. Jack, give me a hand, if you will.'

'What's this, then?'

Eddie was tugging at a rug. 'Help me with this.'

Jack did tuggings, too. They tugged the rug aside.

'Ring in the floorboards,' said Eddie. 'Secret compartment. Lift the trap door, Jack.'

'Oh,' said Jack. 'Exciting. What's down there?'

'You'll see.'

Jack pulled upon the ring and the trap door lifted He held up his candle. 'Golly,' he said.

'Golly? Where?'

'Term of surprise,' said Jack, 'not golly as in gollwog.' And then Jack did awed whistlings. 'This is what you'd call an arms cache,' said he, once done with these whistlings.

'Well, Bill *was* a private eye.'

'And part-time arms dealer?' Jack beheld the stash that lay beneath, steely parts glinting in the candlelight. There were many guns there, big, impressive guns, toy guns all, although toy guns got the business done in these parts.

'Just haul up some weaponry.'

'Okey-dokey,' said Jack, 'will do.' And he lowered himself into the secret hideaway beneath and handed weapons up to Eddie. And as he did so, Jack did thinkings. What exactly was all this about? went one of these thinkings. What exactly happened here in Toy Town that drove its population away at the hurry-up, without their possessions? Why would Bill Winkie really have needed so much high-powered weaponry? And there would have been more thinkings along these lines had not Eddie hurried Jack up and broken the chain of these thinkings.

'It's too much to carry anyway,' said Jack.

'And those grenades,' said Eddie.

'This is ridiculous,' said Jack.

'You'll thank me for it later,'

'What was *that*?'

'What?' said Eddie.

'I thought you bears had special senses,' whispered Jack. 'I heard something.'

'Come on, then, hurry up—gather up guns and let's be off.'

The sound of voices now came to the ears of both Eddie and Jack.

'On second thoughts,' whispered Eddie, now tossing weaponry back down to Jack, 'it might be more propitious for us to hide.'

'But we're all tooled-up.'

'These guns are *very* old.'

'Sling the rest of them down here and follow on, then.'

Eddie did so. Jack climbed from the secret hideaway, extinguished candles, did complicated in-the-dark back-tuggings of the rug and lowerings of the trap door over him and Eddie.

Voices, slightly muffled now but growing louder nonetheless, were to be heard above.

'And *I* say that I locked the door behind us,' said one voice.

'And *I* say that you forgot,' said another. 'And as I'm in charge, that's final.'

'Oh yes, so who put you in charge?'

'You know perfectly well. This operation has to be carried out with military precision. I'm in charge, you are merely my comedy sidekick.'

'I'm *not* a comedy sidekick, I'm a professional.'

'Light the candles, then.'

There came now the sound of a slight scuffle, followed by a heavy thump. Right on top of the trap door.

Eddie flinched, as did Jack, though neither saw the other do it.

'Good comedy falling,' said one of the voices. 'See, you excel at that kind of thing. Stick to what you know. I'll be in charge, you do the comedy falling about.'

'I didn't do it on purpose. Someone scuffed up this rug. Someone's been here.'

'Well, they're not here now.'

'They might be upstairs, asleep.'

'There's no one here. Just you and me and our little cargo, of course. You didn't damage the cargo with your comedy falling, did you?'

'Of course I didn't. I'll put it here on the table—do you want to see it?'

'Best see it, I suppose. Not that I really want to.'

'No, nor me—they give me the creeps, they way they move about in their little jars. They're really horrid.'

Eddie looked at Jack in the darkness beneath.

Jack looked at a spider. He thought he was looking at Eddie.

'One little peep, then,' said one of the voices above.

'One is quite enough. I'll be glad when this job is done. If it ever is done. I can see this job going on for ever. Or at least until everyone in Toy City is jarred-up. They are valuable commodities back home. The boss will have us jar-up the entire city, you see if I'm wrong.'

'It's not right, you know.'

'Right doesn't enter into it. It's business, pure and simple. Gather them up, take them back, that's what we're paid for.'

'But they're living beings.'

'They're toys.'

'Yes, but *living* toys.'

'Well, of course they are. There wouldn't be much point in going to all this trouble if they weren't living, would there?'

'But it's murder when it comes right down to it.'

'Murder of *toys*?'

'Oh, look at that one in the jar at the end. It's really agitated.'

'The bandleader. He's frisky all right, just like those monkeys. Shut the case up, I don't like looking at them.'

Eddie and Jack heard muffled clickings.

Then they heard a voice say, 'Get your stuff from upstairs and we'll be off. We have to deliver tonight's cargo by dawn.'

And then they heard departing footsteps.

Then returning footsteps.

Then departing footsteps again and the slamming of the front door.

'Do you think they're gone?' Jack whispered.

'Hold on a bit longer,' said Eddie. 'Just to be sure.'

Time passed.

'They've gone,' whispered Eddie.

Jack pushed up the trap door, rug and all, emerged from the hideaway, blundered around in the darkness and eventually brought light once more to the late Bill Winkie's parlour.

'Well, what do you make of all *that*?' Jack asked.

'Nothing good,' said Eddie.

'Shouldn't we be following them?' Jack asked.

'No,' said Eddie, 'we shouldn't.'

'Why not?'

'Because we're not ready to deal with this yet, Jack. We don't know what's going on—we have to know more.'

'Then we should follow them now.'

'They said they were delivering tonight's cargo. They'll be coming back tomorrow, I would guess. Let's make certain we're ready and waiting for them then.'

'Sound enough,' said Jack. 'But what were they talking about? What did they have in their jars?'

'Souls, perhaps,' said Eddie. 'The souls of the clockwork band.'

'Their souls, Eddie? What are you saying?'

'You heard what I heard, Jack. Draw your own conclusions.'

'I heard what you heard, Eddie, but did you hear *what* I heard? *What* we heard?'

'I don't know what you mean,' said Eddie.

'Oh, I think you do. The voices, Eddie. You heard the voices.'

'Of course I heard them. Now stop talking, let me think.'

'No,' said Jack. 'You heard them as I did. You heard those voices.'

'I heard them,' said Eddie. 'Now stop.'

'Not until you've said it.'

'Said what?'

'You know exactly what. Now say it.'

'I don't know what you're talking about.'

'Yes you *do*, Eddie. Say it.'

'All right!' Eddie glared at Jack. 'I know what you want me to say that I heard. And all right, I *did* hear it, same as you heard it. Their voices. All right, I heard them.'

'Say it,' said Jack.

'They were *our* voices,' said Eddie. 'Yours and mine. Our voices. All right, I've said it—are you happy?'

'No,' said Jack. 'I am *not*. They *were* our voices. What does this mean?'

'It means,' said Eddie, 'that not only is there a doppelganger of me doing these murders, but there's one of you, too.'

Jack did shudderings. 'I was really hoping that you might have been able to come up with a comfier explanation than that,' he said.

'Comfier?' said Eddie.

'This is really scary stuff,' said Jack. 'Doppelgangers of you and me? I don't know about the soul-stealing business, but murdering doppelgangers is scary enough for me. Were they space aliens, do you suppose?'

Eddie shrugged as best as he was able. 'I suppose so,' he said.

'But space aliens don't go stealing souls,' said Jack.

'Oh, you know all about the habits of space aliens now, do you?'

'I know what I know,' said Jack. 'There's a blinding light and the space aliens abduct you, stick instruments up your bottom and then return you hours later with your memories erased. That's what space aliens do.'

'You do talk twaddle, Jack.'

'Listen,' said Jack, 'that's what space aliens do, if there are space aliens. But as I don't believe in space aliens, I don't care whether you believe me or not.'

Eddie was now thumping his head with his paws.

'I hate it when you do that,' said Jack.

'It helps to jiggle my brainy bits about,' said Eddie. 'Aids cogitation. We have all the clues, Jack, I'm sure we do. We can figure this thing out. *I* can figure this thing out.'

'Let's tell Bellis what we heard here,' said Jack. 'Let him and his laughing policemen lay in wait for these—'

'Doppelgangers of us?' said Eddie.

'Whatever they are.'

Eddie gave his head some further thumpings. 'Something is coming,' he said.

'An idea?' asked Jack. 'An answer? What?'

'Something,' said Eddie. 'Something.'

'Something,' said Jack. And then he said, 'Eddie?'

'What, Jack, what?'

'Eddie, something.'

And then something came upon them. It came upon them in a blinding light, which rushed at them through the windows and up through the cracks between the floorboards and around the trap door and in through the keyhole and down the chimney and even up the plughole in the sink in the kitchen. And this light was white and this light was pure and this light was fearsome.

And Eddie clung to the legs of Jack and Jack held Eddie's head in one hand and shielded his eyes with the other. And Eddie screamed. And Jack screamed. They screamed together. Together as one. And the bright white light engulfed them, surrounded them, and swallowed them up.

And was gone.

'Careful,' said Eddie. 'Look where you're driving.'

Jack swung the wheel; the car all but struck a fence. Nearly went over a cliff and into a river. Jack jammed his foot upon the brake.

'That was close,' he said.

'You dozed off,' said Eddie. 'Fell asleep at the wheel.'

'I'm sorry,' said Jack. 'It's been a long night. I'm tired.'

'You were asleep.'

'I'm sorry, I said. Where are we?'

'Nearly home, I think.'

'Nearly home?'

'Nearly home.'

'But—' said Jack.

'But what?'

'But we weren't driving home. We were—'

'We were what?'

'We were somewhere, weren't we?'

'We were at Tinto's Bar and now we're driving home.'

'No,' said Jack. 'We were somewhere else after Tinto's Bar—we went somewhere else.'

'No we didn't,' said Eddie. 'We had a beer, several, in fact. Many, in fact.'

'I didn't,' said Jack. 'I'm confused.'

'See, you did have beers.'

'Did you have beer?'

'Do my kind defecate in the woodland regions?'

'Then you're drunk.'

Eddie felt at his legs. 'I'm not,' said he. 'My legs are not.'

'Something happened, Eddie, something weird.'

'Jack, you're not making sense.'

'There was a light,' said Jack. 'A very bright light.'

'You *are* drunk.'

'I'm not,' said Jack. He looked at his watch. 'Five a.m. in the morning,' he said. 'The sun's coming up.'

'Five in the morning?' said Eddie. 'That's odd. I thought it was about two.'

'There was a bright light,' said Jack. 'I remember a light. And there's something more.'

'Something more?'

'My bottom's sore,' said Jack.

'Oh,' said Eddie. 'That's funny.'

'It's not,' said Jack. 'It hurts.'

'No, I didn't mean that it's funny like that. I mean it's funny because my bum is sore, too.'

Jack looked at Eddie.

And Eddie looked at Jack.

'Aaaaaaagh!' they both agreed.

9

'No,' said Eddie. 'No, no, no.'

'Yes,' said Jack. 'I think so, yes.'

It was nine of the morning clock now and they hadn't slept, or at least they thought they hadn't slept. They were back in Bill Winkie's office. Eddie sat on Bill Winkie's desk in a bowl of iced water. Jack sat in Bill's chair upon several cushions.

And, 'No,' said Eddie once again. 'It can't have happened, no.'

'I don't get you at all,' said Jack, rootling around in desk drawers in search of a bottle of something. 'You were the one saying that it was space aliens and now we've been abducted by space aliens and returned with our memories erased and you're saying no, it can't have happened. Why are you saying this, Eddie?'

'Because,' said Eddie, shifting uncomfortably upon his sore bottom. 'Just because, that's all.'

'Just because they're *my* kind of space aliens.' Jack shifted uncomfortably in Bill's chair. 'That's it, isn't it? You wanted clockwork space aliens with tin-plate ray guns and now you're jealous—'

'Jealous?' said Eddie.

'No,' said Jack, 'jealous is not the word I mean. You're miffed.'

'That's nothing like jealous at all.'

'But you are miffed, because it was *my* space aliens. Because I was right and you were wrong.'

'Then pat yourself on the back for being right.' Eddie made a huffy face. 'But pat yourself on the shoulders to avoid your punctured bum.'

'Stop. Don't even think about that. What do you think they did to us?'

'If I don't even think about it, then I don't know.'

'We were abducted.' Jack now made a different face from the one he had previously been making, the one that would have turned the milk sour if there'd been any milk around, but there wasn't any, because he and Eddie hadn't got around to buying any, as they spent most of what money they had upon alcohol. The different face that Jack made was of that variety that one sees in those big paintings of the saints whilst they are being horribly martyred in some unspeakable fashion (which often tends to involve certain pointy things being thrust up certain tender places). It is the face of the beatified. There's no mistaking it.

'What does *that* face mean?' asked Eddie

'It means that we have become two amongst the chosen.' Jack linked his fingers, as in prayer. 'It means we're special, Eddie.'

'I was special anyway.' Eddie splashed iced water about himself. 'I have a special tag in my ear to prove it and everything.'

'We were taken up,' said Jack, in the voice of one evangelising. 'We were taken up into the light.'

'By sexual perverts,' said Eddie. 'Don't forget that part.'

'They might have implanted us,' said Jack, in no less evangelising a tone. Well, perhaps just a little less. Perhaps with a hint of a tone of troubledness to it.

'You mean they've made us pregnant?' Eddie all but fell out of his bowl.

'No,' said Jack. 'They stick implants up your nose.'

'Up your bum, up your nose? What is the matter with these people?'

'We can't be expected to understand them,' said Jack. 'Their thinking patterns are totally different from ours. It would be like you trying to communicate with a beetle.'

'Some of my best friends are beetles,' said Eddie. 'But this doesn't make any sense, the way you're talking. I seem to recall that you *do not believe in space aliens.*'

'I've been converted,' said Jack. 'I've seen the light.'

'Just like that? There could be all manner of other explanations. You shouldn't go jumping to conclusions.'

'The bright light. The missing time. The erased memories. The . . .' Jack indicated the area of his anatomy that rested gingerly upon the cushions. 'It all fits together. There's no point in denying it.'

'All right,' said Eddie. 'All right. Something happened to us. Something worrying.'

'We were taken up into the light.'

'Stop saying that or I'll bite you somewhere that will take your mind off your sore bottom. Although not by many inches.'

Jack crossed his legs, said, 'Ouch,' and uncrossed them again.

'Something happened to us,' Eddie continued. 'I don't know what and you don't know what, either. Somehow we will have to find out what. It all has to be part of the case. A big part. Think hard, Jack. Do you remember anything at all?'

'Leaving Tinto's,' said Jack. 'Driving. Then a really bright light, then waking up in the car, which was nearly going over a cliff and into a river.'

'And nothing else?'

'Nothing.'

Eddie dusted at his trenchcoat; its hem was sodden in the water bowl. 'We went somewhere after we left Tinto's. Hold out your hands, Jack.'

Jack gave a doubtful look. 'Why?' he asked. 'You're not going to bite me, are you?'

'I just want to look at your hands. Stick 'em out.'

Jack stuck 'em out.

Eddie examined Jack's hands. 'Interesting,' he said. 'Turn them over.'

Jack turned them over.

'*Very* interesting,' said Eddie. 'Now stand up, turn slowly around and show me the soles of your shoes.'

'Are you having a laugh, Eddie?'

'Please just humour me.'

Jack rose carefully, pushed back the chair carefully, did a slow twirl, with equal care, then lifted one foot and then the other towards Eddie. With insufficient care, Jack fell down in a heap.

'Always the comedy sidekick,' said Eddie. 'What would I do without you?'

'I'm not a comedy sidekick,' said Jack, rising *very* carefully and lowering himself with considerable care back onto the cushions.

'Well, you had an interesting night out,' said Eddie, 'by the evidence upon your person.'

'Did I?' said Jack. 'Go on.'

'You took a walk in the countryside,' said Eddie, 'through gorse and briar, then along a yellow-bricked road. You lit a candle from a tinderbox and you handled several antique weapons.'

'I did all *that*? How can you tell?'

'I could leave you in awe of my special senses,' said Eddie, splashing water at Jack, 'but the evidence is all over you, on your coat, the soles of your shoes, your fingers and fingernails. And lean over here a little.'

Jack did so and Eddie sniffed at him.

'What?' said Jack.

'You need a shower,' said Eddie. 'Your personal hygiene is a disgrace. Typical of teenage boys, that is.'

'Thanks a lot,' said Jack.

'Only kidding. There's a smell about you, Jack.' Eddie sniffed at himself. 'And about me also. A different smell. One I've never smelled before.'

'The smell of space aliens?' Jack took to sniffing himself.

'Very probably so. We have to find out what happened to us.'

'I could hypnotise you,' said Jack. 'Hypnotic regression, it's called. Take you back to the moment when we saw the bright light. That's how it's done.'

'Jack,' said Eddie, 'do you *really* know how to hypnotise someone?'

'I do in theory.'

'But you've never actually done it.'

'I've never had sex with a chicken, but I know how to do it, in theory.'

Eddie looked very hard at Jack.

'Sorry,' said Jack. 'I don't know why I said that. But you know what I mean.'

'I certainly do *not*.'

'No. But you know what I mean.'

'Forget it,' said Eddie. 'Teddies cannot be hypnotised.'

'You don't know that. Don't knock it 'til you've tried it, I always say.'

'And thus the chickens walk in fear.'

'What did you say?'

'Nothing. But teddies cannot be hypnotised. I tried it once and it didn't work on me.'

Jack looked hard at Eddie. 'Why did you try?' he asked.

'I had this theory,' said Eddie, 'that if hypnotists can hypnotise folk into doing anything they want them to do—'

'I'm not sure that's true,' said Jack.

'It is around here,' said Eddie. 'Believe me. Well, my theory was simple: I'd get the hypnotist to hypnotise me into being Toy City's greatest hypnotist, then I'd be able to place anyone I wanted under my control.'

'That's outrageous,' said Jack.

'Naturally, I would only have used my powers for good.'

'Well, naturally.' Jack now made a *very* doubtful face.

'But it didn't work,' said Eddie. 'The hypnotist said that he'd really tried his hardest. I had to go for ten sessions. It was very expensive.'

'Hm,' went Jack. 'Did it ever cross your mind—'

'What?' Eddie asked.

'Nothing,' said Jack. 'So teddies can't be hypnotised. But I'll bet I could be. Shall we visit this hypnotist and see if he can do it?'

'Ah,' said Eddie. 'I don't think he's practising any more.'

'Oh,' said Jack. 'Why not?'

'Well, he gave up when he got out of hospital.'

'Why was he in hospital?' Jack asked.

'He took a rather severe biting,' said Eddie.

'Right,' said Jack, and he recrossed his legs and kept them recrossed, though it hurt. 'So,' said Jack, 'hypnotists are not a happening thing, then.'

'Oh, they are,' said Eddie. 'Though not that one. I know another one. I think we'll pay him a visit.'

'Right,' said Jack once more. 'There's just one thing.'

'What's that?'

'First I think I'll take a shower and then we'll take some breakfast.'

They took their breakfast at Nadine's Diner. They travelled there in Bill's car, via the nearest pawnbrokers, where they pawned Bill's water cooler. Well, money *was* short, and they *were* on an important case. And they *were* very hungry indeed.

And on the way into the diner, Jack purchased the morning's edition of the *Toy City Mercury*.

They took a table by the window, ordered a Big Boy's Blow-Out Breakfast a-piece, with double hash browns, muffins, dumplings, pancakes, cheesecakes, fishcakes, fairy cakes, and Fanny Lapalulu's Fudgecake Surprise. Jack spread the paper before him and perused the front page news. 'DOLLY DUMPLING DEAD' ran the headline, which told it as it was. And beneath it ran text that didn't.

'Freak accident?' said Jack. 'Struck by lightning?'

'Well, what did you expect?' Eddie asked.

'The truth,' said Jack.

'In a newspaper?'

Jack shrugged. 'Well, not *all* of the truth, perhaps.'

'And what is the truth? No one saw anything except a really bright light. It could have been lightning.'

'It wasn't lightning, you know that.'

'I know that, you know that. Oh, damn, *he* knows that, too.'

'He?' Jack looked up. 'Oh dear,' he said.

Chief Inspector Wellington Bellis smiled his perished smile upon them. 'Good morning, gentlemen,' he said. 'Might I sit down and join you?'

'Oh yes, please do,' said Eddie. 'How wonderful to see you again so soon.'

'I thought I might find you here, filling your faces.' Wellington Bellis took a seat. 'You've seen the paper, I see.'

'For what it's worth.' Jack tossed the thing aside.

'It's worth a great deal,' said Bellis. 'We don't want panic in the streets, now do we? We want to get this thing tied up all neat and nice, as quickly as possible, don't we?'

'Of course we do,' said Eddie. 'Jack and I were just planning our next move when you arrived. Such a pity you've derailed our train of thought.'

'Such a pity,' said Bellis, and he reached out and squeezed Eddie's left paw.

'That hurts rather,' said Eddie. 'Would you mind not doing that?'

'I want results,' said Bellis, 'and I want them fast I need the culprit banged up at the hurry-up. And if I do not have the real culprit, I will have to make do with the next best thing. Do I make myself clear?'

'Very clear,' said Jack. 'Please stop doing that to Eddie.'

'Always the little bear's protector.'

'Eddie is my friend. Please let go of his paw.'

Bellis let go of Eddie's paw. Eddie gave it rubbings with his other one.

'You wouldn't want any harm to come to this dear little chap, would you, Jack?' asked Bellis, smiling horribly. 'Such a pity that would be.'

'There's no need for this.' Jack glared daggers at the chief inspector. 'We are doing all that we can. We want to sort this out as much as you do. Especially after what happened to us.'

'What?' said Bellis. 'What is this of which you speak?'

'Jack's talking about Old King Cole's,' said Eddie. 'That's what you were talking about, wasn't it, Jack?' Eddie made a frowning face at Jack.

'Ah,' said Jack. 'Ah, yes. That's exactly what I was talking about. Very upsetting for me, that was. I didn't sleep a wink last night.'

'Yes,' said Bellis. 'You certainly look like shi—'

'Two Big Boy's Blow-Out Breakfasts,' said a waitress. A long dolly waitress, with long dolly legs that went right up. 'Excuse me, sir, if you would.'

Bellis rose from his chair and gazed down upon the two detectives. 'Results,' said he. 'And fast. Or else.' And he drew a rubber finger across his rubber throat. 'Enjoy your breakfasts.'

And Bellis departed.

'What a bastard,' said Jack.

'Language,' said Eddie. 'There's a lady present.'

'Oh, that's all right,' said the waitress. 'I'm not much of a lady. A couple of drinks and I'm anyone's, really.'

'Really?' said Jack. 'What time do you finish your shift?'

'Jack,' said Eddie.

'Sorry,' said Jack.

'Six o'clock,' said the waitress.

'Jack,' said Eddie.

'Might we have a pot of coffee, please?' said Jack.

The waitress departed and Jack watched her do so.

'Please keep your mind on the case,' said Eddie. 'You're as randy as.'

'I think she fancies me,' said Jack.

'Of course she fancies you,' said Eddie.

'I have a definite way with the ladies,' said Jack, preening at his trenchcoat lapels.

'You don't,' said Eddie, tucking into his breakfast.

'I do,' said Jack, now tucking into his. 'Amelie says that she loves me.'

'Well, of course she would.' Eddie thrust breakfast into his mouth, which made his words difficult to interpret.

'Because I'm so handsome and nice,' said Jack, although there was much of the, 'Beccmmnth mmn sm hndsmn and nnnce,' about the way he said it.

'No, Jack,' said Eddie. 'That's not why and you know it.'

'It is why,' said Jack. 'Sort of.'

'Not,' said Eddie. 'It's because you're a meathead, Jack. Amelie could aspire to nothing better than marrying a meathead. *Any* meathead.'

'That's rubbish,' said Jack, spitting muffin as he said it. 'She loves me for me, not for what I am.'

'Don't kid yourself,' said Eddie, spitting pancake back at Jack. 'You have meathead status. Why do you think she wanted you to take her to Old King Cole's? What was that fight you got into about?'

'I never mentioned to you that I'd got into a fight.'

'Evidence,' said Eddie, making a breezy paw gesture towards his partner against crime. 'You punched someone. And someone else—a lady, I presume—struck you several times with a sequinned handbag.'

'You really are a *very* good detective,' said Jack.

'I'm a *special* detective,' said Eddie. 'But believe me, Jack, cruel as it sounds, she loves you for your status.'

'Well, all thanks for *that*,' said Jack.

'*All* thanks? I thought you'd be devastated.'

'Well, I'm not, you cruel little sod.'

'Less of the little.'

'I'm not ready to get involved in another relationship,' said Jack. 'I'm still smarting from the last one. I'll settle for the deeply satisfying shallow sex and have done with it for now.'

'You're a very bad boy,' said Eddie.

'I'm a teenage boy,' said Jack. 'What do you expect from me, sincerity?'

'Stop now,' said Eddie. 'It's too early in the day for such honesty. Tuck into your breakfast, then we'll get this hypnotism thing done. Then—'

'Then?' said Jack.

'I really don't have a clue,' said Eddie.

Their breakfasting done and their bellies distended, the two detectives dabbed at their mouths with napkins and grinned at one another.

'It's not a bad old life,' said Jack.

'It has its moments,' said Eddie.

Jack went up and paid the bill.

And took the waitress's telephone number.

Jack wound up Bill's car and he and Eddie entered it.

'So, where to?' Jack asked.

'The circus,' said Eddie, 'that's where.'

'I don't like the circus,' said Jack. 'I've never been one for clowns.'

'Odd that, isn't it?' said Eddie. 'Clowns are such a popular thing at the circus, but you'll never find anyone who actually likes them. Odd that, isn't it?'

Jack shrugged and said, 'I suppose so. So where is this circus?'

'I'll guide you,' said Eddie. 'But please drive slowly or I'll throw up in your lap.'

Jack drove slowly, with considerable care. He followed Eddie's guidings and eventually drew up the car before a rather colourful funfair affair in a part of the city that he'd never been to before.

Jack looked up at the colourful banner that hung between colourful posts. 'Count Otto Black's Circus Fantastique,' he read. Aloud.

'You'll like the count,' said Eddie. 'Or at least I hope you will.'

'You do?'

'Yes,' said Eddie, 'because then it will sort of balance things out.'

'It will?'

'It will,' said Eddie, 'because I can't stand the sight of him.'

★

The sight of him was something to behold. At Eddie's urging, Jack knocked upon the colourful door of a colourful gypsyesque caravan. This door opened and Jack beheld Count Otto Black.

Count Otto Black was tall. He was beyond tall, if such a thing is possible. Beyond tall and well gaunt with it was the count. High above on his facial regions were wonderful cheekbones, just beneath deeply set eyes of the deepest of sets. And just above a great black beard that nearly fell to his waist, the count's nose was a slender arc; the count's hair, long and black. Count Otto Black wore wonderful robes of rich purple velvet and plush. Mystical rings adorned his long and slender fingers.

'Count Otto,' called Eddie. 'Hello up there.'

Count Otto Black gazed down upon his visitors.

'I must be off now,' said Jack.

'No you mustn't,' said Eddie.

'Oh yes, I really must.'

'So,' said Count Otto Black. And it was a long and deep 'So'. 'So, Eddie Bear, you have returned.'

'Like the old bad penny,' said Eddie. 'You look well.'

Jack looked down upon Eddie Bear. Eddie looked far from at ease.

'Let's go,' whispered Jack. 'I don't like this fellow at all.'

Count Otto Black took a step back and the colourful door began closing.

'No, please, your countship,' called Eddie, 'this is very important. We're sorry to bother you, but it *is* important. You are the only one who can help us.'

The colourful door reopened a tad.

'We need you to use your special powers.'

'Ah,' said the voice of the count. 'You are hoping once more to become Toy City's greatest hypnotist.'

'No,' said Eddie. 'Not that.'

'I still bear the scars on my ankles,' said the voice of the count.

Jack looked at Eddie. 'I thought you said—'

'I did apologise for that,' said Eddie, ignoring Jack.

'Only after I kicked you over the big top,' said the voice of the count.

'I think we're on a loser here,' said Jack. 'And I hate to say this, Eddie, but have you ever considered anger-management counselling?'

The colourful door of the count's caravan slammed shut.

'Let's get out of here,' said Jack.

'No,' said Eddie. 'We have to know what happened. The count is the only man who can help us.'

'*Man?*' said Jack. 'Not *meathead?*'

'He's a bit special, the count.'

Jack raised eyebrows. Two of them. Both at the same time. And both high.

'Stop doing that,' said Eddie. 'You're only doing it because I can't.'

'I'm impressed,' said Jack, 'you showing respect for a meathead.'

'I'm not prejudiced,' said Eddie.

'Well, we're stuffed here,' said Jack. 'Let's get back in the car.'

'No,' said Eddie. 'We must do this. *You* must do this. Leave this to me.'

Jack dusted imaginary dirt from his trenchcoat shoulders. 'Go on, then,' he said.

Eddie called out to Count Otto Black. 'Count Otto,' called Eddie, 'this is very important. You are the one man who can help us.'

The colourful door of the colourful caravan remained colourfully shut.

'The fate of Toy City depends on you,' called Eddie.

The door, colourful as it was, did not at all colourfully budge.

'It's about your monkeys,' called Eddie.

A moment passed and then the door opened a smidgen.

'Your clockwork cymbal-playing monkeys,' called Eddie. 'Jack and I are on the case. Jack is a special investigator. I'm . . .' Eddie paused.

The door didn't move.

Eddie took a deep breath. 'I'm his comedy sidekick,' called Eddie.

The door opened wide.

'Say that again,' said Count Otto Black.

'Jack is a special investigator,' said Eddie, 'investigating the monkey case. He needs your help.'

'No,' said Count Otto. 'Say the last bit again.'

'I'm . . .' said Eddie.

'Again,' said the Count. 'And loudly.'

'I'm his comedy sidekick,' said Eddie.

The colourful interior of Count Otto Black's colourful carnival caravan was very much the way that such interiors are in movies. Although not those of the Toy City P.P.P.s persuasion. Those circus movies, with handsome juvenile leads who are trapeze artistes and up-and-coming starlets who ride white horses side-saddle around the circus ring, but seem to do little else. And there are elephants, of course, and a bloke who gets shot out of a cannon. And those clowns that no one actually really likes. And a fat lady and a stilt-walker, and high-wire walkers and even fire-walkers sometimes. And a head without a body that was dug from the bowels of the Earth. But none of these are particularly relevant to the appearance of the interior of the count's colourful carnival caravan. The relevant point about the interior that gave verisimilitude to those featured in movies was that it was so much bigger on the inside than it was on the outside.

Phew.

'Why are they bigger on the inside than the outside?' Jack asked Eddie.

'That's obvious,' said Eddie. 'So you can get a camera crew in, of course.'

'Be seated,' said Count Otto Black, taking to a big old colourful chair of his own and indicating a lesser. Jack sat down on this lesser chair. Eddie sat down on the floor.

'I feel that you could have seated yourself in a somewhat more comical manner than *that*,' said Count Otto Black.

Eddie sighed. Rose. Toppled backwards. Lay with his legs in the air.

Jack winced and chewed upon his bottom lip.

'Funny enough for you?' Eddie asked.

'I'd like to see it again,' said the count.

Eddie obliged. 'Are you satisfied now?'

'Very much so,' said Count Otto Black. And he extended a long hand to Jack. 'So you are a special investigator,' he said.

Jack took the count's hand and shook it. It was a very cold hand indeed. Very cold and clammy.

The count took back his hand and Jack said, 'Yes, I am a special investigator and I believe that you can help me in my investigations.'

'Into the death of my monkeys.'

'They were all *your* monkeys?'

'Each and every one worked for me. There are not too many openings for cymbal-playing monkeys nowadays.'

'No,' said Jack, 'I suppose not. I never really thought about it.'

'They are a great loss to my circus.'

'I suppose they would be.'

'In what way?' asked the count.

'Eh?' said Jack.

'Shouldn't that be "pardon"?' asked the count.

'Pardon?' said Jack.

'In what way do you suppose they would be a great loss to my circus?'

Jack glanced at Eddie. It was a 'hopeless' glance. Sometimes a single glance can say so very much. Without actually saying anything at all. So to speak.

'Please don't do it to him, Count,' said Eddie, making a rather pathetic face towards Count Otto Black. 'Jack, my . . . employer, *is* a very special investigator, very good at his job, but he's not up to matching wits with you.'

'I'm up to matching wits with anyone,' said Jack. 'Show me a wit and I'll match it.'

'Time *is* of the essence,' said Eddie. 'Please, Count.'

'Quite so,' said Count Otto Black. 'So I suppose you have come here to examine the murder scene. Five of my monkeys gone to dust in their dressing room.'

'Well, not exactly,' said Jack. 'I assume that the laughing policemen have already visited the crime scene.'

'And stomped it into oblivion. What, then?'

'Well,' said Jack, 'it's like this.'

And Jack explained to Count Otto Black exactly what it was like. He spoke at length and in detail.

The count listened and then the count nodded. And then the count finally said, 'And so you wish me to hypnotise you, regress you to the point when you were engulfed by the very bright light and draw out your repressed memory of what happened next.'

'Exactly,' said Jack.

Count Otto Black nodded thoughtfully.

'No, I won't do it,' he said.

10

'No?' said Jack. 'No?'

'No,' said Count Otto Black. And he said it firmly. Definitely. Without reservation or regret.

'No?' said Jack once more.

'Absolutely no.' The count stretched out his great long arms, brushing his fingertips against the opposite walls of the caravan. 'And I will tell you for why: because it would be dangerous, very dangerous, to you, to your mental health. You have to understand this. Your memory was not artificially erased by some piece of advanced space-alien technology. You did it yourself. Your own brain did it.' And Count Otto stretched out a hand to Jack and tapped him lightly on the forehead. 'Whatever happened to you was so appalling, so utterly terrifying, that it was too much for you to take in and retain. Your mind rejected it, spat it out, closed itself to these horrors. The door within closed. It would be folly to reopen it.'

'No,' said Jack, and he shook his head. 'I don't believe that. I've seen horrors enough. Nothing could be *that* bad.'

'Really?' said the count. 'And yet I feel that I could whisper words into your ear that you would wish until the end of your days that you had never heard me utter.'

'That I consider most unlikely,' said Jack.

'Really?' said the count, and he leaned in Jack's direction.

'Don't let him do it, Jack,' cried Eddie, leaping up. 'I saw him do it once to a clown. It wiped the smile right off his face.'

'Big deal,' said Jack.

'A smile painted on a tin-plate head,' said Eddie. 'Wiped it right

off. The smile fell to the ground and a crow swooped down and carried
it off to his nest.'

'Eh?' said Jack.

'Trust me,' said Eddie. 'Don't let him do it.'

'All right, all right, but we have to know what happened, Eddie,
and if hypnosis is the only way, then hypnosis it has to be.'

'I won't be persuaded,' said Count Otto Black.

'We'll give you money,' said Eddie.

'How much money?' asked the count.

And now a period of negotiation began, of bargaining and bartering
and wrangling. It was a protracted period and resting times were taken
at intervals, whilst negotiators sat and smoked cigarettes, or paced up
and down, or worked out calculations on small bits of paper.

It was coming on towards teatime before all was said and done.

'And that's my final offer,' said Eddie.

'I'll take it,' said the count. Palms were spat upon, or in Eddie's
case, a paw, then spitty palm and spitty paw were clapped together.

'Now just hold on,' said Jack. 'I want to get this straight. Count
Otto will hypnotically regress me—'

'Taking no responsibility for the potential damage to your mental
health,' said the count.

'Yes, I understand that. But you will regress me in exchange for
what, exactly?'

Eddie read out the list of the count's demands.

'Bill's car,' he read, and Jack groaned.

'And your trenchcoat.' Further groanings.

'And your hat and your watch.' Eddie paused. Jack groaned doubly.

'Fifty per cent of the reward money.'

'*What* reward money?' Jack asked.

'Oh, there *will* be reward money,' said Count Otto Black. 'When
all else fails.'

'That doesn't make sense,' said Jack. 'That means when Eddie and
I fail.'

'You're right,' said the count. 'I want sixty per cent.'

Eddie sighed. 'We agreed on fifty. And forty on the film rights.'

'Film rights?' said Jack.

'There's a movie in this.' The count mimed camera crankings. 'I
would want to play myself, of course, although perhaps it might be better if I were to play the juvenile lead.'

Eddie shook his head and sighed once more.

'I'll have my solicitor go into all the details of the subsidiary rights, marketing offshoots, merchandising deals and suchlike.'

'How long will *that* take?' asked Jack, whose patience had worn beyond thin.

'No time at all,' said Count Otto. 'I keep him in that box over there.'

'He does,' came a muffled voice from that box.

'Fine,' said Jack. 'Fine—take everything we've got. The car, my coat, my watch. Do you want my shoes, too?'

The count made so-so noddings with his head.

Jack threw up his hands and said, 'Ludicrous.'

'I think the count has been very reasonable,' said Eddie.

'Yes, well, *you* would. He doesn't want your hat, your coat and your watch.'

'I can't wear a watch,' said Eddie. 'Watches fall off my paws—I don't have wrists.' And Eddie made a sorrowful face that almost had Jack sympathising.

'Oh no you *don't*,' said Jack. 'It's not fair. It's not.'

'It is most fair,' said Count Otto Black, 'because I am taking nothing from you that you will want.'

'Oh, I think you are,' said Jack. 'The car. The coat. The watch.'

'No.' Count Otto shook his head. 'You will have no need of these things after I have put you through the period of hypnotic regression. All you will have need of is heavy sedation and the immediate use of a straitjacket.'

'Hm,' went Jack, as 'Hm' usually served him adequately at such times.

'So let us begin.' Count Otto Black linked his fingers together and did that sickening knuckle-cracking thing that some folk take delight in doing to the distress of those who have to watch them doing it. 'To work, to work. And let me ask you this.'

Jack tried to do the knuckle-cracking thing with his own fingers, but failed dismally. 'Ouch,' said Jack. 'It hurts.'

'I have to ask you,' said the count, wiggling his fingers and, unseen, his toes, 'what is the last thing you remember *before* the big white light?'

'Leaving Tinto's Bar,' said Jack.

'Although we know that we did more,' said Eddie. 'Went through a briar patch and along a yellow-brick road.'

Count Otto Black made a thoughtful face, but as most of it was lost beneath his beard, the degree of its thoughtfulness was lost upon Jack and Eddie.

'We will take Tinto's Bar as a starting point,' said he. 'Why did you leave Tinto's Bar?'

'Because Tinto had given a note from a spaceman to what he thought was Eddie, but wasn't,' said Jack.

'And what did that note say?'

'It said that the location of a landed spaceship was Toy Town,' said Jack, 'so we went to Toy Town in the car.'

'Hold on,' said Eddie. 'I don't remember any of *that*. How come you didn't mention that you remembered *that* earlier?'

'He couldn't,' said Count Otto Black.

'Why not?' asked Eddie.

'Because he didn't remember it.'

'So how come he remembers it now?'

'Because I just hypnotised him.'

'What?' said Eddie. 'I never saw you do *that*.'

'You did,' said Count Otto, 'but I hypnotised *you* so you won't remember how I did it.'

'You didn't,' said Eddie.

'Crow like a rooster,' said Count Otto Black. 'You *are* a rooster.'

'Cock-a-doodle-do!' went Eddie.

'And rest,' said the count. And Eddie rested.

'So you left Tinto's Bar and travelled to Toy Town,' said the count to Jack. 'What happened next?'

'We went to Bill Winkie's house,' said Jack. 'Eddie still had the key and we let ourselves in. And Eddie showed me all these weapons hidden beneath the floor. And then we heard someone coming and we hid beneath the trap door.'

'Tell me what you heard then,' said the count.

And Jack spoke of the conversation that he and Eddie had overheard, regarding things in jars and suchlike. And he told the count that the voices they had heard had been their own voices. And then how they'd climbed out of the hideaway and how there had then been a very bright light.

'And what happened *next*?' asked Count Otto Black.

Jack sat in his chair and stared into space. His eyes grew wide and his hands gripped the arms of his chair. His knuckles whitened, as did his face. Eddie looked on and Eddie looked on with a sense of growing fear.

'The light,' went Jack. 'The terrible light.'

'Go on,' said the count. 'The light can't hurt you now.'

'Oh,' went Jack. 'They're coming for us. Out of the light, they're coming.'

'Gently now,' said Count Otto Black. 'You're quite safe here, they can't hurt you here. Who is coming out of the light?'

'Not *who*,' said Jack, and cold sweat formed upon his brow and trickled down his cheeks. 'It's *what*, not who. They are not men.'

'Are they toys?' asked the count.

'Not toys. Oh, now, they're taking us. Up into the light. They have us. In that place, that bright place. They're putting things up our— Ouch! Stop! Ouch!'

'We'll take a little break there, I think,' said the count.

'No, we can't,' said Eddie. 'Painful as this is, we have to finish.'

'It's too painful for me,' said the count.

'Too painful for *you*?'

'Indeed,' said Count Otto. 'I need to take a wee-wee. I should have taken one earlier. I can't hold on any longer.'

Count Otto Black went off to the toilet. Presently, he returned.

'All better now,' he said. 'I took a poo as well, just to be on the safe side.'

'Too much information,' said Eddie. 'And you've quite spoiled the mood.'

'Well, it's neither here nor there,' said the count, settling himself down into his chair and wiggling his fingers at Jack. 'He'll be nothing more than a vegetable when all this is done.'

'No, I won't,' said Jack. 'I'll be fine.'

'See how brave he is?' said Eddie. 'He's as noble as.'

'Please yourselves,' said Count Otto. 'Pray continue, Jack. Tell us all about the rectal probings.'

Over in the big top, high-wire walkers paused in their practisings, struck by the screams from Count Otto's caravan. Pigeons fled their airy perches. Dogs howled in the distance.

'Much too much information,' said Eddie, rubbing at his own bum and feeling rather queasy.

'All right,' said the count, 'they did all that to you.'

'They did more,' said Jack. 'They did . . .'

Count Otto Black leaned close as Jack whispered.

'They never did?' he said. The count's eyes started from their sockets. The count rushed outside and was sick.

'Nice going,' said Eddie to Jack, whilst the count was outside up-chucking. 'Nice to see the count getting a bit of his own medicine. Because, after all, he is an *evil* hypnotist.'

'And worse is yet to come,' said Jack.

'Oh good,' said Eddie. 'I'll just keep my paws over my ears, then.'

'Best to,' said Jack.

Count Otto returned and Jack continued with his tale.

And eventually he was done.

Count Otto Black sat staring at Jack and Jack sat staring at him.

'Are you all right, Jack?' Eddie asked.

Jack said, 'Yes, I'm fine.'

'No feelings of empathy towards members of the vegetable kingdom?'

'Fine,' said Jack. 'Now I've got it all out of my system. I'm fine.'

'Well, thanks very much, Count Otto,' said Eddie. 'Count Otto? Can you hear me? Are you all right?'

Jack drove away from Count Otto Black's Circus Fantastique. He drove away in Bill's Anders Faircloud. Jack was wearing his trenchcoat and his fedora and his watch.

'Well, I wasn't expecting *that*,' said Eddie, who sat once more in the passenger seat. 'Who'd have thought it, eh? Your revelations driving Count Otto Black into a vegetative state? Who'd have seen that coming, eh?'

'Anyone with more than sawdust for brains,' said Jack. 'It was what is called a telegraphed gag. One that you could *really* see coming.'

'So we really *were* abducted by spacemen.' Eddie whistled and kicked his legs about.

'No, we weren't,' said Jack.

'We *weren't*?' said Eddie. 'But we were taken up into the light and terrible bottom experiments were performed on us.'

'True,' said Jack. 'There's no denying that.'

'But you're saying that it *wasn't* spacemen?'

Jack shook his head.

'Then what?'

'Chickens?' said Tinto. 'You were abducted by chickens?'

It was early evening now and they were in Tinto's Bar.

'He's winding you up,' said Eddie. 'And before you say it, *not* in the nice way.'

'I'm not,' said Jack, counting the drinks that he had ordered and trying to reconcile them with the number that Tinto had delivered. 'We were abducted by chickens. Big ones in spacesuits. Horrible, they were, with nasty beaks and evil little eyes.'

'And *you* remember this?' asked Tinto of Eddie.

'No,' said Eddie, tasting beer. 'I do not. The count only hypnotised me to prevent me from remembering how he hypnotised Jack.'

'Oh, slow down there,' said Tinto. 'Too much information.'

'We're done with that line now,' said Eddie. 'It wasn't relevant anyway.'

'I just fancied using it,' said Tinto. 'I'm a barman. I *do* have rights, you know.'

'You have the right to remain silent,' said Eddie. 'Why not use it now?'

'Because I want to hear about the chickens. Could you give me a bit of a wind, please, Jack, I'm running down.'

Jack leaned over the bar counter and turned the key in Tinto's back.

'Howdy doody,' said Tinto to Jack. 'Can I help you, sir?'

'We were talking about the chickens,' said Jack. 'The ones that abducted Eddie and me.'

'Well, yes,' said Tinto. 'You told me that. But I'm rather confused. These space chickens, was it them that blasted the cymbal-playing monkeys with the deaths rays?'

Jack looked at Eddie.

And Eddie looked at Jack.

'Nice mutual lookings,' said Tinto, plucking spent glasses from the bar and giving them a polish, 'but hardly an answer to my question.'

Jack now took to tasting beer. 'I'm rather confused myself,' he said. 'We *were* abducted by chickens, for reasons unknown.'

'They'd have their reasons,' said Tinto. 'They probably stuck implants up your bum.'

'They stick those up your nose,' said Jack.

'Nose, bum, it's all the same to me. Bits of body never do what they're supposed to anyway. Take that sailor doll over there.' Tinto pointed and Jack did lookings across. 'Obviously built upside down,' said Tinto.

'He looks the right way up to me,' said Jack.

'Then how come his nose runs and his feet smell?'

'We should have seen *that* one coming,' said Eddie.

'But it wasn't the chickens, was it?' said Jack to Eddie. 'We heard who did the murderings—it was those doppelgangers of us.'

'Probably in league with the chickens,' said Tinto, and he tittered.

'Did you just titter?' asked Eddie.

'There's a screw loose in my voice box,' said Tinto. 'Are you going to pay for these drinks or engage me in further conversation in the hope that I'll forget to ask you for the money?'

'It's always served me well in the past,' said Eddie.

'Well, not tonight,' said Tinto. 'Pay up. Twenty-five beers and that's . . .' And Tinto named the sum in question and that sum in question was correct.

'How did you work *that* out?' asked Eddie.

'Aha!' went Tinto, and he touched his printed nose. 'Because I have a pocket calculator.'

'So where do you keep it? You don't have any pockets.'

'Who said that?' asked Tinto.

'I did,' said Eddie.

'Well, that just shows you how smart *you* are,' said Tinto. 'I don't need a pocket to own a pocket calculator, because a pocket calculator is a calculator in the shape of a pocket. I thought everyone knew that.'

'Actually, *I* didn't,' said Jack. 'Might we have a look at this calculating pocket?'

'Certainly,' said Tinto, and he rootled beneath the bar counter and brought out something that resembled a bag made out of shiny fabric. 'Wallah,' went Tinto.

'Wallah?' went Eddie.

'Wallah,' went Tinto. 'That's the calculating pocket's name.'

'Wallah?' went Jack.

'Yes?' said Wallah. 'How can I help you?'

Jack looked at Eddie.

And Eddie once more looked upon Jack.

'And there was me thinking that I'd seen everything,' said Jack, 'what with the space chickens and all. Where did you get this calculating pocket, Tinto?'

'I do have a name,' said the calculating pocket.

'Excuse me,' said Jack.

'Won her in a competition,' said Tinto. 'You have to work out the number of gobstoppers in a big jar.'

'And *you* got that right?' asked Eddie.

'Well, I had a little help,' said Tinto. 'I asked to meet the prize first, before I bought a ticket to enter the competition, and I asked her to work it out.'

'That's called cheating,' said Eddie.

'And your point is?' Tinto asked.

'No point at all,' said Eddie. 'But it was dishonest.'

'Possibly so,' said Tinto, 'but then so is engaging a barman in conversation in the hope that he will forget to charge you for your drinks.'

'You can put a "Hm" in about now if you wish, Jack,' said Eddie.

'Hm,' Jack put in.

'So pay up, or you're barred,' said Tinto.

Eddie sighed, pawed his way into a trenchcoat pocket, wormed out a wallet and set it down upon the bar top. 'Help yourself,' he said.

Jack viewed the wallet and Jack viewed Eddie.

Tinto helped himself to money and wheeled himself off to the till.
'Where did that come from?' Jack asked.

'Count Otto's pocket,' said Eddie.

'You stole his wallet?'

'Well, he won't be needing it now, will he? He'll be needing heavy sedation and a straitjacket.'

'I'm sure there's some kind of justice or moral in that,' said Jack, 'but for the life of me I can't think what it might be.'

'I'm sure there must be somewhere,' said Eddie, 'if you think very hard about it. Same again?'

'I haven't finished these yet.'

'Then drink up, it's Count Otto's round once more.'

'I'll have a short, if I might,' said Wallah the calculating pocket.

Jack reached forward and picked up Wallah.

'Put me down,' said the pocket.

Jack shook the pocket about.

'And don't do that, it makes me feel sick.'

'How do you think it works?' Eddie asked. 'It's probably empty— have a look inside.'

'Don't you dare,' said Wallah. 'We hardly know each other.'

'Just a little peep,' said Jack.

'Certainly not,' said Wallah. 'Not until you've bought me a drink, at least. What kind of a pocket do you think I am?'

'A female one for certain,' said Jack.

'Don't start,' said Eddie. 'I know where that line of thinking is going.'

Jack returned Wallah to the counter top. 'This is all very entertaining,' he said.

'Not *that* entertaining,' said Eddie.

'Well, maybe a *bit*,' said Jack, 'but it's not helping *us*, is it? That other you and me will probably be coming back tonight to perform more evil deeds. Suck the life out of more innocent citizens of Toy City. They have to be stopped, Eddie, and we have to stop them.'

'I know,' said Eddie. 'But I don't quite know how.'

'We go back to Toy Town,' said Jack, 'get our hands on those weapons at Bill Winkie's. Lie in wait, then blow the blighters away.'

'Blow the blighters away?'

'Bang, bang, bang,' went Jack, and he mimed blowings away. 'Case closed and we collect the reward.'

'Case closed, perhaps, but there's no reward.'

'Then we'll settle for case closed.'

'No,' said Eddie, taking further beer. 'It's not enough. That other me and you, they are evil cat's-paws for some big boss somewhere, who wants whatever is in those jars. The soul-stuff of the murder victims, or whatever it is. It's the big boss we're looking for.'

'Fair enough,' said Jack. 'I'll hold the cat's-paws at gunpoint and you can bite the details out of them.'

'That does have a certain brutal charm.'

'I hate to interrupt you,' said Wallah, 'but you really are going about this all the wrong way.'

'Excuse me, please,' said Eddie, 'but Jack and I are professionals. We are private detectives. We know our own business.'

'Oh, get you,' said Wallah. 'Too proud to take some kindly offered advice.'

'I didn't say *that*,' said Eddie.

'You did, in so many words,' said Jack.

'Please yourself, then,' said Wallah. 'Don't listen to me. I don't care.'

'We'd like to listen,' said Jack. 'What would you like to tell us?'

'*He* doesn't want to listen,' said Wallah.

Eddie shrugged.

'Yes, he does,' said Jack.

'He doesn't, and he's not even funny. You should get yourself a better comedy sidekick than him.'

'Cheek,' said Eddie, raising a paw.

'Don't hit me,' cried Wallah.

'He's not hitting anyone.' Jack moved Wallah beyond Eddie's hitting range. 'Talk to *me*,' he said. 'You'd like to talk to *me*, wouldn't you?'

'Actually, I would.' Wallah's voice was *definitely* female. Jack gave Wallah a little stroke.

'What a lovely soft hand you have,' said the calculating pocket.

Eddie turned his face away. 'I'm going to the toilet,' he said.

Tinto returned with Eddie's change, but finding no Eddie returned this change to his till.

'I could help you,' said Wallah to Jack. 'I could help you to solve this case.'

'That's very kind of you,' said Jack, and he gave unto Wallah another little stroke.

Wallah the pocket gave a little shiver.

'How *exactly* could you help us?' Jack asked.

'There is an expression,' crooned Wallah, and it was a crooning little voice, 'in crime-solving circles, when seeking a culprit of a crime involving theft. That expression is "follow the money".'

'I don't follow you,' said Jack.

'I haven't finished yet,' said Wallah. 'These present crimes—the murdered monkeys and the clockwork band—your comedy sidekick is right in that you must follow the money, as it were, to the big boss. But doing so will require a degree of calculation that you and your sidekick, and no offence intended here, are not sufficiently skilled in making. And that's where I come in.'

'I still don't *exactly* follow you,' said Jack, but he gave Wallah another stroke. And Wallah sighed. Erotically.

Jack withdrew his hand.

'Please don't stop,' whispered Wallah.

Jack stared down at the calculating pocket. There was something not altogether wholesome about this.

'Further crimes will be committed,' Wallah crooned further. 'And in order to get ahead of the game and succeed, it will be necessary to calculate where these crimes will take place and what they will be. And that is where I come in. Let me help you. I really *can* help you. I *really can*.'

'How, *exactly*?' said Jack once more.

'Lean over a bit and let me whisper.'

Jack leaned over and Wallah whispered.

Eddie returned from the toilet.

'Why exactly,' said Eddie, climbing up onto his barstool, 'do blokes feel it necessary to pull all the toilet rolls out and throw them all over the floor? And will someone please explain to me the purpose of flavoured condoms?'

'Stop, *please!*' said Jack. 'That's quite enough of *that*.'

'Do *you* use flavoured condoms?' asked Eddie. 'And if so, *what* flavour? I'd have thought chocolate was out of the question.'

'*STOP!*' shouted Jack. 'I don't know what comes over you at times.'

'Just idle speculation,' said Eddie.

'Well, be that as it may, drink up your drinks—we're leaving.'

'*We?*' said Eddie.

'We,' said Jack.

'Now that surprises me,' said Eddie, 'because I recall you taking the telephone number of that dolly in Nadine's Diner this morning and asking her what time she got off. I bought you some flavoured condoms, by the way.'

'That dolly will have to wait,' said Jack, although there was a note of regret in his voice. 'Something has come up regarding the case. We have to go.'

'What?' said Eddie. 'And why?'

'Another crime is about to be committed. Another murder. Several murders, in fact.'

'And how did you work this out?'

'It's a *calculated* guess,' said Jack.

They drank up their beers and they left Tinto's Bar.

Tinto waved them goodbye, took their empty glasses and polished them clean.

'It was a real joy to get money out of that Eddie Bear,' he said to the pocket that lay on the counter top. 'And I stiffed him for his change and everything. That's the last time he ever gets one over on me.'

The pocket on the counter top had nothing to say in reply to this.

But then again, trenchcoat pockets rarely do.

11

'No,' said Eddie. '*Not* the ballet.'

He sat in the passenger seat of the Anders Faircloud once more. Jack was once more at the wheel. But for once the Anders Faircloud was not performing high-speed death-defying automotive manoeuvres. It was sort of poodling along and clunking sounds were issuing from the bonnet regions.

'You've overwound this car,' said Eddie to Jack. 'And you've trashed the engine with all your high-speed death-defying automotive manoeuvres.'

'I'll fix it when I have time,' said Jack, ramming his foot floorwards but eliciting little response. 'I know clockwork. And I'll soup-up the engine, spraunch the springs, caflute the cogs, galvate the gears and other things of a workshop nature generally. You wait until you see how fast it will go then.'

'The poodling's fine by me,' said Eddie, 'but as I was saying, oh no, *not* the ballet.'

'The ballet it has to be.' Jack poodled through a red light, causing concern amongst righteous motorists. 'That is where the next murders will occur. We can be ahead of the game this time, Eddie.'

Eddie yawned and shuddered slightly. 'As I am sure you know,' he said, between further yawns, which set Jack off, 'we bears are known for our remarkable stamina, and can go for many days without sleep.'

'Bears hibernate all winter,' said Jack, informatively.

'Yes, but that's because they stay up all summer clubbing 'til dawn.'

'And your point is?' Jack asked.

'I'm knackered,' said Eddie. 'Done in, banjoed, wrecked and smitten. I don't think I can take the ballet.'

'The ballet is soothing,' said Jack. 'You can take a little nap.'

'I'll take a *big* nap, believe me. And that is not professional for a crime fighter. Five minutes of ballet and I'll be gone from this world.'

'You'll be fine.' Jack smiled and drove; the car lurched and hiccuped.

Eddie yawned once more, this time behind his paw, did little lip-smacking sounds and promptly fell asleep.

'We're here,' said Jack, and he woke Eddie up.

There was no real question as to whether when they built the Toy City Opera House, which also housed the ballet, that they had built it for the patronage of toys. They hadn't. This was a man-sized affair, as was Old King Cole's, built for the elite of Toy City. The elite that was man.

Jack had to cruise around for a bit looking for a place to park, but once parked-up, in a rather seedy alleyway, he and Eddie plodded on foot to the glorious, grand establishment.

'It's beautiful, isn't it?' said Jack.

'Frankly, I hate it,' said Eddie. 'It sends out all the wrong messages.'

'Right,' said Jack. 'Well, I don't really recall exactly what the protocol is here. The last time we came was when you were first made mayor, remember? We had some times then, didn't we? We were fêted everywhere.'

Eddie *did* remember. 'Wasn't I sick in the royal box?' he said.

'Yes,' said Jack. 'Just a little. So I think I'd better carry you in under my coat, or something.'

'You *what*?'

'We don't want any unpleasantness, do we?'

'I could wait in the car, I don't mind.'

'Eddie, a crime is going to be committed here. A murderous crime. A multiple murderous crime.'

'You have yet to tell me how you know this to be.'

'I have my sources,' said Jack, and he stuck a hand into his pocket. A tiny sighing sound coming from within went unheard by Eddie.

Because Eddie was now nearly being stomped upon.

The fashionable set, Toy City swells, the fêted glitterati, were hustling and bustling around the two detectives. Exclusive fragrances perfumed the air, diamonds dazzled and shimmered amongst fur stoles, gowns and gorgeousness.

'Do you have tickets?' Eddie called up to Jack.

'No,' said Jack, and he grinned.

'Phew,' said Eddie. 'Then at least we won't get in.'

'We'll get in—I have my special lifetime membership card.'

'You hung on to that?'

'I have a walletful,' said Jack, 'for all those posh places that wanted the bear and his partner who had saved Toy City to patronise their premises.'

'Scumbags all,' said Eddie. 'Scumbags and treacherous turncoats. And my lifetime membership was lost in the post, as I recall.'

'You'll be back on top, Eddie,' said Jack, lifting Eddie from his paw pads and tucking him under his arm. 'Once we've saved the city once more.'

Eddie made a growly groan. 'Just listen to yourself,' he said.

'I'm confident,' said Jack, elbowing his way into the crowd with his free elbow. 'We have the edge, we'll succeed.'

'The edge?' and Eddie shook his head.

The Toy City Opera House owned to a doorman whose livery put that of Old King Cole's severely to shame. This man was magnificent. So much so that thankfully he was beyond description.

He held up his gloved hand against Jack's slovenly approach.

'No tradesmen,' said this personage.

'How dare you,' said Jack, making the face of outrage and adopting once more the haughty tone. 'I am a lifetime honorary member of this here establishment, and can therefore attend any opera or ballet, free of charge, in the very bestest seats that you have, as it happens. Would you care to see my gilt-edged membership card?'

'Dearly,' said the doorman. 'Few things would give me greater joy.'

'That's a smirk on your face,' said Jack, lowering Eddie to the marble flooring and rootling out his wallet. 'We shall see who's smirking soon.' Jack flicked through a number of cards that offered him lifetime privileges, some at certain establishments that really suited Jack.

'There,' said he, presenting the doorman with a grand-looking one.

The doorman perused this grand-looking card. He held it close to his smirking face, inspected it carefully, raised it up to the light. Marvelled at the watermark and the special metallic strip. Checked the ID photo and everything. 'Wow,' he went, and he whistled. 'You weren't pulling my plonker-piece, were you, your princeship.'

'No, I wasn't,' said Jack. 'Now hand it back and stand aside and be grateful that I do not report you for your insolence.'

The doorman whistled once more and returned Jack's card to him. Then he leaned forward, still smirking, and informed Jack in a curt and brusque manner exactly what Jack could do with himself.

'What?' went Jack. 'How dare you!'

'I dare,' said the doorman, 'because your card has no currency here. Shove off.'

'What?' went Jack. 'What?'

'Do you ever read the newspapers?' the doorman asked Jack.

'Actually, I do,' Jack said.

'Well, not too long ago,' said the doorman, 'Toy City was plagued by a mad mayor. A hideous freak, he was, with glass dolly eyes and these really creepy hands—'

Eddie flinched and took shelter at the rear of Jack.

'Well, this abhorrence put into place certain edicts,' the doorman continued. 'He appeared to have it in for his betters, you see. Inferiority complex, inverted snobbery or have it as you will. I've been reading all about that kind of business in this self-help manual I bought. Anyway, this mad mayor did away with all the privileges of the monarchy. Edict Five, as I recall.'

Jack said, 'What?' and Jack looked down at Eddie. Around and behind himself and then again down at Eddie.

Eddie made a foolish face and shrugged.

'Ah,' said Jack. 'Ah, but—'

'Ah, but what?' asked the doorman.

'Ah, but the mad mayor was kicked out. Tarred and feathered.'

'Yes.' The doorman smiled. 'But not all his edicts were rescinded. Actually, the management of the Opera House quite liked Edict Five— they were fed up with the monarchy always poncing free tickets for all the best bashes.'

'Oh,' said Jack.

'So on your way,' said the doorman. 'Scruffy trenchcoated oik that you are.'

'You will answer for this,' said Jack.

'Word has it,' said the doorman, 'that The End Times are upon us, and that all of us will answer soon for something or other.'

'You must let us in,' Jack protested.

'Us?' said the doorman. 'I wouldn't have let you take that tatty bear in with you anyway.'

'But,' said Jack, 'we are detectives. We're here on a case. We have the authority of Chief Inspector Wellington Bellis.'

'Yes, of course you have, sir. Now move along please, we have posh people trying to get in.'

'Let us in!' Jack demanded.

'Please don't make me use force,' said the doorman. 'As enjoyable as it would be for me, I regret to say that it would probably leave you with permanent damage.'

Jack made fists and squared up to the doorman.

The doorman made bigger fists and squared himself down to Jack.

'You haven't heard the last of this,' said Jack.

'I can assure you that I have,' said the doorman, 'because I am no longer listening.'

Posh folk pushed past Jack on either side. Jack retreated down the marble steps with Eddie following on.

'You and your bloody edicts,' Jack said to Eddie.

'Actually, I feel rather justified in imposing that one,' said the bear. 'Can we go home now, please?'

'We have to prevent a crime.'

'I'm still not really convinced.'

'Eddie, evil will be done here and only we can stop it.'

'You could call your associate, Chief Inspector Wellington Bellis.'

'He might not have faith in my source,' said Jack.

'About your source—' said Eddie.

'Damn,' said Jack, and he sat down on the kerb. 'Damn, damn, damn.'

Eddie sat down beside his friend. 'Tell me about this source of yours,' he said.

'Can't,' said Jack. 'I am sworn to secrecy.'

'What?' said Eddie. 'Why? We don't have secrets. We're partners.'

'Look, Eddie, I don't want to go into it now. We have to get inside the Opera House and that's all there is to it.'

'Well,' said Eddie, 'if your mind is made up, and that *is* all there is to it, then you'd best follow me.'

'Where to?'

'Just follow.'

Jack rose and followed Eddie. The little bear led him around the corner and down an alleyway and to the stage door. Several Stage Door Johnnies surrounded the stage door.

'Disgusting,' said Eddie, stepping over one of them. 'You're supposed to flush those things away.'

Jack made an appalled face. 'Was that a condom gag?' he asked.

'Take it as you will,' said Eddie. 'Knock at the door, please, Jack.'

Jack knocked at the door.

The backstage doorman opened it. He was a clockwork fellow, somewhat rusty and worn.

'Ralph,' said Eddie.

'Eddie?' said Ralph.

'Ralph, how good to see you after all this time.'

'All this time?' said Ralph, and he scratched at his tin-plate top-knot, raising sparks.

'We're here on a bit of business,' said Eddie. 'Would you mind letting us in?'

'Again?' said Ralph.

'Why is he saying "again"?' Jack asked Eddie.

'I don't know,' said Eddie. 'Why are you saying "again", Ralph?'

'Because I've already let you in once,' said Ralph. 'And your comedy sidekick there.'

'What?' said Jack.

And, 'What?' said Eddie. And, 'Oh dear,' said Eddie. 'This is bad.'

'How did you get past me?' Ralph asked. 'I never saw you go out again.'

'We didn't,' said Eddie. 'That wasn't us.'

'Oh yes it was,' said Ralph. 'I'd recognise those crummy mismatched button eyes, and the tatty old raincoat and the—'

'Have to stop you there, Ralph,' said Eddie. 'Those were two impersonators. Two very bad and evil beings.'

'Uncanny,' said Ralph.

'What?' said Eddie once more.

'That's what you said to me earlier, when I let you in. You said that two impersonators might turn up and try to get in, but that I was to refuse them entry because they were very bad and evil beings.'

And Ralph slammed the stage door shut upon Jack and Eddie.

And Jack and Eddie stood in the alley.

And Jack said, 'Damn,' once more.

Eddie Bear looked up at Jack. 'It seems,' said Eddie, 'that I was wrong and you were right. We *have* to get into the Opera House.'

'We *should* phone Bellis,' said Jack, 'get him to bring a task force, the Army, whatever is necessary. Everything. What do you think?'

Eddie gave his head a couple of thumpings. 'I think not,' said he. 'And before you ask why, I'll tell you for why. These murderers, or soul stealers, or whatever Hellish things from beyond or above they are, are disguised as *us*. And it does not require the gift of precognition to predict the inevitable consequences, as in when a bunch of overexcited police snipers gun us down by mistake.'

'Ah,' said Jack. 'You think that might happen?'

'I'd give you a very good odds on it,' said Eddie. 'We will have to deal with this on our own. Just you and me.'

'So how do we get in there?'

'Well,' said Eddie, and he cupped what he had of a chin in a paw, 'it will have to be the sewers.'

Jack made a sour face and Jack said, 'The sewers?'

'It's an Opera House,' said Eddie. 'Ergo it has a phantom.'

'A *what*?' said Jack.

'A phantom,' said Eddie.

'No,' said Jack. 'I mean, what's an *ergo*?'

'Most amusing,' said Eddie. 'But every Opera House has a phantom. Everyone knows that. It's a tradition, or an old charter, or something. And the phantom always lives in the bowels of the Opera House and rows a boat through the sewers.'

'And he does this for a living?'

'He's a phantom,' said Eddie. 'Who can say?'

'I don't like the sound of him very much.'

'We really *are* wasting time,' said Eddie. 'Let's find some conveniently placed sewer-hole cover to lift and get down to business.'

'Aren't sewers filled with business?' Jack asked.

'Yes, and Stage Door Johnnies, and crocodiles, too, I'm told.'

'Perhaps if I bribed that doorman . . .'

A sewer-hole cover was conveniently located not many paces before them. Jack looked up and down the alleyway and then took to tugging, then struggling, then finally prying open.

'Here it comes,' he panted. And here the cover came, up and over and onto Jack's foot.

'Ow!' howled Jack. And his 'Ow' echoed down along the sewer beneath them.

'Keep it quiet,' said Eddie. 'And get down the hole.'

'I'll get business on my trenchcoat,' said Jack.

'Time is wasting,' said Eddie. 'You brought us here to save lives, didn't you?'

Jack lowered himself into the unpleasantness beneath, then called up to Eddie and Eddie jumped down. Jack caught Eddie, reached up and pulled the sewer-hole cover back into place.

Eddie and Jack stood in darkness. And in smelliness also.

'Whoa!' went Jack, holding his nose and fanning his face. 'This is revolting—I'm up to my ankles in business here.'

'I'm nearly up to my bottom,' said Eddie. 'But it's quite a pleasant smell. Once you've acclimatised yourself.'

'So, which way do we go?'

'That way,' said Eddie.

Jack sighed deeply. 'I can't see a thing in the darkness. Which way do you mean?'

'*That* way,' said Eddie.

'Oh, *that* way,' said Jack. 'I see.'

But of course he did not. But he did follow Eddie by holding his ear. And Eddie strode forward with confidence, because, as he informed Jack, bears are noted for their remarkable night vision and natural sense of direction.

Presently they reached the inevitable dead end.

'Brilliant,' said Jack.

'Up the ladder,' said Eddie. 'Put your hands out—there's rungs in the wall.'

Jack put his hands out. 'Ah,' he said.

There were strugglings and pantings and it's hard to climb a ladder in the darkness with one hand holding your nose. But at length the two now somewhat ill-smelling detectives emerged into a kind of underground chamber, bricked all around with big stone slabs and lit by flaming *torchères* in wall sconces. There was an old organ in one corner of this chamber and at this sat an old organist, playing an old organ tune.

Jack dusted down his trenchcoat, but demurred at wringing out its sodden hem. Eddie squeezed at his soggy legs and dripped fetid water.

The old organist suddenly burst into song.

> The gulls that circle overhead
> Cry out for crumbs and bits of bread.
> The gulls that circle underfoot
> Are very rarely seen.

'What a wonderful song,' said Jack.

'I hated it,' said Eddie.

'Who said *that*?' asked the old organist. And he turned. And Jack and Eddie beheld . . . the Phantom of the Opera.

'Oh my goodness,' said Jack, and he fell back in considerable disarray.

The Phantom wasn't the prettiest sight, but he wasn't the ugliest, either. He was somewhere in between, but at a certain level in between that made him, or perhaps it was a her, or indeed an it, utterly, utterly . . .

'What is the word I'm looking for?' Jack did whispering to Eddie.

'Search me,' said the bear in reply. 'Average, bland, standard, run-of-the-mill, insipid, dull, middling, trite, mediocre, commonplace.'

'That's enough,' said Jack. 'But that's what it is.'

'Aaagh,' went the Phantom. 'Do not gaze upon my ubiquitousness.'

'And that's a good'n,' said Eddie. 'Possibly the best'n. He's as ubiquitous as.'

'What are you doing here?' The Phantom raised his voice, but it didn't really seem to raise. It droned somewhat. Which was odd as his, or her, or its, singing had been sweet. Although Eddie had hated it. 'Have you come to mock me for my generality? Come to laugh at the cursed one? The one too dull and everyday to be noticed?'

'We noticed you at once,' said Jack. 'And I really loved the singing.'

'You did?' said the Phantom. 'You *really did*?'

'It was a beautiful song. But we're lost. We need to get up into the Opera House. Would you help us, please?'

'I rarely venture above,' said the Phantom. 'My appearance is too lacking in extremity even to draw notice. Folk don't even know I'm there.'

'Who said that?' said Eddie.

'Stop it,' said Jack. 'It's not funny.'

'Oh, it is,' said the Phantom, wringing hands of abundant nonentity. 'They all laugh. It's all the Toymaker's fault.'

'The kindly, lovable white-haired old Toymaker?' said Jack.

'Unless you know of another.'

Jack shook his head.

'He wanted to create a toy that would be loved by all, that would appeal to all. So he took a bit of this and a bit of that and a bit of the other and he blended them all together. But did he create something that would universally be loved by all?'

Jack shook his head slowly. 'No?' he suggested.

'Correct,' said the Phantom. 'I am everything. And by being everything, I am nothing. I am a Phantom.'

'That's very sad,' said Jack.

'But we are in a hurry,' said Eddie.

'That *is* true,' said Jack. 'Do you think, Mister Phantom, that you could be kind enough to show us the way up into the Opera House. It is *Mister* Phantom, is it, or is it *Miss* or *Missis*?'

'If only I knew,' said the Phantom. 'Then, if I *did* know, I'd know whether some of the urges I feel at times are natural rather than perverse.'

'Difficult,' said Jack.

'Time,' said Eddie, pawing at an imaginary wristwatch.

'That bear's no master of mime,' said the Phantom. 'And what is *he*, anyway?'

'I'm an Anders Imperial,' said Eddie. 'Cinnamon plush—'

'That's a beer-bottle top in your ear hole.'

'That's my special button tag.'

'Oh no it's not.'

'Oh yes it is.'

'Time,' said Jack, and he pointed to his wristwatch.

'I'll take you up,' said the Phantom, 'but I'll caution you to take care.'

'Oh yes?' said Jack.

'Something is amongst us,' said the Phantom. 'I can sense it. Something that pretends to be us, but is not. Something other. Something apart. Something from Beyond The Second Big O.'

'We are aware of this,' said Jack, 'and it is our job to stop it.'

'Really?' the Phantom voiced surprise, but in a manner too dull and too monotone to express the emotion. 'Really, I *am* surprised. But you *must* beware. This something, and there is more than one of these somethings—there are two, in fact—these somethings will destroy us all, they will suck the very life force out of Toy City, leaving it an empty shell.'

Jack looked at Eddie.

And Eddie looked at Jack.

'Please lead us up,' said Jack.

The Phantom led the way. He, she or it, or all of the aforementioned, had a certain height to whatever he, she or it was. But it was an indeterminate height that was difficult to quantify. It was neither one thing nor the other; it lay somewhere in between, but beyond.

'If they ever make a movie of *this*,' Eddie whispered up to Jack, 'they'll have a real problem casting this, er, being.'

'They'll probably get Gary Oldman,' said Jack. 'He can play anyone.'

'Who is Gary Oldman?'

'Search me,' said Jack. 'I think my mind's wandering again. It was poetry yesterday. I probably *do* need some sleep.'

'This way,' said the Phantom, leading onward.

And onward the Phantom led and eventually his leading was done with the opening of a secret panel, as is so often the case with Phantoms. 'This is the royal box,' he, she or it said. 'You'll have a good view of the show from here—no one uses it any more. Something to do with Edict Five. Did you ever hear of it?'

'Never,' said Eddie. 'Thank you for helping us, Mister, er, well, Phantom.'

'I do have a name,' said the Phantom.

'Oh,' said Jack. 'What is it?'

'Ergo,' said the Phantom. 'I'll be leaving you now.'

'Nice fellow,' said Jack, once the Phantom had departed. 'Or woman, or whoever, or whatever.'

Eddie shrugged and climbed into a most comfortable-looking queenly kind of a chair. 'All right, I suppose, if you like that kind of a thing.'

Jack dropped down into the chair next to Eddie's, a most sumptuous kingly kind of a chair. Jack gazed all about the royal box. It was all gold twirly bits and gilt wallpaper.

And then Jack looked out from the box and into the Opera House proper. He had been there before, had Jack, as too had Eddie, and this *was* the royal box that Eddie had been sick in. Although it didn't smell of sick now, or possibly it did, a bit. It smelled a bit like sawdust. And Jack marvelled anew at the wonders of the Opera House.

'It really *is* an incredible place,' said Jack.

'Gaudy,' said Eddie. 'Gaudy.'

Jack looked out over the audience.

And then Jack whispered to Eddie, 'They're out there somewhere, our lookalikes, about to strike.'

'Did your, er, *secret* source tell you just *who* they are intending to strike at?' Eddie asked.

'The orchestra,' Jack whispered in return.

Eddie stood up on his chair and peered down into the orchestra pit. And Eddie counted on his paws, which meant counting two at a time. And when Eddie had finished his counting, Eddie turned to Jack.

'The orchestra?' said Eddie. 'The *entire* orchestra?'

'According to my source,' said Jack, 'who calculated the odds. There were twelve monkeys and then there was the jazz trio. Three times twelve is thirty-six and there are thirty-six orchestra members here. The murders are growing in a mathematical progression.'

'Jack, the *entire* orchestra? All of them?'

'That's what my source suggests.'

'Jack,' said Eddie, 'look down at the orchestra, if you will.'

Jack looked down upon the orchestra.

'Jack, count the number of members of the orchestra, if you will.' Jack counted.

'Jack, tell me the number you have arrived at, if you will.'

Jack said, 'Yep, that's thirty-six, including the conductor, I'm afraid.'

'Jack, so many folk. This will be a massacre. What are we going to do?'

'Well,' said Jack, 'I *have* thought about this, and the way I see it is—'

But then Jack's words were swallowed away, for the orchestra struck up.

12

Now Jack felt that he could understand a clockwork orchestra. In a way. Which is to say that he understood the principles involved. A clockwork orchestra was an orchestra of automata—clockwork figures programmed, as it were, to perform a series of pre-planned tasks, to pluck certain strings, to touch certain keys, to finger certain notes. In fact Jack, with his knowledge of clockwork, apprenticed as he had been in a factory that produced clockwork figures, felt confident that he had the ability to personally create a reasonably efficient and melodic clockwork orchestra. It was only down to knowing how clockwork functioned and what it was capable of.

But the trouble was.

The trouble was, as the trouble had been ever since Jack had first arrived in Toy City, in what now felt to him like a distant past, the trouble was that the clockwork orchestra playing beneath him was actually playing. These were not simple (or indeed complex) automata going through their mechanical motions. No, not a bit of it. These were clockwork musicians, but they were *real* musicians. They actually played, and some of them sometimes hit the wrong notes.

They *really* played. They thought. They used their skills.

But clockwork brains? It was a mystery to Jack. It had always been a mystery and it remained a mystery still.

Jack glanced at Eddie. The little bear looked out anxiously over the audience, down upon the clockwork orchestra. That bear, as Jack knew, had nothing in his head but sawdust. Yet he thought, saw, heard, felt. Loved.

It was above and beyond a mystery. And although Jack felt certain that his own senses—those of a living, breathing man—did not deceive him, that he really *was* here in Toy City, a city where toys lived and moved of their own accord, it was beyond his comprehension as to how. And Jack knew that he cared for these ersatz creatures, these living toys. He wished no harm to come to them. In fact, like Eddie, he wished that something could be done to ease their lot, which was for the most part a pretty rotten one.

Jack looked out once more towards the orchestra: they were hammering into the overture. Going at it with gusto. These thinking, feeling clockwork musicians knew nothing of the threat that was presently hanging over them, that at any moment the terrible light might strike and their very essences would be torn from their bodies.

'Eddie!' bawled Jack. 'We have to get down there. To the stage.'

'You *do* have a plan?' Eddie bawled back.

'I need the toilet,' bawled Jack.

'You need *what*?'

Jack and Eddie left the royal box. There was no one in the corridor. Jack located the nearest gentlemen's toilet.

'Bottle job, is it?' Eddie asked.

'Just give me a minute, please. Wait here.'

Jack slipped into the gentlemen's toilet, closing the door behind him. He locked himself into the nearest stall and withdrew from his trenchcoat Wallah the calculating pocket.

'You've a lovely soft hand,' crooned Wallah.

'Yes,' said Jack, 'I'm sure I have. Now, you must help us, please. You were absolutely right about the orchestra being the next target and I'm still not certain how you arrived at your calculations.'

'That's because I haven't explained it to you,' said Wallah, in a husky tone. 'And it's not really necessary that I do, is it?'

'No,' said Jack, 'not at the moment. But please, tell me, what should Eddie and I do next? The murderers are already in the building and they could strike at any moment. Eddie and I have to stop them.'

'Well then, my dearest—' said Wallah.

'Dearest?' said Jack.

'Well, you're such a dear boy.'

'Please tell me,' said Jack. 'I don't know what to do.'

Wallah did snugglings into the palm of Jack's hand. 'You'll need a plan,' she whispered.

'Yes,' said Jack, 'and very fast indeed.'

'Then hold me up to your ear and let me whisper.'

★

Jack emerged from the gentlemen's toilet.

'All right now?' Eddie asked. 'I hope you didn't forget to wash your hands.'

'I have a plan,' said Jack.

'Now, that's a coincidence,' Eddie said, 'for I have a plan as well.'

'Nice,' said Jack. 'But my plan is this—'

'You'll want to hear mine first,' said Eddie.

'No I won't,' said Jack.

Oh, I think you will—mine is a real blinder. It's as brilliant as.'

'Mine is calculated to achieve optimum success,' said Jack.

'Ooh,' went Eddie. 'Optimum success.'

'Time,' went Jack, doing wristwatch tappings, 'time is surely running out.'

'Then we'll run backstage and on the way I will explain to you my plan.'

'And if it doesn't conflict with mine, we'll put it into operation.'

'Jack, there's something you're not telling me.'

'You know there is.'

'Then tell me, please.'

'I won't.'

And the two took to jogging down the corridor.

It's really quite easy to move about unseen, as it were, in a bit Opera House when a production is underway. After all, the audience are in their seats, the front-of-house staff, who are not required again until the half-time rush for the bar, are outside having a fag and discussing what rubbish they think the production is and how much better they could do it themselves. The technical staff are deeply engaged in their technical stuff, gaffers are gaffing and best boys, who don't really have a role to play in the running of a successful ballet, and who would be better off getting back to whatever movies they should be being the bestest of boys on, are generally to be found in the stars' dressing rooms, sniffing the roses and drinking champagne out of glass slippers. But some folk have all the luck and best boys have most of it.

And so it really is quite easy to move about unseen, behind the scenes, as it were, in a big Opera House when a production is under way.

'Up this way,' said Eddie.

'Might I ask why?' Jack asked.

'It's part of my plan. Any objection?'

'Actually, no,' said Jack. 'It's part of my plan also.'

Jack and Eddie were backstage now, that wonderful place where all the flats are weighted down and there are big ropes everywhere and curiously it smells a bit like a stable.* Unlike the front of the stage. Which smells quite unlike a stage.

As a matter of interest for those who have never attended a ballet, or those who have attended a ballet but sat either up in the circle or further back in the stalls, it is to be noted that if you are ever offered front-row stall seats to the ballet, *do not* accept them. If you do attend the ballet, take a look at the front row of stalls seats. Notice how few folk are sitting there, and how uncomfortable these folk look.

Why? you might well ask. What is all this about? you also might ask. Well, the answer is this: what you can smell when you sit in the front row of the ballet is a certain smell. And it is a smell quite unlike stables. What you can smell when you sit in the front row of the ballet is . . .

Ballet dancers' feet.

Why ballet dancers' feet smell quite so bad is anybody's guess. Probably because ballet dancers work so hard that they don't have time to wash their feet as often they should, would be anybody's *reasonable* guess.

But there it is.

Never accept front-row seats for the ballet.

Never.

Understood?†

'Why does this backstage smell of stables?' Jack asked Eddie.

'Because of the hay bales that are used as "running chuffs".'

'Ah,' said Jack. 'But what are—'

'This way,' said Eddie.

'That was the way I was going,' said Jack. 'But what are—'

'Let's hurry,' said Eddie. 'I have a *very* bad feeling coming upon me, and as you know, we bears are noted for our sense of—'

'Let's just hurry,' said Jack.

And so they hurried and presently they found themselves, and indeed each other, upon a high gantry, which held the above-stage lighting rigs. There were lots of ropes all about and wires and cables, too.

'We're here,' said Eddie.

'Yes we are,' said Jack. 'About this plan of yours.'

'Let me ask you just one thing,' said Eddie. 'Does your plan involve a chandelier?'

---

* It really does.

† And I'm not joking here. When I worked in a prop house, I regularly received free tickets from one of the staff who was dating a Covent Garden ballet dancer. The tickets were always front-row tickets. I used to breathe through my mouth.

'Actually, it does,' said Jack.

'Mine, too,' said Eddie.

'Well, what a coincidence that is.'

'Really?' Eddie raised his imaginary eyebrows. 'And yet this is an Opera House, and we did meet the Phantom of the Opera. And the one thing everyone remembers about the Phantom of the Opera, and indeed associates with operas, is the big chandelier that hangs above the centre of the stage. Which gets dropped upon someone.'

'Well, I wouldn't know about *that*,' said Jack.

'Nor me,' said Eddie. 'I just made that bit up to pass some time.'

'Oh,' said Jack. 'Why?'

'Because *that*,' said Eddie, and he pointed with a paw, 'is a *very* big chandelier and I'm not exactly certain how we'll be able to drop a thing that size on anyone.'

'Aha,' said Jack. 'Gotcha.'

'Gotcha?' said Eddie. 'What means this odd word?'

'It means that my calculated plan extends a little further than your own. I know exactly how to drop that chandelier upon the evildoers.'

'Assuming of course they stand directly beneath it when we do the dropping,' Eddie said.

'Eddie,' said Jack, 'let's face it: it's a pretty preposterous idea. But this *is* a pretty preposterous situation. All of this is utterly ludicrous.'

'When you put it like that, how can we fail?'

'Well said. Now bung your furry ear hole in my direction and let me whisper into it.'

And so Jack whispered. And when his whispering was done, which, it has to be said, was quite loud whispering as it had to make itself heard above the spirited strains of the orchestra beneath, Jack straightened and Eddie looked up at him.

And then Eddie said, 'No way.'

'No way?' said Jack.

'Absolutely no way,' said Eddie. 'What do you take me for? You'll get me killed.'

'It will work,' said Jack. 'You'll be fine. It's a calculated risk.'

'I won't be fine, I'll die. You do it.'

'I can't do it. It has to be you.'

'And what do I do it with?'

'You do it with a spanner. This spanner.'

'And where did you find that?'

'Backstage, next to the "thunder sheet".'

'And what's a—'

'Don't start with me. I know you made up "running chuffs".'

'But I've only got paws, Jack. No hands with fingers and opposable thumbs.'

'It'll only take a few turns—you'll manage.'

'Oh, look,' said Eddie. 'The ballet has begun.'

Now ballets and operas have several things in common. Swanky costumes they have in common, and too much stage make-up. And music, of course—they are both traditionally very musical affairs. But the most notable thing that they share is the storyline. The one thing that you can always be assured of if you go to the opera or the ballet is, in the case of the opera, lots of really good loud singing, and in the case of the ballet, lots of really wonderful dancing, and *in the case of both, really rubbish* storylines.

They *are* rubbish. They always are. You always know what's coming next. Who the baddy is and who the goody. The jokes, such as they are, are telegraphed a mile off. Rubbish, they all are. Rubbish.

Eddie watched the dancers a-dancing beneath. Very pretty dancing dolls they were, of the variety that pop out of musical boxes, only bigger.

'What is this ballet all about?' he asked Jack.

'Boy sees girl, villain sees girl, boy meets girl, villain sees boy meet girl, boy gets parted from girl due to villain's villany, boy remeets girl and boy gets girl in the end.'

'And *that's* the story?' Eddie asked.

'Yes,' said Jack. 'Clever, isn't it?'

'That would be irony, would it?'

Jack said, 'We should be doing our stuff!'

Eddie said, 'I don't want to!'

Beneath them, dolly ballerinas twirled. The hero, a wooden dolly who given the bulge in his tights apparently had wood on, did pluckings up on the heroine and twistings of her round in the air and the doing of something that is called a pas de deux. And also a full-tilt whirly-tronce, a double chuff-muffin rundle and a three-point turn with the appropriate hand signals and other marvellous things of a quite balletic nature.

The villain of the piece, imaginatively costumed in black, lurked in the limelight at stage left, posturing in a menacing fashion and glowering 'neath overlarge painted eyebrows.

Eddie said, 'Don't do this to me, Jack.'

Jack said, 'It has to be done.'

And then Jack did it, but did it with care. He lifted Eddie from his paw pads, raised him to shoulder height and then hurled him. Eddie, wearing the face of terror, soared out over the dancers beneath. Jack buried his face in his hands and prayed for a God to believe in and wished Eddie well. And Eddie landed safely in the topmost crystal nestings of the mighty Opera House chandelier.

Unseen by dancers, orchestra or audience.

Jack peeped out through his fingers and breathed a mighty sigh. Eddie clung to the chandelier and growled in a bitter fashion. Jack waved heartily to Eddie.

Eddie raised a paw to wave back and all but fell to his death. Jack rootled the spanner from a nameless pocket and waggled it at Eddie.

Eddie steadied himself in his crystal nest and prepared to do catchings.

And it could have been tricky. In fact, it could have been disastrous. That spanner could have fallen, down and down onto dancers beneath. But it didn't, for it was a calculated throw.

And Eddie caught that spanner between his paws and offered a thumbless thumbs-up back to Jack.

And Eddie peeped down from his lofty crystal eyrie. Through twinkling crystals, which presented the world beneath as one magical, he viewed the dancers, the orchestra and even the backstage, smelling of stables, which lurked behind the flats. It was a pretty all-encompassing overview, and one that brought no little sense of awe to Eddie Bear.

And of course bears *are* noted for their tree-climbing abilities and fearlessness of heights.

Eddie clung to the chandelier, and if he had had knuckles, these would at this time have been white. As would his face. From fear.

Jack grinned over at Eddie. 'Bears are noted for their tree-climbing abilities and fearlessness of heights,' he said to himself, 'so Eddie will be fine.'

Beneath, the villain enticed the heroine. Well, menaced was better the word. But as he did this via the medium of skilful dance, a degree of menace was lost.

And Jack looked down from on high, as did Eddie, and then Jack saw what Eddie saw, although from a different perspective.

Along the backstage the two of them crept, one Jack and the other one Eddie. The Jack carried two large suitcases. The Jack upon high's eyes widened, though the Eddie upon high's could not. Jack now did blinkings and rubbings at his eyes. That *was* him below. It really was. Though of course it really wasn't. But it looked like him and walked like him, or at least Jack thought that it did.

Although it didn't look altogether right. Jack screwed up his eyes and did long-distance squintings. What was wrong with this picture?

'He's the wrong way round,' whispered Jack. 'Oh no, he's not—it's just that I've never seen myself like that. I've only seen myself in a mirror.' And Jack did frantic wavings of the hands towards Eddie. Frantic mimings of a spanner being turned.

But Eddie wasn't looking at Jack. Eddie was looking down upon his other self. 'Damn fine-looking bear,' said Eddie to his own self. 'Anders Imperial. Cinnamon plush coat . . .'

Down below, backstage, the other Eddie and the other Jack were unpacking the contents of the suitcases and assembling some rather snazzy-looking hi-tech equipment.

Above, Jack's motions to Eddie became ever more frantic. Jack sought things to throw at the bear.

Eddie gawped at his other self. It was a damn fine-looking bear, but *what* was it? Spaceman? Space *chicken*? What? Where had it come from? Why did it look like him? Why was it doing whatever it was it was doing? And whatever *was* it doing?

Eddie now glanced in Jack's direction. Jack seemed to be doing a foolish dance.

'Spanner!' mouthed Jack. 'Release the chandelier,' he mouthed also. 'Ah,' went Eddie. 'Oh, yes.'

Beneath the two detectives, their other selves, the other Eddie and the other Jack, appeared to have concluded the setting up of their hi-tech and Hellish apparatus. The Jack was now adjusting settings, twiddling dials, making final preparations.

Eddie on high laboured with the spanner—not easy between teddy paws—at the great nut and bolt that secured the chandelier to the ceiling above.★

Ballet dancers twisted and twirled. The villain, who wouldn't get around to stabbing the hero until at least the third act, did more posturing and glowering with his eyebrows. The orchestra did the slow bit that involved violins.

The other Jack did straightenings up and rubbings of his hands.

Eddie struggled with the spanner. It was a tricky nut.

Jack glanced here and there and everywhere, down at the dancers, up at Eddie, down at their other selves, out towards the orchestra. Jack felt helpless. He *was* helpless.

Eddie continued his struggling, but the tricky nut wouldn't budge.

'What do I do? What do I do?' Jack took to flapping his hands and doing a kind of tap dance.

★ As opposed to the 'ceiling below'—although there is no such thing. Unless of course you live in a flat. But this is by the by.

Something tweaked him hard in the groin. Jack ceased his kind of tap dance.

'Ow,' went Jack. 'Who did that to me?'

His groin got tweaked once again.

'Stop it! Oh, it's you.' And Jack drew Wallah from his trenchcoat and held her to his ear.

'My calculations regarding the nut-turning potential of the bear would appear to be incorrect by a factor of one-point-five,' said Wallah. 'It will be necessary for you to jump from the gantry onto the chandelier and turn the nut yourself. Do take care to cling onto something safe when the chandelier falls.'

'What?' went Jack.

'It's a calculated risk,' said Wallah. 'And as I will be with you and I care about you, believe me, it is the product of most careful and meticulous calculation.'

'I can't do that,' said Jack. 'I can't.'

Eddie struggled hopelessly to turn the nut.

Lights began to pulse on the hi-tech apparatus far below.

'No,' said Jack. 'I can't. I can't.'

A big white light began to grow backstage.

'No,' said Jack. And he climbed onto the handrail of the gantry. 'No, I can't. I can't. I can't. I . . . ooooooh.'

And Jack leapt into the wide blue yonder, as it's sometimes known. And he soared, as in slow motion, and struck the mighty crystal chandelier. And did scrabblings. And did clawings. And did grippings. And did holdings on.

And did sighings.

And.

'Hello there, Jack,' said Eddie. 'I wasn't expecting you.'

'They're . . .' Jack huffed and puffed and clung on also and climbed a bit, too, until he was level with Eddie. 'They're going to blast the orchestra. We have to drop the chandelier upon them.'

'Such was my plan,' said Eddie, 'but I cannot shift the nut.'

'Let me.' And Jack took the spanner.

And down below the other Jack's fingers hovered above a big red button. And the other Jack looked down towards the other Eddie. And the other Jack smiled and the other Eddie smiled back. And those smiles were evil smiles. And the other Jack's finger pressed down upon the blood-red button.

And above, Jack fought with the tricky nut. 'It's a tricky nut,' said he.

'Get twisting,' howled Eddie, looking fearfully below. 'Oh no—something terrible's happening.'

The white and awful light spread out from the hi-tech whatnot. It penetrated the rear of the stage flat, emerged through the painted back-drop and spread out onto the stage. The ballet dancers shielded their eyes, ceased their pirouetting and fled in confusion. The clockwork or-chestra engaged in orchestration played on regardless, regardless.

'Twist the blighter,' Eddie further howled.

The awful light flooded the stage.

Other howls went up now, these from the audience. The explosion of light blinded their eyes and folk rose from their seats in confusion.

Jack got a purchase upon that nut. 'I think it's giving!' he said.

The other Jack adjusted controls, did twistings of his own of but-tons rather than nuts. The terrible light swept out from the stage and dipped down into the orchestra pit.

And it fell upon the orchestra. Musicians rose to take flight, to es-cape from a terrible something. Dread. And panic. And confusion.

'Hurry, Jack, hurry!' cried Eddie.

'I'm hurrying.' Jack put his back to his work. The chandelier swung beneath him. Crystals shook. Jack forced at the nut, and the nut began slowly to turn.

But now terrible cries and screams came from the orchestra.

And terrible cracklings and poppings and sounds of hideous horri-bleness.

'Swing it,' cried Eddie. 'As you turn that nut, swing the chandelier—we have to drop it right on top of these monsters. And quick please, Jack, the musicians are dying. They're killing them, Jack.'

'I'm trying. I'm trying. Oh!'

And off came the nut, away from the bolt.

And . . .

'Nothing's happening!' Jack shouted.

'You'll have to kick the bolt out,' Eddie shouted back.

'And how will I do that?'

'Use this!'

The voice came in a shouted form from the lighting gantry. Upon this now stood the Phantom of the Opera. He held a hammer in his hand.

'Catch it and knock out the bolt.' And the Phantom threw the hammer. And Jack caught the hammer. And Jack used the hammer. And Jack knocked out the bolt.

And then things happened in sort of slow motion. In the way that they would if this were a movie (instead of real life, as it obviously was!).

Jack knocked out the bolt.

And the bolt spiralled away into space.

And the chandelier fell (in slow motion, of course).

And the light beneath penetrated the orchestra, bored its way into their very beings, sucked away at their very soul-stuff.

And the chandelier fell.

And with it fell Eddie and Jack.

And down went that chandelier. Down and down upon the other Jack and the other Eddie, who at its coming down looked up to see it doing that very thing.

And down too went Eddie and Jack.

And the orchestra, writhing and dying in the terrible light.

And the chandelier falling.

And now the Phantom, gripping a dangling rope. Swinging down from the gantry.

And the chandelier falling.

And the other Jack and the other Eddie looking up.

And the orchestra dying.

And the Phantom swinging (normal action now, not slow motion).

And he gathers up Jack and Eddie as they fall, sweeps onward, lands them and himself all safely upon another gantry, just lower down on the other side of the stage.

Nice work.

And the chandelier smashes down (normal action).

And explodes.

Into a million crystal fragments.

Spiralling crystals fly in all directions, which you can do really well with CGI nowadays.

And the awful light dies.

And things go very dark.

And very still.

And cut!

That's a take!

Well done, everyone.

13

'Oh my goodness,' croaked Eddie. 'Are we still alive?'

'You are alive,' said the Phantom, lowering Eddie to the floor of the lower gantry, 'and so is your companion.'

'That is *not* what I mean.' And Eddie craned what neck he had to peer down at the shattered chandelier. It had probably been a most expensive chandelier, but there wasn't much of it left now. 'I mean the *other* we, the other me and Jack—are *they* still alive?'

Jack took to peering, clinging to the gantry handrail, his knees now wobbling somewhat.

'Can you see?' Eddie asked. 'Did we smash those blighters good?'

'I can't see,' said Jack. 'But I can see . . . Oh dear, Eddie.'

'What is it? What can you see?'

'The orchestra,' said Jack, and he said it in a strangled whisper. 'It's the orchestra, Eddie. All the musicians are dead.'

Eddie buried his face in his paws. 'This is as bad as,' he said.

'Oh Eddie, I'm so sorry.' Jack leaned down and patted his friend. 'I'm so very sorry. It's all my fault.'

'All *your* fault?' Eddie looked up with a bitter face. 'It's not *your* fault, Jack. You did everything you could. You were as brave as. It was my fault. The fault of these stupid paws. I couldn't turn the spanner. If only I'd had my hands—'

'You did *your* best,' said the Phantom in his or her (or its) toneless manner. 'And you couldn't be expected to have hands. Hands, indeed? You'd look like that creepy mayor. In fact—'

'It *was* my fault.' Eddie regarded with bitterness his fingerless, thumbless paws. 'Everything has been my fault.'

'Stop it, Eddie,' said Jack. 'You did what you could. I should have leapt over to the chandelier in the first place.'

'You were both very brave,' said the Phantom, 'and you had no care for your own safety.'

'And you saved us both,' said Jack. 'We owe you our lives.'

'Oh, it was nothing. The least I could do.'

'I won't forget this,' Jack said.

Eddie sighed, and he so hated sighing. 'We'd better go down,' he said. 'There is nothing we can do for the orchestra, but if the other me and the other you are still alive down there, I'm going to see to it that they don't remain so much longer.'

'Steady, Eddie,' said Jack.

'I'll lead the way,' said the Phantom. 'It's a bit complicated, but it does involve another secret panel.'

'We could just go down these steps,' said Jack.

'What, and miss the secret panel?'

'It's probably for the best,' Jack said.

And Jack led the way down the staircase to backstage. Much of the backdrop had collapsed beneath the fallen chandelier and Jack was able to look out across the empty stage, over the silent orchestra pit and the deserted auditorium.

Eddie Bear raised an ear. 'I hear police sirens in the distance,' he said.

'Let's make haste, then,' said Jack, and he began to sift amongst the ruination that had been the chandelier.

'Anything?' Eddie asked.

'You might help,' said Jack.

'No, I might not,' said Eddie. 'That's a lot of broken glass—I could cut myself and lose my stuffing.'

Jack did further siftings and added some rootlings to these. 'There's something,' he said.

'Bodies?' Eddie asked. Hopefully.

'No,' said Jack. 'Their machine is here, all broken in pieces. Which is something, though not very much.'

'But no bodies?'

'No,' said Jack. 'Ah, I see.'

'You see bodies?'

'I don't see bodies. But what I do see is the trap door.'

'And it's open, I suppose.' Eddie made low growling sounds. 'They've escaped.'

Jack was dragging ruined chandelier to this side and the other. 'Then we'll go after them,' he said.

'What? When they seem capable of vanishing away in a puff of smoke? Like my one did at Old King Cole's?'

'I don't think they'll find it quite so easy this time,' Jack said. 'Their machine is busted, after all.'

'Their killing machine? What has that to do with them making their escape?'

'It has to double as a means of transportation, surely?'

'That doesn't *really* follow,' said the Phantom, who hadn't said much lately and had done absolutely no rootling or sifting either. 'You are making a supposition there that is not based on any empirical evidence.'

'Please keep out of this,' said Jack. 'You saved our lives and for that we are extremely grateful, but Eddie and I must now pursue these monsters. Pursue them to their lair.'

'And destroy them,' said Eddie.

'Well, apprehend them, at least.'

'Destroy them,' said Eddie. 'At least.'

'Well, we'll see how things take shape when we catch up with them.'

'And how will we do *that*?' Eddie asked.

Jack now made a certain face. 'Now, excuse me,' he said, 'but don't I recall you telling me at some time or another—yesterday, in fact—how bears are noted for their tracking abilities?'

'Ah, yes,' said Eddie. And he sniffed. 'And I have the scent of the other me in my nostril parts right now.'

'Then sniff on please, Mister Bear,' said Jack.

'Mister Bear,' said Eddie. 'I like that, Mister Bear.'

'Then sniff on, if you will.'

'I will.'

Jack thanked the Phantom once more and promised that he would return as soon as matters were sorted and take he, she or it out for a beer, or a cocktail, or a measure of motor oil. Or something. Eddie Bear too said his thanks and then he and Jack descended into the void that lay, uninvitingly, beneath the open trap door.

And not before time, as it happened, for now laughing policemen swarmed into the auditorium. And rushed in the direction of the stage. But there they found nothing, for the trap door was closed and the Phantom had melted away.

'Which way?' Jack asked. 'I can't see a thing.'

'Follow Mister Bear,' said Eddie. 'And I'm here—stick out your hand.'

And Jack followed Eddie and Eddie Bear sniffed the way ahead.

Which just went to show how subtle a bear's smelling sense can be, considering the stink of all that business down there.

'They might be hiding down here,' Jack whispered, 'waiting to get us.'

'They're not,' said Eddie. 'My nose tells me that. But if they're still upon our world, then Mister Bear will find them.'

Jack was about to voice words to the effect that he might soon grow tired of Eddie calling himself Mister Bear, but then he considered that he probably wouldn't. Mister Bear sounded good; it lent Eddie dignity.

'After you, Mister Bear,' said Jack.

And Mister Bear led on. And soon he and Jack were no longer in the Opera House; they were outside in the car park. Police car roof lights flashed around this car park, and Eddie and Jack moved with stealth.

'Actually, why are *we* moving with stealth?' Jack asked.

'Because,' said Eddie, 'this would be the moment when the misidentification scenario kicks in and we both get arrested.'

'I'll bet I can move with more stealth than you,' Jack said.

'And I'll bet you cannot.'

Eddie did further sniffings at the evening air. 'To use one of your favourite words,' he said, 'damn.'

'They took a car, didn't they?' Jack asked.

'That is what they did, but I can still track them. We'll just have to get the Anders Faircloud and skirt around the police cordon until I can pick up the scent again.'

'Right,' said Jack, and he plucked up Eddie. 'Then let's do this fast.' And with that Jack took to his heels in a stealthy kind of a way.

There followed then far more skirting around the police cordon than either Eddie or Jack might have hoped for. Jack drove with his head down, but Eddie had to stick his out of the window.

They were outside Tinto's Bar when Eddie picked up the scent once more.

'That's typical,' said Eddie. 'How dearly I'd like a beer.'

'Beers later, justice first,' said Jack.

'Nice phrase,' said Eddie. 'We could put that on the door of the office. And on our business cards. Put your foot down, Jack, that way.'

Jack now put his foot down, but the car just poodled along.

'I'll paint it on the door of the car, too,' said Jack. 'After I've given it a service.'

And so they moved off, in *cold* pursuit. Which indeed was a shame, because there's nothing like a good car chase to spice things up. A good car chase always has the edge, even over falling chandeliers.

Eddie kept on sniffing and Jack kept on driving.

And sometime later Eddie said, 'We're getting close now, Jack.'

And Jack looked out through the windscreen and said, 'We're approaching Toy Town again.'

'Damn,' said Eddie once more, and he smote his head with a paw. 'It was obvious they'd return here. We should have reasoned it out. We've wasted too much time.'

'We might still have the element of surprise on our side.' Jack switched off the headlights and the car did poodlings to a halt. 'Down the hillside once more,' said Jack, 'and this time we'll keep a careful lookout. Any big bright lights and we run like bitches.'

'Like *what*?' Eddie asked.

'Lady dogs,' said Jack. 'What did you think I meant?'

And down the hillside they went, through those briars and that gorse and even those nettles and stuff. And Jack held Eddie above them all, and troubled not about his trenchcoat.★

'To Bill's house, is it?' whispered Jack.

'That's what my nose tells me,' said Eddie.

Across the yellow-bricked road they went, across the town square and through that darkened alley. Finally, Jack set Eddie down.

'You could have walked the last bit,' he said.

'I was conserving my energy.'

'Still have the key?'

'Of course.'

But Jack didn't need it. The door to Bill Winkie's was open.

'Stay here,' said Jack. 'I'll go inside and see what's what.'

'What's what?' Eddie asked.

'This is neither the time nor the place,' Jack said, and he slipped into the house.

And presently returned.

'They're not in there,' Jack told Eddie.

'No,' said Eddie. 'But all those guns are.'

And so the two detectives went inside and availed themselves of weapons. Jack did mighty cockings of a mightier firepiece.

'The old M134 7.62mmm General Clockwork Mini-gun,' said Jack. 'My all-time favourite.'

'Everyone's all-time favourite,' said Eddie, 'but somewhat heavy for me and tricky to fire without fingers.' And Eddie selected weaponry that was built with the bear in mind.

★ Well, it *was* all soiled with the sewage.

'And now?' Jack asked as he slipped bandoliers of bullets over his shoulders and tucked grenades in his pockets.

'Payback time,' said Eddie.

That full moon was in the sky once more, silver-plating rooftops, and a chill was in the air. Jack turned up his collar and Eddie sniffed the chillified air.

'Follow me,' said Eddie Bear, and with that said led the way.

They threaded their way through alleyways, and up front paths and out of back gardens and finally Eddie said, 'Stop a minute, Jack. That's where they went. Up there.'

Jack looked up, up the hill he looked, the hill that rose up behind the conurbation that was Toy Town. The hill upon which those great letters stood. Those letters that had once spelt out TOYTOWNLAND.

'Up there?' Jack said. 'But what's up there, anyway?'

Eddie shook his head.

'And on the other side of the hill, what?'

Eddie shook his head once more. 'I've never been to the other side of that hill,' he said. 'In fact . . .' and he paused.

So Jack asked, 'What?'

'Oh, it's a crazy thing,' said Eddie. 'A silly thing. It's just what some toys believe.'

'Well, go on then and tell me.'

'No,' said Eddie. 'You'll laugh.'

'I'm really not in a laughing mood right now.'

'It's a silly thing, it's nothing at all.'

'Just tell me, Eddie.'

'Did you say "Just tell me, Mister Bear"?'

'I did.'

And so Eddie told him. 'It's just a belief, a myth, probably, but it's what we were brought up to believe. I was told by Bill when I was his bear never to wander up that hill, because if I did, I'd be lost.'

'That's fair enough,' said Jack. 'Bill cared about you. You were his bear. He loved you, he didn't want you to get lost.'

'Not *get* lost, Jack. *Be* lost.'

'*Get* lost, *be* lost, what's the difference, Edd—Mister Bear?'

'The difference is,' said Mr Eddie Bear, 'that I would *be* lost. The theory was that that hill marks the end of Toy Town—the end of everything, in fact. Beyond that hill is nothing. If you went over that hill you'd fall off the edge of the world and be gone for ever.'

'Well, that *is* silly,' said Jack.

'There,' said Eddie. 'I knew you'd say that. I wish I hadn't told you now.'

'Hang on there,' said Jack. 'Hold on, if you will.'

Eddie didn't know what to hold on to, so he stood his ground.

'Beyond that hill lies the end of this world—that's what you were told?'

Eddie nodded and continued standing his ground.

'Eddie,' said Jack, 'look up there—what do you see?'

'A dark and threatening hillside,' said Eddie. 'Well, threatening to me.'

'Yes, I can see that, but what else?'

'The Toy Town letters, that's all.'

'Eddie, look at those letters and tell me what you see.'

'Not much—most of them are gone. I see "TO TO LA".'

'And beyond that lies the end of this world?'

'Look, it's just what I was told. You believe these things when you're young.'

'Wake up, Eddie,' said Jack. 'Look at the letters. What do they say? What do they tell you about the *beyond*?'

'About the beyond?' And Eddie scratched at his head.

'You're not going to get it, are you?' Jack said. 'Even though it's there, staring you in the face?'

Eddie Bear looked up at Jack. 'I don't know what you mean,' he said.

'Wake up, Eddie,' said Jack once more. 'You've used the phrase yourself enough times. Something about "Beyond The—"'

'Second Big O,' said the suddenly enlightened Eddie. 'Beyond The Second Big O.'

'Exactly,' said Jack. 'And there it is, The Second Big O in what once spelt TOYTOWNLAND. That's where these invaders have come from. They come from Beyond The Second Big O—and *that* is The Second Big O.'

Eddie Bear looked up at Jack. 'You genius,' he said.

'Well, thank you, Mister Bear,' said Jack, 'but I just reasoned it out. That's what we detectives do, reason it out.'

'Or calculate,' said Eddie, 'As in the Opera House business. Do you feel up to confiding in me about that yet?'

'Later,' said Jack. 'For now we have to get after the murderers. What does your nose tell you, Eddie?'

'It tells me,' said Eddie, dismally, 'that that is the way they went. Beyond The Second Big O.' Eddie sniffed. '*Through* The Second Big O.'

'Then that's where *we're* going. Come.' And Jack set off. And then Jack turned. 'Come on, then,' he said.

But Eddie once more stood his ground. Most firmly so, in fact.

'Well, come on then, Eddie,' said Jack. 'Let's go, come on now.'

'Ah,' said Eddie and Eddie stood firm.

'Come on now,' said Jack.

'I can't,' said Eddie. 'I just can't come.'

'What do you mean?'

'I mean that I can't go through there,' Eddie said. 'We must call Bellis, get him to employ troops, send an armed task force through, if he will. If he dares.'

'Dare?' said Jack. 'What's to dare? We've got weapons, Eddie. Stop this foolishness, come on.'

'I can't come on, Jack. I can't. It's the end of my world up there. I don't know what will happen if I leave my world.'

'There's only the two of them. We're a match for them.'

'There isn't just two, Jack. If there's another world beyond that O, then there could be a whole worldful, another whole worldful and not yours or mine.'

'You don't know what's there and you won't know until we've gone through and found out. Those monsters that are impersonating us have killed *your* kind, Eddie, many now of *your* kind. They'll return and kill more if we don't stop them.'

'We'll lie in wait, then,' said Eddie.

'You can walk,' said Jack, 'of your own accord, or else I'll carry you.'

'You wouldn't!' Eddie drew back in alarm. 'You wouldn't treat me like *that*.'

'All right, I wouldn't, but I'm pleading with you, Eddie. Let's go after them now, before the scent goes cold. We'll be careful and I'm damn sure that they won't be expecting us.'

'You don't understand,' said Eddie. 'You didn't grow up here.'

Jack looked down at Eddie Bear. The bear was clearly shivering.

'You *are* afraid,' said Jack. 'You really are.'

'Yes I am, Jack. I *really* am.'

Jack cocked his head from one side to the other. 'You knew,' said he. 'You've known all along.'

'Know what?' said Eddie. 'What did I know?'

'You knew what the phrase meant. Beyond The Second O. If you grew up here and you were told you'd be lost if you went over that hill, you *had* to know what the phrase meant.'

'Well, perhaps I did. But it doesn't matter now, does it?'

'Look,' said Jack, 'whatever is out there, I'll protect you. I'll protect you with my life.'

'I know you will, Jack—you've done it before.'

'Then come with me.'

'I can't.'

'Then I will go alone.' And Jack turned to do so.

'No,' cried Eddie. 'Jack, please don't go up there alone.'

'Then come with me, Eddie. Come with me, *Mister* Bear.'

Eddie dithered and dithering wasn't his style. 'Let's go tomorrow,' he said. 'In the daylight.'

Jack hefted his mighty Mini-gun. 'I'm going *now*,' he said, 'and if you won't come, if you *can't* come, then I understand. You're brave, Eddie. I know you're brave. But if this is too much for you, then so be it. Wait here and I'll be back as soon as I can.'

'Jack, please don't go.'

'I must.'

And with that Jack turned away, looked up the hill, up at the letters TO TO LA, and then Jack set off up the lonely hillside, and Eddie Bear watched him go.

And Eddie Bear made faces and scuffed his paw pads in the moon-lit dirt. He couldn't let Jack go up there on his own, he couldn't. There was no telling what kind of trouble he'd get himself into. Eddie would have to go, too. No matter how great his fear.

And Eddie took a step or two forward.

And then a step or two back.

'This is ridiculous,' said Eddie. 'I *can* do it. I *must* do it. I *can* and I *must* and I *will*.'

But he couldn't.

The figure of Jack was diminishing, as is often the case with per-spective. Eddie watched as Jack climbed higher, bound for that Second Big O.

'Come on, Eddie,' the bear told himself. 'Jack is your bestest friend. You would never forgive yourself if he came to harm and you could have protected him from it.'

'I know,' Eddie now told himself, 'but I've been hoping against all hope that there was another solution. That the murderers *were* simply spacemen, or something. Something not of this world, but *not* some-thing from Beyond The Second Big O. Because beyond there lies a ter-rible, dreadful something. That's what I was taught and that is what I believe.'

'And you're letting your bestest friend wander into that something alone,' Eddie further told himself. 'What kind of bear are you?'

'A terrified one,' Eddie further, further, further told himself.

'Oh, what do I do? Tell me, what do I do?' And Eddie, although no devout bear, prayed to the God of All Bears. 'I don't know what to do,' Eddie prayed. 'Please won't you send me a sign?'

And perhaps it was the God of All Bears, or perhaps it was not, but a sign was made manifest to Eddie. Manifest in the Heavens, it was, as such signs often are.

And Eddie looked up and Eddie beheld. And he beheld it on high.

The moonlit sky was studded with stars, but one was brighter than all the rest. Eddie Bear peeped through his button eyes. 'There's a new star in Heaven tonight,' he said.

And the new star, the bright new star, grew brighter still.

'Is that you, Mister God?' asked Eddie.

And brighter and closer grew this star until it was all over big.

And Eddie looked up at this very big star.

And Eddie Bear said, 'Oh no!'

For this star, it now seemed, was no star at all. This star now grew even bigger and hovered now overhead. For this star, it seemed, was no star at all. It was a spaceship instead.

A proper flying saucer of a spaceship, all aglow with twinkling lights and a polished underbelly.

And the saucer now hovered low above Eddie and Eddie could make out rivets and tin plate and a sort of logo embossed into the underside of the brightly glowing craft. And this logo resembled a kind of stylised, in-profile sort of a head. And this was the head of a chicken.

And a bright light swept down upon Eddie.

And Eddie Bear took to his paw pads.

And onward scampered Eddie with the spaceship keeping pace, and the light, a sort of death-ray one, he supposed, a-burning up the grass and gorse and briars and nettles and stuff.

'Wah!' cried Eddie as he scampered. 'Wah! Oh, Jack. Help me!'

Jack, a goodly way up the hill, turned and looked over his shoulder. And Jack saw the spaceship and Jack saw Eddie.

And Jack was frankly afeared.

And when Jack had managed to summon a voice, this voice cried, 'Eddie, hurry!'

'I *am* hurrying.' And Eddie was, his little legs pounding beneath him. And Jack now hefted his great big gun and flipped off the safety catch.

The spaceship, keeping pace with Eddie, burned up the hillside behind him. The gorse and briars and nettles and stuff took all to blazing away. A goodly fire was spreading now, fanning out to Eddie's rear.

'Hurry!' cried Jack. And then he let rip. Let rip with the Mini-gun.

The clockwork motion hurled projectiles through six revolving barrels. Barrels spat flame and bullets, bullets that tore tracer-like into the moonlit sky.

And the craft moved onward, bullets bouncing from its hull. And the light swept onward, raising fire in Eddie's wake.

And the bear rushed onward, bound for his bestest friend.

'You're a really bad spacecraft,' cried Jack, and he flung the Minigun aside and brought forth a grenade from his trenchcoat pocket. 'Come on, Eddie, faster now,' and Jack pulled the pin and wondered how many seconds 'til *Boom!*

'Ow!' went Eddie. 'Ouch!' And his heels took fire.

'One,' said Jack. 'Two. How many? Ten, I suppose, so three, no, that would be four now, or maybe six, or seven, or . . . damn.'

And Jack hurled the grenade.

And it was a good hurl, but it fell short.

And a big chunk of hillside exploded.

And some of that hillside rained down upon Eddie.

'Don't do that, Jack!' cried the bear.

Jack pulled out another grenade and once more pulled the pin.

'One, two, three, four,' Jack counted. 'Hurry, Eddie, hurry, eight, nine, oh!' And Jack did another hurling and ducked his head as he did so. For the spacecraft was very near now, as indeed was Eddie.

'Quickly, Eddie.' And Jack snatched up the bear and ran very fast indeed.

And next there came an explosion, an explosion on high. And the spaceship swung about in the sky, flames roaring from its upper dome area. And then it began its plunging down, in Jack and Eddie's direction.

'Oh no!' shouted Jack, and he ran and he leapt, a-clutching Eddie tight. And as the spaceship smashed down to the hillside with a mighty explosion, which far exceeded that of the falling chandelier and probably had the edge over even a car chase when it came to exciting spectacle, Jack leapt for his life, leapt with Eddie, up and through and beyond.

Jack leapt through The Second Big O.

And through and out and into nothing.

And down and down and down.

And Jack tumbled down.

And Eddie, too.

And down and down and down.

And, 'Oooh!' cried Eddie.

And, 'Ouch!' cried Jack.

And, 'Ooooh!' and, 'Ouch!' and, 'Ow!'

And then all finally became still and silent and Jack lay upon grass, and so did Eddie, and moonlight fell down on them both.

'Are we still alive?' Eddie asked. 'And this time I *do* mean us.'

'So it would seem.' Jack patted at his limbs. None, it appeared, were broken.

Eddie did flexings at his seams, and none, it seemed, were torn.

'And *where* are we?' And Eddie looked all about himself.

'We went through The Second Big O.'

'Oh no!'

'But we're still alive, don't knock it.'

'And we are . . .' Eddie felt at the ground. 'We're on grass, on a hillside.'

'Because we're on the other side of the hill,' said Jack. 'Which means that you had nothing to fear. I'd like to say, "I told you so," but as I didn't it wouldn't help much.'

'On grass,' said Eddie. 'On grass.'

'On grass,' Jack said. 'Just on the other side of the hill.'

'Well,' said Eddie, and Eddie rose, 'I don't know what you were making all the fuss about.'

'*Me?*' said Jack. '*I* was making all that fuss? Sorry?'

'I forgive you,' said Eddie.

'What?' said Jack.

'It doesn't matter, forget it.'

Jack now climbed to his feet. He dusted down his trenchcoat, sniffed at his fingers and said, 'Yuk!'

'You'll want to get that trenchcoat cleaned,' said Eddie. 'I know a good dry-cleaners. Although I've never understood how dry-cleaning works—do you know how it does?'

'Don't change the subject, Eddie.'

'What subject would that be?'

Jack smiled down upon Eddie. 'It doesn't matter, *Mister* Bear. We're both safe and that's all that matters.'

'You certainly taught those space chickens something,' said Eddie. 'Don't mess with my bestest friend Jack. That's what you taught them. Well done you.'

'It *was* a big explosion,' said Jack. 'Actually, I'm quite surprised that a lot of flaming spaceship didn't rain down upon us. Pretty lucky, eh?'

'Pretty *damn* lucky,' said Eddie. And looked all around and about. 'And so this is it?' he said. '*This* is what I spent my whole life dreading? The land Beyond The Second Big O. And all it is is another hillside—not much of a big deal, eh, Jack?'

Jack didn't answer Eddie. Jack was gazing back up the hillside. Up in the direction from which he and Eddie had tumbled down and down.

'Not much, eh, Jack?' said Eddie once again. 'Eh, Jack?'

But Jack didn't answer.

'Jack, are you listening to me?' asked Eddie.

And Jack stirred from his staring. 'Eddie,' said Jack, 'tell me this.'

'Tell you what?'

'Well, we plunged through The Second Big O, didn't we?'

'We did.'

'The Second Big O in the remaining few letters of what once spelled out "TOYTOWNLAND" and now just spell "TO TO LA".'

'That we did,' said the bear.

'So, looking back,' said Jack, 'at those big letters, we should see the reverse of "TO TO LA". "A⅃ OT OT", in fact.'

'Indeed,' said Eddie, 'but I don't know how you were able to pronounce that.'

'But that's not what I'm seeing,' said Jack. 'Those big letters on the hillside, they're not spelling out "A⅃ OT OT".'

'They're not?' said Eddie.

'They're not.'

'So what *are* they spelling?'

And Jack pointed upwards and Eddie looked up upwards and then Eddie said, 'What does *that* mean?'

And Jack said slowly, 'I don't know what it means, but those letters spell out "HOLLYWOOD".'

14

'Hollywood?' said Eddie Bear. 'What does *Hollywood* mean?'

'Place name, I suppose,' said Jack, a-dusting at his trenchcoat. 'This coat is going to need some serious cleaning.'

'Forget the coat!' And Eddie raised his paws. 'We *are* in another world, Jack. This isn't just the other side of the hill.'

'Seems so.' Jack stretched his shoulders and Jack also yawned, tiredness catching up with him. 'But it looks pretty much like the world we just came from—there's nothing scary here.'

Eddie Bear shuddered and shook his head. 'There is something scary, I know it.'

'You *don't* know it, Eddie. You're just disorientated.' Jack sniffed at the air and Jack took off his trenchcoat. 'It's warmer here at least, which is nice.'

Eddie now also sniffed the air and with these sniffs he stiffened. 'No, Jack,' he said. 'Not nice, not nice at all.'

'You've picked up the scent again?'

'Not the scent, Jack. Not the scent.'

'Then what?'

Eddie gave the air another sniffing. 'Meatheads, Jack,' he said, and there was fear in his growly voice.

'Men?' said Jack. 'Nearby? Where?'

'Everywhere,' said Eddie Bear. 'We're in the world of the meatheads.'

Jack looked back at the Hollywood sign. 'The world of the meatheads,' he said.

★

Now, for those who have an interest in such things as these, it is to be noted that . . . ★

For those who do *not* have an interest in such things, it probably doesn't matter.

'So what do you think we should do now?' Jack asked.

'Go back,' said Eddie. 'Climb through The Second Big O up there and hope it leads back to our own world.'

'Perhaps I put it poorly,' said Jack. 'What I meant to say was, now that we *are here, to stay*, until the job is done, what should we do next?'

Eddie yawned mightily. 'Don't think I haven't noticed,' he said, 'that there is a vast city down the hill, all lit up in the night. How about us finding somewhere safe and taking a bit of a sleep?'

Jack did further yawnings, too. 'Good plan, Mister Bear,' said he.

As going forward was fearsome for Eddie, they tramped back to the Hollywood sign. And from there Jack looked out at the lights of the big city that lay below. And it was (and is) an impressive sight. And Jack was suitably impressed. And behind the sign they located the little hut where the bulb-man who had tended to the lights way back in the nineteen-thirties had spent his illuminating existence.

The door was padlocked, but Jack soon had the padlock picked. The two exhausted detectives crept into the little hut, pulled shut the door and settled down in the darkness upon ancient light-bulb boxes. And in less time than it takes to interpret a Forgotheum conundrum, using as your baseline the Magwich/Holliston Principle, they were both quite fast asleep.

★

★ The Hollywood sign is probably the most famous sign in all of the world. It was erected in 1923 to advertise the housing development beneath it. The original letters, fifty feet high and thirty feet wide, spelled out 'Hollywoodland' and were lit up nightly by more than four thousand bulbs. With a chap living in a little hut behind the sign, whose job was to change them when they needed changing. Nice work if you can get it. In 1932 an aspiring young starlet named Peg Entwhistle threw herself off the H. Others followed her example, but to avoid the bad publicity their names went unpublished in the Los Angeles press. In 1939, the light-bulb chap was sacked, the sign fell into disrepair and all its light bulbs were stolen. But then in 1949, the Hollywood Chamber of Commerce restored the sign, knocking down the 'land' bit at the end. By 1978 it was all knackered again, so the Chamber of Commerce got a fund-raising campaign going, raised enough cash to completely restore the sign and have kept it looking smart ever since. With the aid of sponsorship from Hollywood stars. Apparently Alice Cooper sponsors The Second Big O.

A big smiley sun rose over the Hollywood Hills. It didn't have a big smiley face like the one that rose over Toy City, but it got the job done and its rays slipped in through the dusty panes of the little old hut and touched upon sleeping faces.

Jack awoke with a yawn and a shudder, blinked and sniffed and clicked his jaw. Hopes that the doings of the previous night had been naught but dreamstuff ebbed all away as Jack surveyed his surroundings.

Man-sized shed with a man-sized door. Man-sized tools hanging on a rack. A pile of what looked to be newspapers tied up with string. 'A world of men,' said Jack to himself. 'Hardly a nightmare scenario. I grew up in a town inhabited by men and women; Toy City has to be the only city inhabited by toys. Probably everywhere else, no matter on which world, is inhabited by men.' Jack paused for a moment then, before adding, 'Except those inhabited by an advanced race of chickens, that would be.' A further pause. 'But looking on the bright side, Eddie didn't smell chickens last night, only men.'

'Talking to yourself again?' asked Eddie, awakening.

'Only time I ever have an intelligent conversation,' said Jack.

'Most amusing.' Eddie now looked all about himself. 'Shame,' said he. 'As you know, we bears never dream, but I really hoped that I might have dreamed this last night.'

'I'm sure there's nothing to get alarmed about, Eddie. As I was just saying to myself, I come from a town exclusively inhabited by men.'

'Nice place, was it?' Eddie asked.

'Well,' said Jack.

'Well,' said Eddie, 'I seem to recall that you hated it so much that you ran away from it.'

'Which doesn't mean to say that this Hollywood place won't be nice. Chin up, Eddie, let's look on the bright side, eh?'

Eddie's tummy rumbled. 'Breakfast would be nice,' he said. 'Perhaps there's a farm nearby where we could steal some eggs, or something.'

'Steal some eggs? Have you decided to give up detective work and pursue a life of crime?'

'You possess local currency, then?'

'Well.'

Eddie was up now and peeping through the door crack. 'Much as I hate to do it, then,' he said, 'let's wander carefully into this world of meatheads and see what there is to be seen.'

'Trust me,' said Jack. 'Everything will be fine.'

★

And so down Mount Lee they went,* with Jack whistling brightly in order to disguise his nervousness and Eddie quoting and requoting Jack in his head. 'Everything will be fine,' he requoted. 'What a load of old toot.'

Eventually they reached a fence, climbed over it and found a road.

'See,' said Jack, 'nothing to be worried about.'

'I've never had a particular terror of roads,' said Eddie. 'You gormster.'

'There are houses here, nice houses,' said Jack. 'Should I knock and ask for a glass of milk or something?'

'Let's head on down,' said Eddie. 'We saw all the lights last night—this must be a very big city. Big cities have alleyways, many of them behind restaurants. We'll just rifle through some bins.'

'I'm not doing *that*!'

'Well, you make your own arrangements, then. I'm as hungry as.'

It's a long walk down to LA proper. But you do pass some very nice houses on the way. Homes of the Hollywood stars, they are, although Jack and Eddie weren't to know this yet.

'These are really swish houses here,' said Jack.

'Probably the homes of the local P.P.P.s.' Eddie peered in through magnificent gates, curlicues of bronze and steel, intricate and delicate, held fast by padlock and chain.

'*Ra! Ra! Ra! Ra! Ra!*' It was a most excruciating sound, loud and raw and fierce. Something huge slammed against the gate, causing Eddie to fall back in alarm. A monstrous hound yelled further *Ras!* and snarled with hideous teeth.

'Down, boy,' called Jack. 'Nice doggy, down.'

'Run for your life,' howled Eddie.

'It's all right, it can't get through the gates.'

'I hate it here, Jack, I hate it.'

They walked along the centre of the road. To either side of them now, growly dogs appeared at padlocked gateways and bid them anything but a warm welcome.

'You don't think,' said Jack, 'that you might have got it all wrong, Eddie? We're not in Dog World, are we?'

'Gormster.'

And then they had to get off the road and off the road with haste.

'*Ba! Ba! Ba! Ba! Ba!*' went this scary something.

---

* For it is indeed upon Mount Lee that the Hollywood sign is to be found.

And then something wonderful rushed by.

Jack looked on and he did so in awe. 'An automobile,' he said.

And such an automobile was this. An electric-blue Cadillac Eldorado, circa 1955. Big fins, fabulous tail-lights, all the trimmings. Nice.

'Wow,' went Jack as the Cadillac sped on. 'Did you ever see anything quite like that?'

Eddie shook his shaken head. 'Did you see the *size* of it?' he said. 'I've seen swimming pools smaller than that. And . . .' And Eddie rubbed at his nose and coughed a little, too. 'That wasn't clockwork, was it, Jack? It had smoke coming out of the back.'

Jack shrugged and Jack said, 'Let's keep moving.'

'I'm hungry.'

'So am I.'

And so they wandered on. But for the *Ra*-ing dogs and the *Ba*-ing car they saw no more signs of life.

'Where is everybody?' Eddie asked.

'Sun's just up,' said Jack. 'I suppose it's early yet.'

'What time do you have on your wristwatch?'

Jack checked his watch, shook it, put it to his ear. 'It's stopped,' he said. 'That's odd, it's never stopped before, although—'

'Although what?'

'Well, I never understood how it worked anyway—it doesn't have any insides, just a winder connected to the hands.'

'I thought that was all a watch needed,' said Eddie.

'No,' said Jack, and they wandered on.

And at last reached Hollywood Boulevard.

Eddie looked up and Eddie was afeared. 'Jack,' whispered Eddie, 'Jack, oh Jack, those are very large buildings.'

'A world of men,' said Jack. 'Look—there's a hotel, what does it say? The Roosevelt.'*

Jack looked up with considerable awe. 'I love *that*,' he said.

'I hate it,' said Eddie. 'But there is one thing I do know about hotels: they always have a lot of dustbins round the back.'

Now it is a fact well known to those who know it well, and those who know it well do not necessarily harbour a particular interest in the foibles of architects, that the rears of hotels are always rubbish. Which

---

* The Roosevelt Hotel is a magnificent Spanish-colonial-style affair, built in 1927 and thoroughly unspoilt, and it is to be noted that not only were the very first Academy Awards presented there, but Marilyn Monroe did her first ever professional photo-shoot beside the pool.

is to say that whilst the front façades display all the architectural splendours that those who commissioned their construction could afford, the rears of the buildings are a proper disgrace. They're all waste pipes and rusty fire escapes and dustbins, lots of dustbins.

Jack stood in the alleyways to the rear of the Roosevelt, looking up at the waste-pipe outlets and rusty fire escapes; Eddie sniffed his way along the dustbins.

'This one,' said Eddie. 'Lid off please, Jack.'

'This is disgusting, Eddie.'

'Look,' said Eddie, 'I'm not proud of this sort of thing, but it's a *bear thing*, okay? We bears might be noted and admired for our exquisite table manners, but we do like a good old rummage around in a dustbin now and then. *You* do things that *I* find abhorrent, okay?'

Jack lifted the dustbin lid. 'What things do I do that you find abhorrent?' he asked.

Eddie shinned into the dustbin. 'You shag dollies,' he said.

'I . . . em . . .' Jack sniffed in Eddie's direction. There was a rather enticing smell issuing from the dustbin.

'They must have had a big do on last night,' said Eddie. 'Look at all this lot.' And he passed Jack an unnibbled cake and a piece of cheese.

'It might smell nice, but I could catch something horrible.'

'Wipe it clean on your trenchcoat . . . No, on second thoughts . . .'

There was a remarkably large amount of edible food to be found in that dustbin, and it appeared to have been gift-wrapped in paper napkins and needed next to no wiping off.

Jack had a rumbling stomach, but dined without any joy.

His repast complete, Eddie sat with his back against the dustbin and his paws doing pattings at his swollen belly. 'Now that was what I call breakfast,' he said. 'I couldn't eat another thing.'

'Not even this wafer-thin mint?' asked Jack, which rang a bell somewhere.*

Jack sat down beside Eddie. 'Well, on the bright side,' he said, 'and we must always look on the bright side, much as I loathe the idea of dining from dustbins, it looks like we'll never starve in Hollywood.'

'What the Hell, fella? What d'ya think you're at?'

Jack looked up in startlement. A ragged man looked down.

If Jack had known anything of the Bible, Jack might have described this man as biblically ragged. He was wild of eye and wild of beard, of which he had more than his share. What face of him was to be seen above the beard and around the eyes was tanned by grime and

---

* Yes, *there*, obviously.

sunlight. His clothes hung in ribbons; his gnarled hands had horrid yellow nails.

'My Goddamn trashcan!' roared this biblical figure.

'Excuse me?' said Jack, with exaggerated politeness.

'My Goddamn breakfast, you—'

'Sorry,' said Jack, and he rose with some haste to his feet. 'We're new to these parts, we had no idea.'

The biblical figure pushed past him and rootled around in the open bin. 'You ate my cake! She said there'd be cake.'

'It was very nice cake,' said Eddie. 'I'm not sure what flavour, but very nice nonetheless.'

The biblical figure turned his wild eyes back to Jack. 'So,' said he, 'a wise guy, is it, making growly voices?'

'No,' said Jack, 'I didn't—that was Eddie.'

'Eddie?' The wild eyes looked wildly about.

'Hello there,' said Eddie. 'Pleased to meet you.'

The wild eyes looked down.

The wild eyes widened.

'There is some cake left,' said Eddie. 'I tried to eat it all, but I'm ashamed to say that I failed.'

'For the love of God!' The biblical figure fell back against the bin and floundered about like a mad thing. Jack offered what help he could and eased him once more into the vertical plane.

'Get your Goddamn hands off me!'

'Only trying to help,' said Jack.

'Make it do it again, go on.'

'Sorry?' said Jack.

'That little furry thing, make it talk again.'

'I'm not a *thing*,' said Eddie. 'I'm an Anders Imperial, cinnamon plush coat—'

'Holy Baby Jesus!' went the biblical figure, which was suitably biblical but somewhat blasphemous, because you are not supposed to use the name of Jesus in that fashion. 'How does it do that? Is it on strings?'

'*On strings?*' said Eddie. 'How dare you.'

'You're working it somehow.' The wild eyes turned once more upon Jack. 'It's a Goddamn puppet of some kind, ain't it?'

'Ah,' said Jack, most thoughtfully. 'Yes, you're right, of course.'

'Eh?' said Eddie.

'Knew it.' The biblical figure did a little dance. 'Darnedest thing I ever saw. How much do you want for it?'

'He's not for sale,' said Jack. 'He has, er, sentimental value.'

'Eh?' said Eddie, once again.

'Shush,' said Jack to Eddie.

The ragged man knelt down before Eddie. 'Cute little critter, ain't he?' he said. 'Though real ragged and he don't smell too good.'

'That's good, coming from *you*,' said Eddie, shielding his nostrils.

'Darnedest thing.' And the ragged fellow rose and did another dance.

'Well, nice as it was to meet you,' said Jack, 'and sorry as we are about eating your breakfast, being unaccustomed to, er, trashcan protocol in this vicinity—'

'Eh?' now went the ragged man.

'We must be moving along,' said Jack. 'We're—'

'Carny folk,' said the ragged man. 'Don't tell me, let me guess from your accent. English, is it? Carny man from England, I'll bet.'

'English carny man?' said Jack slowly.

'Here with the circus. I'll bet this is one big midway attraction.'

'That's right,' said Jack. 'And we, er, *I'm* an English carny man and I should be on my way.'

'Can't let you do that, buddy.'

'Sorry,' said Jack, 'but I must.'

'Nope. I can't let you do that.' And from a ragged pocket the ragged fellow pulled a knife. And it was a big one and it looked sharp.

'Now see here,' said Jack, which is what folk always say first under such circumstances.

'You ate my breakfast—you owe me, buddy. I'll take your furry thing here in payment.'

'No,' Jack said. 'You will not.'

The knife was suddenly very near Jack. What sunlight the alleyway gathered fell on its polished blade.

'You don't really want to do that,' Jack said, which is another thing folk say in such circumstances—the brave, tough ones, anyway.

'Don't I really?' The gnarled hand flicked the blade before Jack's eyes.

'No,' said Jack, 'you don't. Because if you do not put that knife away at once, I will have no option other than to blow your balls off.'

'Jack, really,' said Eddie.

The ragged man did wild-eyed glancings downwards.

Jack held a pistol, aimed at the ragged man's groin.

'Now what the Hell do you call *that*?'

'It's a gun,' said Jack. 'Perhaps you've not seen one before.'

'I've seen plenty o' guns, fella, but that ain't a real one—that one's a toy.'

'It will cause you considerable damage at this close range,' said Jack.

'Oh yeah? What's it gonna do, hit me with a little flag with "BANG" written on it?'

'It does *this*,' said Jack, and he aimed the gun into the air and pulled the trigger.

And nothing happened.

Jack squeezed the trigger once more and then once again. Nothing else happened either.

'That's odd,' said Jack, examining the pistol.

'Ain't it just!' And the knife's blade flashed once more before Jack's face. 'Hand me the puppet or I'll cut ya deep.'

'But you don't understand—'

'I understand *this*.' And the knife went up. And the knife went down. And the knife fell into the alleyway. And the wild eyes of the biblical figure crossed and then they closed and the figure fell to the ground.

Eddie Bear stood on the dustbin, holding between his paws the dustbin lid.

'Nice shot,' said Jack. 'Right on the back of his head.'

'His conversation tired me,' said Eddie. 'What a most unpleasant man.'

Jack took the lid and helped Eddie down. Eddie went over and bit the ragged man on the nose.

Jack said, 'Don't do that.'

'I think we had best be on our way,' said Eddie. 'I'll just bet they have policemen in this city too and I don't think I want to meet them.'

Jack shook his pistol about. 'This is really odd,' he said. 'First the wristwatch, now this pistol. I wonder.' Jack pulled a grenade from his pocket and removed the pin.

'No, not *here*,' said Eddie.

'I just want to test a proposition.' Jack hurled the grenade and ducked. And Jack counted, too, up to twenty.

'Doesn't work,' said Jack. And he pulled out his remaining weaponry from his pockets and tested it, too. And none of that worked either.

'This I find worrying,' Jack said, and Eddie agreed.

Eddie tested the gun that he had, and as this didn't work either he tossed it away. 'We'll be in trouble when we finally track down our other selves,' he said. Miserably.

'Well,' said Jack, 'looking on the bright side once again, given that amazing automobile we saw, I'll just bet they have some really amazing weapons here.'

'Well, that we already know,' said Eddie. 'Don't we? The death rays and everything.'

'If they come from here,' said Jack. 'Perhaps they came from Chicken World.'

The ragged man made moaning sounds.

'Time to go,' said Eddie.

They reached the end of the alleyway and looked out at the world beyond, the world of men. And men were moving now, out and about on Hollywood Boulevard. Well-dressed men and women, too. The men wore fedoras and double-breasted wide-shouldered suits. The women wore colourful dresses; they looked most appealing to Jack.

'Now, Eddie,' said Jack to the bear, 'I don't want you to take offence at this, but I think it would be better if I carried you. It would appear that in these parts talking bears are the exception rather than the rule.'

'I'd gathered that,' said Eddie. 'I'm not stupid, you know. I'm as intelligent as.'

'Then if you'll pardon me,' said Jack, 'I'll carry you, Mister Bear.'

And so Jack carried Eddie along the boulevard.

And what Jack saw he marvelled at. And not without good cause. The bright storefronts displayed wondrous things, things all new to Jack, although not perhaps new—different, maybe.

There were electrical stores, their windows filled with radio sets and televisions and record players and washing machines, but all of a style unknown to Jack, as were the garments in the clothes stores. Jack lingered long before a trenchcoat shop. Eddie urged him on.

'Low profile,' whispered Jack. 'Please behave yourself.'

And soon Jack stood before Mann's.★

Jack looked up in awe beyond awe.

Then Jack looked down at the pavement.

'Handprints,' he said to Eddie, and he set the bear down and he gazed upon them. 'Clark Gable,' whispered Jack. 'Shirley Temple, the Marx Brothers—I wonder what this is all about.'

'They're movie stars, of course.' The voice was the sweetest of voices, and it issued from the sweetest of lips.

★ Now, again for those who harbour an interest in such things, it is to be stated that Mann's Chinese Theatre can truly be described as the jewel in Hollywood's crown. Created in the late nineteen-twenties by Sid Grauman, this oriental-style folly, with its sixty-nine-foot-high exotic bronze roof and its wealth of architectural detail, dazzles the eye and is the palace for the 'royalty' of Hollywood.

Jack looked up at the speaker. A pretty girl looked down.

She wore a colourful dress that reached to her knees, beneath which rather shapely legs reached down to elegant shoes.

Jack's eyes lingered on these legs before moving up, with some deliberation, to view the pretty face of the speaker. It was that of a flame-haired beauty with stunning green eyes. A girl who was roughly Jack's age.

'Movie stars?' said Jack.

'Of course. What did you think they were?'

Jack rose slowly to his feet. He did not possess the nose of Eddie, but this girl smelled beautiful and Jack drew in her fragrance.

'You're sniffing me,' said the pretty girl. 'I don't think that's very nice.'

'I'm so sorry,' said Jack. 'If I was rude, will you please forgive me?'

'It doesn't matter, you're funny.'

'Am I . . . I . . .'

'My name is Dorothy,' said Dorothy. 'I'm from Kansas. Where are you from?'

'England?' Jack suggested.

'I knew it,' said Dorothy. 'I recognised your accent at once. England is so romantic. Do you know the Queen?'

'Oh yes,' said Jack. 'Very well.'

'And do you wear a bowler hat and take your tea at three?'

'Every day,' said Jack. 'With the Queen, naturally.'

Eddie made a growling noise.

Dorothy looked down. 'What a sweet little bear,' she said. 'Is it yours?'

'Mine,' said Jack. 'His name is Eddie.'

'Eddie Bear, how cute. Might I pick him up and give him a cuddle?'

'I wouldn't advise it,' said Jack. 'He's a bit smelly.'

'You're a bit smelly, too,' said Dorothy. 'You smell of poo.'

'An unfortunate incident,' said Jack, 'but in the line of business. My name is Jack, by the way, and I'm a detective.'

'A detective, how exciting.' And Dorothy put out her hand and Jack most gently shook it.

'I'm an actress,' said Dorothy. 'Or will be, as soon as I'm discovered.'

'Discovered?' Jack asked.

'By an agent. I've got my publicity shots, and I've been around to lots of agents, but they're not very nice. They want you to do . . . *things*.' Dorothy cast down her eyes.

Jack felt he could imagine what things. 'And so these are the handprints of famous movie stars?' he said.

'Yes,' said Dorothy. 'And mine will be here one day. Once I'm discovered.'

'You're a very beautiful girl,' said Jack. 'I'm sure someone will discover you soon.'

'I hope so. I don't like what I'm doing now.'

'What, talking to me?'

'No, I have to work as a kitchen maid in the hotel just up the road. The Roosevelt.'

'Ah,' said Jack.

'It's very hard work, but at least it allows me to do a bit of good.'

'In the kitchen?'

'Well, not really in the kitchen. I package up all the leftover food that the rich people don't eat and leave it in the trashcan outside for the homeless. There's a poor old man who lives in the alley—the scraps I leave are his only food.'

'Ah,' said Jack once again.

'But I *will* be discovered. And when I am, and when I'm wealthy, I'll feed as many of those poor souls as I can.'

'That's a very wonderful thing to say,' said Jack. 'You are a beautiful person.'

'But tell me about you,' said Dorothy. 'You're a detective. That must be very exciting. Do you catch a lot of criminals? Did they send you over from England on a special case? Are you working for the Queen, or is it the President?'

'Well,' said Jack.

And Eddie growled again.

'It's been lovely to meet you,' said Jack, 'but we, that is, *I* have to be going.'

'Won't you stay for just a little longer, have a cup of coffee?'

'I'm embarrassed to say that I don't have any money.'

'It's only a cup of coffee, I'll pay.'

'No, I couldn't, really.'

'Oh please, it will be my treat and you can tell me all about England.'

'Well,' said Jack.

And Dorothy smiled upon him.

'Just one cup,' said Jack, and he gathered up Eddie.

And then Jack strolled along Hollywood Boulevard. And he felt rather good, did Jack. Rather 'Top of the world, Ma', as it happened. The sun shone down and here was he, with a beautiful girl on his arm. And as Jack walked on, smelly as he was, he caught the occasional envious glance from a young male passer-by.

'Now this *is* the life,' thought Jack to himself. 'I could make a home in this place. Perhaps I could set myself up as a private detective, and take a wife, perhaps a wife who was a movie star. Yes, this *is* the life. I really love this place.'

'We're here,' said Dorothy. 'This is it.'

And Jack looked up and said, 'Ah.'

They stood before the Golden Chicken Diner. It was a symphony of chrome and neon. A neon chicken on high flashed on and off, in profile, pecking up and down.

'It's one of a growing chain,' said Dorothy. 'They're springing up everywhere. The chicken burgers are very popular and the coffee is good, but cheap.'

'Right,' said Jack. 'It looks wonderful. Let's go inside.'

And then Jack stopped. And then Jack stared. And then Jack said, 'Oh no!'

And Dorothy looked at Jack, who now stared wide-eyed. And she watched as Jack took Eddie from under his arm and held him up before his chest.

And Eddie stared and saw what Jack saw, and Eddie Bear mouthed, 'No!'

In the front window of the Golden Chicken Diner there was a garish sign. It was a big garish sign and it advertised the fare on sale.

But not only did it advertise this, it also advertised something else. It advertised special offers and what came free with these.

COLLECT 'EM ALL (said this garish sign)
FREE WITH EVERY FAMILY SPECIAL
A CLOCKWORK CLAPPINGMONKEY or
A CLOCKWORK BAND MEMBER or
A CLOCKWORK ORCHESTRA MUSICIAN
AND COMING SOON
LAUGHING POLICEMEN
AN ENTIRE SET OF TOY TOWN FIGURES
INCLUDING
TINTO THE CLOCKWORK BARMAN
AND
EDDIE THE CUDDLY BEAR

15

When Jack could find his voice he whispered, 'What does it mean, Eddie, what?'

Eddie just stared and Dorothy said, 'What is the matter, Jack?'

'It's this . . . this sign.'

'Free toy figures.' Dorothy smiled. 'Don't thay have free offers in England? These are incredibly popular. They only started a day or so ago, with the clockwork monkey. Everybody's collecting the figures now, not just kids, but grown-ups. There's something about them, something—'

'Special?' said Jack. 'Something special?'

'Yes, that's the word. They're not like ordinary toys.'

Eddie wriggled gently in the arms of Jack.

Jack said, 'This needs thought, much thought.'

'Thought about what?' Dorothy was steering Jack into the Golden Chicken Diner.

Jack held back. 'Let's go somewhere else,' he said. 'In fact, perhaps it would be better if I were to see you later on, this evening or something. I think I should be pressing on with my case.'

'I'm not letting you go that easily.' Dorothy clung to his arm. 'At least let a girl buy you a cup of coffee. And I want to hear all about this case of yours.'

'No,' said Jack. 'I don't . . .'

But Dorothy tugged at Jack's arm and Jack let himself be drawn into the Golden Chicken Diner.

It was within, as without, swathed in chrome and neon. A long chrome counter, behind which at measured intervals were mounted splendid chromium cash resisters, behind which stood personable young women wearing skimpy gold costumes. They sported golden caps and these in turn sported corporate logos: profiled pecking chickens. One of the girls said, 'How might I serve you, please?'

'Two coffees, please,' said Dorothy.

'And a large glass of beer,' said Eddie.

Dorothy looked up at Jack. 'How did you do that?' she asked, and she smiled as she asked it.

'Just a trick,' said Jack, but in a distracted voice, as he was viewing large posters that hung upon the walls to the rear of the serving counter. These were adorned with dozens of pictures of the special-offer free Toy Town figures. Jack instantly recognised Chief Inspector Bellis, and the cigar shop proprietor, monkeys and musicians, several of the laughing policemen that he had recently fallen foul of, Tinto the clockwork barman and . . .

'Amelie,' whispered Eddie.

'Sorry?' said Dorothy. 'What did you say?'

'Amelie,' Jack pointed. 'I know her, she's my—'

'She's your what?'

'It doesn't matter,' said Jack. 'Or rather it *does*, very much.'

Eddie set free a dismal growl. For Eddie could see, as indeed could Jack, Eddie's own picture up there.

'I don't understand it,' said Jack. 'I don't.'

'You are a very strange boy. Ah, here are our coffees.'

'And where's my beer?'

Dorothy laughed. 'That really *is* very clever.'

'Get him a beer, please,' said Jack. 'He needs it and I need one, too.'

'I can't get beer—I'm underage and so are you. Don't be so silly.'

'Bad bad meathead world,' grumbled Eddie.

'Stop it now.' Dorothy paid for the coffees and carried them to a vacant table. 'Come on, Jack,' she called.

With difficulty Jack tore his eyes away from the colourful posters and carried Eddie to the table. He pulled out a chair and seated the bear upon it.

'Horrible world,' grumbled Eddie.

Dorothy looked nervously at Jack. 'You weren't touching him when he said that,' she said.

'Just a trick,' said Jack.

'I'm not so sure.' Dorothy gave Eddie a close looking-at. 'There's something about this stuffed toy of yours. Something—'

'Special?' Jack suggested.

'Different,' said Dorothy. 'Odd, perhaps.'

Jack stared into his coffee cup. He recalled his conversation with the cigar proprietor who had told him, 'I have the special eye and I see trouble lying in wait ahead for you. Trouble that comes in the shape of a chicken,' and also his conversation with Eddie when they first went to Toy Town and had talked about souls being stolen and all of Toy City being under threat.

'Stealing their souls,' said Jack. 'Taking their very essence. And for *this*?'

'Please tell me what you're talking about.' Dorothy looked over at Jack. 'You're frightening me.'

'I'm sorry.' Jack shook his head. 'I'd like to tell you, but I can't. And even if I could, you wouldn't believe me. You'd think I was mad.'

'This is California,' said Dorothy. 'Everyone's mad here. There was an Englishman like you, well, he was a Scotsman, but I think that's the same thing. His name was Charles Rennie Mackintosh, and he said that if you turn America on its side, everything that is not screwed down rolls to California.'

'I'm sure that's very profound,' said Jack, 'but it means nothing to me. Is this California? I thought it was Hollywood.'

'It is Hollywood, but Hollywood is part of LA, which is in California. California is a state in America. But why am I telling you this? You know where you are, surely.'

Jack shook his head. 'Hold on,' he said. 'You said LA.'

'LA,' said Dorothy. 'Los Angeles.'

'LA,' said Jack. 'TO TO LA. To LA. It was a signpost.'

'I'm more confused than ever.'

'And so am I,' said Jack.

'You're coffee's getting cold.'

Jack sipped at it.

'Do you like it?' Dorothy asked.

'It's fine, thank you.'

'Beer would be better,' Eddie said. 'This is a nine-pint problem.'

'You didn't do that,' said Dorothy to Jack. 'You were sipping your coffee when it spoke.'

'I'm not an *it*,' said Eddie. 'I am an Anders Imperial. Cinnamon plush coat—'

'Not now,' said Jack.

'He speaks by himself.' And Dorothy's green eyes grew wide.

'It's just a trick.'

'It *isn't* a trick.'

'All right. It's a small child in a costume.'

'Oh no it isn't.'

'Let's go to a bar,' said Eddie. 'There's bound to be one somewhere that will serve us.'

'It's speaking by itself, it really is.'

'And I'm not an *it*! Get rid of her, Jack. We have to press on now, find our other selves, stop them doing what they're doing and fast.'

'I agree,' said Jack. 'This is bad, very bad.'

'It's alive, Jack! Make it stop!' And tears sprang into Dorothy's eyes.

'Listen,' said Jack, 'please be calm. I'm sorry.'

'But it's alive.'

'Will you please stop calling me an it?'

'Make it stop, it's frightening me.'

'Eddie, please be quiet.'

Eddie made growling sounds.

Dorothy rose to flee.

'No,' said Jack. 'Please don't go.'

'Let her go, Jack.'

'No. Please stay.' Jack rose, took Dorothy gently by the shoulders and sat her back down. 'I'll tell you,' he said. 'I'll tell you everything. But before I do, you must promise me that you will tell no one what I tell you. And I'm saying this for your own good. Murders have occurred—'

'Then *you*—'

'Not *me*. I'm not a murderer. Eddie and I are detectives. We are in pursuit of murderers.'

'That thing is looking at me in a funny way.'

'It's the only way he knows.'

'Thanks very much,' said Eddie, and he shifted in his chair, which had Dorothy cowering.

'Please promise me,' said Jack, 'and I'll tell you everything.'

And Dorothy promised in a shaky voice and Jack then told her everything.

And when Jack was done there was silence.

Except for the background restaurant noise of large Californians chowing down on family chicken-burger meals.

'My head is spinning,' said Dorothy. 'But somehow I always knew it. I used to say to my little dog Toto, before he was sadly run over by a truck, somewhere over the rainbow . . .'

And Dorothy burst into song.

Which rather surprised the diners. And rather surprised Jack, too.

'Oh, sorry,' said Dorothy, bursting out of song. 'I'm rather prone to that.'

'It was very nice,' said Jack. 'I liked the bit about the bluebirds.'

'I didn't,' said Eddie. 'Ne'er a hint of a bear.'

'A land of toys,' said Dorothy.

'Well, a city,' said Jack. 'That was once Toy Town.'

'And the toys on the posters—'

'As I said,' said Jack, 'some of them are already dead and if we don't stop these doppelgangers of us, as you can see on the posters, many more folk in Toy City will die. Including Eddie here.'

'At least I seem to get star billing,' said the bear. 'I'm the last on the list.'

Dorothy smiled upon Eddie. 'He really *is* quite cute,' she said. 'Can I give him a cuddle?'

'You *cannot*,' said Eddie Bear. 'Most undignified.'

Dorothy smiled once more and shook her head. Her flame-red hair glittered in reflected sunlight. 'Let me help you,' Dorothy said. 'I'm sure I could do something to help.'

'I wouldn't hear of it,' said Jack, finishing his coffee. 'It's far too dangerous.'

'Because you're a girl,' said Eddie. 'No offence meant.'

'I think you did mean *some*,' said Dorothy.

'I think he probably meant plenty,' said Jack. 'But in a way he's right. Eddie and I are used to getting into danger. It's just about all we ever do. In fact, I can't imagine how we've managed to sit for so long in this restaurant without someone trying to shoot us, stab us, or blow us up.'

'It can't be danger *all* the time,' said Dorothy.

'Not *all*,' said Eddie. 'The danger is relieved periodically by bouts of extreme drunkenness and bad behaviour. So as you can see, it's no job for a girl. And Jack has a girlfriend anyway.'

Jack clipped Eddie lightly on the ear.

And then withdrew his fingers hastily to avoid having them bitten off.

'I *could* help you,' Dorothy said. 'You are strangers here and I know my way around LA. I could be very useful to you.'

'It's too dangerous,' said Jack. 'You could get hurt, badly.'

'I know how to handle myself.'

'Yes,' said Jack, 'of course you do.'

'Stand up,' said Dorothy. 'Try to attack me, see what happens.'

'Don't be silly,' said Jack.

'I'm serious. Try.'

'Some other time,' said Jack. 'Sit down.'

'Chicken,' said Dorothy.

'Hardly a well-chosen word, considering the circumstances.'

'You're still a chicken. Cluck! Cluck! Cluck!' And Dorothy made chicken sounds and did that elbow thing that people do when they impersonate chickens. As they so often do in passionate bedroom situations.*

'You're making an exhibition of yourself,' said Jack. 'You'll get us thrown out.'

'She's a stone bonker, this one,' said Eddie. 'Give her a little smack, Jack, and make her sit down again.'

'I can't smack a woman.'

'Let me bite her, then.'

Dorothy began what is called in theatrical terms a 'dance improvisation'. Diners looked on briefly, then continued with their chowing down of chicken burgers. Because, after all, this *was* California.

'Just one little smack then,' said Jack, 'and we'll stop all this nonsense.'

Jack rose from his chair.

Dorothy ceased her dance improvisation, extended an arm and with her fingers beckoned Jack nearer.

Jack sighed, took a step forward and swung a gentle slap in Dorothy's direction.

And what happened next seemed to Eddie to happen in slow motion. Dorothy leapt into the air and somersaulted over Jack's head, turning as she did so to boot him right in the side of the gob.

It may have seemed like slow motion to Eddie.

It seemed very fast to Jack.

And as Jack hit the floor with a thunderous blow . . .

Dorothy landed several yards away, right on her feet, light as thistledown.

Eddie buried his face in his paws. 'That's going to hurt in the morning,' he said. 'And as this *is* morning, it will probably be hurting now.'

'Ow, my face.' And Jack did flounderings about. 'That wasn't fair . . . my face.'

'I'll get some ice,' said Dorothy.

'Eddie,' groaned Jack from his floor-bound repose, 'Eddie, bite her, please.'

'Not my battle,' said Eddie.

'But Eddie.'

'Sorry,' said Eddie. 'Count Otto kicked me over the big top. *That* really hurt. This woman could kick me all the way to England, wherever that is.'

Dorothy went and fetched some ice and then she helped Jack up.

---

* What? Ed.

'I can get up by myself.' Jack patted her away.

'I told you I could handle myself.'

'I wasn't ready,' said Jack.

'Well, if you're ready now you can take another shot. I'll close my eyes if you want.'

'Go on,' said Eddie. 'You might strike lucky.'

Jack sat down in a right old huff. Dorothy offered him ice in a serviette. Jack took this and held it to his jaw.

'It's call Dimac,' Dorothy explained. 'The deadliest martial art on Earth. My hands and feet are registered with the police as lethal weapons—I have to have a special licence for them.'

'Dimac?' said Jack.

'I sent away for a course. A dollar ninety-eight a lesson, from Count Dante—he's the Deadliest Man on Earth, obviously.'

'Obviously,' said Jack. And he clicked his jaw.

'So do I get the job?'

Jack sighed and almost shook his head.

'I know my way around,' said Dorothy. 'And I could come in very useful if anyone menaces you or Eddie.'

'Well,' said Jack. And then he said, 'Why? Why would you want to help us?'

'*Why?*' said Dorothy. 'Why? You have to be joking.'

'Jack's not very good on jokes,' said Eddie. 'Actually, as a comedy sidekick he's pretty useless. But it is a valid question. You want to be an actress, don't you? Why would you want to get involved with us?'

'How can *you* ask me that? You are a talking toy bear. Jack says that you and he came here from somewhere over the rainbow. I believe in fate. Our paths haven't crossed by accident—destiny led you to me.'

'Oh dear,' said Eddie, and if he had been able to roll his eyes he would have done so.

'And there's definitely a movie in this,' said Dorothy. 'I might es-chew acting in favour of a role as producer.'

'Hm,' went Jack.

'Hm?' went Dorothy.

'Ignore him,' said Eddie. 'He's had woman trouble. The love of his life left him. I suspect that his "hm" represented something along the lines that your unexpected evolution from the wide-eyed innocent on Hollywood Boulevard to lean, mean killing machine with pretensions to movie moguldom within the space of a short half-hour is somewhat disconcerting for him.'

'You're a most articulate little bear,' said Dorothy.

'And most democratic,' said Eddie. 'I hold no prejudice. I bite man or woman alike if I consider that they are patronising me.'

'That flight of yours over the big top,' said Dorothy. Suggestively. 'I overheard that.'

'I'll get you when you're sleeping,' said Eddie.

'Stop it, please,' said Jack. 'All right, Dorothy, I *am* impressed. If you want to help us, it would be appreciated.'

'Not by *me*,' said Eddie. 'We're a team, Jack. A partnership, you and me, Jack and Eddie, bestest friends through thick and thin.'

'This won't affect our partnership.'

'Yes it will. It will lead to a romantic involvement and then there'll be all the drippy smoochy stuff and that will interfere with the action and the car chases.'

'Rubbish,' said Jack, although unconvincingly. The thought of indulging in some drippy smoochy stuff with Dorothy had indeed crossed his mind. As indeed had some of that get down, get naked and get dirty kind of stuff. 'She *can* help us, Eddie,' said Jack. 'And we need all the help we can get.'

'We were doing fine on our own. What happened to your inspired calculating stuff? It was you who calculated that the murderers would strike next at the Opera House, remember?'

'Ah,' said Jack, who in all the excitement and everything else had quite forgotten about Wallah the calculating pocket. 'About that.'

'We'll manage on our own,' said Eddie. 'Thank you for your offer, Dorothy, but you'll only get Jack all confused and he won't be able to keep his mind on the job.'

'Listen,' said Jack, wringing out his serviette ice pack into his empty coffee cup and shaking his fingers about, 'I'm up for you helping us, Dorothy, but I have to go to the toilet now. Eddie and I are a partnership, and it's a fifty-fifty partnership. If Eddie says no then I have to respect his decision, even if I don't agree with it. But I *am* going to the toilet, so please speak to him. I'm sure you can win him over.' And Jack winked at Dorothy.

It was an intimate kind of a wink and if Eddie had seen it he would have recognised it to be the kind of wink that meant, 'I would *love* you to help us and I'm certain that a beautiful, intelligent *woman* such as yourself can soon win over a stroppy toy bear.' And if Eddie *had* seen it and *had* recognised it, Jack would have received such a biting from Eddie that if Jack had owned a bicycle he would not have been able to ride it again for at least a week.

'I'll be back in a minute,' Jack said. 'Which way *is* the toilet?'

'Over there,' said Dorothy.

And Jack went off to the toilet.

And went into one of the stalls and locked the stall door behind him. And Jack withdrew Wallah from his trenchcoat and gave her a little stroke.

Wallah gave a little yawn and made a sensual purring sound.

'I'm sorry not to have spoken with you for a while,' said Jack. 'As you are probably aware, things have been a little hectic of late.'

'Naturally I am aware. That horrid woman hurt your face—it's all bruised. Hold me against it, I'll make it better.'

'Well,' said Jack.

'Please,' said Wallah.

And Jack held the pocket to his face. And it *did* feel rather nice.

'You don't need *her*,' whispered Wallah into Jack's ear. 'I calculate that although in the short term she might facilitate some success, in the long term disaster awaits.'

'You don't foresee a lasting relationship, then?'

'It looks unfavourable in percentage terms.'

'So I should dump her? Is that what you're saying? You're not being a little biased, are you?'

'Biased?' whispered Wallah. 'I don't know what you mean.'

'Yes you do,' said Jack, 'and *our* relationship, our *special* relationship will only continue if you are totally honest with me.'

'I am dedicated to your success,' said Wallah. 'In fact, our special relationship depends directly upon it.'

'Well, I'm asking for your help,' said Jack. 'I need all the help I can get. Which is not to say that I do not value yours above all others', of course.'

'I wonder,' said Wallah, 'whether a relationship actually exists anywhere that is based upon pure truth, rather than one partner telling the other partner what they think the other partner wants to hear, rather than the pure truth that that partner should hear from someone he or she trusts.'

With his free hand Jack scratched at his head. 'I'm not quite certain what all of that means,' he said, 'but I'm sure it's most profound. So, can you help me out here? Can you tell me what I should do next?'

'Not directly,' said Wallah. 'I can calculate odds. And I can tell you this: if you do not bring the malcontents to justice within one week, not a single soul in Toy City will remain alive.'

'One week?' said Jack.

'According to my calculations the evil is growing exponentially. It's working on a mathematical principle. You have one week at the most.'

'So what must I do?'

'Corporate enterprises such as this Golden Chicken organisation function upon a pyramidal principle. At the base you have the most folk, those in customer facilitation, the counter-service folk, the factory workers, et cetera. Next level up, lower management, supervisors—far fewer. Next level, middle management, then up and up, executive management, board of directors, chief executive officer. And he is not the pinnacle of the pyramid. Above him is a single figure. You must move up the chain of command, seek out this individual—they will be the brains behind it all.'

'That's rather obvious, surely,' said Jack.

'Obvious perhaps, but it's how you do it that counts. How you penetrate the chain of command, find your way to the top.'

'And how do I do *that*?' said Jack.

'I calculate your chances of doing so in your present situation as zero,' said Wallah. 'You will have to take employment with the Golden Chicken Consortium. Infiltrate, as it were.'

'Is there time for *that*?' Jack asked.

'Yes,' said Wallah. 'There is, just. I am susceptible to vibrations, Jack. I pick them up, assimilate them. You are now in a land that you do not understand, and I now *do* understand it. Within three days, if you work hard, persevere and keep your eyes and ears open, you will be able to rise up the pyramid sufficiently to discover who hides upon the pinnacle.'

'I'm hardly likely to get promoted up the management chain in three days,' said Jack.

'Oh yes you can,' said Wallah. 'You are now in a land called America where many things are possible. You will realise what is known as "The American Dream".'

'All right,' said Jack. 'I'll do my best.'

'You will have to do better than that.'

'My best is all I have. And I'll have you to help me, which I appreciate, believe me.'

'Sadly, that is not going to be the case. I calculate that I will only be able to help you for another twelve hours at the most.'

'Why?' asked Jack.

'Because I am dying,' said Wallah.

'What?' and Jack held Wallah out before him. 'What are you saying to me?'

'I'm saying that I'm dying. Me and my kind cannot survive here in this world. This world will kill us.'

'Why are you saying this? How do you know this?'

'Believe the evidence of your own eyes,' said Wallah. 'You were here no time at all before your wristwatch ceased to work, and less than eight hours after that so did your weapons.'

'Yes,' said Jack. 'I suspected that it was something like that when I tested the grenade in the alleyway.'

'I know,' said Wallah. 'The simple things die first, then the more complex. I have perhaps another day, maybe a little more. My calculations cannot be entirely precise.'

'Then I'll take you back right now,' said Jack, 'pop you through The Second Big O onto the other side.'

'And without my help you will fail and all Toy City will die.'

'But I can't let *you* die.'

'It's a percentage thing,' said Wallah. 'I will die so many will live.'

'No,' said Jack. 'I can't have that.'

'Then you will have to do more than your best.'

'Yes I will,' said Jack. 'I promise I will.' And then Jack said, 'Oh no!'

'I know what you're thinking,' said Wallah, 'and yes, it's true.'

'Eddie,' said Jack. 'You mean—'

'Three days at most,' said Wallah. 'I'm sorry.'

'Then I'm taking you both back.'

'And if you do you'll doom all of Toy City. You can't do this on your own, even with the help of Dorothy. You need us to succeed.'

'But I can't risk Eddie's life.'

'He wouldn't hear of you trying to save him at the expense of all the others. You know Eddie well enough—do you think that he would?'

'No,' said Jack. 'I do not. Eddie is—'

'Noble,' said Wallah, 'is the word you're looking for.'

'But I *must* tell him.'

'I think that's only fair. And by my calculations it is something that you should do now. And fast.'

'Fast?' said Jack.

'Very fast,' said Wallah. 'Trust me.'

'I do.'

And Jack slipped Wallah back inside his trenchcoat and then Jack left that toilet at the hurry-up.

And Jack returned to Dorothy and Eddie.

Or at least.

'Dorothy?' asked Jack. 'Where is Eddie?'

Dorothy looked up at Jack and said, 'Why are you asking me that?'

'Because I left him here with you,' said Jack, 'but he's not with you now.'

'No,' said Dorothy. 'That's not what you did. You went off to the toilet and then you returned. And I commented on how impressed I was that you had managed to clean up your trenchcoat in such a short time. Which rather confuses me now, as it is all dirty again. But then you said that you wanted a quiet word for a moment outside with Eddie and then the two of you left. And now you've come out of the toilet again—how did you do that?'

Jack's jaw did a terrible dropping, and then he gave vent to a terrible scream.

16

Jack left the Golden Chicken Diner at the hurry-up.

He sprinted through the open doors and out into the sunlit street beyond. The sunlit Californian street that was Hollywood Boulevard.

Jack was a very desperate lad. He sprinted here and sprinted there in desperation, up this way and down that way, but all to no avail. Passers-by did passings-by, but none paid Jack any heed.

Jack took now to shouting at and accosting passers-by.

'Have you seen him?' Jack shouted at a large man in a larger suit of orange plaid. 'Small bear, about this size? Being led along by me, but it wasn't me?' The large man thrust past Jack, continued on his way.

Jack started on another. Dorothy's hands caught Jack by the shoulders. 'Stop it, Jack,' said Dorothy. 'You'll get yourself arrested.'

'But I have to find him, time is running out.'

'He could be anywhere now—he was probably taken in a car.'

'A car?' and Jack made fists. 'I need a car. Do you have one?'

'Of course I don't have a car. Do I look like I could afford a car? And I'm too young to drive, anyway.'

'I've got to find him. How could you let this happen?' Jack turned bitter eyes upon Dorothy. 'I left him in your care.'

Dorothy's eyes weren't bitter, but they flashed an emerald fire. 'You did no such thing,' she said to Jack. 'You left him with me in the hope that I could win him over.'

'You're part of this.' Jack made fists and shook them all about. 'You're in on it. This is all a conspiracy.'

'Now you are being ridiculous. Come back inside and sit down with me and then we'll talk about this.'

'I've no time to talk. They've got Eddie and if I can't get to him quickly he'll die.'

'If they'd wanted to kill him,' said Dorothy, 'they could have done it there and then in the diner. Ripping a teddy bear apart would hardly have caused the customers much concern.'

Jack put his hands to his head and raked them through his hair. Knocked his hat off, stooped to pick it up, kicked it instead and watched as it rolled beneath the wheels of a passing car to be ground to an ugly flatness.

Dorothy stifled a smirk. This was no laughing matter.

'Let's go inside,' she said.

'I can't.' There was a tear in Jack's left eye. 'It's my fault, I shouldn't have left him. I should have protected him at all times. If any harm comes to him—'

'No harm will come to him.'

'That's a very foolish thing to say.'

'I've said that if they'd wanted to kill him they would have. They've taken him captive, probably as a hostage, probably to use to bargain with you.'

'With me?'

'To get you to stay out of their affairs.'

'That's not going to happen,' said Jack. 'I'll track this other me down and if he's harmed Eddie, I'll kill him. I'll probably have to kill him anyway, but if he's harmed Eddie, I'll kill him worse.'

Dorothy's green eyes fairly glittered. 'You really love that bear,' she said. 'You really, truly do.'

'Of course I do,' Jack said. 'He's my bestest friend. We've been through a lot together, Eddie and me. And he's saved my life more then once.'

'Come back inside, then, and we'll work out some plan together. We'll get him back somehow.'

Jack followed Dorothy back to the diner. 'I'm so sorry, Eddie,' he said.

Eddie Bear was rather sorry, too. Sorrowful was Eddie Bear, puzzled somewhat, scared a bit and quite uncomfortable also.

He was all in the darkness and all getting bumped about.

'How did I let this happen?' Eddie asked himself. 'How could I have been so stupid? I'm as stupid as. How didn't I know that it was the wrong Jack? Why didn't I smell a rat?'

But Eddie Bear had not smelled a rat and neither had he smelled that that Jack wasn't Jack. So to speak.

And this worried Eddie more than most things.

'I don't understand this.' Eddie sniffed at the air. Hot air, it was, and humid, too, as can be the way of it in the boot of a car on a hot and sunlit day. Eddie sniffed the air some more and then he growly grumbled. 'I've lost my sense of smell,' he growly grumbled. 'I can't smell anything. Why has this happened? Do I have a cold? This can't be right—my nose has never let me down before and OUCH!'

The car, in whose boot Eddie was presently domiciled, bumped over something, possibly a sleeping policeman, and Eddie was bounced about something wicked.

'I'll have things to say when I get out of here,' said Eddie Bear.

'And he'll die,' Jack told Dorothy over another coffee. 'He has three days left at the most. If I don't get him back to his own world before then, he'll die.'

'And how did you arrive at this revelation?' Dorothy asked.

'I have my sources,' said Jack. 'Let's leave it at that.'

'So we have to do something fast.'

'*You* don't have to do anything,' said Jack. 'I'll do this on my own.'

'We've been through all that. You need me, Jack. You won't last long here on your own. You'll get stopped by the police, they'll ask you for ID, you won't have any and they'll take you off to juvenile hall.'

Jack did grindings of the teeth. He felt utterly helpless. Utterly impotent. Neither of these were nice ways to feel. The second in particular didn't bear thinking about. So Jack did some heavy thinking about other things. And certain thoughts entered his head. Regarding his most recent conversation with Wallah the calculating pocket.

Wallah's advice to Jack, based upon her calculations, had been that he must take employment at a Golden Chicken Diner and penetrate the higher echelons by utilising the American Dream. Also that Dorothy would prove to be a useful asset during the short term, if ultimately a disaster.

Jack leaned forwards, elbows on the table, and buried his face in his hands.

Dorothy said, 'Let's think about this, Jack. Work together, throw some ideas around.'

Jack groaned.

Dorothy continued, 'I think we have established that whoever is the brains behind the Golden Chicken Diner is the most likely candidate for being behind the murders in Toy City.'

'Yes,' said Jack. 'Of course.'

'Well, not necessarily "of course"—there could be other options to choose from. But he or she—'

'Or *it*,' said Jack.

'He, she or *it* is the most likely candidate. That entity is the one that you have to find and deal with.'

'And I will,' said Jack.

'So the questions is, how?'

Jack nodded through his fingers.

'Well,' said Dorothy, 'the most logical thing to do, in my opinion, would be to gain employment at one of the Golden Chicken Diners, then work your way up into a position that would gain you access to this, er, entity.'

'Eh?' said Jack, and he looked up through his fingers.

'It's the most logical solution,' said Dorothy. 'By my calculations, it's the best chance you'd have.'

'By your *calculations*?'

'Yes. You see, it's an American thing—the belief that anyone in this country can do anything, if they just try hard enough. That they'll get a fair deal if they try. It's called pursuing the American Dream.'

'I know what it's called,' said Jack.

'You do?'

'I do. Do *you* really think it would work?'

'It might with my help.'

'Ah,' said Jack.

'You have no ID,' said Dorothy. 'You're, well, an illegal alien, really. You'd need a work visa. But there are ways. I could help.'

'I have no choice,' said Jack, and he threw up his hands, knocking over his coffee, which trickled into his lap. 'Oh damn,' went Jack. 'I think this trenchcoat is done for.'

Dorothy giggled, prettily.

Jack smiled wanly towards her. 'When I said I had no choice,' said he, 'I didn't mean it in a bad way towards you. I'm very grateful for your help. So how do we go about getting jobs?'

'Just leave that to me.'

Now it is a fact well known to those who know it well that in America, in accordance with the American Dream, you can always get a job in a diner. No matter your lack of qualifications, the fact that you cannot add up to ten, the fact that you have rather strange ways about you, a curious squint, buck teeth, answer to the name of Joe-Bob and hail from a backwoods community where your father is your brother and your aunty your uncle (although it has to be said that there *is* a more than average chance that you will be very good at playing the banjo), you can always get work in a diner.

In England (a small but beautifully formed kingdom somewhat to the east of America) it is the case that you can always get a job in a pub. Here, of course, you will not be expected to be able to count up to ten, as, if you are, like Jack, an illegal alien (probably from Australia, in the case of England), it will be expected that you will short-change the customers. Oh, and be an alcoholic, which is apparently a necessary qualification.

But this is neither here nor there, nor anywhere else at the present.

Twenty minutes passed in the Golden Chicken Diner and when these twenty minutes were done, certain things had occurred.

Dorothy now stood behind counter till number three, all dolled up in a golden outfit. And Jack stood somewhere else.

Jack stood in the kitchen washing dishes.

Jack had his arms in suds up to the elbows.

Jack had a right old grumpy look on his face.

'Back in the bloody kitchen again!' swore Jack, frightening Joe-Bob, who was drying dishes. 'A couple of days ago I was washing dishes in a Nadine's Diner, and now I'm back at it again. Is this to be my lot in life? What is going on?'

'You ain't from around these parts, aintcha, mister?' asked Joe-Bob, spitting little corncob nibblets through his big buck teeth. 'You a wet-back, aintcha?'

'I don't know what one of those is,' said Jack, 'but whatever it is, I'm not one.'

'You must be from England, then.'

'If this is some kind of running gag,' said Jack, really wishing that he'd rolled up his shirt sleeves before he began the washing up, 'then it stinks.'

'Not as bad as that trenchcoat of yours,' said Joe-Bob.

'No,' said Jack, 'but it's washing up nicely.' And he scrubbed at the trenchcoat's hem.

'I don't figure the manager'd like you washing your laundry in his kitchen sink,' said Joe-Bob. 'But I guess I'd keep my mouth shut and not tell him if you'd do a favour for me.'

'Listen,' said Jack, 'I can't lose this job. It's really important to me. But then so is a smart turn-out. I'll soon be done washing the trench-coat. Then we can dry it in the chicken rotisserie.'

Joe-Bob shook his head and did that manic cackling laughter that backwoods fellows are so noted for. 'That's even worse,' said he. 'I'll want a *big* favour.'

Jack sighed deeply and wrung out his trenchcoat. 'You won't get it,' said Jack.

'Then I'll just mosey off and speak with the manager.'

'All right,' said Jack. And he sighed once more. 'Tell me what favour you want.'

'Well,' said Joe-Bob, 'you've got a real perty mouth and—'

Joe-Bob's head went into the washing-up water and then Joe-Bob, held by the scruff of the neck by Jack, was soundly thrashed and flung through the rear kitchen door into the alleyway beyond.

'And *don't* come back!' called Jack.

The head chef, who had been in the toilet doing whatever it is that head chefs do in the toilet—going to the toilet, probably, but neglecting to wash their hands afterwards—returned from the toilet. He was a big, fat, rosy-faced man who hailed from Oregon (where the vortex is)* and walked with a pronounced limp due to an encounter in Korea with a sleeping policeman.

'Where is Joe-Bob?' asked the head chef.

'He quit,' said Jack. 'Walked off the job. I tried to stop him.'

The head chef nodded thoughtfully. 'Tried to stop him, eh? Well, young fella, I like the way you think. You have the right stuff—you'll go far in this organisation.'

Jack did further trenchcoat wringings, but behind his back.

'I'm going to promote you,' said the head chef, 'to head dryer-up.'

'Well,' said Jack, 'thank you very much.'

'Not a bit of it,' said the head chef. 'Loyalty is always rewarded. It's the American Dream.'

By lunchtime Jack had gained the post of assistant to the head chef. He had risen rapidly through the ranks, from dishwasher to dryer-up to plate stacker to kitchen porter (general) to kitchen porter (specific) to head kitchen porter to rotisserie loader to supervising rotisserie loader to assistant to the head chef.

There had been some unpleasantness involved.

There had in fact been considerable unpleasantness involved and no small degree of violence, threats and menace. And a few knocks to himself. Jack sported a shiner in the right-eye department; the kitchen porter (general) was beginning a course of Dimac.

---

* Look it up. It's really weird.

Jack's role as assistant to the head chef gave him a degree of authority over the lower orders of kitchen staff. Who were now a group of boisterous Puerto Ricans whom Jack had seen dealing in certain restricted substances outside the kitchen in the alleyway and asked in with the promise of cash in hand and free chicken for lunch.

Jack stood next to the head chef, decapitating chickens.

The chickens, all plucked and pink and all but ready, barring the decerebration, came out of a little hatch in the wall, plopped onto a conveyor belt and were delivered at regulated intervals to the chopping table for head-removal and skewering for the rotisserie.

Jack put a certain vigour into his work.

'You go at those chickens as one possessed,' the head chef observed after lunch (of chicken).

'What do you do with all the heads?' Jack asked as he tossed yet another into a swelling bin.

'They go back to the chicken factory,' said the head chef. 'They get ground up and fed to more chickens.'

'That's disgusting,' said Jack, parting another head from its scrawny neck.

'It's called recycling,' said the head chef. 'It's ecologically sound. I'd liken it to the nearest thing to perpetual motion that you can imagine.'

'Chickens fed on chicken heads,' said Jack, shaking *his*.

'Well, think about it,' said the head chef. 'If you want a chicken to taste really chickeny, then the best thing to feed that chicken on would have to be another chicken. It makes perfect sense, doesn't it?'

Jack looked up from his chopping and said, 'I can't argue with that.'

'Mind you,' said the head chef as he drizzled a little oil of chicken over a headless chicken and poked a rotisserie skewer up its backside, 'chickens are a bit of a mystery to me.'

'Really?' Jack nodded and chopped.

'I don't know where they all come from,' said the head chef.

'They come out of eggs,' said Jack. 'Of this I am reasonably sure.'

'Do they?' said the head chef. 'Of *that* I'm not too sure.'

'I think it's an established fact,' said Jack.

'Oh really?' said the head chef. 'Well, then you explain this to me. Every day, in Los Angeles alone, in the Golden Chicken Diners, we sell about ten thousand chickens.'

'*Ten thousand?*' said Jack.

'Easily,' said the head chef. 'We'll do five hundred here every day and there's twenty Golden Chicken Diners in Los Angeles.'

Jack whistled.

'And well may you whistle,' said the head chef. 'That's ten thousand, but that's only the tip of the chicken-berg. Every restaurant sells chicken, every supermarket sells chicken, every sandwich stall sells chicken, every hotel sells chicken. Do I need to continue?'

'Can you?' asked Jack.

'Very much so,' said the head chef. 'It's millions of chickens every day. And that's only in Los Angeles. Not the rest of the USA. Not the rest of the whole wide world.'

'That must add up to an awful lot of chickens,' said Jack, shuddering at the thought.

'I think it's beyond counting,' said the head chef. 'I don't think they have a name for such a number.'

'It's possibly a google,' said Jack.

The head chef looked at Jack and coughed. 'Possibly,' he said. 'But where do they all come from?'

'Out of eggs,' said Jack. 'That's where.'

'But the eggs are for sale,' said the head chef. 'We do eggs here. Again, at least five hundred a day. And that's just here, there's—'

'I see where you're heading,' said Jack. 'Googles of eggs everyday.'

'Exactly,' said the head chef.

'Well, the way I see it,' said Jack, 'or at least what I've always been led to believe, is that fertilised eggs, that is those that come from a chicken that has been shagged by a cockerel, become chickens. Unfertilised eggs, which won't hatch, are sold as eggs.'

'You are wise beyond your years,' said the head chef, 'but it won't work. The numbers don't tie up. Unfertilised eggs, fine—battery chickens will turn those out every day for years. Until they're too old to reproduce, then they get ground up and become chicken feed. But think about this—to produce the fertilised eggs you'd need an awful lot of randy roosters. Billions and googles of them, shagging away day and night, endlessly.'

'Nice work if you can get it,' said Jack.

'What, you'd like a job shagging chickens?'

'I would if I were a rooster. And it's probably the only job they can get.'

'Well, it doesn't pan out,' said the head chef. 'I've never heard of any chicken stud farms where millions of roosters shag billions of chickens every day. There's no such place.'

'There must be,' said Jack.

'Then tell me where.'

'I'm new to these parts.'

'Well, don't they have chickens where you come from?'

Jack remembered certain anal-probings. 'Well, they do . . .' he said.

'It doesn't work,' said the head chef, oiling up another chicken and giving it a little flick with his fat forefinger. 'Doesn't work. There's simply too many chickens being eaten every day. You'd need a stud farm the size of Kansas. It just doesn't work.'

'Well,' said Jack, 'I have to agree that you've given me food for thought.' And he laughed.

'Why are you laughing?' asked the head chef.

'Sorry,' said Jack. 'So what is your theory? I suspect that you do have a theory.'

'Actually I do,' said the head chef, 'but I'm not going to tell you because you wouldn't believe it. You'd laugh.'

'You'd be surprised at what I believe,' said Jack. 'And what I've seen. I've seen things you people wouldn't believe.' Which rang a bell somewhere.*

'Well, you wouldn't believe *this*.'

'I'll just bet you I would. Trust me, I'm an assistant chef.'

'Well, fair enough,' said the head chef. 'After all, you are in the trade, and clearly destined for great things. But don't pass on what I say to those Puerto Rican wetbacks—they'll only go selling it to the *Weekly World News*.'

Jack raised his cleaver and prepared to bring it down.

'They are not of this world,' said the head chef.

Jack brought his cleaver down and only just missed taking his finger off.

'What?' said Jack. 'What are you saying?'

'Have you heard of Area Fifty-Two?' asked the head chef.

Jack shook his head.

'Well,' said the head chef, 'ten years ago, in nineteen forty-seven,† a flying saucer crashed in Roswell, New Mexico. The Air Force covered it up, gave out this story that it was a secret military balloon experiment, or some such nonsense. But it wasn't. It was a UFO.'

'And a UFO is a flying saucer?'

'Of course it is. And they say that the occupants on board were still alive and the American government has done a deal with them—in exchange for advanced technology they let the aliens abduct a few Americans every year for experimentation, to cross-breed a new race.'

'Go on,' said Jack, his cleaver hovering.

'Half-man, half-chicken. Those aliens are chickens, sure as sure.'

---

* Yes, *there*. What a good movie, *Bladerunner*, eh?
† Oh, it's the 1950s, is it? YES, IT IS.

Jack scratched his head with his cleaver and nearly took his left eye out.

'And I'll tell you how I figured it out,' said the head chef. 'Ten years ago there were no chicken diners, no fast-food restaurants. Chickens came from local farms. Shucks, where I grew up there were chicken farms, and they could supply just enough chickens and eggs to the local community. Like I said, the numbers are now impossible.'

'But hold on there,' said Jack. 'Are you saying that all these google billions of chickens are coming from Area Fifty-Two? What are you saying—that they're being imported by the billion from some chicken planet in outer space?'

'Not a bit of it,' said the head chef, oiling up another bird. 'Well, not the last bit. These chickens here are being produced at Area Fifty-Two. The alien chickens would hardly import millions of their own kind to be eaten by our kind every day, would they?'

Jack shook his head.

'When I say that they're being *produced*, that's what I mean. Look at these chickens—they're all the same. All the same size, all the same weight. Check them out in the supermarket. Rows of them, all the same size, all the same weight. They're all one chicken.'

Jack shook his head once more and made a face of puzzlement.

'They're artificial,' said the head chef. 'I'm not looking now, but I'll bet you that each of those chickens has a little brown freckle on the left side of its beak.'

Jack fished a couple of chicken heads from the bin and examined each in turn.

They both had identical freckles.

Jack flung the chicken heads down, dug into the swelling head bin, brought out a handful, gazed at them.

And said, 'Identical.'

'Sure enough,' said the head chef.

'This is incredible,' said Jack. 'But why hasn't anyone other than you noticed this?'

'It's only at the Golden Chicken chain that the chickens arrive with their heads on. They don't have their heads on in supermarkets.'

'Whoa!' said Jack. 'This is deep.'

'Do you believe what I'm telling you?'

'I do,' said Jack. 'I do.'

'Well, I'm glad that you do. You're the first assistant chef I've had who did. Mostly they just quit when I tell them. They panic and run. They think I'm mad.'

'Well, I don't,' said Jack. 'But what are you going to do about it?'

'Do?' asked the head chef. 'What do you mean?'

'I mean,' said Jack, 'that you know a terrible secret. You have exposed a dreadful conspiracy. It is your duty to pursue this to its source and expose the perpetrator. All of America should know the truth about this.'

'Well,' said the head chef, 'I'd never thought of it that way.'

'Well, think about it now. Surely as head chef you could follow this up the chain of command. Identify the single individual behind it.'

'Well, I suppose I could. We head chefs are being invited to head office tomorrow. I could make subtle enquiries there.'

'It is your duty as an American to do so.'

'My duty.' The head chef shook his head. It had a chef's hat on it. The chef's hat wobbled about. And now much of the head chef began to wobble about.

'Your duty,' Jack continued, 'even if it costs you your life.'

'My *life*?' The head chef's hands began to shake.

'Well, obviously they'll seek to kill you because of what you know. You are a threat to these alien chicken invaders. They'll probably want to kill you and grind you up and feed you to the artificial chickens that are coming off the production line.'

'Oh dear,' said the head chef. 'Oh my, oh my.'

'You'll need to disguise the shaking,' said Jack, 'when you're at the meeting tomorrow with all those agents of the chicken invaders. I've heard that chickens can smell fear. They'll certainly be able to smell yours.'

'Oh dear, oh my, oh my,' said the head chef once more, and now he shook from his hat to his shiny shoes.

'If you don't come back,' said Jack, 'I will continue with your cause. You will not have died, *horribly*, in vain.'

The head chef fled the kitchen of the Golden Chicken Diner upon wobbly shaking legs and Jack found himself promoted once again.

17

By the time Jack clocked off from his first day at the Golden Chicken Diner, it had to be said that he was a firm believer in the power of the American Dream.

'Head chef?' said Dorothy as she clocked off in a likewise manner.

'Hard work, ambition and faithfulness to the company's ethic,' said Jack, and almost without laughing.

Although Jack didn't feel much like laughing. Jack felt anxious and all knotted up inside. Jack worried for Eddie. Feared for his bestest friend.

Jack's bestest friend was more than a little afeared himself. He was afeared and he was hungry, too. Eddie had spent a most uncomfortable day travelling third class in the luggage compartment of a long black automobile.

There had been some stops for petrol, which Eddie had at first assumed were stops for winding of the key. Until he recalled that the cars of this world were not at all powered by clockwork. And there had been lots of hurlings to the left and the right, which Eddie correctly assumed were from the car turning corners. And there had been slowings down and speedings up and too many hours had passed for Eddie Bear. For as Eddie knew all too well, with each passing hour, indeed with each passing minute, the car was taking him further away, away from his bestest friend Jack.

'I can see that look on your face again,' said Dorothy to Jack. 'You are worrying about Eddie.'

'How can I do anything else?' Jack asked outside the diner as he slipped on his nice clean trenchcoat.

Dorothy shrugged and said, 'You're doing all you can. And my, that trenchcoat smells of chicken.'

Jack made that face yet again.

'I'll tell you what,' said Dorothy. 'I'll take you out tonight, to a club—how would you like that?'

'If it's a drinking club,' said Jack. Hopefully.

'I'll see what I can do.'

'Dorothy,' said Jack, and he looked into the green eyes of the beautiful woman. 'Dorothy, one thing. You only had enough money to pay for a couple of cups of coffee earlier. How come you can now afford to take me out to a club?'

'I stole money out of the cash register,' said Dorothy.

'Oh, that's all right then,' said Jack. 'I thought you might have done something dishonest.'

No further words were exchanged upon this matter and Jack and Dorothy walked arm in arm down Hollywood Boulevard.

Dorothy pointed out places of interest and Jack looked on in considerable awe, whilst wishing that Eddie was with him to see them.

'That's where the Academy Awards ceremony is held each year to honour the achievements of movie stars,' said Dorothy. 'One day I will go onto the stage there and receive my award for Best Actress.'

'I thought you were going into producing,' said Jack.

'Yes,' said Dorothy. 'Best Actress and Best Producer and I hope you'll be there, too. You'd look wonderful in a black tuxedo and dicky bow. Very dashing, very romantic.'

At length they reached the Hollywood Wax Museum.

'Would you like to see the movie stars?' asked Dorothy. 'They are here in effigy.'

Jack shrugged. 'About this drinking club. I've had a hard day and I do like to unwind over a dozen or so beers.'

'All in good time, come on.'

Now wax museums are very much like Marmite.

In that you either love 'em or hate 'em. There's no in between. No, 'I think I fancy a visit to the wax museum today, sort of.' It's either yes indeedy-do, or no siree.

At the door to the wax museum stood the effigy of a golden woman in a white dress, the skirt of which periodically rose through the medium of air-jets beneath to reveal her underwear.

'I like wax museums,' said Jack. 'Yes indeedy-do.'

'That's Marilyn Monroe,' said Dorothy as she purchased the tickets

from a man in the ticket booth who looked like a cross between Bella
Lugosi and Rin Tin Tin. 'She's the most famous actress in the world.'

'Does she have a nursery rhyme?' Jack asked.

'No, silly,' said Dorothy. 'Come on.'

And they entered the wax museum.

It was dark in there—well, they always are, it lends to the necessary ambience. And disguises, of course, the fact that wax museums are
generally housed within crumbling buildings with really manky
decor, faded damp-stained wallpaper and carpets that dare not speak
their name.

But that's part of their charm.

Jack viewed The Legends of the Old West: William S. Hart, Audie
Murphy, Jimmy Stewart, Gabby Hayes, Hopalong Cassidy, Clayton
Moore, Roy Rogers and Trigger.

Jack then viewed The Mirthmakers: Buster Keaton, Charlie Chap-
lin, Laurel and Hardy, the Marx Brothers (whose hand prints Jack had
viewed outside Mann's Chinese Theatre) and Abbott and Costello.

Then The Hollywood Horrors: Lon Chaney Senr., Bella Lugosi,
Dwight Frye, Boris Karloff.

'Oh,' said Dorothy. 'They scare me.' And she nuzzled close to Jack.

And Jack took to this nuzzling and Jack turned up the face of
Dorothy and kissed it, on the forehead and on the cheek and then on
the beautiful mouth. And Dorothy kissed Jack and moved his hands
from her shoulders down to her bottom.

And, as there was no one else around, and the lighting was so dim
and everything, very soon some clothes were off and the two of them
were having sex.

And somewhat sooner that Jack might have hoped, it was over, and
somewhat soon after that the two of them were back in the evening
sunlight of Hollywood Boulevard.

'Well, thanks for *that*,' said Jack.

But Dorothy put her fingers to his lips. 'It took your mind off Eddie for a while, didn't it?' she said.

'Damn,' said Jack. 'I wish you hadn't said *that*. Now I feel worse
than ever.'

Eddie Bear felt worse than ever. He felt hot and he felt sick from all the
bumping about and when the car finally stopped for good and all and
the lid of his prison was lifted, Eddie Bear peered into the sunlight and
felt almost exhilarated. Almost.

'Out,' said the voice of his bestest friend, which came not from
that fellow.

'I'm wobbly,' said Eddie. 'You'll have to lift me out.'

'Out, or I'll kick you out.'

'Well, there's no need for *that*.' Eddie struggled up and over and down. To rest his paw pads on sand. 'If I ask you where I am, will you tell me?' he asked.

The other Jack shook his head grimly. 'Where you'll not be found,' said he. 'Come on, get a move on, that way.'

That way proved to be between the open steel-framed gateway of a tall and barbed-wire-fenced enclosure. Eddie looked to the left and the right of him. The fencing faded off in either direction. This was a large enclosure. There was a guard post by this gateway. A uniformed guard sat in it.

There was also a sign on an open gate. The sign read:

AREA FIFTY-TWO
UNAUTHORISED ACCESS FORBIDDEN

There were some rules and regulations printed beneath these words and these were of the military persuasion.

Eddie looked up bitterly at the other Jack. 'I'm hungry,' said Eddie. 'And thirsty, too. Is there a bar nearby?'

'There's plenty of bars where you're going,' said the evil twin of his bestest friend. 'All made of steel.' And he laughed, in that mad way that supervillains do.

'Most amusing,' said Eddie. 'But why have you brought me here?'

'Because you are *so* special,' said the anti-Jack. And he did more of the manic laughing.

Jack wasn't laughing. He now felt *very* guilty.

'Listen,' said Dorothy, 'you're doing everything you can. Didn't you tell me that as head chef of a Golden Chicken Diner you were invited to the head office tomorrow for a motivational training session?'

'I don't recall doing so,' said Jack, 'but that is what I'm doing.'

'So you'll probably be on the board of directors by lunchtime and in a position to find out where they've taken Eddie.'

'You really think so?' said Jack.

'Just follow the American Dream.'

'I am a little confused by the American Dream, as it happens,' said Jack as he and Dorothy walked on, passing the Hollywood Suit Company, which knocks out really natty suits at a price that one can afford.*

---

* You look a right Herbert in the one you bought. Ed.

'I mean,' Jack continued, 'if it is every American's born right to follow the American Dream and succeed in this following, how come most Americans aren't googlaires living in mansions?'

'It's their right to *try*,' said Dorothy.

And *that* was *that* for *that* conversation.

'Let's go on to a club,' said Dorothy.

Jack took to halting and gazing at her.' Actually, let's not,' he said. 'As you might be aware, I have nowhere to sleep tonight.'

'You can sleep with me if you want.'

'I was hoping you'd say that. Why don't we give the club a miss, go to your place, have some more sex and get an early night? I have a hard day ahead.'

Dorothy looked up at Jack. 'All right,' she said. 'We should both have an early night. There's no telling what might happen to us tomorrow at the Golden Chicken headquarters.'

'Us?' said Jack. 'I will be going alone.'

'I think you'll find that all management staff have been invited. Restaurant management as well as kitchen management.'

'So that's why I'll be going alone.'

'And that's why you won't. I follow the American Dream, too, Jack. I manage *our* branch of the Golden Chicken now.'

'What?' said Jack.

'There was some unpleasantness with the previous manager,' said Dorothy. 'She didn't go quietly. I was forced to use my Dimac.'

'Early night it is, then,' said Jack.

The Californian sun rose once again. As it always does, unfailingly.

Its warmth and golden wonder did not fall on Eddie Bear, however, for he lay dismally in a barred cell, many floors beneath ground level in that Area known as Fifty-Two.

It touched upon the cheek of Jack, though, who lay in the arms of Dorothy in the single room she rented in a house in Blue Jay Way that would one day be rented in its entirety by George Harrison, who would write a rather pleasant song about it. But not yet.

Jack yawned, stretched, rose. Viewed his clothes, all washed, ironed and ready, hanging on a hanger. Looked down upon the sweet sleeping face of Dorothy and kissed her on the cheek.

Dorothy stirred and murmured, 'Not now, Brad.'

'*Brad?*' said Jack.

And Dorothy awoke.

'Brad,' said Jack. 'You said Brad.'

'Brad is the name of my dog,' said Dorothy.

'You said that your dog was named Toto.'

'Bradley Toto,' said Dorothy. 'He's a thoroughbred from England.'

Jack laughed loudly. 'Your first lie,' said he. 'We should celebrate it with some early-morning sex.'

'I'm not in the mood,' said Dorothy.

'Your second lie,' said Jack.

And when the early-morning sex was done and Jack was once more feeling really rotten about himself for having such a good time whilst Eddie was either in peril, or dead, they had their breakfast. Which Jack really hated himself for enjoying so much.

And then they got dressed and went out.

And that sun was still shining. Like it does.

And they caught a downtown train and it took them to downtown LA, where they alighted downtown.

And Jack looked up at GOLDEN CHICKEN TOWERS and Jack went, 'Wow, that's big! Especially the lettering.'

Golden Chicken Towers was located next to the Eastern Building, which remains to this day a triumph of Art Deco and is celebrated for the fact that *Predator 2* stood upon its roof and was not at all concerned when his retractable spear jobbie was struck by lightning.

The foyer, entrance hall, vestibule, lobby or whatever you might wish to call it of Golden Chicken Towers was nothing less than palatial.

It was sumptuous. It was golden. It was chickeny.

To either side of the expanse of golden floor tiles stood golden plinths, upon which rose statues of golden hens. These hens stood in noble attitudes. Some held tall upward-thrusting spears beneath their golden wings, spears capped with golden pennants, each emblazoned with the company logo. Some of these hens wore uniforms decked with golden medals. Others looked defiant, bearing golden guns.

'I don't know about you,' Jack whispered to Dorothy as they joined a queue to receive their official passes, 'but all this is *very* wrong.'

'It's like some temple dedicated to the God of All Chickens,' Dorothy observed. 'Those are very big statues.'

Jack craned his neck and peered along the queue. It was a long queue made up of eager-looking young Americans. They were all spick and span and as near to business-suited as they could afford. They had that scrubbed quality about them that is somehow unwholesome, although it's difficult to explain exactly why.

To Jack they all looked all of a sameness. And this, Jack felt, was odd. And then it occurred to Jack, perhaps for the first time, that they all *were* of a certain sameness. That everyone he had encountered since entering this world that was exclusively peopled by his own kind, even though they had certain superficial differences, they *were* all of a sameness.

They were all of a single race. The human one.

And suddenly Jack yearned to be back in Toy City. This was *not* his world, even if these *were somehow* his people. There was such diversity amongst the denizens of Toy City, the gollies and the dollies, and the teddies and the clockwork folk. Each with their own specific, particular outlook on life, their own ways of being. *They* were Jack's folk. Jack was one of them now. He had always been an outsider, always looking for something. But there was nothing *here* he wanted.

Jack looked towards Dorothy.

No, not even *her*, really.

Jack just wanted to be back with Eddie. Back in Toy City with all of this horror behind him.

'What are you thinking about?' asked Dorothy. 'Eddie, I bet.'

'More than Eddie,' said Jack. 'I was thinking about . . . well, no, it doesn't matter.'

But it did. It really did.

As they drew closer to the desk where they were to receive their passes, Dorothy said, 'Look at that, Jack. I bet you don't like that.'

Jack looked and Jack saw. Behind the desk was a tall glass cabinet. Very tall, very wide, glass-shelved. Upon these shelves were many little figures.

Jack peered and Jack saw and recognised these figures.

The clockwork clapping monkeys. The band from Old King Cole's. The orchestra from the Opera House. And oh so many more.

And right in the middle and larger than the rest sat a bear wearing a trenchcoat. And there was no mistaking *that* bear.

Jack made certain growling sounds and urged on the queue before him.

And presently it was his and Dorothy's turn to receive their passes.

'Name?' said a young tanned lovely, with a great beehive of golden hair.

'Dorothy,' said Dorothy. And then she added her surname. Dorothy received her pass.

'Next,' said the lovely to Jack.

'Jack,' said Jack to the lovely. 'Jack is my name. My name is Jack.'

'And Jack *what* would it be?'

'You have me on that one,' said Jack. '*What* would it be?'

'Your surname. You are Jack *what?*'

'I am Jack the head chef of the Golden Chicken Diner on Hollywood Boulevard.'

'I require your surname.'

'All right,' said Jack. 'I'm Sir Jack.'

'There's no *Sir* Jack on my list,' said the lovely. 'Please leave by the way you came in. Next, please.'

'No,' said Jack. 'Hold on there. I am the head chef.'

'Your name is not on the list.'

'I only started yesterday. I rose up through the ranks.'

'Ah,' said the lovely, batting preposterous eyelashes towards Jack. 'You are a migrant worker.'

'Exactly,' said Jack.

'No work visa, no ID, paid in cash and poorly, too.'

'That kind of thing,' said Jack.

'Then get out before I call security.'

'Now hold on—' said Jack.

'If *I* might explain,' said Dorothy. 'Jack is from England.'

'Oh,' said the lovely. 'England, is it? Where you all wear bowler hats and take tea with the Queen at three? Well, why didn't you say so?'

'Would it have made a difference?' Jack asked.

'Well, naturally it would. We Americans just *love* you English. Our politicians, in particular our President, are so keen to cultivate a special relationship with your Prime Minister. I have the gift of prophecy, you see, and I calculate that in some future time our President will be able to bully your Prime Minister into breaking the Nato Alliance and help him invade a Middle Eastern nation state.'

'Eh?' said Jack, accepting the pass he was now offered. 'What was that you said?'

'You want it *all* again? You see, I have the gift of prophecy. And I *calculate*—'

'That's enough,' said Jack. 'Can I use your toilet, please?'

'Well, you can't use mine, but you can use the men's room—it's over there.' And the lovely pointed with a lovely hand.

And Jack said, 'Excuse me, please,' and made for the door at the hurry-up.

And once inside the men's room, he locked himself into a stall and withdrew from his trenchcoat Wallah the calculating pocket.

'Oh,' whispered Wallah. 'Remembered my existence at last, have you, Jack?'

'I'm so sorry,' said Jack. 'All kinds of things have been happening.'

'Of that I am fully aware,' whispered Wallah. 'I have been plunged into dirty dishwater, then roasted in a rotisserie. Then washed and wrung out once again by your lady friend to get the smell of chicken out of me.'

'It's all been rather hectic,' said Jack.

'Well, all the sex you've been having certainly has.'

'It's just business,' said Jack. Which was a callous thing to say, more callous too because there was a more than even chance that he meant it.

'You are a very bad boy,' said Wallah.

'Eddie sometimes says that,' said Jack.

'And you behave very badly when that little bear isn't with you.'

'I behave *very* badly when he is,' said Jack. 'Often with his encouragement.'

'Time is growing short,' said Wallah, and her voice was faint. 'Eddie has less than forty-eight hours—you must move with haste.'

'I've got this far,' said Jack, 'thanks to you.'

'But I can take you no further. You forgot about me, Jack.'

'I didn't. Everything got hectic. I told you.'

'You forgot about me. But it doesn't matter. I thought I was special to you. But it doesn't matter. What matters is that you find Eddie and together you stop the fiend who would destroy Toy City.'

'I'm on the case,' said Jack. 'I'm trying.'

'I can do no more to help you but tell you this: I calculate trouble by teatime and I calculate that, given the choice, you should duck to the right.'

'Right,' said Jack in a puzzled tone.

'Right.' said Wallah. 'And so goodbye, Jack.'

'Goodbye.'

'Goodbye, Jack. I am fading fast. Time is up for me.'

'No,' said Jack, shaking Wallah about. 'You can't go now. You can't—'

'Die?' said Wallah. 'I'm dying, Jack. Would you do something for me?'

'Anything,' said Jack.

'Anything?' said Wallah. 'Anything I ask?'

'Anything,' said Jack. 'Anything at all.'

'Then kiss me, Jack,' said Wallah, 'and . . .'

Jack emerged from the men's room. He had a rather guilty look on his face. And it was a red and embarrassed face that this guilty look was upon.

'What have you been doing in there?' Dorothy asked Jack. 'You look as if you've been—'

'Don't be absurd,' said Jack. 'I've been in there by myself.'

'Then you were—'

'Stop, please,' said Jack. 'Let's get a move on with what we're supposed to be doing.'

'You *have* been,' said Dorothy. 'Every woman can recognise that look on a man's face, even though most women won't ever admit it to a man. You've been—'

'Stop!'

When all had been issued their passes, all were led by the lovely to a golden escalator, up this and into a great hall (all gold) with seating upholstered in a similar hue. The seating was set up in rows before a stage, which Jack found unsurprisingly to be all over golden panels. And at length blinds were drawn at golden-framed windows and a spotlight, remarkably white in its brilliance, shone on the golden stage illuminating a golden microphone held high by a golden stand.

And into this spotlight stepped a dramatic personage who wore a suit that was not of gold, but was beige.

'Howdy doody, golden people,' he bawled into the microphone.

The sitters mumbled some good mornings/howdy doodys.

The man at the mic shook his head.

Jack peered up at the man at the mic. There was no all-over sameness about this fellow. He had *something*, something more. Just what was it? Jack wondered. A certain overconfidence? A certain *attitude*? He looked even more scrubbed than the sitters.

The man in beige had a big round head, with a big pink face and a kind of cylindrical body. His arms were long and so too were his hands, with very long fingers upon them.

His pink face surely shone.

'I said, "Howdy doody, golden people,"' he bawled.

The 'golden people' sitting replied, this time with a louder 'Howdy doody'.

'A very good howdy doody,' said the man on the stage, 'but not good enough for you golden people. One more time.'

And this time he got a veritable thunderstorm of howdy doodys hurled back in his direction.

With the notable exception of Jack and Dorothy. Although Dorothy did mumble *something*.

'Good enough,' said the man in beige. 'And welcome to Golden Chicken Towers. Welcome to you, the chosen ones. The special ones. The trusted ones. Your labours have brought you here. Your dedication to the company ethic. Your sense of duty. Your pride as young Americans.' And he raised a fist and shook it in a friendly fashion.

'Now who can tell me what *this* is?' he said. And he produced from his pocket . . . an egg.

Hands went up from the sitters.

Jack said, 'It's an egg.'

'It's an egg, well done.' The figure in beige smiled down upon Jack. 'It's an egg indeed. And what is your name, young man?'

'Sir Jack,' said Jack. 'I'm from England.'

'An Englander, is it? Well, up you come onto the stage.'

'And why would I want to do that?' Jack asked.

'Because I have chosen *you* to assist me with this presentation.'

'Well, aren't *I* the lucky one.'

'What did you say, young man?'

'I said, "Well, I *am* the lucky one."'

'As indeed you are. Up, up. Let's have a round of applause for Sir Jack.'

And a round of enthusiastic applause went up.

Jack shook his head and climbed onto the stage.

'Now, Sir Jack,' said the man in beige, putting a long beige arm about Jack's shoulders, 'what I'd like you to do is—'

'Work the slide projector?' Jack asked, as one was now being wheeled onto the stage by the lovely with the golden hair and the big dark batting lashes.

'Precisely.'

'And would I be right in assuming,' Jack asked, 'that the slides will display a sort of potted history of the company?'

'You are a most astute young man—I can see that career opportunities aplenty await you.'

'Splendid,' said Jack. 'And then I assume you will be giving us all a motivational speech.'

'Something of that nature, yes.' The man in beige gave Jack a certain look.

'Followed by a slap-up lunch,' said Jack.

'Why, yes.'

'Followed by more, how shall I put it, indoctrination?'

'Well,' said the man in beige. And he removed his arm from Jack's shoulders.

'Just so,' said Jack. 'But I think not.'

'I do not fully understand you.'

'Then perhaps you will understand *this*.' And Jack pulled from his trenchcoat pocket the cleaver that he had used the previous day for the decerebration of the chickens.

'Oh,' said the man in beige. 'What is *this*?'

'*This*,' said Jack, 'is a cleaver. And if you do not take me, *at once*, to your leader, I will use it to cut off your head.'

Now this caused some alarm, not only from the man in beige and the lovely on the stage, but also from the seated chosen ones, who now unseated themselves, preparing to flee.

'And sit down, you lot,' shouted Dorothy. Pulling, much to Jack's surprise, two pistols from her clothing. 'Anybody moves and you're dead.'

Jack looked at Dorothy.

Dorothy smiled. 'Well, get a move on,' she said.

18

There are moments.

Sometimes.

Special moments. Magic moments. Moments when everything becomes as clear as the air and you can see right through it, into eternity.

These moments are often reached via the medium of alcohol. In
England, for example, where most folk wear bowler hats, take tea at
three and know the Queen well, there are public drinking houses. And
those who frequent these sociable establishments respect something
that is known as the ten-o'clock watershed. It is understood that before
this time, talk is generalised and covers many topics—the day's news,
recent sporting events, trivial this and thats.

But beyond the ten-o'clock watershed, certain matters are deemed
acceptable that would otherwise be considered taboo. Friendship is one
of these and many is the time when two large masculine fellows will be
seen putting their arms about one another and swearing to anyone who
would care to hear, and many who might care not, that 'this is my
bestest friend'. And 'I love this man'.

And although at nine fifty-five this would not be deemed the
thing-to-do, beyond the ten-o'clock watershed it is A-okay.

This is but one example and the cynical reader might lean towards
the opinion that it is in fact 'the alcohol speaking', rather than a moment. A special moment.

But who amongst us has not experienced a special moment? A moment of total clarity. A reality check. A revelation.

As Jack held his cleaver over the beige man's head, Jack experienced
such a special moment.

For Jack it was not peace, or love, or a semi-religious revelation.

For Jack it was more a case of WHAT IN THE NAME OF ANY GOD THAT I MAY CARE TO BELIEVE IN **AM I DOING**?

It *was* a special moment. Jack saw the audience cowering beneath the guns of Dorothy. The beige man cowering, too, beneath Jack's cleaver. The great golden room with its Californian sunlight slanting through the slats of the window blinds.

The sudden terrible reality of it all.

And for one moment, and a special one at that, Jack thought of fleeing, dropping that cleaver and running away. This was real, these were people. What was all the rest of it? Chickens, spaceships, walking, talking toys? Eddie was gone and Jack was here and for one terrible, special moment Jack wondered whether all that stuff, all that mad unlikely stuff, really *was* real. Perhaps, Jack thought to himself, he, Jack, had gone insane, and perhaps now, at this moment, he had reawakened from the nightmare of insanity to this moment of absolute clarity.

Jack hesitated, all in confusion, for there is a problem with special moments: they play havoc with all your previous moments.

And Jack's hand loosened on his cleaver.

And Jack stared into the fearful face of the man in beige.

'I'm . . .' Jack was about to say 'sorry'.

'Hurry up, Jack,' shouted Dorothy. 'Pull yourself together. Eddie is in danger—don't forget that.'

Jack blinked and gazed towards Dorothy.

Had she known what he was thinking?

Jack didn't say, 'I'm sorry.'

Well, he did, but he didn't. He said. 'I'm sorry, Mister Man In Beige, but if you do not take me at once to your leader, I will chop off your ear.'

'No, please have mercy.' The man in beige sank down to his knees. 'Don't hurt me, please, I'm innocent.'

'No one is innocent,' called Dorothy. 'Get a move on, Jack.'

Jack hauled the beige man back to his feet. 'Your leader or your ear,' said he.

'No, please.' The lovely on the stage wrung her beautiful hands. The manicured nails of the slender fingers twinkled in the spotlight. 'Please don't hurt him, please.'

'I'm sorry,' said Jack, 'but my best friend has been kidnapped by someone in this building. Someone in power. I demand to be taken to this someone. Now!'

'But we don't have the authority,' said the lovely. 'We don't know who you should speak to. Mister Tinto here—'

'What did you say?' asked Jack.

'Don't say anything, Amelie,' said the man in beige.

'Amelie?' said Jack. 'Mister Tinto? What is this?'

And then Jack saw it. Because perhaps *this* was the special moment. In fact, the other special moment, which had seemed like a special moment at the time, was, in fact, only a warm-up sort of special moment.

Jack stared hard at the man in beige.

And then Jack saw it.

And had a special moment.

The man in beige was Tinto. Well, he wasn't *the* Tinto, but he was, well, what was he? Yes, he was a human manifestation, a human counterpart—he was the *human* version of Tinto. And the lovely? The lovely? Yes! Jack glanced at her and his glance became a stare. She *was* Amelie. Amelie made flesh.

Jack fell back for a moment, gawping and shaking his cleaver about. It *was* them. Why hadn't he seen it immediately? He'd known there was something . . .

But . . .

'Jack!' shouted Dorothy, most loudly, too. 'Jack, get a grip on yourself.'

'But it's them.' And Jack did foolish pointings all around with his free hand. 'It's Amelie and Tinto. It's them. It's them if they were people. It is.'

Jack's confusion turned to anger. As is often the case.

'Elevator,' said Jack. 'Upstairs,' said Jack.

'Yes,' said Mr Tinto. 'Anything you say.'

'Dorothy?' called Jack.

'I'll follow,' said Dorothy. 'Once I've dealt with this lot.'

'You're not going to shoot them?'

Chefs and managers ducked and flinched.

'I'll just have a word with them.'

'You promise?' Jack had some doubts in his head.

'I promise,' said Dorothy. And as Jack led Amelie and Mr Tinto from the stage, one hand on the beige man's collar, the other holding the cleaver high, Dorothy addressed the shaking, trembling audience.

'Ladies and gentlemen,' she said, 'I am so sorry that this talk, which I'm sure you were all looking forward to, has been brought to a premature conclusion. I suggest now that you vacate the premises and do so in an orderly fashion. I would also strongly advise that you say *nothing* about what has occurred here. We have two hostages and should you inform the police, we will not hesitate to kill them. Do you understand?'

Heads nodded thoughtfully. Eyes strayed to the exit doors.

'Ah, just one more thing,' said Dorothy, 'before you leave. Which one of you is it?'

The crowd, as one, made a puzzled face.

'Come on,' said Dorothy. 'You know what I mean.'

The crowd, as one, shook its head.

'The hero,' said Dorothy. 'The one who will stay behind. The one who although working as a chef used to work for Special Ops, or something, but got sacked through no fault of his own, which led to the break-up with his wife, a bit of a drink problem. But who, rising to such a situation as this, will slip away from the departing crowd, crawl through air-conditioning ducts and bring my companion and me to justice. There's always *one*. We *all* know that.'

'Ah,' went the crowd, as one. Because, after all, *we all* know *that*.

'So come on, then,' said Dorothy. 'Which one of you is it?'

The crowd now took to a collective silence.

'All right,' said Dorothy. 'Then let me put it another way. I will count to ten, and if the hero has not identified himself before this time I will execute two people at random. Come on, now, I'm counting down.'

'Oh, all right,' came a voice from an air-conditioning duct. 'Don't shoot anyone, I'm coming out.'

Jack was making good progress along the corridor. If good progress can indeed be measured by progress along a corridor.

'We really can't help you,' said Amelie, wiggling in front.

Jack looked down at those long, long legs. They were just like re— Oh, they *were* real legs, weren't they?

Jack said, 'Get a move on.'

'Amelie's right,' said Mr Tinto. 'We can't help you. We don't know anything.'

'You know something,' said Jack. 'I've been following the American Dream, me, and I know how it works. You can lead me to the next person in the chain of command. That's how it works, I know it.'

They were approaching a lift. The doors of this were gold.

'That's not how it works,' said Mr Tinto. 'Well, I suppose it is in theory, but not in reality, no.'

'I have no time to debate issues with you,' said Jack, flashing the cleaver's blade before Mr Tinto's frightened eyes. 'I am a desperate man.'

'Well, clearly so, yes. But you are making a mistake.'

'They always say that,' said Jack.

'Who do?' asked the man in beige as Jack hauled him bodily onwards.

'Baddies,' said Jack. 'It's a threatening thing to say, "You are making a big mistake."'

'I don't mean it to be threatening,' the beige man protested. 'I'm just telling you the truth—you *are* making a big mistake.'

'We'll see,' said Jack. 'Get a move on, please.'

And on they went and they reached the lift. And at the lift Dorothy caught up with them.

'Is everything all right?' Jack asked her.

'Yes, it is *now*,' she replied.

'I don't like the sound of that.' And Jack reached out and pressed the 'up' button. 'What happened? You didn't kill anyone, did you?'

'No, I just knocked on them on the head.'

'All of them?'

'No, just the one—the chef who'd stripped down to his vest and bare feet and hidden himself in the air-conditioning system.'

Jack shook his head. 'Do chefs often do that?' he asked.

'They do here in Hollywood,' said Dorothy. 'Going up.'

And the lift doors opened.

'Everyone inside,' said Jack.

'Do I really have to?' asked Mr Tinto.

'Yes,' said Jack. 'You do.'

'But you don't need two hostages. Why not just take Amelie here?'

All were now inside the lift and the lift doors closed upon them. Jack pressed the topmost button. The lift began to rise.

'What did you say?' asked Amelie.

'I'm only saying,' said Mr Tinto, 'that in hostage situations such as this, I'm the one most likely to get shot. They rarely shoot the pretty girl—she'll probably end up snogging the hostage-taker.'

'Snogging?' said Amelie.

'Well, shagging,' said Mr Tinto.

'What?' said Amelie, and she smacked Mr Tinto right in the face.

'Go girl,' said Dorothy.

'Not in the face,' cried Mr Tinto. And he burst into tears.

'She didn't hit you that hard,' said Jack. 'Don't be such a baby.'

'I'm not paid to get smacked,' said Mr Tinto. 'Taken hostage, yes, that was in my contract. But not smacked. I always demand a stunt double if there's any smacking involved. Or being thrown through windows.'

Jack rolled his eyes.

'Well, I've not been paid for any shagging,' said Amelie. 'That's work for a body double. I don't do *that* kind of work.'

'Oh, please,' said Mr Tinto. 'It's common knowledge that you've done stag films.'

'I've done no such thing. And we all know how *you* get work. Whose casting couch did you have to bend over to—'

'Would you please stop now,' said Jack. 'I'm in charge here. I have the cleaver.'

'Yes,' said Mr Tinto, 'and I've been meaning to talk to you about that. That is a *real* cleaver—you could have injured me with that. If I wasn't a professional I would have stopped you dead on the set and demanded a prop.'

'A *what?*' said Jack.

'A soft cleaver. A rubber one.'

'This is a real cleaver,' said Jack.

'Yes, I know, and you can stop threatening me with it now—we're no longer on camera.'

'We might be,' said Amelie. 'The director never called "cut".'

Jack looked towards Dorothy. 'Is it just me,' he asked, 'or is something not altogether right with these two hostages?'

'Oh, come off it, luvvie,' said Mr Tinto. 'Just because you're all Stanislavski method acting to disguise the fact that you can't remember your lines—'

'What?' went Jack.

'It's true,' said Amelie. 'You were far too rough with Sydney.'

'Thank you, Marilyn.'

'Sydney?' went Jack. 'Marilyn?'

'Oh please, sir,' said Sydney. 'As if you didn't recognise us.'

The lift went clunk and stopped. They had reached their destination.

'Now just *stop!*' shouted Jack. 'What is all this about? What are you saying? What is all this Marilyn and Sydney business?'

'You have to be jesting and your jest is in very poor taste,' said Sydney. 'Well, we're here now. Back in character everyone. And cue. Press the open-door button, please.'

Jack shook his head and pressed the 'open' button.

And the lift doors opened.

And Jack beheld.

And Dorothy also beheld. And so did Sydney and so did Marilyn.

And Sydney said, 'Typical, that.'

'Typical?' said Jack, and he stared. There was nothing. Nothing at all. The lift was at the top of its shaft, but there was no floor for them to step out onto. Just a big empty nothing. Four interior walls of the building. And these, it appeared, constructed from canvas and timber. Far, far below them there was to be seen the above parts of a ceiling below—the ceiling of the lecture room they had so recently left. And the above parts of another ceiling that followed the corridor that they had followed to enter the lift they now stood in. And stood in somewhat fearfully. Clinging onto one another now, for fear of falling the considerable distance to their doom below.

'Utterly typical,' said Sydney, pressing himself back from the open lift doors and flattening himself against the opposite wall.

Jack did more slack-jawed starings. Then he turned, shook Marilyn away from his arm and squared up large before Sydney. 'Speak to me,' Jack demanded. 'Explain what is going on here.'

'The set's not finished,' said Sydney. 'Utterly typical. Labour disputes with the union, I expect. I was on *Casablanca*, back in forty-two with Bogart, half the sets weren't finished. We had to double up the Blue Parrot Café with the airport lounge, although I don't think anyone noticed. They were too entranced by my acting.'

And Jack hit Sydney. Right in the face.

And Sydney broke down in tears.

'You beast,' howled Marilyn. 'How unprofessional. How dare you hit a Hollywood legend like that. He came out of retirement to play this part—you have no right to treat him in such a way.'

Jack turned upon her. 'You speak to me,' he said, 'or I'll throw you out of the lift and you can make your own way downstairs.'

'No, stop, please.'

'Then *speak*.'

And Marilyn spoke. 'We are actors,' she said. 'Surely you recognise us. This is Mister Sydney Greenstreet and I am Marilyn Monroe.'

'Marilyn Monroe?' asked Jack. 'But you can't be her. I saw her effigy at the wax museum, although—'

'It *is* her,' said Dorothy. 'But I didn't recognise you—how come?'

'Because when I play a role, I *am* that person.'

Jack looked *most* unconvinced.★

'It is her,' said Dorothy. 'It really is. Could I have your autograph, Miss Monroe? I'm your greatest fan.'

'Now stop all this,' said Jack. 'It doesn't make any sense.'

'Of course it makes sense, man,' said Sydney. 'What is the matter with you? This isn't a real building. It's a set. It's a part of a movie. But why am I telling you this? You're an actor. Although not a very good one, I might add. What have you been in before? Have I seen any of your work?'

'Actors?' went Jack. 'Set?' went Jack. 'What does this mean?' went Jack.

★ As well he might!

'It could mean,' said Dorothy, 'that we have fallen into a very large and elaborate trap.'

'No,' said Jack. And Jack shook his head. 'That's absurd. No one would go to all this trouble, set all this up, this building, the big foyer downstairs, all of this, simply to trap us.'

'Giving yourself airs and graces,' said Sydney, flinching as he said it. 'Who would want to trap *you*?'

Jack shook his head. 'But why?' he asked. 'Why all this? What is it for?'

'You know what it's for,' said Sydney. 'You read your contract, or your agent did. You signed the confidentiality clause.'

Jack was about to say 'What?' once more, but Dorothy, however, stopped him. 'Jack's from Arkansas,' she said. 'I'm sure you recognised his hokey accent.'

Jack said, 'What?' to this.

'Recognised it at once,' said Sydney. 'I can do almost any accent. But then I was classically trained. But then I'm from England, of course.'

'Well,' said Dorothy, 'Jack really *is* a method actor, trained at the New School's Dramatic Workshop with Brando, where he studied with Stella Adler and learned the revolutionary techniques of the Stanislavski System.'

'Overrated,' said Sydney. 'That Brando will never amount to anything.'

'What is this toot?' Jack asked. 'Where is this leading?'

'Just leave this to me,' said Dorothy to Jack. And to Mr Greenstreet she said, 'You see, Jack can't read or write. *I'm* his agent.'

Jack shook his head. He had given up on the 'What?s'.

'A sort of actor–manager,' said Sydney. 'Like Henry Irving.'

'Henry Irving managed a theatre,' said Marilyn, knowledgeably. 'He wasn't an agent.'

'I do it all,' said Dorothy. 'And all my own stunts.'

'Might we close the lift doors?' asked Sydney. 'I have vertigo. Did a rooftop scene in the nineteen forty-nine remake of *Death is a Dame in a Doggy Bag*. A Lazlo Woodbine thriller. Brian Donlevy played Laz in that one and the final rooftop confrontation scene was shot on a real rooftop. *Cinéma-vérité* black and white. I nearly fell to my—'

Jack raised his hand.

Sydney said no more.

Dorothy said, 'I signed the confidentiality clause on behalf of Jack, but I didn't tell him about it. Sydney, please put Jack in the picture. We wouldn't want him blurting anything out—it would not help to advance any of our careers.'

'Oh, it's quite simple,' said Sydney, sighing as he said it. 'Your agent, Dorothy here, signed the confidentiality clause for you, which states that we actors, employed by Golden Chicken Productions, must not discuss the script or contents of the movie prior to its release. There's millions of dollars riding on this, what with the merchandising already being in place and everything. It's a revolutionary concept, the toys being given away free and no one knowing that the movie, with big Hollywood stars playing the parts of the toys, is already in production.'

'I'm very confused,' said Jack.

'No you're *not*,' said Dorothy. 'Think about it.'

Jack thought and thought hard. 'I'm *still* confused,' he said. 'If this is a movie, Tinto is a barman, *not* a—'

'Motivational speaker,' said Sydney. 'I know, I went up for the part of Tinto but I didn't get it. I'm only calling myself Mr Tinto because the "Motivational Speaker" doesn't even have a name. Do you know who got the Tinto part in the end?'

Jack shook his head. Strangely he had no idea at all.

'Gene Kelly,' said Sydney. 'Tinto the dancing barman, I ask you.'

'So let me just get this straight,' said Dorothy, 'for Jack's benefit, because he is from Arkansas. You two were hired for a single day's work on this movie, which is a Golden Chicken Production, a live-action movie based upon the toys that are presently being given away free in the Golden Chicken Diners.'

'There is something special about them, isn't there?' said Marilyn. 'I'm collecting them myself.'

'And the movie will star major Hollywood actors and go world-wide?'

'The talk at the studio,' said Sydney, sighing once more as he spoke, 'is that with the movie's release, the Golden Chicken Diners will also go global. It's a vast commercial enterprise—not one I would normally wish to associate myself with, but such exposure can only advance my career. And let's face it, dear, I came out of retirement for this and even if I never work again, the fact that I was in *this* movie will ensure that I can make money for the rest of my life doing signings at Sci-Fi conventions.'

'Sci-Fi conventions?' Jack asked.

'Well, this *is* a Sci-Fi movie. What with all the spaceships and stuff.'

'Spaceships?' Jack shouted, and his hands were once more on Sydney's lapels.

'Spaceships!' Sydney tried quite fiercely to shake off Jack's manic grip. 'It *is* based on *War of the Worlds*, isn't it? Although having chickens as the saviour of mankind is a bit far-fetched in my opinion. And this strap line—"Eating chicken makes you a winner, too". Gross, but business, I suppose.'

Jack was, as they say, 'losing it', although they probably wouldn't be saying it for at least another ten years, but then of course they wouldn't actually have chaps in vests crawling around inside air-conditioning ducts and bringing criminals to justice for perhaps another forty years, but this *was* and *is* Hollywood, where Dreams become Reality, so Jack 'held it together' and Jack now shouted, 'Show me the script of this movie.'

'I don't have it with me,' said Sydney. 'I learn my lines. I can't be having with improv.'

'Take me to your script,' roared Jack.

'It's all "take me to this" and "take me to that" with you,' replied Sydney, quite boldly, considering. 'Take, take, take, that's all you do.'

'Or it's out and make your own way down.'

'Easy, Jack,' said Dorothy. 'They're only actors.'

'*Only?*' said Sydney.

'Well, not *only*, of course,' said Dorothy. 'Anything but only.'

'I want to see the script,' said Jack. 'I need to see the script.'

'And so you shall, young man. Just calm yourself down.' Sydney freed himself from Jack's grip.

'Is this going to help?' Dorothy asked. 'Help to find Eddie, I mean.'

'What else do we have? All this is fake. There's nothing here.'

'All right, then. Let's go down.'

Jack pressed the ground-floor button. The lift doors closed.

'Thank you for that,' said Sydney.

'I'm sorry,' said Jack. 'I know now that none of this is anything to do with you. I'm sorry I was so rough.'

'I'm a professional,' said Sydney. 'But I wonder, are we supposed to do a second take downstairs? I'm no longer certain what my motivation is. Was I supposed to fight you off? It wasn't in my backstory. Do you have a rewrite?'

Sydney said no more. The lift descended.

Sydney *might* have said more. But he couldn't, for Jack had head-knocked him unconscious. Which wasn't really very sporting, as he *was* a Hollywood legend.

The lift descended.

At length it reached the first floor. Jack thumped at the ground-floor button, but the lift would go no further. It could go no further. There were lift doors on the ground floor, but they were only doors— there was nothing behind them.

'What about poor Sydney?' asked Marilyn as the lift doors opened on the first floor.

'I'm sorry,' said Jack. Who was sick of saying sorry, but felt that upon this occasion he really should say it. 'I lost my temper. He's a nice fellow. You have a copy of the script, I assume?'

'Don't hit me,' said Marilyn. 'I do.'

'Then we'll go and look at yours.'

'Whatever you say, all right?'

And Marilyn left the lift and Jack and Dorothy followed her and Jack gazed once more at Marilyn's legs and thought certain thoughts. And Dorothy, as if, once more, she was able to access Jack's thoughts, dealt Jack a hearty slap to the face.

The lecture theatre was deserted.

But for a fellow in a vest and bare feet who lay all prone upon the floor. Jack stepped over this fellow.

'It had to be done,' said Dorothy.

And Jack just shrugged, as he was beyond caring anyway.

They moved through the lecture theatre, then out onto the mezzanine floor, then down the great escalator into the greater entrance hall with its golden statues and reception desk.

No one sat behind this. Indeed, but for Jack and Dorothy and Marilyn, this great golden area was deserted.

'Gone for lunch?' Jack suggested.

'Let's just get this script,' said Dorothy.

And so they crossed the great golden entrance hallway, passed through the great golden doorway and into the great golden sunlight of Los Angeles.

And here they paused, all well lit in goldenness.

Before the Golden Chicken Towers were many police cars. Many black and white police cars. Which had conveyed many of Los Angeles' finest to . . .

The scene of the crime.

And a voice, coming through what is known as an electric bullhorn, called unto Jack.

And its call went thus ways. And so. And suchlike also.

'Drop your weapons and get down on the ground. You are surrounded,' it went.

Thus ways.

And so.

And suchlike.

Also.

19

LA Police Chief Samuel J. Maggott was having a rough one.

Such is the way with police chiefs, that they are generally having a rough one. Things conspire against them all the time. Things pile up. Often it is that they have just given up smoking, and drinking, and are going through a messy divorce. And that the 'powers that be' are coming down hard upon them, demanding results on cases that seem beyond all human comprehension.

Then there's the matter of their underlings. That feisty new policewoman who doesn't play by the rules but always gets results. And that troubled young detective who won't give up smoking or drinking and has never been married and gets all the girls and doesn't play by the rules, but also always gets the job done.

And then there's that coffee machine that never works properly and it's a really hot summer and the air conditioning's broken down and . . .

So on and so forth and suchlike.

And now there's *this* fellow.

LA Police Chief Samuel J. Maggott sat down heavily in his office chair, behind his office desk. The office that he sat down in was a proper police chief's office. There were little American flags sprouting from his inkwell. There were medals in small glass cases on the walls. Near the picture of the President. And the ones of Sam's family, which included the wife who was presently divorcing him. And there were other American flags here and there, because there always are. And there were framed citations won in the cause of police duty (above and beyond the call of it, generally). And there was a coffee machine and an air-conditioning unit, the latter making strange noises.

And there was *this* fellow.

This fellow sat in the visitors' chair, across the desk from Sam's. This fellow sat uneasily, uncomfortably. His hands were in his lap. His wrists were handcuffed together.

After he'd done with the heavy sitting down, Sam did some puffings. He'd been putting on weight recently. It was all the stress that he'd been under, which had caused him to put more food beneath his belt, which put him under even more pressure to lose some weight.

Sam sighed and inwardly cursed his lot. The things he had to put up with. And he hadn't even touched upon the racial politics, because Sam was, of course, a black man.

As are all American police chiefs.

Apparently.

Sam puffed and Sam sighed and Sam mopped sweat from his brow. He mopped it with an oversized red gingham handkerchief. It had belonged to his mother, who had died last week, and had only yesterday been put under.

And still there was *this* fellow.

This fellow sat, with his hands in his lap, naked in the visitors' chair.

Sam shook his head, which was thinning on top, and said a single word. 'Coffee?'

The naked fellow looked up at Sam. 'Did you say "coffee"?' he asked.

'I'm asking you, do you want coffee?'

'I'd rather have a pair of underpants.'

'Don't be foolish, boy,' said Sam. 'You cannot drink underpants. Unless, of course . . .' And Sam's mind returned to something he'd done recently at a club on the East Side, which he really shouldn't have been at, and wouldn't have been at if he hadn't been so depressed about his dog getting stolen and everything.

'Could I have my clothes back, please?' asked the naked fellow. He was a young naked fellow, rangy and tanned, spare of frame and wiry of limb.

'Are you cold?' asked Sam.

'No,' said the fellow, 'but it's pretty humiliating sitting here naked.'

'You've got nothing that I ain't seen before, fella,' said Sam, almost instantly regretting that he had. What *was* it his therapist kept telling him?

'Well, if men's genitalia are so commonplace to you,' said the fellow, 'I can't imagine what pleasure you will have viewing mine.'

'Pleasure don't come into this,' said Sam.

'I do so agree,' said the fellow.

'But anyway, your clothes are with forensics. We'll soon see what they have to tell us.'

The fellow, whose name was Jack, thought suddenly of Wallah. Suddenly and sadly too thought he.

'My clothes will have nothing to say to you,' said Jack.

'On the contrary.' Sam rose heavily from his chair to fetch coffee for himself. 'They've told us much already.'

'They have?' Jack asked as he watched the large black police chief worry at the coffee machine.

'Oh yes.' And Sam kicked the coffee machine. 'A great deal.' And Sam shook the coffee machine. 'A very great deal, in fact.' And Sam stooped heavily and peered into the little hatchway where one (such as he) who had pressed all the correct buttons above might reasonably expect to see a plastic cup full of coffee.

No such cup was to be found.

Sam peered deeper into the little hatch. 'A great deal of Aaaaagh!'

'A great deal of *what*?' asked Jack.

But Sam didn't hear him. Sam was wildly mopping boiling water from his face with his oversized red gingham handkerchief.

'Goddamn useless machine!' And Sam moved swiftly for a heavy man and dealt the machine many heavy blows.

The glass partition door opened and the attractive face of a feisty young policewoman smiled through the opening. 'Chief,' said she, 'I've just cracked the case that's had you baffled for months. I—'

'Get *out*!' shouted Sam, returning without coffee to his desk.

'Stressful job, is it?' Jack asked. 'The American Dream not working out?'

Sam, now once more in his chair, leaned forward over his desk. Two little flags fell onto the floor along with an overfull ashtray. 'Now just listen here, fella,' said Sam, 'don't go giving me no lip. I don't like a wise guy, understand me?'

'Yes,' said Jack. 'About my clothes.'

'Ah yes, your clothes.' And Sam leaned back and Sam took up a folder. And having opened same, examined the contents therein. 'Fingerprints not on file,' said Sam. 'No ID. No record, it seems, that you even exist.'

'I'm from England,' said Jack, 'and I'm a friend of the Queen.'

'Is that so?' Sam nodded. 'And your name is Jack, no surname. Just Jack.'

'Just Jack,' said Jack.

'As in Jack the Ripper?' asked Sam. 'English psycho, said to be in league with the royal household?'

'I think we're going off on a bit of a tangent,' said Jack, uncomfortably shifting from one bottom cheek to the other. 'Could I please have my clothes back, please?'

'No,' said Sam. 'Those clothes of yours could well be my passport out of here.'

'I'm certain that if I listen long enough,' said Jack, 'I will be able to learn whatever language it is that you are speaking. But I do not have time. I must be off at once.'

'You're going nowhere, fella. Nowhere at all.'

'But I've done nothing. I'm innocent.'

'Innocent?' Sam laughed and loudly, too. And then he coughed, because laughing too much always brought on a touch of the malaria he'd contracted whilst fighting U-boats in the jungles of South-East Asia. 'Cough, cough, cough,' went Sam.

'If you'll unlock these cuffs,' said Jack, 'I'll gladly pat your back.'

'I'm fine.' Sam reached into a desk drawer, drew from it the bottle of bourbon that he'd promised his specialist he'd poured away down the sink, uncorked it and poured away much of its contents down his throat. 'I'm fine. Goddamnit.'

'Can I go, *please*?' Jack asked.

'No, fella, you cannot. You and your girlfriend held a crowd of managers and chefs at gunpoint, beat a chef called Bruce to within an inch of his life—'

'We never did,' said Jack.

'Took two hostages. Famous movie stars—Sydney Greenstreet and Marilyn Monroe.'

'Well . . .' said Jack.

'Beat poor Sydney nearly to dea—'

'Hold on.'

'Sexually harassed Marilyn—'

'I did *what*?'

'And we caught you with your chopper in your hand.'

'Cleaver, please,' said Jack. 'Let's not sink to that level.'

'Resisting arrest, et cetera, et cetera.' Sam closed the file. 'You're looking at twenty to life, if not the chair.'

'The chair?' said Jack, looking down at the chair. '*This* chair?'

'The electric chair, Old Sparky.' Sam mimed electricity buzzing through his own head and then death. And well he mimed it, too, considering that he'd no formal training in mime. Although there had been *that* incident that the department had hushed up, regarding that female mime artist, the raspberry jelly and the bicycle pump. *That* could always blow up in his face if he sought further advancement.

'I don't like the sound of that,' said Jack.

'You won't like the feel, either, or the smell as your brains boil in your head.'

'Listen,' said Jack, 'you don't understand. I've been trying to explain.'

'Explain to me about the clothes,' said Sam.

'Well,' said Jack, 'it's pretty basic stuff, really. The shirt is worn much in the way that you wear yours, although mine doesn't have those large sweat stains under the arms. The trousers, well, that's pretty basic also—you put your left leg in the left-leg hole and—'

Sam brought his fists down hard on his desk. Inkwells rattled, things fell to the floor. Jack was showered with paperclips. Jack ceased talking. And the glass partition door opened once again.

A young male detective stuck his head through the opening; he had a cigarette in his mouth. 'Any trouble, Chief?' he asked. 'Only I've just solved that other case that has had you baffled for months. I—'

'Get out!' bawled Sam. The young detective removed himself, slamming the door behind him.

'Now listen, fella, and listen good,' Sam said unto Jack. 'The clothes, your clothes, the ones with forensics—I have a preliminary report here. Let's deal with the labels first.'

'The labels?' And Jack shook his head.

'The Toy City Suit Company, Fifteen Dumpty Plaza. Explain that if you will.'

'It's the shop where the trenchcoat came from. It's not my trenchcoat.'

'So you stole it.'

'No, it belongs to someone who was murdered.'

'You took it from their corpse. Do you wish to make a confession?'

'I'd like to see a solicitor,' said Jack. 'I believe I am entitled to one.'

'Ah, yes,' said Sam. 'As I recall, your girlfriend shouted that at you when we had to have her carried down to the cells after she injured several of my officers.'

'I warned you not to try to cuff her,' said Jack. 'She knows Dimac.'

'That I know,' said Sam, sipping further bourbon. 'We located the official licence for her hands and feet. Registered here! But no matter. There is *no* Toy City Suit Company. No Dumpty Plaza.'

'It's in England,' said Jack.

'Which part?' asked Sam.

'The whole shop,' said Jack.

Sam didn't smile. But then who would?

'Which part of England is the shop in?'

Jack thought hard. 'The south part?' he suggested.

'The south part,' said Sam. And he said it thoughtfully.

'Next door to the Queen's palace,' said Jack.

'Right,' said Sam, and he plucked at his shirt collar. And, leaning back, he thumped at the air conditioner. Further strange noises issued from this and then it fell silent. Sam took to mopping his brow once more. 'There is no Dumpty Plaza in England,' said Sam. 'There is no Dumpty Plaza anywhere. And as for the fabric of this trenchcoat, there appears to be no such fabric.'

'Could I see a solicitor *now*?' Jack asked.

'Soon,' said Sam. 'When you have answered my questions to *my* satisfaction.'

'I don't think that's how it's supposed to work,' said Jack.

'Tell me again about this bear,' said Sam. 'This . . .' and he consulted the notes he had taken down (before his Biro ran out), 'this Eddie.'

'A valuable antique toy bear,' said Jack, as this was his present stratagem. 'Stolen from my client by an employee of the Golden Chicken Corporation. I tracked the bear to the headquarters of this corporation. I was interviewing two suspects.'

Sam did further big deep sighings. 'Ah, yes,' he said. 'Because you are a private eye, sent here from England to recover—'

'The Queen's teddy bear,' said Jack. 'Like I told you.'

'And the Golden Chicken Corporation stole the Queen's teddy bear?'

Jack made a certain face. It wasn't perhaps the *best* stratagem that he'd ever come up with, but he *was* committed to it now. 'Which is why I am here, undercover,' said Jack. 'With no identification.'

Sam did further shakings of the head. And further noddings, too. 'I wish,' said he, 'I just wish that for *one* day, *one* single day, everything would just be easy.'

'Listen,' said Jack, 'you're not going to believe me no matter what I tell you. If I were to tell you everything and the whole truth and nothing but the truth, you wouldn't believe me. You wouldn't believe a word.'

'But you *won't* tell me the truth.' Sam leaned back in his chair and all but fell from it. 'Because no one tells the truth. No one. Take my wife, for instance . . .' Sam swivelled round in his chair, rose and gazed through the window. Outside, LA shimmered in the midday sunlight, high-finned autos cruised along the broad expanse of thoroughfare, palms waved drowsily, birds circled high in the clear blue sky.

'My wife,' said Sam. 'I gave that woman everything. Treated her like the Queen of England, I did, me. She wanted dance classes, I got her dance classes. She wanted voice tuition, I got her voice tuition. She wanted singing lessons, I got her singing lessons. I paid for that woman to have plastic surgery, breast implants, nail extensions. And what does she do? Becomes a Goddamn movie star is what she does. Signs that contract and dumps yours truly. Is that fair? Is that just? Is that right? I ask you, fella, is that right?'

Sam turned to gauge Jack's opinion on the fairness and rightness of all this.

But Jack was nowhere to be seen.

The handcuffs he had been wearing lay on Sam Maggott's desk, their locks picked with a paperclip.

Now, it's never easy to escape from a police station. Especially during the hours of daylight. And especially when naked.

And Sam set off the alarm, which had police all running about. And Sam opened his office door and shouted at the feisty young policewoman and the troubled young detective who was smoking a fag and chatting her up. And all the other policemen and -women in the big outer office. And he berated them and ordered them to reapprehend the naked escapee *at once*, or heads would roll and future prospects be endangered. And police folk hurried thither and thus, but Jack was not to be found.

Jack eased his naked self along the air-conditioning duct. The one he'd climbed into from the police chief's desk, through its little hatch, which he had thoughtfully closed behind him. He was uncertain exactly which way he should be easing his naked self, but as far away from the office as possible seemed the right way to go.

'I don't bear the man a grudge,' said Jack to himself as he did further uncomfortable easings along. 'And I do think his wife treated him unfairly. But even though I am a youth, in the early bloom of my years, I am drawn to the conclusion that life is *not* fair and the sooner one realises this and acts accordingly, the less one will find oneself all stressed out in later years.

'I think that I will remain single and use women purely for . . . OUCH!' and Jack snagged a certain dangling part upon a bolted nut.

And as chance, or coincidence, or fate, or something more, or less, would have it, at that *very* moment, and many miles south of Jack, and many floors beneath the desert sand, Eddie Bear was having trouble with a nut.

'Nuts?' said Eddie, taking up a nut between his paws and peering at it distastefully. 'Nuts? Nuts? That is what you're offering me to eat?'

The other Jack grinned into Eddie's cage. 'That's what bears eat in the wild, isn't it? Nuts and berries.'

'I wouldn't know,' said Eddie. 'I never associate with such unsophisticated company. I'd like a fillet steak, medium rare, sautéd potatoes—'

The other Jack kicked at Eddie's cage. 'Eat up your nuts,' he said, 'like a good little bear. You're going to need all your strength.'

Eddie's stomach grumbled. And Eddie's stomach ached. Eddie didn't feel at all like himself. He wasn't feeling altogether the full shilling, was Eddie Bear. 'What do you want from me?' he asked. 'Why have you brought me here?'

'You have to pay for your crimes,' said the other Jack.

'I'm no criminal,' said Eddie.

'Oh yes you are. You and your companion shot down one of our spaceships. Murdered the crew—'

'Self-defence,' said Eddie. 'Your accusations won't hold up in court.'

'Would you care to rephrase that?'

'No court involved, then?' said Eddie.

'No court,' said the other Jack. 'No court and no hope for you.'

'What are you?' asked Eddie. 'What are you, really?'

'I'm Jack,' said the other Jack. 'I'm the Jack this side of The Second Big O. I'm the Jack in this world.'

'An identical Jack?' said Eddie. 'I don't think so.'

'Oh, we're all here, human counterparts, reflections of your world—or rather your world is a reflection of ours. We're all here, even you.'

'The murdering me,' said Eddie, peeping through the bars of his cage. 'The me who murdered the monkeys and the band and the orchestra?'

'And all the rest, soon. The contents of your world will be sucked into ours. For our use.'

'But for why?' asked Eddie Bear. 'To be produced as giveaways for promoting the sale of fried chicken? That's as mad as.'

'You eat up your nuts,' said the other Jack. 'I'll be back in a little while. Don't make me have to ram them down your throat.'

And with that the other Jack turned to take his leave.

'Oh, Jack,' said Eddie.

The other Jack turned.

'When my Jack gets here, as he will, he'll really kick your ass.'

And in his air-conditioning duct, Jack snagged his ass on a pointy something. And whispered, Ouch!' once again.

Jack could hear lots of sounds beneath him. The sounds of the alarm and the sounds of shouting and of running feet. And if his hearing had been a tad more acute he would have been able to discern the sound of gun cabinets being opened and pump-action shotguns being taken from these cabinets and loaded up with high-velocity cartridges. But there is only so much that you can hear from inside an air-conditioning duct.

Jack added to the easings along he had formerly done with more of the same, but more carefully. Where *exactly* was he now?

Light shone up through a grille ahead. Jack hastened with care towards it.

'Hm,' went Jack, peering down. 'Corridor, and by the look of it, deserted. Now the question is, how might I open this grille from the inside and lower myself carefully to the floor beneath?'

Good question.

Jack put his ear to the grille. Alarm, certainly . . . Ah, no, alarm switched off. Running feet? Shouting? Not in *this* corridor. Jack took a deep breath, then took to beating the grille. And then beating some more. Then rattling everything around. Then beating some more.

And then screaming, as quietly as he could, as the length of ducting containing himself detached itself from its fellow members and fell heavily the distance between the ceiling to which it had been attached and the floor beneath.

Which was uncarpeted.

Exactly how long Jack was unconscious, he had no way of telling. The police had confiscated Jack's watch. And it no longer worked anyway. Jack awoke in some confusion, crawled from his fallen length of aluminium ducting, climbed to his feet and rubbed at the bruised parts, which comprised the majority of his body. Wondered anew *exactly* where he was.

A sign on the wall spelled out the words:

POLICE CELLS: AUTHORISED ACCESS ONLY.

'I think *that's* fair,' said Jack. 'I deserve a little luck.'

And Jack made his way onwards upon naked feet.

And presently reached the cells.

Now, as we all know, and we *do*, police cells contain all kinds of individuals. And, curiously enough, all of them innocent.

It is a very odd one, that—that *all* police cells contain innocent, well, 'victims', for there is no other word. As do prisons. Prisons are full of folk who have never confessed to any crimes. In fact, *all* of them pleaded innocent at their trials. And even though the evidence piled against them might have appeared, on the face of it, compelling and condemning, nevertheless the 'victims' of 'circumstance' and 'injustice' protested their innocence and were unjustly convicted.

Odd that, isn't it?

Jack peered through another little grille, this one in the door of the first cell.

Here he espied, a-sitting upon a basic bunk, an overlarge fellow, naked to the waist, his chest and torso intricately decorated via the medium of tattoo.

'Wrong cell,' said Jack. Although perhaps too loudly. As his words caused the overlarge fellow to look up, observe Jack's peering face and rise from his basic bunk.

Cell two presented Jack with a small well-dressed gentleman who rocked to and fro on his basic bunk, muttering the words, 'God told me to do it,' over and over again.

'Definitely wrong,' said Jack.

And this fellow looked up also.

In the third cell Jack observed a number of Puerto Ricans. They sported bandannas and gang-affiliated patches. Jack recognised them to be the kitchen workforce he had employed the previous day.

'Hi, fellows,' called Jack.

The fellows looked up towards Jack.

And now Jack's attention was drawn back to the first and second cells. Their occupants were beating at the doors, crying out for Jack to return, shouting things about being the daddy and knowing a bitch when they saw one.

'Shush!' Jack shushed them.

But the cell-three Puerto Ricans now joined in the crying aloud.

'Damn,' went Jack. And Jack pressed on.

And finally found Dorothy.

'Dorothy,' called Jack. And the beautiful girl looked up from her basic bunk.

'Jack,' she said, and she hastened to the door to observe him through the grille. 'You are naked,' she continued.

'Well, yes,' said Jack. 'But—'

'Nothing,' said Dorothy. 'This is California. Please would you open my cell?'

'I certainly will.' And Jack spat out the *other* paperclip. The one he had kept in his mouth to perform this very function. Because he *did* think ahead, did Jack. Because he *was* a private detective.

And with this paperclip and to the growing cacophony of shouting victims of circumstance, Jack picked the lock on Dorothy's cell door and freed her from incarceration.

Good old Jack.

'Here,' said Dorothy, lifting her skirt and dropping her panties. 'Put these on, it will help,'

'Help?' Jack looked hard at the panties. Now in the palm of his hand.

'Unless you really want to run completely naked through the streets of LA.'

'But they're your . . .' Jack shook his head and put on the panties.

'It's an interesting look,' said Dorothy, 'and not one that would normally ring my bell, as it were, however—'

'Time to run,' said Jack.

And Jack was right in this. Because a door at the far end of the corridor, back beyond his fallen length of ducting, was now opening and heavily armed policemen and -women were making their urgent entrance.

'That way, I think,' said Dorothy, pointing towards a fire exit. 'That way at the hurry-up.'

And that was the way Jack took.

20

What they say about doors is well known.

As one door closes, another one opens, and all that kind of caper.

The door that Jack had opened he now closed behind himself and Dorothy and he dragged a dustbin in front of it and caught a little breath. And then he viewed his surroundings and said, 'This does not look at all hopeful.'

Dorothy shook her flame-haired head. 'At least the sun is shining,' she said, with rather more cheerfulness than their present situation merited. 'You'll get a bit more of a tan—it will suit you.'

'A bit more of a tan?' Jack put his back to the dustbin, which was now being rattled about by policemen and -women belabouring the door. 'We're in the police car park. This is not a good place to be.'

Dorothy glanced all around and about. There were many police cars, all those wonderful black and white jobbies with the big lights that flash on the top. All were parked and all were empty.

All but for the one a-driving in.

Two officers sat in this one, big officers both, one at the wheel and one in the passenger seat. They were just coming off shift, were these two officers. Officer Billy-Bob was at the wheel and beside him sat his brother officer, Officer Joe-Bob, brother of the other Joe-Bob, the one Jack had thrown out of the diner's kitchen the day before. (Small world.) They had had an unsuccessful day together in the big city fighting crime and were looking forward to clocking off and taking themselves away to a Golden Chicken Diner for some burgers.

These two officers peered through their windscreen at the young chap in the ladies' panties who was fighting with a trashcan and the flame-haired young woman, who appeared now to be waving frantically in their direction.

Officer Billy-Bob drew up the black-and-white, wound down the window and offered a gap-toothed grin to the flame-haired young woman. 'Any trouble, ma'am?' he enquired in a broad Arkansas accent.

'This maniac attacked me,' screamed Dorothy. 'He's taken my panties.'

'Taken your panties, ma'am?' Officer Billy-Bob took off his cap and gave his head a scratch. 'That's a four-sixteen.'

Officer Joe-Bob took off *his* hat. 'That's a four-twenty-three,' he said.

Jack continued his fight with the dustbin. 'Run,' he told Dorothy.

'Stay,' said Dorothy to Jack. 'I'll take care of this.'

'Take care of it? I'm not a maniac. What are you doing?'

Officer Billy-Bob climbed from the car. Officer Joe-Bob did likewise.

'Four-sixteen,' said Officer Billy-Bob. 'Cross-dressing in a car park.'

'A four-sixteen ain't that,' said Officer Joe-Bob. 'A four-sixteen is a Chinaman in a liquor store stealing liquorice with intent.'

'Intent to do what?' asked Officer Billy-Bob.

'Intent s'nuff,' said Officer Joe-Bob.

'Intense snuff? What you talkin' about?'

'I said, intent is enough. Like a four-thirty-eight, being tall with intent.'

'Being tall? What kind of gibberish you talkin', boy?'

'Excuse me, officers,' said Dorothy, 'but I'd really appreciate it if you'd arrest this maniac.'

'All in good time, ma'am,' said Officer Billy-Bob. 'Law takes due process. If we run him in on a four-fifteen and it turns out to be a three-six-nine—'

'A three-six-nine is a goose drinking wine in a Presbyterian chapel,' said Officer Joe-Bob. 'You're thinking of a six-sixty-six.'

'Goddamnit, Joe-Bob,' said Officer Billy-Bob, 'six-sixty-six is the number of the Goddamn Beast of Revelation.'

'True enough, but you're thinking of it, you're always thinking of it.'

'True enough. But then I'm also always thinking of a thirty-six-twenty-two-thirty-six.'

'That's Marilyn Monroe.'

And both officers sighed.

And then Dorothy hit both officers. In rapid succession. Although there was some degree of that slow-motion spinning around in mid-air. As there always should be on such occasions.

Officer Billy-Bob hit the Tarmac.

Officer Joe-Bob joined him.

'To the car,' cried Dorothy.

And Jack ran to the car.

Dorothy jumped into the driving seat. Jack fell in beside her.

'I should drive,' said Jack. 'Climb into the back.'

'*I* will drive,' said Dorothy. And down went her foot. And Jack went into the back. Rather hard.

'Ow,' and, 'Ouch,' went Jack, in the back. And, 'Arrgh!' as the car went over a speed bump, which is sometimes known as a sleeping policeman. And, 'Oh!' went he as his head struck the roof. Then, 'Wah!' as Dorothy took a right and Jack fell onto the floor.

And now all manner of officers burst into the car park. The feisty female one with the unorthodox approach to case-solving. And the troubled young detective, with whom at times the very letter of the law was something of a grey area. A Chinese officer called Wong, who was in LA on a special attachment from Hong Kong and who spoke with a cod-Chinese accent but was great at martial arts. And there was a fat officer who got puffed easily if the chase was on foot. A gay officer, whose day was yet to dawn. And an angry, sweating black police chief by the name of Samuel J. Maggott.

'After them!' bawled Sam. 'Taking and driving away a squad car. Add that to the charge sheet.'

'And two officers down,' said the feisty young woman.

'And add that, too. Someone get me a car.'

'Come in mine, Chief,' said the troubled young detective. And as various officers leapt into various black-and-whites, the troubled young detective leapt into an open-topped red Ford Mustang (which he called Sally). It was an unorthodox kind of vehicle for police work, but the troubled young detective did have a reputation for getting the job done in it.

'No Goddamn way!' bawled Samuel J. Maggott.

'Then come in mine,' cried the feisty young female officer, leaping into an open-topped AC Cobra. Lime green, with a number twenty-three on the side.★

Samuel J. Maggott weighed up the pros and cons. The feisty young female officer did have a very short skirt. And he *was* going through a very messy divorce. 'I'll take my own Goddamn car,' declared Sam.

★ Number twenty-three being *that* number which always turns up in American movies. On hotel room doors, on the sides of freight train carriages. Here, there, everywhere. Why? Well . . .

And he would have, too, had he not been run down by a very short-sighted officer with thick pebblelensed glasses, who was rather quick off the mark but not at all good at backing up.

'Did I just run over a sleeping policeman?' he asked.

And out into the streets of LA they went.

Dorothy with her foot down hard and Jack bouncing around in the back. The troubled young man in his Ford Mustang, Sally. The feisty young woman in the Cobra. And black-and-white after black-and-white and finally Sam Maggott, who was at last in a squad car.

Now it could be argued that the streets of San Francisco are far better than the streets of LA when it comes to a car chase. They have all those hills and the tramcars that get in the way. And the sea views are nice, too. And in the 1960s, Owlsley *would* produce the finest LSD that any generation had ever experienced, which although having nothing particularly to do with car chases (although you can have them on acid without actually leaving your armchair) ought to be taken into consideration when it comes to the matter of deciding whether to shoot the car chase for your movie in LA or San Francisco.

Although it could well be argued, in fact it is difficult to argue against, that the best car chase ever filmed was filmed in Paris.★

But this *was* Los Angeles and this was where *this* car chase was occurring. Now!

And at this point. Before things get very hairy. It might also be worth mentioning that anyone who has never visited LA knows what the headquarters of the Los Angeles Police Department really looks like. It *doesn't* look like that big building with the great columns and everything that you see in virtually every crime movie that's set in LA. That building is, believe it or not, the General Post Office.

The genuine headquarters of the Los Angeles Police Department is housed in an ivory palace that looks like the Taj Mahal, but with feathered wings and pink bubbles and . . . †

Dorothy swung a hard right.

'Speak to me, people, speak to me now,' demanded Sam from his squad car, which was being driven along at some speed by another officer. 'Speak to me, what's happening?'

'Escaped prisoners moving west on Wilshire Boulevard,' came a voice to Sam, the voice of the feisty young female officer. 'Am in pursuit. Hey, get back there.'

'Leave this to me,' came the voice of the troubled young detective.

★ Ronin. And what a great movie *that* is!
† Well, it would in the 1960s on Owlsley acid.

Sam heard the sounds of a Mustang called Sally striking an AC Cobra.

Dorothy put her foot down and glanced into the rear-view mirror. 'They seem to be trying to drive each other off the road,' she told Jack, who had struggled up beside her. 'This is Koreatown, by the way.'

'Very nice,' said Jack. 'Look out!'

A police car travelling south on South Western Avenue crossed their path. Dorothy struck its rear end and sent it spinning around. The feisty young female officer crashed into this car, which put her out of the chase rather too quickly for her liking. The troubled young detective, however, kept on coming and behind him Officer Wong, the fat officer, the gay officer whose day was yet to dawn, but sadly not the short-sighted officer, who was now travelling south on South Broadway and heading for the beach.

Samuel Maggott was close upon the rear of the gay officer, though. Which was something that he would have to discuss with his therapist at a later date.

Dorothy took another turn to the right, north onto Beverly Boulevard.

And what a nice neighbourhood that is.

Although.

A chap in a uniform jumped out in front of the speeding automobile, hand raised, face set in an expression of determination. Dorothy tried to swerve around him, but he jumped once more into her path. Dorothy slewed to a stop. The chap in the uniform with the determined expression on his face came around to the side of the car.

'Sorry, ma'am,' he said, 'but this is Beverly Hills. We don't allow car chases here, nor tourist buses. You'll have to go back the way you just came.'

Dorothy glanced once more into the rear-view mirror. The troubled young detective and all the other squad cars had halted at the Wilshire/Beverly intersection. They knew the rules. Some things were just *not* done.

'Sorry,' said Dorothy, backing up the car.

'What?' went Jack. Astounded.

'It's an American thing,' Dorothy explained.

'Speak to me, people. Oh, Goddamn!' Sam Maggott's car slammed into the rear end of the gay officer's.

And then Sam said, 'Goddamn,' once again as Dorothy shot past him, returning the way she had come. 'Will somebody shoot that woman?' cried Sam, and he drew out his gun and did it himself.

'Duck to the right,' cried Dorothy.

And Jack ducked to the right.

Bullets sang in through one side window and exited through the other.

'Duck to the right?' said Jack to himself. 'That's what Wallah said to me this morning. "Don't forget to duck to the right." ' And Jack felt sad once more. And somewhat scared, of course.

Police cars were swinging around in further pursuit. Officers in passenger seats, who had mostly non-speaking parts and so needed no particular characterisation, were sliding cartridges into pump-action shotguns and looking forward to firing these.

'This is Chinatown,' said Dorothy to Jack as she took a left to head north on the 110.

Officer Wong overtook Sam Maggot's car. 'This job for me,' he said in his cod-Chinese accent. 'This call for much dangerous stunt work performed by me to much applause.' And he climbed out of the window of his speeding car and up onto its roof.

'What is that damn Chinee up to?' Sam asked his driver.

His driver just shrugged, for his was a non-speaking role.

'Whoa! Get down, Jack,' shouted Dorothy as Officer Wong's car drew level and Officer Wong leapt from the roof of his car and banged down onto theirs.

'That was impressive,' said Jack, 'although somewhat above and beyond the call of duty, I would have thought.'

'They'll give him a medal,' said Dorothy, slamming on the brakes.

Officer Wong flew forward, rolled over the bonnet and fell into the road. Dorothy drove carefully around him. 'And a neck brace, too,' she said.

Other police cars were now joining the chase. They do have a lot of police cars in LA. Mostly because during every police chase, they lose so many as they smash into one another and roll over and over into storefronts.

Dorothy swerved. Two police cars smashed into one another. One of them rolled over and over into a storefront.

'South Pasadena,' said Dorothy. 'Look—there's Eddie Park.'*

Eddie Park made Jack feel even sadder.

The big fat officer opened fire.

'Duck,' shouted Dorothy as shotgun shells blew out the rear window, causing Jack much distress and considerable ducking.

There was of course much to be enjoyed in all the excitement, in the screaming of tyres upon asphalt and pedestrians leaping out of the

---

* And there is!

way and the motor cars of innocent motorists slamming into one another. And why shouldn't there be, eh? That's what car chases are all about. And given their longevity, they probably *do* have the edge on explosions. Even really big ones.

'Ouch!' went Dorothy as the Mustang called Sally, being driven by the troubled young detective, shunted *her* rear end.

'Oi!' shouted Jack. 'That's *my* girlfriend's rear end you're shunting.'

And then Jack sort of vanished into the back of the car. Another impact crumpled up some of the boot, causing the rear seat to lift and Jack to roll into the boot.

Dorothy slammed on the brakes once more and the troubled young detective's Mustang Sally struck her rear end once more, then travelled onwards, travelled upwards, and . . .

In slow motion (praise the Lord).

Sailed forward.

And, as they had now reached a place known as the Santa Fe Dam Recreational Area, it sailed over the dam and down and down and down.

'Nasty,' said Dorothy. 'But I'm sure he leapt from the car in time.'

They were now, and praise the Lord for this also, travelling along Route 66. They were, they *really* were. Not that they were running from St Louis down to Missouri, taking in Oklahoma City, which everybody knows is oh so pretty. They were in fact passing Horse Thief Canyon Park, La Verne, Cable Airport and now Rancho Cucamonga, where a young Don Van Vliet, who would later change his name to Captain Beefheart and become a legend in his lifetime, would as a teenager try to sell a vacuum cleaner to Aldous Huxley.★

It's a really long straight road there, above San Bernardino. You can get up an unhealthy speed if you really put your foot down. Which was what the gay officer, whose day was yet to dawn, was doing. His police car overtook Sam's, much to Sam's disgust, because *his* police car had just overtaken *his*. The gay officer's police car now drew level with Dorothy's. The gay officer addressed Dorothy through his public-address system, which is located somewhere on police cars, although no one has ever been able to ascertain exactly where.

'Give yourselves up,' came his amplified voice through the special speaker in the radiator grille.† 'There's no need for all this kerfuffle. You don't really want to behave in this fashion. It's not your fault—you

★ Absolutely true.
† Ah, that's where.

are a product of your upbringing, you are programmed to behave in this way. I have this self-help manual I could lend you—'

Dorothy swerved the car and drove the gay officer off the road. His car, once again in glorious slow motion, sailed from Route 66 and down onto the famous California Speedway, where numerous speeding motorbikes, with very nice leather-clad riders, the gay officer noted, before all things went black for him, came all a-mashing into his rear parts and everywhere else.

'Right,' said Sam. 'I'm angry now.' And he leaned out of his window and fired his gun once more.

And there at last it was.

Because we *have* been expecting its arrival for some time now, if only subconsciously. But there it was at last, that great big truck, with its great big dangerous cargo on the back. It was being driven towards them at considerable speed by a trucker called Joe-Bob, who was, coincidentally—

And who was also chatting on the CB to a fellow trucker called Joe-Bob, who was, coincidentally—

'Well, that's a big ten-four,' said driver Joe-Bob. 'Heading for the City of Angels on Route Sixty-Six. Pulling turkey with a shorthaired rabbit. Doing a manky dance rattle on my blue suede shoes.'★

'Come on?' said the driver called Joe-Bob at the message-receiving end.

'I said . . . Oh, Goddamn!'

And, 'Goddamn!' also went Police Chief Sam Maggott as Dorothy swerved around the on-rushing truck and Sam Maggott's car struck it dead on.

Boom.

In slow motion.

Of course.

Some time later, Dorothy drew the raddled, bullet-pocked black-and-white to the side of the road, climbed from it and opened the boot.

Jack peered out. 'Are we still alive?' he asked.

'We're fine,' said Dorothy. 'We've shaken them off.'

Jack climbed out in a wibbly-wobbly way. 'How did you learn to drive like *that*?' he asked.

'My daddy won the Indianapolis Five Hundred,' said Dorothy. 'Oh, look, there's a police uniform in the trunk.'

★(For there is much jargon involved in being a trucker in the USA and chatting on the old CB.)

'I know,' said Jack, dusting down his all-but-naked self. 'I've been fighting with it for several miles. It smells really bad.'

'Well, you'd best put it on. Then you can drive for a bit. We don't want to arouse suspicion.'

Jack's jaw dropped. 'Well, no,' said he. 'We wouldn't want to do *that*.'

And Dorothy smiled upon Jack and said, 'Well, hurry up now, come on.'

Jack dressed himself in the uniform, and but for its acrid qualities it did have to be said that he cut a rather dashing and romantic figure. He settled down into what was left of the driving seat.

Dorothy sat beside him. 'Mmm,' she said to Jack.

'Mmm?' Jack asked. 'What means "Mmm"?'

'As in, "Mmm, you look cute."'

'Cute?' said Jack. 'A teddy bear looks cute.'

'Not your one,' said Dorothy.

And Jack once more thought of Eddie. Not that Eddie had slipped Jack's mind, but what with all the excitement and everything . . .

Eddie Bear lacked for excitement. In his cage many floors beneath the Nevada desert in Area Fifty-Two, Eddie Bear was having a bit of a snooze. And then things suddenly became exciting for Eddie, or perhaps 'alarming' was better the word.

Eddie awoke as hands were laid upon him. Rough were these hands, although not in texture. Rough as in violent and forceful.

'Ow!' went Eddie. 'That's as rude as. Get off me.'

But Eddie was hauled from his cage by the other Jack and flung to a concrete floor.

'There's no need for that!'

And then the other Jack kicked him.

'Oh!' went Eddie, climbing to his paw pads. 'You are *so* going to get yours when *my* Jack gets here.'

'No one is going to rescue you.' The other Jack took a big step forward. Eddie took several steps back. 'Along the corridor, hurry now.'

Eddie turned and plodded up the corridor. It was one of those all-over-concrete kind of jobbies with bulkhead lights at regular intervals. The number twenty-three* was painted on the walls at similarly regular intervals. Eddie assumed, correctly, that this meant that he was on the twenty-third level beneath the ground.

'Where are you taking me?' Eddie asked.

'To meet your maker,' said the other Jack.

---

* There it is again. Weird, isn't it?

'My maker was Mister Anders Anders,' said Eddie, 'the kindly, lovable white-haired old Toymaker.'

The other Jack laughed and his laugh all echoed around. 'He'll soon have his work cut out for him,' he said.

'And what does *that* mean?' Eddie asked.

'In twelve hours from now,' said the other Jack, 'Toy City will be wiped from the map. If there *is* a map with it on. My employer will suck it dry of all life. Lay it to waste. Oh yes.'

'Why?' Eddie asked. 'To what purpose?'

'Why?' asked the other Jack. 'Because we can. And to what purpose? To further our own ends.'

'Now, I'm only guessing here,' said Eddie, turning and peering up at the other Jack, 'but would these "own ends" be of the world-domination persuasion?'

'You'll know soon enough.' The other Jack nudged Eddie with his shoe. 'Now get a move on. To the elevator.'

'Where am I?' asked Eddie. 'Tell me where I am.'

'Where are we?' asked Jack. 'Exactly.'

He was making good progress, considering he had never driven a car with an internal combustion engine before. He'd almost got the hang of the gears.

Dorothy flinched as Jack changed from second to fourth.

'Exactly?' she said. 'We are travelling North on Interstate Fifteen. We just passed Las Vegas, which you would probably have liked, lots of lights and things like that. We are heading towards the Nevada desert.'

'And is that good?' Jack asked. 'Only I'm not sure what we should be doing next. The plan was to follow the American Dream. Find the top man. Beat the truth out of him.'

'Perhaps you were over-hasty bringing that meat-cleaver into play. But look on the bright side—at least we got to meet Marilyn Monroe and Sydney Greenstreet. I wish I'd got their autographs. And the names of their agents and—'

'Stop now,' said Jack. 'We'll have to go back to LA. We need the movie script. I'm sure a lot will be explained when we read it.'

'LA is no longer an option,' said Dorothy. 'And I don't know where this leaves my career. I know that it's expected of starlets to do disreputable things that will later come back to haunt them when they become famous, but I might just have stepped too far over the line this time.'

Jack sighed, changed from fourth to first, changed hastily back again and said, 'You do talk some toot at times.'

'Not a bit of it,' said Dorothy. 'The people who get to the top in this world do so because they are risk-takers. They thrive upon risk. Every woman or man at the top has a shady past. They've all done things that they wouldn't want their contemporaries to find out about. They wouldn't want these things to come out once they are famous, but they're not ashamed that they did these things. They did them because they got a thrill out of them. They did them because they are risk-takers.'

'So what are you saying?' Jack asked, as he performed another interesting gear change. 'That it's all right to do bad things?'

'It's never right to do bad things. Bad things hurt good people.'

'I don't mean to be bad,' said Jack.

'You're not bad,' said Dorothy.

'I am,' said Jack. 'I'm selfish. I put myself first.'

'*Everyone* does that.'

'Eddie doesn't,' said Jack. 'Eddie would risk anything to protect me, I know he would.'

'And you would do the same for him.'

'Of course I would,' said Jack. 'But time is running out for Eddie and if I don't find him soon and take him back to Toy City he will die.'

'You'll find him,' said Dorothy. 'Somehow.'

'Somehow,' thought Eddie, 'Jack will find me somehow.'

'Into the elevator,' said the other Jack. 'Go on now.'

Eddie entered the elevator. The other Jack joined him, pressed a button, the doors closed, the elevator rose. Eddie Bear fumed. Silently.

And then the doors took to opening and Eddie Bear gazed out.

And wondered at the view that lay before him.

It looked to be a big round room with shiny metal walls. There were all kinds of strange machines in this room. Strange machines with twinkling lights upon them, being attended to by men in white coats who all looked strangely alike.

'Where are we now?' asked Eddie.

'Central operations room,' said the other Jack. 'Go on now.'

'I do wish you'd stop saying that. It's as repetitive as.'

'Go on *now*.' And the other Jack kicked Eddie.

'But where shall we go *now*?' Jack asked.

'How about somewhere to eat?' asked Dorothy. 'Lunch would be nice.'

'I'm really not hungry.' But Jack's stomach rumbled.

'We do need a plan of some kind,' said Dorothy.

'Plan?' said Jack. 'What we need is a miracle.' Jack hunched over the wheel.

Presently they approached a route-side eatery. It was a Golden Chicken Diner. Jack drove hurriedly past it.

Somewhat later, with the police car making those alarming coughing sounds that cars will make when they are running out of fuel, they approached another eatery: Haley's Comet Lounge.

'This will do us fine,' said Dorothy.

The car clunked up to a petrol pump.★

A tall man with short hair smiled out from the shade of a veranda. He wore a drab grey mechanic's overall that accentuated his drab greyness and wiped his hands upon an oily rag, which implied an intimate knowledge of automobiles.

'Howdy, officer,' said he as Jack wound down what was left of his window. 'Suu-ee, what the Hell happened here?'

'Nothing to concern yourself with,' said Jack.

Dorothy leaned over him. And Jack sniffed her hair. 'Fill her up,' said Dorothy, 'and check the oil, please, and the suspension.'

'Have to put her up on the ramp for that, ma'am.'

'Fine, please do it.'

Dorothy led Jack off to eat as the drab grey mechanic drove the stolen police car into the garage. †

'It's best out of sight,' said Dorothy to Jack as they entered the eatery.

'Do you have money?' Jack asked as he patted his uniform pockets. 'Because I don't'

'Leave all the talking to me.'

The eatery was everything that it should have been. Everything in its right place. Long bar along the right-hand wall. Tables to the left with window views of Interstate 15. A great many framed photographs upon the walls, mostly of men in sporting attire holding large fish.

There were some trophies on a shelf behind the bar, silver trophies topped by figures of men in sporting attire holding large fish.

Behind the bar counter stood a short man with tall hair. He wore sporting attire and held a large fish.

'Good afternoon, officer, ma'am,' said he. 'Would you care to take a number?'

★ This being one of those roadside diners that had a petrol pump in front. Which was quite convenient really.

† And a garage too. How convenient was *that*?

'A number?' said Jack. 'What do you mean?'

'So that I can seat you. In the right order.'

'But there's just the two of us.'

'In the right order to be served.'

'There's still just the two of us.'

'Take a number,' said Dorothy.

'Can I have *any* number?' Jack asked.

'You can have *this* number,' said the short man with tall hair. And he placed his fish upon the countertop, peeled a number from what looked to be a date-a-day calendar jobbie on the wall next to a framed picture of a man in sporting attire holding—

'Can we sit anywhere?' Jack asked. And he viewed the tables. All were empty.

'What number do you have?' asked the short man.

'Twenty-three,'* said Jack.

'Then you're in luck. Table over there, by the window.'

Dorothy and Jack sat down at this table.

'Was I supposed to understand any of that?' Jack asked.

'What's to understand?' asked Dorothy, and she took up a menu. It was a fish-shaped menu. Jack took up one similar.

'So,' said the short man, suddenly beside them, 'allow me to introduce myself. My name is Guy and I will be your waiter. Can I recommend to you today's specials?'

Jack looked up at the short man called Guy. 'Why don't you give it a go?'

'Right,' said the short man called Guy, and he drew a tall breath. And sang a jolly song.

> We have carp from Arizona
> And perch from Buffalo,
> A great big trout
> With a shiny snout
> From the shores of Idaho.
>
> We've a pike called Spike
> And I'm sure you'd like
> A bowl of fries with him.
> There's a shark called Mark
> That I'll serve, for a lark,
> With salad to keep you slim.

---

* Damn me, not *again*!

I've monkfish, swordfish, cramp fish, cuttlefish,
Goby, goldfish, gudgeon.
I've sperm whale, starfish, bottle-nose dolphin,
I ain't no curmudgeon.

If you like salmon, perch or bass,
Mullet, hake, or flounder,
Dory, plaice, or skate, or sole,
Try Guy, he's a great all-rounder.

And there was plenty more of that, twenty-three* verses more of that, all sung in the 'country' style.

'Well,' said Jack, clapping his hands together when the song was finally done, 'I quite enjoyed that.'

'Enjoyed *what*?' asked Guy.

'The song,' said Jack.

'What song was that?'

'The one about fish.'

'Oh, *that* song. I'm sorry, officer, it's been a rough morning, what with all the toing and froing.'

'Yes,' said Jack. And added in as delicate a fashion as he could, 'Do you have anything other than fish on your menu?'

Guy looked puzzled. He *was* puzzled.

'Meat,' said Jack. 'Any meat?'

'A burger,' said Guy.

'A burger,' said Jack.

'Certainly, officer. One mackerel burger coming up. And for your lovely daughter?'

'Daughter?' said Jack.

'So sorry, officer, it's these new shoes, the insteps pinch.'

'I'll have the sardines,' said Dorothy, perusing the menu. 'Do they come with the quahog sauce?'

'Surely do, ma'am. And whiting mayo and chingree chitlins.'

'Mahser on the side?'

'With hilsa and beckti?'

'That's the way I love it.' And Dorothy smiled at Guy and he smiled back at her.

'And a mackerel burger for your uncle,' said Guy.

'Yes,' said Jack, 'With snodgrass and mong-waffle and pungdooey.

---

* If it's going to become a running gag, it's already becoming tedious. (Ed).

Oh and add a little clabwangle to my little chikadee while you're about it.'

Guy bowed and departed.

'You made all that up,' said Dorothy.

'Well, so did you.'

'Here you go then,' said Guy, presenting his discerning patrons with an overloaded tray.

'That was fast!' said Jack.

'This *is* America,' said Guy, and he placed the tray upon the table and lifted food covers from two plates.

'That's not what I ordered,' said Jack.

'Nor me,' said Dorothy.

Guy burst into tears.

Dorothy reached out and patted his shoulder. 'There's no need to go upsetting yourself,' she said. 'I'm sure that whatever this is, it will be very nice.'

'What *is it*?' asked Jack, taking up a fork and prodding at the items that lay steaming up on his plate.

'It's chicken fish,' said the sobbing Guy. 'Locally caught and as fresh as the day is long.'

'It's chicken,' said Jack. 'There's no fish at all involved here.'

''Tis too,' said Guy.

''Tis not,' said Jack. 'It's chicken. That's a chicken leg.'

'It's a *fish* leg,' said Guy.

'Fish do not have legs,' Jack informed him.

'Chicken fish do.'

'I don't believe that there is such a thing as a chicken fish,' said Jack.

'There's one there on the counter,' said Guy. 'I was petting it when you came in.'

'It doesn't have any legs.'

'I de-legged it earlier. That's what's on the plates.'

'Fish don't have wings, either,' said Dorothy. 'There are wings on my plate.'

'Well, that's where you're wrong,' said Guy. 'Flying fish have wings, everybody knows that.'

'This is definitely chicken.' Jack sniffed at the chicken on his plate.

'Mine's definitely chicken, too,' said Dorothy.

'You're sure?' Guy dabbed at his running nose with an oversized red gingham handkerchief. 'You're absolutely sure?'

'Jack here *is* a police officer,' said Dorothy, 'so he knows these things.'

'I knew it!' Guy beat a right-hand fist into a left-hand

handkerchief-carrying palm. 'I knew it. Chicken fish be damned. I've been cheated, officer. I wish to register a complaint.'

'Do you have *any* fish in this restaurant?' Jack asked.

Guy sniffed.

'That wasn't an answer,' said Jack.

Guy shrugged.

'Nor was that.'

'All right! All right!' Guy fell to his knees, although given his short-comings in the tallness department the difference in height that this made was hardly perceptible. 'I'm so sorry,' he wailed, and he beat his chest with diminutive fists. 'Thirty years I've been in business here. Thirty years in these parts, winning every fishing competition, known in these parts as Guy Haley, Champion of Champions. I took an eighty-pound buckling up at the creek in forty-seven. Never been beaten. Never been beaten.'

'Where is this leading?' Jack asked. 'Only we *are* hungry. And we *are* in a hurry.'

'I'll leave you to your chicken fish, then.'

'No,' said Jack, 'you won't. I don't want chicken. I will eat any-thing that you have, but *not* chicken.'

'All right! All right!' Guy was back on his feet.

'Get up,' said Jack.

'I *am* up.'

'Then please, in as few words as possible, offer us an explanation.'

'For what?' asked Guy.

'Would you like me to hit him?' asked Dorothy.

Guy flinched.

'No,' said Jack. 'He's only little.'

'I'm not *that* little,' said Guy.

'True enough,' said Jack. 'I'll hit you myself.'

'No, please.'

'Then tell us. Everything.'

'Well, like I say, I've been fishing these parts for—'

Jack raised his fist.

'No, please, officer, no.'

'Then tell us,' said Jack. 'Everything. And you know what I mean by that.'

'It's not my fault.' Guy wept. 'The chickens made me do it.'

'The chickens?' said Jack. *'The chickens?'*

'Out there.' Guy pointed with a short and trembly finger. 'Out there in the desert, twenty miles from here in Area Fifty-Two.'

21

'Area Fifty-Two?' went Jack, a-falling back in his seat. 'Chickens from Area Fifty-Two?'

'It's as true as I'm sitting here, although I'm actually standing up.'

'Chickens,' said Jack to Dorothy.

'Area Fifty-Two?' said Dorothy to Jack.

'Where the crashed flying saucer was taken. The head chef at the Golden Chicken Diner told me all about it.'

'It's a "chef thing",' said Guy. 'All chefs know about it.'

Jack looked very hard at Guy. '*What* did the chickens make you do?'

'Did I say *chickens*?' said Guy. 'I meant *chicken people*. The people who produce the chicken for the Golden Chicken Diners. It all comes from Area Fifty-Two, up the Interstate. The toxic waste from their factory out there in the desert polluted the creek, so I couldn't catch fish anymore. And I complained. I went out there. And their guys said that if I just kept my mouth shut they'd see to it that I had free supplies of chicken for life to sell as fish.'

'No one is ever going to be fooled by you passing off chicken as fish,' said Jack.

'No one's ever complained before,' said Guy.

'No one?' said Jack. 'How long have you been serving this chicken?'

Guy looked down at his wristlet watch. 'Since ten this morning,' he said. 'You're the first folk in the diner today.'

'Right,' said Jack, and he nodded. Thoughtfully.

'Listen, officer,' said Guy, 'this is my livelihood. Could you not just eat the chicken and pretend it's fish? What harm could it do?'

'Mister Haley,' said Jack, 'I'm going to ask you a question and I'd like you to think very carefully before you answer it. Do you think you can do that?'

Guy Haley nodded also. Perhaps even a little more thoughtfully than Jack had.

'My question is this,' said Jack. 'Why don't you just sell chicken as chicken?'

'Sell it as chicken,' Guy said. Slowly.

Jack did further noddings.

'Ah,' said Guy. 'You mean *not* pretend it's fish?'

Jack made an encouraging face. And did a bit more nodding.

'If I might just stop you there,' said Dorothy, with no head noddings involved. 'I feel that this conversation has gone quite far enough. Which way is it to Area Fifty-Two, Mister Haley?'

'Not pretend it's fish,' said Mr Haley.

'Which way?' asked Dorothy.

'Say it's chicken,' said Mr Haley.

'Which way?' asked Dorothy once more.

'Now let me just get this straight,' said Mr Haley. 'What you're suggesting is—'

But suddenly he was up off his feet and dangling in the air. Dorothy held him at arm's length and then shook him about. 'Which way is it to Area Fifty-Two?' she demanded to be told.

'That way. That way.' Guy Haley pointed. 'Five miles up the Interstate there's a turn-off to the right, a dirt road. It goes all the way there.'

'Thank you,' said Dorothy, lowering Guy to the floor. 'We'll pass on the lunch, I think. Farewell.'

And she and Jack left Haley's Comet Lounge.

'Well,' said Jack as they stood in the sunlight, 'fancy that. What a coincidence, eh? Area Fifty-Two being just up the road. And it being the place where all the chickens for the Golden Chicken Diner are produced.'

'Yes,' said Dorothy. 'Fancy that.'

'If I believed in a God,' said Jack, 'I would believe that he, she or it was smiling right down on me now. That he, or she, or it, had provided me with the miracle that I'd hoped for earlier.'

'Would you?' said Dorothy. 'Would you really?'

'Yes,' said Jack. 'I would.'

'Hey, officer,' the tall drab grey man with the short hair called out to Jack from the garage. 'Your auto's all done. Shall I bring it out?'

'Thanks,' said Jack. 'Please do.'

Sounds of engine revvings were to be heard and then the tall man drove the black-and-white from the garage.

Jack gawped somewhat at the black-and-white. It had been totally repaired. The bodywork was perfect, resprayed and waxed, too. The windows had been replaced. There was a shiny new back bumper.

The tall man climbed from the car and tossed the keys to Jack.

Jack was all but speechless.

'There's still a bit of rust inside the tailpipe,' said the tall mechanic. 'I hope you don't mind about that.'

Jack shook his head. 'You fixed it all up,' he said. 'That is incredible.'

'It's nothing,' said the mechanic, getting to work on his hands with an oily rag. 'After all, this *is* America.'

'Yes,' said Jack. 'Quite so. So, er, what do I owe you?'

The tall mechanic winked. 'Nothing at all,' he said. 'You scratch my back and I'll scratch yours, if you know what I mean.'

'Not exactly,' said Jack.

'Well,' said the tall mechanic, 'I have been guilty of one or two minor misdemeanours, and if you, as a police officer, could turn a blind eye to them, then we're all square. Is that okay with you?'

'Absolutely,' said Jack, settling himself back behind the steering wheel and taking a sniff at the Magic Tree that now hung from the rear-view mirror. 'This is America, after all. Consider yourself forgiven in the eyes of the law.'

'Why, thank you kindly, officer.' The tall mechanic closed the driver's door upon Jack. Dorothy sat herself down on the passenger seat and patted at the refurbished upholstery.

'I mean, it's no big deal,' said the tall mechanic. 'And I only did twenty-three* of them.'

'Twenty-three,' said Jack, sticking the key into the ignition and giving it a little twist. The engine purred beautifully.

'And they all had it coming, those daughters of Satan. High-school girls with their skirts all up to here,' and he gestured to where these skirts were all up to. 'Flaunting themselves. And those nuns, too.'

'Excuse me?' said Jack, looking up at the tall mechanic. All shadow-faced now, the sunlight behind him.

'Killed 'em quick and clean. Well, some not so clean, perhaps, but after all the torturing was done, they was begging for death anyway,' said the tall mechanic. 'And I only ate the good bits.'

'Right,' said Jack. 'Well, we have to be on our way now. Thank you for fixing the car.'

'No sweat!' The tall mechanic took a step back.

'Goodbye,' said Jack, and he drove away.

---

* Make that the last (Ed).

The tall mechanic sidled out onto the road, where he waved farewell with his oily rag.

'Twenty-three,' said Jack to Dorothy. 'Did he just say what I thought he just said?'

Dorothy said, 'Yes, he did.'

'That's what I thought.' Jack halted the car.

The tall mechanic stepped out into the middle of the road. 'Everything okay up there?' he called. 'No trouble with the engine?'

Jack looked at Dorothy.

And Dorothy looked at Jack.

And then Jack put the car into reverse, revved the engine, let out the clutch and reversed at considerable speed over the tall mechanic.

And then to be sure, as you *have* to be sure, drove over the body once more.

Then backed up a couple more times to be *absolutely* sure.

And then proceeded on his way.

No words passed between Dorothy and Jack for a while.

And when words *did* pass between them once again, these words did not include any reference to the tall mechanic.

'Slow down a bit,' said Dorothy. 'We must be almost there.'

Jack slowed down a bit. 'There?' he asked. '*That* dirt road, do you think?'

That dirt road had a big signpost beside it. The signpost read:

DON'T EVEN THINK ABOUT DRIVING UP HERE.

'I think we should drive up there,' said Dorothy.

Jack steered the spotless police car onto the dusty dirt road.

'What are you planning to do,' asked Dorothy, 'when we get there?'

'Rescue Eddie,' said Jack.

'But we don't know for certain that he's there.'

'I do,' said Jack. 'He is.'

'But you can't know for certain.'

'Oh yes I can,' said Jack. 'I can feel him. In here.' And Jack tapped at his temple. 'The closer we get, the more I can feel him. I can feel him, and he's hurting.'

And Eddie Bear *was* hurting. He'd been kept waiting about in a concrete corridor outside a big steel rivet-studded door for quite some time now. The other Jack had passed this quite some time by kicking

Eddie up and down the corridor. So Eddie was *really* hurting. And hurting more than just from the kickings.

Eddie felt decidedly odd. Slightly removed from himself, somehow, as if he didn't quite fit into his body any more. It was a decidedly odd and most disconcerting sensation. And it was not at all helped by the kickings.

The other Jack squared up for another boot. Belts clunked and clanked and the big steel door slid open.

'Thanks for *that*,' said Eddie.

The other Jack kicked him through the opening.

Eddie came to rest upon a carpeted floor. It was most unpleasantly carpeted. With poo. Chicken poo.

'Urgh,' went Eddie, and he struggled up from the floor.

Eddie was now, it had to be said, a somewhat unsightly bear. He was thoroughly besmirched with sewage and cell dust and now chicken poo. Eddie was *not* a bear for cuddling, not a bear to be hugged.

'So,' said a voice, and Eddie searched for its source, 'So, Mister Bear, we meet at last.'

Eddie could make out a desk of considerable proportions and behind this a chair, with its back turned to him. Behind this chair and affixed to the wall were numerous television screens and upon these were displayed numerous scenes of American life. Most being played out via the medium of the television show.

The shows meant nothing to Eddie and so he did not recognise George Reeves as Superman, Lucille Ball in *I Love Lucy*, Phil Silvers as Sergeant Bilko or Roy Rogers on Trigger.

On one TV screen, Eddie viewed a newscast. It showed scenes of devastation, crashed police cars, a wrecked AC Cobra and a Ford Mustang called Sally. And a photograph was being displayed also. A mugshot of a wanted man. Eddie gawped at the mugshot: it was a mugshot of Jack.

The desk and the chair back and the TV screens, too, were all besmutted with poo. Chicken poo. Eddie Bear sniffed at the air of this room. It must have smelled pretty bad. But Eddie Bear couldn't smell it. Eddie Bear had no sense of smell left whatsoever.

'Who are you?' asked Eddie. 'Who is this?'

The chair behind the desk swung around and Eddie Bear viewed the sitter.

The sitter on the chair was no chicken.

The sitter was Eddie Bear.

★

'Whoa,' went Jack and he shuddered.

'Are you all right?' asked Dorothy.

'Yes,' said Jack. 'I suppose so. I went all cold there. Have you ever heard that expression about feeling as if someone just walked over your grave?'

'I've heard it, but I've never understood it.'

Jack peered out through the windscreen. He had the wipers on now—there was a lot of dust. 'Are we nearly there yet?' he asked.

Dorothy did peerings also. 'There's something up ahead,' she said. 'It looks like some big military installation with a big wire fence around it. What are you going to do?'

'Bluff it out,' said Jack. 'This is a police car. I'm a policeman. We'll get in there somehow.'

'Seems reasonable,' said Dorothy. 'Let's just hope that there's no real policemen around.'

'I don't think that's very likely out here,' said Jack.

'Out *where*?' asked Police Chief Samuel J. Maggott, shouting somewhat into the mouthpiece of his telephone. Sam was considerably bandaged, but back behind his desk. 'Speak up, boy, I can hardly hear you, what?'

Words came to him through the earpiece.

'You're saying what? You saw the midday newscast? The wanted maniac, Jack? That's right. Dressed as a police officer, at your lounge? Left without paying for his chicken-fish lunch? Drove over your mechanic? How many times? That many, eh? And he's gone on to where? I see.'

Samuel J. Maggott replaced the receiver.

And then picked it up again.

'Get me Special Ops,' he told the telephonist. 'Get me Special Ops, get me a chopper and put out an all-points bulletin.'

'You look put out,' said the Eddie in the chair. 'In fact you look all in. You look as wretched as a weevil with the wobbles.'

'What are you?' asked Eddie Bear. 'You're not me. What are you?'

'I'm the you of this world,' said the other Eddie.

'No you're not,' said the Real McCoy. 'Toys don't live in this world.' Eddie Bear paused. 'Or do they?'

The other Jack loomed over Eddie. 'Would you like me to knock him about a bit, boss?' he asked.

'That won't be necessary. Eddie and I are going to get along just fine, aren't we, Eddie? We are going to be as cosy as two little peas in a little green pod.'

Eddie looked down at his grubby old self.

'Yes, you're right,' said the other Eddie. 'You really are in disgusting condition. You're as foul as a fetid fur-ball. We'll have to get you all cleaned up. Jack, take Eddie to the cleaning facility, see that he gets all cleaned up.'

'Can I hold his head under the water? Or use the high-pressure hose?' asked the other Jack.

'No, Jack, I want Eddie in tip-top condition. He's very precious, is Eddie. After all, he'll soon be the last of his kind.'

'What?' asked Eddie. 'What do you mean?'

'Hurry,' said his other self. 'The countdown has already begun.'

The other Jack picked Eddie up and hurled him out into the corridor.

The *other* other Jack, the real Jack that was, drew the police car to a halt before a little guard post. A little guard issued from this post and made his way to the car.

Jack wound down the window.

The guard wore a rather stylish golden uniform with a Golden Chicken logo picked out in red upon the right sleeve. He took off his golden cap and mopped at his brow with an oversized red gingham handkerchief.

'Good day, officer,' he said. 'It's a hot'n, ain't it?'

'Very hot,' said Jack. 'Would you open the gates, please?'

'Have to ask the nature of your visit, officer.'

'Official business,' said Jack. 'I'd like to say more, but you know how it is.'

'Not precisely,' said the guard. 'Could you be a little more explicit?'

'Well, I could,' said Jack, 'but frankly I just don't have the time. Would you mind dealing with this, Dorothy?'

'Not at all.' Dorothy left the police car. Walked around to the guard's side. Dealt the guard a brutal blow to the skull and returned to the passenger seat.

'Thank you,' said Jack. 'Would you mind opening the gates now?'

'Why don't you just smash through them with the car?' asked Dorothy. 'It's so much more exciting, isn't it!'

'This is an exciting machine,' said the other Jack.

He and Eddie now stood in another room. One of an industrial nature. There were conveyor belts in this room and big, ugly-looking machines into which they ran in and out again.

'Prototype, this,' said the other Jack. 'Chicken cleanser. Chickens go in this end,' and he pointed, 'through the cleansing machine, out again, along that belt there, then through the drier, then out of that, then through the de-featherer, then out again. Just like that.' And he ambled over to a big control panel, threw a couple of switches and pressed a few buttons. Great churnings of machinery occurred and conveyor belts began to judder into life. 'Never went into mass production though, this model. The chickens kept getting all caught up inside. Came out in shreds, some of them. Didn't half squawk, I can tell you.'

'Now just you see here,' said Eddie. 'I don't think that I—'

But Eddie was hauled once more from the floor.

And Jack in the car gave another terrible shudder.

'Through the gates it is, then,' said he, and he put his foot down hard.

'And put your foot down hard,' said Samuel J. Maggott to the pilot of the helicopter that now stood upon the rooftop of Police Headquarters, slicing the sunlit sky with its blades.

Horrible slicing, mashing sounds came from the chicken cleanser.

And terrible cries from Eddie Bear.

And then he was on the conveyor belt again.

And into the drying machine.

And great puffs of steam and smoke belched from this machine.

And further cries came from Eddie.

Cries of vast despair.

And the other Jack clapped his hands together.

And Eddie cried some more.

And the stolen police car smashed through the gates and Jack did further shudderings.

Ahead lay a long, low concrete bunker kind of jobbie. Jack swerved the police car to a halt before it.

'Looks rather formidable,' he said to Dorothy. 'I can only see one door, and it appears to be of sturdy metal. Should I try to smash the car through it, do you think?'

'No,' said Dorothy. 'Best not. We might well need to make a speedy getaway in this car. I'd use this, if I were you,' and she handed Jack a plastic doodad.

Jack examined same and said, 'What is it?'

'Security pass key card,' said Dorothy. 'I took it from the guard.'

Jack smiled warmly at Dorothy. 'Come on then,' he said.

★

'Come on then,' said the other Jack. 'Up and at it, Mister Bear. Oh dear.'

Eddie Bear looked somewhat out of sorts. He was certainly a clean bear now. Very clean. And dry, too. And sweetly smelling, although he wasn't personally aware of this. But there was something not quite right about Eddie. His head seemed very big and his body very small. And his arms were all sort of flapping sleeves, whereas his legs were thickly packed stumps.

And as for his ears.

'What have you done to me?' he asked, in a very strange voice.

'Your stuffing seems to have become somewhat redistributed,' said the other Jack. 'But no matter. I'll soon beat you back into the correct shape.'

And outside Jack gave another very large shudder.

And now up in the sky in the police helicopter, Samuel J. Maggott remembered that he had this pathological fear of flying, which his therapist had assured him stemmed back to a freak pogo-stick/low-bridge accident Sam had suffered as a child.

'Fly lower,' Sam told the pilot.

'Really?' said the pilot. 'Can I?'

'Of course you can—why not?'

'Because it's not allowed,' said the pilot. 'We're not allowed to fly at less than two hundred feet, unless we're landing or taking off, of course.'

'Why?' asked Sam.

'Helicopters have a tendency to crash into power lines if they fly low,' said the pilot.

'Fly low,' said Sam. 'And look out for power lines.'

'Can I fly above all the police cars and the military vehicles that are now speeding along Route Sixty-Six?' asked the pilot.

'That would be preferable,' said Sam.

'Splendid,' said the pilot. And he flung the joystick forward.

And Samuel J. Maggott was sick.

And so was Eddie Bear. He coughed up sawdust and nuts.

'Not on my floor,' said his other self. 'You'll soil my chicken droppings.'

'Sorry,' said Eddie, 'but this joker punched me all about.'

'But you look much better.'

Eddie patted at himself. 'I don't feel very well.'

'Then perhaps you'd like a drink?'

'If it's beer, I would,' said Eddie.

'Jack,' said the other Eddie, 'fetch Eddie here a beer, and one for me, too, and one for yourself.'

The other Jack looked down at Eddie Bear. 'I don't think I should leave you alone with him, boss,' said he. 'He might turn uglier.'

'He'll be fine. Eddie and I have much to discuss. Hurry along now.'

The other Jack saluted and then he left the room.

'He never makes me laugh,' said the other Eddie. 'Some comedy sidekick he is, eh?'

'Eh?' said Eddie. 'Eh?'

'Well, he's as funny as a fart in a lift.'

Eddie nodded and said, 'I suppose so.'

'Sit down,' said his other self.

'What, here, in the chicken poo?'

'Quite so—they are rather messy, aren't they? But they do call the shots, as it were, so who are we to complain?'

'I'll just stand then,' said Eddie.

'You do that, good fellow.'

And so Eddie stood. 'And while I'm standing,' he said, 'perhaps,' and now he shouted. Loudly. *'Perhaps you can tell me what in the name of any of the Gods is going on here?'*

'Quietly, *please*.' The other Eddie put his paws to his ears. 'It's a quite simple matter. And I am certain that an intelligent bear such as yourself, one skilled in the art of detection, has, as these Americans would say, figured it all out by now.'

'Are you in charge here?' Eddie asked. 'Are you the one in control?'

The other Eddie inclined his head. 'I'm in charge,' he said.

'And there's only the one of you? Not more than one, no other copies?'

'Just me,' said the other Eddie. 'Just me, just you.'

'And so *you* are the murderer,' said Eddie. 'The one who murdered the clockwork monkeys, and then the band at Old King Cole's, and then the orchestra at the Opera House. I saw you there.'

'And I saw you, and I applauded your enterprise, risking all to enter this world. Very brave. Very foolish, but very brave all the same.'

Eddie Bear made a puzzled face. 'Why did you do it?' he asked. 'Murder your own kind? To reproduce them as free giveaways to sell chicken? It doesn't make any sense.'

The other Eddie laughed. 'You call it murder,' he said, 'but here we call it franchising. Your kind are not my kind, Eddie. I am not of your world. Your world is very special. To those in this world it is a land of dreams, of make-believe, where toys live and have adventures. A world of fantasy.'

'It's real enough for me,' said Eddie Bear

'But it's a mess. Every world is a mess, every world needs organisation.'

'This one certainly does.'

'Which is why *we* are organising it. Let's face it, you tried to organise yours, didn't you? When you were mayor of Toy City?'

'Ah,' said Eddie, 'that. Well, that didn't go quite as well as it might have.'

'But you tried your best and we observed your progress. You tried your best but it just didn't work. And so we decided that the best thing to do would be to wipe the slate clean, as it were. Out with the old and in with the new, as it were. Take the best bits out of the old, employ them in this world. Then do away with the worst.'

'I don't know what you're talking about,' said Eddie, 'but I know I don't like it, whatever it is.'

'I'll explain everything,' said the other Eddie. 'And then you can make your comments. Ah, here comes Jack with the beer.'

Jack entered bearing beers. He gave one to Eddie and Eddie took it between his paws and gave it a big swig.

'I spat in it,' said the other Jack.

And Eddie spat out his swig.

'That wasn't very nice,' said the other Eddie, accepting his beer.

'I know,' said the other Jack, 'but it made me laugh. Cheers!' and he raised his bottle.

'Cheers,' said the other Eddie. 'Oh and by the way, I saw a little light twinkling on my desk a while ago. It would seem that someone has penetrated the outer perimeter.'

'That's right,' said the other Jack. 'His friend,' and he cast a thumb in Eddie's direction.

'My Jack?' said Eddie.

'*Your* Jack,' said the other Jack, 'smashed through the gates in a stolen police car, in the company of some young woman, and entered the bunker using the guard's security pass key card.'

'Most enterprising,' said the other Eddie. 'And where are he and the young woman now?'

'In the elevator, on their way down.'

'Really?' said the other Eddie. 'Well, we can't have that, can we?'

And he reached out a paw and pressed it down on a button on his desk.

★

And in the elevator all the lights went out.
    'Oh dear,' said Jack. 'I don't like this.'
    And then the elevator juddered.
    And then it began to fall.
    And Jack in the darkness went, 'Oh dear me.'
    And the elevator plunged.

22

Down went the elevator, down and down. Down and down in the dark. And up rushed the ground, it seemed, in the dark. Up and up and up.

And then there was a sickening sound that echoed all around and about.

Eddie heard something and felt something, too.

'What did you do?' he asked.

'Nothing to concern yourself with,' replied his other self, taking up his beer between his paws and draining much of it away. 'These paws are a real pain at times, aren't they? No opposable thumbs—'

'I had hands with those once,' said Eddie sadly. 'But tell me, *what* did you do?'

'Just switched off the elevator. Don't go getting yourself upset.'

Eddie rocked gently upon his paw pads. He felt upset, he felt unsettled, he felt altogether wrong.

'You look a little shaky,' said his other self. 'But never mind, it will pass. Everything will pass. But it is a great shame about the hands. They were very nice hands you had. I can't understand why everyone thought them so creepy.'

'What?' went Eddie, raising a now droopy head. 'How did *you* know about me having hands? I don't understand.'

'I know all about you,' said his other self. 'It is my job to know all about you. Learn every subtle nuance, as it were. *Be* you, in fact. I told you, we kept a careful eye on you when you were mayor.'

'I'll tell you what,' said Eddie Bear, 'I really hate sighing, you know. Sighing gets me down. I have a normally cheerful disposition, but once in a while I really feel the need for a sigh. And this is one of those times.' And so Eddie sighed. And a deep and heartfelt sigh it was, and it set the other Jack laughing.

'And so why sigh you, Eddie Bear?' asked his other self.

'Because,' said Eddie, 'I don't understand. I consider myself to be more than competent when it comes to the matter of private detective work. I pride myself upon my competence. But for the life that is in me, I do not understand what is going on around here. I don't understand why you've done what you've done, what you intend to do next, nor why you look just like me, and why this gormster—' Eddie gestured towards the other Jack '—looks like my best friend Jack.'

'And so you would like a full and thorough explanation, couched in terms readily understandable to even the simplest soul?'

Eddie sighed once more. 'Please feel free to be condescending,' he said. 'I've never been very good with subtle.'

'Nice touch of irony.' Eddie's other self finished his beer and set his bottle aside. 'All right, it is only fair. I will tell you all. Jack, you may leave us now.'

'Oh, I don't think so.'

'I think so, Jack. Take your leave at once.'

'But he'll go for you, sir—he's a vicious little bastard.'

'Language,' said Eddie's other self. 'Eddie needs to know and it is right that he should know. Bears have a code of honour, don't they, Eddie?'

'Noted for it,' said Eddie. 'Along with their sexual prowess. And their bravery, of course. Bears are as noble as. Everyone knows that.'

'And so if I ask you to swear upon all that means anything to you that you will make no attempt to harm me during the time that I am explaining everything to you, I can rely on you to honour this oath?'

'Absolutely,' said Eddie Bear.

'Because you see, Jack,' said the other Eddie, 'bears can't cross their fingers behind their backs, so when they swear they have to stick to what they've sworn.'

The other Jack made non-committal sounds.

'So clear off,' the other Eddie told him.

And, grumbling somewhat, that is what he did.

'Care to take a little trip?' asked Eddie's other self.

Eddie Bear did shruggings. 'Is my Jack all right?' he asked.

'Don't worry about your Jack. Would you care to take a little trip?'

'It depends where to.'

'I could just kill you,' said Eddie's other self.

'I'd love to take a little trip,' said Eddie. 'Teddy bears' picnic, is it?'

'In a manner of speaking. Step a little closer to the desk, that's it. Now, let me join you.' And Eddie and his other self now stood next to each other. 'And if I just press this.'

And then.

The horrible chicken-poo-carpeted floor fell away.

Eddie and his other self hovered in the air, borne by a silver disc that, it seemed, shunned the force of gravity.

And this disc, with these two standing upon it, slowly drifted downwards.

Eddie peered fearfully over the rim of the disc. 'What is happening here?' he asked in a rather shaky voice.

'Fear not, my friend, fear not. I am going to take you on a tour of this establishment. You will see how everything works and why it does. We shall chat along the way.'

'Hm,' went Eddie. And that was all.

And the slim disc drifted down.

'The technology that drives this,' explained the other Eddie, 'is years ahead, centuries ahead, of the technology that exists upon this particular world. And the denizens of this particular world will never catch up with such technology. That will not be allowed to happen.'

'The chickens from space,' said Eddie Bear.

'Well, hardly from space, but in a way you're right. There are many, many worlds, Eddie Bear, many, many inhabited worlds. But they are not out in space somewhere. They are all here, all next to each other, as the world of Toy City is next to the world of Hollywood, separated by a curtain, as it were, that only those in the know are capable of penetrating.'

The flying disc dropped low now, over a vast industrial complex, great machines attended to by many, many workers.

'And what is this?' asked Eddie.

'Chicken production,' his other self explained. 'Humankind has this thing about eating chickens. But as logic would dictate to anyone who sat down and thought about it for five minutes, it is simply impossible to produce the vast quantity of chickens required for human consumption every day. It would require chicken-breeding farms covering approximately a quarter of this world's surface. So all the chickens that are eaten in the USA are produced here. They are artificial, Eddie, cloned from a single chicken. The pilot of a chicken scout ship that crashed here ten years ago. Soulless clones—they are not *real* chickens.'

'From space?'

'No, not from space. Do try to pay attention. Recall if you will the various religions that predominate in Toy City. You have The Church of Mechanology, followed by clockwork toys who believe that the universe is powered by a clockwork motor. The cult of Big Box Fella, He Come, a Jack-in-the-Box cult that believes that the universe is a big box containing numerous other boxes. There is more than a hint of truth to their beliefs. But what I am saying is this: all these religions have a tiny piece of the cosmic jigsaw puzzle. The chickens just happen to have a far larger piece.'

'Yes, well,' said Eddie, 'everyone is entitled to believe whatever they want to believe, in my opinion, as long as it causes no hurt to others. I happen to be an elder in an exclusive teddy bear sect, The Midnight Growlers.'

'You are its one and only member,' said the other Eddie as the flying disc flew on over the seemingly endless faux-chicken production plant. 'My point is this. All religions are correct in one or other respect. All religions possess a little part of the whole. The followers of Big Box Fella are about the closest. All life in the entire Universe exists right here, upon this planet. But this planet is not, as such, a planet. It is the centre of everything. The centre of production, as it were. There are countless worlds, all next to each other, each unaware of the existence of the world next door. Sometimes beings from one world become capable of penetrating to the world next door. And do you know what happens when they do?'

'Bad things,' said Eddie. 'That would be my guess.'

'Well, there have been *some* bad things, I grant you. But I will tell you what the beings from the world next door discover when they enter a new world. They discover that, but for a few subtle differences of belief and appearance, things are exactly the same. There are the many who toil and the privileged few who control their toiling and profit from their toil. This is a universal truth.'

'And so you and whoever or *whatever* you represent are going to do something about this injustice?' asked Eddie.

'You are seeking to be ironic, I suppose?'

'Very much so,' said Eddie.

'And not without good cause. It is not possible to change the status quo with anything less than force of arms. You tried, Eddie, when you were mayor. You tried to put your world to rights. And what came of your good intentions?'

'Bad things,' said Eddie, sadly. 'Hence the loss of my hands.'

'Exactly. You tried, but you failed. But it was the fact that you were trying that drew our attention to you. One of our craft penetrated the world Beyond The Second Big O. To your side of it. And we observed your efforts. And we thought to ourselves, things *could* work out in this world. Things could be better. And so *I* was created, to replace you, so that smoothly and without incident I could be substituted for you and run your world for our own ends.'

'You thorough-going swine,' said Eddie. 'And I mean that offensively, as some of my best friends are pigs.'

'But after all the effort of creating the perfect facsimile of you, what happened? As I was on the point of eliminating you in order to take your place, you made such a foul-up of being mayor, because in your naivety you thought that things could be changed in a nice way, that you were kicked out of office. Leaving *me* redundant.'

'Poor old you,' said Eddie.

'It was touch and go,' said his other self. 'They were all for melting me down, me and the Jack they'd created to substitute for your Jack. But I had a plan.'

'I often have a plan,' said Eddie, sadly.

'Of course you do, which is one of the things I like about you—we have so much in common.' And the other Eddie patted Eddie on the shoulder.

And Eddie considered just how easy it would be to push him right off the flying disc.

But then there just might be a problem getting off that disc himself.

And there was the matter of the bears' code of honour.

'So I came up with this plan,' said Eddie's other self. 'Why not clear out Toy City? It could become a decent environment, with a lick of paint and a bit of rebuilding. And what with the ever-expanding population of Chicken World—'

'Chicken World?' said Eddie. 'There really *is* a Chicken World?'

'Of course. And one with no natural predators. And you *would* be surprised at just how many chickens a single rooster can, how shall I put this, "get through" in a single day. The chickens are looking to expand—to your world, to this one. Once all the indigenous inhabitants have been, how shall I put this?'

'Murdered?' Eddie suggested.

'That's probably the word. Or a least subdued. So I took an overview of the denizens of Toy City. In this world, the young, and indeed the old, just love toys. Especially *special* toys. Collectables. They just love them. And so, I thought, why not have the toys of Toy City work for us, to aid us in our plans for expansion.'

'You sick, and how shall I put this? *Bastards!*' said Eddie.

'Tut, tut, tut. It's business—and survival, of course. Imagine, if you will, travelling to another world and discovering that its inhabitants feasted upon your kind. Bred them, slaughtered them and ate them.

That is what the pilots of the first chicken craft, the one that crashed here in the desert near Roswell in nineteen forty-seven, discovered. One lone survivor was brought here to this establishment. Happily he was able to communicate, to make deals in order to ensure his survival. And when he offered an alternative to all the eating of his own kind that went on here, by demonstrating that it was possible, using advanced chicken technology, to mass-produce ersatz chickens and eggs at a fraction of the cost of real ones, the humans went for it. Fools that they are. And there you have it.'

'No,' said Eddie. 'That's not fair. I assume that you intend to have me killed. Am I correct in this assumption?'

The other Eddie shook his head.

'No?' said Eddie Bear.

'No,' said his other self. 'You will die—and shortly, too—but not at my hands. Your kind cannot survive in this world. There is a certain, how shall I put this, magic to your kind. We remain unable to discover just how the kindly, lovable white-haired old Toymaker imbues toys with life. But toys cannot live here. Surely you noticed when you arrived here—your companion's watch ceased to work, then his weaponry.'

'You *saw* that?'

'We see all. Remember, you and Jack were abducted and implanted with homing beacons up your bums. We've known where you were from the start. Jack's watch soon failed, then his weaponry and then that calculating pocket of his—'

'Wallah,' said Eddie. 'He nicked it from Tinto. I should have known. That's how he figured out about the Opera House.'

'Wallah is dead and you will soon die,' said the other Eddie. 'Sad but true. So I suppose it will do no harm to explain the rest. By channelling the very essence, the very soul-stuff of those toys, the monkeys, the band, the orchestra, and soon *all* of your kind, by drawing out their essence and funnelling it into free giveaways to promote the sale of our *special* chicken, we eliminate all competition. No real chickens will be eaten on this world again. And within one year, after the release of the movie, when the Golden Chicken chain goes global and every chicken that is eaten is one of our special chickens, this world will be ours.'

'I don't quite follow how,' said Eddie.

'Because,' said Eddie's other self, 'our special chicken has rather special qualities. It is, for one thing, highly addictive. The more you eat, the more you want to eat. The population of this world will grow fatter and fatter and they will also grow more and more aggressive as we up the dosages of certain hormones. By the turn of the next century this country, so well known for its love of democracy and justice, will begin to invade Middle Eastern states. And here, the religion of this world, well, at least one of them, which prophesies something called Armageddon, will prove correct in its prophecy. The world of men will wipe itself out. There will be no more men. And then the chicken population, having already expanded into *your* world, will take over this one as well. There's plenty of room here for a long time yet.'

'And when there isn't?' Eddie asked.

'Then the chickens will continue onwards.'

'Well, bravo to the chickens,' said Eddie Bear.

'What?' said Eddie's other self.

'I said, bravo. What else can I say? I suppose that whoever is at the top of, how shall *I* put this, the "food chain" wins the race for survival. And why would I expect chickens to respect my kind? Men do not respect my kind. The men of Toy City, the P.P.P.s, have no respect for toys. Bravo the chickens, I say.'

'You are taking this very well, considering.'

'Considering *what*? That I am soon to die? I'm resigned to it now, I suppose. How long do I have, by the way?'

'A few hours, perhaps.'

'I thought so,' said Eddie. 'I've been growing weirder ever since I got here. I'm not inside myself for much of the time. But then what can I say? I've had a good life, really, a long life, and I've done interesting things. Dying won't be so bad, I suppose.'

'I find that really quite moving,' said Eddie's other self.

'It comes to us all,' said Eddie. 'It will come to you too, eventually.'

Eddie's other self gave Eddie Bear another shoulder pat.

'Could I have a bit of a hug?' asked Eddie.

'Yes, indeed you can.' And Eddie's other self gave a big hug to Eddie.

'And could I ask you just one little favour?'

'Go on then, just ask.'

'Well,' said Eddie, 'I know that Jack shot down one of the chickens' flying saucers. But I personally didn't have any part in that, so I was wondering, do you think I could meet to one of the chickens before I die? Just to say hello, just to try to understand. The King of all the chickens, perhaps.'

'It's the Queen, actually.'

'Then do you think I could meet her, perhaps? Is she here, in this complex?'

The other Eddie grinned from ear to furry ear.

'She *is*,' said Eddie. 'She *is* here, isn't she?'

The other Eddie nodded his grinning head. 'Oh yes she is,' he said.

'And do you think she might grant me an audience?'

'Well, she *might*. But I'm not quite certain why she would. You see, she's a little busy at the moment.'

'I wouldn't take up much of her time,' said Eddie. 'Because I don't have much time, do I?'

'No, that's true. But she *is* very busy, coordinating the final phase of the Toy City project.'

'The final phase?' asked Eddie.

'Tonight—well, within the hour—the task force will fly from here, through The Second Big O of the Hollywood sign, into your world and gather up the remaining denizens of Toy City. To be franchised.'

'All of them?' said Eddie.

'So you see, she *is* rather busy.'

'Well, it was just a thought.'

The other Eddie looked hard at Eddie Bear. 'You really *are* taking this *very* well,' he said.

And Eddie Bear shrugged.

And then a sound was to be heard. A terrible sound, as of sirens.

'What was *that*?' asked Eddie.

'A breach of security.'

'Jack?'

'*Not* Jack. I will have to take us aloft.'

'Do what you have to,' said Eddie.

And through some means that Eddie did not understand, but which evidently involved the application of advanced chicken technology, Eddie's other self took the flying disc aloft and soon they were back in the chicken-poo-splattered room.

And the other Eddie was back behind his desk and viewing TV screens.

'Most inconvenient,' he said. 'It would seem that we have a heavy police presence above.'

'Really?' said Eddie. 'Why?'

'Well, *that*,' and the other Eddie pointed to a screen that displayed the sweating face of a large and bandaged black man who was struggling from a grounded helicopter, 'is LA Police Chief Samuel J. Maggott. He arrested your chum Jack, who later escaped from police custody and found his way to the Haley's Comet Lounge. It was from there that your chum was directed to come here.'

'I don't quite understand *that*,' said Eddie. 'In fact, I don't understand it at all.'

'Mister Haley is in our employ. As are many others. However, it appears that Mister Haley overstepped the mark and reported your chum to the police. Mister Haley is what is known as a hick. He's as dumb as a dancing dingbat.'

'So what do you intend to do?' Eddie asked.

'I am not altogether sure.' The other Eddie pressed buttons on his desk. Other TV screens lit up to display many black and white police cars, all within the confines of the wire-fenced compound, and many armed officers climbing from these cars.

'Tricky,' said the other Eddie.

'Very,' said Eddie. 'And at such a difficult time for you. Do you think I might make a suggestion?'

'Well, you *might*—go on.'

'Well,' said Eddie, 'my end is near. I understand that and I *have* come to terms with it. Would I be correct in assuming that my Jack plunged to his death in that elevator?'

'Well . . .' said the other Eddie.

'I thought so,' said Eddie. 'But no hard feelings. You were doing what had to be done. I understand that.'

'You really *are* a most understanding little bear.'

'Most,' said Eddie. 'So, the police have come for Jack, haven't they? So why not give them what they've come for?'

'Give them his body. That's a good idea.'

'No,' said Eddie. 'That's a *bad* idea. That would attract much suspicion. Questions would be asked. Policemen would hang around the crime scene. Bad idea, don't do it.'

'No,' said the other Eddie. 'You're right. Then what?'

'I'll tell you *what*.' And Eddie Bear smiled. And it was a broad one. It was an ear-to-ear.

The other Eddie pressed another button. He had so many buttons on his poo-flecked desk. 'Jack,' he called into an intercom. 'Jack, are you there?'

'Yes,' said the voice of the other Jack. 'I'm here, boss—what do you want? Does that bear need further roughing-up?'

'No, Jack, no. But we have a bit of trouble upstairs. A lot of policemen have arrived. Would you mind going up to speak to them?'

'What do you want me to say to them, sir?'

'Well, you'll find a big sweaty black one puffing away next to a helicopter. Go up to him and say these words: "I give myself up." Do you think you can remember that?'

'Well, of course, sir, but I don't quite understand.'

'All will become clear. Just do it, please—it is a matter of the utmost importance. *And* a direct order. Do you understand *that*?'

The voice of Jack said, 'Yes, boss.'

The other Eddie switched off the intercom. 'I suppose you'd like to watch this on the TV screen,' he said to Eddie. Eddie Bear nodded. 'Could we watch it on *all* the screens?' he asked.

And Eddie Bear *did* enjoy the screenings. He enjoyed watching the other Jack shambling over to Police Chief Samuel J. Maggott. He enjoyed the look of surprise and shock on the face of the other Jack, which the other Eddie brought into close-up, when the other Jack found himself surrounded by *so* many armed policemen. And although he couldn't actually hear the remonstrations, he enjoyed the shouting faces. And then the truncheonings down and the police boots going in. Eddie did enjoy those boots going in.

Very much indeed.

'Now you see,' said the other Eddie, clearly enjoying it, too, '*that* makes me laugh. In fact, *that* is the first time that my comedy sidekick Jack *has* made me laugh.'

'I'm so pleased that I could be of assistance,' said Eddie, and he rocked somewhat as he said it.

'Oh,' said the other Eddie. 'You're all but gone, aren't you?'

'All but so,' said Eddie Bear.

'And do you know,' said the other Eddie, 'I *do* feel for you. Somehow. I *do*, really.'

'Thanks,' said Eddie Bear.

'And look.' The other Eddie pointed to the TV screens. 'They're leaving. All the police are leaving.'

'Glad to be of assistance. Like I said.'

'You're as genuine as a golden guinea,' said the other Eddie. 'I'll tell you what. As you haven't much time, I *will* let you meet Her Majesty. In fact, I will take you to her now. It's only fair—I owe you. Okay?'

'Okay,' said Eddie. 'Thanks.'

'Come on then,' said the other Eddie. 'Let's do it.'

And he pressed yet another button on his desk.

And they did.

23

The flying disc dropped down once more through the floor hole in the poo-splattered office. It drifted downwards and downwards and as it did so Eddie made enquiries regarding its motive power.

He received in reply a stream of technical data, which, even though he repeatedly smote his head in order to aid cogitation, passed over his head, due to its intricate nature.

'And these chickens created *you*?' asked Eddie as his knee parts wobbled uncertainly. 'How did they do *that*, exactly?'

'You weren't abducted only the once,' said his other self in reply. 'They took you off several times during your tenure as mayor. They grew me from bits of you as one might grow a plant from a seed. Although the technique used was considerably more complicated than that. Would you like me to explain it?'

'No,' said Eddie. 'I'm fine, thank you.'

'And of course, during your periods of abduction the chickens put a few ideas into your head regarding social reform in Toy City.'

'What?' went Eddie, in some alarm. 'You put ideas in my head? How?'

'It was somewhat easier than you might think—we just added our own special sawdust.'

Eddie now whacked at his furry head. 'I feel somehow . . . *dirty*,' he said.

'Dirty?' And the other Eddie laughed. 'If you think that us messing about with your head makes you feel somehow dirty, we won't broach the subject of the tracking device we stuck up your bum.'

'No,' said Eddie. 'I don't think we will. So where are we going now?'

'To the launch site, of course.'

'Well, of course, where else?'

'We'll be there in just a moment.'

The flying disc drifted downwards. Eddie viewed once more the massive engines and machinery of the ersatz-chicken production lines and shortly this was above them, as down they continued to the lowermost level of Area 52.

'Now let me ask you this,' said Eddie, 'as some bright spark might, if he, she or it were observing this—why would the "launch site" be on the lowermost level of Area Fifty-Two?'

'Good question,' said his other self. 'But then why some things are underneath other things has always been a mystery, hasn't it?'

'Has it?' asked Eddie.

'I watch a lot of TV,' said the other Eddie. 'They have these programmes on about archaeology, digging up ancient sites. But the ancient sites are always underground. Along with the ancient roads. How do you explain that, eh? Why are ancient walls always four feet deep in the ground? Where did all that earth come from that has to be dug away? Does it mean that this world is getting bigger every year? Growing and growing? Perhaps that explains why there are so many worlds all next door to each other. What do you think?'

'I think I'm not very well,' said Eddie, and his knee parts gave out.

'On your feet, soldier,' said the other Eddie. 'We're nearly there now, see?'

And Eddie saw and Eddie was impressed.

Afeared also was Eddie Bear, but very much impressed.

They were dropping down now into a massive underground compound, a vast concrete expanse lit by many high-overhead lights, a concrete expanse on which stood at least a dozen spacecraft.

These were of the variety that Eddie had seen before. Like unto the one that had pursued him up the hillside of Toy Town.

Fine-looking tin-plate craft were these, with many rivets, many portholes and those big dome jobbies on the top that proper flying saucers always have.

'The propulsion units are fascinating,' said the other Eddie. 'They employ a drive system powered by a cross-interflux, utilising the transperambulation of pseudo-cosmic anti-matter. Imagine *that*.'

And Eddie tried to. But did not succeed.

'You have to hand it to the chickens,' said the other Eddie, 'I think it must have been that eternal question that sparked them into advanced technology.'

'You mean, "What came first, the chicken or the egg?"'

'No,' said the other Eddie. '"Why did the chicken cross the road?" I feel that the answer must be that the chicken needed to know what was on the other side. *Really* needed to know. And now they know what's on the other side of so many roads and barriers between worlds and almost everything else. And one day there will be no life in the universe except chicken life and there's no telling what they'll do after that. Travel beyond death or beyond time, probably.'

'Well, bravo to those chickens,' said Eddie Bear once more. 'Are we nearly there yet, by the way?'

'Nearly there, and . . . yes, we're here.'

And Eddie had been watching as the disc came in to land. He had been watching all the activity around and about the flying saucers. All the comings and goings, all the liftings intos of stuff and fiddlings with all sorts of things. And Eddie had been viewing those who were all engaged in this industrious enterprise. For all and sundry engaged thus so were indeed of chicken-kind.

But somehow these were no ordinary chickens. No farmyard peckers, these. They were of a higher order of fowl. Clearly of superior intelligence, clad in uniforms and capable of using their wing-parts as a passable facsimile of hands.

Eddie viewed these dextrous appendages and wished like damn that his own hands had not been denied him.

As the flying disc settled onto the concrete floor, the other Eddie stepped nimbly from it and bid his wobbly counterpart to follow if he would.

Eddie stumbled onwards after his other self.

'Twelve spaceships,' the other Eddie told him as Eddie stumbled along, 'each equipped with a thousand jars to store the essences in. It was felt prudent to speed up operations. Take all in a single gathering. Which ironically enough will fulfil certain prophecies promulgated by the various religious factions in Toy City. So I suppose there must be something to religion, mustn't there?'

Eddie nodded slowly. There were no prophecies of doom to be found in the religious credo of The Midnight Growlers. There was love, there was laughter and indeed there was beer. But there was none of the grim stuff.

'The spaceships will fly out there,' said the other Eddie, pointing with a paw, 'up that tunnel, out and through The Second Big O.'

'Surely they will be seen,' said Eddie Bear.

'By humankind? Probably. But it doesn't matter. Those who believe in flying saucers are so vastly outnumbered by those who do not that their sworn testimonies are always laughed at. And as for those on the other side, they will never know what hit them. Fear not for them, Eddie. Their ends will be swift and painless. Their misery and enslavement will be over.'

'Will the chickens be hitting the meathead P.P.P.s?' asked Eddie, hopefully.

'Not yet. They'll crash a single saucer, as they did here. The "survivor" will wheel and deal with the P.P.P.s. Set up a production plant. Then they'll add a few ingredients to the ersatz chickens, something to make the P.P.P.s and all the humankind on that side of the barrier compliant. The chickens will need their services as a workforce to redecorate Toy City. After that they will be redundant. Then they will be disposed of.'

'It's all figured out,' said Eddie, 'isn't it?'

'Years and years of planning.'

'I am impressed,' said Eddie. 'Now can I meet Her Majesty?'

'All in good time.'

'But I don't have much in the way of good time left.'

'This is true,' said the other Eddie. 'This is true indeed.'

And back beyond The Second Big O and up the Yellow Brick Road, a clockwork barman called Tinto said, 'This is true indeed.'

'It is certainly true,' said Chief Inspector Wellington Bellis. 'But what do *you* know about it?'

'Not much,' said Tinto, polishing furiously at a glass that needed no polishing. 'I know Eddie's missing because he hasn't been in here for two days. And I think that's a bit poor. It's always me who helps him out on his cases *and* I wish to report the theft of my calculating pocket Wallah. Between you and me, I think that big boy Jack nicked her. Do you want me to fill out a form, or something? I have really nice handwriting.'

'That will not be necessary.' Wellington Bellis quaffed the beer that he wouldn't be paying for, because chief inspectors never have to, which is a tradition, or an old charter, or something, no matter where you might happen to be in the known, or indeed the unknown Universe.

Along Tinto's bar counter, laughing policemen laughed amongst themselves, poked with their truncheons at things they shouldn't be poking at and laughed some more when these things fell to the floor and broke.

'And I'd really appreciate it if you'd stop them doing that,' said Tinto to Bellis.

'So you're telling me,' said Wellington Bellis, 'that you put a lot of ideas into the head of this wayward bear?'

'More than a lot,' said Tinto. 'Most.'

'You are the source of inspiration to him, as it were?'

'Yes, you might say that.'

'Same again,' said Wellington Bellis, offering up his empty glass.

Tinto hastened without haste to oblige.

'You see,' said Bellis as Tinto did so, 'we have a positive ID on the mass-murderer who did for the orchestra at the Opera House. The backstage doorman identified him.'

'Then you arrest the blighter,' said Tinto, 'and do so with my blessings. If you need them, which in my opinion you probably will, as I am lately informed by the vicar of the local Church of Mechanology that The End Times are imminent.'

'Yes,' said Bellis, 'word of such seems to be reaching me from all sides of late. But let us apply ourselves to the matter presently in hand.'

'The mass-murderer,' said Tinto.

'That very fellow. You see, it is my theory that he is not working alone. In fact I suspect he is an evil cat's-paw working on behalf of some supercriminal. A sinister mastermind behind his vile doings.'

Tinto nodded thoughtfully, though his printed face smiled on.

'A criminal mastermind who put ideas into the head of this monster. Who is the source of his inspiration as it were. Do you understand what I'm saying?'

'Well,' said Tinto. 'Ah, excuse me, please, I have to serve this lady.'

The lady in question was Amelie, the long-legged dolly from Nadine's Diner. The dolly well known to Jack.

Bellis looked on approvingly and made a wistful face. Now *there* was a good-looking dolly, he thought. A dolly who could certainly bring a fellow such as himself a great deal of pleasure. And solace, too, of course, because Chief Inspector Bellis was, in his *special* way, a police chief. And so he was, as with all police chiefs, having a rough one today. What with all the pressure being put upon him from his superiors to get results. And his wife in the process of divorcing him and everything. And him trying to give up drinking, and everything. And his India rubber self now being so perished that bits and bobs of him kept regularly dropping off. And everything.

'Bring me something long and cold with plenty of alcohol in it,' said Amelie to Tinto.

'I don't think my wife's available,' said Tinto.*

---

* The old ones really are the best.

'Just get me the drink, you clockwork clown.'

Tinto did as he was bid, chuckling as he did so.

Amelie turned to Chief Inspector Bellis. 'And have *you* done anything?' she asked.

'I've done all manner of things.'

'About my boyfriend. I reported him missing. The gormsters on your front desk just laughed and looked down the front of my frock.'

Bellis, doing likewise, ceased this doing. 'We're on the case, madam,' he said.

'Well, you'd better get a move on. I've just come from a chapter meeting and from what I've heard there's not going to be much time left to do anything.'

Tinto placed Amelie's drink before her. It was short and warm, but it did have plenty of alcohol in it.

'Chapter meeting?' said Bellis to Amelie, averting his eyes from her breasts and straying them down to her legs.

'Chapter meeting, you dirty old pervert, I am a member of The Daughters of the Unseeable Upness.'

'Ah,' said Bellis, 'one of those.'

'And according to our Chapter Mother, tonight is the night of the Big Closing. After tonight there will be no more nights, ever.'

'Really?' said Bellis. 'And you personally hold to this belief?'

'I do,' said Amelie. 'Which is why I intend to get very, very drunk tonight and, if given the opportunity, fulfil my wildest fantasies.'

'Really?' said Bellis. 'And might these fantasies include having sex with a hero?'

'Women's fantasies generally do. When they don't include having sex with an absolute villain.'

'Interesting,' said Bellis. 'So would these fantasies include having sex with a police hero? One who brought to book the evil mastermind, the source of inspiration who puts ideas into the head of a mass-murderer?'

'Undoubtedly,' said Amelie, tipping her drink down her throat.

'Well . . .' said Wellington Bellis.

And, 'Well,' said the other Eddie to his failing counterpart. 'As time is now rapidly running out for you and the chickens are on a tight schedule, we'd better let you say hello to Her Madge, eh?'

'That would be nice,' said Eddie, tottering somewhat as he did so. 'Then I could wish her well and everything.'

'You are such a well-adjusted bear,' said Eddie's other self.

'I try my best,' said Eddie. 'Oh, and might I ask you something?'

'Indeed, my friend, you might.'

'Well, I was just wondering—what would happen if something were to happen to Her Majesty?'

'Happen?' said the other Eddie.

'Something bad,' said Eddie. 'Some accident or something.'

'That is *not* going to happen. Believe me, it is not.'

'No,' said Eddie, 'of course not. But say it did. Say the unthinkable occurred, something that you were unable to prevent. Some tragedy, resulting in Her Majesty's untimely demise.'

'Such is unthinkable, of course.'

'But imagine if you did think it. How would it affect the chickens' plans for inter-world domination?'

'Rather hugely, I imagine.' And the other Eddie laughed. 'You see, there is no royal line of succession in the chicken queendom. Too many princesses, you see. The chicken queendom is a matriarchy, democratically elected. But a queen will live for hundreds of years—chickens do if they're not interfered with. But it is the tradition that a new queen will overthrow and reverse all the policies made by a previous queen.'

'And why is that?' asked Eddie.

'It's a tradition,' said the other Eddie. 'It is, of course, the tradition everywhere amongst politicians. Here, for instance, in the USA, each new candidate for the presidency promises the people that should he gain the position of power, he will dump all his predecessor's policies and begin anew. And if the population believe him, they vote him in.'

'And so he does what he says?' said Eddie.

'No,' said the other one. 'He does nothing of the kind. Because he lied to the people. The problem with this world is that everyone lies to everyone else. Nobody tells the truth. Nobody. That's another reason why things are in such a mess. But chickens cannot lie. They always tell the truth. Should this Queen die, the new Queen would reverse everything. Not because she wanted to, but because it is tradition. Which is why it's a very good thing that chicken queens live for such a long time, or there would be no progress.'

'Interesting,' said Eddie Bear. 'So can I meet the Queen now, please?'

'Now, *I'm* saying please,' said Samuel J. Maggott, Police Chief of LAPD, 'because I'm such a nice man, and because I bear you no malice for the mayhem you wrought upon the personnel of this precinct.'

'Really?' said the other Jack. 'That's nice all round then, isn't it?'

They were in Sam's office, the other Jack handcuffed to the visitors' chair, a goodly number of knocked-about-looking officers standing around looking 'useful'. A troubled young detective smoking a cigarette. A feisty young female officer paring her fingernails with a bowie knife.

'All I want to know is *why*?' said Sam. 'Why the kidnappings at the Golden Chicken Headquarters? Why all the mayhem during your escape? And why flee to a secret military establishment, of all places? The mysterious Area Fifty-Two? What were you doing there?'

'I demand my phone call,' said the other Jack. 'I am entitled to my phone call.'

'And you'll get to make your phone call. As soon as you've answered my questions. Would you care for some coffee?'

'The coffee machine's still on the blink, Chief,' said the troubled young detective, putting his cigarette stub out on Sam's desk with a bandaged hand. 'We could send the feisty female officer here out to the diner to get some.'

'You could *try*,' said the feisty female officer, adjusting the arm that she had in a sling.

'And you'll do it if I tell you,' said Sam. 'So, young man, Mister Jack-no-surname, from wherever you come from—are you hungry, would you like something to eat?'

The other Jack said, 'Yes, I would, before I make my phone call.'

'Then pop out to the Golden Chicken Diner, would you, honey?'

' "Honey"?' said the feisty female officer, flipping Sam 'the bird'.

'Get us in coffees all round. And eats, too. We'll all have chicken burgers.'

'Chicken burgers?' The other Jack flinched. 'I don't want chicken burgers.'

'Don't want chicken burgers? Are you some kind of weirdo, buddy? No, don't answer that, I know you are. But don't want chicken burgers? What kind of madness is *that*? Everyone *wants* chicken burgers. Everyone *needs* chicken burgers. You'll *have* chicken burgers and you'll *love* chicken burgers. Just as everyone does.'

'Oh no I won't,' said the other Jack, struggling in the visitors' chair. 'I'm getting out of here. Let me go, you have the wrong man. You're making a big mistake.'

'Get the burgers, feisty lady,' said Police Chief Sam.

'No!' The other Jack fought fiercely.

'Don't go hurting yourself,' said Sam. 'Those cuffs are made of high-tensile steel. You'll not break out of them.'

'Oh really?' And the other Jack fought. And as Sam looked on and the officers looked on and a chap from the ACME Coffee Machine Company who had come to fix the machine in Sam's office looked on (through the glass of Sam's office door), the other Jack rose from the visitor's chair. The steel cuffs ripped down through his hands, ripped his hands most horribly from his wrists. The ankle cuffs restraining his feet fell down to the floor and the other Jack's feet fell, too.

Sam Maggott made a horrified face, which matched all others present. He fell back in considerable alarm as the handless, footless other Jack rose up before him. And then the officers fell upon this Jack and awful things occurred.

'Let us not speak of awful things,' said the other Eddie, leading the wobbly Real McCoy towards a flying saucer. 'Come aboard the mothership and you will meet Her Madge.'

'I think it had better be quick,' said Eddie, 'for I am all over the place.'

'You're doing fine. You're doing fine.'

'I'm not doing fine. I'm all in and out of my body.'

'Soon,' said the other Eddie, 'there will be peace for you. Peace for you and all your kind. Eternal peace. What better peace than that, eh?'

'None much better,' said Eddie. 'None much . . . better.'

'Come on then, up the gangway. This way, come. Come on now.'

And Eddie was led to the mothership.

And it had to be said that the interior of the mothership looked just the way that the interior of a mothership should look. Your basic pilot's seat, of course, in the cockpit area, with the steering wheel and the gear levers and the foot pedals. And the computer jobbies with the blinking lights. And the coffee machine.

'Whoa,' went Eddie. 'So this is what the inside of a spaceship looks like. What does *that* do?'

'You don't really have the time to concern yourself with *that*,' said the other Eddie.

'Does it matter?' Eddie asked. 'What does *that* do?'

'*That* does the steering. *That's* the steering wheel. Those are the foot pedals. Those are the weapons panels. That button there activates the, well, how shall I put this? Death ray, I suppose. It's as accurate as a time-clock at a Golden Chicken Diner. And they are really accurate, believe me.'

'Oh, I do,' said Eddie. 'All the controls look so simple.'

'Oh, they are. They really are. You can complicate things to death, but it's not necessary. The more advanced technology becomes, the more user-friendly it becomes. The more simple to use.'

'I'll bet I could have flown this,' said Eddie. Wistfully.

'I just bet you could have, too. But never mind.'

Eddie sank down heavily into the pilot's seat. 'I think I'd like to go to sleep now,' he said in a very drowsy, growly kind of a voice.

'Well, perhaps you should,' said the other Eddie.

'But I really would like to meet Her Majesty. Do you think I could have a glass of water, or something? Or better a glass of beer. My very last glass of beer. I'd like that very much.'

'Oh, I think that could be arranged.'

A chicken in a uniform clucked words into the other Eddie's ear.

'And at something of the hurry-up,' said the other Eddie. 'It's two minutes to take-off. Her Majesty is already on board and we must prepare for Operation Take Out Toy City.'

'Well done on the name,' said Eddie Bear.

'I'll just get you a glass of beer. You just sit and relax.'

And the other Eddie took his leave and Eddie sat and sighed.

And, 'Oh,' sighed Amelie also as Chief Inspector Wellington Bellis presented her with another short warm drink with plenty of alcohol in it.

And, 'Oh,' sighed Tinto, as he knew that Chief Inspector Wellington Bellis had no intention of paying for this or any other drink.

And, 'Oh-oh,' went laughing policemen as they knocked other things to the floor and laughed more as they broke.

And, 'Oh,' went the feisty female officer in Police Chief Sam Maggott's office as a blur of blood and guts enveloped her.

And, 'Oh,' went Eddie Bear as he sank lower and lower over the flying saucer's dashboard.

And oh it was to be hoped that there might have been some kind of something, some kind of solution to all this trouble and strife.

And then, 'Oh,' and, 'Holy Mother of God!' Sam Maggott drew his gun from his shoulder holster. And the feisty female officer and the troubled detective did their own particular forms of Oh-ing as a fierce metallic skull-type jobbie burst out through the top of the other Jack's head.

★

And another 'Oh' was heard, and this from the other Eddie. It was an 'Oh' of surprise, and one of alarm also. Because in the cockpit of the flying saucer, Eddie Bear had slammed his paw onto the ignition button and caused the engines to roar and the chicken crew to panic and flee.

And then all sorts of extraordinary things occurred.
Which caused more Oh-ings all round.

24

'Oh no, no, no,' said the other Eddie, returning to the cabin with a beer. 'The last thing we need right now is for something extraordinary to occur—we are running to a tight schedule.' And he lifted Eddie's paw from the ignition button. And the powerful engines stuttered and died and all was at peace once more.

Much peace.

'You see,' said the other Eddie, and he grinned at Eddie Bear, 'it is this way and . . .' The other Eddie paused. Eddie Bear was slumped back in the pilot's seat. His button eyes were crossed and his mouth drooped oddly at the corners.

'Eddie?' went the other Eddie, shaking Eddie Bear. 'Eddie, wake up now. We can't have you dying on us just yet. We haven't kept you alive all this time, when we could simply have killed you, for no purpose. There are things we need to know from you. Eddie, wake up. Eddie?'

But Eddie Bear would not wake up.

Eddie Bear could not wake up.

His head rolled forward, his shoulders sank.

Eddie Bear was dead.

25

'That is most inconvenient.' The other Eddie called out to the chicken crew who had now returned to their duties tinkering with electronic doodads and ticking things off on clipboards. 'Toss him out of the hatchway, will you? No, on second thoughts, dump him in the hold. We'll deliver him home, toss him out when we make our first pass over Toy City.'

The chickens cackled with laughter, the way chickens will, and two of their number hauled the lifeless Eddie from the pilot's chair and carried him away to the hold.

'Right then,' said the other Eddie, seating himself in the pilot's chair and strapping himself in for good measure. Because you should never pilot a flying saucer without following all safety procedures, which include wearing your seat belt, putting your beer into the little holder on the arm of your chair, extinguishing your cigarette, of course, switching off your mobile phone and knowing where the exit doors are in case of a crash. Oh, and that business regarding the inflatable life jacket with the little whistle attachment, although no one ever really pays any attention to that because everyone knows full well that when whatever means of flying transportation you happen to be travelling in falls from the sky and hits either the ground or the sea, there really aren't going to be any survivors to inflate their life belts or blow their little whistles.

'Calling all craft,' said the other Eddie, slipping a pair of bear-stylie headphones over his ears. The ones with the little face-mic attachment. 'Calling all craft.'

Headphone speakers crackled, chicken voices cackled.

'Oh goody,' said the other, well, now the *remaining* Eddie. 'All present and correct, splendid. Well, ladies, you have all been briefed for this mission. It is of the utmost importance, in order to put overall plans for the domination of this world and our imminent expansion into the world of Toy City into action, that this mission goes without a hitch. I want this done by the numbers, ladies, smooth formation following my lead. Through The Second Big O of the Hollywood sign, full speed ahead to Toy City, then on with the evil soul-sucking death rays, hoover up the population. And then nuke Toy City.'

Rather surprised chicken cackles crackled through the remaining Eddie's headphones. There had been no previous briefings regarding any nukings.

'I know, ladies, I know. But let's face it—Toy City is something of a dump. The clean-sweep approach is probably for the best. Negotiating with the humans there will be such a long-winded process that I feel we should simply take the lot of them out in one fell swoop and have done with it. What say you?'

Chicken voices cackled in the affirmative.

'Splendid, splendid. My call sign will be Great Mother-Henship and this operation, as you know, is Operation Take Out Toy City. So, gangways up, hatchways sealed and then we'll run through the safety procedures. I want everyone to be certain that they know how to inflate their life jackets and use their little whistles. These things matter.'

Although it might appear to be a somewhat tenuous link, it did have to be said that certain *things* were at present really *mattering* to Samuel J. Maggott of the LAPD.

Staying alive in the face of a mad robot's onslaught being foremost amongst these.

Sam pumped bullets at the robot's head, but the thing was moving so swiftly about that he mostly missed and shot up the coffee machine.

'You've broken that for good this time,' said the engineer who had come to fix it. Ducking as he did so to avoid being struck by the troubled young detective as the robot Jack flung him through the glass of Sam's partition door.

Sam ducked down behind his desk as an officer flew over his head and left via a window, taking much of the faulty air-conditioning unit with him.

'Eat lead, you son of a bitch!' cried the feisty young female officer, bringing out her own special weapon, the one that was *not* police issue, and blasting away like a good'n.

The robot Jack, impervious even to such superior firepower due to the nature of his hyper-alloy combat chassis,* flung officers to every side, stormed straight through the partition door, causing much distress to the coffee-machine engineer, then stormed through the outer office and through the outer wall.

'After it!' bawled Sam to those who still remained conscious. 'Get that motherfu—'

But none seemed too keen to oblige.

Sam snatched up what was left of his telephone receiver and shouted words into it. 'Is my helicopter still on the roof?' he shouted. 'Right, then rev the son of a gun up,' he further shouted. 'And call every car, call everything—there's a robot on the loose.'

There was a moment's pause. As well there would be.

'Yeah, you heard me right!' shouted Sam. 'I said *robot*! No, I *didn't* say *Robert*. Yes, I *have* been taking my tablets. Get the . . . what? Oh, you can see it now, can you? It just burst out through the front of the building. Right. Then get everything you can get—we're going after it.'

'Generally speaking,' said Wellington Bellis to Amelie as he accepted two more free drinks from Tinto, a triple for Amelie, a diet swodge† for himself, 'on the surface, as it were, police work might seem mundane and everyday—petty theft, toys pulling bits off each other, that kind of thing. But once in a while something really big happens. And that is when I get personally involved. I'm a *special* policeman, you see. Super-criminals fear my name. Is that drink all right, my dear?'

Amelie hiccuped prettily. 'Do you have your own car and a *special* expense account?' she asked.

'Oh yes, I'm well taken care of. Don't be put off by all these perished bits, by the way. I've booked in for a makeover with the kindly, lovable white-haired old Toymaker.'

'I'll bet you're not perished *all* over,' purred Amelie.

'Excruciating,' said Tinto.

'Quiet, you,' ordered Bellis. 'I'm only postponing your arrest for crimes against toyanity until closing time because I am so enjoying my conversation with this fascinating young dolly here.'

---

* It might well be asked why, if the other Jack was in fact an armoured robot, he didn't simply do away with the officers when they arrested him at Area 52. It might well be asked, but it's as sure as sure that it won't be answered. Surely he was ordered not to cause a commotion near the launch site, and at all until the launch time was up and he was sure that the operation was under way! It's possible, so let's stick with that.

† A soft drink popular amongst rubber toys.

'Fascinating?' purred Amelie. 'Jack never said that to me.' *And what of Jack,* Amelie wondered.

What of Jack, indeed.

The other Jack, or perhaps he should now be referred to as the *remaining* Jack, was making good progress through the streets of Los Angeles. He was doing all the things one might reasonably expect, in fact, unreasonably demand, of such a robot in such a situation. He was thrusting innocent passers-by aside, some, with inclinations to seek positions as Hollywood stuntmen, through plate-glass windows, and others of a frailer disposition into those piles of cardboard boxes that always seem to be there to conveniently cushion one's fall in such situations. Should such situations occur.

And then there was the lifting up and overturning of automobiles that got in his way. There's always a lot of mileage to be had from that kind of thing.

And then there was the kind of thing that we all really like. In fact, if it didn't come to pass, we'd all be bitterly disappointed.

And that is, of course, the climbing into the cab of a great big truck, flinging the driver out of the door, settling down behind the wheel and taking-and-driving-away.

Oh, and it needs to be a truck with a *significant* bit-on-the-end sort of jobbie, a great long canister on the 'bed' containing twenty tonnes of liquid oxygen, or highly volatile solvents, or toxic waste, or even nuclear nasties.

Or something.

Joe-Bob, the driver of the Sulphuric Acid Truck, made loud his protests as the robot Jack hurled him out through the windscreen and took the steering wheel.

Now in his helicopter, Police Chief Sam heard the call-in from the traffic cop who had witnessed the taking-and-driving-away. Witnessed it while parked on his bike beside a Golden Chicken Diner, munching upon a Golden Chicken burger family meal and admiring the little clockwork giveaway cymbal-playing monkey toy that he intended to take home for his daughter. There was something really special about that monkey.

'Westbound on Route Sixty-Six,' Sam told the pilot. 'I'll bet the S-O-B is heading back to Area Fifty-Two. After him.' And Sam thrust on headphones of his own with the little microphone attachment and shouted orders to all and sundry. Adding for good measure, 'And call up the Air Force, just to be sure.'

★

Call up the Air Force, just to be sure! Well, why not? You always have to call up the Air Force sooner or later. And there's always this troubled young pilot, who might well be black and want to be a space pilot, but keeps getting kicked back and is looking to prove himself and . . .

'Calling all craft,' went the remaining Eddie through his little fitted microphone. 'Follow my lead. Open outer launch doors.'

Up, up on the desert floor, great doors slid aside.

'And away we go!' And the remaining Eddie pawed the ignition, *brrmmed* the engines, put the saucer into gear and with a hum and a whiz and a whoosh and a swoosh, the saucer did its liftings off and dramatic sweepings away.

'Tally ho!' shouted the remaining Eddie. 'Onward, follow me.'

And up they went, those saucers all, off up the underground runway.

It was night-time now and the Californian sky was sprinkled over with stars. Were there worlds up there, one might wonder, with folk like us looking out at our sun and wondering, just wondering, were there folk like them down here? Well, perhaps, or then, perhaps not. Perhaps the Universe *is* nothing more than a great construction kit, given by God to his offspring and awaiting the day when his offspring will grow tired of it just sitting there and pack it up and put it back into its box.

Or is there really no Universe at all? Is it just an illusion, a dream, which, when the dreamer awakes, will cease to be?

Or perhaps the world *is* just an apple turning silently in space. Or a great big onion. Or a melting pot. Or perhaps, as has been mooted in many a public drinking house, some time after the ten-o'clock watershed, the real truth is that . . .

'Weeeeeee!' went the remaining Eddie as his lead craft shot up through the opening in the desert floor and into the star-speckled sky. 'Now *this is* a rush!'

And up came the other craft one by one, up into that sky.

'Full speed ahead,' cried the remaining Eddie. 'Make me proud of you, ladies.'

And aboard all the craft, the chicken crews did cluckings and cacklings and such.

'And such a night,' said Wellington Bellis, standing in the doorway of Tinto's and looking up at the dark and star-sprinkled sky. 'Hardly the night for an Apocalypse, I think you will agree, my dear.' And his perished rubber arm strayed about the waist of Amelie. And laughing policemen peering out from the bar counter nudged each other, did lewd winkings and made suggestive remarks.

'Now, I just want to make this clear,' said Tinto, 'in case any of you lot are thinking of truncheoning me senseless, I am *not* a supercriminal. I am a barman. And to prove this, I propose that I waive normal licensing hours on this occasion and continue to serve you fellows until all of you are too drunk to do any arresting at all. In fact, until you all agree that you are my bestest friends. What say you to this?'

The laughing policemen laughed some more and ordered further drinks.

'I don't suppose you have any drink in the glove compartment?' Police Chief Sam asked the helicopter pilot, 'because, by God, I could use some.'

'Certainly not,' the pilot replied. 'That would be most unprofessional. We pilots *never* drink on the job. We do a bit of Charlie, of course, but who doesn't? Piloting a helicopter is a very stressful job, what with all those power lines you might crash into and everything. I always have a couple of lines before I go up.'

'Got any left?' Sam asked.

'In the glovey, help yourself.'

'Why, thank you . . . Oh my God, what is he doing *now*?'

He, the robot Jack, was doing what one would expect of him. He was bothering other road users. The great big truck with its highly dangerous cargo swerved from lane to lane on the highway, swiping cars to left and right.

'So,' said Sydney Greenstreet to Marilyn Monroe, whom he was driving home after the meal they'd just had together, 'my agent says that the producers are very pleased with my performance so far. They thought that the scene where we were taken hostage at the Golden Chicken Headquarters might well be the one that earns me an Academy Award for Best Supporting Actor.'

'Did he say anything about *me*?' asked Marilyn.

'He said you were okay.'

'Okay?'

'That's a compliment coming from him, dear. Oh, and they're changing the name of the movie now—did you hear that? They're calling it *The Toyminator*, whatever *that* means. And we're to do one last scene together. I have the revised script right here.'

Sydney handed Marilyn the revised script.

And she read it. '"While driving home after a night out at the Golden Chicken Diner, where they enjoyed the Big Bird Munchie Special with extra fries on the side, the merits of which they are discussing whilst marveling at the special qualities of the giveaway clockwork pianist toy, they are run off the road by a speeding Sulphuric Acid Truck."'

'I said no to that bit,' said Sydney. 'That's work for a stunt double, I told my agent.'

Marilyn perused the script. 'There isn't any actual dialogue,' she said. 'It simply reads, "They scream."'

'I know—it's outrageous, isn't it?'

And then Sydney and Marilyn were run off the road by a speeding Sulphuric Acid Truck.

They screamed.

And out into the desert went that truck. And after it in hot pursuit came many a black-and-white. And overhead now came Sam Maggott's 'copter, all thrashing blades and bawling Sam.

And so on and suchlike.

And . . .

'Whoa!' went the helicopter pilot. 'Would you take a look at *that*?'

And Sam looked up and Sam looked out and Sam said, 'What *is* that?'

'*That* and *those*!' The pilot made a troubled face. 'They're coming towards us . . . They're flying saucers. Oh my God—and oh!'

And the fleet of saucers swept over the helicopter, spinning it all around. And on the desert highway below the robot Jack saw the saucers, slammed on the brakes of the big truck and swung *it* around.

'Going without me, eh?' he went. 'Well, that's not fair for a start.'

On-rushing police cars swerved and smote one another. The big truck ploughed through several of these, mashing them fiercely to this side and the other.

'Get back after him,' cried Sam. Hanging on for the dearest of life, as the helicopter clung to the air. 'Get after him and get after those flying saucers.'

'This really *is* a job for the Air Force now,' said the helicopter pilot. 'Although in all truth, I'm prepared to have a go at them myself. I've been applying to be a space pilot for years, but I keep getting kicked back. If I could take out a few flying saucers, I'll just bet that NASA will give me a chance.'

'You go for it,' said Sam. 'I've lost the plot good and proper now anyway. I didn't even notice you were black—I thought you were from Arkansas.'

'What *is* all this Arkansas business anyway?' asked the pilot as he steered the helicopter around in pursuit of the departing truck and similarly departing saucers. 'Some kind of lame running gag, do you think?'

'Like all that stuff that weirdo Jack told us about following the American Dream? Before he turned into a robot, of course.'

'Well, he did say he was from England. And as all we Americans know, the English have no sense of humour.'

'Well, I'm glad we've got all *that* out of the way,' said Sam. 'On with the chase, if you will, Mister Pilot.'

'Ten-four, Chief, ten-four.'

And on flew the flying saucers, low now over the outer suburbs of LA. The bits that tourists never see. Many gap-toothed fellows called Joe-Bob, who sat upon their verandas drinking from earthenware demijohns and smoking corncob pipes, viewed the saucers' passing. And many shook their dandruffed heads and said things to the effect that they were not in the least surprised, as they'd been abducted so many times, but could find none to believe them.

'Onward, onward!' cried the remaining Eddie. 'On through The Second Big O.'

And as there had been no apparent response from the Air Force, which was a shame because a really decent UFO/Air Force battle outclasses ground-based explosions, shoot-outs and car chases (no matter how extreme and prolonged) any old day of the week (with the obvious exclusion of Tuesdays), Sam's pilot said, 'Check this out!' and pressed certain buttons on his dashboard.

'What do you have there?' asked Sam.

'A special something,' said the pilot. 'Fitted it myself. State of the art. It's called an M134 General Electric Mini-gun. 7.62 mm. Full-clip capacity of 5,793 rounds per minute. 7.62 × 51 shells, 1.36 kg recoil adapters. Muzzle velocity of 869 m/s.'

'Nice,' said Sam. 'Then open fire on those alien sons of bitches.'

'Ten-four, Chief,' said the pilot, and he opened fire.

And down below and through the streets of Hollywood now roared that truck with the robot Jack at the wheel and all that dangerous acid on board. Along Hollywood Boulevard, past the Roosevelt Hotel, and Grauman's Chinese Theatre and the Hollywood Wax Museum.

And, 'Rat-at-tat-at-tat-at-tat-at-tat,' went the M134 General Electric Mini-gun. And Sam Maggott cheered as tracer bullets scoured the sky. And he bawled, 'You've hit one. You've hit one.'

And the pilot had.

A saucer wobbled, spiralled, span. The chicken pilot squawked.

And down and down the saucer went to strike the home of Sydney Greenstreet. Who was presently being loaded into an ambulance with many broken bones. Which really wasn't fair. But there you go.

'Well done,' cried Sam, patting the pilot. 'Oh no, one's turning around.'

And a single saucer was. The helicopter did nifty manoeuvrings. Hollywood residents looked up from their poolside soirées, rubbed at *their* rectal probings and said, 'I told you so.'

'Whoa!' went Sam, once more clinging on for the life of himself. 'Shoot that mother, will you?'

'Doing my best, Chief, doing my best.'

And down below the robot Jack drove onward in his stolen truck. Up now and towards the Hollywood hills in pursuit of the saucers. And police cars screamed after him, all flashing lights and wailing sirens. And cars swerved and passers-by took to their heels.

'Onward, ever onward,' cried the Eddie in the Mother-Henship, 'and engage the fiendishly clever miniaturisation units that will enable us to sweep through The Second Big O without touching the sides.' And his paw pressed the special button and in other craft wing tips did likewise.

'And did you see *that*?' shouted Sam. 'Did they just get smaller, or are they suddenly very far, far away?'

'Bit of both, I think, Chief.' The pilot rattled away with the M134 General Electric Mini-gun.

The robot Jack's truck bumped up the grasslands, but lost neither speed, nor size.

'Onward!' cried the remaining Eddie. 'Onward, ladies. Onward into the future pages of chicken world history. God of All Chickens, I love this job.'

And onward they swept towards the Hollywood sign.

And onwards too swept the robot Jack, his truck bouncing all about, but roaring ever onward.

And after him the black-and-whites, doing what black-and-whites always do in situations like these: crashing into one another, flying off cliffs in slow motion, having the occasional bit of comedy relief with blackened-faced officers staggering from wrecked police cars to the sound of incidental music going, 'Wah–waaaah.'

'They're going through, Chief,' cried the helicopter pilot. 'They're going through The Second Big O.'

'Then pull up. We'll get them on the other side.'

The pilot yanked back on the joystick. 'Oh my God!' he shouted. 'The controls are stuck. Oh my God! Oh my God!'

'Don't go without me, you rotters!' And the robot Jack put his foot down harder.

And then it all happened.

As it always does.

In slow motion, with some really great shots.

Picture it if you can.

The flying saucers moved from the horizontal into the vertical plane and swept one after another towards The Second Big O of the Hollywood sign.

The great big truck with its dangerous cargo did its own kind of sweeping up, which involved its wheels leaving the grasslands and the performance of a rather spectacular flying leap forward *into* the Hollywood sign.

To be joined there, at that very moment, by Sam Maggott's helicopter, big guns blazing and controls all gone to pot.

And then that explosion.

With the flatbed canister-load of sulphuric acid crumpling forwards, releasing its lethal load, swallowing up the robot Jack.

That *big* explosion. As of truck and sign and helicopter. And of a few surviving police cars, too.

And of the lone Air Force jet, which hadn't actually been scrambled but had been taken aloft by a young black pilot who was hoping for a job in the space programme with NASA.

And, by golly, at least a good half-dozen flying saucers that hadn't quite done the sweeping through The Second Big O thing.

And what a big explosion *that* was!

And all in slow motion, too.

And cut, and print, and that's a wrap.

Hooray for Hollywood.

26

'What was all *that*?' The Eddie at the controls of the Great Mother-Henship, which had now swelled back to its regular size, glanced into the rear-view mirror and called out in alarm. 'What happened back there? Speak to me, ladies.'

Chicken voices clucked into his headphones.

'How many ships lost? Six? No, seven! That's outrageous, impossible.'

Further chicken voices confirmed the sad news.

'Oh well, never mind,' said the remaining Eddie. 'There will never be a shortage of chickens. And they died nobly in a glorious cause. Their names will be forever remembered. Whatever they were. Does anyone remember?'

Further voices clucked.

'What, no one? Well, never mind. Onward, ladies, on to victory. You'll have to double up in all the soul-sucking-jar jobbies. Beam down those rays, suck up those souls and then we'll nuke the place.'

Chicken voices cackled in a merry kind of a way.

'And then you'll nuke the place?' asked a certain voice, which did not come through the headphones.

The remaining Eddie swung around in his chair. '*You?*' he went. 'How's this?'

'How's this?' said Eddie Bear. 'It's me, that's how it is.'

'But you're dead.' The other Eddie pawed the autopilot. 'You're as dead as a donkey dodo.'

'The rumours of my death have been greatly exaggerated,' said Eddie, padding his way to the centre of the cockpit.* 'As you can see, I am in remarkably fine fettle. And not too dead at all.'

'No!' And the other Eddie threw up his paws. 'This cannot be, it cannot.'

'Well, it can be and it is,' said Eddie, squaring up before his other self. 'And personally I think I deserve an award for my acting. I certainly had *you* fooled. And do you know what? Now that I'm back on my side of the barrier, back in my own world again, I feel fine. I'm as healthy as, and it's time to set matters straight.'

'Time for you to die properly,' said Eddie's other self.

'I think not,' said Eddie, making the fiercest of faces. 'Now land this craft or know my wrath—I'll bite your blinking head off.'

'Land this craft?' The other Eddie laughed.

'I really hate it when you laugh like that,' said Eddie Bear.

'Well, it is of no consequence to me. Guards, take this resurrected bear and throw him out of a porthole, or something.'

'Guards?' said Eddie. 'What guards?'

'The guards that I summonsed by pressing the special "guards" button next to the "autopilot" button. I pressed them both simultaneously, as it were, when you made your appearance.'

'You fiend,' said Eddie Bear.

'Yes, I can really be a stinker at times.' And the other Eddie laughed once again. And as he did so, chicken guards dressed in figure-hugging golden uniforms (which displayed their breasts to perfection), sleek golden helmets with beak-guards, high-heeled boots and the inevitable heavy weaponry jogged into the cockpit and surrounded Eddie.

'Ah,' said Eddie. '*These* guards.'

'Out of a porthole with him,' said the other Eddie. 'And if his fat belly gets stuck, shoot him up the bottom, that will do the trick.'

'I don't think that's a nice idea,' said another voice.

The guards and the other Eddie glanced towards the source of *this* voice. And Eddie Bear did glancings, too. And Eddie Bear said, 'Jack!'

'Nice to see you again, Eddie.' Jack brandished a large gun of his own. He aimed this at the other Eddie. 'Let Eddie go,' said he.

'Jack?' said the other Eddie. 'Now I'm damned sure that I killed you. You plunged to your death in the elevator.'

'Not quite so.' Jack brandished the large gun some more. Because in such situations as this you can never do too much brandishing of a big gun. He had acquired this particular big gun from a chicken guard

---

* Or *hen*pit, possibly. Or possibly not.

at the launch site, whom Jack had taken by surprise and overcome through the employment of a handy spanner.

'I like the uniform,' said Eddie. 'Very dapper, it really suits you. Although it smells a bit.' And Eddie smiled as he said this, for his sense of smell had returned.

'Why, thank you,' said Jack. 'And you've had a wash and brush-up, I see.'

'I'd rather not think about *that*,' said Eddie.

'Now just stop this nonsense,' said the other Eddie Bear. 'You really should be dead!'

'I certainly would have been,' said Jack, 'if it hadn't been for Dorothy here.'

'Hi, Eddie,' called Dorothy.

'Hi, Dorothy,' called Eddie.

Chicken guards swung their weapons about, some aimed at Dorothy, some at Jack and some at Eddie Bear.

'Dorothy is not what she at first appears,' said Jack. 'Which I am a little sad about, but we won't go into that here. But she saved my life, pushed me out of the roof hatch in the lift, helped me cling to a dangling cable, that sort of thing. It was all very exciting.'

'Sounds so,' said Eddie. 'It's a shame I missed it. I spent the time being booted about by your doppelganger.'

'I know,' said Jack. 'I felt your pain. I could feel what you were thinking.'

'And I could feel you too, Jack,' said Eddie. 'Something to do with my condition on the other side of The Second Big O.'

'Yes, yes, yes,' said the other Eddie, 'all *very* interesting, I'm sure. But how did you get aboard this craft?'

'We sneaked on while Eddie kept you talking,' said Jack. 'And now you must ask the guards to drop their guns or I will take great pleasure in shooting you dead.'

'Shoot *me* dead?' The other Eddie laughed some more.

'Oh, just shoot him, Jack,' said Eddie. 'I'm sick of all his laughing.'

'Tell the guards to drop their weapons and land the craft now,' said Jack. 'Oh and order all the other ships to turn back, tell them that the mission is aborted.'

'You have no idea what you're dealing with,' said the other Eddie. 'I will *not* land the craft, *I* will *not* abort the mission. In fact.' And he swung about in his chair and disengaged the autopilot. And also swung the steering wheel, which caused the craft to swing.

And chicken guards went tumbling and so did Eddie and Jack.

And Dorothy went tumbling, too.

The other Eddie didn't tumble; he was strapped into his chair.

But he put the craft through a triple roll and the tumblers whirled all about.

'Kill them all!' shouted the other Eddie. 'Fly, you foolish guards. Fly and shoot them, toss them off the ship.'

And squawking guards went fluttering.

And unpleasantness occurred.

'Such a pleasant night,' said Wellington Bellis, his perished arm now tight about Amelie's waist. 'Such a night for romance.'

'Calling all cars. Calling all cars,' the radio crackled in Bellis's parked police car.

'Calling all cars?' said Wellington Bellis. 'Now what might this be, I wonder?' And he detached himself from Amelie and shuffled over to the car, reached in through the open window and took up the toy microphone that was attached by a length of string to the dashboard. 'What is all this commotion?' he said into it.

'Sir, sir—is that you, sir?'

'It's me, yes. Is that *you*, Officer Chuckles?'

'*Special* Officer Chuckles, yes sir. Calling all cars, I am.'

'And why are you calling all cars?'

'Because we are under attack, sir, from spaceships. They just blew up the remains of the old Toytownland sign. Half a dozen spaceships, sir, flying towards the city.'

'Have you been drinking, officer?'

'Of course I've been drinking, sir.'

'And where are you calling from?'

'From Tinto's Bar, sir—I'm looking out of the back windows. The saucers are coming. We're all gonna die. I'm converting to Mechanology. Out.'

'Out?' asked Bellis.

'Out,' said the voice of Tinto. 'This is my telephone and it's for use-of-barman only. Aaagh! Stop hitting me!'

'Flying saucers?' said Bellis.

And suddenly there they were.

Large as life in the Toy City sky. Great big saucers with blinking lights. The lead craft doing a sort of victory roll, the others flying steadily.

Bellis reached into his car and pressed buttons on his dashboard. 'Action stations. Fire at will. Operation Save Our City is *go*!' And then he replaced the microphone and smiled towards Amelie. 'Have no fear, my dear,' said Bellis. 'Everything is under control.'

'The End Times are upon us,' gasped Amelie. Huskily. Sexily.

'Not a bit of it,' said Bellis, re-establishing himself at her side and offering her a comforting hug. 'All will be attended to. I received a tip-off this morning from a clockwork spaceman. He told me an extraordinary tale, which I did not at first believe . . . Oh, duck, if you will.'

And Amelie ducked as a bolt of light swept down from above and carbonised Bellis's car.

'As I was saying,' said Bellis, 'an extraordinary tale. But I felt it prudent to take it at face value. So I put the Toy City Army on red alert. They'll soon shoot those aliens out of the sky.'

'My hero,' said Amelie.

And the words of Bellis were no idle words. Well, he hadn't risen to his present position of power through not being able to rise to the occasion. In fact, he intended to rise to the occasion with Amelie, quite shortly, when all the mayhem was over and done with.

'Excruciating,' said Tinto once more.

But then *he* had cause to duck.

A blinding light bore down into the bar.

Swept along the counter.

Crispy-crunchy husks of policemen toppled to the floor.

'Oi!' cried Tinto, rising from his duck and shaking a dextrous fist towards the ceiling. 'There was a slight chance that they *might* have paid for their drinks.'

The saucers now criss-crossed the sky, beaming down their rays. And to the great surprise of the chicken pilots and death-ray crews, fire was now being returned at them from below.

'Go to it, lads,' cried the Grand Old Duke of York, who may not have *actually* had ten thousand men, but had been given command of a legion of clockwork tanks.

Tank barrels spat their shells towards the sky.

And as this *was* Toy City, those toy shells carried force.

'I'm hit,' squawked a pilot, but in chicken tongue.

The other Eddie levelled his craft. 'Kill them all!' was the order he gave. 'Prepare the nukes and kill them all.'

Eddie and Jack and Dorothy rolled about on the floor. Chickens fluttered above them, but they still held onto their guns.

Somehow!

'And please shoot this troublesome trio,' ordered the other Eddie. 'And get it over and done with.'

And guns trained down on the troublesome trio.

And one of these leapt up.

She leapt up with a great degree of style, so stylish it could almost be called balletic.

And, as with all the best bits so far, it happened in good old-fashioned slow-mo—which, although it could be argued that there has been rather too much of it lately, it is exactly the way that this bit *should* and *did* happen.

Dorothy cartwheeled into the air and spun around, her left foot describing a wonderful circle, striking beak after beak-guarded beak, striking chickens from the air.

Eddie, in slow-mo, also leapt, towards his other self. He caught him a decent enough blow to the ear with the special tag and knocked him from his seat and seat belt. The two bears bowled across the cockpit. Things now became a bit tricky.

From beneath came vigorous gunfire. Toy cannons added to the tanks' assault. Toys of all varieties issued into the streets, many, in the more disreputable parts of town, toting illegal weaponry that they too discharged skywards.

A stricken saucer plummeted down and struck Toy City Town Hall.

Gunfire ripped into the undercarriage of the Great Mother-Henship.

The Great Mother-Henship, now pilotless, slewed hideously to port.★

The Eddies bowled over and over, punching and biting and suchlike.

Dorothy dropped down nimbly into the pilot's seat.

'Do you know how to fly this?' asked Jack, swaying about in an alarming fashion.

'Now would be the time to learn.' And Dorothy yanked back the steering wheel.

The craft shot upwards, narrowly missing another craft that was rapidly on the descent.

This one struck police headquarters. Mercifully empty. Although Chief Inspector Bellis's entire collection of dolly porn went to ashes.

'Whoa!' went Jack, a-steadying himself.

The Eddies did further tumbling.

Separated.

★ As opposed to starboard. As ships of all varieties are wont to do in this kind of situation.

Fell in different directions.

Dorothy took control of the craft, levelled it out and put it into a circular holding pattern.

Jack snatched up his weapon as the two Eddies prepared to engage in further battle.

Explosions burst all around the circling saucer.

Remaining saucers poured down fire.

Greater fire was returned.

'Stop it, you two,' Jack told the squaring-up Eddies. 'It's all over now—will you stop.'

The Eddies glared at one another. 'Shoot him, Jack,' said one.

'Don't shoot *me*,' said the other one. 'I'm the real Eddie. Shoot *that* one.'

Jack's big gun swung from side to side.

'I'm not shooting anyone,' said Jack. 'Land the craft, please, Dorothy.'

'That might be a problem,' said Dorothy. 'The controls appear to be jammed.'

'Let me have a go at them,' said an Eddie.

'No, let me.' And an Eddie snatched up a fallen big gun.

The other Eddie rapidly did likewise. 'Drop that gun,' he said. 'Drop your gun or I'll shoot you dead.'

'Shoot him, Jack,' said an Eddie.

'No, shoot *him*, before he kills us all.'

Jack's gun moved backwards and forwards and back.

Explosions rocked the craft.

Dorothy struggled at the controls. Said, 'I think we're going down.'

Eddies cocked their big guns both.

'Jack, shoot him,' said one. 'I'm your bestest friend. You know it's me. Shoot him, Jack.'

Guns were turning in all directions now. Upon both Eddies. Upon Jack. Even upon Dorothy.

Jack dithered, rightfully.

One Eddie said, 'Jack, after everything we've been through together, you must know *me*. I'm your bestest friend. The bestest friend you've ever had.'

'Jack, don't let this monster fool you. If you shoot me, he will shoot you, then both of us will be dead.'

'It's a dilemma,' said Jack. And he flinched as another explosion rocked the ailing ship.

'It's not a dilemma,' an Eddie said. 'Go with your feelings, Jack. Do the right thing. You've always done the right thing, really. You can do the right thing now—it's as simple as blinking.'

And there was another explosion.

And Jack's big gun went off.

And Eddie looked down at another Eddie. This one with a hole in his belly. It was a *big* hole. A lethal hole. Smoke rose from this hole. Which went right through to the other side.

'You did it, Jack,' said the vertical Eddie. Turning his gun upon Jack. 'Good boy.'

And . . .

Eddie dropped his gun. 'How did you know for sure?' he asked.

'Because I know *you*,' said Jack. 'He said, "As simple as blinking." You'd say, "As simple as." '

'Well, that *was* simple,' said Eddie. 'Well done.'

'Well done, nothing.' The perforated Eddie struggled to its feet and stood swaying on the swaying floor. 'It's not as simple as *that*,' said this Eddie. 'I don't die *that* easily.' And this Eddie put its paw to its head. And lifted it. Raised it from its shoulders, cast it aside.

Where it bounce–bounce–bounced across the cockpit floor.

And Jack looked on.

And Eddie looked on.

As the head of a chicken rose through the neck hole of the decerebrated bear. 'I cannot be killed so easily,' said this head, 'for I am Henrietta, Queen of all the hens.'

'Henrietta?' said Jack. 'Well, you're a dead duck now.'

And he squeezed the trigger.

But nothing came from the barrel.

'Sorry,' said Queen Henrietta, and wing tips sprouted through the Eddie paws, and these scooped up a fallen gun and levelled it at Jack. 'You have no idea what you've done,' said the Queen of all the chickens. 'Were I to die, all my policies would be reversed by my successor. That cannot be allowed to happen. This craft must return to Area Fifty-Two. We will return here tomorrow and destroy every inch of Toy City. But for now, you and this abominable bear must die. Right now.'

And the Queen of all the chickens squeezed the trigger.

And then gave a sudden shriek and fell in a jumbled heap.

'Dorothy,' said Jack. 'You—'

'Wrung its scrawny neck,' said Dorothy. 'Well, you'd have done the same for me. Wouldn't you?'

Jack was about to say, 'Yes.'

But he didn't.

Jack instead said, *'No!'*

Because fire from below rattled into the craft.

And the craft turned upside down.

★

And then the Great Mother-Henship, the sole surviving member of the chicken strikeforce, dropped from the sky.

And, 'No!' shouted Tinto. As it was coming his way.

And then there was another of those terrible explosions.

But no, not in slow motion.

Enough is enough is enough.

27

Chief Inspector Bellis looked all around and about himself.

A very great deal of Toy City appeared to be ablaze.

The bells of fire engines came to his ears.

The wreckage of his car once more to his eyes.

And the wreckage of the spaceship beyond.

'Well,' said Bellis, 'that would appear to be *that*. Job jobbed, but goodness, I dread the paperwork.'

Amelie looked through her fingers. 'Did we win?' she asked.

'Naturally, my dear. Most naturally.'

Amelie shook her beautiful head, beautiful, but drunk. 'I am *so* impressed,' she said. 'You saved Toy City. You are *so* a hero.'

'He wouldn't have done so if *I* hadn't tipped him off,' said a clock-work spaceman.

'Then *you* are *so* a hero.' And Amelie threw her arms around him.

'Oi!' said Bellis. 'Not so fast. He would never have tipped me off if he hadn't . . . How did you put it, spaceman?'

'Received a telepathic message,' said the spaceman. 'From the other side of The Second Big O. A bear spoke unto me. Told me what was to occur. Said he kept going in and out of his body, whatever *that* meant.'

'Well, let's not worry about *that*,' said Bellis. 'And get your space-man's hands off my girlfriend.'

'Do you think there are any survivors?' asked Amelie, stroking the spaceman's tin-plate chest. 'And do spacemen have credit cards, by the way?'

'Big shiny gold ones,' said the spaceman.

'Survivors?' said Bellis, prising the hands of Amelie away from the spaceman's helmet. 'Aliens in need of shooting, now there's a thought.' And reached towards his car, then reached away, for it smouldered.

'Shoot 'em with *this*,' said Tinto, wheeling through the doorway and presenting Bellis with a shotgun that he, as indeed do *all* barmen, kept hidden beneath his bar counter.

Just in case.

Bellis took the shotgun and approached the craft.

It was pretty buckled up and smoking.

Some laughing policemen who had escaped annihilation through being in the toilet when the mayhem occurred backed up Bellis at a distance.

The fallen craft had flattened several shops. It lay half upon its side.

And as Bellis approached, and so too the policemen, the hatchway slowly opened.

'Hands up, you aliens,' cried the chief inspector.

And struggling down from the hatchway came a tattered trio.

Jack was helping Eddie Bear. And Dorothy helped Jack.

28

And Tinto served drinks on the house.

Jack toasted Eddie.

And Eddie, Jack.

And Bellis toasted himself.

'You did brilliantly, Jack,' said Eddie Bear, balancing upon his head on the barstool in order that he might really benefit from the beer. 'You are as brilliant as.'

'We both did okay,' said Jack. 'We're a team, you and me. We're the business.'

'And we should be back in business now.' Eddie struggled to pour further beer down his inverted throat. Jack gave him a little helping out. 'We can open for business big time now.'

'You think we've seen the last of the chickens?'

'I reckon so. The portal between the worlds is destroyed.' Eddie hiccuped. 'And from what we both know about the chicken matriarchy, the new Queen will reverse the policies of the old. Pretty daft system, I grant you, but they *are* chickens. And so I suppose that means that not only is our world saved, but the world of men also.'

'I didn't take much to *that* world,' said Jack, draining his glass and ordering several more. 'Things are problematic here, but out *there* . . . That place is mad.'

'I thought it held some appeal for you.' Eddie tried to remain on his head and did so with some style. 'What with that Dorothy. Where is she, by the way?'

'She's gone,' said Jack. 'She left.'

'Left?' said Eddie. 'Left for where and why?'

'She returned to the soil,' said Jack. 'I dug her in.'

'You did *what*?' And Eddie fell from the barstool.

Jack helped Eddie to his feet. 'She wasn't human,' he said. 'She was something else entirely. The last of her kind. She was, well, *is* a vegetable.'

'And you're kidding me, right?'

'No,' said Jack. 'I'm not. The chickens conquered her world a couple of years back. She escaped through another Big O, this one in a big sign that spelt out "SPROUTLAND". She escaped to Hollywood. She was waiting there for someone like me—well, someones like us, as it happens—to help her take her revenge against the chickens for wiping out her kind.'

'And you "dug her in"?'

'Into Tinto's garden. She'll take root. She'll bloom here. She's, er, been fertilised.'

'Excruciating,' said Tinto.

'That almost makes me want to cry,' said Eddie. 'But I'll fight the sensation and drink more beer instead.'

'I *really* liked her, you know,' said Jack, making a wistful face.

'A bit more than *liked*, I suspect,' said Eddie, climbing back onto his stool.

'Nothing of the sort,' said Jack. 'I'm as hard as nails, me. Women are just women.'

'Leave it out, Jack, you're as romantic as.'

'Yeah,' said Jack. 'I suppose I am. Now where is Amelie?'

'She went to the toilet,' said Eddie. 'To throw up, I suspect. Ah, here she comes now, wobbling somewhat. And, oh look there's the Phantom of the Opera.'

Eddie waved towards the Phantom and the Phantom waved back.

And there indeed came Amelie. And she *was* wobbling somewhat. And she swayed up to Jack and gazed into his eyes.

And then she flung her arms about him.

And gave that Jack a snog.

And Jack for his part snogged her in return.

And Jack, as he would soon find out, was really, truly in love.

'And so all's well that ends well,' said Eddie, resuming his inverted position on the barstool and enjoying the sensation of all that alcohol draining back into his head.

'All's well indeed,' said Wellington Bellis, looking with distaste towards the snogging Jack and then with even greater distaste towards Eddie. 'And now I feel it is time to bring matters to a satisfactory conclusion. And make my arrest.'

'Your arrest?' asked Eddie.

'Bring the malcontent to justice,' said Bellis. 'To whit, arrest *you*, Eddie Bear, cat's-paw of the evil criminal mastermind, Tinto—'

'What?' went Tinto.

'Eddie Bear, mass-murderer, and clearly commander of the alien strikeforce, I arrest you in the name of the law. You do not have to say anything, but anything you do say will be twisted around and used against you as damning evidence. In order to condemn you to prison, or worse; and I can think up far worse.'

Eddie Bear said, 'Hold on there.'

And Bellis said, 'You're nicked.'

'No, hold on,' said Eddie, tumbling from his stool. 'It's not the way you think—I'm the good guy. I sent this telepathic message to the spaceman to warn you what was going to happen. You see, there were these chickens. You don't understand . . .'

Wellington Bellis laughed and laughed. 'Had you going there,' he said to Eddie. 'You're not really nicked, I was only joking.'

Eddie Bear looked up and huffed and puffed.

'Do you know what?' said Bellis. 'I feel you deserve some special reward for your services to Toy City. In fact I feel that you deserve some special position, or rank. I have the necessary clout to pull a few strings around here. How would you fancy taking on the job of Mayor?'

'Well . . .' said Eddie Bear.

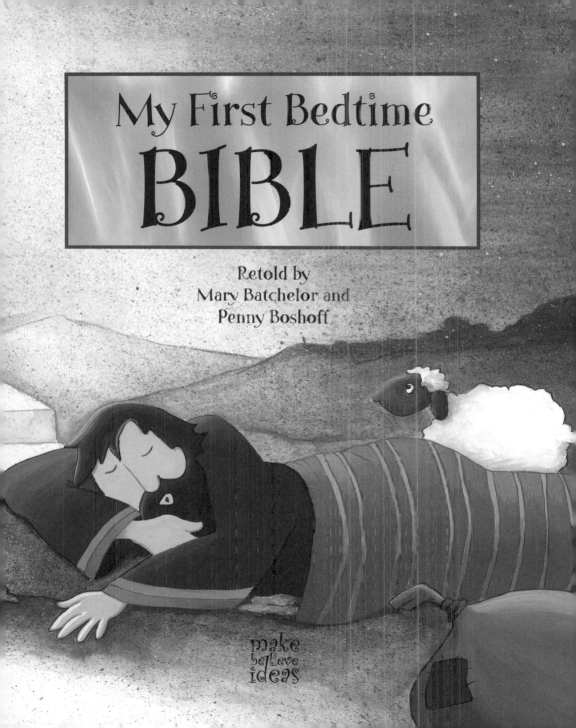

My First Bedtime
BIBLE

Retold by
Mary Batchelor and
Penny Boshoff

make
believe
ideas

First published in the US in 2005
by make believe ideas
27 Castle Street,
Berkhamsted,
Hertfordshire, HP4 2DW

Designer: Belinda Ellis
Illustrators: Sara Baker,
Jo Goodberry, Nikki Loy,
Helen Parrott, Cathy Shimmen,
Q2A, Rachel Stevens
American consultant:
Claudia Volkman

Printed and bound in Singapore

CONTENTS

The Old Testament

The Old Testament is full of wonderful stories. They tell how, long ago, God chose Abraham and his family after him, to be his special people and to tell the world about God. They often disobeyed and failed, but God always kept his promises. And he is still the same today.

Long, long ago, when God began to
make everything, our world, called
Earth, was in a terrible mess.
Everywhere was dark. Storms
raged and the seas roared.

God said, "Earth needs light."
And he made the sun to shine
by day and the moon and stars
to give light at night.

Then he said to the sea, "Don't go
any further than the seashore."

Earth began to look good.

8

Dear God,
thank you
for making our
beautiful world.
Amen.

God was pleased with Earth but it looked very empty.

So God said, "I will make grass and flowers and trees to cover Earth."

Then God made creatures of every kind to fill the sea and the air and the land.

Soon there were fish swimming in the rivers and seas, birds singing in the trees and animals running and playing together.

Everywhere God's Earth was busy and happy.

Thank God for all the different birds and animals and the sounds they make.

God needed someone he could love and be close to. So he made Adam and Eve to be his friends and take care of his Earth.

God said: "Eat and enjoy all the fruit in this garden you're living in." But pointing to one tree he said, "Never eat that fruit because it will poison you."

Thank you, God,
for making
people and for
making me.
Amen.

Every evening God came to the
garden to talk to Adam and Eve.
They were very happy.

Genesis 2

13

One day the snake saw Eve near the forbidden tree.
"Why not eat *that* fruit?" he asked.
"Because God said 'No,'" Eve said.
"Don't listen to God," the snake whispered.

The fruit looked delicious, so Eve picked
some and shared it with Adam.

Dear God,
I'm sorry for
sometimes being
disobedient today.
Please forgive me.
Amen.

They had
disobeyed
God and
they were
miserable.

"I made you to love me and be my
friends," God told them sadly. "But
now you must leave the garden."

GENESIS 3

15

Adam and Eve had two baby boys – Cain and Abel.
When they grew up, Cain became a farmer and
Abel a shepherd. Cain thought that Abel was
God's favorite.

When they both gave
presents to God, God
said: "Cain, I can't take
your present because
you are angry inside.
Don't be jealous of
your brother."

16

Dear God,
help me not
to be jealous of
other children.
Amen.

But Cain hated
Abel more and
more. One day
when they were
out together,
Cain killed Abel.

God was very sad.
Hate and murder
were spoiling Earth.

GENESIS 4

God was sad. Everyone in his world
was doing bad things – except Noah.

"Noah, build a big boat," said
God. "It's going to rain and
water will flood the earth."

Everyone laughed as
Noah built his boat far
from the sea.

When the boat was ready, God said,
"Noah, go onto the boat with your family. Take
two of each kind of animal and bird with you."

18

Please, God,
keep *us* safe too.
Amen.

Then it rained
and rained – until
all the land had
disappeared.

But Noah's boat floated safely.

GENESIS 6, 7

At last the rain stopped. Noah waited and waited . . . .
20   When the land was dry Noah opened the door.

Out flew the birds and off scampered the animals.

Can you name all the colors in the rainbow?

Noah was so happy. He said a special "Thank you" to God.

"Noah," God said, "look at that rainbow in the sky. It will remind everyone that I promise never to flood the whole earth again."

GENESIS 8, 9

21

Abraham and Sarah lived happily together.
But they really wanted a baby!

Then God said: "Abraham, I've chosen you – you're special!"

"One day everyone in the whole
world will be happy because of you
and the family I shall give you."

"But now you must leave your house and live in
a tent, ready to move on whenever I tell you to."

Thank you,
dear God,
that we are all
special to you.
Amen.

Abraham said "Yes" to God.

GENESIS 12   23

The desert sun was burning down as Abraham sat outside his tent. When he caught sight of three tired strangers, he called out: "Welcome! Please stay here and rest!"

Thank you,
God, for mothers
and grandmas.
Amen.

So they sat in the shade while
Abraham hurried off to get them
food and water. He didn't know
that they were God's messengers.

After dinner one of them said, "Next year
Sarah will have a baby."

Sarah laughed – why, she was old enough to be a
grandmother! Could God *really* give them a baby?

GENESIS 18

25

Sure enough, God kept his promise, and Baby Isaac
was born. Abraham and Sarah were so happy!

But one day, years later, God said, "Abraham, will you give Isaac back to me?" Abraham's heart sank, but he made up his mind to obey God.

Help me, God, to trust you always, no matter what. Amen.

They set off to a faraway place and Abraham got ready to give Isaac to God. Then God called out, "Abraham, I'm *not* going to take Isaac away. I know now how much you love and trust me."

GENESIS 22

27

Isaac married Rebecca and they had twin boys.
Esau, the older twin, liked being outdoors with
his bow and arrows while Jacob stayed at home.

Esau cared nothing about God,
but Jacob listened eagerly
to the story of God's
promises to his
grandfather Abraham.

One day Esau came back from hunting,
tired and hungry. Jacob was cooking
soup and it smelled delicious!

"Give me some, Jacob!" Esau shouted. "I'm starving!"

Thank you, God, that we're all good at different things. Amen.

"Only if *you* give *me* your special place as eldest son," Jacob bargained. "All right!" Esau agreed.

Years later Jacob tricked Isaac too. Isaac promised Jacob all the good things he had to give, because he thought Jacob was really Esau. Esau was furious. "I'll kill Jacob!" he muttered. Jacob was scared and ran away.

All day he walked, and at night he lay down under the stars.

In his dream he saw a staircase.
Angels were hurrying up and down, busy for God.

Thank you, God,
for being with us
all night long.
Amen.

Then God came close to Jacob.
"I will be with you," he promised. "I'll never leave
you. You and your children's children will have good
things, just as I promised to Abraham."

GENESIS 28

Jacob had lots of children but Joseph was his favorite. He gave him a beautiful colored coat

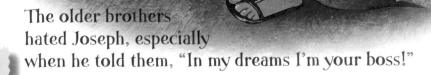

The older brothers hated Joseph, especially when he told them, "In my dreams I'm your boss!"

One day Jacob sent Joseph to find his brothers, who were caring for the sheep far from home. They saw Joseph coming.

Draw and color Joseph's special coat.

"We've got him now!" they boasted. They seized Joseph, ripped off his special coat and threw him down an empty well. GENESIS 37

33

Soon Joseph heard shouts –
his brothers were back. They
hauled Joseph up and sold him to
some merchants traveling to Egypt.

The merchants
sent Joseph to
the slave market
where he was sold
to an important
man called
Potiphar.

34

Joseph worked so hard that Potiphar soon put him in charge of everything he had.

Help me, dear God, not to tell lies about other children. Amen.

One day, Potiphar's wife told wicked lies about Joseph, so he was sent to prison. But God was still with Joseph.

GENESIS 37, 39

35

The king of Egypt
had upsetting dreams.
"Send for Joseph," a
servant who knew him
suggested. "He explains
what dreams mean."
Joseph was rushed
from the prison to
the palace.

"I dreamed about
seven thin cows who
ate up seven fat cows
but still stayed thin,"
the king told Joseph.

Dear God, please help me to have good dreams. Amen.

"God says seven good harvests are coming, followed by seven poor ones," Joseph explained. "Save corn from the good years to feed your people when the bad years come."

"I will put you in charge of saving Egypt," the king told Joseph.

GENESIS 41

37

When there wasn't enough food, everyone came to Egypt to buy corn.

One day Joseph's own brothers arrived. They did not know it was Joseph – alive and in charge! He pretended to be angry.

"You are spies!" he shouted. His brothers were very frightened.

At last, he told them, "I am your brother, Joseph! Don't be frightened. I won't pay you back for selling me. God brought me here to save everyone! Bring the whole family to live with me in Egypt."

GENESIS 42–45

Dear God, help me to be forgiving like Joseph. Amen.

God gave Jacob the name "Israel." Israel's people lived in Egypt, but a cruel king made them his slaves.

Next the king ordered: "Throw their baby boys into the river!"

One mother said, "God will save my baby." She put Moses in a little floating basket, then pushed it out among the river reeds.

The princess came along.
"What's in that basket?" she asked.

A servant waded in and fetched it. The princess
opened the lid and little Moses smiled at her.
"What a beautiful baby!" she exclaimed.
"I shall keep him."

EXODUS 1, 2

41

When Moses grew up he longed to save his own people. The king found out and was furious, so Moses ran far away.

One day, as Moses looked after his sheep, he saw fire coming from a bush. It was no ordinary fire and he stopped to look.

God spoke from the bush
Moses stood very still and quiet.

Draw and color
the burning bush.

"Go back to Egypt," God told him,
"and rescue your unhappy people."
"I can't!" Moses exclaimed.
"Yes, you can," God told him,
"because I will be with you."

EXODUS 3

43

Moses packed his bags and left for Egypt.

"God says you are to let his people go," he told the king.

"Certainly not!" the king replied. "I don't know or care about your God. I'm keeping your people here."
He gave orders: "Make the Israelites work harder!"

44

"You've made things worse, not better,"
the Israelites complained to Moses.
"Wait and see what God will do,"
he told them.

Please help
me, God, to
be obedient.
Amen.

Then Moses warned the king: "Obey
God or bad things will happen."
"I won't!" the king replied.
EXODUS 4, 5

45

Everything happened as Moses had warned.
First, frogs ran everywhere, then flies came, then storms.

Every time the king told Moses he was
sorry, God made things right again.
Then the king would change his mind.

At last Moses said, "No more chances! God *will* rescue his people, but because of *you*, all Egypt will be sad." "Go away!" the king shouted.

Thank you, God, for keeping your people safe. Amen.

Then Moses told the Israelites, "Cook a special meal to thank God for saving us. Tomorrow we'll leave Egypt!"

EXODUS 4–12

47

The Israelites left with all their belongings, traveling along the desert road. At night they camped beside the Sea of Reeds. Suddenly they heard noises – the Egyptian army was coming! They were terrified.

God said to Moses, "Calm down! Stretch your stick over the water, then tell the people to go forward."

Sing a "Thank you" song to God.

Moses obeyed God. The waters rolled back and the Israelites crossed on dry ground.

"Hurrah!" they shouted on the other side.
"The Egyptians are gone for ever."
They thanked God with dances and songs.

Exodus 14, 15

"We're on our way to the country God promised us," Moses told the Israelites. But first they had to go through the desert, and soon the people were asking,

"What can we eat?"

God told Moses, "I will feed them."

Next morning the ground was covered with small, white flakes. "This is the food God will send each morning," Moses told them.

The Israelites didn't know what the food was, so they called it "manna" which means "What is it?" It tasted good, like honey biscuits.

Exodus 16

51

The people kept on grumbling.
"We're thirsty, Moses," they
moaned. "Give us water!"

"Trust God – he'll give us all
we need," Moses told them,
but they got angry with him.
Moses told God all about it.

"They're *really* grumbling at me," said God. "Now go to the special rock that I will show you and hit it with your stick."

Thank you, dear God, for clean water. Amen.

Moses did as God told him, and cool, refreshing water gushed from the rock. There was plenty for everyone.

EXODUS 17

53

God gave Moses rules to help the
Israelites live as his special people.

God said:
Put me first and love me best.

Keep one day a week special for me –
take a holiday from work.

Obey your father and mother.

Keep your special love for your
husband and wife.

Don't take what isn't yours.

Don't tell lies about other people.

Don't be jealous of other people and
want what they have.

These are good rules for everyone.

Exodus 20

55

After many months, Canaan –
God's promised land – was near.

Moses sent twelve men as spies to explore it.

When the spies came back they said,
"It's a wonderful country, BUT
we'll never own it! The Canaanites
are huge and strong!"

Please God,
make me brave
like Rahab.
Amen.

"Hang a red rope from your window,"
the spies told her. "When we take
Jericho, we will keep you safe."
Then they escaped.

JOSHUA 1, 2

God told Joshua: "I will give you Jericho. Just do as I say. Tell the soldiers and priests to march once around the city walls every day for six days.

"On the seventh day, they must march round Jericho *seven* times while the priests blow their trumpets. At the last long trumpet blast, everyone must shout!"

The people obeyed God's strange orders.

Be an Israelite soldier and march round Jericho.

On the seventh day, at the trumpets' last, long blast, the people shouted at the top of their voices – and the city walls fell flat! But Rahab was kept safe.

JOSHUA 6

61

The Israelites settled in Canaan – God's
promised land – but they forgot about God.
Then enemies attacked them, and God told
young Gideon,

"You must rescue Israel. I'll show you how."

Gideon wasn't very brave, but he obeyed God.
He gave every soldier a trumpet in one hand and,
in the other, a lighted torch hidden inside a jar.
That night they crept to the enemy camp.

Please, God, help me to be brave. Amen.

At Gideon's signal, every soldier smashed his jar, blew his trumpet and shouted, "For God and for Gideon!" Their frightened enemies ran for their lives.

JUDGES 6, 7

Once more Israel had enemies, and God chose Samson to fight them. But he often spoiled God's plans by wanting his own way.

One day Samson asked his enemies, the Philistines, to solve this riddle:

Out of the eater came something to eat

Out of the strong came something sweet.

What *could* it mean? The Philistines were puzzled.

Can *you* guess the word that answers Samson's riddle?

Then they found out that strong-man Samson once killed a young lion with his bare hands.

Later he found a bee's nest in the lion's dead body and greedily swallowed the honey.

Judges 13-16

65

After many adventures, the Philistines seized
Samson and blinded him. Then they celebrated.
"Dagon, our god, is the greatest!" they chanted.

A boy fetched Samson, so the
Philistines could tease and bully him.
"Guide my hands to the big pillars,"
Samson whispered to the boy.

"Please God, help me once more to
beat the Philistines!" Samson prayed.
He put one hand around each pillar
and pushed – and pushed!

Help me, God,
not to bully
other children.
Amen.

Suddenly, the pillars that held up the roof gave way
and the building collapsed. God's enemies were
crushed to death and Samson perished with them.

JUDGES 16

Naomi lived in Bethlehem with her husband and two sons. But when there wasn't enough food, they moved to the country of Moab.

Poor Naomi! Her husband and her sons died. But their Moabite wives, Orpah and Ruth, looked after her.

One day news arrived:
"There's food again in Bethlehem."

Thank you, God,
for everyone
who takes care
of me.
Amen.

"I'm going back,"
Naomi told the girls.
"But you belong here."

So Orpah sadly hugged Naomi good-bye. But
Ruth said, "I'll come with you and stay with
you always. I love you and I love your God."

RUTH 1

69

Naomi and Ruth arrived in Bethlehem at harvest time. They were so poor that Ruth collected stray ears of corn from the fields to make bread.

The owner of the fields, Boaz, asked, "Who's that stranger?"

The farmworkers told him all about Ruth's kindness to Naomi. Boaz said, "Look after her, and drop extra corn for her to find."

Then Boaz discovered that he was related to Naomi's husband! So he decided to look after Naomi and marry Ruth.

Thank you, God, for everyone who takes care of me. Amen.

How happy Naomi was when she held her first little grandson in her arms!

RUTH 2–4

71

Hannah's husband loved her very much, but she did long for a baby!

One year when they visited God's house for a celebration, Hannah felt really miserable. She went off by herself, crying.

"Please God," she prayed, "send me a baby. I promise I'll give him back to you."

Eli, the old priest,
heard her and said,
"May God give you
peace and answer
your prayer!"

Thank you, God,
for listening
when we feel sad.
Amen.

How excited Hannah was when she had her baby!
She called him Samuel, which means "I asked
God for him".

1 SAMUEL 1

73

Hannah remembered her promise, and took little Samuel to stay with Eli, the priest at God's house.

One night, when Samuel was nearly asleep, he heard: "Samuel!"

"It's Eli," he thought, and ran to answer him. "I didn't call," Eli said. "Go back to bed!"

Three times Samuel heard his name called and three times he ran to Eli.

74

Dear God, help me to listen when you speak to me. Amen.

Then Eli said, "It's God's voice. Next time he calls, say you are listening."

God called again. Samuel listened – and heard God's message.

1 Samuel 3

When Samuel grew up he looked after
the Israelites and taught them about God.
But the people wanted a king instead.
"I will choose their king," God told Samuel.

One day a young man arrived to see Samuel.
"My name is Saul," he told Samuel.
"My father's donkeys ran away and I can't
find them anywhere. Can you help me?"

"Don't worry," Samuel said,
"they found their
own way back!"

Then God whispered to
Samuel, "I have chosen
Saul to be king of Israel!"
1 SAMUEL 8–10

Please, God,
help me when
I'm worried.
Amen.

77

How the Israelites loved King Saul! He was tall
and handsome. But he did not always obey God.
One day the Israelites were
getting ready for battle.
"Wait for me to pray
before you fight,"
Samuel told the king.

Saul waited and waited. The soldiers fidgeted and complained, and Saul decided to say the prayers himself.

Please, God, help me to learn how to wait. Amen.

Just then Samuel came back.

"Why didn't you wait?" he asked Saul sadly. "Because you won't obey God, he will have to choose another king."
1 SAMUEL 13

"The next king will be one of Jesse's sons," God told Samuel.

Samuel visited Jesse and met his handsome eldest son. "He looks like a king!" thought Samuel. But God whispered, "No! You're going by looks, but I see what a person is really like!"

Samuel met seven more of Jesse's sons. Every time God said, "No!"

"Do you have another son?" Samuel asked.

"Only young David," Jesse replied. "He's looking after my sheep."

Thank you, God, for loving us whatever we look like. Amen.

"Go get him!" Samuel ordered.
David arrived, breathless.
"He is the one!" God told Samuel. "My chosen king!"

1 SAMUEL 16

81

David's brothers were soldiers in Saul's army. David
was visiting them when Goliath – a giant of a man –
bellowed from the Philistine camp: "Israelites,
choose a man to fight me!"
There was a terrified silence.
"I'll fight him!"
volunteered David.

He refused to
borrow Saul's
armor, and
took only his
shepherd's sling.

Goliath roared with laughter when he saw David.

"I'll feed you to the birds," he jeered.

"I come in God's strength!" David shouted.

Please, God, help us to stand up for what is right. Amen.

He aimed – and the stone from his sling hit Goliath's skull . . . crack! Goliath crashed to the ground.

David had won the battle for God.

1 Samuel 16

Saul invited David to live at his palace. Sometimes
Saul was miserable, and David would sing and play
his small harp to cheer him up.

David and Jonathan, Saul's
son, became great friends.
But Saul grew jealous of David
because everyone loved him.

Thank you, God,
for best friends.
Amen.

One day Saul hurled
his spear at David,
who dodged it just in time!
"Go!" Jonathan warned his friend.
"Or my dad will kill you!"
They hugged each other and sadly said good-bye.

1 SAMUEL 18

At first, David hid in a cave where Saul wouldn't find him. All sorts of people joined him and made him their chief. But Saul kept chasing him, so David found new hiding places.

One night Saul and his men were camped nearby. David and his nephew, Abishai, crept up on Saul's sleeping soldiers.

David picked up the spear
lying beside Saul.
"Kill him!" Abishai
whispered eagerly.

Dear God, help
me to forgive
people who treat
me badly.
Amen.

"Never!" David replied. "We'll take Saul's
spear and water jug, and go! One day Saul
will die – *then* my time will come!"
1 SAMUEL 26

87

Finally Saul died in battle and David became king. But David was sad – Saul's son, his friend Jonathan, had died too! "I want to care for someone in his family," he said.

So David sent for Mephibosheth, Jonathan's son.

Servants carried Mephibosheth in because he couldn't walk. He had been hurt in an accident when he was little.

88

Mephibosheth was terrified. Would David punish *him* because of Saul's unkindness?

Thank you, God, for kind people. Amen.

But David said, "Mephibosheth, welcome for Jonathan's sake! Live here, and have dinner with me every day."

2 SAMUEL 9

89

When David died, his son
Solomon became king.
Solomon asked God to
help him rule well, and
God made him wise.

One day two mothers arrived with a baby.
"This is *my* baby!" one of them said.
"No, he's mine!" the other one shouted.
"Please decide who the mother is," they
begged Solomon.

90

"Get a sword," Solomon ordered.
"Cut the baby in two and give each
mother half!"

One mother cried out, "No! Don't hurt
him! I'd rather you gave him to *her!*"
"That's the real mother," Solomon
declared. "Give her the baby."

1 KINGS 3

91

God made Solomon rich as well as wise. Every year ships brought him wood, gold, ivory, and monkeys and peacocks for his palace and gardens.

But Solomon planned to build a special, splendid home for God – the temple. Thousands of builders got busy with fine wood and huge stones to build Solomon's temple. Inside, in God's special room, even the floor was paved with gold!

When it was finished, everyone celebrated.

Thank you, God,
for listening to us
wherever we are.
Amen.

God promised to listen to his people when they
prayed to him there.

1 Kings 5–10

Some kings of Israel were bad
kings. King Ahab was married to
wicked Jezebel. She killed many
of God's friends and prayed to a
pretend god, Beal.

One day a man visited Ahab.
"I am Elijah, servant of the true
God," he said. "Be warned! No
rain will fall until I say so!"

Thank you,
God, for brave
people who stand
up for you.
Amen.

So that's just
what happened.
Plants and
animals began to
die and everyone
was hungry.
But Elijah was
kept safe from
Ahab. God
looked after him.

1 KINGS 17

95

After many months, Elijah came back. "Bring everyone, especially Baal's servants, to Mount Carmel," he told Ahab. "We'll prove who's *really* God!"

On the mountaintop, Elijah said to Baal's followers, "Take wood and build a fire. But don't start it yet." Elijah built a fire too. "Now ask Baal to send fire," he told them.

Baal's followers prayed and prayed but *nothing* happened!

Thank you, God, that you are real. Amen.

Then Elijah said: "Please, God, send fire! Let everyone know *you* are God!" At once, flames streaked down and set Elijah's wood on fire. The Israelites all shouted, "Our God is the real God!"

1 KINGS 18

Jezebel was furious with
Elijah and wanted to kill him.
But God looked after Elijah.
"Find Elisha," he told him. "He
will help you. One day he will
take over your work for God."

One day when Elijah
and Elisha were walking
together, they heard a
rushing noise.

Suddenly, a chariot of fire, drawn
by fiery horses, swooped down
between them. A great wind
whirled Elijah off his feet. He
was lifted up, up and away – until
Elisha could see him no more.

Thank you, God,
for friends who
help us.
Amen.

At the same time, a wind whirled Elijah off
his feet, lifting him up, up and away —
until Elisha could see him no more.
2 KINGS 2

One day a woman came to see Elisha. "Please help me!" she sobbed. "My husband is dead and they're taking my sons away because I owe money."

"What have you got at home?" Elisha asked.
"One small bottle of oil," she said.
"Borrow lots of bottles," Elisha told her.
100 "Then fill them from your oil."

The boys found bottles of all kinds and the woman poured and poured . . . ..

The oil didn't run out until every borrowed bottle was full! Only then was there no more oil. "Sell the oil to pay your debt," kind Elisha told her.

2 KINGS 4

An Israelite girl was captured by Naaman, chief of
the Syrian army. He took her to his home. When she
discovered that he had a terrible skin disease, she said,
"Elisha – God's man in Israel – could make him better!"

So Naaman journeyed to see Elisha.
"Wash seven times in the River Jordan," Elisha ordered.
Naaman was furious. "There are cleaner rivers to wash
in back home!" he shouted.

"Please do as Elisha says!" his soldiers pleaded.

Thank you, God – you're great! Amen.

So Naaman dipped in the water seven times – and his skin was smooth again! "Your God is the *real* God!" he told Elisha.

2 KINGS 5

103

Athaliah – daughter of wicked Jezebel – killed all the royal children so she could become queen! But baby Joash was rescued by his aunt, who hid him safely.

Six years later his uncle and aunt called all the people together. Uncle Jehoida led seven-year-old Joash out, placed a crown on his head and gave him a copy of God's Law – their Bible.

Everyone cheered and shouted,
"Long live King Joash!"

Thank you, God,
for aunts
and uncles.
Amen.

Then Athaliah arrived! She gave one
horrified look, and screamed, "Treason!"
"Take her away!" Jehoida told the soldiers.
So Joash became the rightful king.

2 KINGS 11–12

105

One day God said to Jonah, "Go to the wicked city of Nineveh and tell the people to change their ways." Jonah didn't want to help his enemies, so he ran away and went to sea.

But the wind began to roar and the waves grew high as mountains.

Please help
me, God, to do
as I'm told.
Amen.

The terrified sailors cried out.

"We're going to sink!"

"It's my fault," Jonah said.
"It's because I'm running away from God.
Throw me out of the boat and the storm will stop."
Reluctantly the sailors threw Jonah overboard
and the sea grew calm.

JONAH 1

As Jonah sank beneath the waves, a big fish swam by and swallowed him in one gulp.

Inside the fish Jonah prayed, "Please help me, God!"

God listened.
He told the fish to spit
Jonah out onto the beach.
"Go to Nineveh, Jonah," God said again, and Jonah went.
Jonah told the people how wicked they were, and they
promised God that they would change their ways.

"I won't punish them," God told Jonah, "because they are truly sorry."

Thank you, God, for forgiving me when I'm truly sorry. Amen.

Jonah was angry. He wanted God to forgive *him*, but not his enemies.

Josiah was a good king who loved God.
The temple – God's house in Jerusalem –
was falling apart, so Josiah sent for
builders and decorators to fix it.

While they were working on one of the rooms, they
came upon the lost copy of God's Law – their Bible.
They read it to King Josiah. He burst into tears.

"We haven't obeyed God!" he exclaimed.

Thank you, God, for the Bible. Amen.

But God sent a message to cheer Josiah up. Sad times *would* come, but after good Josiah's days were over.

2 CHRONICLES 34, 35

Bad kings followed King Josiah. God's man, Jeremiah, warned everyone that if they kept disobeying God, their enemies would fight them and win.

"We must stop Jeremiah!" said the wicked leaders. The king let them throw Jeremiah into a deep, muddy hole.

But Ebedmelech said to the king, "Your Majesty! We can't let Jeremiah die!"

"Then get him out," the king ordered.

Please, God, help me to be kind and thoughtful. Amen.

Ebedmelech grabbed some old clothes
and rushed off to rescue Jeremiah.
He peered into the hole.
"Jeremiah," he shouted. "Put these rags under
your arms, so these ropes won't cut you."
Then Ebedmelech and his helpers pulled
Jeremiah up to safety.

JEREMIAH 38

113

No one listened to Jeremiah's warnings.
Then Nebuchadnezzar – the mighty king of
Babylon – brought his army against Jerusalem.
They knocked down the city wall, stole all the
beautiful things from the temple and took all the
people off to their own country.

How sad the people were as they marched away from the land God had given them!

Please, God, help me to take notice of warnings from good people. Amen.

Then Nebuchadnezzar told his soldiers to burn the palaces and the gleaming temple. Nothing was left.

If only the people had listened to God!

2 Chronicles 36

115

The brightest young men from Israel
were taken to Nebuchadnezzar's
palace in Babylon.

Daniel and three friends –
Shadrach, Meshach and
Abednego – were among them.

"You will be served the king's food,"
the chief servant told them.
But to share the king's food would
116   mean obeying *him* rather than God.

So Daniel begged, "Give us vegetables and water instead." "Just for ten days," the servant agreed.

Please, God, help me to obey you. Amen.

After ten days, they all looked healthy and bright. "These men are the best!" Nebuchadnezzar said. "They shall be members of my court."

Daniel 1

Nebuchadnezzar set
up a huge, gold statue.
He ordered everyone
to bow down to it when
the band played.

The music began.
Everyone fell flat
except Shadrach,
Meshach and
Abednego.

"Bow down to my image!" Nebuchadnezzar
shouted furiously. "Or I'll throw you into the fire!"

"We bow down only to God!"
the three replied bravely.
Guards tied them up and
threw them into the furnace.

Thank you, God,
for angels who
look after us.
Amen.

Suddenly Nebuchadnezzar exclaimed: "We
threw three men in – now there are four
walking about in the fire! Their God has sent
his angel and kept them safe!"

DANIEL 3

119

The new king liked Daniel. This made the people jealous.
Daniel's enemies persuaded the king to make a law.
"Command everyone to pray to no one but you —
or be thrown to the lions," they said.

When Daniel went on praying to
God, his enemies told the king.
Sadly, the king had to throw
Daniel into the lions' pit.

All night, the king lay awake worrying.
The next morning he hurried back to
the lions' pit.

Thank you, God,
for keeping
Daniel safe.
Amen.

"Daniel!" he shouted.

"Your Majesty!" Daniel called back.
"My God closed the lions' mouths! I'm safe!"

The king of Persia wanted a queen, so the prettiest girls in the kingdom were sent for. One of them was Esther, the niece of a Jewish courtier called Mordecai.

Out of them all, the king chose Esther and made her queen. But Haman, the king's favorite, hated Mordecai. "Those Jews from Israel are troublesome," he told the king. "Have them killed!"

"Yes," the king agreed. He did not know that Esther was Jewish.

Please, God, show me how to help others. Amen.

Mordecai sent an urgent message to Esther: "Help us!" he begged. "I believe God made you queen to save your people."

ESTHER 1–4

123

Esther was scared. She wanted to help, but suppose the king was angry? "Pray!" she told Mordecai. "I will too."

Then, trembling, she went to the king.
"Ask whatever you want, Esther," he said kindly.
"Please come to dinner – and bring Haman," she added.
After a good meal, Esther said, "Your Majesty, an enemy is plotting to kill me and my people!"

124

"Who is he?" the king asked, furious.

Esther pointed to Haman. "This wicked man!" she replied. "He shall die!" the king decreed. "And Mordecai will take his place."

ESTHER 5, 7

After many years, the Jewish people
came home, as God had promised.
But Jerusalem was in ruins.

First, the people began work on the temple.
Ezra, the priest, helped them finish it,
and he taught them the Bible.

But Nehemiah wanted to rebuild the city. "We must start with the walls," he said, "to keep out our enemies. God will help us!"

Help us, dear God, to work well together. Amen.

Nehemiah gave each family a strip of wall to build. Some watched out for enemies while the rest went on building. They worked hard all day, until the stars came out.

EZRA, NEHEMIAH 3, 4

At last the wall was finished!
Nehemiah called everyone to celebrate.

All the singers and band
members were divided into
two groups to march right
around Jerusalem.

There was singing, music,
dancing and giving thanks to God.
Everyone met up again at the temple.
All the mothers and children came too.

Please make us
happy, God.
Amen.

Everyone was happy because
God had kept his promise. The
people of Israel had come home!

NEHEMIAH 8, 12

129

The New Testament

The wonderful stories from the Old Testament showed how God loved and cared for his people, just as he does today. God also made many promises – promises that he always kept. One was that he would send a special king to rescue them. In the New Testament we meet God's king – his name is Jesus.

Mary lived in the little town of Nazareth. One day
God sent the Angel Gabriel to see her.

"Don't be afraid, Mary," said Gabriel.

"God has a special plan for you.
You are going to have a baby. You must
call him Jesus. He will be a great king."
Mary looked puzzled.

Thank you, God,
that Mary was
glad to do what
you asked.
Amen.

"The baby will be God's Son," Gabriel explained.

"God is great; he can do anything."

Mary smiled. "I will do whatever God wants," she said.

LUKE 1

133

Mary was going to have God's baby. She couldn't wait to tell her cousin Elizabeth the news. She packed her bags and off she went.

"Elizabeth, Elizabeth!" she called, running up to the house.

Elizabeth hugged her. "Oh, Mary. As soon as I heard you coming, I knew that God had chosen you to be the mother of his promised king! How wonderful!"

Sing a "thank you" song to God, just like Mary did.

Mary was so happy she sang "thank you" to God.

LUKE 1

135

Joseph was going to marry Mary.
When he heard about Mary's baby,
he was worried.

That night, while Joseph was sleeping,

God sent an angel with a special message.

Dear God, help
me to be like
Joseph and listen
to what you say.
Amen.

"Joseph," the angel said. "Don't worry! God wants
you to marry Mary and look after her. Mary's baby has
been made by God's Holy Spirit. The baby's name will be
'Jesus.' One day he will rescue God's people."
Now Joseph was happy to marry Mary.

MATTHEW 1

137

Bethlehem was busy. People had come to be counted, just as the Roman emperor wanted. Mary and Joseph had traveled all the way from Nazareth. They needed somewhere to sleep but all the inns were full.

"There is a place where you can stay," said an innkeeper at last. He showed them to a warm, dry stable.

Dear God,
I'm very glad
Jesus was born.
Thank you for
sending him.
Amen.

That night, Jesus was born. Mary wrapped him
up warmly and laid him to sleep in the hay.

LUKE 2

139

The shepherds were busy looking after their sheep.
Suddenly an angel appeared, surrounded by God's
dazzling light. The shepherds were very frightened.

"Don't be afraid!" the angel said. "I have good
news for you! Today, in Bethlehem,
God's special king has been born.
You will find the baby lying
in a manger."

140

Then the sky was filled with lots of angels singing to God.

Dear God, thank you for sending your angels with the good news about Jesus. Amen.

The shepherds ran to Bethlehem. They were so happy when they found Jesus!
LUKE 2

One day Mary and Joseph took Baby Jesus to the temple.

There they met an old man called Simeon.

Old Simeon had loved God all his life
and God had made him a special promise.

He took Jesus gently in his arms. "I'm so happy today!"
he said. "Thank you, God, for keeping your promise
and letting me see the king who will rescue us all."

LUKE 2

143

One night, far away in the East, some wise
men saw a bright new star. "It means that a
great king has been born!" they said excitedly.
"We must go and find him."

So they followed
the star until it
stopped above a small
house in Bethlehem.

The wise men were so happy
to see Jesus.

Look up at the
stars. Thank God
for making the
stars, especially
the one that led the
wise men to Jesus.

They bowed down low and gave him precious
gifts – gold, frankincense and myrrh.

MATTHEW 2

After the wise men had left, an angel appeared to Joseph in a dream.

"Joseph! Get up! Hurry! You must leave at once.

"King Herod knows there is a new king. He wants to kill Jesus. Take Mary and Jesus to Egypt. You will be safe there. Stay there until I tell you to come back."

Joseph jumped out of bed. He woke Mary and Jesus. They packed their bags and left at once.

MATTHEW 2

Dear God, you kept Jesus and his family safe. Please keep my family safe too. Amen.

Mary, Joseph and Jesus had been worshiping
God at the temple in Jerusalem. Now it was
time to go home to Nazareth.

"Have you seen Jesus?" Mary
asked. Joseph shook his head.
Oh no! Jesus had been left behind.

Mary and Joseph rushed back to Jerusalem. They searched everywhere.

When I get lost, you're always there, When I'm alone you always care. Please keep me by your side, God. Amen.

Finally, they found Jesus in the temple, talking with the important teachers. "Didn't you know I'd be here in my Father's house?" said Jesus.

LUKE 2

"Come back to God!" John shouted. "God will forgive you for the things you've done wrong. Say you are sorry and get baptized in the water. God will make you clean inside and out!"

So the people told God they were sorry.

Then John baptized them in the river.

Jesus was good. But he came to be baptized too. He always did what God wanted.

When Jesus came out of the water, God said, "You are my own dear Son. I am pleased with you!"

MARK 1

Dear God, I've done wrong things too. I'm sorry. I'm glad that you make me clean inside. Amen.

Before Jesus began God's special work he had to stay in the desert. After many days he was hungry and tired.

Suddenly God's enemy, the devil, came to see Jesus. He wanted Jesus to disobey God.

He tried to trick Jesus, but each time Jesus chose to obey God.

Then the devil said, "I'll give you the whole world, if you bow down to ME."

Dear God, please help me be like Jesus and do what you want. Amen.

"Go away!" said Jesus. "God has told everyone to bow down and serve only him." So the devil left.

MATTHEW 4

153

Andrew and his friend were following Jesus.
They had heard that he was special.

Jesus turned
around. "What
do you want?"
he asked.
"We want to
know where
you live,"
Andrew replied.
"Come and see!"
laughed Jesus.

So they went to Jesus' house and talked with him all afternoon.

If you could spend an afternoon with Jesus what would you talk about?

Now, Andrew *knew* that Jesus was special. As soon as he got home, he told his brother, "Peter! You must meet Jesus – he's the king God promised us!"

JOHN 1

Jesus had been telling
people about God's good news.
Now he was sitting in Peter's
boat. "Let's go fishing!" he said.
"I've already been fishing.
I didn't catch *anything*!" Peter
replied. But he did what Jesus said.

Jesus, Peter did what you told him. Please help me to do what you say too. Amen.

Suddenly the nets were bursting with leaping, wriggling fish. Peter was amazed.

"Peter," Jesus said, "from now on, we're going fishing for people!"

So Peter and the other fishermen – Andrew, James and John – left their boats and followed Jesus.

LUKE 5   157

Mary and Jesus were at a wedding. Mary was worried. "Jesus, they have run out of wine!" she said.

Jesus looked around. He pointed to six huge stone jars.

"Fill those jars with water," he said to the servants. "Then take some out and give it to the man in charge."

Jesus, you can do amazing things. You are wonderful! Amen.

The servants filled the jars with water.

When they filled a cup, they were amazed. Jesus had turned ordinary water into the very best wine! It was a day to remember.

John 2

159

"Jesus can make you walk again," said the men as they carried their friend to Jesus' house.

But when they arrived, the house was so full they could not get in.

So they went up on the roof, dug a hole and lowered their friend down.

Jesus smiled at the friends. Then he said to the man, "My friend, everything you have done wrong is forgiven, so get up and walk home!"

Do you have a friend who is ill? Why not ask God to help them?

Then, to everyone's amazement, the man stood up and began to walk!

MARK 2

Everybody loved Jesus' stories. They gathered around and Jesus began:

There was once a wise man and a foolish man. The wise man dug deep and built his house on solid rock. But the foolish man built his house on the sand.

One day a great storm came.
The wind howled, the rain poured
down, the floods rose and the
house on the sand fell . . . CRASH!
But the wise man was safe in his
house on the rock.

You are stronger
than the strongest
storm, God.
Please keep me
safe with you.
Amen.

"You will be safe too," said Jesus.
"Just listen to me and do what I say."

LUKE 6

163

One day an important
soldier came to
see Jesus.

"My servant is
very ill!" he said.
"I will go and make
him well," said Jesus.
"But I am not good enough for you to come to
my house," said the soldier. "Just give the order.
When I give orders to others, they do it. So, if
you give the order, my servant will get better."

164

Dear God, the soldier trusted Jesus. Help me to trust Jesus too. Amen.

"I'm pleased you trust me!" said Jesus. "Go home and see, your servant is better."

MATTHEW 8

165

"When you find God's kingdom, you never want
to let it go," Jesus said to his friends one day.
And he told them this story:

A man was digging a field
when he found some treasure.

"If I buy this field,
the treasure will be
mine," the man
thought happily.

166

So off he went. He sold everything he had. Then he took the money and bought the field. He was so happy, because now the treasure was his for ever.

God, you are the best treasure of all. Amen.

MATTHEW 13

Some people didn't listen carefully
to Jesus, so he told this story:

A farmer went to sow his seeds.
Some seeds fell on the path
and hungry birds gobbled
them up.

Some seeds fell on stony ground where
the little plants died in the hot sun.

Some seeds fell among the weeds. At first, the plants grew well but then the weeds got in their way.

Help me to listen, God. I want to grow to be good like you. Amen.

And some seeds fell on good soil. There, the plants grew tall and strong. They gave the farmer lots more seeds.

MARK 4

It had been a busy day and now Jesus was fast asleep in his friends' boat.

Suddenly a storm hit the lake.

The wild wind whipped up the waves and they came crashing over the boat.

"Wake up, teacher!" Jesus' friends shouted. "The boat is sinking. We're in danger!"

Jesus got up.
"Waves! Calm down!" he ordered. "Wind, be quiet – now!"

Dear Jesus, thank you for looking after your friends in the storm.
Amen.

All at once it was safe and still.

"Look, even the wind and waves do what Jesus says!" said the friends in wonder.

MARK 4

171

One day an important man came to see Jesus.
"Please come to my house," he begged.
"My little girl is dying. Come quickly!"

Just then the man's servant ran up.
"Jairus," he said sadly, "your daughter is dead."
Jesus looked at Jairus. "Trust me," he said gently.
"Your little girl will get well."

At Jairus' house everyone
was crying. The little girl
was lying pale and still.

Jesus took her hand.
"Little girl," he said
softly, "get up!"
The little girl
opened her eyes
and stood up –
alive and well!

LUKE 8

173

As Jesus left Jairus' house, two
blind men called after him,
"Jesus, be kind and help us!"
"Do you believe I can make you
better?" Jesus asked them.
"Oh, yes!" they replied.

"Then because you believe in me,
it will happen," said Jesus as he
reached out and touched their eyes.

At once the men could see!

Dear God, it's great that Jesus made the blind men see. Amen.

"Don't tell anyone about this," said Jesus. But the men couldn't help telling everyone they met about Jesus and what he had done for them.

"Let's give these hungry people some food," said Jesus, pointing to the huge crowd that had come to listen to him.

"But we can't!" his friends replied.
"We don't have enough money!"

"This boy has five little loaves and two fish," said Andrew, "but that won't feed many people."

Thank you, God, for all our food. My favorite food is _____ . Amen.

Jesus smiled. He took the loaves and the fish and thanked God for them.

Then he began to hand the food out. Jesus' friends were amazed – Jesus had turned one boy's picnic into plenty of food for everyone!

JOHN 6

177

One evening Jesus went up the hill to pray.
His friends set off across the lake in their
boat. They puffed and panted as they rowed
against the strong wind.

Suddenly one of them whispered, "Look!"

They looked and saw someone walking
on the water. They were terrified.

"It's a ghost!" they screamed.

Jesus, no one else can walk on water. You are really special. Amen.

The man walked towards them. "Don't be afraid!" he said, getting into the boat. "It's me, Jesus!" The friends were amazed. It was Jesus!

MARK 6

179

Jesus took Peter, James and John up a
mountain to pray.

As Jesus was talking to God, he grew
brighter and brighter until even his
clothes shone dazzling white.

Jesus' friends looked on in amazement as
Moses and Elijah, two of God's special friends
from long ago, came to talk with Jesus.
Suddenly a misty cloud surrounded them and
they heard a voice. They knew it was God's voice.

"This is my Son," said God. "Listen to him."

Dear God, please help me to listen to Jesus. Amen.

LUKE 9

181

Jesus told this story to remind people to be kind to everyone:

A man was lying on the road, groaning. Some robbers had jumped on him and hurt him badly.

After a while a man came along, but he crossed over and walked away! Then another man walked by, but he did not stop to help either.

At last a kind stranger from another
country came by. He gently bandaged
the man's body. Then he took him to
an inn and looked after him there.

Please, God,
help me to be
kind to others.
Amen.

Then Jesus said,
"Go and be like
the kind man too."

LUKE 10

183

One day Jesus went to Martha and Mary's house. Mary stopped what she was doing and sat down to listen to Jesus. But Martha rushed around getting the food ready. "Oh, there is so much to do!" she thought. "Why isn't Mary helping me?"

"Jesus!" said Martha crossly. "Don't you care about me? I'm doing all the work by myself. Tell Mary to help me!"

"Oh, Martha," said Jesus gently, "Mary wants to be with me. Nothing is more important than that!"

Dear Jesus, I'm sorry when I am too busy to listen to you. Amen.

LUKE 10

185

One day, as Jesus finished praying, one of his friends said, "Please teach us how to talk to God." So Jesus taught them this prayer:

Our Father, you are good and perfect.
May everyone honor your name.
Come and be our King.
Give us today the food we need.

Forgive us for the bad things we do.
Help us to forgive everyone who has
done bad things to us.
And when we want to do something bad
help us choose to do good instead.

Why not use
Jesus' prayer
to talk to
God today?

One day Jesus met some men
with a nasty skin disease.
"Please make us well!" they called out to him.
Jesus looked at them kindly. "Go and see the priest;
he will check that you are better."

So the men set off. As they were on their
way, the disease disappeared and their
skin became as good as new!

God is pleased when we thank him. What can you thank him for today?

"Thank you, God!" shouted one man, as he rushed back to Jesus.

"Where are the others?" asked Jesus. Then he smiled. "I'm glad you came back to thank me."

Luke 17

189

Jesus knew that God invites everyone into his kingdom. So he told his followers a story.

A man was getting ready for his party. The decorations were up and the tables piled high with delicious food.

But the important people he had invited did not come. They sent messages saying, "I'm sorry, I'm too busy."

So the man said to his helpers, "Go into the town and the country. Find all the people who nobody invites to parties and bring them here."

Soon the man's house was full of people having fun.

Tell God what you like best about parties.

LUKE 14

191

Everyone crowded around as Jesus began another story.

There was once a shepherd who had one hundred sheep.

The shepherd carefully counted his sheep.
One, two, three, four . . . 97, 98, 99 . . . oh no!
One of his sheep was missing!

The shepherd searched up and down, near and far. He looked everywhere for his lost sheep. At last, he found it. He was so happy, he carried it all the way home!

"I've found my lost sheep!" he called to his friends, "Let's have a party!"

Have you ever lost something and found it again? Tell God all about it.

LUKE 15

193

"God is so happy when we come back to him," said Jesus. "Listen."

There was once a son who left home taking his share of his father's money. Before long he had spent everything. He had no money for food and was very hungry.

"I'll go back and say I'm sorry to my father," he thought. "I'll ask him for a job – his workers have lots to eat." So he set off.

God, thank you for loving us even when we make mistakes. Amen.

As soon as his father saw him, he ran to hug him. "My son has come home!" he called to his servants. "Let's have a party!"

LUKE 15

There were some people who thought
they were better than everyone else,
so Jesus told them a story.

Two men went to
the temple to pray.

One of them was
very pleased with
himself. "God,
I keep all your
rules," he said,
"and I don't steal
or cheat like that
man there."

196

The other man stood sadly at the back. "I know I'm a bad man, God," he said. "Please forgive me."

Dear God, I'm sorry for the bad things I've done today. Please forgive me. Amen.

"Guess which man God was pleased with!" said Jesus. "The one who said he was sorry."

LUKE 18

Martha and Mary were very sad because their brother Lazarus had died.

"If you had been here," they said to Jesus, "Lazarus would be alive now."

"Lazarus will live again," said Jesus, "because I give new life. Anyone who trusts me will never really die."

Then Jesus told the people to move the stone away from the place where Lazarus was buried.

"Lazarus, come out!" shouted Jesus.

Jesus, you are good and powerful. You have done so many wonderful things. Amen.

And to everyone's amazement Lazarus walked out alive and well!

JOHN 11

199

Some people brought their children to see Jesus.
"Go away," said Jesus' friends. "Don't bother Jesus.
He's much too busy."

Jesus was cross with his friends.

"Let the children come to me," he said.

"Don't try to stop them. God wants children in his kingdom."

So the children ran to Jesus' open arms. He picked them up, hugged them and asked God to take special care of them.

MARK 10

Jesus likes us to spend time with him. What do you want to tell him today?

"I'll never see Jesus from here," thought Zacchaeus, standing on tiptoe. So he climbed a tree.

As Jesus walked by, he stopped and looked up at Zacchaeus.

"Hello, Zacchaeus!" said Jesus. "I want to come to your house today!"

The crowd gasped. Zacchaeus was
a cheater; nobody liked him!
Zacchaeus gasped. Could Jesus
really want to be his friend?

Dear God, I've
done bad things
too. I'm glad you
still want to be
my friend.
Amen.

Zacchaeus had a wonderful day with Jesus.
"I'll give back the money I took and
more," Zacchaeus promised.
"Today you've come back to God,"
said Jesus, with a smile.

LUKE 19

203

As Jesus and his friends were having supper, Mary came in carrying her most precious bottle of perfume. Very quietly, she poured the perfume over Jesus' feet and wiped them gently with her long hair.

Everyone stopped eating as a wonderful sweet smell filled the room.

"What a waste, we could have sold that perfume and given the money to the poor," complained Judas.

"Leave Mary alone," said Jesus. "Soon I will die. Tonight she has done something very special for me."

What is your favorite smell? Tell God about it.

"It's time to go to Jerusalem," Jesus had said to his friends. "Find me a young donkey to ride."

Now the donkey was plodding along the road to Jerusalem, with Jesus sitting quietly on its back. Some people ran ahead, spreading branches and coats on the ground like a special carpet.

Crowds came to cheer and shout and wave branches to welcome Jesus.

Hooray, God. I want to say "thank you" for Jesus. Amen.

"Hooray, for God's special king!" they shouted. "Hooray, hooray!" "Who is this," asked some people. "It's Jesus, of course! God's messenger!" the crowds replied.

MATTHEW 21

207

Jesus told his friends a
story about being ready
for God's kingdom.

Ten bridesmaids were waiting
for the bridegroom to arrive.

The wise ones took extra oil for their lamps.
The foolish ones did not. At midnight the
foolish girls' lamps flickered and faded.
So they went to buy more oil.

While they were gone, the bridegroom arrived and took the wise bridesmaids to the wedding party. But the foolish girls missed the party altogether.

Jesus said to his friends, "Make sure you're ready for God's party."

MATTHEW 25

209

The temple was busy when Jesus arrived. People were buying and selling animals to give to God or waiting to buy temple money.

"Buy a good lamb here," shouted some sellers. "Doves for sale!" yelled others.

Jesus was very angry. There was so much noise that no one could talk to God. He pushed over a stall piled high with money.

Dear God, thank you for quiet places to pray. Amen.

"God's house is a special place to pray," said Jesus, "not to buy and sell and cheat!" Then he chased them all out of the temple.

MARK 11

One evening while Jesus and his friends were eating, Jesus got up, tied a towel around his waist and began to wash his friends' feet.

They were shocked – it was the servant's job to wash feet. Their feet were smelly and dirty from walking along the hot, dusty roads.

"Jesus, you mustn't wash our feet!" said Peter.

Dear God,
please help me
to be loving
and helpful
like Jesus.
Amen.

"I'm washing your feet because I love you," said Jesus.
"Now copy me. Love and help each other."

JOHN 13

213

Jesus and his friends were eating a special meal together. Jesus took some bread, thanked God for it, then broke it in pieces and gave it to his friends.

"This is my body," he said. "I give it for you."

Then he took a cup of wine, thanked God and passed it around.

"Drink this — it is my blood. When I die it will be poured out so that many people will be forgiven."

Thank you, Jesus, for giving your life for everyone. Amen.

Then they sang a song to God and went together to the garden to pray.

In the garden Jesus became very sad and afraid.
He knew he was going to die.

He knelt down
and prayed.

"Father, please don't let me suffer.
But if it is part of your plan,
then I will do what you want."

Suddenly Jesus and his sleepy friends saw blazing
torches and glinting swords. Jesus' friend Judas
was leading a crowd of Jesus' enemies!

When you are sad or afraid you can talk to Jesus about it. He knows how you feel.

Judas went up to Jesus and kissed him. At once the soldiers surrounded Jesus and took him prisoner.

LUKE 22

217

The soldiers took Jesus
to the High Priest's
house. Peter stood
outside by the fire.

"You're one of Jesus'
friends, aren't you?"
said a servant girl.
Peter shook his head,
"No, I don't know him!"

218

Two more people
asked him if he
knew Jesus.

"No!" said Peter. "NO!"

Dear God, please
help me when
it's hard to be
your friend.
Amen.

Just then a cock crowed, and
Peter remembered Jesus'
words: "Before the cock
crows you will say three times
that you're not my friend."

Peter burst into tears.
He knew he had let Jesus down.

LUKE 22

219

Jesus' enemies took Jesus to the
Roman leader of Jerusalem.
Pilate asked Jesus lots of questions.
Then he said to all the people,
"Jesus has not done anything
wrong. I will let him go."
"NO!" the people shouted. "Kill
Jesus! Nail him to a cross!"

So Pilate told the soldiers to take Jesus to Skull Hill. There they nailed him to a cross and left him to die.

Jesus, thank you for loving everyone enough to die to save them. Amen.

Jesus knew that he had done what God wanted. "My work is finished!" he cried. Then he died.

JOHN 18–19

221

Jesus was dead. His mother Mary stood crying as the soldiers took Jesus' body down from the cross.

Nicodemus and Joseph were standing nearby. They had been afraid to say they were Jesus' friends, but now they showed that they loved him.

They wrapped Jesus' body in cloth with precious perfumes.

Do you know someone who is sad? Ask God to help them.

Then they carefully carried the body and put it in a new tomb in a garden close to Skull Hill. Together they rolled the huge, heavy stone across the doorway. Then they walked sadly away.

JOHN 19

It was the first day of the week. Jesus' friend, Mary, was standing outside Jesus' tomb, crying. The heavy stone had been rolled away, but the tomb was empty. Jesus' body was gone! Someone had taken it away!

A man was standing nearby.

"Why are you crying?" he asked.

Mary thought he was the gardener. "Have you taken Jesus away?" she sobbed.

"Mary!" he said gently.
Mary stopped crying and looked up.
It was Jesus!
Jesus smiled.

Thank you, God,
for Easter time.
It's wonderful
that Jesus
is alive!
Amen.

"Go and tell
my friends,"
he said.

Mary ran back to
her friends. She
couldn't wait
to tell them the
good news –
Jesus was
ALIVE!

JOHN 20

225

As Jesus' friends were walking back to
their village, a stranger joined them.
"What are you talking about?" he asked.

Jesus' friends were surprised. "Haven't you heard?
Jesus was killed three days ago. Today his body is
missing. But our friends say he is alive!"

226

"God said that this would happen to his special king," said the stranger.

Dear God, help me to know every day that Jesus is alive. Amen.

Later that evening, while they were eating together, the stranger thanked God for the bread and gave them each a piece. Jesus' friends were amazed – the stranger was Jesus! He really was alive!

LUKE 24

227

The two friends ran back to Jerusalem. "We've seen Jesus!" they said to all Jesus' friends. Everyone was excited; talking and asking questions.

Suddenly Jesus was there in the room! Everyone stopped talking. They were very frightened. "Don't be scared," Jesus said. "It's me. Touch me; I'm not a ghost!"

Jesus' friends were so happy to see Jesus alive again.

Thank you, Jesus. It's great that I can be God's friend. Amen.

"You must tell everyone, everywhere, what happened to me," Jesus told them. "Because of me they can be God's friends again."

LUKE 24

229

The next day Jesus' friends met Thomas.
"We've seen Jesus!" they said.
"I don't believe you," said Thomas; "I need to see and
touch Jesus for myself. Then I'll believe he's alive."

A week later Jesus came again.
"Thomas," he said, "look at my hands
and feet; touch them. It really is me."
Thomas gazed in wonder and said, "My
Lord and my God."

Dear God,
please help me
to trust you.
Amen.

"You believe because you've seen me," said Jesus.
"God will be very pleased with people who believe
without having seen me."

JOHN 20

231

"Stay in Jerusalem until God sends you his special helper," Jesus told his friends. Then he took them to a hilltop near the city.

"God's Holy Spirit will help you tell the whole world about me," he said, smiling. Then, before their eyes, Jesus was taken up to heaven.

Suddenly two angels appeared beside them. "Why are you standing here looking at the sky?" they asked. "Jesus will come back – one day."

Dear Jesus, you are coming back one day. That's so exciting! Amen.

So the friends walked back to the city and waited . . . . .

One morning Jesus' friends were praying together.
Whooosh! A sound like a rushing wind roared
through the house.

A flickering flame rested gently on each head and
Jesus' friends began to speak in many languages.
They were so happy! They knew that the helper
promised by Jesus had come. God's Holy Spirit was
with them to help them tell others about Jesus.

Thank you, God, for sending your Holy Spirit. Amen.

People from different countries came to listen. They understood what Jesus' friends were saying! And when they heard what God had done, they wanted to be Jesus' friends too.

As Peter and John were going to the temple to pray, they passed a man who could not walk. "Please give me some money!" begged the man.

"I don't have any money," Peter said kindly, "but I know that Jesus is God's king. And Jesus tells you to get up and walk!"

Dear God, thank you for your power to make people well. Amen.

Peter took the man's hand and helped him up.

Suddenly the man's feet and legs were strong again – he could walk, he could jump, he could run and leap! "God you are great!" he shouted. "Thank you! Thank you!"

ACTS 3

One day an angel sent Jesus' friend Philip
to a dusty, desert road. As he walked along,
a chariot rumbled by. On board was an
important man from Ethiopia.

"Keep up with
that chariot,
Philip," God's
Holy Spirit
told him.

As Philip ran beside the chariot, he heard
the man reading from God's book.
"Do you understand it?" asked Philip.
"No," sighed the man. "What does it mean?"
238 So Philip climbed up.

Thank you, God, for the Bible. Amen.

"These are words about Jesus," he said. Then he told the man all about Jesus. And that day the important man became Jesus' friend too.

ACTS 8

Paul hated Jesus' friends. He did not believe that Jesus was God's special king or that Jesus was alive.

One day Paul set off for Damascus to find Jesus' friends and put them in prison.

FLASH! All around him there was a bright, white light! Paul fell to the ground.

"Paul," said a voice. "Why do you hate me and hurt me?"

"Who are you?" asked Paul.

"I am Jesus!"

Thank you, Jesus, that you want to be friends with everyone. Amen.

Paul was shocked. But from that moment he became a friend of Jesus. And Jesus gave him an important job – telling everyone that Jesus was alive!

ACTS 9

241

Peter was in prison, chained to King Herod's
soldiers who guarded him night and day.
One night, as Peter was sleeping, an angel came.

"Wake up," he said,
prodding Peter.
Peter's chains fell to
the ground.

"Quick, put on your sandals,"
said the angel.
"Follow me."

So Peter followed the angel, right past all the guards, through the gate and into the street. Then the angel disappeared.

When I'm in trouble, God, please help me like you helped Peter. Amen.

Peter blinked. It wasn't a dream – he really was free! He rushed to tell Jesus' friends how God had rescued him.

ACTS 12

243

Paul had been given a special job. He travelled to many places telling people about Jesus.

One night a man called to Paul in a dream, "Come to Macedonia! Help us!"

The next day Paul got on a boat and set sail. "I must tell the people in Macedonia about Jesus," he thought.

There he met Lydia, a rich lady, and her friends. He told them about Jesus.

Thank you, God, for all the people who tell me about Jesus. Amen.

"Come to my house!" said Lydia. "Tell me more about Jesus." And so Lydia and many others became friends of Jesus.

ACTS 16

Some people would not listen to Paul. One day, when Paul was at the temple, Jesus' enemies grabbed him. "Paul tells lies!" they shouted as they tried to kill him.

Just then, the Roman commander and his soldiers marched in. The soldiers stopped the people from hurting Paul.

"What's going on?" asked the commander. Paul began to explain about Jesus – that he was alive and that God wanted everyone to know about him.

Thank you, God, for being my friend, even when others are unkind. Amen.

"NO!" shouted the crowd. "Get rid of Paul." So the commander took Paul to the prison.

ACTS 21, 22

"The Roman emperor must decide if I am right," Paul said.

So the soldiers took Paul
and set sail for Rome.

Before long the
ship was caught in a big storm and blown along
by a raging wind. Everyone on the ship was terrified.
248 "Don't be afraid," said Paul. "God will keep us all safe."

As the ship broke up, everyone swam for the shore or floated safely to land.

Thank you, God. You always keep your promises! Amen.

At last, they all lay on the sand – cold, wet and safe. God had kept his promise.

ACTS 27

249

Finally Paul and the soldiers arrived in Rome. The emperor let Paul live in a house, but sent a soldier to guard him day and night.

Paul was not allowed to go out, so he wrote letters to Jesus' friends. He had met so many of them on his travels. He wanted them to continue to love Jesus and love each other.

Jesus' friends wrote to Paul too. They told him their problems and asked him questions. And Paul wrote back to help them. They were always happy to get Paul's letters.

Talk to God about your best friend. Then draw a picture and send it to her.

"Write to my friends!" John heard a voice say.

He turned and saw a man – strong and good
and shining bright. It was Jesus!

252

Jesus had come to cheer
up his friends who were in
trouble. He showed John
God's wonderful plan, and
John wrote to all Jesus'
friends with this good news:

"God is going to make a new heaven and a
new earth where no one will be hurt or die!
God will wipe away our tears and all God's
friends will live with him for ever!"

REVELATION 1: 1, 2

One day, God,
all your friends
will live with
you for ever.
Hooray!

253

Index

This index shows where to find some favorite Bible stories in this book and also shows groups of stories that link together.

First mention of people in this book